THE PATRIOTS

BY SANA KRASIKOV

One More Year

The Patriots

THE
PATRIOTS

a novel

SANA
KRASIKOV

GRANTA

Granta Publications, 12 Addison Avenue, London W11 4QR

First published in Great Britain by Granta Books in 2017
Published by arrangement with Spiegel & Grau, an imprint of Random
House, a division of Penguin Random House LLC, New York

A CIP catalogue record for this book is available from the British Library.

1 3 5 7 9 10 8 6 4 2

ISBN 978 1 78378 181 2 (hardback)
ISBN 978 1 78378 364 9 (trade paperback)
ISBN 978 1 84708 834 5 (ebook)

Book design by Barbara M. Bachman

Offset by Avon DataSet Ltd, Bidford on Avon, B50 4JH

Printed and bound by CPI Group (UK) Ltd, Croydon, CR0 4YY

www.grantabooks.com

For
T. Friedman

CONTENTS

PROLOGUE

ON A SUNDAY IN AUGUST, A BOY AND A ONE-ARMED MAN APPEARED ON the platform of the Saratov train station. The train they awaited was due to arrive at six. In that early-evening hour the air was beginning to cool. The sunlight shifted, deepened and turned to gold the dust suspended by the shoes of hurrying passengers. Leading the way through milling crowds, the man drew a handrolled cigarette from his jacket and gripped it between his teeth. He worked a match out of a box with his one hand, struck it up with the flesh of his thumb, and leaned down on the flame. Sucking his cigarette, he glanced back to see that the boy had not been swallowed up by the masses.

All summer had found the railway stations mobbed as they hadn't been since the war. To contain the stench of public toilets, the sanitation workers poured bleach powder in the latrine pits. The man forbade the boy to go alone into one of these facilities, knowing they were full of *urki* ready to slit your throat for the money you carried in your underwear. A wave of crime had hit the cities two years prior, for the first of the condemned to be let out were the pickpockets and prostitutes, the murderers, thieves, and onanists. Only now, three years after the tyrant had croaked, were the others being released—the fifty-eighters and counterrevolutionaries and enemies-of-the-people whose number was too absurd, too enormous for the bosses, with their abiding fear of chaos, to free all at once.

From Vorkuta they came, from Pechora and Inta, from Kolyma and Kengir and Perm. They arrived that summer moving south with the trains, like logs down a swollen river. Entire forests of people felled, bound and piled and now cast adrift into the rising water. A winter's cut, carried aloft with frightening rapidity.

A signal blasted from the locomotive up ahead. A click and switch of iron rails brought the final filling of teakettles. When the second wail sounded, the boy wished he hadn't heard it, then reproached himself for the cowardice of this wish. All week long he'd been failing to conjure her up in his head. Now, as he prepared to recognize his mother among the strangers rapidly streaming from the wagon, he felt swamped by despair. "Car nine," said the man, and let the boy walk ahead.

His hair, freshly cut, fell across his forehead in a fringe that made him look younger than his twelve years. His clothes, though not new, were ironed and starched.

A woman stepped off the train, her mouth frozen in an imploring smile. Her olive padded jacket reminded the boy of the one worn by the farmer who delivered potatoes to his orphanage. Her thick sweater hung over a coarse-hemmed dress. The suitcase she set down on the platform was cardboard, reinforced with metal corners, and so small he couldn't imagine it holding anything besides a few papers. The light that entered her face as she recognized him sent a twinge of nausea down his throat.

She was older, of course, her face pale and puffy. Her once-sculpted features were altered by an odd short haircut: parted on the side in two dove-gray streaks. Only her eyes, those heavy-lidded blue eyes that had always been the striking focal point of her face, were troublesomely familiar.

The man gave him a shove.

She squatted and cupped her hands around Julian's face. "Let me look at you, my precious, sweet boy." He caught the meaning of her words at the last moment. She had spoken them in English—a language he hadn't heard or uttered in almost seven years. As if teasing, she said, "You don't recognize me?"

"Of course I do, Mama!" he answered in Russian.

"That's all right. I've turned into an old crow, haven't I?"

He wasn't sure how to answer this, and in a voice full of falseness said, "Let me carry your bag, Mama!"

The train was leaving. Bits of sky flashed between wagons. But where was her hair? The long, thick curls he'd buried his small face in, which he'd pictured for years in his sleep, all he'd been able to preserve of her—their loss felt like betrayal. He held her suitcase as she approached Mark Pavlovich, the children's home director, and took his one hand in both of hers. She was thanking him for everything he had done for her son all these years. Now that she'd reverted to Russian, Julian was suddenly stunned: her voice, surprisingly loud and clear, was afflicted with the thick lilt of an American accent.

How could he have not remembered this?

"We'll be sorry to see him go," said the director. "Yulik has been a real helper." Briefly he glanced at the departing train. "You'll see for yourself what a fine boy he is. An outstanding worker."

"I'm certain I will," she said, putting a hand on Julian's shoulder. He felt his body go rigid. He'd have to leave school now, forsake the games behind the cowshed, say goodbye to his friends, to his whole life. The thought that he would have to go live with this woman made him want to crumble in angry tears. But the director, seeming to read his mind, said, "I hope you won't mind that we'll keep him a little longer. . . ." It was less a question than a promise to look after him until she could get back on her feet. It had all been arranged beforehand. It was done this way for all the prisoners' children.

His mother's eyes filled with bitter gratitude, but still she looked at Julian to make sure he approved. He felt a pang of shame. It was clear she had no means to take him with her. Mark Pavlovich asked whether she wanted to stay that night, but she said she'd wait for the nighttime connection to Moscow. There she would sort out her life—obtain her rehabilitation papers, look for work, find a room for the two of them to live. "But everything should be in order by December," she said with an effortful, slightly bronchial laugh. "Then we can celebrate the New Year together. Won't that be something?"

For years he had rehearsed what he might say to her once they were together (*Sit down, Mama, rest, I will take care of you*). Now he felt like a conscript who'd evaded the draft.

"What's a few more months after all this time?" she said. And with these words, his mother—the phantom of his exhausted imagination—reentered his life.

BOOK I

1.

___

QUALITATIVE LEAPS

New York, 1934

BREAKING YOUR FAMILY'S HEART WAS THE PRICE YOU PAID FOR RESCU-ing your own. Florence had committed herself to this credo, letting it carry her through the cruelty of the past six weeks—so that she was surprised, on the upper deck of the *Bremen*, to feel her faith recede. From under her narrow palm she gazed down at the people crowding the dock. A May sun accosted the harbor and coated everything with a blinding shine. The air smelled of coal and rotted fish. Small green waves raced from the hull back to the pier, where her parents and her little brother stood squeezed in among strangers. She would have shouted out to them but knew her voice could not carry over the screeches of gulls and the intermittent bassoon of the ship's tremendous whistle.

ONLY AFTER SHE'D BOUGHT her ticket had Florence told her parents she was leaving. Then she braced herself for the family volcano.

"Cleveland was not enough!" Her father's shouts had rattled their Flatbush living room. "*Russia!* You want to go where they're shooting people dead for eating their own grain?"

She'd fought back. "No one who's traveled there ever reported seeing any such thing."

He turned to her mother. "Never reported! They're being duped, Florie. And *you're* being duped."

"Sure, and the factories are only burning straw to make smoke come out the chimneys?"

"You think I'm such a dummy that I don't know what kind of hoodwinked world my own father left. A young person such as yourself, ripe for recruitment . . ."

"No one has recruited me!"

But his eyes were wild with lunatic distrust. "Let me see your Party card!"

"I don't have one!" she shouted, her voice caving from tears. "For Pete's sake, I am not a communist!"

"Then why, Florie? Just tell me *why*. What kind of madness is this, for a girl to want to leave her family, her home, all the people who love her? To the other end of the world!"

She could not tell him the truth. Could not show him the photograph of the dark-eyed man with the Apache cheeks, tucked in the back of her dresser drawer. Better they think her a communist than a *nafka*. "I am not leaving forever, Papa!" she said in a voice hoarse from shouting.

"Then tell us how *long?*"

"I *can't* tell you. A year, maybe more."

"And throw away another year of your life?"

"I want to *live* my life."

"Go, then! I've had enough of you," her father said. "May the day never come when you feel the pain we feel now."

Despite their threats, her parents had come to see her off. Her mother gave Florence her own fur coat to brave the snowy Russian winter. Her father bought her a traveler's trunk. They stood watching as it was tossed by a ship's attendant into the hold, where it took on the size of a matchbox beside all the other cargo—enormous boxes and barrels, chrome automobiles, upright pianos. Her brother Sidney had given her his beloved BSA Taylor compass, whose cold beveled edges Florence now dug with torturous pleasure into the soft flesh of her thumb. She'd discovered it in her purse only after she boarded the ship. She wanted to walk off the boat and give it back to Sidney, whose muskrat's hard hat of hair was still visible in flashes among the bodies on the dock. But it was too late; the third-class passengers were boarding, blocking the gangway with awkward bundles. Danes, Poles, Germans, stocky in their winter overcoats and rubber boots. With their American children in tow, they were returning to their homelands in search of work. Observing them trudge aboard, Florence suddenly felt she was watching an old Ellis Island film reel flipped by the Depression into reverse: masses of immigrants returning to the ship, being herded backward through that great human warehouse as Lady Liberty waved them goodbye.

Her reverie was interrupted by an argument on deck. Somebody was demanding to carry a poultry incubator aboard ship rather than abandon it to the hold. Into the fray came the noises of a hen cock crowing in defiance of the third steamer signal. Taking advantage of the clamor and tumult, one of the Poles was making the rounds with a collection box. When he saw a tall, handsome girl in a tailored green suit, he mistook Florence for a wealthy young lady and approached her with a heavily accented speech about penniless deportees. It was impossible to hear the story in the flapping of ropes and echoes from port. She thought she heard her name being called—her father's voice a hallucination conjured by the wind's eddies. Florence opened her purse and gave the man a coin.

She felt ready for the ship to cast off, but a fresh commotion had seized the crowd. On the gangway ramp, a girl of about eighteen had dropped her glasses and was now palming around for them, interrupting her search only to toss angry defenses at those she was holding up behind. In her myopic squint Florence recognized the feral defiance of someone who'd learned to carry her awkwardness brazenly. A girl accustomed to being out of place. But it was her physical appearance that most struck Florence. The girl might have been Florence herself—younger, shorter, and plumper, but otherwise bearing an almost familial likeness. Her skin was equally pale; her curls, only slightly darker than Florence's, had the strong kink that Florence had learned to tame out of her own hair with relaxers and combs. Someone from the boat was sent to help the girl, and soon her spectacles were retrieved from between the gangplanks. The commotion was drowned out again by a final signal from the ship's heights. The chimneys belched coal smoke, and the engines of the tugboats began to turn. At last the *Bremen* made its imperceptible slide backward into the Hudson.

A flock of gulls with black-edged wings circled the ship as it churned and split the water. Slowly by slowly the crowd on the pier receded, her family along with them. Only the gulls stayed close. Trailing the *Bremen*, they rose and fell on a tunnel of air which seemed to propel the ship and everyone on it down a course that stretched irreversibly into a bright, portentous sea.

THE FOLLOWING MORNING THE SUN'S RAYS WERE UNOBSTRUCTED BY any buildings or trees. An ocean chill drew bumps on Florence's arms as she sat on a lounge chair in the scalloped shade of an awning. She drew on her round sunglasses and attempted to read a book she'd brought for the journey: *Red Virtue: Human Relationships in the New Russia* by Ella Winter. Winter's prose was making it hard to get past page 2. And another human relationship was presently competing for her attention: on the top deck, in first class, a tall madam with sunken cheeks and a greyhound's ropy body was promenading on the arm of a much younger, darker-skinned gentleman. The man's hair was gelled back like Valentino's. His spine stayed rigid with military aplomb even as his companion petted his shoulder and brushed his ear with her thin lips.

"So—what do you make of her?"

Florence turned to find the girl she'd seen the day before. Her tortoise-shell glasses were now affixed firmly on the short bridge of her nose. Atop her curly head a woven beret was tipped at a precarious angle.

"Pardon me?"

"Ella Winter. Your book. Another phony Margaret Mead, if you ask me."

Florence frowned and took a glance at the cover.

"It must have been real disappointing for her to discover her Russians weren't illiterate savages like the Samoans," the girl resumed with no preliminaries.

"Have you read it?" Florence said mistrustfully.

"I read all I needed to in the essay they printed in *The American*. They'll print any so-called scholarship as long as it's penned by Mrs. Lincoln Steffens. *You* like it?"

It wasn't a question so much as a preemptive dismissal of her tastes, and therefore, Florence decided, undeserving of a response. In fact, the book was astonishingly dull. Yet this odd girl's exuberant abrasiveness now compelled Florence to defend it. "And what about Dorothy Thompson—you won't read her, either, 'cause she's Mrs. Sinclair Lewis?"

"What kind of false comparison is that?" The girl plopped down on the neighboring lounge chair. "Thompson's queen of the press corps. Winter is just another suffragette born twenty years too late."

The girl's eyes—as blue as Florence's own—glowed with a lust for debate that Florence found all the more irritating having once had it in good measure. She sensed that entering into a conversation with this creature would return her to a version of herself that she had struggled to shed. In high school and college Florence had earned good marks but a part of her knew that the educators she admired did not admire her back. Her history teacher once applauded her to other students as being the kind of girl "who could chop down an oak with a baseball bat." She cringed to think how tone deaf she'd been to this double-edged praise.

"Why a suffragette?" she now inquired with careful nonchalance.

"The place of the working-class woman is beside the men of her class, not beside women of other classes. It's basic Marx, if *she'd* ever bothered to crack him."

"If you'd bothered to crack *her,* you'd see she acknowledges that Marx claims it's only true for societies that haven't eliminated class. Anyway, I'm not reading it for the theory."

"I knew it! You're heading to Russia, like me." The girl jutted out her hand. "Essie Frank."

"Florence Fein."

In less than a minute, Florence was assailed by an artillery of questions. Which class was she traveling? Where was she from? Where had she gone to school? Where did she plan to stay once she arrived in Moscow?

"The Intourist Hotel?" Essie sounded horrified. "They'll fleece you. They overcharge all foreigners." Essie, evidently, would be lodging at a workers' dormitory at the Foreign Language Institute, where she already had a job lined up.

"I'm only staying in Moscow till I can get a ticket for Magnitogorsk," Florence said, in a way she hoped both sounded mysterious and discouraging of further inquiry. The *Bremen* was making stops in Copenhagen, Danzig, and Libau, and Florence had yet to meet anyone who, like her, was disembarking in Latvia and taking the train to Moscow. Judging by her talk, Essie had undertaken the journey with more preparation, carrying extra passport photographs as well as items to trade or gift. Her preparedness felt like a challenge to Florence's faith in the future. "Magnitogorsk, all the way out in the Urals!" Essie said, either impressed by Florence's bravery or stunned by her foolhardiness. "Have you got a job there or something?"

Florence was uncertain how to answer. She was hardly sure herself what dream she was pursuing: one of Soviet Mankind, or of one particular dark-eyed Soviet man.

At that moment, a coterie of passengers from steerage emerged on deck. One of the men waved to Essie.

"Is that your group over there?" Florence said.

Essie seemed embarrassed. "No, no, I'm not really with them. . . ." Having intruded on Florence's privacy, Essie now seemed to be jealously patrolling her own. "See, there was a vacancy, and, last minute, I got the ticket on the cheap. . . . They're all getting off at Danzig."

"Oh." Florence turned her gaze back to the couple in first class. The greyhound in her silk pajamas was arching her long torso in a swooning laugh, while her tanned and ascotted paramour clutched her waist as if to keep her from throwing out her back. "It's like they're posing for pictures," Florence remarked.

"And wouldn't you know it's the press she's trying to escape," Essie said unexpectedly.

"You *know* who she is?"

"Everyone on this steamer knows it. It's Mary Woolford, the utilities heiress, and that's her new Alfonse, an Argentine polo player of legendary prowess. Oh, don't look so shocked; he's far too dark to be American. He's husband *número tres* for her."

Florence *was* shocked, not at the shade of the new husband's skin but at Essie's superior command of ship gossip. "Look, she just fixed his shirt again."

"I hope she doesn't get it greasy after touching his hair," Essie quipped.

"Ick!" they sang in unison, and nearly choked laughing.

"You know what they say," Essie said. " 'From the back a damsel fair, from the front a wrinkled mare.' "

"Well, he *does* like ponies," Florence said, before a second convulsion of laughter made the two of them collapse, red-faced, in their chairs. Essie removed her glasses and wiped her eyes, and Florence now found herself battling the powerful sensation of feeling won over by this girl, whose dimples looked like they'd been poked out with a gimlet.

"Don't look now," Essie said, grabbing Florence's wrist, "but there's a couple of Joe Colleges about to waltz over."

Florence glanced back and recognized two young men in cable sweaters who'd been circling the deck since breakfast time. "More like Joe Grammar School," she said, then stretched her legs for an extra precious inch of sun, letting the boys get a good look. The two young men consulted each other quietly before making their approach.

"We don't mean to lean into your conversation, girls," said the shorter of the two. He had a large-eared, cheerful face. "But my friend was convinced you were Norma Shearer."

It wasn't the first time a boy had made the comparison. On her good days, Florence could notice the similarity in the mirror: her deep-set blue-gray eyes, the aquiline profile people called "regal," features that hovered somewhere between innocence and arrogance. "I'll be Al Jolson if you want, darling," she said, "as long as you have a Lucky. We're all out of smokes, as you see." On the courage of the sea air, she sounded like a hardened flirt.

The young man turned out his pockets. "Sorry, Miss Shearer, no gaspers before tournaments, coach's orders. But we could bring you some desert horses from the restaurant. . . ."

And so they did. They said their names were Jack and Brian and they were traveling to Germany with the New Haven Tennis Club, as guests of the Rot-Weiss Tennis Club. With her nail, Florence opened the pack of Camels they'd brought and shared one with Essie.

"Russia! That's *really* jumping the blinds," said Brian when they told him where they were heading. "Off to build the Red Paradise?"

"As a matter of fact," Essie remarked unplayfully.

The boys gave her a confused smile and turned again to Florence. Whenever Essie opened her mouth, Florence noted, it was plain to see how inadequate she was at saying anything that might hold a man's attention. Soon the boys had to go to practice (somewhere in the ship's labyrinth was a full-sized tennis court), but they asked if the girls would join the team for a drink after dinner. "If it isn't past our bedtimes," Florence said, waving them goodbye with a cigarette between her fingers.

THAT EVENING, AFTER THE second dinner bell, Florence met Essie in the carpeted hallway outside the Kronprinz Lounge. She took a look at Essie's skirt, and at her shoes, and said, "Come with me."

From the lower berth in Florence's cabin, Essie looked around with undisguised envy. "You've got this all to yourself?"

"They don't normally sell out of second-class tickets. What's your shoe size?"

"Six-and-a-half. They pack *us* eight to a room, but it's really nine because there's a four-year-old, too, and the others are all Social Democrats who debate in Polish all night, so you can't catch a wink of sleep."

"I only have size eight. We'll have to stuff the toes. Here, try this for size." Florence threw her a loose dress with wide kimono sleeves.

"What's the matter with the shoes I got on?"

"Nothing's the matter if you don't care to tell which one's left and which one's right, they're so boxy." She squinted at the dress and said, "We'll have to cinch the waist," though Essie hardly had any waist to speak of.

"The trouble's my hair," Essie said despondently. "All the salt in the air makes it a bird's nest. If I had your curls . . ."

"You can. Just roll 'em around a hot pair of scissors. I'll show you after," she said. "Right now we're late."

THE NEW HAVEN PLAYERS, about half a dozen of them, were assembled at one of the high tables near the bar. Collectively, they gave off an almost menacing air of good health. Essie and Florence's arrival aroused from them no interest apart from Brian's cheerful dragging of more chairs. "Two Joe Rickeys over here." He tapped his glass. "They claim to be out of gin, so we're nursing bourbons."

"Three Rickeys," corrected a pink-cheeked six-footer beside Florence.

"You've had enough to wash the decks, Kip," someone said. Unpersuaded, Kip lifted a finger to the waiter.

"I'll tell you one thing, the Davis Cup's become too big," said a young man by the name of Leslie. "No one hears his own name called anymore.

You hear 'advantage, States,' or 'France four, England two.' The fate of the whole damn country's on your neck."

Florence didn't have the remotest idea what they were talking about, and was glad when Brian asked if the two of them were really headed to Russia. "Don't we look it?" she said.

Kip cast a bored look over them and said, "The Frenchies don't seem to be feeling the heat."

"The Germans do, I can promise you," said Leslie. "And they've got Hitler breathing down their throats about their physical superiority."

"So long's they've got von Cramm, they can still take the Cup. One champion horse is all you need."

"Which one's von Cramm?" Essie said, entering the conversation late, but the men went on talking.

"*If* von Cramm plays."

"Why won't he?"

"He and Old Hitts aren't exactly chums. Last year he called Herr Führer a house painter."

"I heard Ribbentrop was trying to get him to sign up with the Nazis but von Cramm told him to go eat hay."

"Too much an aristocrat for them, eh?"

"No, he's sore about them kicking his buddy Daniel Prenn off the team."

Florence saw Essie's eyes grow bright with angry comprehension. "It's revolting," she said, "the way they've been expelling the Jewish athletes."

"They're crippling themselves without Prenn," said Brian.

"Prenn's an all-right player," admitted Kip, "but no one's irreplaceable."

Florence was considering a proper rejoinder to this when Essie jumped in ahead of her. "It's imponderable to me," she pursued, "how Germany can even be permitted to host the Olympics when they're driving out the Jewish players. . . ."

"Just *imponderable!*" Kip mimed cruelly. "Prenn can go play for someone else if he doesn't like it."

"The Brits will snap him up."

"Or the Russkies. He's one of theirs, right?"

"They ought to toss Germany out of the games," Essie declaimed.

"So you don't like their politics. Well, I don't like the Bolshies and theirs," said a sharp-nosed boy with a crew cut. "Let's toss *them* out. And the goat-sniffing Greeks while we're at it, why not?"

Taking the bait, Essie launched into an attack on this reasoning. But no one was listening to her. Even to Florence, she looked like a schnauzer among Dobermans. "I'd say your friend's a wet fish on dry land, but there ain't any for miles," Brian said in a whisper to Florence. Florence felt a sense of shame for her silence—letting Essie take a beating from these *shkotzim*.

"Come on, chaps, no politics tonight," someone pleaded. "Let the Olympic Committee sort it out."

"They *have* sorted it out," said Kip. "Brundage said all this talk about the Jewish athletes was pure booshwash."

"And these committees always do such a *fine* job," Florence replied, seizing her opening. She washed down the dregs of her Rickey. Her gaze fell coldly on Kip. "It ain't *booshwash* when half the world's calling for a boycott."

"Not half the world, just a few Jews and commies who want to get us into a fresh war. Good night, everyone," he said, rising to his full Aryan height.

"Auf Wiedersehen!" Florence called after him, and took hold of Essie's hand before her friend could drop any more cinders from the hot cavity of her mouth.

"AND THAT'S WHAT COUNTS for loyal patriots these days, Florence! First-class American flag-waving bigots. That's who's in charge, and that's why I'm through with the fine U.S. of A."

Florence could hear heavy tears gathering behind Essie's nasal passages. Essie hadn't stopped talking since they'd entered Florence's cabin.

"You don't have to tell *me*," Florence happily assured her. She wondered why Essie's dismay made her so buoyant. Then it occurred to her that, for the first time since separating from her family and boarding the ship, she was absolutely convinced of the rightness of her decision. America had nothing to offer her.

"High-minded swine with their muzzles in their fancy drinks and their heads in the sand. Hypocrites making nicey-nice with the fascists while they arm against all of Europe," Essie went on. "And it's people like that who'd be the first to call *my* parents traitors."

"Don't cry, Essie, or can you at least take off my dress?"

"Sorry," Essie said, wiping her dripping nose on her bare arm. She removed Florence's dress, revealing the girders of her yellowed brassiere and drawers. "Oh, look at me," she cried. "I didn't even have new bloomers or a proper girdle to bring along with me. If my mother was still alive, she'd have taken me to get one, but I didn't want to ask my father for the money. Oh, Florence, he didn't even come to see me off. And the worst part is, I'm to blame. It's true, because I *told* him not to come. I didn't think he'd listen. . . . Don't make that face!"

"I'm not."

"I thought he'd come anyway. But I said so many nasty things to him. Such *awful* things . . . See, we were all supposed to be on this ship together. My papa, my little sister Lilly, and my mother too . . . Oh, you'll think I'm horrible if I tell you."

"Sweetie, I wouldn't." Florence picked up Essie's old clothes off the floor and sat down beside her. "Whatever it is, it's all behind us now."

2.

AGNOSIA

FOR MOST OF MY LIFE PEOPLE HAVE CALLED ME YULIK, THOUGH I GO BY
Julian now. In spite of my coming into the world on the black banks of the
Volga, my birth certificate unambiguously states my nationality as "American." This honor I owe to my mother, Florence Fein, who at the time must
have thought it wiser to have me catalogued as a Yankee than a Yid. (She
herself could claim both heritages.) In 1943, on the cusp of a not at all
certain victory against the Nazis, her decision might have been driven by
the same logic that ensured that all the Jewish boys of my generation
would proceed through life with their foreskins intact. Then again, maybe
it wasn't the invading fascists that Florence was nervous about, but her
own Soviet comrades.

Who the hell can say?

I never asked my mother what was behind her decision, and I doubt
she would have given me a straight answer if I had. Suppressions and
omissions were an unshakable habit of hers, as they are of so many who
carry on unreciprocated romances with doomed causes. As camouflage,
"American" turned out to be about as good a cover for "Jew" as a sweater
on a Chihuahua. It did, however, alter my life in one important respect: it
gave a clear shape (a sovereign border, you might say) to my feelings of
apartness. Maybe there is nothing remarkable about this today, when no
worse fate can befall a child than to be ordinary. But in my time, when a
modest, inconspicuous presence was a useful commodity, my American-

ness was the port-wine stain that made me a freak and aristocrat. Even at the state children's home, where I was terrified of the other boys learning of my difference, I nursed a bitter pride at my secret connection to the avocado-colored portion of the map about which our teachers spoke with such reverent loathing.

It was not until I actually set foot on American soil in 1979 that I was suddenly turned back into another Soviet pumpkin. The polite confusion on my patrons' faces told me that the English I'd been speaking (largely in my head) since I was a child was about as comprehensible to them as Mandarin. I'd like to think that in my three decades as an American citizen I've come far in reclaiming my patrimony. I drink my beer chilled. I floss. I tip at least 15 percent. My accent is now of indeterminate origin. On the occasions when I'm obliged to travel back to Russia, I'm pleased to discover that my former countrymen identify me first and foremost by the blue color of my passport.

So why have I been traveling back? The simplest answer is that I am now employed in a business that has done more to advance the cause of Cooperation and Friendship between our two glorious nations than have decades of international peace talks and nonproliferation treaties. I am speaking of Big Oil. For the past four years I've been employed by one of the half-dozen oil-and-gas firms whose Washington offices form a tight little semicircle (or noose, some might say) around our nation's capital. My own expertise is in icebreakers—those thousand-ton megalosauruses that chew through glaciers so that you and I can get our tanks pumped with the dregs of Paleozoic graveyards. Now that several of these graveyards have been discovered in the Russian Arctic, I have no shortage of work. Every few months, I pack my polycarbonate Rimowa and board the red-eye for Moscow. By morning, I'm clearing customs at Sheremetyevo under the wordless gaze of a matron whose exquisite contempt in comparing my face with the mug shot in my passport reminds me that in Russia I am, like any other national, a nobody. For this refreshing humiliation I am handsomely compensated.

Lest it seem that money is the only reason I fly back, it isn't so. What I most count on is the chance to see my son, Lenny, who for the past nine years has been chasing his own fortune in Moscow. Chasing, indeed. There are a few things Lenny hasn't told me that I happen to know anyway. But persuading my son to cut his losses in Russia and come home has proven even harder than extricating my mother was thirty years ago. Wanderlust and stubbornness are homologous traits in our family. Were Florence still alive, she would be impressed with how her grandson has managed to dig in his heels. Her own refusal to budge was a masterpiece of dignified mutiny as monumental as one of Gandhi's hunger strikes. In 1978, as we were getting ready to exit, she not only declined to emigrate with the rest of the family; she even refused to utter the word "America." Only after a brush with incapacity did she start timidly, testingly, bringing up the topic. "Are you still planning to go to . . . *that place?*" was how she put it. *That place.* A couple of years ago, I read about a neurological condition that can afflict victims of stroke. A person suffering from this condition can look at a lightbulb and tell you its components—the filament, the wire, the glass. He can describe the shape and its properties. But for all the gold in Araby he'll never be able to screw it in and turn it on. "Agnosia" is the formal name of the condition. Ancient Greek for "not-knowing." There is no injury to the senses, no loss of memory. Simply, a person has lost the ability to recognize something for what it is. I've often wondered if a similar kind of menace had gotten its fingers around Mama.

Maybe I would have been less hard on my mother had she been another ordinary Russian afflicted with that national form of Stockholm syndrome they call patriotism. But she wasn't. She was, like I am now, an American. More so. She had grown up on the elm-lined streets of Flatbush, Brooklyn, debated the Federalist Papers at Erasmus Hall High, studied mathematics among the first emancipated coeds at Brooklyn College, tuned in to Roosevelt's Fireside Chats, and watched Cagney kiss Harlow on the projection screen at the Paramount. No matter how much she pretended to have forgotten it all, I was never convinced that all that New York upbringing could be stripped from memory like so much scabbed paint. Surely, I insist even now, she must have once known what freedom smelled like.

3.

BROOKLYN

SHE WOULD HAVE DONE ANYTHING TO ESCAPE FLATBUSH, GONE ANY-
where to find a life of meaning and consequence that surely existed beyond the pale of Brooklyn—a territory that, like Ireland or Poland, was
always doomed to lie in the shadow of a superior power.

As salutatorian of her class at Erasmus Hall, she'd set her sights on attending one of the esteemed private women's colleges, where she would
spend four years mingling with other intellectually curious and uncon-
ventional young women. That Florence had believed her father would finance this plan said less about her self-regard than about Solomon Fein's
ability to shield from his family certain obvious financial realities. Her first
year at Hunter College was largely spent getting over her disappointment.
Then, in October of her sophomore year, the stock market collapsed, and
her unhappiness was replaced with astonishment at her good fortune to
be attending college for free. The following year saw another unexpected
turnabout: the Brooklyn branch of Hunter merged with the City College
of New York, and was spun off into Brooklyn College, the first coed public
campus in the city. To call it a "campus," as Florence observed, was a
stretch; having as yet no buildings of its own, the college rented class-
rooms in five different office buildings in the restless business district that
circled Borough Hall. Dodging trolleys and manning the obstacle course
of Fulton Street, Florence soon discovered the cafés and cafeterias of
downtown Brooklyn, where lawyers from nearby courts popped in for

corned-beef sandwiches, as did congregations of curly-headed students who formed, if not the brain center, then a close synapse of the student movement. She hadn't even known there *was* a student movement. But here they were, arguing Lenin versus Marx, Stalin versus Trotsky, not arguing so much as yelling at one another across the long wooden tables while brandishing slices of rye. At first she had been intimidated by these kids from New Utrecht High who'd read William Foster's *Strike Strategy*, who knew how to set up a committee, how to print a pamphlet, how to organize. While the girls and boys at Erasmus were reenacting the Lincoln-Douglas debates in civics class, these Bensonhurst kids were staging milk boycotts to protest the price hikes of their high-school lunches.

It struck her as crazy that she'd ever considered attending a college where the girls adopted finishing-school attitudes and the teachers tried to govern their morals and behavior. At Brooklyn College, the girls were no less militant than the boys, cutting their hair, wearing sacklike dresses and sandals without stockings, knocking on doors to advocate birth control to the Irish housewives. And they were militant in another way that Florence had yet to follow. Under the blessing of their patron saint, the anarchist Emma Goldman, they felt the need to give away their virtue freely, so as not to commit the more venial sin of trafficking their virginity under the hypocritical code of Capitalism.

EACH WEEK, FLORENCE STOPPED to examine the Help Wanted section of the campus bulletin board. "Part-time work for Physical Science majors," a posting might read. And when she, a mathematics major, would inquire, the job would turn out to involve not physics or chemistry or astronomy, but lugging trash cans or mopping snow slush. The administration would post jobs by major to prevent the whole college from applying.

She learned of the job at Amtorg from a professor for whom she did occasional secretarial work. He told her an organization uptown was seeking a secretary with a head for numbers. "You know a bit of Russian, don't you? That could be helpful."

It was her father who had insisted she study mathematics, with the advice that the insurance business sailed on an even keel even in the severest economic storms. Florence was fairly sure, however, that the job the professor had in mind had nothing in common with the life-insurance company where Solomon Fein spent his days as an actuary.

"The Soviet Trade Mission?" She had a vague recollection of it from reading the newspapers. It operated as a de facto embassy, since America didn't officially acknowledge the Bolshevik government. "Aren't they mostly . . . spies?" she inquired uncertainly.

The professor, a grizzled old progressive who smelled of tobacco and menthol, did his best not to look disappointed. "I didn't peg you for a reader of the yellow press, Florie. Anyway, the contracts department is staffed mostly by Americans," he said reassuringly. "And if you're nervous that they'll ask you to present your Party card, not to worry. No American who works at Amtorg is permitted to be an active communist. The diplomacy is too delicate. Mainly, they put together import-export contracts for companies selling goods to the Russians—tractors, cars, factory equipment, and so on."

"I thought we didn't do business with the Bolsheviks."

Again the man indulged her with a downturned smile. "During the Napoleonic Wars, ships traveled along the English Channel, carrying goods back and forth between England and France. This, while the two nations were locked in bloody battle. Are we at war with the Russians?"

THE SOVIET TRADE MISSION—otherwise known as Amtorg—maintained its quarters on tony Fifth Avenue, keeping up a legal fiction as a private corporation of the State of New York. It was common wisdom in diplomatic circles that the Americans who staffed its posts, including Florence's boss, Scoop Epstein, took their orders straight from Moscow. But if this were so, Florence wouldn't have been able to guess it from the speeches Scoop delivered at luncheons in the Financial District to the managers of American import-export firms. He spoke not about the world proletariat but about the "Soviet awakening to the value of American technology and efficiency." He told American businessmen of the million Russian peasants who had never heard of Rykov or Bukharin but who all knew the name of Henry Ford. It was a fact not lost on Florence that, although the American government continued to deny the U.S.S.R. official recognition, American businesses were happy to provide their newly flush Bolshevik customers with steel and lathes and roller bearings and rebar and tractors while their American clients remained cash poor.

At Amtorg she was not much more than a secretary, but the tedious work reliably filled her with excitement for its proximity to the cranking gears of power. Even modest acts felt momentous. Blue-penciling a contract for nine thousand tons of steel for export to the Ural Mountains seemed an act of more heft and consequence than all the angry noise made by a hundred cafeteria commies. In a single week she might place an order on behalf of Russia's AMO factory with the Toledo Machine and Tool Company for a hundred thousand dollars' worth of cold-stamping presses, and another order with the Greenlee Company in Rockford, Illinois, for multi-cylinder lathes, or call up the Hamilton Foundry and Machine Company of Ohio to commence talks for a technical-assistance agreement to help the Russians produce two hundred thousand chassis for their new ZIS-model automobiles.

Now that she was free of the spell of the college dining halls, she was willing to admit how little she'd enjoyed the fulminations and rhetoric. All that talk of smashing the bourgeois machine of the state offended her values of discipline and hard work. It seemed pointless to desire to overthrow something old when you could help build something new. In the pragmatic tranquillity that underlay the chaos of the busy office, she felt the peculiar pleasure of a world shedding its bruised skin and admitting her into some inner sanctum—a chamber in which the steady whoosh and hum of typewriters and telefax machines was like the muffled murmur of a heart pumping blood through a powerful arterial system.

Scoop Epstein, a rotund, soft-featured boy in his fifties, was many things at once: generous, sly, boastful of his connections, and adoring of his young assistant, sometimes taking Florence along to his meetings with Manhattan financiers and Indiana manufacturers. But before her first luncheon on Wall Street, he had plainly addressed her legs: "We'll need to find you something different to wear. Wool stockings won't do."

"But it's still winter!" she protested.

"Is it? I must not have noticed. You have perfectly lovely legs, Florence. May I be frank with you? Wool stockings are for nuns and apple sellers. There's no harm in making yourself attractive." Because Scoop's frankness felt less like a come-on and more like the confidential guidance of a mentor, she followed him that morning from Fifth Avenue to a wholesaler he knew on Seventh, who turned out to be a cousin. Atop a footstool, Florence raised her arms while this other, quieter Epstein circled her waist with tape and worked his assertive fingers under her bust and around her narrow hips, molding stiff fabrics to her body. Her new wardrobe included a felt jacket with velvet piping and a pencil skirt tailored high against her waist, a silk crepe blouse in cream, and another in apricot satin. The cost of these clothes, heavily discounted, would be deducted from her salary. At the sight of this new Florence in the mirror, she experienced the vexing pleasure of at last seeing her own true self.

"Beautiful," Scoop reassured her.

"Hah. They'd crucify me if I showed up at campus like this."

"The fellows we're meeting aren't looking to lunch with Mother Jones."

"I feel like a banker's moll," she said in an anguish of self-admiration, turning sideways to an even more flattering angle.

"Florie, honey, if you're going to wear your politics on your sleeve, you'll get further with nicer sleeves."

But at home, her mother said, "You think those clothes make you special? They make you as common as dirt." Her parents knew whom she was working for and didn't approve. Still, with her older brother Harry out of work and expecting a baby, they could hardly advise her to quit her job. Only, in the evening, she could hear her father arguing with her mother; it was Zelda, after all, who'd pushed *his Florie* out into the world to earn a piece of bread, out into the workplace, with all its moral dangers. And why? Were they starving? He had been against it from the beginning. With Florence, he was more careful. "Florie, why do you need these people? They're snakes. A girl with a head like yours—you learned to read and write before you were five," he reminded her. "And I remember in first grade, when all the parents came to school to watch the children read poems, you could recite yours and everyone else's, too. The other kids forgot their lines and you'd whisper them. Whole verses you learned by heart." He offered to help her find a job in his company. But at a time like this, when Metropolitan Life had recently given the axe to a quarter of its agents, they both knew that a girl—even one with a mathematics degree—would do little more than fetch coffee and take dictation. And so, in the end, it was not her mother's scorn but her father's unrelenting praise, his stubborn belief in her specialness, that felt the most infuriating.

Florence's small salary was not enough to plug the hole in the dam of changes that were taking place on Beverly Road. One evening, in the kitchen, Florence was pulled from her reading by the sound of dishes being stacked in the dining room. The angry clang of her mother's tidying made her pause, but it was her father's voice Florence heard first: "You haven't told her yet?"

"You said after Rosh Hashanah."

"And after Rosh Hashanah there's Yom Kippur, and after that . . ."

"Yes, Sol, I need help those weeks! You think our daughter is going to cook for all your relatives?"

"Okay, but we have to give the woman warning *now*. It's only right."

The clanging stopped. "I don't know how I feel about this whole idea, Sol."

"We used to get on fine without a maid. She only comes in three days a week, now that the kids are big."

Florence set down the apple she'd been chewing. The mention of Sissy—her old nanny, who only months earlier had been willing to endure listening to her rehearse lines for the college's production of *Dido* while she mopped the floor—made it painful to swallow.

"I'm not twenty." Her mother spoke from the other side of the kitchen door. "You can't expect me to bend on my knees and scrub those stairs."

"Florie can help."

"Florence? She can't wring out a rag. Maybe if you had ever let her lift a finger around here. God forbid—'Don't trouble Florie, she's reading. Let the girl study.'"

"All right, then," her father said in a reasoning voice. "If you don't want to let Sissy go, we can stop the synagogue dues."

"Have you lost your mind?"

"We hardly ever go."

"Sidney has his Bar Mitzvah in April."

"He can have it at the Community Center. At least their rabbi doesn't have three assistants writing his speeches while he goes off playing golf."

"How ungrateful would it make us look, Sol, after Cantor Kleiner has worked so hard with Sidney on his stutter?"

A silence came from Sol—a silence in which Florence could hear all her father's grievances with organized religion in general, and with the fancy Midwood congregation in particular. As an actuary who had spent his years tabulating the most meaningful occurrences in people's lives—their births and marriages, their children, their accidents, their sicknesses, and, in the end, their deaths—Sol no more believed in the God of Abraham than in a God that behaved like a blackjack dealer. But the atheist Jew was, nonetheless, a Jew, and so he answered, "Only until April, Zelda."

ZELDA LET SISSY GO just before the Christmas holiday. To Florence her mother gave a shoebox of items Sissy had left behind and asked her to send it by post. The box was shockingly light and contained little: a pair of Bakelite hair combs, a pocket Bible stamped with the "Active Service" seal of 1914, and a square headscarf of crepe de chine. Perhaps it was the air of hermitry these items radiated, or the odor of Sissy's bergamot hair oil still lingering in the scarf—the smell of Florence's own recent childhood—that kept her from sending it back immediately. But what Florence now felt, as she gathered these orphaned objects in her hands, was a sense of such astonished guilt and solidarity that she could barely breathe. Her parents were away, visiting Harry in Riverdale, while Sidney was getting dressed for Haftorah class. Adjusting his collar, he followed Florence from room to room, talking about the Cardinals' new roster. "They shouldn'ta traded Grimes to the Cubs," he complained with his amateur's astuteness. Ever since the Yankees had hammered his beloved Dodgers, he believed it was time for them to pay. The only team in the league with a shot at beating the Yanks were the Cardinals, but they were pursuing a bad strategy. "They're picking off veteran players from the minors and raiding old guys from the clubs. It'll give 'em a few easy wins. But it's no way to build a team." He trotted after Florence down the stairs, his hair molded to his head like a cornhusk. Her brother's nonstop talking normally entertained her; talking and thinking were not, for Sidney, separate acts, just one revolving mechanism. But this morning his chatter was like the noise of a foghorn in her ear. She placed Sissy's package in her book bag and strapped it shut.

"Where are you going?"

"To mail Sissy's things back to her."

"Why can't she take them herself when she comes back?"

Florence paused long enough to turn and stare at him. Had their mother not *told* him? "Where have you been, Sidney? She's not coming back."

"What do you mean, not coming . . . ?"

"Mom fired her. Why do you think she hasn't been around?"

"I thought she was on vacation, like us."

"Vacation?" She rummaged her bag for the scrap with the Harlem address.

"Did she do something to make Mom mad?"

"Don't you have to get ready for Hebrew school?"

But he wouldn't quit. "Did she steal something?"

"No, idiot! Why would you say that?"

"I don't know. Why did Mom fire her?"

"Because we can't afford house help right now, *capisci?* Or haven't you noticed? Harry is unemployed, and we have to pay dues at the synagogue for the rest of the year so you can stand in front of everyone for ten minutes and stutter your way through three verses of Torah."

The distress on his face was out of proportion to what she'd expected. The green-brown of his eyes seemed to shatter like the glass of a medicine bottle. "It's not my f-f-fault! I don't even want to d-do it!"

He was nearly shouting at her.

"Too late, lemming. You'll be made a man whether you like it or not, even if we have to eat turnips all year round."

Maybe it was rotten to break it to him like that, but he deserved the truth. "I've got to work today. I'll be back by dinner," she said, and placed her gloved fingers on his head in a way she hoped was affectionate. When he didn't move, she had no choice but to leave him, like a collapsed puppet, and let herself out into the cold February morning.

SHE UNLOCKED HER BOSS'S office, expecting solitude, and instead found Scoop with his feet up on his desk, turning the fresh pages of a new *Daily Worker.*

"You're back early!"

"It appears so."

He had been gone all week, traveling through the Middle West by Pullman and brokering deals with steel manufacturers. Now he removed his buckskins from the corner of his desk and said, "You know what I love about America?" He smiled up at the ceiling fan and quoted Whitman: "'I am large! I contain multitudes!'" Stopped at a station somewhere in Ohio, he told Florence, he'd watched as a woman and child emerged from a tent camp across the tracks. The woman led the boy carefully across the planks so the child could crouch and do his business. Then, with a glance at the train car, she lifted up her own dress and squatted nearby, offering the passengers a defiant view of her bony bottom. Florence could hear in Scoop's retelling an exuberance for the bountiful contempt his beloved America had brought upon itself.

He tossed down the *Daily Worker* and steepled his fingers. "Florence, I have a proposition," he said. A group of Soviet engineers were journeying to Cleveland for eight weeks, to receive training in the construction of steel plants by the engineering firm McKee and Co. The delegation was due to arrive in mid-June. The men were in need of a translator and intermediary. "We both know you're tired of being just a secretary."

"You're asking me to go to Cleveland?"

"You'd have a new title, sweetheart." He framed his fingers as if around a banner. "Commerce Liaison."

"But, Scoop, I don't know anything about steel mills. And my Russian is only so-so."

"Some of the guys speak English. And they don't need another engineer—just someone to assist them in the more practical aspects of American life, keep 'em out of trouble."

She wondered how exactly she was meant to keep a group of grown Russian men out of trouble, but she didn't want to disturb Scoop's faith in her by asking. Instead, she said, "Where would I live?"

"We'll set you up in a place of your own."

"An apartment?"

"Sure, if that's what you'd like."

"I'm not sure my parents would approve. Living so far away and all."

Scoop turned up his hands. "Florie, we both know this Trade Mission won't have its doors open forever. It's only a matter of time before they open up a real embassy in Washington. Roosevelt's no Hoover. He knows the Bolsheviks aren't going away. And a smart girl with field experience in diplomacy . . ." His eyebrows lifted suggestively. "She could be a useful asset. A real contender for an embassy job."

THE IMMEDIATE DIFFICULTY, FLORENCE realized while riding the high rail back to Brooklyn, was how to break the news to her parents. Even if she

could convince them that being a chaperone to six foreign men was a legitimate occupation for a twenty-three-year-old girl, even if she were to
contrive some smooth elision denying the political nature of her work and
claim she was merely a bookkeeper, even then Sol and Zelda would certainly take charge of her accommodations. They would call up the roster
at Midwood Synagogue until they found a family with respectable relations in Cleveland who could install her in a spare room and chaperone
her *in loco parentis*. But what choice did she have? A paycheck could not
win a girl's independence.

THE SKY ABOVE THE ELMS was turning violet by the time she got back to
Flatbush. She let herself in through the kitchen door. Hearing her parents'
voices coming from the dining room, she braced herself to plead her case
on the subject of Cleveland. But someone else was in there with them—a
familiarly didactic voice declaiming loudly. "We understand that some of
the boys this age might have certain *injudicious* reactions to the more sensitive materials in the *Toy-rah*—the laws dealing with bodily purity, dis-
charges, and so on and so on. . . ."

Florence pushed the door a crack and saw Rabbi Soffer sitting at the
table, his huge palm squeezing Sidney's bony shoulder. "Jokes have their
place, but we also expect the boys to exercise certain mah-*toority*, especially given this important preparation for entry into Jewish adulthood."

"What exactly did he say in class, Rabbi?" her father inquired cau-
tiously. "Sidney?"

The accused was silent.

"Shmuel?" the rabbi asked, calling Sidney by his Hebrew name. Having brought the boy before justice, he now appeared to be acting in lieu of
counsel, trying to persuade Sidney that if he only paraded his contrition
everything would be righted. But Sidney was taking the Fifth.

"What he told the boys was that a 'kosher' woman was one who waited
three hours after the butcher leaves before, er"—the rabbi cleared his
throat—"engaging in relations with the milkman."

A single snort of laughter escaped her father's nose. "I don't know
where he heard that, Rabbi."

"It does not matter if he heard it in the street, or at home. . . ."

"Certainly not at home," Zelda objected.

"Rabbi, he's usually a good, respectful boy," said Sol. "I don't know what's gotten into him."

It pained Florence to see her brother on trial. She of all people knew what a mouth the kid had on him, yet she also knew that Sidney was usually wise enough to keep his jokes out of earshot of his teachers. She tiptoed unnoticed up the stairs to her room. Soon she could hear her parents, full of apologies, escorting the rabbi to the door. The minute the door was shut, the full force of their rage erupted on Sidney.

She went quietly to her bed, lay down, and squeezed her eyes closed, the better to shut out the sounds of the shouting downstairs. She awoke a half-hour later to find her mother standing over the bed. "Did you tell Sidney it was his fault we let Sissy go?"

Florence sat up.

"Did you tell your brother we were going to be eating turnips all year because of his Bar Mitzvah classes?"

With small blue eyes and thin lips, Zelda's was a face made for disappointment.

"I meant we had to tighten our pockets. I heard Daddy say so himself."

"What you *meant*, I don't know. I know that child listens to everything you say. He does whatever you tell him, and now he's trying to get himself kicked out of Hebrew school on your account."

"I didn't tell him to do that!" But there was no uncowardly way to defend herself. "Can I talk to him?"

"Don't you dare! Do you know what that boy feels the absolute worst about?"

Florence said nothing.

"Telling on you." Her mother's face was heavy with disapproval as she left the room, as though to suggest that even her brother's loyalty was evidence of her selfishness.

And where, Florence wondered, was Sissy now—the woman who had practically raised her? Was it so selfish to care about others besides her family?

As she heard the resolute sound of a door closing in its jamb, Florence felt an equal resolve in her heart. She would not ask. She would not plead. She would not argue or supplicate. The next morning, she let Scoop buy her a ticket for Cleveland.

4.

GRAPHOMANIACS

"FUELING THE FUTURE"—THAT'S OUR SLOGAN, HANGING RIGHT ABOVE the doors I walk through each morning into our lobby, an acre of black and white marble that runs past Reception and up to a back wall of blue and red pixels pulsing with the movements of Continental Oil's three hundred–plus ships as they set sail from ports all over the globe. This breathtaking lobby is the first place I took my old friend Yasha Gendler when he paid me a visit in D.C. In hindsight, this was an error.

Half a decade had passed since Yasha and I had seen each other. He had flown in from Haifa, a trip he undertook every few years to visit his adult son in Bethesda. "Come downtown, I'll show you where I work," I offered when he called. If anyone could appreciate the wild course my life had taken, it was Yasha, the one person alive who not only knows my childhood nickname—Yul'ka—but feels it necessary to repeat it at every opportunity. As boys of six and seven, we'd played jacks and *nozhiki* on the same common hallway, over oak floorboards ruined with lye soap. By 1945, when my parents brought me from Kuibyshev to Moscow as a teething toddler, the apartment (whose original owners had escaped the Bolsheviks in 1922) had been partitioned and subdivided so many times that there were seven families sharing it in schismatic harmony. My mother had been in the Soviet whirlpool for eleven years by this point. Enough time, I imagine, to unlearn the bourgeois habits of her native Brooklyn, to accustom herself to the farting and shouting of her neighbors, to doing her wash by hand in the collective tub, to keeping her dry food locked up in her wardrobe. But where Florence was alien, I was native—Yasha and I both products of that pinnacle of evolution known as the Communal Apartment. Western scholars like to say our Soviet *kommunalki* were places devoid of personal space. This is not true. What better testament to private dominion could there be than the dense tangle of seven separate buzzers on the front door? The seven separate kerosene burners in the kitchen? The seven separate wooden toilet seats, which each tenant scrupulously tucked under his arm as he marched to the single communal toilet?

Those were the good days, before our real troubles began. Before the disappearances.

The next time I saw Yasha was in 1962, when we were reunited as students at the university. We both sat in a course called Fundamentals of Cybernetics, taught by an aging redheaded asthmatic who'd been tossed out in the early fifties for pursuing research in computer science, a field banned by Stalin for being one of the mercantile whores of imperialism. A decade later, it occurred to someone up top that the country was too far behind in its race with the Americans, and the disgraced professor was tracked down (he was mixing resins in an industrial-paint plant) and reinstated to teach the very subject he'd been fired for pursuing. The little man's impiety revealed itself on the first day of class, when he wrote his full name on the blackboard: Arnold Peysakhovich Lubarsky. "Most people call me Arnold Petrovich," he said, turning to face us. "You can call me whatever you prefer." But that enormous "Peysakhovich" stayed on the board for the rest of the lecture, a patronym not merely Jewish, but so boldly and undauntedly Yid that I couldn't keep myself from twisting my neck to glance at the faces behind me. Lubarsky might as well have announced he was Ben-Gurion himself come to read us a lecture on Zionism. Thus glancing backward, I locked eyes with the stunned face of Yasha Gendler, possibly the only other Jew in the room who'd also managed to pole-vault the university's invisible quotas.

Lubarsky was the only professor at the university who dared mock that to which the state had given its approving stamp. One afternoon, he interrupted his own lecture to interrogate the lyric of a popular song. " 'I love you, Life, and I hope that the feeling is mutual' . . . Can anyone tell me what in the world this *means*?" He removed his spectacles to scan our timid faces.

Each time Yasha and I walked into his lecture, we were entering a universe whose plane geometry held nothing in common with the contorted realities of our daily lives. With each theorem and arched brow, Lubarsky seemed to be saying to us, "Young people, what sense is there in these 'laws' that are violated by the very officials who issue them? How can they compare to the eternal, immutable laws of Newton, Pascal, Bernoulli, Einstein?"

Neither Yasha nor I ever forgot our little redheaded professor. Lubarsky immigrated to Israel and died a few years thereafter. This was the sort of news that Yasha stayed abreast of and reported to me faithfully in our annual New Year's Eve phone call. In this way, he was more like a relative than a friend, our relationship cemented by mutual history. Years could pass without our seeing each other, but then we'd meet and Yasha might say, "Remember that New Year's party when your father made costumes for the kids? We were both crows—he made us caps with cardboard beaks. It was the Year of the Ox, and everyone hung a picture of a bull on their door?" And just like that, I would remember.

The technological revolution arrived at the perfect time for brainy kids like Yasha and me. Strategically indifferent to politics, but not as yet perceiving ourselves as anything other than loyal Soviet citizens, we chose technical fields that seemed relatively immune to propaganda yet unimpeachably useful to society. Though we smirked at slogans, we were no less idealistic or enamored of ourselves than that first generation of revolutionaries. Instead of barricades, we believed in satellite launchers. Instead of marches, we had particle accelerators.

But, as I was reminded upon our reunion in D.C., I had long shed my idealistic notions, whereas Yasha's had multiplied, like barnacles on a stranded vessel.

"Well, it's what you always wanted, isn't it?" He yawned, affecting a grand lack of interest in the pulsing spectacle of Continental's lobby, and the view of the National Mall from my office window. "A big-time career. That's why you left, after all."

The boy who'd once been as lanky as a telephone pole was now a telephone pole with a gut. He'd let his stringy gray hair get too long, and now raked it back like a pompadour across his high forehead.

"Why I *left*?" I tried to clarify.

"Sure. They denied you your Ph.D., so you said, 'Nothing more to do here, time to pack up and go to Ah-merica.'"

"I would have left sooner or later. We all did."

"Ah, but if they'd given you your fancy doctorate, you're telling me you wouldn't have happily stayed and built ships for *them*? Hell, who do you think you're building your ships for *now*? Who are you making rich? The same bastards who had red telephones on their desks."

"I see," I said. "So you left for the *right* reasons, and I left for the *wrong* ones."

"Hey, I applied to leave before the *word* 'refusenik' was invented. I'm not boasting. I'm just talking about principles. When they finally let me leave I'd been working six years as a janitor, not a physicist. A little bird whispers and suddenly you're tossed out of your department and the only work you can find is cleaning elevators. But I'll say this: in all those years I never compromised my convictions. I never gave up my activity like they wanted me to."

Yasha loved alluding to his dissident "activity," which as far as I knew was limited to attending a few underground Hebrew lessons to meet girls. He hadn't gotten much past the Aleph-Bet, either with the Hebrew or with the girls. "Yasha, is it my fault," I said, "that 'out of principle' you elected to immigrate to a country that enjoys a Euro-socialist lifestyle of month-long vacations and forced unemployment? If you wanted a career in research, you could have had one. Picked up where you left off."

"Oh sure, with all the kids graduating every year from the Technion."

But Yasha became more animated at the Air and Space Museum. Forced early retirement had given him abundant time to obsess over Israel's parliamentary politics while attacking various theorems whose proofs he had abandoned as a young physicist. He was also, he informed me, writing a "popular book" on the lives of the great mathematicians. At present he was working on a chapter about Niels Henrik Abel, a Norwegian who had invented group theory by age nineteen, yet died, penniless and rejected by the Academy, of pulmonary tuberculosis at the age of twenty-six.

Yasha was still talking about this unheralded genius when we arrived at the upscale restaurant that I'd carefully selected for our lunch. But then he abruptly switched topics, from the underappreciated dead to the overrated living.

"A few weeks ago, I open *Vesti*, our Russian paper," he said, "and there's a review of some book. Some samizdat press, but the author's name I recognize. You remember our apartment neighbors, the Vainers? Their two girls, Dita and Marina . . ."

I conjured up a vague memory of blue hair-bows and white pinafores. "The family that had the Ukrainian relatives staying for three weeks at a time?"

"The same one. The father with the drooping mustache. Dita immigrated to Israel, and a couple of years ago, she writes the father's 'memoirs.' Full of inaccuracies. Forget the small ones. She writes that, because my mother was never arrested, she must have been the informer in our *kommunalka*. Can you imagine drawing that conclusion? Very scientific. I wanted to pick up the phone and call the publisher."

"What's the point?"

"The point? To ask what this Dita's process of deduction was! And *mezhdu prochim*, by the way, if there was an informer, it was probably Vainer himself. Or Flora Solomonovna."

This was the point where I stopped hearing. The sounds of the restaurant rushed into my ears like an ocean roar. Flora Solomonovna. Florence. My mother. Yasha was still talking ecstatically, gesticulating with his French fry. He must have forgotten for a moment who his audience was. "What are you talking about?" I interrupted. "You're saying *my mother* was the apartment informer?"

Yasha reluctantly bit his fry. A familiar twitch at the corner of his mouth told me this was no slip. He'd meant to say it. But his voice carried a note of regret, even sympathy. "Look, I wasn't there. My mother, she lost her mind a little by the end. I don't know who was right, who was wrong—and I don't care. But to put it on paper like that! That's what got me."

"Come on, now, Yasha, I didn't pull you by the tongue. You started, please finish. What did she say?"

"Who, Mama?"

I was silent.

He palmed back his untidy gray hair. "Flora used to talk to her . . . when all the chaos started in that apartment with the arrests. Flora told her, 'Rosa, if you're taken away, they can send your boy to live with relatives. If it happens to me, where is Yulik going to go? Lord knows they won't send him to *my* relatives in America. What will happen to him?' Mama said Flora was ready for anything. Ready to go to any length."

"Well, that's certainly more deductive." I felt something cold and stern taking hold of me. "A conversation over a kerosene burner."

Yasha was avoiding my eyes, wolfing down his brisket like a sword swallower, though the effort of it seemed to be causing him some difficulty now. "She said some things. What does it matter now? I'm sure you could get all the facts, if you wanted." I could see satisfaction wearing through his apologetic grin. "They've opened up the archives again. Didn't you tell me you always wanted to get your mother's classified files?"

I stared at him. He certainly never forgot a thing. It was true: I'd once lamented to him about missing my chance to obtain my parents' dossiers. That had been some time after '92, when Yeltsin had decreed that the KGB's old archives could be opened for anyone who'd had a relative arrested, killed, or sent away under Stalin. But a few years after the announcement, access to the files was again restricted, without warning or explanation, as is our Russian way.

Yasha mopped up the sauce on his plate. "You must have read about it. It was in all the papers."

"I haven't had much time for reading," I said.

"Of course." He gazed around at last, taking in the view with a look that said, *I can see you've kept yourself busy*. "Well, if you're still *interested*, you ought to do it soon. You never know, they could start reclassifying everything tomorrow. That's how it is—a few years of so-called freedom and they turn the screws tight again."

I smiled. "I'll give it some thought." I raised two fingers to signal for the check.

"Better to light one candle than to curse the darkness, right?" Yasha said, giving me a shrug and a half. "Especially if you're already traveling there for business."

"My trips are scheduled pretty tightly," I said.

He took another bite of beef. "Oh, I'm sure you'll find the time."

THAT NIGHT, I COULDN'T SLEEP, THINKING ABOUT ALL THE COUNTER-arguments I'd failed to make to Yasha's face. My mother, going "to any length" to save her child? Was he kidding? The defining tragedy of my mother's life was that she'd never had an instinct for family preservation. I recalled a conversation around our small kitchen table in Moscow. We'd been reminiscing about my old babysitter, Avdotya Grigorievna, the old woman who'd lived down the hall and was fond of me. Mama and I were laughing at old Auntie Dunya's queer way of rolling her "o"s when Florence suddenly said, "Her family was from one of those Volga villages, outside Gorky somewhere. She offered to help us get there, stay with her relatives for a while, keep low after Papa was arrested."

"So why didn't we go?" I said.

But she'd laughed at my dismay. "What was I going to do in a village? Pick turnips? Grow potatoes?"

"And what were you doing that was so special in Moscow? Writing letters to Comrade Stalin? Dragging me out before dawn so you could get a better spot on the prison lines?"

"I wasn't going to abandon your father. I had to find out what happened to him."

"You *knew* what happened to him. You were just drawing attention to yourself."

At this, her face acquired that gloss of incomprehension she liked to retreat behind when challenged. "I couldn't have just left him," she said irritably.

"And what about *me*, Mama? Did you ever think about what would happen to me when they came for *you*?"

She chewed her food for a while before answering. Then she said, "Yes, I did think about it. Your father and I talked about it." This was a surprise to me. "We knew that, no matter what happened to either of us, they would never let anything bad happen to the children here. The children were always going to be taken care of."

Then it was my turn to laugh. Taken care of, indeed! It was a miracle my arm hadn't been emancipated from its socket when I was six years old by my state-appointed caretakers.

"No matter what *happened* to you, Mama?"

"Yes, no matter what happened to us, the country would always look after the children," she repeated like a robot.

"But, Mama," I said, "it didn't have to happen to you at all! Don't you get it? None of it *had* to happen to you, or to anybody."

Again the fact-proof screen was raised. Once more her eyes acquired the perplexed look that indicated all communication had ceased.

The list of subjects to which my mother could apply her famous silence was bounded by neither taste nor logic. I could understand her not wanting to elucidate on her years in the labor camp. But later, in the seventies, I almost never heard her speak about our family in America, though we were regularly in receipt of packages filled with sweaters, denim Levi's, instant coffee, and sneakers. And still later, in Brooklyn, she refused to let me change the name tag on the intercom in the vestibule of her Section 8. For the next eight years, I would buzz myself up to the flat of one deceased "Marquita Muñiz." If I asked Florence for whom all this subterfuge was intended, she simply answered, "Whoever needs to find me knows where I am."

Her tight-lipped-ness I'd long made my peace with. Why, then, after my lunch with Yasha Gendler, did it set my teeth on edge that there might be things about my mother—humiliating, atrocious things—that others knew, or believed they knew, and that I did not? Over and over I'd weighed every word I'd spoken to Yasha and felt ugly about the indifference I'd affected. "Touch shit and you're the one who smells"—that had always been my motto in dealing with unsavory innuendo. Not for a moment did I believe Yasha's suggestion that Florence had betrayed her friends and neighbors to the Soviet secret police. And yet I was pained by the unfair impression my mask of amused silence must have made on him.

And so, at midnight, with a glass of Rémy in my hand and wearing only my pajama bottoms, I found myself climbing the eight steps up to my attic office and booting up my Dell. I cracked open the skylight above my head and let in, through the liquid reaches of the night, the restless summer screeches of the cats and raccoons.

I called up a browser and in the search window, in Russian, typed "repressions," "stalin," "FSB," and "archives." In .45 seconds, the search engine returned 48,535 entries. Most of the links were to articles or academic texts, though those gave way to personal accounts: unpublished stories, poems, and screeds pertaining to brothers, fathers, uncles swallowed up by Stalin's terror. The Internet was undeniably demonstrating that the affliction of graphomania, to which Dostoyevsky claimed every Russian was predisposed, had blossomed into a disease as contagious as it was incurable. I shivered at the thought of adding my number to that roll of countrymen sucked back endlessly into the past.

When I limited my search to recent news stories I found what I was looking for—articles in several prominent newspapers covering the announcement that the Russian government had made just months earlier: The FSB had declassified millions of documents on victims of repressions. Relatives could now request information about those who'd been executed in prison or deported to camps.

I'd missed that window in '92. Traveling back *there* had been the furthest thing from my mind. I had work to do, and my mother's growing list of ailments to manage. And *she*, I was sure, had no desire to reopen chapters of her life she'd so carefully forgotten. Now I wondered if my failure to raise the topic with Mama had been inspired by a fear of trespass. Our relationship was fraught enough without adding this to the mix. That summer was still entangled for me with the memory of our last fight, which it anguished me now to recall. My mother had suffered a stroke. For days, her right side was paralyzed. Gradually, she began to recover her speech and movement. But there was no longer any question of her living alone. With unsettled feelings, Lucya and I relocated her to a nearby group home. She'd been at the facility for almost a year when doctors operated on her leg. A few days after she was released from the hospital, I visited Mama in the nursing home and discovered that the undersides of her legs and her backside were covered with bedsores. The so-called caretakers were clearly neglecting to sponge-bathe her in a timely manner and properly apply ointment to her sores. Enraged, I started berating the nursing assistant on duty—an imperious imbecile who continued to insist, even as I pointed to the subclean sheets, that everything had been done properly and "according to procedure." I informed the woman that only a mental incompetent could fail to see my mother was in serious discomfort. I demanded to speak with the doctor in charge. That was when the nurse stormed out, maybe to find her superior, more likely to complain about me while she sucked a cigarette or whatever it was she normally did instead of tending to her patients.

But all of this is only the backdrop to the crucial part of the story: While I had been chewing out the nurse, Florence, reclining in her metal bed, would not stop interjecting that everything was "just fine." Why was I making a fuss, she demanded, when she was feeling "absolutely all right" (though she had confessed quite the opposite to me minutes earlier)? There was "no need to make trouble," she kept insisting to me, smiling wanly at her idiotic caretaker.

I could understand her impulse to appease when the nurse was within hearing range, but she continued defending her own abuse even after the woman had stormed out. "These people know how to do their job."

"If these people were doing their jobs," I said, "your backside wouldn't be covered in sores."

As if not hearing me, she said, "They take care of it their own way. They know best."

They know what they're doing. *They* know best. It was the refrain I'd been hearing from her all my life. *For heaven's sake,* I thought, *you are eighty-two years old. You've been living in a free country for thirteen years now. Why must you compulsively parade your loyalty to whatever cruel and indifferent master happens at this moment to be pressing his boot on your neck?*

What I did in fact say was "Enough, Mama. I'm doing the talking now."

We remained locked in disagreement until the day she died, less than a year later. Now, with my mother buried along with her silences, I googled the names of activists quoted in the news articles, and came upon the object of my search: a website called MEMORIAL. Apparently, it was a Russian society dedicated to the rehabilitation of victims of Stalin's repressions. The website was forlorn-looking, a Gulag of defunct links, many of which, like the victims the site represented, were themselves "under rehabilitation." But toward the bottom was the name of the webhost, listed simply as Yevgeny@memo.ru. For a full minute, I let my cursor hover uneasily over the address. I pictured Yasha's gloating face. His invitation had been a challenge. What was I afraid of?

I double-clicked on the link and composed a short email asking how and to whom I was supposed to address my request for my parents' documents. Judging by the site, I didn't expect an answer. I pressed *send* and closed the window. Now Yasha could be satisfied.

Only I wasn't. If there were any secrets to be found, there was one person I knew who might reveal them. And I was overdue to pay him a visit.

THE AVALON WAS UNLIKE ANY PLACE TO WHICH ONE MIGHT ATTACH THE words "retirement" or "home." The reception area, with ferns and planted palms, large armchairs, carved wooden side tables with exotic ironware artifacts, and a grand Steinway in the corner, resembled a waiting room in some far-flung U.S. embassy. The residents looked like vacationers shuffling about in their loafers and Bermuda shorts. On my way out to the patio I consulted the calendar, on which the weekly activities were mixed in among such notable events as:

AMELIA EARHART IS LOST OVER THE PACIFIC, 1937 * Sundaes on Sundays 2:00. THE BIKINI DEBUT IN PARIS, 1946 * MARC CHAGALL BORN, 1887 * Morning Stretch BR 10:30 * Mind Boosters BR * MILTON BERLE BORN, 1908 * Caribbean Party w/Gary Lovett * JOHN DILLINGER KILLED BY THE FBI IN CHICAGO, 1934 * Spanish for Beginners BR 4:00 * Poker Pals GR 2:00 * JFK JR. CRASHES OFF MARTHA'S VINEYARD, 1999 * Shabbos Service * 10:30 Schmooze & News BR

Out on the brick terrace, I sat down on one of the striped-cushioned chairs and tilted my head back to drink in the sun. It wasn't long before my uncle Sidney emerged, sockless in espadrilles, with an issue of *The Wall Street Journal* tucked under his arm. He was moving more stiffly than I remembered. "Julian, my boy, good to see you! Sit back down."

"How's the colon, Uncle Sid?" I said.

"Very good. Doctor says I have the longest colon he's ever seen in a man my size. A spool of kishkes a mile long. Apparently, I've got plenty more to snip if the day comes again."

He was letting me off the hook. I felt terrible for not coming to see him sooner. Despite the easygoing way he managed to speak about it, the physical signs of his recent surgery and chemo were difficult to disguise. His lightweight khakis hid the sticks of his legs well enough, but his polo shirt couldn't do the same for his thin arms and wrists, his sharply protruding shoulders. My mother's brother Harry had passed away before we'd arrived in America; his children now lived in California. Sidney was the only one who remained who still remembered Mama.

"So you're feeling good?" I said.

"That's a different question."

"Looks like they keep you busy as a cruise line here. Spanish lessons. Board games."

"I skip all that kindergarten stuff."

"Poker your game?"

"Gin. I'll play a hand with anyone. What do you want for lunch?" he said when a member of the staff appeared. "Get him a cup of coffee, Deborah," Sidney instructed. "With cream, and some herring. You like herring? Good. An egg-white omelet for me, and a coffee, black."

The scrub-attired Deborah smiled and left with our unopened menus.

"How's Judy?" I said.

"My daughter and her husband are in Myanmar. Last spring it was Turkey. Each year a more exotic destination. I don't think middle New Jersey is far enough away for them to visit. But you know what they got here now?" he said, almost perking up. "Computer tutors! Twice a week, they teach us how to email our grandchildren, like nobody can pick up a telephone anymore. But me—I've started doing my stock trading on the computer now—just *a bissele*."

"I didn't know you still played the market."

"I don't *play*. I read the papers, I look at the numbers, and I only listen to myself." Talking about stocks always got Sidney animated. "Last week," he rushed to add, "my broker called, said he had a tip for me. I told him, 'Jeff, you've known me for twenty years. You know my name and you know where I live. The day you start giving me advice on trading is the day you're no longer my broker.'"

I'd loved Sid's disarmingly gruff manner since the first time I'd met my uncle, back in Moscow in 1959. I was fifteen; he, thirty-nine, a dapper vision in a gray flannel suit, brimmed hat, shiny black wingtips, striding to greet my mother and me in Sokolniki Park. As an executive at Dow, he'd managed to score himself a visa that year as a delegate to the Moscow World Exhibition, an enormous trade show intended as a technological pissing contest between Nixon and Khrushchev. My first memory of him is still engraved in the Kodak colors of that day, along with all the panoramas of American houses and automobiles, the "model kitchens" and washer-dryers of tomorrow and the other marvels of domestic technology meant to teach us Soviets about the humanity of our rivals. I saw him again twenty years later, at JFK Airport, upon our arrival in America. It was Sidney who, along with his now departed wife, Stella, had welcomed my family that first cold evening in New York, with his reassuring warning that the United States was just a labor colony with better food. And

Sidney who, while giving Lucya and me our first nighttime car tour of luxury Manhattan, told me, "You'll do all right here, Julian, as long as you don't let envy clog up all your senses." We'd found a mutual language right away; all the things I'd never had in common with my mother, I finally had with Sidney. Like me, he was no justice crusader. After he'd gotten out of the army, he'd taken his GI money and picked up a master's in chemical engineering at Northwestern, then spent the next forty years pragmatically embracing the American Dream his sister had turned her back on.

"It's good to trust only yourself. I guess that's why you haven't lost money," I said to him now.

"Oh sure, I've lost. Never enough to break the bank. I'm not a gambler. I grew up during the Depression, when folks was tossing themselves off buildings."

"So did Florence," I said. "I guess it taught her a different lesson."

Sidney took a moment to think and finally shrugged. "I was a kid. Florie, she was older. Folks who lived through that time, they were like survivors of a war. And your mother was always very sensitive to all the injustices. She'd get into fights at the dinner table with our father every night. At the Sabbath dinner, we all had to agree not to talk about politics."

"What would you talk about?"

"Well, I remember they once argued about the Harlan County miners who were getting beat up by the police for striking. Dad said, 'Nobody got jobs nowadays, and those ones are striking!' Well, Florie, she was quick, she said, 'They starve while they work, they might as well strike while they starve!' Every night it was something like that."

"Sounds like a slogan she probably heard," I said.

"Yeah, maybe," Sidney said charitably. "But she believed it. Once, she came home all bruised up after some demonstration. She claimed she struck a policeman who'd grabbed her. Clocked him with her pocketbook. We were just happy she didn't land herself in jail."

"Speaking of the police, Uncle Sid," I said, "I was wondering if she ever had any run-ins with the police in Russia. I mean the secret police. They would have kept tabs on American expats."

"What makes you wonder about that?" Sidney asked, a groove of disapproval forming between his brows.

"Just curious. Did she ever mention anything to you about that?"

"You mean when they tossed her in that dungeon?"

"Or . . . before that." I hesitated. "Did she ever say anything about getting harassed by the NKVD, or, I don't know . . ." I wanted to say "recruited," but couldn't get my lips to form the word. ". . . intimidated," I uttered at last.

Again Sidney's mouth got that sewn-up look of displeasure. "No, no, no. Florie wasn't scared of anything," he said.

He seemed to have misunderstood my question, and I felt somehow that I had lost my chance. To go back to the sensitive matter seemed impossible.

"Whatever or whoever she got involved with, she went into it *all the way*," Sid said. "Everybody in the family said it was that job at the Trade Mission that screwed her up. That it was all the Russians she got involved with. That she had some lover she followed there. In those days it wasn't nothing, you know. Not like today, a woman jumping into bed with any man like it's hopscotch. Everything done out in the open, like in a Macy's window. They talked about free love and all of that in my day, too. But I'm talking about among respectable people. Proper young women. It was *a shandeh un a charpeh*. You know what that means?"

I nodded sagely.

"A shame and a disgrace. A *Pah*-zor!"

"Po*zor*," I corrected.

The Yiddish Sidney and my mother had picked up growing up in Brooklyn was so mixed in with Russian, likely because of their grandparents' Litvak roots, that Sid sometimes mistook one for the other.

"She always had to be ahead of the train, your mother. And you know what happens to people who are ahead of the train?" He steadied his eyes on me once more. "They get run over!"

Uncle Sidney was not one for being figurative.

"But you're sure she wasn't a communist herself?" I asked.

"Nah! Look—all those people she knew were a little screwy in that respect. They had Sacco and Vanzetti's birthdays marked up on their calendars along with Christmas and New Year's. But, no, she wasn't a communist. Just restless. Wanted to do something *grand* with her life. She was always rubbing elbows with important people, politicians and so on. She met Senator Borah once—a big shot, head of the Foreign Relations Committee in the Senate. You know what he said about her?"

"What?"

" 'It's gals like Florence Fein who make the world go round.' What do you think of that?"

I tried to look impressed. I'd heard it before.

A grimace passed across Sidney's face. "Eh," he said, swiping a hand. "All those fools are in the ground now."

5.

___

DANGEROUS LIAISON

SHE STEPPED OFF THE TRAIN IN CLEVELAND INTO A WALL OF
101-degree heat. The sun had seared the crops and cooked the gardens.
The air smelled of cement and smashed tomatoes. The apartment Florence was promised turned out to be a boarder's room off an elevated porch
in a house belonging to a retired couple named Shulte. Nothing had been
fixed before her arrival. Three days into her sojourn, the collar around her
shower head came loose, falling in a cascade of rust mixed with a miserly
stream of water. It was 8:00 A.M., and she was late for work.

In her damp housecoat, Florence marched around to the Shultes' front
door. Her loud knocking brought forth no response. Through the door she
could hear the loud asthmatic voice of Father Coughlin on the radio barking about Jewish Bolshevism. Florence took a calming breath and knocked
more insistently. After a moment, Alva Shulte opened the door and offered
Florence her pinched, inhospitable smile.

"Is Mr. Shulte in? The shower's broken, and there's no pressure again."
Florence tried to peek into the darkened hall, but her landlady's broad
back blocked the view. "I have to be at work in twenty minutes."

Alva Shulte made no motion to summon her husband. She continued
studying Florence, and finally called back into the house without turning
around, "Mr. Shulte, we got a water problem!"

"Getting my tools, Mrs. Shulte!" Florence heard from within the bleak interior. The two women stood waiting, Alva wearing an odd grin that suggested she half-expected Florence to pick her pocket. Old Shulte finally appeared in the light, holding his toolbox. "Don't know if I can do much, with the whole neighborhood keeping its water on," he spoke while Florence followed him up the back stairway to her quarters. "The fire siren's been going all morning, and when that fire department comes with its hose, nobody can get any pressure at all."

Alva, who'd followed them, now stood watching Florence in the little green-painted room while Dwayne Shulte went down the hall to fix the shower. "You a secretary up there at McKee?"

"Not exactly." Florence peered down the hall. Let the old cat stew in her curiosity.

"Dwayne said you do some bookkeeping."

Florence turned to her. "I'm a liaison, actually. For a group of foreign business clients." She sounded idiotic to herself. Who was she showing off to?

"*Lays-on,*" said Alva. "Heavens, me. Sounds awfully important."

Florence shrugged. "It just means I'm an intermediary. Like an arbiter."

"I know the word, hon. Didn't know they had such big titles for young girls nowadays, with so many of our boys out of work."

Dwayne Shulte shuffled out of the bathroom, wiping a hand on his pants. "I tightened that neck, so it's got more force, but I wouldn't run that shower too long now." He glanced at Florence's face, then at her hair, and his eyes seemed to dim at the thought of the water required to wash it. He looked disappointed, for reasons entirely different from his wife's, that the tenant they'd been sent wasn't a man.

INSIDE THE SIXTH-FLOOR CONFERENCE ROOM of the McKee building, a Midwestern sun cut through the blinds and fell in penal bars on the oak conference table. In New York, the canyons of high-rises had offered Florence some protection against the summer heat, but here there was no such cover. A stalemate was in progress among the Russians and McKee's engineers. The Soviets claimed that the blueprints McKee had drawn for their rolling mill in Magnitogorsk were unusable. Moscow was refusing to sign off on any construction requiring so much iron and concrete.

"Hold on, now, we worked all this out three months ago," said Kyle Clement, a dimpled Minnesotan. "You said you wanted a mill like the one in Gary, and that's what we've given you."

"You promise us mill 'modified for *Magnitostroy*,'" said a Russian named Fyodor Zimin.

"A modified *floor* plan, not a plan that called for wood and brick!"

"Bricks and wood is what we have in Magnitogorsk. If we had iron, we would not need iron *mill*, yes?"

On her steno pad Florence tried hastily to give some order to the cross-fire. She'd been sent to make sure the two sides got along, but was failing remarkably at this task. The McKee men, distrustful of the Russians and concerned about litigation, insisted she record every word of their meeting.

"Here's how it is: We aren't going to risk this company's reputation on a structure that's goin'a collapse before the last stone is mortared," said a lipless engineer named Knur Anderson. "You can just telegraph your boys in Moscow and tell them we aren't changing one centimeter of these drawings. We've got our building codes to mind by."

Across the table the Soviets were conferring in mumbles too rapid for her to understand. She'd arrived aiming to improve her Russian, but her role as translator had turned out to be largely redundant, since two of the delegates spoke passable English. Now those two—Zimin and a massive-boned, tan-faced engineer named Sergey Sokolov—returned the Americans' challenge with bored smiles. A whirring ceiling fan chopped up the silence that threatened to settle like dust over the room. The silence lasted a good eleven seconds before Florence rushed in to fill it. "Gentlemen, I'm sure we can come to an agreement that satisfies everyone."

Sergey Sokolov rolled his eyes, presumably at her use of the bourgeois term "gentlemen." He adjusted himself in his chair as though it were the saddle of a motorcycle. "Your codes," he said, aiming a cynical grin at the Americans, "include many steel reinforcements we do not need. These codes were written by your steel industry *kapitans* to skveeze money, nothing more."

Knur Anderson removed the lead pencil from his pocket and knocked it several times against the unshakable structure of the tabletop. "We showed you those mock-ups three weeks ago, and you said nothing. Maybe if you'd come to work a little less hung over . . ."

"And if we were not being cuck-holdened to make profit for steelmakers . . ."

"Cuckolded—now, that's a gas!" objected Clement.

"But, then, I suppose in Soviet Russia, where you all got full employment," Anderson continued, "anyone can show up to work half soused."

"Everyone, let's just focus on the matter at hand," Florence begged. Both sides of the table ignored her.

"You're welcome to break the contract," Clement suggested.

Again Sokolov looked amused. "Yes, but it would be you who are breaking it."

AT McKEE SHE'D BEEN given a desk with her own telephone in the personnel department, beside an unaccountably ebullient personnel director named Claude. She was waiting for Claude to leave for the day so that she could telephone Scoop in New York.

"Hear the news, Florence? Brick-road explosion near Frankfurt a few hours ago," Claude said cheerfully.

"Awful," she said, not listening.

"From the heat, they say. Sent a poultry truck flying twelve feet. Chicken crates everywhere."

"That's a shame."

"Not for the hens that got free. You can bet it's Independence Day for them. Say, are you going to the Independence Day Fair in Buford?"

"Still got a lot of work here, Claude. I'll do my best."

"Well, you have a good Fourth, now, Florence."

"You too, Claude."

"You bet I will."

Once she was sure Claude had left, she dialed her boss.

"Scoop, you have a minute?"

"For you, Florie, always! How's life on the High Plains?"

On the street below, dust-covered sweating men were mending the road.

"I'm not getting anywhere with these people, Scoop. The Soviets want to modify the blueprints. They're claiming McKee is foisting more beams on them than they need. And now both sides are threatening to revoke the contract!"

Fumes from melted tar and hot gravel mixed in a dizzying bouquet in her head. "God*damn* it." She tried to slam the window shut and almost severed her fingers.

"Whoa, slow down, Florence. No one is going to be revoking any contracts. The Soviets are just driving a sharp bargain."

"But McKee's men are saying they weren't paid to do the job twice."

"Forget McKee. The Soviets' contract is with Burlington Steel in Pennsylvania. McKee is just working on commission from Burlington."

"I don't understand. . . ."

"Moscow doesn't want to order six thousand tons of steel from Burlington if they can get most of it on the cheap somewhere closer, like Germany. They promised to buy from Burlington if McKee did their plans, and Burlington is probably paying McKee extra for every foot of beam they can stick into those drawings."

"That wasn't in the contract . . . and it hardly seems fair."

"Fair is a place where pigs win ribbons, sweetheart. The real trouble is that the Soviets have run out of money."

"How can they *run out?*"

"Their grain exports have been falling. Guess they've had a few years of bad crops."

None of this was easing her anxiety. "So what do you want me to do, Scoop?"

"Well, look—I'm guessing McKee can make some cuts, but they don't want to bite the hand that's feeding 'em. Get them to compromise a little. McKee doesn't want to lose the whole commission."

She felt a knot in her throat at his suggestion that she use persuasion. It was never her strong suit. She could imagine no words she could say that would get the stiff-necked men of McKee to bend. "It's just . . . sometimes I don't even know what I'm doing here."

"You're seeing that our Soviet friends don't get ornery. Keep them busy. Didn't you plan to take them to some county fair this evening?"

"Fourth of July fair. Just some local boosters trying to keep up morale."

"Sure. Beautiful. Why don't you go home, make yourself pretty, and then go and show our friends a slice of real American heartland?"

She hung up and let her eyes fall shut. With the window closed, she could hear Claude's radio playing quietly on his desk. He'd forgotten to switch it off. From where she sat by the window the radio seemed to be playing two stations at once, alternating between a gabble of news voices, advertisements, foxtrot music, and static. Florence let her eyes behold the sweaty lumbar exertions of the workmen outside. Before arriving here she had never thought much about "men" as a species. But now the sight of these well-muscled Polacks and Slovenians filled her head with the echo of her mother's injunctions about a girl living on her own "developing a taste for that kind of life." Of course, Zelda, not being Christian, would never have called it "a taste for sin," but burning, sulfurous sin seemed very much to be the path her own mind was veering down. She was still picturing the smirking Sergey Sokolov sitting irreverently astride his backward chair. Her brain was like the radio stuck between stations—on one frequency was the serious chanting of hard news, but turn your head a little and all you heard was seedy, sweet jazz.

THERE WAS BARELY ENOUGH ROOM FOR THE FOUR OF THEM PLUS HERself in the old Buick steered by a short man the others called "Kotik." He was the leader of this ragtag delegation and wore a serious face, either from the strain of driving or from the importance of his position. Florence had to squeeze in the back, between the pickled Fyodor Zimin and the broad-shouldered Sokolov, who'd come wearing a large straw hat that Florence guessed belonged to "the missus" who rented them a bungalow in Tremont. On his head the hat looked just shy of absurd, like a silk shirt on Paul Bunyan. Catching her looking, Sergey narrowed his eyes into a sly smile of familiarity, mistaking her surprise for admiration. And because it was Sergey that she'd taken speculative notice of that afternoon, Florence felt herself flush with the effort of avoiding bumping his knee with her own and instead pressed closer to Fyodor, who smelled like the back side of a brewery.

They left the car outside the fairgrounds and picked their way through the maze of battered trucks and trailers leading to the entrance. Only a

handful of towns from Cuyahoga County were participating in the events
this drought-stricken year. Nevertheless, Florence saw housewives setting
out their rhubarb pies and jams and the air resounded with the murder-
ous screeches of boys practicing their hog hollering. A welcome coolness
was starting to settle over the field, the cow-plop smell of livestock giving
way to a spicy evening scent of clove. The deference and friendly attentions of the foreigners were giving her a pleasurable awareness of herself—
her height, the crisp, fitted feel of her cotton dress, the wild hair she'd
pinned up at her temples. She'd been afraid the Russians would find the
fair hokey, but even the unsmiling Kotik was getting a good laugh out of
watching the sawing contest and tractor pulls.

Only when she'd led them to the miniature rodeo at the far edge of the
grounds did she realize there were only two men in her company instead
of four. "Where are the others?!" she said in a panic.

"Don't be afraid," Sergey said behind her. "They are exploring."

"We need to find them."

"Why? They will find us," said Fyodor.

Sergey removed his straw hat and wiped the sweat off his low brow. His
face might have looked dull-witted were his dark eyes not so alert. It struck
Florence as a face that could belong to a criminal or to a poet, and she
couldn't look at it openly for more than a few seconds without feeling self-
conscious. Beside him, the towheaded Fyodor sat down on an overturned
crate and withdrew some furry tobacco. Absently rolling his cigarette, he
watched some teenaged cowhands in the field. "Cowboys—like in film!" he
remarked. "This is *real* America."

"Hardly," Florence said, unable to stop herself. "More like a dog-and-
pony show."

"A dog and what . . . ?"

"A circus," she said.

"I do not like the American circus," Sergey spoke. "They take us to Bar-
num & Bailey. There is no"—he rubbed his fingers, as if the friction might
generate a word—"*art.*"

"I'm sure it isn't as fine as your circus," said Florence. "You do have a
longer tradition."

"I am not talking of acrobatics. Why you Americans want to see
aborted fetuses?"

For the first time she let herself stare at him. "Pardon me?"

"Cripple girl with tiny head the size of apple dancing like she is at a birthday party."

"Oh—you mean the pinheads in the sideshow!"

"This entertains people? Black man in cage scratching himself like a monkey? He is not come from Africa."

"Good God, those exhibits are just awful. Is *that* what they showed you? Well, that's Ohio for you."

"You are not from Ohio."

"No. *I'm* from New York."

"New York—whah!" Sergey said, showing an appropriate amount of awe. "They take us around New York City when we came off the ship— first three days. Whah! The trains always making noise on top of your head. They look like they are rolling on buildings."

"What else did you see in New York?"

Sergey consulted with Fyodor. "Aquarium? Rockefeller Center."

"Radio City Music Hall," Fyodor chimed in.

They might have gone down the entire list of attractions if she hadn't interceded. "The usual tourist trumpery." There was a silence, during which she worried that she'd come across as unbecomingly cynical.

"You don't like New York?" said Sergey finally.

"I didn't say that. It's a grand city but they showed you the kid stuff. They might have shown you Greenwich Village. They might have taken you to the piers."

"Cleveland: it is not New York." The bored aplomb with which Sergey uttered this snooty bon mot forced her to laugh. He raised his prominent brows in clownish surprise.

"Well—that's true," she said. "It's just that . . . you sounded like some-one *from* New York just now."

He evidently found the laugh an encouraging sign, for his next ques-tion was: "You have young man in New York?"

"I don't have a 'young man.'"

"Old man?"

"Pardon?"

"Why did you run away to Cleveland?"

She looked dumbstruck at him. "I didn't *run away*. I took a job. Same as you." But he didn't seem altogether convinced. "For a crust of bread," she said, and to make sure he understood, she switched to Russian. *"Zarabotat' na kuska khleba."*

This amused Sergey. *"Na* kusok *khleba,"* he corrected, and patted her on the head.

Fyodor eyed her more suspiciously. "How *you* know Russian?"

"My father's mother was from Litva. She lived for Russian novels. She used to read to me from *Evgeniy Onegin* when I was sick in bed."

Fyodor looked at her inquisitively. She tried to think of something to convince him she wasn't spying on them. "I also took a class at the university. I understand better than I speak. I would like to improve."

Fyodor tossed what was left of his cigarette into the dry dirt and got up from his crate. He seemed convinced enough to say, in Russian, "We better watch it with this one," with a wink at Sergey.

Sergey turned to Florence. "Very well. You talk to us in your language, and we'll talk to you in ours. And if that doesn't work, we'll switch to French."

AFTER THE FIREWORKS, they drove back through the midland darkness until they could see Cleveland light up on the interstate's horizon like a glowing ember at the end of a long cigarette. So much had Fyodor and Sergey enjoyed the outing that they extended an invitation for Florence to join them the following Sunday, to smoke fish they intended to catch at the lakefront. Taking a trolley uphill, Florence could see, in the abandoned furnaces and mills along the river, signs of a once-brawny city. The men's bungalow was the last on a block of disused houses once occupied by mill workers and their families. She found Sergey seated on a bench inside the covered back porch, scaling a trout over that day's copy of *The Plain Dealer.* A few steps down, in the tiny backyard, Fyodor was stoking a fire in a smoker he'd fashioned out of a trash can and an oven grate.

"To your health," said Sergey, pouring her some cloudy liquid from a milk jug.

She wasn't prepared for the burn that went all the way down her throat as she swallowed. "Where did you get this? It tastes like rotten bread!"

"Our new Ukrainian friends on the West Side," said Sergey.

"Where did you meet these friends?"

"Church," Fyodor answered from his post at the trash-can grill.

"Your friends crooked you. Have you got any cola to water this down?"

"The missus does not keep cola."

"Or salt," said Fyodor.

"I saw a general store a few blocks back," Florence offered. "I'll go fetch some."

Sergey cleaned his knife and dropped the rest of the fish into a water bucket. "I will go with you."

They walked quickly, crossing the little park on Lakeside. It was five o'clock, but the sun was still beating down. She could smell the tang of her own perspiration through her linen dress. "How does anyone live in this heat? I feel destroyed by it," she said, trying to keep one step ahead of Sergey so he wouldn't smell her.

"If you want—you come to the lake with me and Fyodor?"

"Last thing I need is those crowds," she said, panting.

"Your young man in New York—he is married?" said Sergey out of the blue. In the colonnaded shadow of a courthouse that dwarfed the other buildings, Florence stopped walking.

"What kind of person do you take me for?"

"You are a woman from New York. New York is jazz music." He did a little jig. "Flapper girl like Louise Brooks?"

"Louise Brooks? Is that what you've been sold about American women—that we're all craven and erotically obsessed?"

He shook his head. "Yes."

"Well, then, you're playing the wrong number," she said, walking again. She wanted not to be enjoying this conversation as much as she was. All week long, thoughts of Sergey had been hovering on the edge of her consciousness, as though waiting for some acknowledgment from the rest of her mind. Now the two of them were walking in lockstep, his hand casually within an inch of her arm, his audacity annulling all of her mental discipline.

"But it is not true . . . ," he said wistfully. "I can see now. American women are, we say, potatoes without salt. Young women dress same as grandmothers. Not interesting like in Russia. Women here are . . . *prundes.*"

"Prunes?"

"Proo-d's!" he said, biting down on the "d."

"First we're vamps, and now we're prudes."

"Yes."

"Well, which is it?"

"You are *both*. You either grandiotize sex or you say, 'Is cheap!' In Russia—it is more simple. We say: sex is unimportant as drinking a glass of water when you are thirsty."

If he were someone else, she might have given him a slap. Instead, she said, "Is that so? How nice for the Bolshevik men."

"But it is a *woman* who said this. Alexandra Kollontai. She sleep with many men," he said, gallantly opening the door of the general store for Florence.

Florence gazed over her shoulder at the two men outside, spitting tobacco juice out of the corners of their mouths.

"Shh. You can't talk like that here."

"Why? Kollontai talked about this to *Lenin*."

"Maybe your leaders discuss things like that," she whispered, "but we don't. Salt, please," she requested, and smiled chastely at the grocer behind the counter. At a sedentary speed the man took his stepladder and began his catatonic ascent up to the dry-goods shelf.

"Because in your country everything is comm-yerce," Sergey whispered loudly. "Commerce and bourgeois morality make sex 'decadent.' When sex is only part of healthy spirit of youth."

He smiled sinlessly, delighted to be scandalizing her.

The high-waisted grocer gave a little headshake, as if beleaguered more than offended by this low-mindedness. "Iodized is what you want?" he said.

"Yes, sir. And two colas, please," Florence answered in a wholesome way. Once they were outside again, she turned to the still-smiling Sergey. "I'm not as bourgeois as you think."

"I knew it. You have a man in New York."

"What if I did?"

"But you did not marry him."

"I despise the whole institution of marriage," she said with implausible vigor.

"Whah—the whole institution!" Sergey did a good impression of being impressed.

"I mean, most girls marry for expediency rather than love. It's just so hypocritical. Plus, it seems like sheer madness to marry at a time like this, with the whole country falling apart."

"So you are not interested in men?"

"What? Yes. I mean no." She was starting to feel light-headed from the speed of their walk and conversation. "I just feel my energy would be better spent on . . . a less narrow purpose."

"What is a 'narrow purpose'—your pleasure?"

"Pleasure? Goodness, Sergey. I didn't have you down for a hedonist."

"Why I am *hedonist*? Hedonists live *only* for pleasure. In Russia we live for other things also. This is why sex is not so important."

"Yes—I forgot—it's like drinking a glass of water."

He gave her a sad look that seemed to say, *You mock me, fair lady.* "I am like you," he said. "I live to work. To build. I believe: when you do not satisfy desire, it is like you are pouring sawdust into engine of your mind."

A surf of prickles washed up and down her flesh. The heat of the sun couldn't explain away the pinkness of her cheeks. "Spoken like an engineer," she said, picking up speed to keep his remark from gathering too much meaning.

"Spoken like a human being," said Sergey.

SHE DRANK HER COLA on the porch swing while Sergey gutted the last of the fish. Underneath the pine, Fyodor poked at the coals in his smoker with a branch. "Do you know what I love about the Europeans?" Florence said, stretching her toes. "A man can cook for a woman, and cook just as well."

"You hear that?" said Fyodor. "We're Europeans!"

"That one can cook and sew and geld a horse," Sergey said in Russian. "A Cossack!"

"Not like *him*," said Fyodor, as if responding to a slight.

"A real war hero," said Sergey.

"I wonder if we'll have anything like that here," said Florence. "I mean a civil war, like you did."

"America had civil war to end chattel slavery," Fyodor said. "Same law of history will work in overturning capitalist order of wage slavery."

She glanced over at Sergey, who said nothing and went inside to wash his hands.

"But our communists aren't like your communists. In New York, they're always on the street demonstrating, but their demands are absurd. Slash rents! Free groceries and electricity for the poor! They demand that landlords open up their vacant apartments to house the unemployed. They even demand that the Communist Party distribute unemployment relief instead of the Labor Department. They might as well demand cake and champagne."

"I don't know about 'your' communists. I only know what is scientific laws of history," Fyodor said.

"Well, if that sorry bunch is who's bringing us the revolution, then we can wait another hundred years," Florence said. The Coca-Cola and moonshine were sending a primal warmth down her veins. She felt a combative urge to keep talking. "What riles me is how we pretend in this country that everything is just dandy. 'Good Times Just Around the Corner!'" she said, quoting the headline on the fish-stained *Plain Dealer* that had been lying at Sergey's feet. "And now everyone is cheering Mr. Roosevelt. Praise be! *He's* signed the Agricultural Adjustment Act! *He's* putting Americans back to work! But tell me *what* Americans. Not the women. No one's talking about the women who've been *losing* their jobs thanks to the anti-nepotism laws he's signed. If your husband works in the government and so do you, well, then, you can kiss your job goodbye. One of the spouses has to go, but do you think anyone's discharging the men? No, sir. It's the wives who are being given the boot. Because in this country, if a woman works, she's un-American. A money grubber."

She was conscious of Sergey listening from inside the screen door. She raised her voice. "It's the whole damn attitude here. The eminent Mrs. Gompers, widow of the leader of the biggest union that's ever looked out for the rights of workers—that silk-stockinged ninny has the nerve to tell women: A home no matter how small is large enough to occupy a woman's mind and time. And *this* from one of the so-called *progressive* women in our country—the heroic first lady of the AFL!" She felt unable to stop herself. How delicious was the pleasure of letting your convictions *rip*, of holding nothing back. Washing down the last of the booze and cola, she said, "And my own landlady, she says to me: 'Sweetie, I don't see how it's right for a girl to work when so many of our fellas have to feed their families.' She looks at me like *I'm* the reason all the fine boys of Cleveland aren't making a living."

"You are the reason," said Sergey, coming back out to the porch.

"How?"

"Because women will work for less money. Your bosses keep them when they cut payrolls. And men then also have to accept low pay to stay. Marx wrote about all this already. When wages are set by your 'free market,' men and women are natural enemies." Sergey delivered these self-evident principles without passion, as if he were reciting building codes.

"If you want to work so bad, come to Russia," Fyodor suggested. "We'll put you to work in no time. Our gals are regular horses—you ought to see them shoveling gravel, slapping paint on buildings. We've put them into production and taken them out of reproduction."

"What he means," said Sergey, "is that a woman with your energy would be valued, not made ashamed."

"You don't have to translate, Casanova," Fyodor responded. "I know what I meant. All right, children, our fish is ready." He laid the last of the trout on a wooden board, sat on a porch step, and washed back his second glass of moonshine. "Why does a girl like you want to work so much, anyhow? I know girls your age been married and divorced twice already."

"Let her be," said Sergey.

"Why? She ought to be able to find herself a fellow."

"Not every woman can find herself a Fyodor," Florence said, smiling at Sergey.

"My wife's not complaining," rejoined Fyodor. "Lives in our engineers' compound in Magnitogorsk, doesn't lift a finger. Spends half her morning putting on perfume, and the afternoon bossing around the maid."

Florence took a piece of fish. "Lucky her."

"Don't get smart. She's damn lucky. I got her set up like a countess in an English cottage."

"An English cottage in the empty Russian steppe," remarked Sergey.

"Listen to this high-hat! Member of the former exploiting classes!"

"You're drunk stiff, Fyodor."

"Sure, I am. Sure, I am." He turned to Florence. "Ask this exploiter why his English is so good."

"Never stops babbling, does he? He'll gab his whole life away."

"I know what I'm talking about," Fyodor said, turning away petulantly. "I don't wish to have this chat in front of our female company." He refilled his glass and lifted it once more. "Let us drink to women. When they love us, they forgive even our crimes! When they don't, they do not credit even our virtues!"

Florence raised her nearly empty glass. "I'll drink to that."

Fyodor smacked his lips and looked at Sergey again. "You know who said that, lyceum boy?"

"I don't have any idea."

"Honoré de Balzac!" Fyodor pursed his lips to mimic French.

"Enough posturing, Fyodor. Why don't you play us something already?"

Fyodor finished what was left in his glass and went inside. By the amber backlight through the screen door, Florence watched him take down a guitar from the wall. He carried it out under his arm and sat down to tune the strings. And then he began to strum a soft, melancholy tune. From the plaintive gravel of his voice, she could make out a few stray words of a love song.

Sergey had seated himself on the floorboards by her feet. "Do you understand what he's singing?"

She shook her head.

Quietly, over the sound of the music, he said: "My dear, please do not deceive me so my heart does not break. Geese—swans in the sky—it was not your fault that we cry."

Fyodor's eyes were closed as he strummed, and the chirping of grasshoppers seemed to grow louder as he sang, as though they feared being outdone. Moths circled the porch lantern and made weird shadows. She stared at the top of Sergey's head. In the dim porch light his hair looked like baled hay. Her fingers tingled with an almost irresistible desire to comb it.

"I have put on my old vest," Sergey translated quietly. "Sweetheart, where have you gone?" He circled his thumb and forefinger around Florence's naked ankle and, smiling, closed and released his grip around it as if he found its narrowness a structural curiosity. And she let him, as they both listened to Fyodor's tune of unrequited love.

6.

STEEL

COMING BY A BOTTLE OF HOOCH HAD NEVER BEEN A PROBLEM FOR MOST Clevelanders. From the first days of Prohibition, cases of quality liquor had been floated down Lake Erie from Canada in cabin cruisers and delivered to drop-off points all along the Huron River. From there they were trucked to basement bars and clandestine saloons all over the city. It was in one of these dusky establishments that Fyodor, having just been told to move his elbows off the bar by a prodigious Clevelander of Polish extraction, turned to Sergey and spoke audibly in his native tongue, "Fat Polish hairbag smells like a sewer pipe." At which point the fat hairbag landed a rabbit punch on Fyodor's neck to exact retribution for every repression suffered by Poles under Russian rule since the failed November Uprising of 1831. Staggering forward, Fyodor managed to dodge another punch and throw one himself—his first and last before the Pole landed an uppercut to his jaw, this time in memory of the failed January Uprising of 1864. The final punishment (in payback for the disastrous Polish-Soviet War of 1919) was a cut so low it slammed into Fyodor's groin and lifted him clear off the floor. A moment later relief arrived in the form of a bouncer—an ape in a suit who pinned Fyodor's elbows to his sides and dumped him in the street with a warning that the next time his Red ass would be hanging from a meat hook.

It was past midnight when Florence discovered the two men at her back door, scratching at the screen. Turning on the porch light, she found a bloodied Fyodor draped around an unhappy Sergey. Florence touched her face, tight with egg whites she'd rubbed in for the night. She pulled her housecoat tighter. "My God—what happened?"

"Let us in." Fyodor's heavy shoes scuffed the threshold as Sergey dragged him inside. Blood had dried under Fyodor's nose. His eye was swollen and turning a livery purple.

"You can't stay here," she said. "My landlords will be up. . . ."

"It is another two kilometers to our house. I cannot carry him myself."

Left and right, the three of them veered down a lampless street. The moon, moving through clouds, reflected off the faces of public buildings. From the alleys came smells of things fecal. "The cavalry's arrived!" shouted Fyodor, his arms draped around their shoulders. "So you've brought your Levantine beauty to show her what drunks and scoundrels we are?"

"You're showing her well enough without my help. Grab his arm," Sergey instructed.

"You've got this pony eating out of your hand."

"She understands what you're saying, you fool."

A freight yard appeared in the shadow of a sinister-looking warehouse.

"All the better." Fyodor turned his head to Florence and gave her a drunken grin. "All you intelligentsia girls, vowing you'll only love a real proletarian, a real worker—and then you go off and start making eyes at fakes like him. This careerist." She could feel the sharpness of Fyodor's nails digging into her shoulder as they dragged him. "See for yourself, little girl," he slurred, his breath like kerosene. "We Russians get drunk, sing songs, cry like children. While you Jews keep yourself busy scheming how to make a ruble."

"There's plenty of poor Jews," Florence muttered.

"But they're always trying to get rich. Or powerful—look at Litvinov, Kamenev, Zinoviev, all the big wheels."

"You already have one black eye tonight, Fyodor," Sergey warned. "Would you like another?"

"What am I—insulting her honor? Who said I didn't like Jews? I knew a Jewish girl in Leningrad, before the Revolution. She wasn't allowed to live in the city, because of the quotas. So she got herself a yellow pass"—he turned to Florence—"that's what the prostitutes used, to get across the bridge and do their business. Imagine! Pretending to be a prostitute, so she

could be a student at the university! You Jews—if there's a way, you'll find
it. So why don't you ask her to help us out, Seryozha?"

"You want to ask, you ask."

"Why should I? It's not me she's got eyes for. We go home with lint in
our pockets and the whole plan is thrown. Whose heads are on the chopping block then?"

"That isn't her problem."

"What's the harm in asking—*she'll* find a way."

AFTER SERGEY HAD STRIPPED off Fyodor's big shoes, peeled his pants, and
dumped him on the sagging mattress in the bedroom, he returned to the
main room, where Florence sat waiting at the table with her palms between her knees.

"Is he all right?"

"He won't remember it tomorrow."

She edged her palms on the table and raised herself abruptly.

"I will walk you home," Sergey offered.

"I'll be fine."

"You cannot walk alone."

"How could you take him to a place like that?"

Sergey looked back without speaking.

"You're lucky he's not at the bottom of the river. You're lucky he wasn't
picked up by the police! Did you think what a nightmare that would be—
for *me*, if not for you?" And because he gave no sign of speaking, she lit in
more. "You're not in *your* country—do you understand? There are some
sacrifices you have to make."

"Okay, I will go buy sheep and slaughter it tomorrow."

"What?"

"You said: sacrifices."

"Is this all a joke to you?"

He slammed his fists on the table. "What do you want me to tell you?"
He got up and made his way to the kitchen cabinets, where he searched
through some drawers until he found what he was looking for: the folded
yellow pages of a letter. He slapped it on the table as he sank back onto his
chair.

"Fyodor's wife—she has left him. He received this letter today: She writes she does not want anymore to live in Magnitogorsk. Uncivilized. Dirty. No culture. She has gone back to Leningrad, to live with his friend."

Florence lifted the pages and tried to make out the tiny, delicate hand. She glanced at Sergey. "Are you afraid of getting a letter like that?"

He was sitting in his motorcycle-saddle way again, his knees apart. "I am not married. You know that."

"I don't know much about you."

"I was married. Now I am not. It was only one year. We tried. We ended it." This explanation seemed barely to interest him.

"Just like that."

"Divorce, marriage—these are simple things where I am from."

She held the letter in her hand. "Many things seem more simple there."

"No," he said in a bored voice. "Only that."

Their exchange had become a wilted echo of their earlier conversation. From the other side of the bedroom door came moaning sounds and a hacking cough. "I need to go," she said. But his hand reached out for her wrist.

The compulsion to *work, to be useful, to escape futility's grip*—maybe these things foretold a deeper wish to be used up. Eradicated. Maybe the pleasures of being backed up against the wall, of having your head wrenched back by its curly hair until you puffed shallow breaths, perhaps these satisfactions and others came from the same obliterating impulse that made the soul search for a cause worthy of consuming it. The varied delights of being lifted and flung across a sofa bed, and having your raw backside pressed into its scratchy fibers while a man pinned back your fists and crushed his erection into your thigh, and washed the dusty residue of your thoughts away with a roughly stroking tongue on your nipple— maybe it all arose from a primordial yearning to be completely *spent*.

Sergey's face, hovering over her, was deadly serious. No jokes now. None of the outlandish, hick excitement of the foreigner. His claim over her body was that of a man who might have been her lover for years. When he came, his back broke out in one fierce sweat. But in that very instant he was off of her, for even in this paroxysm of passion he had the foresight, or experience, to pull out and roll down onto the floor. He lay there in his gorgeous natural state for several minutes while Florence stretched out lengthwise on the cushions and let her head fall back. In her ears was the unexpected loudness of birds at dawn. The soreness between her legs brought curious fulfillment, if not exactly pleasure. She placed her hand between her thighs and confirmed the loss of her innocence with the ferric smudge on her fingertips. Sergey was lying on the floor, his eyes still shut. He seemed to have noticed nothing. Her head was pounding from sleeplessness, she had bits of egg white in her hair, her breath very likely stank, and she was shivering as if from a chill. And yet she had never felt so light-headed in her own desirability, so awakened to herself, so animated and frightened by the awareness of her own freedom. Despite her veneration for Emma Goldman, with boys her age she had never done anything more than neck. Only five hundred miles from home could she have allowed this to happen. She tried to summon up some sense of solemnity for the loss of her prolonged girlhood, but came up with nothing but a bird's song.

Through the upside-down window Florence could see the first pale prairie light entering the sky. She got up and found her bloomers, a big cotton pair that suddenly mortified her. She watched the movement of his chest, the rise and fall of the soft dark hair on his belly, and the thicker hair around the impressive but now harmless member that Sergey, his eyes closed, displayed with uninhibited candor. She had an overpowering urge to cup her fingers around it, to test its reality with a touch.

Her hand did not get a centimeter past his stomach before Sergey cracked open one eye. He peered up at her like a smiling Cyclops, then abruptly curled himself up and planted a kiss between her collarbones.

"Your smell—what is it?"

She hesitated. "I don't know. Eggs? I should go."

"Why?" he said, trailing his prickling cheek down her sternum.

"I don't want him to find me here."

"Don't *worry*. He will be sleeping until noon."

Quickly, she slipped her dress on over her arms and head. "What was Fyodor going on about last night?"

Sergey had found his trousers and put them on without bothering to look for his underwear. "He doesn't believe half of what he says, and the other half he can't remember."

"I mean about you coming back with lint in your pockets?"

Sergey took a thoughtful breath and buttoned his pants. "McKee is still refusing to change the mill plans. We cannot agree to the terms that make us buy all the steel they require. They claim there isn't enough time to make the changes we want."

"Will it really take that long?"

"Maybe for them. For me and Fyodor, we could do it in three weeks—while we have original plans to work from."

"Then they ought to let you do it. They complain that you sit around doing nothing."

Sergey gave her an indulgent smile. "Flora, you lovely girl. It is not enough to have blueprint. We also need manuals."

"What manuals?"

"With specifications—strength, density, material properties." He sighed. "For conversion."

"McKee's got a whole library of technical manuals on the sixth floor."

Sergey sighed again, as if communication was impossible. "But who will let *us* on the sixth floor?"

"It's not classified material. Just ask permission."

"It is easier, I find, to ask for forgiveness than for permission, Florence."

"What are you saying?"

He touched his temple. "I should not have said anything."

The sober, reasonable part of her mind told her not to pursue this any further. She watched Sergey button his shirt over his splendid chest.

"Wait," she said. "Tell me."

Sergey rubbed his chin thoughtfully. "They do not want to lose their commission from Burlington Steel. They do not want to admit the plant can be built from cheaper materials. There is only one way to defang their argument, to *show* them—yes, it can be done!" He'd gotten to the top button of his shirt. "So you see now—our difficulty."

The difficulty, as Florence saw it, was that the Russians needed desperately to industrialize, while McKee and Burlington were conspiring to inflate the costs and squeeze them out of their last kopek. "It's hardly fair to you," she said.

Sergey shrugged. " 'Business is business' is the expression, no?"

"I suppose I could obtain those manuals for you," she heard herself say.

He looked up at her with an almost loving surprise. "You would really do this?" He seemed unsure suddenly. "No, I cannot ask you. . . ." But there was in his imploring eyes already that joyful mix of gratitude and admiration that some part of her seemed to need like oxygen.

"We'd have to be careful," she said.

7

DEPARTURES

```
Nonquota Immigration Visa  609
Sec 4
Quota  No.
Dated .Cleveland...........
                    1933
Issued in ..... .....-....
              (Name)
```

COMING UP AS AN ONLY CHILD IN PRE-REVOLUTION PETERSBURG, SERGEY Sokolov had never thought of himself as a member of the proletariat. His father, Arkady, a toolmaker's son, had risen to the rank of foreman at the Petrograd Metal Works, where he adapted designs of Rateau turbines and boilers of Vulcan destroyers that the foundry was commissioned to make for the French and Germans. Sergey's mother, Yelena, was a sought-after seamstress to society ladies. Together the Sokolovs brought home enough money to enroll Sergey in one of the city's top boys' schools: the Second Petrograd Gymnasium, near St. Isaac's Cathedral. Attending class with the children of civil servants, doctors, merchants, clergymen, and a few of the lesser nobles, Sergey was expected to further his father's ascent, to become a top engineer in one of the many factories that were rising like a brick shadow around the marble-colonnaded city. By the time Sergey was in the sixth form, Arkady was in his fifties, occupying his own office in the workshop, fixing workers' hours and pay and waiting for his chance to retire on the family-owned plot outside the city. Then the Revolution came, and Arkady's dreams of moving to the countryside were cut short. The Metal Works were nationalized, the Sokolovs' plot was requisitioned by the government for a workers' sanatorium, and the Sokolovs were forced to suffer mutely as their five-room apartment was subdivided and stuffed with shrill, illiterate workers who promptly destroyed their floors and furniture.

To the young Sergey, whose classes had dwindled with the sudden emigration of his classmates, the Revolution was a mixed prospect. He'd seen the cretins it brought to power, endured his father's complaints about the new Metalworkers' Union, dominated no longer by master craftsmen like himself but by unskilled dolts; he had watched his mother suffer as their new "neighbors" flung muddied boots on her brocade chairs. At the same time, he thrilled at Russia's industrial ambitions: building steel mills in Siberia and oil refineries on the Caspian Sea, laying out factories in Stalingrad. As a boy enamored of machinery, he shared the Bolsheviks' love of bigness. His parents' weariness could not dampen the boy's wonder at the great dams thrown across broad rivers, the awesome machines so complex he couldn't imagine how human hands had built them or how human minds had conceived them. He knew that, to ensure a place for himself in the new order and among the rising ranks of young engineers, he would need to join the youth division of the Party: the Komsomol. But at the Petrograd Polytechnic Institute this proved to be far from simple.

Not long after he entered, the first purge of the student body was conducted. He was called into a room and questioned by an unfriendly troika including the flabby-faced Party Committee secretary in a worker's leather jacket. They asked him questions about his mother and father, his grandparents, uncles, his former classmates at the gymnasium. With a father who had been a foreman in a tsarist factory, there was now some doubt as to whether the Sokolovs were true proletarians or "hostile class elements." Sergey tried to answer the questions modestly and directly, concealing his fear and pretending to show no insult. He said that his father, a simple man, had been promoted gradually from the shop floor to the lowest rung of management because of his skill. He spoke of how he himself had worked for a year on the same factory floor, in a cold-shop, before attending the Polytech. At the end of the purge, all students with a bourgeois class background were expelled. He had been spared, though barely. From that moment on, he understood that he would have to work harder than the others to keep his nose clean. His first two attempts to join the Komsomol were unsuccessful. It wasn't until his penultimate year that he was given another chance, thanks to the endorsement of a girl—a combustible little blonde named Olga, a Komsomol organizer he'd somehow become involved with. Taken with his impressive height and aloofness, she'd pursued Sergey as a conquest. He had discovered early on that, though the tall, slender beauties were shy around him, something about his size provoked the scrappy ones to want to climb him like alpineers.

It was the year the government had started collectivizing the farms, and Olga told him she'd help him get his Komsomol ticket in the fall if he did "social work" with her brigade over the summer. That June, he exchanged his britches for a pair of overalls and traveled with a student brigade to the town of Tikhvin to educate the peasants in the surrounding villages.

In many of the villages that were forced to collectivize, the peasants had already slaughtered their animals so that they would not have to hand them over to the collectives. He'd never seen a town market so full of meat. Shanks of cow and pork attracted hordes of flies. In the village of Luginy, the peasants were prosperous and did not want to join the commune. Inside a church that had had its steeple lopped off, the young communists showed the peasants pictures of buxom women in wheat fields with full baskets on their shoulders, and the gleaming tractors and combines they'd get when they joined the collective farm. "First give us the machines; then we'll think about joining your collective," one silver-haired farmer had said, drawing cheers from the others.

"Old kulak thinks he's clever," Olga had remarked afterward.

"What makes you think he's a kulak?" Sergey had wondered. "He doesn't hire anyone—he's got his three huge sons to help him till his land."

"Don't be naïve, Seryozha. No one does that well working the land with his own hands. The man is a kulak, and we will find someone to testify to it."

At the following week's meeting of the Regional Party Committee, a skinny, half-drunk peasant had shown up to say the old man had hired him during harvests, and to throw in that the farmer was a speculator who bought pig bristles from the villagers, made them into hairbrushes, and sold them at a profit in town. The whole thing had been a farce. Olga had practically fed him the script; Sergey guessed that she'd bought him off with a few bottles of vodka. He had not challenged her at the meeting, but protested to her privately afterward: "Plenty of peasants do a little trading on the side. It's not the truth to call him a speculator."

"You're so silly, Seryozha. What gets recorded at our meeting, *that's* the truth." The troublemaker was going to poison the whole village. Sergey's impulse to defend him showed only that he didn't have "real class consciousness," just intellectual idealism—the cowardice of the bourgeoisie, Olga said. "You want your Komsomol ticket, but you're afraid of building socialism." He never learned what happened to the old peasant who'd stood up at the meeting. Most likely his house and land had been requisitioned, and he, along with his three sons, had been shipped off to Siberia.

That summer he had learned how the Revolution was really made.

And so it was strange that, so many years later, so far away from home, he was thinking about Olga again. Something in Florence reminded him of her. Not a physical resemblance—though both fit his type: mouthy women who knew how to look good in a dress. What they shared was a certain impulsivity, like little girls wanting to dispense with some chore as quickly as possible. Unlike himself, who weighed every word and action carefully, they acted first and thought afterward. Florence had helped them outwit the engineers at McKee. And for what benefit to herself? None, as far as he could see. And now, with her landlords away visiting family, she'd helped herself to their Chevrolet, without so much as thinking to check the oil or bring a proper map.

They had set out in the morning to beat the upwelling of heat, a jug of water in the back, and a flask of gin on the seat between them, of which she'd already dispatched at least a quarter.

"I'll tell you what I won't miss when I leave this place," she said as he drove out of the city. Ringlets around her ears flapped in the wind made by the car's bumping speed. "I won't miss hearing those hideous radio sermons the Shits are always listening to." "The Shits" was what she'd taken to calling the Shultes—Dwayne and Alva—whose car they'd temporarily appropriated. "Bad enough the Shits keep the radio on at all times, but when that Father Coughlin comes on with his gripes against the Negroes and the 'Jewish Conspirators'—then they play it full-volume, probably so I'll hear upstairs. And if it's not him, it's the 'Reverend' Smith. Always with an honorific, these cranks, these men of God, ready to tell us on whose account we're suffering. Blame someone, just don't question the whole rigged capitalist setup that is the U.S. of A. No, sir!"

In reply, he had laid his hand on her bare leg where the chiffon of her dress was hiked up. They stopped for an early lunch at a farmer's roadside stand, where a chalked sign advertised peaches and baby chickens. She was so soused by then that he had to convince her to take the peaches and leave the chicks. And then she decided she wanted to see the country, so they turned the car onto a sandy road that cut through farmland. Another mistake.

The heat had started thickening. As the distance from Cleveland grew, the furrowed countryside got browner and dustier. Singed weeds leaned away from the blacktop, and crops lay flattened where thunderstorms had battered them a few days earlier. She gazed off into the distance where corn stubble met flat-bottomed clouds, and said, "I heard it all smelled like coffee roasting around here last winter."

"Coffee—why?"

"'Cause they were burning corn instead of coal." She turned to look at him, eyes glazed with drink. "Imagine *that?*"

He had no desire to imagine it. He was in no mood to engage in another discussion about the absurdities of "the whole capitalist setup," or to listen to another harangue about the American Way, with its unwanted goods and unwanted people.

What he wanted, in the time he had left, was to soak in the physical grandeur of a country he would surely never see again. Frankly, he had been surprised they'd given him the exit permit, considering his less-than-impeccable class origin. It was a testament to how few specialists they had to choose from—the ones who knew a screw from a lightbulb, who could speak proper Russian, let alone converse in English. Where were they? Run out. Exiled. Shot. Who was left? *Narod*—the sentimentalized horde known as "the People" in whose name all this epic work was being carried out. He doubted he'd receive much gratitude from *them* once he'd completed his duty. All he wanted now was to savor the texture of the leather seat, feel the polished wood of the steering wheel turning lightly under his fingers. Fleetingly, he allowed himself to wonder what it might be like to have a car of his own. The engineers who worked at McKee all drove the latest Fords and lived in their own houses. They weren't better engineers than he was. It was true that the crisis of capitalism had degraded the country, but if one had a few pennies to one's name, one was still a free man. If *he* were living here, *he* would do fine, he knew, just as these men were doing quite fine. He'd briefly considered defecting, but that was no option. They'd arrest his parents in Leningrad and exact punishment in some gruesome way he could not imagine. He stole a glance at Florence in the passenger's seat. Her eyes were shut, as if against some pain. Her skin was flushed—from the heat or the gin, he couldn't tell.

———

THE SUN FELT HEAVY on her head, like a manhole cover. In another week Sergey would be returning home and she would go back to New York. She wanted him to display at least a small sign of regret about leaving her. She opened her eyes and gazed out the windshield. They were in another town, almost exactly like the one before, only emptier: a single street with a browned church steeple, vacant storefronts with orange Nehi and Coke advertisements dangling in dust-streaked windows. She too was thinking about the McKee men. It was improbable that any of them had seen her with Sergey. Though it didn't matter now. Her mood of irritation, with herself and with Sergey, had started taking on a distinctly McKee-like flavor. The "heist" that she and Sergey had contrived, to get their hands on those manuals, do the conversions of the plans, and demonstrate that the mill in Magnitogorsk could be effectively constructed with cheaper materials, had come off almost flawlessly. They had "defanged" McKee's arguments, in Fyodor's words. "I hope you're happy with yourself" was what Knur Anderson had said to Florence afterward. Clement had only shaken his head. Deducing that she'd been the one who'd helped the Russians, the American engineers looked at her as though she was either immeasurably conniving or unfathomably dumb. Her conviction that she'd only leveled an unjust playing field dulled the distress she felt at knowing they were talking about her behind her back as a turncoat. Harder to ignore were the smirking looks. It rankled her that the McKee men assumed she was sleeping with one of the Russians, and galled her all the more that they'd guessed right. She'd been feeling a kind of moral asphyxia in Cleveland for weeks now. She wanted Sergey to redeem her despair, redeem the sacrifice she'd made on his behalf—but how? Love was a thing you couldn't get a receipt for, if this could even be called love. And the things they'd said to each other in the dark—well, those were part of the game too. "Could you imagine us, together—if you didn't live over there and I didn't live here?" "Yes, why not?" "Oh, but then you wouldn't be who you are. You'd be somebody else, and I would, too." It was astonishing how this nonsense could arouse them. Lately, she'd even wept afterward, and let him console her with kisses, all of these dramatics somehow necessary to give meaning to what was otherwise just a lot of dirty business.

For most of the summer, they hadn't spoken about what they were doing. But her body, it turned out, needed no help in understanding the signs of its hungers. She might be falling asleep in her room, but the quietest sound of Sergey's finger scratching at her screen door late at night could rouse her to full wakefulness. Just the sight of him in her porch light could revive her body to that weightless yearning it had spent all day suppressing. He never rushed her. They could kiss until her chin was raw and her lips were numb, until she was utterly immobilized by desire. She understood now what people, including her mother, meant when they spoke of girls getting themselves "caught." There seemed to be no ways but dangerous ways to be in love, no ways to satisfy your heart without deforming your mind.

The road had narrowed and they had to drive slower. A sputtering knock could be heard in the engine with every few revolutions of the wheels. On the right another churchyard appeared, this one with sagging willow trees. Behind its neatly whitewashed fence several picnic tables were set out in a long snake. Florence pointed to the sign: "Come unto me, all ye that labor and are heavy laden, and I will give you rest."

"They must be running a soup kitchen out of there."

"The missus who rents to us makes soup for her church, too. A kind woman."

"God bless America. Soup kitchens as far as the eye can see."

"Why are you being nasty?" he said. "Give me the map." The road signs made no sense to him. He looked for something that might lead them back to the motorway.

"I'm not being nasty." She spread the flapping map between them. "I'm only saying philanthropy in this country is a way for some people to alleviate their sins. Morgan, Rockefeller—all they're doing is tossing a few pennies back to the people they've robbed." She knew she was being a shrew, souring whatever pleasure was left in their time together.

"I was not talking about Rockefeller. I was talking about old ladies making soup," he said impatiently. He took the map and studied its network of blue veins.

"This map won't help you. It's of Ohio, and we entered Indiana twenty minutes ago."

"Why did you not tell me!"

"Didn't you see the sign?"

Sergey shut his eyes.

"We're fine," she said, trying to sound reassuring. "We're just along the side here. It's like what Fyodor was saying: these are the same people protecting their interests with guns and . . ."

"Fyodor! Really? This is who you've been listening to?"

Her eyes were radiant with anger and embarrassment. "What's wrong with that?"

"Nothing. I am thinking it is better if you stop so much blah-blah-blah, and look at the map," he said in a voice thick with irritation.

She averted her face and tried to swallow the knot of tears in her throat. The car's engine was laboring louder as they mounted a slope. Sergey stepped down on the accelerator, but the Chevrolet only climbed stiffly while the rear wheels turned dirt and rocks with an alarming squeal. "What's happening?" she said. Sergey strained his jaw and threw the car into high gear. It lunged distressingly. He clamped on the brake and turned off the ignition. Steam was rising from the engine. "*Chyort!*" he muttered. He climbed out and stood looking blindly under the hood. "You drive," he ordered suddenly.

He put the car into neutral and Florence moved into the driver's seat. She clamped her heel on the gas pedal while Sergey pushed from the back. The Chevy bucked forward, then died with another pounding sputter. On the edge of the field, crows were picking at the corn stubble. She felt weak and watered down from the heat. Doom was starting to settle over everything. She gazed around for some sign of human life but saw only the distant silhouette of a barn against the low clouds. Sergey cursed louder and kicked a tire. "Now we walk," he announced. He grabbed his jacket and the water jug from the back seat. Only a few drops remained, and he let Florence swallow them. As she stepped out, she glimpsed the oily leak under the chassis, a trail of black drops as far as her eye could see.

"We've been leaking this whole time?" she yelled, limping after him. "How could you not notice?!"

He turned to her with a look of stone. "*You* want to yell at me?"

She continued trudging, half lamely, behind him. The field and mesh fence along the road were beginning to spin. "Where are you taking us? You don't know where this road leads!" A wave of dizziness overtook her. The sun in the west blotted out her vision. Through the haze of airborne dirt, she sank to her knees.

"Get up, Flora."

"No," she whimpered.

"Up!"

She shook her head.

"I am leaving."

"Leave! Go!" She hated the need that her voice betrayed. "Go back to Russia. Go on!"

Sergey turned around and watched Florence for what seemed like a long time. She let her eyes fall shut and opened them again. Sergey was squatting on his haunches beside her. "So here it ends? In a cornfield?"

She felt sick. Sick of making him comfort her. Sick of her weak flesh. Sick of griping. Sick of her need to have all their humid late hours in her bed produce in him an equivalent in words.

"Forgive me." She wiped the side of her wet face with her arm. "This isn't how I want you to remember me—as some silly American woman."

He frowned sympathetically. "Silly? You are the opposite of silly, Flora. What would I have done without you here?" He looked at her more seriously now. "But you are too moved by everything wrong in this world. You feel it too *much*," he pleaded. "It is madness to burn up inside about things you cannot change."

She felt almost idiotically flattered by his words—by his possibly false belief that her heart, her sense of justice, was capacious enough to embrace the world.

"So what is this, that you cannot go?" He touched her face and moved aside a curl. "A little dust? A little heat? A little gin?" He stretched out his hand.

She let him pull her up. On the horizon, the light had become malt-colored. A dark, backlit figure was walking along the dirt road toward them, a man in denim and a hat. In the sidelong evening rays he appeared to be surrounded by a halo.

THE FARMER'S HOUSE WAS only a mile south, and he soon returned with his truck and a tow chain for the Chevy.

She sat on the farmer's porch step, a chunk of wrapped ice tucked in her armpit. Like the car, she'd suffered sunstroke. Now the ice, and the sugar water she was sipping, were restoring her back to herself. In the ginger-colored field, Sergey and the farmer worked over the engine. Soot had gummed under the seat of a valve and sprung the leak. Florence watched Sergey scrape off carbon deposits from the cylinders. He removed his shirt and placed it delicately over the valves, to protect them from the carbon's dust. The amber light gave a deep tan to the flexed muscles of his back, a blond sheen to the hair on his chest and stomach. She could never respond indifferently to his body.

Shadows cast by the clouds moved down the earth. A bird flew over her head, trailed by its reflection. She could hear the farmer chattering while he handed Sergey tools. He was telling Sergey about the way things had changed since the war. How people used to help out one another, lending corn if someone's crop was low. "A handshake was as good as an IOU. No more." The farmer lifted his hat to reveal his balding, closely cropped head. "Now it's only the bank, making you sign twenty pages for a bag of seed." Sergey, bent over the open hood, murmured something that made the farmer laugh. Even here he could find a common language with people. How was this so simple for him, she wondered, yet so complicated for her? Did it have to do with coming from a place where egalitarianism was lived and not just talked about?

A murky little creek wound through the farmer's front property. That was what she felt like—that nameless little rivulet. To the surface of her memory now rose a line from *Middlemarch:* "Her full nature, like that river of which Cyrus broke the strength, spent itself in channels which had no great name on the earth." She had copied it into her notebook at sixteen, moved by the tragic poignancy of a mighty river forced to expend its energies into nameless streams. Even at sixteen, she had nursed visions of a great destiny for herself. Had she realized that Eliot was simply mourning the tragedy of being a woman? If she had, then she, Florence, believed she'd be spared. All around her, women were bobbing their hair, raising their hemlines, enrolling in universities, blowing cigarette smoke at a whole lot of stuffy Victorian commandments. Feminine disobedience was in vogue, and she had been too young, she saw now, to understand that vogue was all it was. She had mistaken style for matter, fashion for progress. America had not changed at all. The promise that had been dangled before her at sixteen—the possibility by which a free-spirited girl might grow up into a free woman—had, in the years since she'd actually become a woman, been withdrawn so gradually that she'd barely noticed its passing.

In her lap lay Sergey's jacket. He'd asked her to hold it, along with the documents he kept there. She dug into the cool lining of the pocket and removed his passport. It was heavier than she expected. She cracked open the booklet and unfolded the tissue-thin "Zagran passport" stapled to one of the pages. A portrait of him, serious and pale, was glued to the bottom. A part of his face was branded by one of three identical purple stamps, applied to the page at various pressures. The paper was cool and brittle to the touch. Here it was—the engine of his mobility. Holding it made her feel landlocked. She slipped it back in his pocket. Out in the field, she watched Sergey turn the motor over a few times. It came to life with the sound of an artillery round. He climbed out of the car and strode toward her, wiping his grease-stained hands on a rag. "Princess," he announced, "your carriage is ready."

FLORENCE RETURNED HOME A week later, while the passport she'd cradled accompanied its owner on a steamer to Europe. At the Finnish border, it was thumbed and inspected by a Soviet official whose spectacles gleamed with sedate hostility. Sergey was taken into a small penal room and questioned about his voyage. His answers did not matter. There was nothing he could say that could dispel the permanent cloud of suspicion he had earned for his service to his country. This was the price he would pay, forever, for his American summer. On the table between Sergey and his interrogator lay the items he had brought back: a set of fine drafting tools, a Gillette shaving kit, bone cufflinks, cologne. They had been vigorously picked out of his bloated suitcase. In America, each purchase had beckoned to him with its promise of sophistication and quality, but on the table, the items seemed to be coated with shame, proof of his lust for the gaudiness of a decadent nation. The customs agent had him sign for them. "Something's missing," Sergey said suddenly. It was a carved Lucite brooch he would not have dared to mention had he not bought it for his mother. "File a complaint," the agent said, his eyes radiant with mockery.

Clouds began to storm as his train crossed into Russia. It was late September, the intimate warmth of summer erased by a cold haze of rain. He shut his eyes. The thunder above was like the sound of an enormous door closing shut behind him.

In March, while snows were still falling on the half-excavated hills of

Magnitogorsk, Sergey received a letter from Florence. This was not a complete surprise. He had written her first himself, care of the Soviet Trade Mission in New York, a holiday greeting timed to arrive just before New Year's. He had discovered that he missed her after all, or at least missed their Cleveland summer, the heat and abandon of it, Florence's careless daring and outspokenness. In Magnitogorsk, things were not going well; construction of the rolling mill had been bedeviled by delays and breakages, thanks to the new management's cutting corners to appease Moscow's unrealistic norms. He had made the mistake of speaking up openly about this and run afoul of the wrong people. None of this did he report to Florence in his letter.

THE ENVELOPE THAT ARRIVED at her desk at Amtorg was as thin as cigarette paper, and when she unsealed it, a photograph fell out. It was Sergey—a small figure standing in front of a great brick building. He was wearing a white undershirt tucked into a pair of high-waisted dungarees, shielding his eyes from the strong Central Russian sun. He wished her a happy new year, and hoped his letter would arrive before 1934 did. The construction of the rolling mill was coming along tremendously. He wished to thank her for her help with its design, everything she had done for him, for being his guide and a beacon of kindness in a foreign country, and especially for making his summer in America a time he would never forget. He had just finished reading a novel by "your great American writer Jack London." *A Daughter of the Snows*, it was called, and its heroine, Frona Welse, had reminded him of Florence. A "brave, natural woman" was how he described either Frona, or Florence, or both. He saw now how lucky he was that life's twists of fate had brought them together, if only for a short time. It made him very happy to think about those weeks.

Reading these lines, Florence felt overtaken by a strange impulse to cross and recross her legs. Her body's intuitive response to the words on the page—merely to the Cyrillic bend of Sergey's penmanship—was like the pulse of a looping current. Hearing his voice in her head, Florence felt haunted by the ghost of every kiss, every touch from the summer. Was this open flow of feeling on his part a quirk of translation? she wondered. Were the unmistakable romantic notes quite standard fare in Russian? She scanned the rest of the pages. With a heroic-sounding enthusiasm that seemed somewhat uncharacteristic, Sergey described the mighty furnaces and plants rising up from the steppes. "How far we've come. How much work there is still to do!" The picture, he wrote, did not convey the proper scale of the work being done. She would have to see it herself one day, with her own eyes.

Florence reread the last line with a turbulent flip in her stomach. Was this an invitation?

IN THE COURSE OF the next several weeks, she attempted to compose a response. She could not manage to match the broad spirit of Sergey's letter. Her bid to strike the same easy romantic note seemed shot through with lovesick desperation. She wished to pour out her whole gloomy heart, but did not want to compromise his image of her as Jack London's physically splendid and brave heroine. It was late in January when she finally managed to write something on her portable.

JANUARY 23, 1934

Dear Sergey,

Your letter arrived like a diamond from the sky. It brought me joy to again see the triumphant and carefree face that I remember so well from Cleveland. All that now seems part of a dream. Looking at snow on top of dead leaves, or smelling the rain, I've sometimes wondered if it was a dream. Perhaps this is only because, ever since I've returned, it often feels to me that the real and important portion of my life is happening elsewhere.

You may have read in the newspapers that our President has declared an end to the odious dry laws. So our New Year was quite merrier than last. Aside from that, there's little that's changed—I won't bore you with all of that. People say things are improving thanks to Roosevelt. Maybe so, but not fast enough for me. You often said I ought to see with my own eyes the majesty of Magnitogorsk. I think I shall.

She had not planned to write this, but as soon as she put down the words, she knew they were true.

I fear if I stay I may fall into the ranks of the indifferent, or, worse, the eloquent malcontents. This thought frightens me more than anything else. Whatever the name of this new craving in me—to see the world firsthand—it's finally come into bloom. Now that I have diligently resolved to see the Soviet Union with my eyes, it should not be too difficult to secure a visa through Amtorg connections. I hope to set sail by Spring.

Perhaps you and I might meet again after all.

Yours,
Flora

8.

ARRIVALS

Moscow, 1934

HER LETTER HAD NOT BEEN ENTIRELY TRUTHFUL: HER DESIRE TO LEAVE her job and country did not come about wholly voluntarily. The word of Florence's breach of loyalties had traveled back to New York before she had. Scoop was sympathetic but unhelpful. "You've got a good heart, Florence; you did what you thought was the right thing, the fair thing, at the time." Only, the first rule of diplomacy, he reminded her, wasn't to say or do the right things, but to avoid saying and doing the wrong things.

"But I thought you wanted me to help the Russians," she'd said, sounding more helpless than necessary.

"What I said," he clarified, "is to try to get the McKee men and Magnitogorsk boys to find a compromise."

It occurred to Florence that Scoop would have solved the problem by inviting men like Clement and Knur Anderson to palaver over roast pig and home brew—the sort of male statecraft it would have been impossible for someone like her—rigid, appeasing, Eastern-born, young, a woman—to carry off. Yet, were she to point this fact out to Scoop, she knew she would sound even more pitiful. Already the disappointment in her boss's voice was more painful than any reproach.

Amtorg would soon be closing its doors. Roosevelt had recognized the Soviet Union over the protests in Congress. As Scoop predicted, there would soon be a consulate in Washington, with trade no longer having to be laundered through a complex web of executive and Amtorg emissaries.

Scoop had succeeded in getting himself hired by a group of export managers to lobby Roosevelt's new people for lower tariffs and open trade. "It appears this old sled dog is going solo," he told her. There was no question now of his getting her a job at the new embassy.

"I can make some calls to old friends after the New Year," he told her when she'd reached him on the phone in Washington.

She didn't remind him that he'd twice pledged to do this.

"I'm starting to think I might have an easier time finding work in Russia," she suggested, expecting him to contradict her.

Instead, he said, "You might. Moscow's swarming with Americans."

"The new Paris," she said in a tone between wistful and sardonic.

"Better than Paris if you can get them to pay you in dollars. You got to be firm—tell them you won't accept anything but legal tender." And his voice filled again like a sail with the instructive rhapsodizing that never cost him a penny.

TO ESSIE, ON THE *BREMEN*, Florence left out most of these details of her failures and said only that she was traveling to Magnitogorsk to meet the man who'd opened her eyes to the opportunities in Russia.

"Does he know you're coming?"

"I wrote to him, but I didn't hear back before I left."

"Hmm. The mail can be quite unreliable in that part of the country. Maybe you oughta telegraph first." They were in their nightgowns. Essie had relocated her meager suitcase to Florence's second-class cabin. Florence waved off Essie's practical suggestion, but this simple idea, for reasons she couldn't explain to herself, stirred more dread in her than the thought of boarding a train and riding it for a thousand six hundred kilometers to the Urals. "Magnitogorsk is a small pond," she said to Essie. "I don't think he'd want me to draw attention with a wire. I'll find him once I get there."

"Well, that's also a plan," said Essie with worrisome geniality.

IN THE WEEKS OF TRAVEL, Essie told Florence her story. While Florence had attended Sunday school at Midwood Synagogue, Essie had spent her Saturday mornings at the Workmen's Circle in the Bronx, studying the lives of the patriarchs Marx and Trotsky. In the mildewed, newsprint-smelling milieu of the Frank apartment, the only holidays observed were the Seventh of November (anniversary of the October Revolution) and the First of May (International Workers Day), when Essie and her little sister joined their parents in taking to the streets and singing "The Internationale" at the tops of their voices, together with other Socialist Youths, whose ranks Essie had joined by the time she was eleven. Summers were spent at Camp Kinderland in Massachusetts, the "Summer Camp with a Conscience." True to the Soviet model, the campers adopted the semi-autonomous role of the proletariat, while their adult counselors assumed the guiding role of the Party.

During the school year, however, things were different. "I always thought it was okay, you know, being poor and having no smart clothes, and gum being stuck in my hair 'cause I refused to say the Pledge of Allegiance," Essie said. "And the other kids calling me a bastard on account of how my parents didn't properly marry till I was six. I could endure it because I knew my mother and father had more guts and principles in their pinkie fingers than any of those pishers had in their whole body."

It seemed that Max Frank's employers, however, saw things differently; after being fired from several factory jobs "on account of his spotless convictions," and certain that the workers' government would never be established in the United States, Essie's father had decided to scrape together money and take his family to Russia. The family had been all set to make the move when Essie's mother fell ill with a harmless tooth infection that rapidly spread to her heart. The trip was delayed and the money used on "fool doctors" and, later, on a cremation. But the plan was still on, with Max again professing to save money for their journey.

A year went by. Then another. Essie worked in a dog-collar factory while taking night classes in Russian. One day, she fell asleep on the factory floor and almost had her thumb chewed off by a leather punch. She came home hysterical after being docked by the boss for jamming the machine, and demanded to know when the family was leaving for Russia.

"And that's when my father says to me: Essie, I wanted to wait until you were ready to hear this, but I'll just come out with it—I'm getting married. Who to? I say. Melmy Skolnik from the fourth floor, he says. My heart falls to my stomach, Florence. She's not seven years older than me! A real cooking spoon, mixes into everybody's business. Started coming by with meals for us when my mother fell ill, making with the tears like a finger wringer.

"I say to him: What about everything you and Mama used to talk about, our dream? He says, *Nit mit sheltn un nit mit lakhn ken men di velt ibermakhn*—'Neither with curses nor with laughter can you change the world, Essie.' Gives me a shrug and a half. Why go to the end of the world? Let's us make the best of it here, he says. He has a nerve to tell me, 'You know Lilly needs a mother,' when I'm the one who's been mothering her all this time!

"So I say, to hell with you, I'm going. I already had a visa, just needed the ticket. Before I left, I told him I knew all along it was my mother who had the principles and guts, and never him. He was just going along, like he was going along with that *tsatske*. Mankind doesn't come any weaker or stupider, I told him. Oh, I said so many horrible things, Florence. I told him not to bother seeing me off, and he just hung his head like a child and said he was going to respect my wishes. But I never wanted him to respect them, I wanted him to fight, Florence, to fight for *me*."

Florence sat nodding attentively. Essie's tears and misery had the agreeable effect of making Florence feel kindhearted and serene. She said, "I'm sure he knows you love him, and so does Lilly." She enveloped the girl in her arms, inhaling a whiff of the bodily sourness that bespoke Essie's torment. And then, suddenly, the feeling she'd had the day before—that she'd been mistaken to leave her family, who *had* fought for her, and mistaken about so much else—returned with a nausealike force so powerful that she had to lie back on the bed to alleviate it.

"Are you ill?" Essie looked worried.

"I think it's just the ocean." Florence sat up and glanced at the porthole. A frothy green-and-black curtain of foam was slapping against the glass. In her throat she recognized the taste of that evening's Stroganoff, and felt herself pitch forward. "Wait!" Essie cried helplessly. "I'll fetch the pan!"

ESSIE HAD BROUGHT ALONG sour drops and saltines to prevent seasickness and fed them to Florence while enormous waves pounded the side of the ship. When the storm abated, she took Florence under an umbrella up to the deck for fresh air. Scaly purple clouds filled the sky. Florence held on to her friend's arm and tried not to look down into the churning black water. She was glad to have Essie there. Clumsy as she'd appeared at first, Essie proved herself to be uncommonly knowledgeable in all practical matters involving travel. She forbade Florence to stay indoors all day and told her to look at the horizon as often as possible. Once the sea calmed, she advised her on everything else. Not to convert her dollars at the Russian border: "They'll give you a standard rate of two rubles for the dollar. Don't take it. Once you're inside, you can exchange them for twenty-five on the dollar." She instructed her not to let the Russian border guards confiscate her typewriter: "Tell them you've got official papers for it. Make a fuss and say you'll call the embassy." A little palm-grease always helped: "Have you got any jazz records, or some pretty tins of face powder?"

Florence bit her lip. She'd packed some rouge and perfume, but had planned to use them when she saw Sergey.

"The guards will give you some line," Essie went on, "about how they're decadent and spread moral corruption. Don't argue. Just let them take something home to their wives or mothers."

AFTER MOST OF THE PASSENGERS disembarked at Danzig, the ship was quieter. By the time they reached the Latvian coast, the sea had acquired a softer, Baltic hue. In 1934, the Baltic States had yet to be absorbed into the Soviet Union under the gentleman's swap of the Molotov-Ribbentrop Pact. Florence would have seen neither Soviet boots nor German ones on the large, broken cobblestones that paved Libau's narrow streets. In Riga, no red banners marred the high-pitched ochre roofs. Florence and Essie took a room in an old-fashioned boarding house and woke up to the clear, reverberating toll of church bells. In the freshness of morning everything around them suggested a miniature kingdom. In Riga, they purchased tickets for the Rizhsky railroad station in Moscow. The train that arrived for them was bright red, fitted with polished brass ornaments—one of the grand old locomotive models that no longer ran in America. Instead of coal, it burned wood, and had to stop frequently in the dense forest to re-fuel. Along the tracks, men in logger boots and woolen hats piled pyramids of timber to sell to the railroad. Closer to the Russian border, Florence noticed, the wood sellers all had vanished.

Dark pine forests flashed by, drew closer, retreated. "Look, Florence! Red Army soldiers," Essie cried excitedly as the train slid into a wooden depot supporting a roof with painted letters that urged workers of all lands to unite. Inspectors dressed as soldiers in khakis strutted onto the train and commenced with their searches. They confiscated Essie's *Life* magazines and *Silver Screens*, which she'd packed strategically toward the top of her luggage. (In fact, Florence was quick to note, Essie looked positively exultant with the privilege of giving away her "anti-Soviet" literature.) When the search was over, Essie assured Florence that she too had made out well, losing only her last pack of Camels and a bottle of Shalimar. Nevertheless, the first feeling Florence experienced upon crossing the Soviet border was a sense not of wonder but of violation. She told herself it was foolish to be angry when most of their American money was still safely tucked in their brassieres. Equally foolish was to believe that such searches didn't occur at every border station in the world. Any other kind of reasoning would have required too severe a downgrade of her hopes about the new land she was about to enter.

Soon her eyes were once more alighting on the majestic pines and flickering birches, little houses with carved windows like those she'd seen in her grandmother's storybooks. But it wasn't long before this mythic countryside peeled away abruptly to reveal the great hammering, bumping, screeching city.

In no time, the swaying train corridor filled with people, and Essie and Florence were funneled along with their trunks into the echoey swarm of Moscow's Rizhsky Station. Out on the huge square, the chrome fenders of Soviet Fords flashed reflections of horses and wooden carriages. Bearded coachmen from the era of Tolstoy mingled on the curb with pomaded taxi drivers. Essie did the haggling, in a rough Russian the drivers attributed to Baltic rather than Bronx origins. And soon the girls were off, rolling at deadly speed along the Prospekt Mira, their GAZ nearly colliding with rumbling trams overloaded with people flattening their bodies against doors and windows.

It was June in Moscow, a late-afternoon hour thick with brick dust from torn-up cobblestones and drifting fluff from ripe poplar trees. On the curbs, crowds ten and fifteen deep jostled in front of shops.

"Oh, Florence, did you ever think it would be so tremendous?" Essie remarked. And, indeed, its proportions seemed to Florence Mesopotamian. Moscow appeared to her as an Asiatic sprawl of twisting streets, wooden shanties, and horse cabs. But already another Moscow was rising up through the chaos of the first. Streets built to accommodate donkey tracks had been torn open and replaced with boulevards broader than two or three Park Avenues. On the sidewalks, pedestrians were being detoured onto planks around enormous construction pits. Derricks poked out of excavated trenches where a vast underground rail system was being drawn. A smell of sawdust and metal filings hung in the air.

Essie was dropped off first, at Baumanskaya, a neighborhood their driver called the German District. "I'll miss you so, Essie!" Florence said, embracing her friend tightly. She was afraid that if she let Essie go she might start sobbing and not stop. She knew no one else in this city, and suddenly felt that fact in all its overwhelming terror. Essie did no better at holding in her tears. "I wish you were staying, Florie. Be my sister here. You could get work at the institute. Well, I can see your mind's made up." She removed her tear-streaked glasses and handed Florence a slip with her address. "Find me when you're back from Magnitogorsk." And then she stood on the street a long time as the black GAZ pulled her friend back into the currents of late-afternoon traffic.

THE HOTEL NOVOMOSKOVSKAYA WAS in the very heart of the old city, and the attention Florence received from the concierge was in every way swift and agreeable until she was told to pay four nights in advance.

"But I'm only staying one or two nights."

"Four nights, minimal for residence registration in Moscow. Rule of Intourist."

The reception manager obligingly took her money before assuming his official capacity as notary, stamping her papers with four identical seals, just as she'd seen on Sergey's documents. In her room, with the curtains drawn, came the payoff: a view so brazenly triumphant that her eyes couldn't accept it as anything but a picture plucked from a postcard rack. Sunset was just then settling over Red Square, turning the cobblestones to radiant ripples. Above St. Basil's, the domes shone like barber's poles, like custards, virtually burlesque against the walls of the granite mausoleum. There seemed, in the contrasts of this panorama, some hidden vision to be gleaned. A message about man's chaotic spirit and his somber dignity. His dignity and his power. His power and his purpose. She was sure that there was some thread there, but the burden of decoding it made her feel too tired. Consciousness was draining out of her in a low tide. For almost a month, she had been in transit, on boats and trains and cars and carriages. Had she really stopped moving, she now wondered, or would her feet take it upon themselves to start walking again? A fly buzzing atop two mandarin oranges stirred Florence out of her reverie. She lifted one orange from its saucer and held it in her palm, feeling its weight and the texture of its waxy skin. This, it seemed, was proof that she had really arrived. She raised the fruit to her nose and inhaled its tang. Forever after, she would associate her arrival in Russia with the smell of tangerines, even when there were none to be found.

BOOK II

9.

THE GREAT COMMUNICATOR

MY BLACKBERRY PUTS THE TIME AT 7:04 A.M. THROUGH THE PLANE'S ovoid window the half-moon dissolves like a watermark. The Finnair stewardess muscles shut my overhead with a smile just short of coquettish. And to think I once found them *frosty*, these Nordic darlings of the sky. What did I know? Nothing, before flying business class. Soon one of them comes by and asks whether she can bring me a drink. A little Scotch would be just fine, I tell her. She leans in and smiles, conveying the impression that the two of us arc conspirators in some delicious secret that it would be impossible to explain to the dollar-counting hordes in the rows behind.

If only these charms could extend to my fellow passengers. But it's just the opposite, I've discovered. My seatmate's all right—a mute Finn. A nation that, thank heaven, sees no need for chat. Two rows ahead of me is a different story: a Russian blueblood with a duck's-ass haircut who's employing the last minutes before takeoff to abuse some hapless underling on his Motorola. So far, he's labeled whoever he's talking to an *urod*, a mutant, and an aborted fetus. I can already feel my chest constricting in response to his voice, as I brace myself for the week ahead.

I let my eyes fall shut. Today I have the uneasy sense that the fluttering in my stomach is not just the consequence of my body anticipating breaking its bonds with gravity. In the compartment overhead are the five-kilo study guides my wife has insisted I deliver to our son. Next to them is an almost weightless folder containing my birth certificate, my mother's old passport, and her Soviet-era bankbook. The thought of presenting those brittle proofs of my mother's time on earth at the FSB archives office—around the corner from the prison where I used to stand for hours with Mama, carrying packages of food for my father (packages never opened, always returned)—doesn't kindle my enthusiasm. It's enough for me to be traveling to Russia without also having to make a sojourn into the still-warm bowels of the Soviet Union. Between that, my meetings with L____ Petroleum, and trying to get my son's head screwed back on straight, I'll have a busy week indeed. At last we take off, and soon enough Miss Finland comes around with my Dewar's—two shots of Scotch and a twist of lemon—and sets it down gently on my ample armrest. It tastes excellent, like garden patios and cypresses.

MY LATE CAREER TURN with Big Oil began five years earlier, in March 2003. I'd driven from my office in Annapolis to D.C. to meet my friend Tom for lunch. Tom Boston, who heads the marine arm of Continental Oil, is an Ohioan, broad of hand and gut, with a fleshy face possessing the sort of pop-eyed wonder that makes all of smug Europe and sneering Russia reliably underestimate the American breed. Continental was then still my client. The official purpose of my lunches with Tom was for me to catch him up on the status of various technical and design projects that my engineering firm was handling for his department. After the debriefing, which usually lasted the seventeen minutes that it took for the waitress to arrive with our salmon or steak, we'd relax and begin to talk about what really interested us, the flight hours Tom had logged on his Cessna, or my tournaments in Tae Kwan Do—I was, at the age of fifty-nine, pursuing my black belt. "The trick is to pretend the kicks and punches are happening to someone else," I told him, suddenly remembering that this was something I had learned long ago, at the children's home.

"That's the upside of coming from a family like the Bostons," Tom boasted. "Today they pummel you, tomorrow they've got to go up against your four siblings and six cousins."

Tom's childhood had been in every conceivable way different from mine, except for the central fact that both of us had grown up poor without knowing quite how poor we were. Also, after boyhoods deprived of the sea, both of us had dedicated our lives to big ships. Among the things, I think, that had drawn together this outsized, amiable Midwesterner and me, the compact, contrarian Jew, was that, for both of us, life was a long show of mastery over our childhoods. That day, Tom had chosen a restaurant inside the Park Hyatt Hotel, a more impressive setting for our lunch meeting than the burger-and-steak houses to which Tom was inclined. He didn't bother with preliminaries. "I've got some interesting news," he said as soon as we sat.

"Do you?"

"Continental has made a deal with L___ Petroleum to buy a six-percent stake in the company from the Russian government."

"And this is *good* news?"

"What do you think? We've just been given access to a billion barrels in oil reserves. Our stock's about to get a nice little spike."

"Okay, I'll call my broker right now."

"Don't joke. At the moment it's still very *sub rosa*. Very buttoned up."

"And how much did you pay for such a privilege?"

"No more than two billion."

I picked up the menu.

"What you should be asking," Tom suggested, "is how much we're going to make."

"I'm sorry to tell you, my friend, but you're going to lose money on this thing. It's been—what—five, six years since every oil company has hurried to Russia. And name me a single venture that's making a profit. Their tax laws are always shifting. They violate contracts. They renege on debts. It's easier to get a drunkard off the ground there than a business." I had been trying to say the same thing to my son for the past four years, but Lenny insisted on taking the "long view."

"How about you don't worry about Continental's money," Tom said. "We aren't going bankrupt. Aren't you curious where we're drilling? I'll give you a hint—it's cold."

"That's very good, Tom. *Very* good."

"What are you smiling about?"

"The penguins."

"What penguins?"

"The penguins that the Kremlin will claim you poisoned when they decide to kick you out."

"There aren't any penguins where we're drilling."

"Putin will fly them in personally."

Tom leaned back in his chair and wrapped his meaty hands behind his head.

"In five years," I resumed, "they will claim you have been drilling in an ecologically delicate habitat, announce that you've poisoned all their fish, or polar bears, and demand you hand over half your profits or get the hell out. They'll give you a warning first—it is, after all, a Christian country."

"If you know so much, maybe you should work for us at Continental."

"You can't afford me," I demurred.

His hands still interlaced behind his head, Tom said, "Name a number. How much are they paying you at Herbert Engineering?"

Were we negotiating? Tom's question was enough to raise the color in my face. It was like a blunt proposition after a courtship so prolonged that all erotic possibilities had been drained from it years ago.

"I like working for Herbert. They let us bring our dogs to work."

"You don't have a dog."

"People play Frisbee on the lawn at lunch."

"You can play Frisbee on our lawn." Tom went on looking at me unblinkingly.

"What do you want me for?" I said. "I'm old."

"Reagan was sixty-nine when he was elected president." He didn't need to remind me. Among the assortment of things Tom and I happened to share was an abiding love of Ronald Reagan. With little Bush in office, there were not too many people to whom I could admit that one of the first actions I'd taken as a freshly minted American (being granted citizenship de jure upon arrival) was to cast my vote for Ronnie.

"What are you doing at Herbert now?" Tom proceeded. He had prepared his pitch. "Retrofitting Coast Guard vessels running thirty years past their prime? Performing life support on icebreakers commissioned in '65. Is that what you want to be doing when you retire?"

The mention of retirement reliably made my skin break out in a prickle. At fifty-nine, I wasn't quite done with ambition. Quite the contrary. At fifty-nine, I found that my ambition was inoculated with the strains of past disappointments, a drive to make up in the second half of the game the chances I'd lost in the first.

Tom explained the opportunity: L-Pet was very interested in tapping its Arctic potential. They wanted to launch a joint venture with Continental to build an offshore terminal in the half-frozen Barents Sea, from which crude could be ferried to the warm port of Murmansk.

"The Arctic is frozen eight months of the year, Tom. You've always claimed shipping across the Arctic isn't economically viable."

"Not yet—but soon."

"I thought you oil folks didn't believe in global warming."

"Nonsense. Our position is merely that 'climate change' is a natural rather than a man-made phenomenon. The area of open water in the Arctic is increasing rapidly, and the Barents Sea is gradually thawing. L-Pet has the oil, and we have the technology."

"What technology?" I said. Murmansk might be a warm port, but it was surrounded by two-foot-thick ice. You still had to get your crude up there, and those passageways were too tight for conventional icebreakers.

"That's the beautiful part. We're going to make our own dual-acting shuttle tankers. Three shuttle ships that'll carry the oil *and* break the ice. A totally new concept."

I couldn't believe it. A year ago, this idea had been mine. Now Tom was selling it back to me. When I pointed this out to him, he said, "You could make it real. You fiddle with other people's ships all day. No more of this Frankenstein business—it's time you designed your own."

"But I can do that from Herbert. You can get me to do it *cheaper* from Herbert."

"Yes, but at Herbert you're also potentially working for Exxon and Chevron, and who knows who else. Maybe we want to take you out of circulation."

Against appeals to my wallet I'd been able to put up some resistance, but against appeals to my vanity I was defenseless. Fool that I am, I've always suffered from the intellectual's weakness for praise.

He employed all his forceful charm and Reaganesque persuasiveness on me that afternoon. He needn't have worked so hard. Underneath my sarcasm was the unalterable fact that I would be turning sixty in seven months, and there were not going to be many more offers like this in my future.

Tom told me not to give him an answer right away, to sleep on it. But a formal offer arrived at my house by fax by the time I parked in the driveway. And once I saw that number, how *could* I sleep?

Had I known Tom's real motivation for wanting to hire me away, I might have had the guts to ask for double. It wasn't a master shipbuilder that he was after, but a person with my more accidental qualities. That evening, however, with the offer still warm in my hands, it occurred to me that the lucrative liaison Tom was proposing might present a rare opportunity to make a few late-stage adjustments for my parental neglect. Maybe, I wondered, the only way to get my son out of Russia was to take myself back to her.

10.

INDEPENDENCE DAY

UNTIL HIS THIRTY-FOURTH BIRTHDAY, LENNY BRINK BELIEVED THAT A man who did not have a million in the bank by the time he turned thirty-five was a failure. But adjustments had to be made. When he arrived in Moscow, nine years earlier, the age number in this equation had been thirty. The problem, as he saw it, was that the forces of globalization, like the forces of entropy, moved stealthily and unchecked across national and social membranes until everything began to resemble everything else. Today this problem was evident all over the leafy premises of Kuskovo Estate—Moscow's miniature "Versailles"—where the expatriate classes and their cohorts had congregated to celebrate America's independence. The summer residence of the Sheremetyev counts had been built to flatter the European aspirations of Russian nobility, but today, on either side of the baronial gardens, the white bosoms of marble statuary were garlanded with the decidedly American banners of Kodak and Avon. An inflatable Ronald McDonald hovered, Zen-like, on the bank of the koi pond. Helium balloons in primary red-white-and-blues were tangled with the branches of the ancient Russian pines. In the distance, the rose-hued central palace hung back from the festivities, slightly embarrassed, like a stout and unobtrusive chaperone. Here, along the geometric grounds of the city's imperial inheritance, the corporate sponsors of the American Chamber of Commerce had erected their food tents and concession stands for the annual Fourth of July celebration.

Pungent gusts of the aroma of shashlik wafted to the pine-shaded area where Lenny sat at a picnic bench, his large shoulders hunched in the task of consuming a second hot dog. The sky was turning the color of champagne, and snatches of Japanese, German, Dutch, and Texan floated on the grill-flavored air. "If dumb was dirt, he'd cover an acre. You wanna convert that to metric for the ladies, Dmitri," a Gulliver-sized oilman standing not two feet away was saying to his Russian companions. The ease with which these American belugas enjoyed their white-god privileges irritated Lenny all the more for the ways he felt incapable of enjoying them himself. Still, even the Texans' sturdy vulgarity offered greater comfort than other conversations he was overhearing, conducted in an unnervingly colloquial English that shielded its speakers' origins (Moscow? Bern? Cleveland?), no longer the stiff Esperanto of Europe's business class, but an all-purpose jargon that could be absorbed by osmosis through DVD marathons of *Lost* and *The Wire*. Its profusion at this picnic was adding a headachy panic to the gut-rumbling anxiety he'd been feeling since morning. In the nine years he'd been coming to AmCham's Independence Day party, the Russian-born had never been as hard to distinguish from the foreign expats as they were today. Lenny could still spot a few Hong Kong suits and more than enough baptismal crosses, but the once-reliable cohort of bleached denim and Adidas mafiawear had so dwindled that it could no longer be counted upon to restore his sense of superiority. In its place had proliferated a swarm of oxford button-downs, preppy pastel knits, and boating shoes, the summertime uniforms of the global elite. For a brief moment Lenny worried that his own wrinkled linen blazer might cause others to mistake him for a native.

His companions at the picnic table were two junior associates at his equity firm: a prematurely balding New Zealander, who was giving a spittle-laced facts-of-life lecture to a young Virginian brooding over his Ukrainian ex-wife. The ex-wife, with whom the Virginian still occasionally slept, was bleeding him for capital for her window-dressing business. "It's like Pavlov, mate, you've *conditioned* her to want your cash." The Virginian nodded sagely, almost as if it were some badge of honor to be so tormented and exploited by Slavic women. It struck Lenny that neither of these fools had any idea that Abacus Group was about to sack both of them upon the successful conclusion of the company's imminent buyout by Westhouse Capital Partners. He was, he assured himself, safe, being a senior associate

on a track to partnership. He listened to his companions just long enough
to vow to take a tougher stand with his own Slavic tormentor, Katya, then
crumpled his napkin resolutely into an overflowing trash can and resumed
his trek across the lawn. Since they had broken up three weeks ago, he had
gallantly assumed the couch while Katya continued to claim their bedroom. Almost a month had passed without her finding, or seeming to look
for, a place of her own. This morning he'd raised the topic at breakfast
only to be reminded by a sobbing Katya at the stove that he had *dragged* her
to this city, away from her beloved *mamochka* and little sister in St. Petersburg. Was she to leave her job, her whole life, now that she'd become for
him an *unnecessary person?* Perhaps it was the sight of her tears and mucus
dripping unhygienically into the kielbasa omelet she was frying for him
that prompted Lenny's spontaneous promise to subsidize her new rent, at
least for a few months. In addition to quieting her sniffles, this promise
had the virtue of being underwritten by the plump little bonus he was
anticipating from the WCP move and buyout, a bonus that, even with his
renewed obligations to Katya, would help him restore his depleted savings.
His only real concern on this bright afternoon, aside from the question-
able meat in the hot dog he was having trouble digesting, was that three
days had passed since his friend Austin had told him in strictest confidence
about the forthcoming deal, and so far no one else had mentioned anything about it. It was, of course, still too early for a formal announcement,
but Austin had all but assured him that as an almost-partner he'd certainly be brought along once Abacus got absorbed by the larger firm.

He had left Katya at home in the hope that he might more stealthily
scope out what was happening. Now he was rethinking this wisdom, given
Katya's propensity to chat up the people he was suddenly finding himself
too nervous to approach. Only a half-hour earlier he had spotted Abacus's
chief partner, Alex Zaparotnik, a man three years his junior, fraternizing
with some pink-shirts who were giving off a *very* Big Four vibe. Alex,
clearly seeing him, had not so much as raised his chin in acknowledgment.

Now, crossing the expanse of Kuskovo's beer-soaked lawn, Lenny kept
his eyes open for potential allies. Pulsing electronica from several sets of
speakers was assaulting his ears. Through these spasmodic house beats
and cycling loops of female moaning, he barely managed to make out the
reassuringly shrill vocalizations of his friend Noah, holding court among

some Alpha Capital folks under one of the red Coke umbrellas. "You would be wasting your money," Noah was testifying in his foghorn voice, "because you can get all the same wonderful things in Pattaya that you can get in Dubai: opium, exotic firearms, little girls, little boys, white sharks. The Thai, you see, are a very open people, like . . . playful cats." The recipients of Noah's wisdom were two giggling young women, whose combined waist sizes did not add up to Noah's own generous girth. Noah's hand was pruriently clutching at the hip of one, a brunette with a minuscule ass outlined nicely by a pair of jeans with lace-up calves. "You walk into any club in Pattaya, they got dancers squeezing ping-pong balls out of their minges." He squatted to demonstrate while his consorts shrieked with laughter. "I'm absolutely serious. I know a guy who had his eye poked out that way. Ask my friend here, he'll tell you all about it," he said, gripping Lenny's arm.

"I don't know what the hell he's talking about," Lenny assured the girls, both of whom, he quickly decided, were too young for his tastes. The blond one, though cute, still had her adolescent acne. He had no idea why these nymphets were so reliably drawn to Noah, a blob of fat who looked like Garfield the Cat. Lenny's only explanation was that, in Noah's years in Moscow, he'd made boatloads of cash managing the American investments of Mikhail Fridman, a job, Lenny believed, his friend had secured because of his uncanny physical resemblance to the oligarch himself. Perhaps being even an ugly oligarch's American doppelgänger somehow accounted for Noah's unnatural confidence with women.

"The girls and I have been comparing our travels. Yulia and Marina have just returned from Sochi, isn't that right?"

"The Saint-Tropez of Russia," Lenny remarked.

"And now they're on the way to . . ."

"Cairo!" announced Yulia.

"Better steer clear of the Arabs," Noah advised. "You know what the sight of white virgin flesh does to those Alis."

Instead of looking horrified, Yulia and Marina giggled once more and agreed that Egypt would indeed be much better if it wasn't so full of Arabs.

"Why don't you like Arabs?" said Lenny.

Yulia shrugged. "I danced next to an Arab in club. They have . . . a smell." The casual racism of Russian women never failed to impress him.

He'd heard the stink argument leveled at Africans, Arabs, everyone from the Caucasus, and even at apocrinely challenged Asian men. Prejudice on the Eurasian continent traveled eastward like the jet stream.

"Marina doesn't mind how they smell. She wants to be a stewardess for Emirates Airline."

"Emirates is not Arab!" Marina protested cheerfully. "It's Dubai!"

"Can I talk to you?" Lenny said.

"The girls have invited us to a party."

"I need to speak to you. Excuse us, please." It took some force to pull Noah aside. "I think something's up with the WCP deal. I just saw Zaparotnik. He acted . . . I don't know . . ."

"How many times have I told you to forget that guy? Let's go to a party. It's the Fourth of July, bay-bay."

"It's the sixth of July. I need to find Austin. Shit. Where is this party?"

"I don't know. On Kuznetsky Most, at the apartment of some BP faggot their friend Dasha lives with."

"No-hua!" Marina called across the grass. "Are you coming! Dasha is waiting at the gates!"

Noah motioned toward the porta-potties. "We're just gonna hit the unemployment line and meet you there."

"It was like I was some girl he was ignoring."

"You're sweating over that mayonnaise eater when you should be asking why you want to be a drone at WCP in the first place. You probably have enough clients by now to go independent."

"It's not that simple. . . ." Lenny couldn't remember what exactly he'd said to encourage this view of himself. Maybe he'd preserved the illusion by letting Noah go on assuming that he, Lenny, always looked out for number one as surely as Noah would have in his place. He scanned the hordes that populated the field. "I gotta find Austin; then we can go."

"He's over there at the whack shack." Noah pointed his chin at a stage by the Procter & Gamble raffle pavilion, which Lenny recognized as the source of the repeating loop of techno. The DJ had evidently abandoned his station long ago, and in his place two Russian dancers in Day-Glo bikinis had continued performing for an oblivious, hypnotized crowd of old white men.

"Wait here, will you?"

"That's not an order, I hope, because my plan right now is to piss and go to a party."

But Lenny was already picking his way across the minefield of red plastic cups and scattered bottles into the thick crowd around the stage where the bikinied dancers were doing go-go moves under strobe lights. Above the human sea facing the stage, Austin's red baseball cap bobbed like a buoy. "Hey, man!" Austin's face lit up with a reassuring flicker of genuine happiness. "Didn't think you were coming."

"Why not?"

"What?"

"Forget it. What are you doing after this?"

Austin took off his cap and wiped his bald and shaved head. "Maybe heading to Bleachers to watch the Rays screw up their shot at the playoffs."

Sometimes Lenny wondered why people like Austin even stayed in Moscow. Aside from professing an old-fashioned reverence for "other civilizations," Austin was drawn neither to the city's high culture nor to its copious depravity. His favorite activity on any given night was to sit in one of the Canadian pubs and follow the score of a Florida–Florida State game.

"Are you kidding me? It's not even a live game," Lenny said.

Austin gazed around. "Is Katya here?"

"No, she stayed home."

"You two all right?"

"Yeah, we're fine. You talk to Sasha Zaparotnik today?"

"Um . . . yeah, I saw Alex." Austin's smile seemed to pass from good-natured to impervious at the mention of Zaparotnik's name.

"So what's up with him chatting up those guys from WCP all afternoon . . . ?" Lenny hoped he was wrong. He was making a wild guess as to who the pink-shirts were, hoping that Austin would now contradict him.

But Austin did not.

"So have they made an offer, or what?" He tried to sound optimistic.

"Yes," Austin said wanly. "They've made an offer."

"Okay, then. So—we're keeping all our old clients, right?"

"Lenny . . ."

"The condition is they all keep us together in one department, right? Full autonomy . . ."

"Lenny, please stop talking."

But he could not stop. He was afraid at this moment that if he stopped his mouth might swell like a Novocained dental patient's and he would be unable to speak another word.

"Lenny. WCP isn't taking anyone except the partners."

"I'm on track to be partner."

"You aren't one right now, is what I'm saying."

"And why is that? *You* told me I'd be partner in a year when we started."

"Lenny, I brought you on. I can't hold your hand every step of the way. And, anyway, Alex is the one who's putting this deal together, not me, and *you* know how things between the two of you have been lately."

"I *don't* know. Why don't you tell me how they've been? He seemed pretty happy the day I brought in Actophage."

"Everybody appreciates what you've done."

"Oh shit, Austin . . ."

"Lenny, it's not my decision."

"Oh shit, please tell me you took my side in this. This is all so much bullshit, Austin."

Austin let out a long breath and looked out at something in the distance. "Of course I did, but you know you've pushed the guy's buttons."

"Like, what did I do!"

"Like calling him Sasha, for one."

"That's his fucking *name*."

"Whatever. Letting some of the clients think you're a partner. He didn't think that was cool."

"There are four of us. The clients *assume* we're all partners."

An unconvinced look stole over Austin's face. He was a person who often disagreed but seldom argued.

The truth was, Lenny *had* thought of himself as a partner. In all but name. And the fact that he hadn't yet been made one officially was an oversight that he was sure would be rectified in a matter of time. "Okay, okay, don't go," Lenny said. "Just . . . help me understand. What did he say?"

"Why are you doing this to yourself, Len?"

"You owe me at least that."

Austin wiped his head again with the side of his cap, and then seemed absorbed in studying the sweat stain. "He thinks you don't always have a sense of the importance of the mission, that sometimes you think like a, like a . . ."

"Like a what?"

"Like a Russian."

"*He* called me a Russian! What the hell does that even mean?"

"The way you're always talking about 'the Big Picture,' and paying for everyone's drinks, and—"

"What's wrong with a little generosity?"

"Nothing's wrong with it. It's just all the glad-happy *tovarisch* stuff you do with everyone, with the clients. It's typical Manilovism."

"You're losing me, Austin."

"Manilov in *Dead Souls*. Gogol—you read it."

Lenny was caught by the twin surprise that Austin *had* read it and that he assumed that Lenny would be at least equally literate in his own heritage. "Yeah, fifteen years ago," Lenny lied, "what about it?"

"Manilov—the one who's always daydreaming about building a bridge over the river where the merchants will set up booths and sell goods to the peasants. But then, when someone interrupts his daydream with a practical request, his brain can't digest it."

"I don't need a fucking book report."

Austin put his cap back on and adjusted the visor. "Lenny, you'll find something. I'm sorry." He appeared to see someone in the distance and lifted his arm in recognition. "I have to go," he said, manfully gripping Lenny's shoulder in parting.

Lenny was finding it hard to move his legs. His feet were suddenly very heavy, or else his knees couldn't be fully trusted not to buckle if he took a step. Not three feet from him, two little girls—five or six years old—were gleefully imitating the libidinous gyrations of the dancers onstage. Lenny heard the sound of his own laughter, a madman's giggle.

BACK IN 2001, WHEN "Alex" was still "Sasha," a pasty-cheeked graduate of Moscow State University whose stoop and pallor spoke of innumerable hours in front of the gelatinous glow of computer screens, the two had been paired up on a mission to do standard analysis on a turbine factory outside the eastern-Siberian town of Plusinsk. The factory was a dud that had languished in negotiations with three other consulting firms in four years. By the time Lenny had arrived in Russia, the choicest plants had all been cherry-picked by the big investment funds, the least choicy ones snapped up on the cheap and stripped for assets. A venturesome young private equity associate had to be more enterprising to find a true investment gem. The turbine factory was their first scouting assignment following a flimsy six-week training program in which they'd been taught to fill out financial and risk reports. The "business jet" WCP had booked for them turned out to be a Yak-40 with a wheezing engine. Their driver and guide in Plusinsk, Kostya, was a five-foot hustler with a junkie's frame and an unheated van that would have required a blowtorch to thaw out, but which Kostya managed to navigate with terrifying skill through the run of potholes that was the Plusinsk road system. Watching a Tarkovsky-esque tableau of rotting utility poles, shell-shocked farmers, and orange snow through the window of Kostya's van, Lenny felt happier than he'd ever been in his life. He thought about all his friends in America with their office jobs and their weed and their HBO. Fuck *The Sopranos*, he thought. Fuck *The X-Files*. He was fuckin' *living* that shit. A cowboy on the frontiers of private enterprise.

The Plusinsk Turbine Factory turned out to be in far better shape than he or Sasha Zaparotnik had expected. It had once been a premier Soviet manufacturer, producing mainly defense-related turbines and generators. Its fatal flaw was neither its debt (modest compared with the typical Russian factory), nor its outdated equipment, which was still viable, but the fact that its management, coddled for years by the plant's defense-industry status, was unwilling to sell a majority share to any foreign firm. The factory was like a moderately attractive woman who'd become an old maid because her expectations were overinflated.

Lenny and Sasha were not expected to score where other matchmakers had failed. Their assignment was not to usher the factory's managers into a shotgun marriage with foreign investors, but merely to crunch some numbers and report whether the plant was worth taking on the buyer's side. Such a job would require an afternoon and a half, which meant that the remaining time could be spent at the local *banya*, partying with some cheap Plusinsk girls. (Lenny had already worked this out with their guide, Kostya, who had offered to arrange both for the *zakuski* and the girls.) But Sasha Zaparotnik had other plans. He had spoken with one of the turbine engineers and learned of a "nearby" geothermal plant some five hundred miles away.

The small thermal field had been abandoned early in the previous decade by the Soviet government, after it had drilled boreholes and set up grid connections and before the nation had run out of money and dropped the project altogether. It now belonged to an oil-and-gas conglomerate which was making so much from its petroleum sales that it had let the plant languish without adding any new investments to it. The conglomerate could be easily convinced to sell the facility, Sasha reasoned. And this was where Lenny lost him. Zaparotnik could be forgiven for thinking that five hundred miles was a short distance by Russian standards, but the kid had to be either a fool or a nationalist to want to ride in the stale heat of the Trans-Siberian just to poke his head down a thermal hole. Sure, it had to hurt to see his motherland's once-robust industries ground to dust, painful to watch legions of uncles and grandpas with advanced degrees made redundant. But thermal power? Seriously? When the country was literally bleeding oil? No, thanks.

That, more or less, was what Lenny told Sasha when he left him at the Plusinsk train station and took a flight alone back to Moscow. He didn't speak to Zaparotnik much until they presented their findings together to the company partners. And that was when Sasha made his surprise case for the little geothermal plant. Counterintuitive as it seemed to try to find a buyer for a thermal plant in an oil-rich country that subsidized its citizens' gas bills, if WCP took another look, it would notice that the field was in a part of Russia where there was an unmet demand for energy, and where the electricity prices were among the highest, since much of the fuel had to be transported from a long distance away. The plant had been overlooked because everyone believed it was too expensive to complete it in the harsh climate. But there was a simple solution: the plant could be designed in modular pieces, which would be manufactured in warmer western Siberia, then airlifted and assembled right on the spot. The most difficult part—the drilling—had already been done by the Soviets. The plant could even start producing electricity immediately and finance the drilling of new boreholes with the money. If a buyer was willing to make, say, a sixteen-million-dollar investment, the project could start financing itself practically overnight. With only a dozen permanent employees,

Sasha reported, its operational costs were actually quite low. Most of the other work could be done with cheap seasonal labor.

Sitting through Sasha Zaparotnik's presentation with virtually nothing to add, Lenny had felt his mouth go dry with cottony sourness. The fetus-face had thought of everything. He'd even found a company in Japan that might be a willing investor. He'd choreographed it all without giving Lenny so much as a heads-up while the two of them had assembled their PowerPoints the night before.

BUT THAT HAD BEEN seven years ago, and much had changed since. Lenny had gone on to have a few successes of his own. He had some talent for drumming up business on the road, and he was a guy the clients could depend on to organize some fun. Part of him had been surprised when he'd gotten the offer from Abacus. It might have been a peace offering on Zaparotnik's part, and there was also the fact that the other two partners, both close friends of Lenny's, were numbers guys in need of a salesman. By this time, Sasha was going by "Ah-lix" and had transformed into one of those de-Russified Russians who sported Anglicized names and certificates from the London School of Economics. Lenny knew that to give voice to his disdain for the "Ah-lix"es was only to make himself vulnerable to an equal and opposite disdain Alex had for him. Zaparotnik always seemed to be looking straight through Lenny's best attempts at business chumminess down to his neurotic immigrant core, as if it were a tragedy to belong to that confused breed of expats whose families had escaped the Soviet Union only to have their children return, salmonlike, to dip their heads into the fecal pool of a *newly democratic* Russia.

UNDER A SKY TURNING from champagne to magenta, Lenny slouched onward in the direction of the front gates, the tacky, sweet odor of burnt grill fat leaving in its wake an odd nostalgia. It made him recall his two years of college fraternity life at Rutgers—the lawn cookouts watched enviously by the unaffiliated freshmen and sophomores. He hadn't stayed in touch with his "brothers" or particularly missed them. What he missed was the fact of affiliation itself, its code of loyalty. It was the promise he had seemed to rediscover in Moscow. In their own way, he and his expat friends had formed a kind of fraternity. The familiar haunts—Bourbon Street, Molly's, Mishka Pub—the all-night benders, the instant friendships over shots, the inexhaustible supply of willing girls, all of it had the same collegiate flavor of life moving fast and yet somehow placed on hold. And, with a bit of maturity and a little money in his pocket, he had at last been able to enjoy it. He had always assumed that he and his American friends in Moscow shared this code of loyalty. When had everything changed? When had guys like Austin started taking Sasha's side? Or was it possible—and this terrified him most of all—that he had been wrong about it from the beginning? That he'd been alone on the lawn all along?

At the front gates, Lenny found Noah bumming a cigarette off some strangers, even though, Lenny was sure, he had a pack of his own somewhere on his body. "Where the hell have you been?" Noah said, gesturing threateningly with the smoke. "You told me five minutes."

"I'm sorry. Are the girls here?"

"They left!"

"I'm out of the WCP deal."

"We're both out of luck, then. Damn it, boy, I hate throwing back my catch."

"I'm sorry."

"You're always sorry. Make it up to me with some food. My stomach's turning from this cafeteria slop."

IT WAS NOAH'S IDEA to take them to Night Flight to lift Lenny's spirits, though a day of stuffing himself on oily hot dogs and soggy corn had not left Lenny in a gustatory mood for rosemary reindeer or elk carpaccio in truffle sauce. Nor was he in the proper state of mind to fend off the coercive friendliness of a roomful of model-level chicks throwing him kittenish glances. For the past twenty minutes, one auburn-headed seductress in the corner had been giving him sad little twists of the smile that only you and she can understand. A year ago this might have worked its magic, but these days all Lenny ever felt around a hooker were vague guilty stirrings and an overwhelming desire to *save her*. That so many impossibly proportioned beauties should have to ply their trade in a restaurant catering to saggy-breasted middle-aged foreign fatsos also attested, in his mind, to a deep flaw in the world's balance of justice.

"Cheer up," said Noah, sawing a knife into his elk flank.

"Why did we have to come here? There's plenty of legitimate restaurants we could have gone to."

"This is a legitimate restaurant. It's got a website!"

"It's a brothel attached to a restaurant."

"A five-*star* restaurant with one of the best Scandinavian chefs in the world. And the girls here are all independent. No pimps threatening to blade their face. I'll have you know that some of them have even gone home with me for free."

"I'm glad you're proud of it."

"I am proud, and I'll tell you why—because it speaks to my powers of persuasion. I told you three months ago, when you had your hands on that Actophage deal, to go to Zaparotnik and tell them all you were walking out unless they made you a partner. And what did you do? You took it like a woman and let them pay you in compliments. You were thinking corporate—keep everyone in the loop, share the bounty, get a little reciprocal action down the line, right? And where did that get you? That doesn't even work in America. And with guys like Zaparotnik, forget it! These people haven't believed in the collective spirit since Collectivization."

"Thank you for the lecture."

"*Na zdorovye.*"

"It's not just Zaparotnik. It's this whole place. I remember when it used to be *exciting*. And now it's become so"—Lenny groped for the words—"pissily bourgeois. Maybe it's time I went back to the States."

"And do what—paste numbers from financial statements onto a spreadsheet for twelve hours a day? Make cold calls while you wait for a corner office?"

"My mom's pushing grad school."

"Of course she is. All immigrant parents want their children to be second-generation nobodies with framed degrees on the wall. It's a stagnant pond over there, my friend. They just don't want to face it."

"I don't know. I was walking home the other night, and suddenly I'm in this pack of dogs, all these scary stray bitches with their six tits, jumping up and barking at me, baring their teeth like I stole their last piece of ham. I swear to God, Noah, that's never happened to me before. Either this city has become overrun with them or they can smell the weakness on me."

Noah waited until Lenny was finished talking, then glanced up with one eye from his respectful position of nodding at the table. "Look, Misha Fridman's got friends putting together some interesting deals. I'll ask around, see who's hiring. But before we venture so deep into Sartre Land, can we just agree tonight to relax? I am having a very good cut of meat, and there is a beautiful, vibrant woman on the other side of this room who is flashing me a 'glaze-my-face-like-a-doughnut' smile." Noah now took a moment to glance over Lenny's shoulder and wink.

"Great. Now she's going to come here and sit with us, and we'll have to buy her dinner."

"Don't worry, cheapskate, this one's on me."

"I'm sorry if I don't feel like spending the evening chatting up a hooker."

"These ladies are not 'hookers.' Hookers are what you find on the side of the Leningradskoye Shosse with a bunch of Dagestanians lining up for blow jobs. These are inviting, mysterious creatures making use of their bankable advantage in life. Or would you rather be sipping on a faggy daiquiri in a strip club where every chick has a copy of the club's rules tattooed on her ass? Now, behave yourself, because she's coming over."

"Dobriy vecher," the girl said, smiling, and then, more formally in English, "May I join you?" Noah gestured gallantly to the chair, then stood and pulled it out for her. She lowered herself onto it like a snake coiling back into a charmer's clay pot. She wore snug black pants, a colorful butterfly pendant, and a backless, shoulderless top that looked like a pool of mercury held up by threads of silver.

"My friend wants to guess your name," said Noah as Lenny made denying headshakes. "Come *on*."

"Vika."

"No."

"Zhana."

She shook her head.

"I give up."

"You are warm." She patted Lenny's hand in an encouraging way. "Yana."

It could not be denied that Yana was indeed stunning. She had light-brown eyes and a small aquiline nose, as well as a snaggletoothed smile that lent a sweet, slutty twist to her otherwise pneumatic beauty.

Noah gestured for the waitress to bring an extra menu for their guest. Barely looking at the offerings, Yana picked two starters and a glass of one of the better wines, dispatching her order with unsettling familiarity. "Yana, my friend Leonard and I were just discussing the stray dog population in this city. I always think better of a city when its stray animal population is cats rather than dogs."

"Is that so?" said Lenny.

"Yes. It speaks to a more refined culture."

What in the world was Noah doing? An hour ago he'd been leching up two teenagers, and now he was playing his worldly gentleman act? To impress whom? A paid escort?

"They're a fucking nuisance either way," Lenny heard himself say, just to cut the shit-thick air of pretension.

"Watch your mouth."

"All of them ought to be shot so they don't go around biting people."

Yana's face assumed a beautiful look of horror. "No, it is the other way! Dogs are good, it is *people* who are cruel. There was a dog, he lived in the metro, very friendly. The people fed him and gave him name Mal'chik—like, 'little boy.' And famous fashion model was walking with her dog, who started biting Mal'chik. This was *many* people watching," Yana said with adorable insistence. "And this model, she took out knife and—phoof!—into Mal'chik's back!"

"You mean she stuck a knife in the dog's back?" Lenny exchanged frightened looks with Noah.

"Yes, yes, yes! Then she ran away from Russia! And many people, they were angry. Actors and important personages, they asked metro administrators to make a sculpture to Mal'chik."

"A monument, for the dog?"

"*Statue of the Fallen Mongrel*," Noah said.

"Yes, they shown it on the television."

"Wow," said Lenny. "If this city has enough money to put up sculptures to stray dogs, why don't they neuter a few, do us all a favor?"

Once again Yana regarded him as if he were deranged. "Neuter, like," she turned to Noah and made a snipping gesture to make sure she understood. "*Uzhas!* If they neutered a man, he would not anymore be a real man! If they neuter a dog, he is no more a *real* dog."

Noah's eyes were dancing. It was evident to Lenny that Yana's line of reasoning was making him ever more enchanted with her. He proposed they take the conversation somewhere more comfortable, such as his château, and motioned for the check. Yana, smiling in agreement with this idea, told them to wait a minute while she went downstairs to get her things.

On the rain-slicked neon street, trying to flag a gypsy cab, Lenny saw that by her "things" Yana had meant not a dainty purse but a much larger object that, from the look of its hard case, appeared to be a violin.

WASHING ONE'S HANDS AFTER a piss in Noah's bathroom proved to be a difficult task. The sink, a giant piece of hand-blown art glass, was cleft by a giant crack. "Your sink's broken!" Lenny hollered over the flushing sounds.

"So use the one in the kitchen!" Noah called back. Lenny shook his head and wiped his hands on his jeans. Noah's proclivity for pretentious novelties always struck him as absurd. And still there was little comfort in the thought, as Lenny walked into the kitchen, that if *he* had Noah's money he would put it to better use. Rinsing his hands in the kitchen sink, he watched Noah and Yana through the open bar. They were seated on the couch, comparing the sizes of their palms, Noah concupiscently gushing over the delicacy of Yana's hands while Yana bemoaned how she had been diagnosed at age six with fingers too short to play the piano and therefore had taken up the violin. "And my mother—she would not let me go outside and play with my friends, or with balls, because my fingers would break."

"Poor Yana." Noah frowned sympathetically. "Poor, poor Yanochka."

"I think I'm gonna take off," Lenny announced.

Noah looked up. "No, stick around! Yana's going to play for us."

"Yes!" Yana said, briskly pulling back the fine exposed muscles of her shoulders as she stood up from the couch.

"I will be right back." Noah left them alone while he went to fix drinks.

Yana was standing by the wall-sized window, admiring the view of Tsvetnoy Boulevard below. Her fingers, which did not look at all short to Lenny, touched the cold glass.

"Klass!" she said, somewhat blandly. "This is best view I see of Moscow."

Briefly, Lenny let himself wonder how many such views she had to compare it with. "Where are you from?" he said.

"Voronezh."

"Voronezh is nice."

Yana turned and leveled him with a sarcastic look. *"Ochen'."* As if. Her sudden switch to Russian had the effect of puncturing the low-key mood of urbanity and intimacy. How did they always know, Lenny wondered? Even when he hadn't spoken a word of Russian to them, these girls could always tell he was from the old country.

"What do you do? I mean, during the day?" he said idiotically.

"Student. Gnesinka." She pointed to the violin case.

"That's a very impressive school."

"Yes, very."

"Do you want to be a concert musician—like, play in the Bolshoi Orchestra?"

Yana gave him an inscrutable look. She didn't appear pleased with the familiarity and seriousness this conversation was taking. "As we say here, the colonels have their own children. And so do the musicians, as it happens." She shrugged and turned back to the window.

Jesus, what was wrong with him? Why did he always try to chat up these birds of paradise and drag them down to the level of ordinary girls? Yana looked relieved when Noah waltzed back into the room with a tray of three cognac glasses and said, "Let the concert begin!"

WHEN YANA WALKED BACK into the living room, she wore her butterfly pendant and four-inch heels and nothing else. Her hair hung like Lady Godiva's over two hard little tits, and she was guarding her lower half humbly with the polished violin. At her thigh, the bow swayed back and forth in her hand like a riding whip. "I will play for you Dvořák," she announced, and in a single motion lifted the violin to reveal a prim, slender isosceles. She set her small chin down on the saddle and, with a quick intake of breath and a gaze out at the enormous city night, began to play.

In all his life, Lenny felt he had never heard such music. Snatches of high-pitched chords cut the silence and disappeared, radiantly, violently, like lightning punishing the earth. The music seemed to take possession of her body—rising from Yana's painted toes up through her bent, pale leg, where a tender brown bruise bloomed. It vibrated up her long, slim torso before being released by her taut wrist to unlock the violin's resonant moan. Only Yana's face stayed pinched and vacant as her playing gathered momentum and shifted, with each turn of the bow, from wild defiance to something proud and almost scornful, to unfathomable sadness. She swayed on her teetering heels like a bridge, and from time to time her knee did a little gallop, as if to keep her from pitching forward. Her pale breasts, the pencil-eraser nipples pointing bashfully away from each other, bobbed along with her flushed performance.

Noah shook his head. "State of the fucking art," he whispered. "I can't tell if these chicks are sent from heaven or from hell."

Lenny wished he'd shut up. He was battling both unspeakable heartache and a budding boner, all of which only added to the exquisite shame and loneliness he'd been feeling all afternoon. He watched as Yana—if that was even her name—attacked the violin. A sheen of sweat had formed above her lips and between her heartbreaking breasts. Lenny let his eyes fall shut and concentrated on each wailing phrase as it stacked up into a ladder of sound that went all the way up, up. . . . To where? He wanted to follow the notes to their highest and thinnest abyss and dwell there forever. God, he hated this city. Yet he couldn't bear the thought of leaving. Where else on earth could he ever find so much mercy?

11.

___

HOMECOMING

MY PLANE TOUCHES DOWN JUST BEFORE EIGHT IN THE EVENING. MOS-
cow's sky is still lucent, the undersides of the copper clouds catching the
last of the long day's sun.

I call Lenny from my cab. He's spirited in his usual way as we talk about
where to meet for dinner. "You like sirloin, Pop? Good, good. Or maybe Italian, pasta 'n' clams?"

Great, I say, leaving out the fact that I'm never hungry after a long
flight.

"Or, no, Armenian!" he pursues. "I know just the place." He tells me
he'll take me to the most *prikol'ny* spot in my neighborhood. By the time I
arrive at my hotel, he's listed off a couple more places we can go, demonstrating his expertise in the local cuisine and hinting at his personal
knowledge of the chefs. For a moment I wonder if he's forgotten who he's
talking to and thinks I'm a client. Then again, maybe it's all to remind his
old papa what an undislodgeable native—what a Muscovite—he's become.

Within an hour I'm out of my steaming, sanitized hotel shower, towel-
ing off and preparing to meet my son for our late dinner. Outside, the air is
warm, pleasantly intimate, as if a sea is lurking somewhere behind all
those blazing pastel façades. Tverskaya Street is immaculately groomed,
almost Swiss in its cleanliness. Not a stray cigarette butt about, even
though every person who passes me seems to be smoking his little heart

out. The mood is almost—how can I say it?—*festive* enough to make me regret my earlier cynical thoughts about Lenny. His manic enthusiasm on the phone was probably just a sign that he's pleased to see his dad. For all my son's muddled allegiances, he has always been sincere about wanting everyone around him to be happy. Only, tonight he has no idea about the bucket of ice water that I'm obligated to toss on his variety show. In my briefcase, I'm carrying ten pounds of glossy paperback GMAT text-books—a present from Lenny's mother, who's told me I shouldn't bother coming home until I've convinced our son to do the "only reasonable thing."

I console myself that I'm only following orders while I inhale the flatu-lence of car exhaust, the faint reek of wet varnish, the after-scent of spilled beer, which remind me that I am in a city that I know far better than my son does. In the course of my visits I've started to think of Moscow as a complicated woman I was closely entwined with in my youth, but who, in our late-life encounters, has surprised me by not aging gracefully (as I have) but instead rejuvenating herself with a succession of increasingly more expensive face-lifts. Each time we meet, I notice some new augmen-tation: A Canali boutique where once stood a pharmacy. Gaudy casino lights in place of a familiar pawnshop. Even the glass pyramid atop the mayor's new office, which I spied on my drive here, is as obscenely radiant as a marquise-cut diamond on the finger of an oilman's dame. Tverskaya in particular was so collagened and siliconed that I've long stopped think-ing of her as the Gorky Street of my youth. Tonight I pass whole blocks under renovation, girdled by scaffolds, corseted and draped in jade-colored nets beneath which all sorts of nips and tucks are being discreetly per-formed.

I'm the first to arrive at the restaurant, a cheerily domestic, half-empty Armenian joint. A furry-browed waiter leads me in and hands me, inexpli-cably, a second menu in English.

Lenny arrives, looking freshly shaved and ten pounds heavier than I remember. I point to the English menu. "What gave me away? I don't look or sound any more foreign than the maître d'."

"Look around you," says Lenny. "Who else asks to be seated in the non-smoking section?"

He's right! We're the only ones in our dungeony corner of the dining room. Which is probably for the best: At the other end of the hall is a noisy party of six trunk-necked gentlemen, their banquet table looking like it's about to snap under the weight of a forest of bottles. Across the room I can hear one of them pursuing some pointless slurring story about a time he boxed a kangaroo.

"You look good," I tell my son, not entirely truthfully.

"I'm trying to stay fit," he says, to my surprise.

"Oh yeah?"

"Been playing a little tennis."

I take his word for it, though he looks more like a tennis ball than a tennis pro. Also, he's let his hair get too long at the neck, combing it back like a pimp's. A shame. Lenny is a good-looking guy when he takes care of himself. "So what's your plan for the week?" he says.

I tell him: I'm here just until Monday, together with my boss, Tom, who's arriving tomorrow. We're reviewing bids for shipping contractors. "We're looking for a charter company to pilot some shuttle tankers from the Nanatz coast to a terminal near Murmansk." I'm surprised Lenny doesn't remember. "It's the joint venture I was telling you about, with L___ Petroleum."

He cocks his eyebrow. "L-Pet? You're in business with them? Those guys are the Kremlin's lapdog. They're practically a branch of the FSB."

"We don't get involved in their politics. This should be pretty straight-forward."

Then, just to remind me how much better he knows this place than I do, he says, "Nothing here is straightforward."

There's a vitreous crash at the other end of the dining room. "Now look what you've done, Sava," says one of the bald gentlemen, a gorilla in a lavender shirt. The waiter is called in to clean up while poor Sava tries to finish his kangaroo story. He doesn't have a chance. The lavender-clad *gospodin* announces he's tired of the whole circus and tells the others to "clean him up."

"How is Katya?" I ask while Sava is dragged out of the room between sets of oak-sized arms.

Lenny makes a sucking breath. "It's over. More or less."

I try to do a good impression of looking upset by his news. Katya is a perfectly nice girl. I've even gotten used to the little baptismal cross she is never without, and her affection for interpreting dreams and reading the future in the dregs of her Turkish coffee. Ever since he's moved to Moscow,

I've given up on a woman of character for Lenny. But is it too much to ask for someone whose perspective on twentieth-century history is not that "the monstrosity of Soviet communism was a curse delivered on the Russian people for the crime of slaying their tsar"? Yes, my son is dating a monarchist.

"So which is it?" I say. "More, or less? Has she moved out?"

"No, but we've agreed to see other people."

"Now, how does that work? Does one of you take the couch while the other has a date?"

He looks more upset by this joke than I think is called for. "She'll move out as soon as I can help her get her own place."

"Well, that shouldn't be too hard," I say encouragingly. "It's a big city. Plenty of apartments."

"You kidding? The rents here are worse than in New York."

I study his face for a moment. "Lenny, you haven't told her that you'll be paying her rent. Right?"

He recites once more the story of how Katya "abandoned" her family and job in St. Petersburg to move to Moscow for him. She can't afford to live on her own and can't go back to Peter because her mother's lover has recently moved into the family apartment. "Everything's become very complicated."

"Complicated for her, not for you."

"You don't understand how it's done."

"Is there a protocol?" I inquire. "I mean, for paying the rent of a woman you don't want to live with anymore? Are you a don who needs a goomah to shtup once a week? Even that I might understand. At least it's *logical*. But what I'm hearing is you don't want this person at *all*."

"Drop it, Pa," he says. Only *he* doesn't. Instead, he starts enumerating Katya's myriad virtues—her kindness and gentleness and dedication to him. I dare not ask why anyone would want to leave such a saint. "You and I are different people," he tells me stoically.

I grin and bear this. "All right, Lenny," I say, "but even decency has to be matched by means. Where are you going to get the funds to pay this alimony? Are you working right now?"

The color leaves his face. He rakes his bitten fingers through his hair. "I knew it. Nobody in this family can keep their goddamn mouth shut."

"So your sister told us. So what? If you're in trouble, we want to help."

"Did she tell you how Austin and the rest of my friends sold me down the river?"

"At least now you know who your friends are. *Druzhba druzhboi a taba-chok vroz'*."

"Yeah, well, I'm not crying over it. I've already got some opportunities lined up."

I bite my lip. "Maybe you shouldn't be rushing into something so soon. Take some time. Think about all your options."

He doesn't answer right away. "What do *you* suggest?" he says at last in a tone mistakable for either despair or sarcasm.

I seize my opportunity and remove the two GMAT tomes from my briefcase. Lenny winces as if he's just watched me drop soiled underpants on the table. "Let me guess whose idea this was."

I smile. "I've got another two in my hotel room."

"Is this supposed to be some kind of bait?"

"It's a serious offer, Lenny. You come back home. Live with us for a few months, or as long as you want. Study. Once you get into business school, we can help pay for the first year."

"And Mama can bring cucumber-and-bologna sandwiches up to my room, right? I'm thirty-four, for chrissake, not sixteen."

Before I can bite my tongue, I say, "And what's your plan? To stay here and compete with the homegrown phys-mat geniuses?"

The hurt on his face is more immense than I expected.

"You and Ma still think a framed degree is the answer to everything. It's your fucking immigrant delusion."

"Come on, Lenny." I try to smile.

"And anyway, I'm too old to go back to school."

I see a chance to redeem myself. "You're not too old. I was two years older than you when I left this country and started over." But I can already hear my wife's admonishments about talking about myself. According to her, all my advice to Lenny boils down to "how you're a something and he's a nothing." I suspect some of this is the influence of our daughter, Masha, a champion of Freudian analysis, who likes to say that my upbringing by a single, psychologically "damaged" mother has made me "second-generation dysfunctional."

"Look," I say, "you've been here—what—nine years? I happen to know that every seven years a man is released from all his obligations. He can wipe his hands, walk away, start clean. Take a look in the Torah if you don't believe me. It's called the Sabbatical Year."

He stares at me like I've lost my mind. "Since when have you been cracking the Torah?"

I smile. "You don't have to decide right now. Just—consider it." I get up, beckoned by the men's room, and leave Lenny to do just that.

When I get to the toilets, I find my entry blocked by a tiny babushka with a short-handled broom. I step right. So does she. I make a move to the left, but she's one step ahead of me, serenely determined not to let me pass. She flashes me an apologetic gold-toothed grin and points to the women's room. I decide I'd rather hold it in. I turn around and rejoin Lenny at the table.

We eat in silence for a while, the GMAT books between us like the Berlin Wall. Finally, he says, "What the hell is going on over there?" I look up. One of the stooges who'd dragged Sava to the men's room is back. His hand seems to be bleeding. He plucks a cloth napkin from the table, wraps it tourniquet-style around his meaty palm, and upends half a bottle of vodka on the wound. Then, like nothing, he sits back down with the others and resumes drinking. The gentleman in lavender tosses some bills into the general chaos of the table and within a minute the rest of them take their cue and are heading for the door. I figure it's as good a time as any to revisit the little boy's room. To my relief, the babushka isn't standing guard anymore. But when I swing open the door she's right there, perched on a footstool and sponging the mirrors above the sinks. A clean arc of crimson spatter covers both of our reflections. I shut myself in the stall. From the neighboring stall issue retching sounds, punctuated by almost prim gasps of strangled respiration. As I leave I give a captain's salute to the babushka sponging blood off the tiles.

"All right, I'll take the books," he says when I come back. "*If* you promise to stop bugging me about coming home."

"I have my orders, Lenny."

He slides them back to me.

"Please, just keep them. I can't take them back to your mother."

He shakes his head. And then, as if on cue, drunken Sava is back. From the men's room he weaves his way between the empty tables like a passenger swaying in the aisle of a train. His misbuttoned shirt is covered with unspeakable stains. A cloud of panicked disappointment steals over his face as he realizes his friends have all left him. Lenny and I trade glances as bruised, bloodied Sava staggers out through the glass doors, then pauses to look left and right, searching in vain for his friends and tormentors.

A grin opens up in Lenny's face. *"Velkom home,* Dad!" he says, opening his arms ceremoniously. *"Velkom home."*

12.

LITTLE ENEMIES

SARATOV
1951

ПОЧТА
СССР

MY WIFE MIGHT BE RIGHT WHEN SHE SAYS, IN HER MOMENTS OF IRE, THAT I make so many missteps in communicating with our grown son because I had no father to walk me through to manhood. But what she scornfully calls my "hands-off approach" isn't a consequence of ignorance, as she believes, but of too much knowledge. What lessons there were to be fished from the black hole between my abruptly aborted childhood and my premature young adulthood were not the sorts of things I was eager to pass on to my own children. The little I learned that *was* worthwhile . . . well, I can't say for certain it has any value in the world we all live in so innocently and publicly now.

Whenever I tell anyone that I spent ages six to thirteen inside of public orphanages, they tend to arrange their face in a reaction I call the Purple Heart Ceremony. It's as if they've discovered that my legs are actually prosthetics. They want to see the stumps but are careful to maintain eye contact. Their voices grow pious with sympathy.

It's to avoid all this that I usually don't talk about those years. Once the fact is laid out, everything I say or don't say about it grows heavy with heroic implication. And, in the end, the sound of my own voice irritates me even more than the delicate inquisitiveness of others. Mostly, though, I just don't want to go through all the trouble of correcting their Dickensian notions of orphanhood. The persistent hunger, the heartless punishments—all those were part of my story, but they weren't the only part. By grace or luck, I wound up in a home where we children were treated with civility, even affection.

I was lucky for another reason: my tenure as an orphan happened to coincide with the period after the war, when the national sentiment was swinging in our favor. No longer were we the seeds of kulaks, criminals, and counterrevolutionaries. Our vagrancy, no more the mark of criminality, was a badge of patriotic sacrifice. All over the country, children's homes were swelling with the war's little victims, and it was among the dead heroes' offspring that we—the littlest enemies—sought camouflage. Perhaps that's how it started for me, my earliest lesson in keeping secrets.

The postwar years were a time of rations and shortages, and yet the variety of food at the Memory of Krupskaya Children's Home was remarkable: wheat bread, oatmeal, buckwheat, barley, honey, conserves, eggs, Dutch cheese, cottage cheese with raisins, compote, peas, cucumbers, cabbage, carrots, tomatoes, and on occasion even kielbasa and watermelon. How did we manage it? We had sponsors—the orphanage was patronized by the local kolkhoz as well as the trade union of a local factory. But the real secret was our director, Mark Pavlovich Guchkov, who was uncommonly deft at courting patronage of this sort.

I picture him clearly, a week into my arrival at the Krupskaya Home. He stands before us in the assembly room, a kind of gymnasium with an old upright piano at one end of a small stage. He is young, no more than thirty-five or thirty-six, and already balding. His wispy brown hair is combed back from a tall forehead. He wears a pulpy brown suit that smells strongly of tobacco. The sleeve of his missing arm is not pinned up to his shoulder, as I've seen other war invalids do; it hangs down loosely, tucked into a pocket of his jacket. In his able-armed hand he holds up something small and white. "This is the kind of soap French women use," he informs us, lifting it up higher so that all us children can see. "French women are ladies, with a high level of culture, measured by how they treat their things. They don't let their soap sit in puddles of water. When they are done using it, they *clean it off* and leave it like this—completely dry."

I am there in that room, sitting in a row of other seven- and eight-year-olds, our heads cocked back, our mouths hanging open. All the boys have the same haircut: cropped close to the scalp to discourage lice, short fringes of bangs falling across our foreheads.

Mark Pavlovich paces between the piano and the flagpole. Above him hangs a portrait of our Illustrious Leader and Teacher, the Gardener of Human Happiness, the one to whom we owe thanks for our happy child-hoods. The room is filled with light—the bottom halves of the windows are not painted over, as they were in my last orphanage, to prevent us from looking out or others from looking in. The hall is filled with a fine bitter scent of September leaves, as if somewhere a door has been left open. None of this seems quite real to me yet. It all feels like part of a dream I recognize from some already fading, pre-institutional life. Guchkov speaks and the children repeat after him: "Because we are fortunate to receive it . . . and because we are not pigs, we will care for our soap like civilized people and not let it get covered with scum." I mouth the words, entranced by the soap's whiteness, so pure it too can almost be smelled at a distance.

AT THE FORMER CHILDREN'S HOME at which I'd been warehoused, we'd been scrubbed down with coarse ammoniac laundry soap that left our skin chafed and itching. Like a chain gang we were overseen by bullishly built wardens who didn't fail to conceal their scorn. "Congratulations! So they've brought us another shipment of the little enemy bastards." "These parasites suck our blood while we break our backs over their ilk." In their own crude way, our minders were only repeating Marx's Theory of Sur-plus Labor: *they* worked all day—changing, feeding, bathing us—while we produced nothing. The taunting from other children started soon thereafter.

"How did your papa die?"

"He was shot in the war."

"No, he wasn't. He was shot like an enemy dog."

Nothing could be hidden from them. They'd been told and knew everything—that my father had never served in the war, and that my mama had been sent off to do penance for her treason with hard labor.

I hadn't quite completed the first grade when all this happened to me. From my first day I had loved school; I yielded easily to the classroom's discipline, to the elevated diction of my teacher, Lydia Varlamovna, to the clearly laid-out path to achievement and reward. I craved distinction but instinctively understood the collective ethos, that I could not seek it out for myself—that its bestowing was the teacher's privilege. I raised my hand often, but not excessively. I was helpful to the slower kids. I was on my way to becoming a master at pleasing grown-ups.

None of this education served me in that first children's home. In my first week I lent my one pair of extra underpants to a boy who'd soiled himself. The act was discovered and both the other boy and I were punished by being made to kneel on cracked dried peas. This turned out to be one of the less bizarre and more tepid punishments I would receive in the next six months.

If I was given any academic instruction during this period, I don't remember it. I remember only the physical-education component: military drills that both boys and girls had to perform together, without wearing our tops, even though a few of the girls were already beginning to develop breasts.

We were hit for anything—for throwing up the rotten food we were fed, for whistling indoors, for forgetting ourselves and sucking our thumbs—for displaying any childlike frailty or need. Before my mother was arrested she'd promised to buy me new shoes; I'd started outgrowing my last pair of leather loafers. Nobody noticed this, of course, and during the shuffle when my old things were taken away and the new things handed out, I'd been too petrified to speak up. But within a week of my arrival, my feet were sore and blistering. The big toe on my right foot was developing an ingrown nail that caused me to squeeze my eyes shut against the pain of each step I took. Favoring my left foot, I developed a slight limp, of which I hoped the grown-ups around me might take sympathetic notice. Finally one of them did. She was one of the younger child minders, a skinny girl with limpid blue eyes and acne scars. She might have been raised in the orphanage herself—a "graduate." If this was the case, her experience did not soften her toward us.

"Why are you dragging your feet like a donkey?"

I told her that my shoes didn't fit well and my toe hurt.

"So what we give you isn't good enough?"

I objected and tried to explain that the shoes were my own, not a pair I'd been handed out. That was my second mistake. Her eyes filled with murder. I'd argued with her in front of others. "All right," she said, and began to undress me. She stripped off my shoes and socks, then my shirt and pants, my undershirt, and, finally, my underpants. She threw open the window and made me stand in front of it while the others watched. It was mid-February. Outside, in a play yard that was mostly mud, crusts of snow clung to half-frozen dirt. I stood naked in the wind as she lectured the others on the sacrifice the country was making, taking in such undeserving children.

I remember shivering. The skin of my arms and thighs and buttocks became a carapace of gooseflesh. I tried to keep my eyes from welling—not from the humiliation of standing naked, but from the sting of being so misunderstood. I steeled my seven-year-old body, already stiff from the cold, with mute and rigid rage—rage at my absent mother for not buying me new shoes when I'd asked her to, at myself for failing to explain that the shoes were my own—my own!—that I was not an ungrateful or bad boy.

I don't know how long she made me stand in front of that open window. As always, I was lucky and only caught a cold and not full-blown pneumonia. "I hope you learned your lesson," she told me when it was all over. I did. I learned that when your toe hurts, it hurts only you and no one else.

I suppose that, to keep their conspicuous enmity of us alive, they had to destroy in themselves any innate sympathy for a child's suffering. We felt their disgust but could not guess its source: in their eyes our malfeasance was predetermined. That was why the cruelest punishments were always brought on by seeking sympathy, as I'd sought with my toe. For such monstrous innocence regarding ourselves, there could be no pardon.

Our wardens' belief in our criminality was convincing enough to make it true. We picked up the code from the older children almost as soon as we arrived. My turn came when I was told to sneak into the kitchen and steal two bottles of kefir. Were I to be caught, I would certainly be beaten, and yet to refuse to do the bidding of the older kids made punishment just as sure. In the end, I chickened out and came back in the dark empty-handed. I took my penalty stoically in the morning, when I was buttoned inside a duvet cover and rhythmically kicked with a series of fast, blunt blows. It was only one of our barracks-style "games," called "Cat in the Bag." By then I knew better than to plead for mercy. Any attempt at seeking compassion would only excite their belligerence. Not long thereafter I saw another boy suffer this punishment. He was older than me, but slender and small-boned. I remember walking in on him, after the duvet had been unbuttoned, and finding him still crouching inside it, his shoulders jerking as muffled sobs escaped him. I recall him looking at me, his eyes blurred, imploring. What did he want from me? Comfort? Probably not even that. He wanted what I'd wanted from my acne-scarred child minder: the barest nod of compassion. But there is no greater demand you can make of another than asking him to suffer with you. I went cold around the edges, felt myself being filled with revulsion for the boy's quivering, naked need. It does not please me to think that my heart could be such a desert. I wanted to go to that boy, and I knew what it would cost me. I was already becoming inoculated against my own human impulses. Though "inhuman" is not the right word. What is more human than having our cruelty incited by another's weakness?

I've tried hard not to imagine my moral or mental disfigurement had I been left in that place. But fortune smiled on me again. My ejection from the grim asylum whose name I've since forgotten happened after an incident involving a maroon rag. Another enemy parasite and I were ordered to wash the floors of a long corridor. A thick-armed janitress brought us a bucket of water and then disappeared without telling us where to find the mops and brushes. Or maybe she did tell us and we couldn't find them. In any case, we went in search of a broom closet, peeking behind the various doors, until I discovered, on a table in an empty room, a maroon rag sufficiently plush to work as both a duster and mop. We took turns dragging it across the floor, sticking it between the walls and the oily radiators so that we would not be impugned for cutting corners. We employed it to swab the grime out of moldings, the residue of shoes off stairs. Filth clung to its felty texture like magic.

The janitress returned not long afterward and dropped her broom when she saw what we'd done. There was an almost audible gust of wind as she ran toward the rag and fell on it in horror. She attempted to wash it out in the bucket, but the water was already dank with old scum. When she turned the rag inside out, I saw that it was not a rag at all but a velvet banner of the sort that hung in so many of the rooms, emblazoned with the profile of our magnanimous mustached Leader, his eyes as always crinkled in a smile. "You turn your back and what these little Abrams don't think up!" she cried.

Two days later, I was pulled out of morning lineup and put on a train to Saratov. I believed I had been tossed out for polishing the floors with

Stalin's face—the only explanation my child's mind could conjure. I couldn't know how absurd that was. The janitress would have told nobody of my crime; she would have cleaned the banner and never spoken of the incident, knowing full well whose head would roll first if she did. This much I understand now, but at seven, alone on a train, hungry, I did not know where I was going or what awaited me there. I thought of leaping off, getting lost in the crowd and living on the street. Only my cowardice saved me.

The Krupskaya Home was in the countryside, in the village of Soko-lovy, built by the Volga Germans. Its rooms did not smell of mice, and its windows were neither whitewashed nor covered with bars. Its original building was squat and long, constructed from the unsawn logs of houses appropriated from the kulaks who'd been exiled to Siberia. With the number of arriving children growing in the war, a new wing had been built. The nearby kolkhoz had given the orphanage two acres of its most arid land. There, on our "farm," was an old cow with weak udders and a horse that wouldn't move without constant prodding, but which we kids loved for the solemn rides it occasionally gave us. Somehow, with continued effort, the staff managed to make a few things grow on the little household plot. In the spring all of us pitched in planting wheat, potatoes, and vegetables with the seeds we received from the collective farm.

What kindness of fate had landed me in this refuge? My mind goes naturally to Avdotya Grigorievna, our old neighbor and my babysitter. I picture her searching for me, checking the city's child-sorting centers until she discovers where I am. I imagine her finding whoever is handling my case—some clerk with blond hair heaped atop her proud head—and imploring her: "Find the boy a good home. Russia is vast—somewhere in the South, maybe."

"Where there is an opening is where we send 'em."

Maybe there is a compassionate crack somewhere in the woman's exterior that Avdotya can pry. "He's like a child of my own flesh. My son was killed at Stalingrad. You have a Christian soul, I can see it."

"Please, stop it at once," and then, "I'll take a look; come back next week."

The following day, Avdotya returns with a meter of Boston wool wrapped in newsprint. My old nanny knows something I don't yet: that this boy must be sent far, far away from Moscow. Far from the great meat grinder that's swallowed his parents. But perhaps dear Avdotya played no such role. I have not the slightest idea what changed my fortune. All I remember is the plump blond clerk—the last in a succession of nameless bureaucrats—putting me on the train and calling me a "lucky boy" before pointing me out to the conductor. And so I was.

The Krupskaya Home was, on the whole, a place of simplicity and cleanliness. The rules were strict but not arbitrary: food couldn't be taken out of the dining hall, nothing was to be left on the plates, nothing was to be wasted. Often Mark Pavlovich joined us for meals. This was when, at our pleading, he would tell us about the war, in whose distant echoes we would hear stories about our own real or imagined fathers. He was a marvelous storyteller. With his voice he could render the terrible inferno of grenades exploding behind embankments. He repeated conversations between commanders and their platoons as though they'd happened yesterday. In every tale brave acts were performed, mettle tested, impossible promises made and kept. In each dramatic pause we would hear the crack of artillery so loud that blood would rush in our ears.

Everybody knew the story of how he'd lost his arm: guarding a position one night when the Germans went on the attack and threw a mortar shell behind his cover. He was buried in earth; his friends dug him out and saved his life. All of Mark Pavlovich's stories invariably ended this way—with a lesson about the value of friendship. During these meals the boys whose fathers had died in battle would assume the poses and coloration of heroes. The ones whose parents had disappeared in less honorable ways would be filled with silent jealousy. And what about me—what thoughts were coursing through my little brain as I sat in a trance, listening to all these chronicles of courage? I knew my father had done something heroic too in the war, something involving papers but not guns. Yet against Mark Pavlovich's tales of robust manhood, Papa's peaceable heroism seemed unimpressive. Like every boy of my era I was already nursing powerful fantasies of my own—dashing scenes depicted in the vein of *Chapayev*, showing my devotion to the cause, Stalin's name on my enameled lips. Whether I lived or died was not the important thing; what mattered most was the redeeming image I longed for others to remember. Here at last, in the new children's home, such a redeeming future seemed within reach.

I'd never bought the line that my parents were enemies, a word I could associate only with German fascists. Yet I also knew they were not true

Russians. They spoke another language with me and with each other. Could I have put it in words, I would have admitted to believing that one or both of them had simply made some sort of outsiders' mistake—a careless, absentminded error that a *real* Russian would never have committed. It was this carelessness that had landed them in the infernal cycle of misunderstanding that held us all captive. My job, while it was all being sorted out, was to keep my nose clean until the moment when I could be called on as a character witness for my mother and father. My parents' abiding and abject loyalty would be underwritten by my evident patriotism. My courage and honesty, my gifts as a leader of men, could all be introduced into evidence. That, at least, was my plan once I started attending school again. I was resolved to be the good boy I hadn't been allowed to be at the first orphanage. To this end I immediately joined several "hobby circles"—an art club sponsored by our teacher, and a "young technicians" club for kids interested in learning to make farm tools. I hoped, with my illustrational talent (I was a gifted artist of realistic and bloody war scenes) and my practical enthusiasm, to make myself eligible for the Young Pioneers. My goodness was not entirely altruistic: If I should fail to redeem my parents, I could, at the very least, redeem myself. If I no longer had a family, I was prepared to let myself be reclaimed into the great communist family. Very likely I was taking my cue from the adults around me. At the new home, our parents were not spoken of disparagingly; they were not mentioned at all. If a child should forget herself and accidentally utter the word "mama" or "papa," the outburst was treated with chilly indifference by the child minders. It was a breach of ctiquette. This should have put me at ease, but it only turned my fears inward. In the old place, where I could be beaten for such a misstep, I'd been physically alert for snares and traps, like a hunted animal. Here, passing myself off as a "regular" Russian boy, I was terrified of being discovered for who I really was.

But who was I? Something strange had started happening to me since I'd been removed from my home. My body had started feeling foreign to me. I heard my own voice as if it belonged to someone else, and watched myself as if with a stranger's set of eyes. I listened to this boy as if to learn who he was, but also to appraise him and take his measure. In time this boy I observed was not "me" but a different boy, one whose father had died in the war, and whose mother, perhaps a nurse, had also perished in some heroic fashion. I watched this boy's body file in with the other bodies to the cafeteria. I watched it in the common bath, sprinkling cold water on itself. I felt myself becoming sentimentally aroused by this intrepid, lonesome creature's struggle to abide austerity and remain modest and unflinching despite life's cruelties. My waking life consisted of secretly playing this character. I clung to him as to a brother and was terrified of having him taken from me.

My fear of being discovered was not totally new. The day I started school, I'd stopped answering my mother in English. She already knew better than to speak English around the neighbors, but even in private I didn't like it. Only after dark did I relax my vigilance and let her sing me to sleep with lullabies she'd sung to me since I was a baby—"Little Bo Peep," "Farmer in the Dell," "Row, Row, Row Your Boat"—as well as others, such as "Angels Watching Over Me," "Roll the Old Chariot Along," "He's Got the Whole World in His Hands," songs that at the time I had no way of knowing were the same Negro spirituals my mother's nanny had sung to Florence when she was a little girl. In my metal cot in the children's home, I continued to hum some of these songs under the thin covers, as quietly as humanly possible. What else did I have? We slept alone, with no rag dolls or stuffed rabbits to press into. The songs and their melodies were all that remained for me of my mother, whose image was already fading.

My two existences—nocturnal and diurnal—were clearly demarcated for me by a rule that forbade us children from reentering the dormitory rooms during the day, after we'd made up our beds. (Ever since, and for most of my life, I have avoided the temptation of walking into the bedroom in the middle of the day.) And yet, one day early on in my stay, I broke the rule and sneaked back into the sleeping wing after breakfast. What for? I can't remember now. Did I leave something inside I'd forgotten? Whatever the reason, I had walked only as far as the door when I heard voices coming from inside.

"They'll disgrace this home!" This voice belonged to a woman we called the Sergeant, a child minder who dragged some unfortunate kid or another out of the lineup every morning to make him or her confess to a fresh sin (dirty hands, pilfered cigarettes). This time, I gathered she'd discovered evidence of depravity under an older boy's pillow. I knew I ought to scram, but my curiosity kept me glued to the spot, unable to breathe or move. The item the Sergeant had discovered, it emerged, was a letter. Specifically, a love letter from a girl at the orphanage. She read some lines of it aloud, before giving her assessment: "Vile stuff! Not even like the songs on the radio."

"I told you, I'll handle this myself." I recognized Mark Pavlovich's baritone, the light gravel in his throat.

"It is *my* job to see they come out of here . . . *intact*," the Sergeant said. "We are running an orphanage, not a brothel. What happens tomorrow when there's another mouth to feed?"

"Stop scaring me, and stop scaring yourself."

"You need to make them an example, before the others get ideas."

"I won't do any such thing, and neither will you."

Crouching behind the open door, I watched the Sergeant stalk out. She didn't even see me. The set of her pincerlike mouth showed how she felt about having such orders forced down her throat.

Did I understand what I had just observed? Only dimly. I sensed that Mark Pavlovich had made it clear who was in charge, which gladdened me, since I feared and disliked the Sergeant as much as the others did. Nevertheless, the exchange unsettled me as well. It confounded some credo in which I'd long been instructed. At school, our teacher had a portrait of Pavlik Morozov hanging alongside portraits of Lenin and Stalin. Each day, "monitors" would be chosen from among us to examine the dirt under all the children's nails and the wax inside our ears. Those who were too lenient and gave their friends a pass were themselves informed on, usually by the little girls who appointed themselves our class disciplinarians. The art of squealing on each other's deficiencies was drilled into us early, and I was unfortunately not immune to its allure.

Not long thereafter I was sent into Guchkov's office for getting into a dirty fight. My resolve to be a model citizen had temporarily deserted me when another boy toppled the only available chessboard, which I'd painstakingly set up after awaiting my turn to play. The kid was a malicious little creep who'd tried to bring trouble down on me before and, worse, treated me like the fraud I feared I was. Usually, I was inclined to let his smart remarks pass, but this was a clear provocation. If I'd learned anything from my first children's home, it was that scores had to be settled at once or never at all. I didn't know how to fight. I went for the boy's face with my hands, knowing the only chance I had was to go completely crazy on him before he could respond. I dug my nails into his chin, about as high as I could reach. He punched me in the stomach, but by then I had the bottom half of his face in a claw hold and wouldn't let go. Blood squirted from his lip. A second blow caught me dead in the eardrum, thundering inside my skull as if I were a deaf man experiencing the percussive shock of a snare drum. Darkness rose up from the bottom of my vision. I might have been smiling as I fell.

THE DOOR OF THE OFFICE OPENED, and I was led in by my sore ear. The door was closed behind me. The director pointed to a chair. The room had a scent—a thick odor of pipe tobacco, wool, and masculine sweat.

The undersides of his eyes were rimmed with dark circles. A day's growth of beard clung to the slack flesh of his not unhandsome face. When he spoke I could feel his voice in my chest. "Stick out your hands, Yuliy." With his one hand he turned over my palms. "I see they've cut off your claws. What do you think you were doing?"

His saying my name made me feel strange. Guchkov walked our halls with an air of celebrity. Now I'd gotten a private audience. Yet it was not for doing anything outstanding, or even for being an honorable outlaw, but for a dirty, opportunistic maneuver.

"Well?"

"I didn't start it . . . ," I said, and launched into the story about the chessboard, leaving out the boy's earlier mockery. I could feel Guchkov making a study of me as I blathered on. Every word that left my mouth I regretted as soon as I spoke it. Even as my nostrils streamed snot, I tried to summon my alter ego—that fine, austere boy who'd never abase himself with excuses. But my doppelgänger had abandoned me. I felt my face getting wet. Something had come loose in me.

Finally, Guchkov stopped me. "Here we don't use our claws to settle matters. Is that understood?"

I nodded.

"Speak up."

Now that I was expected to speak, I fell mute.

"You understand plain Russian?" he snapped.

I managed an affirmative.

"And English, too?"

I felt my body go stiff.

"You're an *amerikanchik*, aren't you?"

Inside my chest, my heart was pounding like a canary trying to get out of its cage. I couldn't take a normal breath.

"What are you afraid of? We aren't sending you there."

"I'm not."

"Not afraid?"

"Not American," I said. The taunts still rang in my ears. I could hear them now. *Enemy. Enemy.* "My mother and father were," I said.

His half-hooded eyes watched me. "Why 'were'?"

"They're dead," I told him without blinking.

I might have even believed it. At that moment, I might have even wished it.

Mark Pavlovich said nothing. He reached his hand underneath his collar and from some recess under his shirt produced a long chain with a brass key. Deftly, he removed the chain from around his neck, and I watched as he crouched to open a drawer in his desk. Above the horizon of the desk I saw his shoulder and limply hanging sleeve. For the first time I understood that even simple movements were not totally natural to him, that he had to turn his whole body to work the lock, as though he were twisting a stubborn screw. At last he got the drawer open and removed something—a heavy leather ledger that he placed on the desk. He found a piece of paper and slid it across to me. "You're old enough to write."

With my heart still pounding I understood what the ledger contained. The page he'd turned to was full of addresses.

He stood up and walked around to where I sat. He placed the inkwell beside me. I held the pen he'd given me tightly, but my mind was blank.

Mark Pavlovich began to dictate. *"Zdrastvui dorogaya mamochka . . ."*

I took down his words like a scribe. He glanced down at my uneven penmanship. "There is a 'v' in the first word. . . . Oh, it's not important. Let's keep going."

My first letter to my mother turned out to be four sentences long. "It is warm here," it began, and concluded with: "I have made a friend. His name is Kolya."

"What now?" I said.

"What do you think? Write, 'Kiss you, your son Yulik.'"

From another drawer in his desk, Guchkov produced an envelope. Finding the right entry in the ledger, he copied over the infamous address of the prison where the letter was to travel. Once he was done, he placed the ledger back inside his desk and locked it with his key.

I watched the long chain and the glint of brass disappear again under the director's rough linen shirt, secreted to a place to which only he could gain access. "That's enough for today," he said. "You'll have more to write next time."

AS FOR MY FRIEND KOLYA—I'd met him in the mess hall. He was two years older, though one wouldn't know it. He was thin, stalk-necked, and albino-pale. His slitty eyes ought to have made him look furtive, but instead he seemed to glance out of them almost serenely, as if wherever he found himself was just a place to pass through. I tried to start a conversation with him by praising the food.

"Yeah, a real health resort. Are you going to eat your candies?" he said.

I looked at my tin plate, where lay two wrapped *barbariski*. It was Sunday, and this was our treat for the Seventh of November holiday. I'd watched him spend the meal biting off little bits of his sausage and stuffing them in his pocket. Since I hadn't objected, he grabbed my candies and did the same.

"Hey!"

"Too late. What's fallen off the wagon is gone."

I was loath to start a fight with a runt, especially since his swipe seemed almost like a gesture of friendliness, and a friend was what I needed most. Taking food out of the cafeteria was against the rules. "They'll make you turn out your pockets," I warned him.

"And what are you, House Management?"

Within a few weeks, he was hoisting me over the metal gate behind the broken-down cattle shed. On the other side of the gate was the wooded path that led to the main road that went to the town bazaar. On this day— some time after my audience with Guchkov—the recent snow had melted and the ground was muddy, tracked with boots and hoofprints. It sucked at our shoes as we walked. Once we were out of view of the children's home, Kolya pulled down his trousers to piss in a stand of black pines. He tucked his shirt back into his underpants, and then unhooked something from inside his pants. It was a mitten attached with a bobby pin to the inside of his trousers, just beneath the pocket lining. He stuck his finger through the hole at the bottom of his pocket and wiggled it to show me how he'd sneaked out the food. Inside the pinned mitten were pieces of kielbasa and the candies. Also, a piece of a broken comb, a cigarette butt, and some matches. Now that we were out in the elements, Kolya smoked openly, like a grown-up, offering me a few drags on his cigarette in thanks for my sweets.

"What are you going to do with the candy?"

"Trade it."

"For what?"

"A whistle."

"Did you trade for the pin?"

"No, I took that from my aunt Marusia's house. Found it in her box of buttons. She doesn't live too far."

"Why aren't you with her, then?"

"I like it here. Anyway, when Mama comes back from the nick, I'll live with her."

I felt myself go cold again. Never before had I heard a kid talk about his mother being in lockup, let alone volunteer it as casually as Kolya did.

"What did she do, your mother?"

"She pulled babies out of women."

"Delivered them."

"No, she pulled them out with her knitting needles before they got to be big. If the women didn't want 'em."

"Did they scream?"

"The women, sure. Not the babies. They were just guts and blood by the time she pulled 'em out."

"You mean you saw it?"

"Sure. I'd look when she went to toss out the slop bucket. There was hair sometimes, but mostly guts."

"And your papa?"

"Froze in a snowbank. Yours both dead?"

I hesitated. "My father might be," I heard myself say. "My mother, she's in a camp." My honesty surprised me. Kolya had gotten the truth out of me without anything like the invasive procedures of which he'd spoken so casually.

"She an enemy?"

"I don't know."

"Well, they had to send her off for *something* or another."

I felt the old feeling of unworthiness attach itself to me again. I'd been asking myself this very question for many months. In my mind, one explanation overshadowed the others. Now I wanted to test it out, to see if it could survive in the open air. "We had an iron bust of Lenin in our room. Mama used to crack walnuts with the bottom of it." The solid iron bust had made a perfect nutcracker. I remembered my father once warned her that if anyone saw her cracking nuts like that she'd be thrown "inside."

"With Lenin!" A reassuringly horrified look came over Kolya's face. "My mama said she loved Lenin more than life!"

It wasn't my first time at the bazaar. We were permitted to walk there on Sundays when chaperoned by older kids, who'd be given a few kopeks to buy us ice cream or a newspaper funnel's worth of sunflower seeds. It was everyone's favorite place, an ever-changing landscape—orderly and energetic in the morning, filled with crowds all afternoon, disheveled like a street after a parade by early twilight. Kolya, however, was going there not as a spectator but to engage in commerce. I followed him from stall to stall as he attempted to barter.

"Babushka, a few coins for the sweets?"

No sooner had we embarked on our bartering project than a shriek came from one of the sellers.

"Thieves! Robbing their children's home." She was shouting from behind a pyramid of carrots and beets, waving her pink, frostbitten hands in the air. "They feed and clothe you vermin, and you steal from the state!"

"Calm down, Auntie! This is mine. I didn't steal from anyone."

"Liars and thieves! They come here to hawk the clothes off their backs for cigarettes. Another one of them was here already, selling off his scarf."

"Not us, Auntie," Kolya said. "Someone shut this horse up."

"Who do you think it was?" I wondered aloud as we walked back in the dimming light. I already had my own suspicion.

"Baldy, I bet."

Baldy was more like a savage dwarf than a real child. I'd seen him torture the stray cats that prowled around the play yard—binding their limbs and tossing them against tree trunks. He'd paralyzed one by bursting its pelvis. He'd chase smaller kids away from the swings and merry-go-round, before suspending himself from the playground equipment derisively. His wild laugh marked him with the unmistakable brand of the criminal. We all suspected him of mental deficiencies, but this only gave him a kind of superiority over the others.

"How did he get a name like Baldy if he isn't bald?" I said.

"His head was covered with bloody wounds when he arrived," Kolya explained. "He lived in a train yard and gambled with the hobos *na volosianku*." He elucidated the rules of this game: "If he won, they gave him food; if he lost, he'd let them yank a tuft of hair from his head."

When I first arrived at Memory of Krupskaya I had found it difficult to keep my eyes off of Baldy, though I was careful not to glance so long as to provoke a fight. To look at Baldy too long was to nurse a desire for suicide. Instead of making him civilized, the children's home had only given him free rein to become more rabid. Lately, he had started flouting the rules of fair fighting, which mandated using only fists and ceasing at the first sign of blood. To pull a knife, as Baldy had done during his latest fight with a new boy, was a violation of the order. It necessitated an immediate intervention. Someone had run to Guchkov, and soon the director was there, parting the oglers and dragging Baldy off by the collar with his one, surprisingly strong arm. When Guchkov returned, he removed his fedora from his head and said that anyone else carrying any kind of weapon should place it in his hat immediately. Two boys stepped forward to drop in their tiny, dull blades, the ones I'd sometimes seen them tossing like darts at the trees. "The next knife I confiscate, you'll be doing more than just shoveling pig shit all month," he'd warned.

It was bitterly cold as we walked back toward the children's home. The frozen ground crunched underfoot. "Should we tell?" I asked Kolya.

"Why stick our necks out?"

A few days later, Baldy was pulled out of morning lineup. "Where's the scarf we issued you?" Mark Pavlovich inquired.

A scornful smile played on the boy's lips. "Lost it."

"We pay money for everything here," the director said, pacing down the lineup. Still addressing Baldy, he added, "You liked picking potatoes so much last month. This month you can enjoy chopping our winter firewood."

Pretending to look at Mark Pavlovich, we were all really trying to watch Baldy, who had tucked his left arm behind his back in order to mimic the strutting step of Guchkov's march. A lewd snicker spread among a cohort of the older kids. Baldy had caught the director's pedantic walk and the uneven wiggle of his behind. Even those who thought the imitation vicious tittered unwillingly. It pained me to see the war hero Guchkov mocked behind his back. Since being reassured that the secret of my mother's penal address was safe with him, I was more devoted to him than ever. Now I felt my body go prickly with a desire to pounce on Baldy. His malice I could stomach, but not his passing off his spite as noble rebellion. For that I vowed to make him pay.

THE NEXT MORNING I stood in my school uniform with my back pressed to the thick, rounded logs of the old building. I was hidden from view by the utility shack. I listened as the other kids filed out for the daily three-kilometer trek to school. I knew I would be punished for being late, but what I'd set out to do was more important than class. I waited for the ring of voices in the crystalline air to fade, and sneaked back to the main building. Observe now the young hero: my earflaps blowing in the wind, the yarn at the bottom of my sweater (already too short) coming loose as I pull on it nervously. The cold air stabs my lungs. As my shoes crunch on the frozen snow, I try to warm myself up with a vision of Mark Pavlovich and me, writing a second letter to my mother (I have yet to receive an answer to my first). The mistaken first impression he had of me as a liar has been corrected now that I've shared with him what I know. Putting his hand on my shoulder, he tells me I'm a boy who can be relied on. The warmth on my shoulder lingers as I compose the letter to my mother.

When I reached the director's office, I found him not alone. Through the door, left partly open, I could hear voices—one gruff and serious, another carefully accommodating. From my vantage point I glimpsed the polish of military boots, the swish of heavy greatcoats of a blue-gray color normally identified with members of the *militzia*. My eye followed the coat upward to its lapelled shoulder. There were two of them inside: one leaning over Guchkov's desk in a way that seemed vaguely threatening, while the other paced the room, brushing hoarfrost from his ursine hat. Their heavy boots had left tracks of melted snow on the floor. Holding my breath,

I tried to hear what these policemen were saying. The story seemed to be that a local boy in town had been sent to the hospital after a bloody knife fight. The director asked if the boy had identified the assailant. One of the policemen smiled and assured him that they had gotten all the information from him they needed. "Then I suppose you're free to do your work," Mark Pavlovich said. The tone of their voices demonstrated dissatisfaction with this decoy answer. The one who had not spoken before began talking about "habitual recidivists" whose ages would not shield them from the full force of the law.

In an instant, like lightning illuminating the night, I knew they were talking about Baldy. Inhaling the scent of their damp army coats, I could feel my pulse quicken. Yes, that's what Baldy had sold his scarf for—to buy another knife! It was as though, walking onto the stage for a simple audition, I'd suddenly found myself in front of a packed house. If ever there was a chance to show myself to be the upright and courageous boy I wanted the world to know, it was this. I felt I had to knock on the door at once and tell these uniformed men all I knew.

I could hear Mark Pavlovich responding with his agreeable yet firm note of protest: "We do not allow knives or any weapons on the premises, and our children do not carry them."

For reasons I couldn't explain, I felt crippled, unable to make myself knock on the door. Even now it's hard to explain, but somehow the presence of these *militzioneri* unmanned me. Something about their boots, their cold, damp smells inside that old tobaccoey cupboard of an office, but most of all their voices. I was haunted by the memory of my mother's arrest. Even as I stood paralyzed, I feared that they would start hounding Mark Pavlovich to produce his secret ledger, in which my own name appeared beside the name of a woman imprisoned for treason. If I walked in now, I would lose my cover for good. They would want to know who I was, and Guchkov would have to tell them. Perhaps for the first time in my life I perceived what it meant to be a "hero" in the original, Greek sense of the word: one for whom any victory must be rewarded by some punishing irony from the jealous gods.

I did nothing. I listened to the rising and falling pitch of the trio inside, letting the minutes lapse. At last the voices resolved into a kind of tense agreement, with Mark Pavlovich allowing that all rooms would be made available for searching. I could tell this was not a satisfying answer for them. One of the policemen smiled sardonically. "You can be certain we'll do that," he said.

Mark Pavlovich escorted them out. Their heavy coats brushed against me, but they took no notice. Only the director's eyebrow lifted as he passed me by. One of the policemen roughly kicked away the snow that was piled up on the back steps before closing the door. When the director turned, I saw the dark circles around his eyes. "How long have you been standing there?"

Something in his face made me too frightened to speak.

"What is it? Did you swallow your tongue?"

"I know something."

He let me enter his office. "All right."

I told him about the screaming woman at the bazaar and about Baldy's missing scarf.

My confession seemed to make him more tired. "His name is Lyova, not Baldy. Is that what you came to tell me?"

"It was *him*."

"*You* saw him sell his scarf and buy a knife."

"No, but she *said* . . ."

"That's enough. We don't trade in empty accusations here. You've let your imagination carry you away. Who else have you shared this fantasy with?"

"No one . . . !"

"Then keep it to yourself. Understood? Now, go."

THE FOLLOWING DAY MORE snow fell in large wet flakes. I watched it sift down as I walked, dejected, from the schoolhouse back to the children's home. What good had come of being "good"? The clownish look of superiority still hovered over Baldy's face. He was afraid of no one and recognized no authority. That was the insight underscoring his mockery: Mark Pavlovich wanted to boss us around like he was our father, but he wasn't our father. And he was no hero. All the real heroes were dead. I removed my gloves and felt the stinging cold on my fingers. From the side of the road I scooped up a handful of sharp pebbles and sculpted it into a hard snowball. Without conscious effort I beamed it at a kid walking two meters ahead of me. To my surprise, it hit him in the back of his hat, pitching him facedown into the snow.

"SO NOW YOU'VE DECIDED to become a hooligan." Mark Pavlovich locked the door behind him. "I can assure you that it's a profession you won't succeed in."

On the director's desk a glint of metal caught my eyes. Guchkov walked to his desk and picked up the knife by its hard celluloid handle. "I confiscated it several days ago." His eyes were not impressed with me: Had I really believed he would let the police search here before doing his own sweep? "They wanted to call in different boys, one by one, and talk to them. Would you have told *them* what you told me?"

"They said if we didn't help catch hooligans we're as bad as them." Even as I spoke these words I regretted them.

"So you would have fingered Lyova?"

"I don't know," I said challengingly.

He lifted his chin, but his eyes did not wander from my face. His gaze was like a piercing shaft of light, searching around for some object at the bottom of a murky pond. I didn't know what the director was looking for, only that the object he sought had a dangerous power of its own.

"I know he did it," I said.

"Let's suppose he did. By our laws, a child of twelve can be imprisoned for ten years. Have you thought of what happens to someone when he's shipped to a juvenile colony? They leave you in a dirty barracks with no heat or light and you huddle at night over a kerosene lamp like a dog. And the others will beat you—or worse—for a stale piece of bread. Lyova won't get any better at a place like that."

But I didn't care about Lyova. I recognized this and knew that Guchkov knew it too. As though reading my mind, he said, "As for you, Yuliy Brink, you are a thinking boy. You can put two and two together. Your cleverness will make people want to use you. So let me give you some advice: Beware of your first impulse. It's always the most noble and the most dangerous."

No better counsel has ever been given to me.

However dimly, I sensed that the object Guchkov had been looking for in the murky pond of my being was *that*. My noble impulse, he called it.

Until then, I'd never been aware of my power to hurt someone, only of being hurt myself.

Guchkov pulled back his gaze. He looked confident that I understood him. What made him so sure of me? I still can't say.

The director let me out through the back door, the same way the *militzia*-men had gone the morning before. The brief winter day was rapidly turning dark. The smell of wood smoke hung in the icy air. A few winter birds made their sounds high up in the treetops. In between their distant squawks, I could hear another song. I followed the path that led from the back entrance to the animal sheds. There, behind a fence, I could see Baldy, wearing a hat with its earflaps pulled down, shoveling manure with a metal spade into a bucket. He was humming a melody, some jovial obscene tune about six burglars screwing an old lady to her great delight. Hearing someone come near, he stopped and rested the shovel under his elbow. His eyes met mine in a knowing, lewd grin. "Can't get enough of that stink?" he said in an almost friendly voice. "Betcha wanna take a few swings at the slop yourself, eh?" And then, aware that he now had an audience, he sang his song with more gusto, letting his voice be carried up to the treetops.

BOOK III

—

13.

MAGNETIC CITY

MAGNITOGORSK
1934

ПОЧТА
СССР

IT WAS THE FATE OF MAGNITOGORSK TO FOREVER PULL THINGS TOWARD itself. Long before the mountain's mythical magnetite lured the first Bolshevik scouts on horseback; before the twitch of compass needles enticed prospectors to ride to the barren frontiers of the tsar's empire; before the day when the Bashkir nomads fighting off their Mongol invaders watched, astonished, as their attackers' arrows flew backward, attracted by the magnetic hill; long before the hill itself was even a wrinkle on the lower lip of the Urals—an invisible force was already pulling Europe into its inescapable collision with Asia, drawing the continents toward their millennia-long turbulent marriage.

Florence Fein was neither the first nor the last pilgrim to be called into the city's orbit. By the time her train came to the end of its long crawl through the steppes and rounded the city on the mountain, the sight she took in through her dust-smeared window was of a gargantuan anthill of crisscrossing rails, refineries, and furnaces rising out of a fog of their own making.

The train's corridor was cluttered with the bundles, baskets, and trunks of those who'd arrived looking for work. Before her journey, Florence had imagined the Russian East to be something like the American West: a territory filled with swells of settlers. What she discovered instead was a boundless emptiness that went on without beginning or end. The few people she'd seen at by-stations along the tracks stood silently, holding up their strings of onions or parsnips, pushing the food through the train windows for a kopek. Their eyes had a mad, hollow look that shamed and frightened Florence. At Amtorg she had heard rumors of a famine in the South but could not imagine that these bearded invalids could be its refugees. The passengers on her pilgrimage were of a reassuringly different sort: they'd come on board with hard-boiled eggs, bread, and sugar cubes that they sucked while they sipped their tea, happy to share. Her trip had required four changes and taken eight days and nights. Florence's response to the sight of the Magnetic City was physical: she scratched her itching scalp. Her sebum-ripe hair, her pimple-sown chin, her bile-shriveled stomach, and the swampy mess in her underwear were all ready for the relief of urban comforts. Her body would be disappointed.

At the brick fortress of the arrival center, a tiny, beetle-browed woman rattled off a series of rapid questions about Florence's point of origin and skills, and placed her name on a list of construction trusts. She would be commanded to go where *they* wanted her, the woman informed Florence when she offered herself up as a translator. She was given a slip with the number of her barracks, which proved impossible to find even for the boy assigned to help her. Residential Magnitogorsk, it was becoming clear, was one giant barracks, composed of identical rows of whitewashed huts. In the pink evening air, mosquitoes and flies swarmed and hummed, taking nips at Florence's unaccustomed flesh as she picked her way through puddles of mud. "Your villa," the boy said, leaving Florence and her trunk in front of Dormitory 19. From between a pair of laundry lines, a woman stared at her. In reply to Florence's timid smile, she looked Florence over unceremoniously, pulled down her sheet, and walked back into her darkened quarters. Perhaps it was at this moment that Florence understood how truly lost she was. That she had no idea what she was doing here was a simple fact that her previous two months of travel had somehow kept hidden from her. To survive the ship and train journeys she had told herself that her real problem was that she'd lived too comfortably for too long. It was her love of comfort that had kept her, as Marx warned, in a bourgeois prison and out of the galvanizing medium of History. Now, looking around her makeshift, sordid habitat, she clung to this idea as fiercely as she'd clung to the railing on the *Bremen*, to keep her stomach from going weak with recoil. The barracks, she discovered, had no amenities at all—no kitchens or bathrooms or showers. Water came from an outdoor pump that was now broken, forcing the women and men who shared the "dormitory" to walk a half-kilometer to the next pump. The outhouse was nothing more than a covered shed, split by an immodest partition that divided a row of five holes for men from the five for women. One couldn't step into this so-called toilet without opening one's mouth to breathe. Closing one's nose and eyes was a necessary measure, not only to avoid the stench and sight but to keep the mucous membranes from being stung by a thick cloud of powdered chloride. After this exquisite persecution it was a relief indeed to return to the overcrowded barracks, where a dozen makeshift Primus stoves sent the odor of cabbage soup and kerosene fumes down the hallways.

Her room was shared by three others: a mother and daughter, and a village girl whose pregnancy was already showing through her heavy overalls. The mother, who might have been thirty-five or fifty, touched Florence's navy wool jacket on the first night, tactlessly fingered her houndstooth blouse, and immediately offered Florence two hundred rubles for them. Florence's shock at this mercantile greeting was offset only by the greater shock that a working-class woman would have so much cash. Florence had as yet no idea that money was plentiful in Magnitogorsk. There was simply not much on which to spend it. The shelves of the workers' store abounded with loaves of black bread but had no butter. Boxes of artificial coffee were stacked in pyramids, but sugar was a rarity. The mother, who was in fact thirty-nine and old enough to remember the civil war, claimed that the store clerks who tore off the coupons in her food book were lying when they told her that the sugar industry had underfulfilled its plan for the year. There had been sugar during the war, after all. And now there was no war! She found much in the Magnetic City preposterous. "A confirmed *amerikanka* in one bed, and in the other, this one who got herself knocked up by the king of England," she sneered.

"And you can fuck off, you dirty old Troktist!" the village girl spat back.

"It's 'Trotskyite,' you imbecile! She ought to learn to write her name before she takes mouthfuls like that," the woman said to Florence.

They asked her why she did not live in the foreigners' settlement at Beryozovka, a cozy cul-de-sac tucked between two hills and rumored to be equipped with running water. Her best answer was that she had come not on a specialist's contract but as a volunteer. "No straw mattresses and broken stools in America that you were so eager to come here?" inquired the daughter. Florence tried, in reply, to paint a bleak picture of the hardships of the working class in the United States (she now counted herself among their number). But neither the mother nor the daughter could take her eyes off Florence's laced leather boots. Had she simply said she'd come to Magnitogorsk looking for an old sweetheart, they might have happily drawn her into the warm comfort of their bosoms. But she was too proud to admit to herself, let alone to them, a fact that might recast her entire noble journey not by the lantern of courage but by the murkier bed lamp of longing.

Her foreign credentials did have some advantage: she was sent to work for a foreman supervising construction of a chemical plant. The American consultants assigned to oversee the plant's assembly had abruptly returned to Pennsylvania when the Russians had started paying them in worthless rubles instead of gold dollars. Similar exoduses were happening all over the chaotic camp. Foundation pits yawned in the earth like primordial craters, filling up with rain and larvae. Around them, excavators and gravel washers with torn gears stood abandoned, like tired beasts at watering holes. Florence saw work that should have been done by machines being performed by human hands. Men with sharp-cornered faces and women with fleshy ones excavated dirt with short shovels, tossed gravel with ungloved hands, put into practice the doctrine of sexual equality by lugging equal loads of bricks on their equally bent backs.

Though work on the chemical plant had stalled for two months while the foreman struggled irately to make sense of the Americans' assembly instructions, he looked less than eager to discover Florence ready to help. Pumping his short, burly arms in the air, he accused the Americans of sabotage. He denounced their designs and demonstrated his Soviet allegiance by altering them freely. In spite of his harangues he was not a frightening man. Every day the foreman informed her that a German firm would soon be taking over the work. In the meantime, he had to abide Florence.

Since the foreman had little use for her except as a Greek chorus, Florence was largely free to roam Magnitogorsk's countless construction trusts in search of Sergey. At high noon she picked her way through brambles of barbed wire, negotiated her lace-ups down steep banks of gravel, crouched under the ungodly clanking of cranes. She inquired about Sergey at the Metalworks Park and at the coke ovens, at the lumberyards, at the Novomagnitsky Settlement and the October Settlement. Word began to spread about the foreign woman prowling for her tomcat of an engineer. Clerks eyed her from under censorious brows. On their desks were newspapers from the capital that warned of wreckers and foreign saboteurs, of capitalist spies. It was a testament to their distance from Moscow that the speculations Florence inspired took on a prurient rather than political innuendo.

She was in the Engineers' and Technicians' Club, idly looking at the notices pasted on the wall and waiting to speak to an organizer, when she heard a familiar voice behind her. "Do my eyes deceive me? Flora? Flora Solomonovna?"

A shiver came over her. In the incandescent glare of the gloomy entryway Florence saw a man in a tweed cap, his face covered with thick blondish stubble. "Yes, I am Flora."

The man clapped his hands. "The belle of Cleveland! At first I thought, *It can't be,* so I came closer. I'd remember your face anywhere," he said, and then, in a quieter voice, "Fyodor Zimin—don't you recognize me?"

Florence's pulse quickened. Yes, she did recognize him. His cheeks were unshaven and sunken in, but it was the same man, the small blue eyes and long nose. "Fedya, of course! You've changed. You're thinner."

"Enjoying the benefits of our health-resort diet," Fyodor said, patting his flat stomach. "As are you, it appears! Oh—this is unbelievable!"

Florence smoothed down her hair. After two weeks in Magnitogorsk, her clothes had become loose on her body, but she had not taken a look at herself in anything but the small pocket mirror she'd hung above her cot.

"I promised you I'd come," she said, taking a light, foolish tone.

The noon whistle rang. Men in vests and greasy pants began to file in through the doors. Girls with colorful rags over their hair headed for the canteen. Fyodor took her arm. "Let's get in line before these philistines empty the trough."

The dining room was thick with bodies. Waitresses wove between wooden tables, ferrying enormous trays of soup bowls and mashed potatoes. A smell of fermenting cabbage cut the air. There were no spoons left for Florence. Fyodor gave her his. "Don't worry, I always bring my own," he said, and pulled a second aluminum spoon from his pocket. "I'm sorry our cuisine can't be more gourmet," he apologized while polishing his spoon with the inside of his vest.

"It's gourmet enough for me."

His face registered surprise at watching her hungrily slurp her fish soup. "This is better than in our cafeteria, actually," she said. "At least the bones in your soup still have some meat on them."

"You can't be serious. Surely, you take your meals with other foreigners—there ought to be a few who haven't gone home yet."

"I'm not on a *valyuta* contract like the specialists."

Fyodor's face looked puzzled, concerned. But he didn't investigate. "Still, you're entitled to an Insnab book for the foreigners' store," he advised. "You can get all sorts of delicacies there. Butter, fish, a little Georgian wine."

She didn't have the heart to tell him that she hadn't known to ask for one. "It doesn't seem entirely fair, though, does it," she said, "to be demanding special privileges when everyone else is making such sacrifices?"

Fyodor looked her over from under his merging brows. "You always were an odd one, Flora Solomonovna. Wait for what's fair and soon you'll be begging like a cripple at a cross."

She was about to laugh when a sudden din in the rear made Fyodor whip his head about. A loud scraping of chairs and dropped plates made one corner of the hall thunderous while the ordinary clamor elsewhere died to a silence. Two men had jumped to their feet over some altercation Florence couldn't hear. The atmosphere in the dining room had become theatrical. The men were pulled off each other, cursing and spitting on the floor.

"And there you are," Fyodor said, turning around, "the Man of Tomorrow. As our pamphleteers like to say, 'We are not remaking ore into steel here, we are remaking *people*!' It's all true: they arrive on the train as yokels in birch-bark shoes, and we turn them into genuine proletarian jackasses."

Florence laughed. "How I've missed the pleasure of your company, Fedya."

"Have you really?" he said, and something like mournfulness misted his eyes. "Some sense of timing you have, little girl," he said suddenly. "To come when all the rest of your kind is leaving. Even Sergey is gone."

She could feel a knot in her chest, an embolus of woe sinking down like a lead ball into her stomach. "Sergey isn't in Magnitogorsk?"

Something of her shock was reflected back in a pantomime on Fyodor's face. "And here I was, thinking you'd come all this way for me."

She stiffened, before realizing he was joking. But the naked effort of her laughter wasn't lost on Fyodor. "Yes," he said, nodding woefully, "our mutual friend has left for good. To Moscow. A fortunate development, considering where else he might have ended up."

"How do you mean? Did he get on the wrong side of someone?"

"A perceptive bird you are," Fyodor said and lowered his voice so that she had to lean in to hear. "Our Sergey made the mistake of complaining about under-allotment of materials, and this new director of ours said, 'If *you* need them, go and find them.'"

"What does that mean—'go and find'?"

Fyodor cast her a tender look. "Make friends, Florochka. Find the right fellow in the supply chain, split a bottle or something else, until he promises to help."

"But that wasn't Sergey's job," she said defensively.

"Well, he didn't think so. He thought the man was just trying to take him down a notch for being a specialist who'd worked in America! He wrote a letter to Moscow that got returned to the same people it sought to expose. Anyway, he must have had one or two friends upstairs, because he got a transfer before things really got ugly."

"Where is he now?"

Fyodor sighed. "Something in light industry. Maybe auto or metallurgy. It was a strange appointment."

She gathered from Fyodor's tone that, in spite of Sergey's rescue, the assignment he'd been given was a kind of demotion.

"I thought I'd tell you before you mentioned our friend's name to someone else you shouldn't," Fyodor said.

It took Florence a moment to register the meaning of his words. Blood flushed her face. She could feel herself dying of shame at the thought of Fyodor looking for her all over Magnitogorsk, the same way she'd been looking for Sergey. But he was only trying to spare her embarrassment, and now he said no more about this; his face stayed tender and serious. "Look around this place, Florochka. My suggestion: get yourself a train ticket before your last pair of stockings runs."

In the end, it was a relief to discover that Sergey was gone. It allowed her grim adventure to remain untainted by defeat. She hadn't, after all, arrived and then, weak-spined, turned back. She'd stayed and weathered the appalling sanitation, battled her nausea and endless hunger, endured her bullying superiors, forgiven the barracks drunks who had kept her up all night with their howling accordion songs. Now that she was saying goodbye, Florence could let herself feel some affection for the place.

She returned to her barracks to find the women outside, beating their straw mattresses with sticks. In her room she discovered the mother washing the walls with a steaming rag. All the cots had been moved to the center of the room and stripped of bedding. "July's arrived," the mother announced. Her daughter came in, carrying a boiling kettle. She climbed on a chair and attempted to pour boiling water on a moldlike spot in the corner of the ceiling.

"What's up there?"

"*Klopi!* What else?"

Florence had never heard the word, but its meaning struck her instantly with terror: bedbugs. The girl tossed some boiling water against the wall, then got down to pour what was left onto the window casing. This was pasted with old newsprint, which was also stuffed in the frame to keep out the draft.

"Peel it all off," the mother commanded. "And you"—she turned angrily to Florence—"go boil more water instead of gawking like a flytrap."

"No use washing the walls," muttered the pregnant girl, who was just walking in. "All they'll do is crawl up onto the ceiling."

"According to you there's no use in washing our hands, neither," said the mother.

THEY SLEPT WITH THE BEDS in the middle, close enough to give and receive one another's body heat. Florence's dream was an extension of her reality: sleeping, she fantasized about the public bath, of washing herself and her clothes before her train journey. Drops fell on her face, tickled her mouth. In the near-perfect blackness, she opened her eyes and saw the iron-colored night in the cockeyed window. Another drop fell on her cheek, just under her eye. Then it moved.

The first sign of madness is a howl that, once uncorked, cannot stop. Such was the sound that exploded in the room's snore-filled darkness.

Someone was scrambling to turn on the light, as Florence flailed, shrieking and grabbing at herself.

"They've gotten in her hair!"

"Serves her right. She ought to have covered up a thicket like that. Go calm her down."

But no one did. Under the swinging electric bulb they all stood watching as Florence scratched her face and pulled her hair. "It's useless," remarked the pregnant village girl. "They've gripped in good now."

14.

GOLD

ON A HOT MORNING IN THE SUMMER OF 1934, AS FLORENCE WAS STUM-
bling through Magnitogorsk and the American economy was still stum-
bling through the Depression, President Roosevelt sat upright to take
breakfast in his mahogany bed and to light the first of the day's forty
Camel cigarettes in their ivory holder. It was a fact widely known among
FDR's advisers that the best time to seek the president's audience was in
the early morning, between the time the maid delivered his hash and eggs
and the arrival of the valet, at ten o'clock sharp, to dress the president and
strap him into his braces. A lesser-known fact was that the first person to
enter Roosevelt's private chambers each morning was not Mrs. Roosevelt
but the stiffer and more morose figure of Henry Morgenthau, his secretary of the treasury. Were a casual viewer to catch a glimpse inside the
presidential bedroom, he might take the balding man in the clerically high
collar to be a priest administering last rites, for there was an unmistakable
air of solemnity to Roosevelt's meetings with Morgenthau. The president,
having recently failed to raise food prices with his agrarian reforms, and
facing another farmers' revolt, had of late undertaken a more radical
strategy: raising prices by rapidly devaluing the dollar. The ritual Morgenthau was performing that morning, and every morning that summer, was
the more profane rite of setting the day's bid price for gold.

It was an elementary game of supply and demand: having snipped the
dollar's link to gold, the government was employing its enormous new

powers to buy up gold on the world market, in order to drive down the value of the dollar and raise the price of everything else. There was but one wrench in this elegant mechanism. For some time now, inexplicable surpluses of gold were swelling the markets in London, Paris, and New York. And not corrupted gold, but ingots so pure that biting into one was like sinking your teeth into hardened fudge. The ingots were stampless, anonymous. Only their smoothness distinguished them—a gravy softness identical to that of imperial tsarist coins. Gold, in other words, that could come only from the prison mines of the Russian Arctic.

"What do these Russians think they're playing at, street dice?" inquired the president. "Are they stupid enough to kill their own market by dumping so much gold?"

"I'm inclined to believe so, sir," replied Morgenthau dyspeptically. "Their understanding of the commodities markets is quite primitive."

"Nonsense, Henry! These Bolshies are ready to saw off their snouts to spite their faces. It's pure sabotage!"

"Or it may simply be that . . ."

"What?"

"That they need the cash, and fast."

"Well, then, someone ought to tell them that, if they want to spend their easy cash on our American machines and in our American factories, they'd best put an end to these shenanigans."

"Received and understood, sir."

Departing the president's quarters, Morgenthau began to pen a letter in his head. He had no authority to stop American firms from doing business with Russia, and neither did the president. Even at the top, power consisted not of a single giant switch but of a myriad of delicate levers that needed to be pulled discreetly.

THE LETTERS THAT BEGAN arriving at the Foreign Currency Department of the Soviet State Bank in Moscow were confounding in their tone of obscure threat and even vaguer appeal. A sentence teetering on the edge of solicitude might turn abruptly to blackmail, or vice versa. The task of reading this cavalcade of memos from the U.S. Treasury, Russia's various creditors, and foreign export firms fell on the shoulders of one Grigory Grigorievich Timofeyev, director of the Foreign Currency Desk. Responding to so much hostile correspondence required, in Timofeyev's view as a former diplomat, a certain aggressive delicacy, and much more time than he had to spare. But one clear and chilly afternoon in September, his answer walked in the door. The pretty, serious-looking woman who entered his office made a clumsy effort to smile as she adjusted her ruffled blouse. But it wasn't her overdressed appearance that gave her away as a foreigner so much as her walk, an athletic stride that even her flouncy clothes couldn't hide. Her complexion was still burnished pink from the summer's sun. But her eyes, blue and downsloping, announced her industriousness and eagerness to please. She'd been sent by the Office of American Trade, formerly Amtorg.

Timofeyev motioned for her to sit.

"You worked at the Soviet Trade Mission in New York?" He was reading a letter from the Mission signed by one Scoop Epstein.

"Yes. My specialization was in trade contracts," the young woman replied in stiff but serviceable Russian, "steel, industrial machinery, special equipment. . . ."

"You don't need to summarize. What is your intention in coming to the Soviet Union?"

Florence had been asked this question many times over in Magnitogorsk and found that, whatever her answer, it did not satisfy the Russians. Since her motives would always be suspect, she settled at last on flattery. "I'm very impressed with everything that's been accomplished in the Soviet Union in such a short time. I want to contribute my labor to a society that's moving forward, not stagnating like—"

Timofeyev cut her off. "There are many people who come to the U.S.S.R. with no intention of living and working here other than to denounce us to the bourgeois press as soon as they leave. As you know, there have already been plenty of such slanderous so-called eyewitnesses."

"Respectfully, Comrade Timofeyev, most of these people are deceived by their unrealistic expectations. My decision to come to Russia was not a light decision. I have no illusions."

"No illusions, eh?" He seemed to like this, but raised a hand to keep her from talking as one of the two telephones on his desk began ringing. While Timofeyev took the call, Florence let her eyes settle on different points around his office. A glass-fronted mahogany bookcase occupied one wall, and a large blue globe stood on a tripod in the corner. On a green blotter beside Timofeyev's elbow, a tea glass in a filigree holder caught the morning sun arriving through the open curtain. Under her shoes the floor was polished to a high gloss. Everything about the balding, dapper Timofeyev seemed as elegant and polished as his office. He had calm, intelligent eyes, a long bony nose, and a neat, somewhat pointy beard. The look he was emulating might have been V. I. Lenin's, but the person he actually resembled, Florence realized with a start, was Shakespeare. Above Timofeyev hung an enlarged portrait of Comrade Stalin, also seated and working at his desk. Florence compared the two mentally and found Stalin lacking. Timofeyev laid down the receiver and regarded her with sharp, tired eyes. "Your references allege you are sincere and reliable," he remarked in an unconvinced, flattering way that made Florence glance down modestly. "What about your eyesight?"

"Pardon me?" She was still thinking about whether Timofeyev meant "reliable" professionally or politically.

"Do you wear glasses, Miss Fein?"

"I've never had the need."

"Good. Then you can read this." He slid across the desk a scrap that looked like a freshly printed dollar. "In the corner," he said, pointing.

"This note is legal tender for all debts private and . . ."

"What kind of stupidity is this—'legal tender'?"

"*Here* it says 'redeemable in lawful money at the United States Treasury or at any Federal Reserve bank.' "

"Is it some kind of word game? Paper money redeemable in . . . paper money! This is what they write above Mr. Washington's head. An English economist called Keynes has convinced your government and half of Europe to float their currencies. But America wants it both ways, as usual: your treasury sets a new price for the dollar every day and then *demands* to know how much gold *we* have in reserve." He pointed to a pile of envelopes on his desk. "You can write these excellent people and tell them politely that we await this information every morning as eagerly as they do. I assume you can type, Comrade Fein. Very good, then."

The questions on the employment forms Grigory Grigorievich gave her started simply enough—"name," "patronymic," "date and place of birth," "nationality" (she wrote "American"), "education," "foreign languages"— before, like a sudden drop in the seafloor, they became utterly confusing.

"What should I say for 'social origin'?" she asked Timofeyev. She hadn't come from "peasants" or "workers" or "gentry" or "clergy." Her father was an insurance man. Was that a trade or a speculation activity?

"Write 'middle-class,'" said Timofeyev impatiently, then frowned, thinking better of it. "*Lower*-middle-class." But before she had the chance, he took the papers from her hand and told her it was better if he completed the questions on her behalf. "The important thing is not to cross anything out," he explained mysteriously. In addition to her class origins, the State Bank seemed to be interested in Florence's marital status, every place she had lived since birth, what political groups she had ever belonged to, whether anyone in her family had been to jail, her height, her hair color, and any distinguishing characteristics she had, such as moles, limps, or a low hairline. Had she not known better, she would have thought she was filling out her own criminal docket. Hearing her uncertain, complicated replies, Timofeyev stopped consulting with her altogether and wrote out his own answers.

"Place of residence."

"I'm staying in a dormitory at the Foreign Languages Institute, on the condition that I start teaching there next week. But with this job, I thought I'd get another—"

"I'm sorry to tell you that Gosbank can't provide you with housing. Approval for another room normally takes months. You can rent something in a communal flat."

"You mean a *speculation* rental? I don't want to do anything . . . improper."

Timofeyev rolled his eyes. "Who teaches you foreigners this bunk? Open the papers; they're full of advertisements. Price set by the square meter. Whatever else you work out with your host is your business. All right, don't look so terrified. I'll have my Klavdia Alekseyevna call around. Heaven knows, if they hear you talk, they'll charge you more than your salary."

Once the paperwork was completed, he walked with her out into the common hall. All around, bank clerks and bookkeepers were busy typing and blotting, clicking abacus beads with a speed she'd only seen in Chinese laundries. Timofeyev's Shakespearean eyes twinkled in a benevolent mockery of her anxiousness. He put out his hand. "Welcome to Gosbank."

For Florence there now began a time of such permanent motion, such epic hustle, that she could never recall afterward how many weeks had passed before the numberless obstacles of her days began at last to take the shape of a familiar routine. Eight A.M. found her running along Solyanka Street to catch the overcrowded trams rolling down to Kuznetsky Most. By nine she was at her desk, surrounded by ringing telephones and chattering typewriters. Once more she felt the reassuring proximity of the immense and inscrutable levers of Power. Her morning hours were spent reading through the world financial papers, keeping abreast of the prices of precious metals and making reports on their movements to Timofeyev. After lunch in the canteen with the other clerks, she ascended the marble steps back to Timofeyev's tobacco-fragrant office and organized her boss's correspondence with foreign treasuries and banks, then typed up his dictations in her good English—not so much translating the words themselves (simple enough with the aid of a financial dictionary) as transmogrifying his tone (Soviet, autocratic) into the more cheerful and paternalistic American style that Scoop Epstein had taught her while conducting business with Midwestern executives.

IN ALMOST EVERY WAY Florence found her work at the Foreign Currency Desk to be a mirror image of the work she'd done at Amtorg: instead of facilitating the procurement of American steel via Russian gold, she was now midwifing the exchange of Russian gold into currencies to buy up American steel—a reverse alchemy of deposits, notes, and receipts. Her new boss, Timofeyev, though less florid in his praise than Scoop, was showing himself to be a more benevolent benefactor. Having solved the question of Florence's housing by finding her an adequate, if overpriced, room in a communal flat, he took on the matter of her Soviet education, enrolling her in a "political-pedagogy" class at the Moscow Electric Lamp Factory. From then on, Florence left work an hour early twice a week to race through the riotous crowds of the factory district and take her seat in a lecture hall full of factory girls and young construction workers. She was relieved to discover that among her peers were students even more poorly schooled in grammar and diction than she, girls and boys only a few years younger who were eager to erase their village pasts and absorb into their vernacular all manner of hyphenated idioms: *klass* and *dialektika; materializm, induktsia,* and *radiofikatsia.* They chewed on these words like young horses with a mouthful of feathers in their hay. And still there was something touching, even epic, in their collective effort to groom their speech into proletarian respectability. Not even at Hunter College, among the sons and daughters of immigrants, had Florence seen so much singular, fused attention, so much passion for self-betterment. She was dimly aware of a similar metamorphosis taking place in herself. Only now, while struggling to express herself simply in a new language, did she feel the burden of her lifelong exceptionalism cast aside. It was as if the very substance of herself was finding new form in a new tongue—not as polished, certainly, but somehow freed from the grip of her nervous hurry, her qualifications and apologies: undistinguished, rough, and plain as freshly cut gingham cloth. She found that the challenge of fitting in could be more exciting than the burden of standing out. She was discovering in herself a talent for picking up clichés, localisms, platitudes, and banalities of all sorts, and stringing them together so adroitly that to an unpracticed ear she sounded almost like a Muscovite. It was rudeness she courted now, for only the rudeness of strangers, cloakroom attendants, and store clerks could assure her that she was no longer regarded as a delicate, confused alien but a bona-fide Soviet.

From outward appearances, it would have seemed she'd forgotten all about Sergey. This was far from the truth. It had taken Florence only a little asking around to extrapolate from Fyodor's hint about "metallurgy" that Sergey could only be employed by one factory: the giant Hammer and Sickle plant near the Yauza River. But now that she was almost certain of where he was, something strange happened: her wanderer's heart, always so resolute, wavered. Like Odysseus with Ithaca so close in sight, she found herself unable to proceed. She knew she was changing, becoming a new person, unburdening herself from her old individualistic hunger for special attention. She wanted him to see how different she'd become, and yet this very desire made its fulfillment impossible. The very act of seeking him out savored of desperation. A year had passed, after all. Maybe he had a woman. Maybe he was remarried. Deep down, she wasn't ready for any meeting with Sergey that didn't involve his lifting her up off her feet, kissing her passionately on the mouth, and shouting "Hurrah!" And so, like napping Odysseus, she stayed put, waiting for some final, mysterious change to come.

15.

A MAN OF THE PEOPLE

FLORENCE'S WISH TO MERGE FULLY WITH THAT TITANIC ABSTRACTION known as the People finally came true on November 7, 1934. She'd woken that morning to the distant sounds of parade music coming from the street's loudspeakers. Below her window an army of women had been deployed with twig brooms.

Florence was meeting Essie on a prearranged corner of Maroseyka Street, where Essie was marching with a column of American workers from the AMO Factory. Florence, as an employee of Gosbank, was not required to march. Nonetheless, she wanted to catch a glimpse of Stalin and other Heroes of the Revolution. The procession was making its creeping progress to the center of the city before it passed through Red Square. Florence elbowed her way alongside the crowd until she caught sight of Essie's red-mittened hand waving at her. "You're late," she said, pulling Florence in.

"I'm sorry."

"We were about to start running again."

Above Florence's head, figures of the great leaders were mounted like giant paper dolls along the sides of surrounding buildings. Everywhere, red pennants flapped in the wind.

"This is Joe and Leon," said Essie, introducing Florence to the two men beside her. One, a middle-aged mechanic in a padded jacket, wore the thin red armband of a parade marshal. Next to him stood an unshaven younger man wearing a gangster's tweed cap and a coat with a raised collar. A cigarette dangled from his fleshy, too-pink lips. The horn blew, indicating that everyone needed to get back in formation. "Get in line! Get in line!" the organizers were shouting. "No stops from here on!" The young gangster spat out his cigarette and got into lockstep with Florence. His cheeks glowed in the winter cold. He looked her over twice before addressing her in English. "Your first time. I can tell."

The confidence of this assessment made her disinclined to answer. Undiscouraged, he studied her with a pair of sardonic black eyes. "You don't work at the AMO, either."

"Lucky guess," she said.

"I won't tell, don't worry. Neither do I. I did, but not anymore." He took a step toward her and flashed open his coat. "Kept my old pass, though. Any piece of paper you get in this city, better hold on to it."

"How about we don't speak English so loud," Florence suggested.

The gangster shrugged and turned to Essie. "Where you from?"

"Park East, Bronx."

"No kiddin'. And her?"

"Florence is a Brooklyn girl," Essie answered.

Florence wished she hadn't, because the next thing the boy said to her was "Oh yeah. Which corner?"

"Beverly," she said, not looking at him.

"Beverly and what?"

She was getting irritated by this summary exam. "What do you care, you planning to go there?" she heard herself say.

"Touchy."

"Florie is from Flatbush," volunteered Essie.

"Florie from Flatbush," the young man repeated with insinuating satisfaction, as if he'd wheedled some dirty secret out of her. "Where is that, Prospect Park? Millionaire Park?"

"South of that. Flatbush is all sorts of people."

"Yeah, all sorts of doctors and all sorts of lawyers. Don't be so sensitive," he said, and gave her a familiar pat on the back. He was looking ahead into the crowd, but the triumph of this discovery brought a smile to his face, and the pleasure of the smile seemed to spread outward, past the corners of his mouth to where the unkempt black hairs of his temple cropped down into a curling sideburn.

There was no response Florence could think of that didn't involve smacking him. A protest tried to take shape in her mouth, but at that moment a wave of music and cheering from the loudspeakers drowned out all talk on the street. The brick pavement was engulfed by workers from other factories around the city. "It means *he's* there if they're cheering," shouted Essie. Their column began to move forward at a jogging pace to catch up with those ahead. Florence felt her shoes touching cobblestones as the colossal expanse of Red Square opened up before them. Columns of people in front of them were spreading outward, swallowing the Kremlin like sea foam around a sand castle. She had been to demonstrations, but nothing like this, and her powers of observation fell short of its immensity. She was just one of thousands now, one of tens of thousands. It was a carnival of conformity. Above the singing and shouting crowds, transmissions of the official announcer boomed like thunder, saluting the marchers, extolling the selfless effort of the Great Soviet People, the potency of their constructive labor, the leaders of their Party—vanguard of the proletariat. With every step closer to the Mausoleum, the atmosphere in the crowd became more theatrical. They were conscious of Stalin in their midst, and held themselves as though he were conscious of them. Young women suffered spasms of ecstasy, their eyes watering. Men overcome by fits of poise held their shoulders as if at any moment Stalin himself might single out any one of them. "There he is, with his arm in the air!" someone behind Florence shouted.

"That's Voroshilov, you idiot!"

"No, over there, standing by Budyonny!"

The Bolshevik leaders perched atop the Mausoleum were no easier to tell apart than chess pawns. But Florence too was certain that she could recognize the twinkling eyes of Joseph Stalin, which looked down at her each workday from the oil painting above Timofeyev's desk. She slowed her pace to catch a better view, but the Red Army soldiers were prodding rubberneckers with the butts of their gleaming rifles, and the marching crowd pressed her forward.

"Get a good look, Flatbush?" the young man said once they'd crossed to the other side of the Mausoleum.

"You gonna call me that from now on?"

"What would you like me to call you?"

Even this seemingly innocent question made her feel like she was about to have her pockets picked. "Florence," she said, as a long cheer rose up behind them. Stalin had saluted the workers. Florence tried to involve herself in the "Hurrah!", but her voice suddenly lacked conviction. The self-forgetfulness she'd experienced only a moment earlier was gone. The music from the loudspeakers no longer carried her ahead toward some glorious future, but backward into a memory: sneaking off with one of her girlfriends from school to Midnight Mass at St. Francis. She was fifteen. She went out of curiosity, hid the expedition from her parents, and felt like an impostor the whole time. The Catholics had smiled kindly at her and her friend, thinking them pious girls worshipping Christ. Now, as then, some dark, subversive corner of her heart was threatening to overturn her awe and deem the whole scene a farce. It was the "Flatbush" remark, she was sure, that had broken the spell: his sly suggestion that she was an interloper among the true proletariat inheritors of the Revolution. She turned to find his pretty mouth still curled in its infuriating shape of wit. Another loud cheer rose from the crowds, and this time he joined it loudly, whistling and whooping like a wino at Mardi Gras.

THE FOREIGN WORKERS' CLUB ON HERTZEN STREET WAS CRAMMED WITH expatriates of every kind that evening. Austrian Schutzbunders and stiff-necked German socialists danced the foxtrot. Hungarian and Czech *polit-emigrants* swung each other out in big rumba turns. American Cominternists rushed the floor whenever the band began to play a Lindy Hop. Even the thin, bearded Italian anarchists were having a go on the footworn parquet. The political frenzy of the afternoon had been all but drowned in a flood of cheap champagne. Out in the cold, those who'd started celebrating early now staggered through the icy streets or lay in gutters. From half-frozen mouths could be heard the discordant slur of patriotic hymns.

Because Florence knew few other foreigners, she found it necessary to attach herself to Essie. She had yet to dance, and now it seemed too late: all the amateur dancers were vacating the floor to make room for a professional performance. A few feet away from them Florence recognized loudmouthed Leon from the parade. Before she could turn, Essie shouted at him over the music, "We lost you at the bridge!"

"Sorry about that," he said, approaching, though he didn't sound very sorry.

"We looked, but there were too many people on the embankment!"

"My friend had to go load the trucks and return all the props to the plant. I got pulled in. I had a hunch you'd end up here." His eyes flashed back and forth between Florence and Essie.

Florence, having resolved never to speak a word to this person again, kept her eyes on the dance floor. A duo—a young black man and a petite Russian girl—was warming up its act to the whistles and encouragements of the crowd. It struck Florence that in most parts of America this pairing would likely be objected to, if not on legal then certainly on moral grounds. The black man sported a thin Frenchman's mustache, and his blond partner, a plain-featured girl with a perfect figure, wore a polka-dot dress that fanned to show her underwear as he rotated her in a few fast, sleek turns.

"That's Jumpin' Jim Cosgrove and his girl, Polly," Leon informed her, though Florence hadn't asked.

"You know him?" Essie said with naked eagerness.

"Everyone knows Jimmy. He's been tearing up the floors of all the hotels—the National, the Metropol. Dancing for all the big wheels."

"Jeez—he's terrific! Is he a professional?"

Florence watched silently while Jumpin' Jimmy beat out an elaborate tattoo on the floor with his clicking heels. The top half of his body remained perfectly, effortlessly erect.

"Actually, he's a student," said Leon. "At the KUNMZ—the Communist University of the National Minorities of the West. But I don't think he ever goes to class. The hotel restaurants pay him a pretty sum to do the Lindochka every night for their guests. And that doesn't include the free drinks. He can drink it faster than they can pour it. These Russians can't get enough of him. Especially the communist wives. Most of 'em never seen a black man before in their lives. One time, a couple of 'em came up to him after a number and tried to touch his hair, then asked if he could speak a few words in 'Negro.'"

"I hope he told them to keep their hands to themselves," Florence said, breaking her vow of silence.

"It don't bother him," Leon replied. "Jimmy makes more dough here in a week than in a month in Chicago. Guys like him are ten a nickel over there, and here he's a true original."

She turned to him with a cold look. "You mean a novelty act? Maybe we should ask him how he feels playing Sambo for the Russians like some dancing bear. . . ." Her tone startled her.

"Take it easy. The man has a gift. Why shouldn't he make a little something from it?" He turned to Essie. "Your cousin always such a stick?"

Florence had no chance to correct him, on factual or philosophical grounds, because Leon's next question was to ask Essie if she wanted to dance.

Clusters of piano chords throbbed through the ether of body heat while Florence stood alone, watching Leon and Essie move around in a box step on the dance floor. Essie was half his height, but Leon was managing to swing her elegantly in a glissade and pull her back into the crook of his arm. Florence had no idea why she'd felt like being so mean. Everything around her seemed strange, including the music. Spotting her alone, one of the Austrian Schutzbunders approached and asked if she cared to dance. She didn't, but accepted. She permitted the Austrian to hold her tightly while they moved around in wide, graceless circles, but managed to keep her head turned slightly away to elude the sour waft from the Schutzbunder's mouth. As soon as the music ended, she extricated herself and found Essie, who was still catching her breath while her fingers lingered on Leon's elbow. "Where'd you learn to dance like that?"

Leon wiped his forehead. The top buttons of his shirt were unfastened to reveal a prolifically sprouting tuft around a bony sternum. "Where I come from, if you got hungry on a Saturday night, you'd go find whoever in the neighborhood was having a wedding. My friends and I would tell the man at the door, 'Our mother's upstairs. It's an emergency. The icebox is melting.' And he'd let us up. And five minutes later we'd be slipping around on the floor. Pretty soon everyone would get up and start dancing. That's when we'd sneak into the kitchen and load up on the rugelach, the fruit, the herring, fill our mouths with seltzer and get the hell out of there."

"Didn't you have food at home?" said Florence.

"Sure, we did," he said, apparently having forgotten her earlier slight. "Potato soup for breakfast. Potato pancakes for dinner. Potato pudding for dessert . . ."

"So you grew up in New York too," said Essie.

"Allen Street. But 'grew up' I don't know about. More like got *dragged* up."

Essie apparently found this hilarious, and Florence, for her part, did a fair impression of looking amused, if only to encourage the view that their earlier disagreement could still be written off as a misunderstanding. And this, to her surprise, had the unexpected effect of making Leon lift his eyes in a kind of shy, canine affection at her, before pulling his shirt straight. It was only a slight tug, but it laid bare what Florence had been looking at, and managed to make something awkwardly intimate of their truce.

Chords of dance music were rising up again over the tumult of the room. Essie was the first to recognize the tune. " 'Stardust!' " she shouted suddenly. "They're playing Hoagy Carmichael, on accordion!" It was true. Florence realized that this was what had been strange about the music: all the numbers were out-of-season tunes that had somehow made their way to Russian soil and settled into a kind of wandering-Gypsy version of themselves, just like her and Essie. It was obvious to her that Leon now felt obliged to ask one of them to dance, but this quandary was resolved by a tall figure bounding toward them. The figure turned into the shape of a lanky, bespectacled man who seemed almost to be rising on his toes as he shouted Leon's name.

"If it isn't Seldon Parker!"

"Greetings, Comrade!" announced Seldon, with the sumptuous inflections of an Englishman. He shook each girl's hand in turn. "Forgive me, I'm terrifically tight tonight."

"I expected you were at the old Metropol," said Leon, "drinking rounds with the Alpha and Omega boys."

"I wouldn't speak those syllables *too* loudly, my friend. Anyhow, there's been a change—they go by 'the Christian Brothers' now."

"Since when?"

"Since the YMCA is easier to remember than the OGPU."

"I thought they were called the NKVD now," said Leon.

Seldon removed a handkerchief and blotted the bullets of sweat from his forehead. "Too many damn abbreviations in this city to keep track of. And they're always changing," he said, turning to Florence. "Personally, I preferred it back when everyone simply referred to the secret police as the Red Cheka."

"What about 'the SPCC'?" suggested Florence.

"What's that, now?"

"The Society for the Prevention of Cruelty to Communism."

"Hey, that's got a nice ring to it. I think I'll write that one down."

"Seldon is going to write a big important book when he leaves this place," said Leon, "only he can't seem to leave it."

"What's your book about?" said Essie, and was rewarded with an elaborate explanation of Seldon's interest in the question of *proizvol*, the notion of "arbitrariness itself!" While Seldon turned Essie into a blinking victim of his theories about "the Russian lack of seemly proportion between cause and effect," Leon, taking a step toward Florence, said, "I keep telling him to hurry up and go back to London so he can start enjoying Moscow."

"How does that work?"

"The problem with writers is they don't know how to have their fun while they're having it. Only in retrospect."

"I take it you're not a writer."

"I do write, as a matter of fact. Seldon and I work together. We write for TASS."

"The Soviet wire service? In that big building up on Gorky Street?"

"So you've heard of it," Leon said with a specious modesty.

"Don't the Soviets have their own reporters?"

"Ah, but you see, we write news for *export*."

"In English?"

"In what else—Tagalog? We write and print a whole magazine. It's even read in the States. It's called *Sovietland*."

"*Sovietland*?" She gave him a sidelong look. "Is that an actual place?"

"Certainly. Sovietland has all sorts of marvelous things. Fresh new department stores with gramophones and vacuum cleaners. Cafés for the workers, where payments are made *strictly* on the honor system."

"Sounds like a wonderful place to live," she said.

"Patience, Florence. Patience."

"It's no wonder so many people who come to the Soviet Union return disappointed," she said. "First they read that baloney, then they go back to America and write all sorts of slander about the U.S.S.R."

Leon grinned innocently, expecting nothing less than this very reaction. He turned his palms out at his sides. "Okay. So let those *ligners* tell their lies."

"HE'S TRULY SOMETHING ELSE," ESSIE SAID, TOSSING OFF HER SHOES and falling backward onto Florence's bed. For a moment, Florence thought she was talking about Leon, but then Essie said, "The way he speaks, it's like he's talking . . . right to *you*."

It was past midnight. Florence pointed to the door to remind Essie that they weren't alone, that she had neighbors on every side.

"At least you've got your own four walls," Essie said. "Try living with twenty-eight others on a dormitory floor." She gathered her dress and pulled it up over her head. Florence unrolled a stocking and held one leg in a pose in front of the mirror before unrolling the other one.

"It's all the rest of it," Florence said, "the handkerchief waving and fainting spells. Everyone trying to outdo each other with the clapping when he speaks. I can do without it." From the wardrobe Florence removed a set of sheets along with a spare nightgown and handed them to Essie.

"But *that* isn't Stalin's fault," Essie objected. "*He* doesn't want the adulation. He ridicules it in all his own speeches. He makes fun of people who idolize him instead of getting on with their work."

"I'm not disagreeing," Florence said, taking the sheets back and spreading them on the bed. She was annoyed at Essie's inability to perform simple tasks while talking.

"And anyway," Essie pursued, "he knows perfectly well that it isn't 'Stalin the man' they're celebrating—it's what he *represents*, the Party and everything that's been done for the people—the way the whole country has been united."

A clean, starched odor rose up from the linens as they turned over the comforter. They sidled into the narrow bed, toe to head, like jacks on a playing card. Essie giggled in the darkness as Florence grabbed hold of the cold flesh of her foot. "Oh no you don't, not without socks."

"My shoes were soaked through," Essie protested.

"It's not the cold! Your little piggies are sharp as clamshells." Florence turned on the shaded lamp and slid out. From a locked drawer in her desk where she kept dollars and valuables, she removed a small sewing bag, then laid Essie's dimpled toes across her lap. "No one sees my feet in the winter," Essie said.

"No one sees your bloomers, either. Doesn't mean you shouldn't wear clean ones."

Essie winced but kept her mouth shut while Florence went on clipping with terrifying concentration.

"I can't find a pair of good scissors in any of the stores," Essie said defensively. "And I've looked too. Not even embroidery scissors. All I can find is fabric shears; the girls at the dorm use them, but I'm afraid to. They say the hairdressers' union works some deal under the table to get all the scissors first, so there's none left for anyone else."

"You can get a pair at the Torgsin shops. They take foreign currency, you know that."

"I can't squander my dollars on vanity, Florie."

Florence stopped cutting and looked up. "Suit yourself. I've always said: there's no such thing as a Plain Jane, only a Cheap Jane."

"And I think it's a bit unfair," Essie said, "that *we* can buy imported goods at those stores, but no one else can."

But Florence had been down this road of reasoning and knew where it led. "What's so unfair about it?" she said now. "The country needs foreign currency, and I need nail clippers. All I'm saying is, the Party Committees have their special shops, and so do the Kremlin doctors, and so on down the line. We aren't the only ones." She laid down her scissors. "These people's labor is valuable to the state. Maybe they don't have time to stand in lines. Our labor is special too, Essie. We should take pride in it, not turn ourselves into aesthetes."

"I think you mean *ascetics*."

"Whatever." Florence was aware that there was, perhaps, a capitalist strand in the fabric of her logic. Still, she felt justified in her reasoning. The work she was doing *was* valuable, and important. Why shouldn't it entitle her to an occasional bar of chocolate?

"I guess you're right," Essie intoned sleepily and settled back on her pillow. Florence turned off the light and the two lay in bed quietly, kneading each other's tired feet. From Essie's side of the bed came a hum Florence recognized as the swaying, Gypsyish melody of "Ochi Chornye." "Black and burning eyes," Essie hummed. "Black as midnight skies . . ."

Softly, Florence joined her, "Burn-with-passion eyes, how you hypnotize."

"I'm in love with you, I'm afra-yd of you!" they sang in unison. "Day that I met you, made me sad and blue."

Then Essie was quiet, and Florence knew why.

"Whose black eyes were you singing about?"

From Essie's side came more silence. But in the tension of her instep, Florence got her answer. Encouragingly, she said, "You danced well together."

"He made it easy; any girl would have looked good dancing with him."

"Mr. Dragged Up sure can drag a hoof, even if he's a little full of himself."

"Why full of himself?" said Essie, sitting up slightly.

"Oh, I don't know—maybe a little mouthy, is all I mean."

"That's funny. He asked me if he'd said something that upset you."

"He asked *you*?"

"He might have asked you to dance, Florie, if he thought you'd've let him." Essie's toes seemed to be at a kind of stiff attention again. "Do you like him?"

"Oh, *please*, Essie."

"What's wrong with him?"

"Nothing's *wrong* with him. I'm not saying he's bad-looking." Florence was suddenly unsure if she was admitting that Leon was attractive to hide the fact that she thought he was. "He's just not my type."

"What's your type?"

"Not American, for starters."

"Oh."

"I'm not saying *you* shouldn't. . . . It just seems silly for *me*, you know, to have come all the way here just to . . ."

"To what?"

"To get all *keyed up* about some guy from across the East River."

If hurt or relief flickered on Essie's face, the darkness hid it. After a while, Florence felt Essie curling herself toward the wall.

"'Night, Essie."

"'Night," she heard in return, and lay staring into the darkness for some time before falling asleep.

16.

THE HEATBIRD

MOSCOW,
1934

TWO DAYS LATER FLORENCE SET OUT TO FIND THE MAN WHO'D LED HER
to Moscow. Along the crumbling edge of the Yauza's asphalt embankment
her streetcar swayed from side to side. She was headed to the outskirts of
the city, up past coal sheds and warehouses and the stone fortifications of
monasteries requisitioned for workers' dorms.

Florence had imagined the Hammer and Sickle metallurgical plant to
be an enormous brick factory like the ones in New York. But as she approached she saw it was in fact a small city of its own. Florence stepped
out of the streetcar and was almost knocked down by the chaotic flow of
people. She had worn, over her narrow skirt, her mother's old fur coat. In
the swarm of padded cotton jackets she felt like Anna Karenina's foppish
heir. One glimpse through the open gates confirmed that each shop within
the factory grounds had its own security guard. Whatever mistake she'd
made in coming here, Florence knew it would be a greater mistake to announce herself to these ursine-hatted sentries. Bodies stampeded past
while Florence stood in a stupor of indecision. She could feel the last bit of
warmth from the trolley leaving her limbs. The crowd was thinning and
the gates would soon close. She didn't know what to do, and so it was like
reaching out for a piece of floating driftwood when her hand of its own
accord took hold of a passing elbow. The elbow belonged to a woman—
gaunt, with a face the color of a dying lightbulb that ignited with a menacing brightness at Florence's touch.

"Pardon me," Florence said, stepping back. "I'm looking for some-one—an engineer at this factory."

"The bell is about to ring. I can't find you no engineer."

"What does she want, Inna?" said a second girl, with a healthier complexion, in a bandanna.

"I'm looking for an engineer named Sokolov."

The girl peered about curiously. "Engineers are all in that far building."

"We can take you through the personnel office," suggested the skinny girl, as though she'd been trying to be helpful all along.

"No—I don't want to make trouble," said Florence.

"Everyone has to be declared," said the first woman.

"I—maybe I'm in the wrong place."

"Do you know who it is you're looking for or not?"

"Yes, he's"—she heard her own words clearly—"my cousin."

"Cousin, eh?"

Against their crude but effortless Russian her foreign accent was as baroque as her coat. "I'm his cousin," she resumed. "From Armenia. I got off at the train station this morning. He was supposed to meet me. Maybe he forgot." She was surprised at how easily this lie came to her. "Maybe I got off on the wrong side—everything is so big and confusing in this city." She sighed in a naked ploy for sympathy. "Maybe one of you could just tell him I'm here. The name is Sergey Sokolov."

"All right, wait over there," said the girl in the bandanna, making a sign to her friend to head in alone and cover for her.

"Tell him it's Flora," Florence called after her. "He'll know!"

SHE WAITED IN THE COLD while the striped shadows of the factory gates faded under a cover of clouds. The sun had been deceptively bright that morning, and without it the winter day was baring its teeth. Florence, berating herself for no reason at all, barely noticed when a tall figure approached the gates.

He was thinner than she'd been expecting, and his face wasn't visible under the cap he'd pulled low on his head. But the unmistakable stoop of those tremendous shoulders could only belong to Sergey. He squinted between the bars as the guard opened the gates for him. The rich summer tan that had been Florence's strongest memory of him was no more. His eyes, too, had dimmed and paled; they looked down at her as though at a specter, a stranger he couldn't place.

"Don't you recognize me?" Florence said, holding her hands together.

He permitted a tiny smile to cross his lips. "Cousin Flora?" But it was when the corners of his brows lifted, satyrlike, that Florence truly recognized *him*. "So," Sergey said, "you found me."

IN HER ROOM THAT EVENING they undressed quickly, removing each other's winter clothes like stiff gauze bandages. "Why are you laughing?" he said. But she couldn't stop. The absurdity of finding themselves together made her delirious.

On the walk over from the tram station where she'd met him, Florence had entertained him with tales of the bewildered American girl she'd been when she'd disembarked at Magnitogorsk, a Red Riding Hood out of her depths in the woods of socialism. Sticking a hand on her hip, she mimed her peasant roommates and remade of them trusty, rough-and-tumble guides in the forest, her confidantes. In the street-lit darkness, Sergey's laughing eyes settled on different points of her face, and soon he was tossing in a few choice details of his own about his "pioneer life" in Magnitogorsk, so that finally a common thread began to weave itself between their past and present. But as soon as they were in her room, he'd shut the door and pulled her roughly to himself. On the tiny metal bed they made cramped, rapid love, shoving everything else to the side. The sensation of his hair in her fingers, the quick hydraulic jolt of him inside her, was a paralyzing shock, like diving into a cold pool, and yet, within moments, strangely familiar. When they recovered, stunned and spent, they were as famished as two people getting over an illness.

Fortunately she was prepared: before going out to meet him at the trolley station, Florence had thrown a tablecloth over her desk. She'd laid out a spread of brined mushrooms, pickled tomatoes, sturgeon, cold cuts, caviars, wine, and brandy. Now, wrapped in her big tartan bedcover, she watched him spear one of the small pickled tomatoes—a tiny red globe—and raise it to eye level, as though studying it. He swallowed it whole, grimacing at its sourness, then flushed it down with a shot of brandy. Florence sat rediscovering the curve of Sergey's back with her fingertips as he bent low over the desk to make an elaborate sandwich of butter, caviar, and cucumbers.

"Red caviar *and* black; how did you manage that?"

She smiled. An entire month's allotment of Insnab coupons had gone to the purchase of these singular delicacies in the well-lit aisles of the exclusive foreigners' store, where her Caspian sturgeon, Georgian wine, and off-season tomatoes were efficiently wrapped by a smiling girl whose obliging nature bore no resemblance to the white-coated guardians of Moscow's common store counters.

"This is ossetra quality," he said approvingly.

"How can you tell?"

"Come here, I'll show you." He spooned more black roe and spread it thinly across the buttered bread. "You see, the eggs are plump, not sticking to each other in the juice. The last time I had this was—oh, let me think"—he stared up at the ceiling—"1928. No! Twenty-seven! New Year's Eve."

She slapped his shoulder. "Sergey, always joking."

"Not at all!"

"I've seen caviar in the grocery stores."

"Grocery stores? Oh yes! I remember those too. We used to have places by that name before they were converted."

"Converted?"

"Yes, to museums."

"What museums?"

"Museums dedicated to the memory of taste! You don't think I'm serious? Last week, I walked into one of these . . . museums. They had cheese in the window—just like this cheese. I went in and asked for half a kilo, and the store clerk—pardon me, the tour guide—told me it wasn't for sale, only for show."

He took a whiff of bread and tossed back a drink. "How long will you be in Moscow?"

"A year. Who knows? Maybe longer."

A crease appeared between his brows. Lest he think she'd come to hang on his neck, Florence added quickly: "I have my own four walls. I have a job. Beyond this, I have no plans. Though I'm taking classes."

But he seemed uninterested in that. "And your visa?"

"That's a simple matter. An overnight train to Helsinki, and the embassy there extends it another six months or a year."

"So you really mean to stay?" he said.

"Is that so strange? I feel like I'm a part of everything here. What was I doing at home that was so tremendous?" There seemed to be no way for her to talk about what she was doing in Moscow without coming across as discontented and defensive. "Here I get letters on my desk from some of the most important people in the world," she continued. "Economic advisers, prime ministers. Did you know that I've helped raise funds for the building of the new House of Culture? I'm helping build socialism."

In the vacuum of Sergey's amused silence, her earnestness sounded hollow and boastful. Sergey was trying to do a good impression of looking impressed, but his friendly effort was starting to irritate her. It was time to change the subject. "I'm not going to ask if you missed me," she said, more irritably than she'd aimed for.

Sergey tipped back another brandy. "Disastrously," he said, in a tone both avid and ironic. "It has not been an easy year."

Before she could stop herself, she said, "And did you drown your sorrow with many girls, or just one?"

He wiped the corner of his mouth thoughtfully with the back of his hand. "I'm not a monk, if that's what you're asking."

"What does it matter, really? Even if you're married . . ."

"I'm not married."

"But you have someone."

His silence suggested an affirmative answer.

"I didn't expect you to clear your evenings for me," Florence resumed. "You're here now, and that's good. Come when you want."

He examined the shot glass in his hand, turning it between his thumb and forefinger. He set it down, refilled her cup with wine, and offered it to her.

"No more. This wine is making my head spin." She brushed a moist strand of hair off her face. She felt cold suddenly. Anyhow, she was glad she'd said what she'd said. Glad it was out in the open. Let him be the one to think about it now.

Sergey shook his head sympathetically. "For a headache, only one cure." Delicately he tipped a porcelain pot to pour tea into Florence's cup, before raising his brow in disappointment at the contents. "What is this piss? Are we rationing?"

"I always make it like this."

"Florentsia, my dear, in Russia you must know two things: how to drink vodka and how to brew tea. Where is it?"

Florence found the black lacquered box in which she kept her loose tea leaves. Sergey took a generous pinch to demonstrate. "Tea has to be thick, like blood, and dark, like the soul." He closed the box, and turned it over in his hand. "This is where you keep tea?"

"Yes, why not?"

As the tea steeped, he turned over the object in his hand, as amused by its prosaic use as he might be by a child wearing a stethoscope. Florence had bought the oval box at an outdoor market, picking it from among similarly gorgeous items. In tiny brushstrokes on its black lacquer veneer, a young man clutched the tail feathers of a flame-colored bird. "It's the Firebird, right?" she said.

"Zhar-ptitsa," Sergey corrected. "Not Firebird. It means *Heat*bird. You know the story?"

She poured herself the darkened tea and reclined in her chair, ready to listen. Sergey scraped his chair closer to Florence and, with a breath warmed up with spirits, began to tell her the legend of the Heatbird.

"In a faraway kingdom," he began, "there lived a brave prince named Ivan. He'd been chosen by the king to guard the tree of golden apples that stood in the center of his father's orchard. Ivan's lazy brothers had already failed at the task by falling asleep. So, when Ivan's turn came, he tied bells to the branches so he'd be woken up when an intruder approached. In the middle of the night the bells sounded. Ivan opened his eyes and thought the sun must be shining. A great flame-colored bird with a hawk's talons was picking the apples. Ivan, leaping to grab at its tail, caught hold of a single feather before the bird flew away. Captivated by this glorious animal and hypnotized by his still-warm souvenir, Ivan vowed to follow after the Zhar-ptitsa.

"With his single feather lighting the way like a torch, he entered the forest, and after much wandering he arrived at a clearing where a princess was bathing with her maidens. Forgetting temporarily about the bird, he began to frolic with these alluring creatures. But soon darkness crept over the forest, and the princess told the smitten prince that she and her companions were obliged to return to the castle of an evil magician-king who turned trespassers to stone. 'Don't follow us,' warned the princess, 'for it will bring you nothing but pain.' Ivan, heeding no warnings, sneaked in after the maidens just as the gates of the castle were closing."

Here Sergey paused to refresh himself with another drink. Florence waited for him to resume the story, but he seemed content to let things conclude there.

"So who was Ivan following—the princess or the Heatbird?" asked Florence.

"Maybe one. Maybe the other."

"But then what happened?"

"What happened," Sergey said dryly, "is, Ivan was captured by the magician." He folded the rest of his sandwich into his mouth and chewed it.

"There's got to be more."

"Oh, there is much more. Do you want the version with the gray wolf or the talking bear?"

"Does Ivan rescue the princess? Does he get the Firebird?"

Sergey nodded, chewing. "Yes, yes, much later. After many misfortunes."

"Does he return home?"

"Many years later. In beggar's clothes. Nobody recognizes him."

She stopped stirring her tea and wiped some caviar off the corner of his lip.

"Go home, Flora," he said.

She stared at him. "What?"

"Believe me when I say socialism doesn't need your help."

She gave a weak laugh. "It was you who wrote to say I should come and see everything that's being built in the Soviet Union."

"Is *that* where you think you are? You go out and buy food in your restricted stores, and you think you're living in . . ."

"Wait a second, I don't need any of this." She waved her arm over the table with its demolished cornucopia. "And I don't see you declining a second helping. If you didn't want me to come, you shouldn't have advertised so enthusiastically. . . ."

He looked at her as at an idiot. "That was for whoever was going to steam open my letter. I expected you to know the difference."

"Well, I'm sorry you think I'm so awfully naïve. The stupid American woman who's come here to saddle you. . . ." She couldn't look at him. She could feel the shame rising up, prickling her under her skin.

"Flora."

She could no longer form a sentence without first suppressing the tremor in her jaw. "What's keeping you here?" she said. "You're free to leave."

Slowly, without protest, Sergey stood up. She stared out the window, at the mute drama of falling snow, while he put on his clothes. She wrapped the tartan tighter around her shoulders.

"I *can't* leave," he said suddenly. "Flora, look at me." And when she did she knew he wasn't talking about her room. "Can't you understand what I've been telling you?"

But now it was her turn to give nothing away.

Picking up his hat, he let his fingers slide with something like tenderness across the smooth leather handle of her trunk. But when he spoke, his voice had the sound of an order: "Take your treasure chest to the station tomorrow, get on a train to Helsinki, and get the first boat out."

She watched, dumbfounded, as Sergey tucked his shirt into his pants. And then, in a voice eerily like those of her instructors at the political-education class, she said, "The only train I'm getting on is the locomotive accelerating into the future. And if you want to jump off that train, watch out you don't break your legs!"

As soon as this declaration was out of her mouth, she wanted to take it back. But part of her was glad she'd said words that finally had some effect on him. Sergey looked—no longer repulsed, but panicked. She'd accused him of being disloyal. The sober disbelief in his eyes gave her an exhilarating, brief feeling of power. It settled the score between them. And yet a tiny part of her was already aware that this power had a cost: that it was the last, impassible barrier between them.

"Happy travels, Flora."

They were the last words he'd ever speak to her.

17.

A NEW MENTALÌTĒT

MOSCOW,
1934

GO HOME, FLORA.

For weeks, the words floated up into her consciousness at inappropriate times. She did not tell anyone of her meeting with Sergey, not even Essie. With the same power of will with which she would, decades later, shove the word "America" into a locked drawer of her mind, Florence resolved now not to utter Sergey's name again. She was convinced that if she let it pass her lips he would continue to be the reason she'd come to Russia.

But his words lingered, and resurfaced in the frequent letters from her mother and father: "Come home, Florence." "Come back, kindeleh." Before her encounter with Sergey, she'd been able to skim over her parents' slanting, pleading script. Afterward, even touching the parchment paper of those letters made her feel sickeningly alone. Just a week earlier her brother had written her about starting high school at Erasmus, lampooning the same teachers whose classes she'd once endured. His words resounded from the page in Sidney's best Eddie Cantor voice. Now, as she sat at her office desk, working into the evening on a dictation Timofeyev had assigned that afternoon, the upwelling of loneliness was so sharp and so pure that it took all her will to clamp her jaw against the pain. She'd already gone through three drafts of Timofeyev's memorandum, each more error-scarred than the last. Glancing up with her tear-lensed eyes, she saw

that the wooden desks around her stood empty. Everyone had left for the
day. She pulled out the incomplete dictation with its carbon copy and
rolled a clean sheet of paper into the carriage.

Dear Siddy,

*Ahoy. By the time you receive this letter, your Thanksgiving gut will
long have shrunk. It appears that the mail travels twice as speedily from
there to here as vice versa, so I'll indemnify myself early and wish you
and the gang a HAPPY NEW YEAR!! What am I doing for Gobbler-day,
you ask? I will tell you. Turkeys here are hard to come by, but I did manage to get myself a chicken. They were "handing them out" (as we say
here) half a block from where I work. The food here is good, and cheap,
so that no one ever has to go hungry. But sometimes you don't know
what they'll be handing out till you're in line. I've gotten much better at
what the Soviets call the hunting-gathering game. As there is a separate
line in a shop for every type of item—butter, bread, bologna—the trick
is to know what each thing costs in advance, go straight to the cashier
and get your receipt, then jump in the slowest line and ask the person behind you to hold your place. While they're holding it, you jump to a line
that's moving faster, get your bread or butter, and run back to the first
line! If the person behind you isn't a gargoyle, you can get away with up
to four runs, like in baseball. Only trouble is when everyone decides to
use the same queue as home base! Then your game goes into overtime,
and the bread you came for is eaten by the time you get the bologna.*

*Don't show this to Mom, as she will send me another tear-smudged
letter telling me how red her eyes are from crying and adding another illness to the list of Papa's ailments that he has already written me he
does not have. I am taking care of myself well here. (And if she does
read this, am eating well also.) In fact, things are getting better and better. My Russian is good enough that I can pass for a not very bright
local. The city is getting bigger and better, too. The future everyone talks
about is really happening here! Soon we will have our very own first-
class subway. I say "we" because a great number of Moscow inhabitants, including your sister, have participated in building it during
"subbotniks" or voluntary days, shoveling earth and rocks, carting de-*

bris, and so on. Even if it is just a little help, when everyone pitches in,
they feel that the metro is their very own. When it finally opens, it will
have columns of marble, beautiful lighting, and escalators so long that
boys will want to ride up and down on them all day. I hope you will visit
and see for your

Her fingers would not obey the order to keep typing.

Lying to her parents was simple. She had done it all her life. But the chipper veil did not go down so easily with Sidney. He would never visit her. She pictured herself going down one of those deep escalators, alone. The interminable ride. Forever.

The deep, buffering silence that surrounded her tiny whimpers made Florence realize it was snowing again. Her eyes lifted to the cathedral gloom of the enormous windows, inky with night. In the grainy darkness, she could detect the stirring motion of floating snowflakes. How many mornings, seeing the snowy web on her windowpanes, had she wanted to crawl back under her blanket to let her bruised heart hibernate like a daffodil bulb?

Tell me what to do!

She heard herself whisper this, though she didn't quite know to whom. To God? It had been years since she'd prayed. To her little brother? Or . . . Between the tall cathedral windows hung a portrait of *Him*. She'd sat under the mustachioed Leader's all-seeing gaze for so long she barely noticed it anymore. Her failure to feel the obliterating devotion to Joseph Stalin that others professed seemed to be one more symptom of her foreignness. She felt she could escape her own unspeakable loneliness if only she could believe with a less uncertain heart. Now, in the wintry, humming silence, she heard: *I believe in one thing only: the power of human will.*

They were Stalin's words and they rang in the chamber of her head like an indictment. Grow up, Florie, she told herself sharply. But self-pity exerted its own allure. She understood, as she never had before, how exquisitely satisfying it was to drink your own misery, and how tasteless it was to everyone else. Perhaps if she had sat there longer it might have occurred to her to see Sergey as something other than a spurning lover. That in cutting her loose he was trying to offer her rescue. But the chrysalis of her melancholy was broken by an unexpected sound. It was the scrape of Timofeyev's door opening. Florence had presumed he'd gone home with the others, but he was only now coming out of his office, buttoning his long coat and fixing his black Astrakhan hat on top of his head.

She yanked the letter from the roller, but it came out only after a long hiccupping squeal.

"Flora?"

"Grigory Grigorievich—I didn't see you."

"The building is going to close soon."

"I was just sorting out my . . . Lost track of the time."

"Have you been crying?"

"Oh no. It's just the snowfall—it's so . . . beautiful."

His sharp eyes squinted in concern behind his amber-tinted spectacles.

"Have you ever eaten solyanka?"

In one gesture she shook her head and wiped her face with her arm.

"My wife makes the best solyanka in Moscow. Tonight you'll try it, all right? We're having guests for dinner; I'd like you to join us."

"Oh, I'm not dressed for dinner."

"You'll do just fine. Get your coat."

TIMOFEYEV'S APARTMENT BUILDING, a sand-colored Art Nouveau mansion on Prechistenka Street, stood equipped with a liveried doorman and an ancient elevator attendant who escorted them in the ornate cage up to the top floor. When Timofeyev opened the door the warmth gathered inside caused Florence to sweat in her heavy coat. The sound of her heels was absorbed by a woven rug that buffered the glare of a varnished entry hall. Two steps below, in a sunken living room, a few guests had already gathered. On an elegantly overstuffed sofa were seated a well-fed gentleman and a tall woman whose blond-gray head and dusty complexion recalled to Florence a species of exotic moth. "It's only natural that the new theater should wear new clothes," the man was saying in a voice rife with discernment.

"I recall you saying something quite different last year, Max," spoke a redheaded beauty Florence took to be the young Madame Timofeyev. Her unbrushed ringlets hung down to the middle of her back. Her mouth was full and painted. Over one naked shoulder she wore a silk smock that clung to the flex and sinews of her body. Her threadbare, embroidered houseslippers only seemed to add to the effect of careless elegance.

"I haven't changed my mind, Ninochka. I've always said that our theater should avoid an *archeological* approach. It achieves nothing new with restorations of former plays."

Florence hadn't yet taken off her shoes when a shaggy dog began sniffing at her skirt. "Stop that at once, Misha!" Ninochka said, dragging the dog roughly by his collar. "I'm sorry about this fat fool," she said. For a moment Florence thought she was talking about the man on the sofa.

"What a lovely dog! What breed is he?"

"He's a mutt. We found him on the street," Timofeyev answered, taking her coat.

"There is no breed of dog in any part of the world that corresponds precisely to the Russian family hound," chimed in the man on the couch. "He is a mixture of all the worst varieties. They sleep all day and bark all night."

Nina, having taken the dog into the kitchen, now came back with cognac. "Grisha, you didn't tell me your American was so adorable," she declared before making effusive introductions of her two guests—Max, a theater critic and "absolute genius," and Valda, who, as Nina explained, had only just come back from Denmark, where she had been traveling with an all-Soviet delegation to the Scandinavian nations.

"Are you a diplomat?" Florence inquired.

"No, no." The woman crinkled her eyes modestly. "Only a translator."

"Valda is a specialist in the Nordic tongues. She knows a dozen of them—Finnish, Swedish, English, Dutch. . . ." Nina might have gone on to include Portuguese and Basque in this list if she hadn't disappeared again into the kitchen to give loud orders to the elderly maid whom she addressed as Olga Ivanovna. It struck Florence that, like every good hostess, Timofeyev's wife knew how to trade in lavish indiscriminate praise. And yet it was almost physically impossible for Florence not to be warmed by her enthusiasm.

"My position has always been," Max said, now addressing Timofeyev, "that, no matter how great the role of the classics, they can't fully satisfy the demands of the new audience. There must be new themes for the new *mentalitēt*."

"I have nothing against the new *mentalitēt*, but why must these adaptations always be so dull?" said Timofeyev. "Why does *Hamlet* need to be set in Uzbekistan? Why should Molière's plays be set on the floor of a factory?"

"There are no *new* themes, Maxim darling," Nina said, coming in with glasses. "There is but one immortal theme."

"And what's that, my dear?"

"Love!"

"Love will always be an absorbing *subject*," said Max, "but it has to be subordinated to more complex social questions."

The moth-faced Valda, listening to this in amused silence, smiled at Florence from the couch.

"Love is subordinate to nothing!" declared Nina, pouring for herself a drink that Florence guessed was not her first that evening.

"Why not combine the two," suggested Timofeyev. "Set *Romeo and Juliet* on a collective farm."

"What a spectacular idea, Grisha," said Valda.

"To our health!" Nina proclaimed.

Timofeyev splashed some wine into Florence's glass as they took their seats at the table, and urged her with a wink to have a drink. She wet her lips on the edge of the glass and for the first time felt such a genuine sensation of enjoying the company she was in; it was like a flash of her childhood memory of being allowed to stay up late with the grown-ups and discovering that despite all the exoticism of forbidden late-night fun, the adults she knew were doing nothing more remarkable than talking and eating and laughing! How much easier it was to be around these jaunty, ironic intellectuals—the exceptional people who had privilege heaped on them—than the simple, salt-of-the-earth, great Russian *narod*, against whom she had to jostle and shove every day as though through some hostile, obstructive medium.

"It's a question of *emphasis*," Max went on, refusing to drop his topic. "Look at our new production of *Resurrection*. The story is even more brilliant than Tolstoy realized when writing it. The playwright saw beyond all the religious moralizing and now it's no longer a story about a love affair between a servant girl and a wealthy cad, but a splendid social canvas! A picture of the oppression and ignorance of the peasantry! The corruption of the aristocracy and the hypocrisy of the church!"

Florence surprised herself by speaking. "But how many changes can be made to a story," she began, and hesitated—everyone at the table was looking at her—"before Tolstoy becomes, well, propaganda?"

"Our guest has a point," said Nina, looking at Max, who now addressed the question without actually addressing Florence.

"Yes, our foreign visitors are often remarking on the 'propaganda' in our theater, but they are entirely blind to the propaganda in their own. Take the chorus girls in Paris or New York, your *Follies*. Young women and, I might add, not such young ones, advertising their legs and breasts for two hours, without so much as an intermission. What do you call that if not sexual propaganda? We boycott such displays here and have a healthier theater for it."

"You might change your mind about that if you ever caught one of those chorus productions yourself, Max," Timofeyev said.

Grinning off this slight, Max resumed: "I find it charming that foreigners show such concern about the influence on the arts by propaganda when in fact Moscow's theaters continue to produce more classics than any other capital's, and do a finer job of it. A Chekhov production that was recently applauded in London would have met only polite toleration by Moscow's public."

"How do you know this?" said Florence.

"The play was reviewed in our theater press here, as well as in the foreign press."

Emboldened by wine, she pursued the impulse to challenge him. "But you didn't see it yourself. You're repeating what you read."

This remark induced in Max a laugh full of scorn and unease. His reply took the form of a mumble that Florence could not entirely make out, but which suggested the absurdity of what she was proposing.

Then it was her turn to feel uneasy. She'd wanted to impress the others with her wit but instead had succeeded in silencing the whole table. It was Timofeyev who broke the awkwardness. "Flora, you of all people, working in our Foreign Currency Department, ought to know that every citizen who goes abroad is a direct burden to the country. He requires foreign currency, which can otherwise be used for importing items of social value. Naturally, our government can't allow every citizen to travel abroad unless the money spent on him brings an equal return. . . ."

"Grigory Grigorievich, I didn't mean to suggest . . ."

"The government would gladly let every theater lover travel to watch a show in London, but, besides the expense, each Soviet citizen in a capitalist country is, as you know, liable to be made a cause for a diplomatic incident. . . ."

"Stop lecturing the poor girl, Grigorievich," said Nina, rising up from her chair. "She meant nothing by it. This whole conversation is getting too complicated for our simple female brains. Come, Florochka, help me in the kitchen."

Florence excused herself. But the relief of Nina's invitation was followed by the surprise of being led not into the kitchen, partially shielded by a view of Olga Ivanovna's ample behind, but farther down the hall, into the bedroom. At Nina's touch a ceiling lamp illuminated a satin lair of creamy coverlets and tasseled lampshades. In the center of the room, a mirrored vanity supported an elaborate collection of perfume flasks and jars of cream such as Florence had not seen in any store.

"Don't feel too awful about Max," Nina said, removing a small brass key from her vanity. "He is a genius, of course—a genius for glomming on to whatever's current. He needs to be taken down a notch once in a while."

"I didn't mean to say anything disagreeable. . . ."

"No need to apologize, dear, but let me give you some teeny advice." Nina stood working the key into a door in her sizable oak wardrobe. "I only say this because your Russian, though it's very good considering . . . Well, I don't want you to miss the nuances of etiquette, either."

The steamy warmth of the bedroom couldn't account for how hot Florence suddenly felt. A vision of unrenewed invitations to the Timofeyevs' spirited home struck her as a consequence of her big mouth.

"Frankly, I don't care to talk politics in this apartment," Nina said, finally getting the wardrobe door opened. "After all, who are we to think we can fathom everything that goes on up top? Right? We have the Party to settle these questions for us, so that we can get on with more lively matters." She bent toward the mirror inside her wardrobe door and fixed her lipstick, as though to demonstrate what livelier matters there were for her to attend to. There came a tap on the door.

"Come in," sang Nina, not taking her eyes off her reflection.

The bedroom door opened, and Valda tiptoed in. "I had to get away from that peacockery."

"Of course you did."

Florence now saw that Valda was holding a small suitcase. "Should I come back with this?" she spoke tentatively.

"No, I want Flora to take a look, too. Let's see the goodies."

Valda unlocked the suitcase and began to spread out on the bed blouses and dresses, gloves and hats. Pressing one of the pieces to her wireframe of a body, Nina twirled around to face Florence. "Is this what they're wearing in New York?"

"I really can't say."

Nina frowned. This was not the answer she was seeking. Her face suggested that Florence ought at least to learn to play the sophisticated foreigner, even if she in fact was not one.

"It's from Finland," said Valda, to vouch for the dress's quality and style. "And, look, it has a zipper, like the Elsa Schiaparelli dresses."

"I don't know." Nina moved the dress back and forth across her body.

And then, so simply, Florence understood what was happening. How dumb she was! Valda and Nina weren't playing dress-up. They were negotiating. Valda, having just been abroad for the social good of her nation, was now performing another social good by refreshing Nina's imported wardrobe.

"It's nice, but the waist is a bit tight, for New York," Florence heard herself say now, with the expert air expected of her. "We wear it looser, like this."

"It can be let out," Valda offered eagerly.

"All right, I'll have my seamstress have a look. How much do you want for it?"

"Oh, let's settle all that later," Valda suggested.

"As you wish." Nina carried the dress to her wardrobe and returned with a black tasseled shawl emblazoned with carmine roses. "And this," she said, wrapping the light wool kerchief around Florence's face and shoulders, "is how we wear things in Moscow. Keep it forever, dear."

IT WAS PAST ELEVEN when Florence left the Timofeyevs' apartment. The filigree of the iron gate, opened for her by the doorman, was dusted with snow. In the stinging, scentless cold, she felt aglow with wine and happiness. No longer Florie from Flatbush. No longer the lovelorn wanderer.

Some invisible barrier between herself and the city had been removed. In the cozy oasis of Timofeyev's salon she felt a sense of rarity and belonging that her life back in Brooklyn had stingily withheld. She had only to play the cosmopolitan role requested of her to gain admission. Even her blunder at the dinner table had been treated as a forgettable faux pas. In the future, she'd be more careful. How unnecessary her tears had been earlier that evening, how illusory her loneliness. She had merely to quiet her doubts, and life would open its doors.

In some secret corner of her heart, where she was less of an atheist than she liked to admit, she was certain that the prayer she'd made in the office had been spontaneously answered. But who exactly had answered it—Timofeyev, Stalin, or God? In her tipsiness, the three had somehow merged into distinct facets of a single divine force. A holy trinity. In the iodine sky, telephone wires swung with a trim of shaggy icicles like the fringe of her new shawl. They clinked like chimes in the wind. She was almost twenty-five years old and she'd never witnessed anything so marvelous. She stuck out her tongue and tasted the falling snow, sure that if she could only let herself embrace this feeling her happiness might last forever.

18.

SOCIALIST REALISM

It is startling to realize how much unbelief is necessary to
make belief possible. What we know as blind faith is sustained by innumerable unbeliefs.

—ERIC HOFFER

I HAVE THIS QUOTE COPIED INTO A FILE ON MY LAPTOP. I CAME ACROSS
it some years ago in a book, *The True Believer,* left for me by my daughter.
She read it in a college class and presented it to me as a badly needed addition to what she claims is my holy trinity of old white men: Clancy,
Grisham, and Dershowitz. When I finally opened Hoffer, I was struck with
a cold shudder of recognition at the words above, and those that followed:

> All active mass movements strive, therefore, to interpose a
> fact-proof screen between the faithful and the realities of the
> world. . . . It is the true believer's ability to "shut his eyes and
> stop his ears" to facts that do not deserve to be either seen or
> heard which is the source of his unequaled fortitude and con-
> stancy. He cannot be frightened by danger nor disheartened by
> obstacles nor baffled by contradictions because he denies their
> existence. . . .

It was *her*. And here I'd been thinking all these years that I was the only one burdened by the "innumerable unbeliefs" that formed the brickwork of my mother's pyramid of pure conviction.

She didn't even have the excuse of being a communist. After all her decades in the Soviet Union, she was proud of never carrying a Party card (though joining the Party in Russia was not as easy or automatic as many imagine, certainly not for foreigners). But this did not mean that my mother was any less blindly dedicated to the Grand Idea. More so, even, than the legions of card-carrying Stalinists and Trotskyites who remained in New York to duke it out among themselves for the next forty years. All those shabbily dressed Reds who refused to talk to one another (out of principle!) well into the 1970s were just that—talkers! My mother had no interest in their rabbinical hairsplitting. She wanted to leap over all that talk straight into the future.

Why she came to Russia never struck me as odd. Why she *stayed* is a different question, and one I've often found myself wondering about. Under what (or whose?) spell did the colorless landscape around her transform into one of those vivid proletarian mosaics that still decorate this mercantile city?

In her recollections of her arrival, one person rises most often in my mother's retelling: the man she called Timofeyev, her boss at the State Bank. (Throughout her life, my mother had few female friends, and seems to have preferred the role of ingénue to a certain sort of older gentleman.) I have no reason to suspect anything incorrect went on between them. From her account, Grigory Grigorievich Timofeyev was married to a theater actress sixteen years his junior—a Georgian princess from Tbilisi whose love of luxury frequently caused her husband awkwardness. One of Timofeyev's virtues, according to Mama, was that even in company he never drank anything stronger than Georgian mineral water, a trait acquired from his Old Believer ancestors—that Russian analogue to the American Quakers, merchants and capitalists and resisters who secretly bucked the autarchy of the tsar by giving runaway serfs refuge and work in their factories.

By the time Florence met Timofeyev, what remained of the old religious discipline and merchant spirit of his ancestors had assumed the narrower forms of strict sobriety and an energetic pursuit of socialist efficiency. I am convinced it was Timofeyev's eloquence regarding the latter that swayed my mother toward the unimpeachable rationality of the Soviet system. I once asked her what she'd thought of the complete lack of freedom in the press when she arrived. "You must have noticed that the newspapers failed to provide any real information," I said. "And didn't you find it odd that the papers carried no opinion columns? No comic strips? No crosswords? Didn't you think all those official pronouncements and statistics were just a tiny bit *relentless?*"

Her answer: "Well, Timofeyev used to say that it was all nonsense about foreign magazines' being 'forbidden.' They were just like any other luxury—to import them would mean the government would have to pay for them. And, yes, the Russian national press was often dull—that was a pity—but . . . you have to appreciate how much had already been accomplished in the country since the Revolution. Of what use to the people would all this *debate* in the press have been? Most of them still signed their names with 'X's. The language they read had to be clear and simple . . . clear and simple." I remember her repeating this in the schoolteacher's way that Timofeyev might have used with her. "You can't feed hard-to-chew meat to an infant, can you? The fact that they were reading the papers at all was a triumph."

I suspect the last bit about infants needing to swallow pre-chewed meats is a direct quote. Mama seemed attached to this explanation well into her sixties, like a duckling that gets imprinted on a farmer's boot and keeps thinking the boot is its mother, even while its neck is being cracked under the weight of the rubber sole.

I can imagine these early-winter evening walks my mother and her mentor take from the office on Neglinnaya Street to his home on Prechistenka, where Madame Timofeyev is hosting one of her salons. At this hour Moscow is at the height of its pristine gray beauty. I can see the thin layer of oil glistening like mother-of-pearl on the surface of the river. They pass a massive foundation for a stone bridge, yet unbuilt. Florence has watched a gang of men working on it for more than two weeks. Now she sees that the work has been abandoned, and the men and their wheelbarrows have moved eighty meters down the riverbank, to break ground for yet another foundation. Can they really be building a second bridge so close to the first? she asks Timofeyev.

To the practiced eye, it's clear what has happened: The river's curve makes it impossible for the first bridge to connect with the street on the other side. A typically sloppy Soviet drafting error that was ignored until it was too late. But Timofeyev only laughs it off as he adjusts his Astrakhan hat. "My dear Florochka, if you're ever to be a real Soviet, you must first understand that the great Russian people are a nation of maximalists. Our ambition is like love—it is impatient of delays and rivals. We built the world's largest warplane—it crashed on its first flight. But we've built others just as large, and they're still in the sky. We challenged France and constructed the mightiest stratospheric balloon, but couldn't get it to lift. Then we tried again, and broke all the world records!"

This is not empty boosterism. He is already developing in my mother that critical Soviet ability to see life not as it is, but as it is becoming. Or better still, as it *ought* to become. Everything they pass is something else in potential: A muddy culvert clogged with garbage is transformed through words into a future aqueduct. A block of demolished houses from which residents have been forcibly removed is not a vacant, brick-littered lot, but a People's Palace in the making. In my mother's mind, the future and the present are already becoming agreeably fused together.

She has no idea that they're about to explode apart.

19.

_____

CONSPIRACY THEORIES

THE WINTER OF 1934 WAS MONOTONOUSLY SNOWBOUND, AND SO FLORENCE could not be blamed for failing to experience the more mercurial political weather around her. On the morning of December 2, she walked into her office at Gosbank to find it a place of mourning. Heavy vapors of bereavement and alarm hung over every desk. Bookkeepers' tears fell in thick drops into giant ledgers. Florence's first reaction was confusion. "What's happened?" she asked, turning to a clerk beside her.

"For heaven's sake, don't you listen to the radio?"

This was not a question so much as an incrimination. Indeed Florence listened to the radio all the time. The radios of Moscow's apartments, like the megaphones in Moscow's streets, were devices apparently manufactured with no off switch. Within a month of her arrival in Russia, she had almost entirely stopped paying attention to the staticky bulletins issuing at all hours of the day from the radio in her communal kitchen. She was hardly the only burgeoning Soviet to acquire the gift of listening-and-not-hearing. Yet to succeed in missing the news of "the Crime of the Century"?

Very simply, she had overslept. Catapulting from her room to the trolley stop without so much as stopping in the kitchen to boil an egg, she'd failed to notice her communal neighbors bowed around the tombstone-shaped LKW radio from which a very real eulogy was just then issuing.

At the office, her colleague now said: "Where have you been, girlie? They've killed Sergey Kirov!"

"Who's killed him?" Florence said, with an alarm she hoped would conceal the question she was too embarrassed to ask: Who was Sergey Kirov?

For those not acquainted with the mother of Russia's political murders—an assassination of JFK proportions, which launched a thousand conspiracy theories—the murder of Sergey Kirov, Leningrad Party secretary, was much like the Kennedy affair, a murder complete with its own lone gunman (killed almost instantly), and its impenetrable cloud of conflicting testimonies and forensic evidence. Not to mention the obvious parallel with Kirov himself—a figure of Kennedyesque looks and charisma, a man whose political popularity was on its way to eclipsing even the Great Leader's. Consider the comparison: on one side, a handsome strapping Slav; on the other, a pockmarked Caucasian; the Leningrader, a dynamic and sociable leader; the Ossetian, a reclusive and paranoid sociopath who kept his Politburo colleagues up for half the night drinking vodka while he himself sat sipping water.

"Damned butchers!" The bookkeeper across the aisle now opened her mouth. "How can the earth spawn such villains!"

But why the plurals? Florence wondered. Hadn't a killer already been apprehended? The answer seemed to be in the newspaper the bookkeeper was holding. " 'The double-dealers, the craven vipers,' " she resumed, no longer declaring her disgust but merely reciting aloud from the *Pravda* on her desk, " 'sworn enemies of Socialism raised their hand against not one man, but the whole Proletarian Revolution. The working people now unanimously demand justice for the killers!' "

The news of the murder had charged the room, herded everyone together in somber, excitable communion. It was as if a great audition were taking place around Florence: a chorus being handpicked for *Oedipus Rex*. But who was doing the handpicking? And just then our heroine took notice of a figure she had not seen before, a woman in a white blouse buttoned high over a grand bosom. A bosom as well strapped in and fastened as a parachutist's.

"Enough dawdling, Comrades," the parachutist commanded—an order that sent the girls scattering to their desks. To everyone but Florence, the identity of this woman, the head of the bank's Party Committee, was well known. "Enough mewling," she chided a girl still tearily reading the paper. "On with your business." Florence took the order at face value by knocking, as she did each morning, on Timofeyev's door. After several knocks, she twisted the knob. Her error became apparent as soon as her boss's red-rimmed eyes fastened on her. "What do you want?" he said curtly, even rudely. His beard was unkempt; his normally placid eyes were so irate they looked wild. "The reports on the silver markets are in," she declared idiotically, pointing to the portfolio under her arm.

It was at this moment that, from behind the open door, a blind spot in Florence's vision, a back as broad as a rhino's and sheathed in a thick hide of black leather turned slowly to take stock of the intruder. Holding one of Timofeyev's books, the man in the leather coat eyeballed her, not unpleasantly. Florence had only just begun to understand the significance of the leather jacket in Soviet life. The knee-length leather coat, perhaps the first and only fashion statement communism ever gave the world (aside from Mao's notable collar), the quintessential symbol of proletarian ruggedness and revolutionary masculinity, was adopted first by the Bolshevik defenders of the working class, before becoming the favored apparel of the secret police. It did not diminish the coat's vanquishing effect that its current wearer had a middle-aged, bloated, and slatternly face. Florence took a step backward.

"Does this look like a suitable time, Comrade Fein?" said Timofeyev.

"Forgive me."

"Next time, knock."

But she had knocked! Walking back, she felt like a church bell that had been violently struck. Her head and fingers were still concussing in humiliation as she sat down at her desk.

The possibility that her boss and mentor might not wish to appear, before the Chekist in his office, to be on too-friendly terms with the foreigner in his employ did not enter her mind. Had she taken a look at that morning's *Pravda,* she might have noticed that tarred among the "craven vipers and sworn enemies of Socialism" were also "camouflaged enemies in the employ of foreign intelligence." Instead, still struggling to think of what she'd done wrong, she laid her cheek down on the cover of her typewriter and began to sob quietly. Her despair could not have been more appropriate to the occasion.

"*Nu, nu . . .*" Somebody was standing behind her and patting her shoulder. Wiping the water from her eyes, Florence turned to see that it was the office manager. "Tears won't bring back even saints, my dear," the woman said. Then, still comforting Florence, she added, "They'll clean up those vermin good now; then it'll be their turn to cry."

Florence will recall this prophecy three weeks later, packed in a room within the bank's bureaucratic bowels with other workers. The room, a small auditorium, is blossoming with the heat of winter sweat. Only one casement window has been left ajar; the morning breeze is stirring the leathery leaves of three giant ficus plants perched on the windowsill. The *Ficus elastica,* commonly known as the rubber plant, a hateful symbol (during earlier years of the Revolution) of petit-bourgeois domesticity, has now been rehabilitated by the mighty proletariat. No other plant, it turns out, thrives quite so succulently in the stale radiator heat of Soviet meeting rooms. Before this tropical background appear, like the heads of a tribal council, the faces of the bank's Party Committee and All-Union Committee. Against the opposite wall hangs a black-bordered flag of mourning.

The headlines have followed one another so forcefully over these past weeks that even Florence can't help paying attention. A week following the assassination, 103 "White Guardists" have been arrested and summarily executed. Their names have not been made public, and the only information disclosed about them is that they smuggled their way into the Soviet Union through Latvia, Finland, Poland, and Turkey for the purpose of assassinating Kirov and other leaders. More recently, Grigory Zinoviev, old revolutionary and comrade-in-arms of Lenin, has been arrested as well, his guilt already gospel though his trial is still two weeks away. But the roll call is just beginning. In two years' time the number of parties responsible for a single man's murder will grow to include 104 Leningrad counterrevolutionaries, 78 conspirators of the "Moscow Center" (to evolve into the nefarious "Trotskyite-Zinovievite Terrorist Center"), 12 Leningrad Chekists, and more. Kirov's death is the golden goose that keeps bearing suitable new enemies, all the way up to 1941, when its fertility is interrupted temporarily by the war.

But let's now return to the auditorium with its rehabilitated ficuses. Surely, if an ideologically incorrect rubber plant can be rescued from bourgeois vulgarity then the young woman on trial today can also redeem herself in the eyes of her co-workers. Florence can just make out the bobbing bun of the stenographer recording the enumerated charges:

"Regression."

"Blunted political diligence."

"Failing to break off contacts."

"But how?" says the ginger-haired girl, her voice quivering. "How could I break off contact? He's my father, after all." She does not pose the question rhetorically. Her small eyes flicker up briefly at the audience as though there might be a genuine answer out there somewhere. Seeing those desperate eyes, Florence feels her flesh go cold.

The girl, it turns out, is a daughter of one of the "Zinovievites." For the first time, Florence learns that Zinoviev and Kamenev were part of a political opposition years ago.

"Truly, you surprise me, Golubtsova," says the woman Florence recognizes as the parachutist with the formidable bust. Her tone is far from belligerent. On the contrary, her words have an almost joyful feel. "When the conspirators' arrests were made known, you did not come to the committee to declare your association with the enemies."

"I didn't believe it all myself."

"You didn't believe they were guilty?" says a man at the end of the table.

"No . . . Yes."

"You thought the Party picks people up for nothing?"

"I . . . was confused."

"Yet not confused enough," the woman resumes, "to contact your old friends in Leningrad and see to it that your name was not on any roster of activists at the Smolny Institute."

"I was an organizer there four years ago, but I've been residing here since."

"But in all your time here you never called anyone in Leningrad to ask to have your name whitewashed from any lists—how do you explain it?"

"In all honesty, I confess, I knew nothing of the schemes that have been suggested by . . ."

"What do you mean by 'suggested by'?" says another man. "You persist in refusing to denounce the terrorists in the face of a mountain of evidence."

But the woman in charge raises her palm to politely silence him.

"Whether you knew or didn't know is beside the point here. Instead of coming clean with your associations at once, you first made plans to cover your own back, going to your uncle for help. . . ."

"It was he who suggested it, only because I was no longer a member of—"

"Nobody here is interested in your alibis," protests the man at the end.

Florence is still struggling to follow what the girl is being asked to confess to, though it is already clear that, whatever new confession she offers, the court will immediately cast it aside as inadequate and insincere. For the past two weeks, Florence has been trying to make sense of the cascade of unmaskings in the newspapers, but she keeps being confounded by the same stubborn paradox: There seem to be too many Iagos hiding in the wings. If the White Guardists have already killed Kirov, then surely the "Zinovievites" are off the hook. Or vice versa. It's a heretical logic of elimination that the mathematical branch of her intelligence persists in performing. And what does it say about the Party, she wonders, that all those Bolsheviks were involved in this business—members of the Central Committee? Did they have no other way of speaking up, that they had to resort to a murder? She longs to bring up these questions with Timofeyev. But her boss has been giving her the brush-off. His days are now taken up with meetings, and Florence has found it difficult enough to borrow his time to clarify his increasingly convoluted morning dictations, let alone ask him to unriddle politics. Instead, it's the voice of Timofeyev's wife, Nina, that Florence now hears in her head: "Who are we to think we can fathom everything that goes on up top?" Her mind returns to this answer as to a lucky amulet. There's enormous comfort in reminding herself that she doesn't—that she can't possibly—have all the answers. Who is she, after all? Not a member of the Party. Not even a Russian. She repeats this mantra to ward off any guilt she might be tempted to feel for not speaking up in defense of the poor girl on the stand. What can she do, really, but watch the ginger-haired sacrificial lamb get slaughtered? One wrong move and Florence might be on the chopping block herself.

Her silence is only a symptom of the collective muteness permeating the nation. By 1934, crimes of passion have all but ceased in the Soviet Union. Likewise accidents, criminal negligence, and any act committed in the sweet shade of opportunism. Every malfeasance reported in the newspapers is an act of collusion.

Industrial accidents? Wreckers!

Production below plan? Saboteurs!

Murder and, yes, even rape—all guerrilla maneuvers in the war against the toiling classes. An overlooked headline on the back page of *Izvestia* just a week before the Kirov affair reads: "Young Pioneer Girl Dragged and Defiled in Wheat Field." Who are her attackers? Kulaks!

The question remains: Did the bullet that punctured Kirov's neck and, in its figurative way, go on to puncture the skulls of countless others, make at least a small dent in the membrane of Florence's enthusiasm for the land of her choosing? All evidence suggests that the events of the winter of '34 led her to draw no permanent conclusions about the *système soviétique*. Or maybe it was all simpler than that. Florence had other things on her mind that December: she was falling in love again.

AS HE'D PORTRAYED HIS CHILDHOOD to their group of friends, Leon Brink had inherited his revolutionary consciousness in utero. "Dragged up," as he told Florence, by a headstrong, lunatic mother and no father. From the age of three, when other Jewish boys in his neighborhood were starting *kheyder*, he'd been taken along to strikes and demonstrations and left to wait amid the raucous sidewalk crowds while his mother pummeled scabs with her lead-weighted umbrella and sharpened hairpins. Batia Brink, a garment worker and follower of Clara Lemlich, raised her son on a diet of contempt for economic despotry, which, she liked to say, boiled in the cauldrons of capitalism and rose like scum to the top.

Her hostility to capitalism was a uniquely American product, but her hatred of religion harked back to her youth in Polish Russia. At nineteen, she'd been married off to a young man, poor but brilliant, who as his mother's only son could claim exemption from the army draft. The following year, all exemptions were lifted. Fearing his death in the service of Tsar Nikolai, she had sold everything and sent her young husband to America. His first correspondence had been to say that work was hard to find and he could send her nothing to live on. She suffered reading his letters and suffered more when months passed without a word. It seemed he had no interest in paying her way over, though she had paid his. In time she went to the town's rabbi and begged him to write the young man in New York so that he'd agree to give her a divorce, which as a woman she had no power to grant herself. The rabbi had instead told her relatives to collect money and put her on a ship to America. In New York, she tracked down her husband, and for a short time the two lived together in a tenement room where, according to Leon, "he filled her full of semen" and disappeared again, this time going out west, and deserting her with debts at the butcher's and the grocery store. From that day onward, working in airless rooms six and seven days a week to feed and clothe her only child, Batia never stopped railing against the cowardice of men and the hypocrisy of the "rabbinical overlords" whose authority had laid waste her innocence. Her fanatical contempt—as it was comically relayed by Leon in his unflagging efforts to keep his audience entertained—appeared to Florence so out of proportion to the benevolent atheism of her own father as to seem a kind of exotic faith all its own. What else but fervent devotion could explain the fragrant four-course meal his penniless mother scraped together once a year on Yom Kippur, the fasting day, so as to scandalize and mock her pious neighbors?

Leon Brink was one of those men naturally gifted at turning his own life into a kind of vaudeville, even a kind of myth. It was a talent not so rare, in fact, among the sort of rebel misfits cast up in Moscow in the thirties—unfettered spirits proudly disinheriting their capitalist homelands. Young, mostly Jewish, hailing from the Bronx or Manchester, England, but coming also from places as exotic as Missoula, Montana. Observe them now: Florence and her friends at the Moscow Café on Pushkin Square, ordering nothing but coffees for the girls and a carafe of vodka for the fellows, so as to be allowed to sit for hours and talk and talk (the socializing, like everything else, being done collectively). So much of their talk centers on America, as if in profaning their birthplace they are performing a kind of ritual to relieve homesickness. See them filing one by one onto the skating rink at Petrovka, still so busy debating, discussing, that in a moment the whole bunch of them will land on their asses, as the natives swerve ably around them.

Leon Brink is the only one of the Americans to keep his balance. A lit cigarette hangs from his mouth. Florence shakes away his outstretched hand and hoists herself up without help. He extends it next to Essie, who takes it gratefully.

Was she still sore about his calling her "Flatbush"? Did she find his stories of sleeping on fire escapes and using the East River as a public toilet a kind of bragging? After all, like the rest of them, he was now a privileged foreigner insulated from the chronic shortages, the waiting in line, and the moral harassment that passes for customer service in Russia. To this upgrade of status they had all accommodated themselves quite swiftly. Out of the dead-end bog of American poverty and obscurity Leon had risen to the privileged post of "journalist" for a foreign outlet of TASS, a privilege that came with a standing table at every hotel café, a pair of tickets for each new concert, play, and film. How had a poor boy from a hard neighborhood managed to pull off such a transformation? Insane Batia, it seemed, was not without some pragmatism. She'd sent her son, at age twelve, to work for a pince-nez-wearing typesetter named Meyer Levitsky, who paid Leon by teaching him the printing trade and lending him books, so that by fifteen young Brink had read his way through most of the Russian classics and political philosophers. At the Foreign Workers' Club and the Moscow Café where his fellow expats gathered, he was not shy about quoting at length from Bakunin, Tolstoy, Jabotinsky, Marx. The only author he failed to cite in this revolutionary company was Horatio Alger, whose books had played no less a role in consummating the great maneuver of metamorphosis that was Leon Brink's life.

Florence could not explain the unease that snuck over her when he regaled their crowd from the corner of some table, not quite seated and not quite standing, either, gripping the back of a chair or someone's shoulder as if half expecting to be pulled up at any moment into the blue clouds. Even the spindles of his hair, the tufts of his sideburns seemed exempt from gravitational pull. Whatever it was, Florence could hold out for only so long.

The beginning of her capitulation came one silvery Moscow evening when, having run as fast as she could toward the fortress of the Bolshoi, she found Leon waiting for her in front of one of its creamy pillars. None of their other friends were there.

"Where is everybody?"

"You asking me?"

"I thought Essie was coming."

"Isn't she with you?" Leon said innocently.

"Where's Seldon?"

"Indisposed this evening. We were the honored guests of some Georgians last night. I warned him that wine was an unreliable mistress who doesn't leave promptly in the morning. Good old vodka, on the other hand . . ."

"We're going to be late," Florence said with perceptible impatience. "Do you have the tickets?"

From inside his meager overcoat, Leon pulled out two tickets for *Lady Macbeth of the Mtsensk District*.

In the grand vestibule, a furious footrace had started for the cloakrooms. The public wardrobes of Russia were, then as now, no optional convenience. To sneak into the opera without first checking one's overcoat would have been an unthinkable offense even for rebellious spirits like Leon and Florence. Seated with her program, Florence attempted to read the libretto of the production she was about to hear. In 1934, before the avant-garde was to be squeezed out completely by Stalin, Russia was enjoying the final days of a period of artistic innovation begun in the revolutionary era. These last explosions of the experimental Belle Époque, of which Florence caught the tail end upon her arrival, helped lull her into believing the country she'd come to was freer than the one she'd left. Florence made an effort to absorb herself in the plot of Dmitri Shostakovich's tragi-satiric opera about a merchant's wife who falls for a charming farmhand. In adapting Nikolai Leskov's dark story to music, Shostakovich had struggled to conform to the encroaching dictates of Sots-realism, but, to his own peril, he had been unable to repress his artistic idiosyncrasies. This might have explained why, inside the opera house, Florence was having trouble with the music. Onstage, the wild-eyed Katerina, lusting after her farmhand Sergey, writhed and convulsed as she murdered first her father-in-law, then her husband. The music groaned and panted along with her. A good deal of the action took place on the merchant's velvet-covered double bed, stage right.

No less agitating than the humid atmosphere of the opera was the potent stillness of the man beside her. The maritime tartness of his eau de cologne enveloped her in the draftless theater air. For the duration of the opera, Florence's knee remained locked in a position intended to prevent accidental brushing. She had nothing to worry about. Leon kept his hands to himself and left the seduction to Shostakovich. The opera had already had a run in Leningrad and rumors of its aphrodisiacal properties had reached Leon well in advance. It was no coincidence that he'd arranged to meet Florence alone for this engagement.

"What did you make of that?" Leon inquired after the lights were raised.

They had given their tickets to the cloakroom attendant by this point and collected their outerwear. Her two-hour effort to quell her arousal was now bringing on a kind of backwash of matronly disapproval. "It's a fine opera," she said, letting Leon help her into her coat, "if you don't care for things like melody, or cadence, or a sympathetic hero."

Florence's criticism of *Lady Macbeth of the Mtsensk District* would echo the scathing still-to-come review in *Pravda:* "coarse," "primitive," "epileptic." "Comrade Shostakovich presents us with the crudest naturalism . . . ," the reviewer wrote. "The composer has clearly not made it his business to heed what the Soviet public looks for in music and expects of it." This blast of official wrath would result in the opera's being taken out of circulation for the next three decades. "You mean you didn't find Katerina lovable?" Leon said, cocking his head, an edge of mockery in his voice.

"The lady is a monster."

"How about a clever, electrifying woman perishing in the nightmarish conditions of an oppressive society?"

"She's a calculating manslaughterer!"

"So she kills a couple of fellas."

"For the love of a confirmed philanderer!"

"That's where you're wrong, Comrade Fein. Katerina's crime is not a crime of love. A crime of love would be a spiritual sin. She, on the other hand, is possessed by pagan furies. Hence the title of *Lady Macbeth. . . .*" And here Leon did a most unexpected thing: he quoted Shakespeare. " 'I dare do all that may become a man; Who dares do more is none.' "

For a moment Florence stood observing him in the lit Moscow evening, her mouth exuding icy silver breaths. "So you've read Shakespeare . . . ," she said.

"Ay, good lady. I was even cast as Macduff in the City College production."

"You never told me you went to City!"

Having perhaps overreached in his claims at erudition, Leon issued a quick retraction. "I quit after less than a year."

"How come?"

"Figured college had nothing to teach me."

His continual boasting was like an endless brief in his own defense.

"I ran out of money, besides," he amended. "Even if the learning's free, life wasn't. Figured I'd learn more by traveling, anyway. I had a magnificent idea to ride the trains across America, but it turned out about a thousand guys had already beat me to it. I might've ended up in Argentina, but they had a military coup."

"So Russia was left."

"As a matter of fact, I was on my way to China. But then I read about Birobidzhan, the Jewish Autonomous Republic . . . Stalin's own Siberian Zion! And I wouldn't even have to learn Chinese."

"I didn't peg you for a homesteader."

"You kidding? I love the frontier! It was the pictures in the pamphlet that sold me—this youth who looked like some Berdichev Hercules lifting a wheat sack. And a big-calved Levantine princess strumming her balalaika. The only thing they forgot to put in the pamphlet was a picture of the mosquitoes."

"It sounds like paradise."

"I wasn't expecting the French Riviera. But here I get off the Trans-Siberian and the train platform is nothin' but a wooden plank in the middle of a mud field. I turn to the conductor and say, 'How much farther to Birobidzhan, Comrade?' He's already laughing at me. 'Two years, son!'

"So I get there, and they put me to work draining swamps. After two nights I have mosquito bites on my mosquito bites. Now, I wouldn't't've minded being eaten alive if at least I'd had something to eat. But I think the zookeepers forgot about us."

"What do you mean, 'us'?"

"They stuffed all us foreigners into one commune—Polacks, Bulgarians, Krauts, South Americans. I wouldn't have been surprised to find a Zulu in there. Guess someone wanted to see if we could build another Tower of Babel. If we weren't all so busy running to the latrines with dysentery, we might've even succeeded in killing each other."

"How long did you stay?"

"Almost four months I stuck around, if you can believe it. And those *mamzers* threatened to throw the book at me when I finally told 'em I was quitting. Said I'd never get a job in the Soviet Union if I didn't finish 'serving my time.' "

"What did you do?"

"I told them *Zai gezunt,* and *Va-fan-gulo* in my best Italian."

"So much for the dream of a Jewish republic," Florence said.

"How can I put it? It wasn't that there were too many Jews, it was that there was insufficiently everything else. See, the way I figure it, every place where there's just a few of us, we're like fertilizer. But all in one place?" He shook his head. "That's just a big pile of manure."

Florence laughed despite herself. Before she could catch her breath, Leon said: "What are you doing tomorrow evening?"

From that point on, it became the winter Florence started lying again. She blew off Essie, claiming committee meetings after work. At work, she skipped the meetings by claiming she had to attend her political-education class (the only permissible excuse), then played hooky from her class to go to the Udarnik Theater with Leon for the new film *Chapayev*.

Purges and politics aside, there was plenty of fun to be had in Moscow in 1934. Florence listened to her first symphony and attended her first ballet. She was astounded by how much high culture was available so cheaply. In the audiences, she saw people who looked and dressed like ordinary workers. Their hunger for culture flattered her sense of pride at being a resident of a city that had declared the differences between high culture and low, classic and current, elite and popular, to be merely bourgeois distinctions. She told herself that these dates with Leon were not really dates. This was egalitarian Russia, after all; no reason men and women couldn't be friends. There was no smooching, or even hand-holding—Florence kept it all on the level of talk. She even tried to prime the pump a little, do a bit of matchmaking.

"What do you think of Essie?"

"She's a nice girl."

"She has such pretty eyes, doesn't she?" Florence suggested encouragingly.

"Yes, and so close together, too," said Leon.

THEIR COURTSHIP UNFOLDED IN two settings, a Russian reality overlaid with New York memories. Passing over the cobblestones of the Arbat District, he'd tell her about his childhood working as a puller in the garment stalls on Canal Street.

"You know why all those suits on Canal have so many little price labels?"

"Why?"

"There's a hole underneath every one of them!"

Sipping mugs of foaming kvass in Gorky Park under a banner proclaiming that "Life Has Become Better, Life Has Become More Cheerful," they recalled the egg-cream sodas they'd drunk in Brooklyn.

"What I wouldn't give for a little chocolate syrup in this!"

"Won't help. You gotta know the formula," said Leon.

"*You* know it, I suppose."

"Sure do. This bartender on Greene Street showed me the secret recipe."

"You alone."

"Yup. Felt sorry for me 'cause I never had a Bar Mitzvah. He took me back into the kitchen and showed me how he done it. Told me, 'Today you are a man.'"

She never knew if he was making it up as he went along. After a while, she didn't care.

"I never see you drink very much, Leon."

"Alcohol interferes with my suffering."

With Leon she went to lectures at the House of Culture and to the State Jewish Theater on Bronnaya Street to watch Solomon Mikhoels perform his famous King Lear. But it was at the Metropol that Leon finally got his chance.

The restaurant of the Metropol Hotel deserves a place among the pantheon of the century's great pleasure dens. Its ceilings were, or appeared to Florence upon first inspection, thirty feet high. Palladian doors circumscribed the enormous dining room, rising to a colonnaded balcony under a stained-glass ceiling. Like the Ritz or the Copacabana, the Metropol could successfully pass off its garishness as timeless. Its ornate brass carvings and red plush furnishings had, by the 1930s, already acquired an air of departed glory, a feel of slightly frayed and shopworn luxury that was of a piece with the gold-braided uniforms of its liveried waiters, some of whom had been around since the days of the tsar.

Like the restaurants of other *valyuta* hotels, the Metropol was the sort of place that had been allowed to stay open to satisfy the bourgeois tastes of Moscow's foreign residents and visitors, especially the members of the press, who liked to loiter in its well-stocked bar, nursing whiskeys and eyeing the hotel's spectacular barmaids. Thus it was at the Metropol that the motley crew of correspondents, in whose number Leon counted himself, had chosen to ring in the new year.

On a dance floor teeming with naked shoulders and bare backs, projectors animated a sparkling fountain in autochrome. The smoky mirrors around the dining room were like steamy windows into another world. Outside, in the twenty-below weather, abounded the usual wintry spectacle of proletarianism: men in spartan sheepskins hurrying down the sidewalk with string bags. But inside, the Tropics: Feathers sprouted from eye masks. Carnations bloomed in buttonholes. Pomaded heads rested on downy décolletages. Outside, shuttered stores guarding meager rations of black bread and salted lard. Inside, wild duck with solyanka, herring in a "fur coat" of beets and horseradish. On the street, snow. Inside, confetti. Out there, the slurred pugnacious howling of national hymns. In here, jazz!

Florence and Essie had arrived just as the conversations at the table were acquiring the lunatic, reckless clarity of an all-night bender. The six-piece orchestra, retuning their instruments, had given the stage over to a pair of Gypsy fiddlers, a man and young woman in embroidered vests.

"You fancy she's a real Gypsy?" said a man named Alistair.

"Don't be ridiculous! The real ones are as cross-eyed as inbred kittens!" said Seldon Parker, beside whom Florence had sat down with the aim of ignoring Leon.

"I thought they banned Gypsy music," said a bald-pated Australian who went by Michaels.

"That was last month," corrected Seldon. "This month they repealed it."

"Seldon's turned sour on them after covering the big Gypsy trial last summer," Leon assured the table.

"There's no criminal in the world lower than a horse thief!" Seldon proclaimed decisively. "Or an automobile thief, which is all the same, really. The government has been trying to make decent Soviets out of them for years, but it's a failure. They hang posters of Lenin in their tents, and just keep thieving."

Now Seldon turned to Florence. "Have you ever noticed they're never satisfied with how many coins you give them? I once gave a hag the last of my pocket change, and she asked me where the rest was. The nerve."

"Why should she suffer just because you've had a bad week?" Leon called out from across the table. He blew a smoke ring and let it fade before he looked for the second time at Florence.

She had seated herself at the opposite end of the table hoping to let Leon down easy. Now her stomach was palpitating, her brain rehearsing reasons for putting an end to whatever was going on between them. Three days earlier, when she had met Leon at the theater on Bronnaya Street, he'd informed her that he was turning twenty-one in the summer.

Merely twenty! She had tried to hide her alarm, and succeeded in wresting just enough control of her face to keep him from guessing *her* age (she'd be twenty-five in a month). It certainly explained the combative way he'd tried to win her attention, the humble bragging and flinty arrogance. She believed it amounted to a failure of will, a failure of her imagination, that, having come all the way to Moscow, she'd allowed herself to become entangled with an American—from the Lower East Side, no less. Now it shamed and panicked her that this American had turned out to be no more than a boy, afflicted with rootlessness and cheerful wanderlust. She experienced her panic as an inability to touch the rich foods on the table. She'd let herself get distracted after the fiasco with Sergey, but hadn't intended to get in over her head. Now that she was in a more sober state of mind, it was time to stop procrastinating and be the serious person she'd come here to become. From an assorted platter of smoked fish, displayed in a pinwheel, a pair of beady piscine eyes stared up at Florence accusingly. It was time to cut bait.

"Essie, did you know," Florence said encouragingly, "you and Leon both attended the Workmen's Circle School."

"Yeah, what branch?" said Leon, slipping a dumpling in his mouth.

"Bronx East," Essie said, perking up. "What about you?"

"East Broadway," said Leon indifferently, "but I didn't stay around long."

And here the parallel dried up. Florence's anxiety was spreading to encompass her friend. Essie might have found Leon's indifference easier to handle were all the other men at the table not so conspicuously smitten with the barmaids who slithered back and forth between tables with their trays of cigarettes and Bengal lights. Yet another difference between the Metropol and the world outside: the gender relations inside the restaurant were patently mercantile. Michaels beckoned a Tatar-eyed beauty and purchased from her a dozen sparklers in exchange for a dollar and a pat of her satin-clad bottom. The Australian was let off with a wagging finger for his naughtiness.

"Are they always so . . . friendly?" Essie inquired with visible horror.

"Certainly!" said Seldon. "Some of them will even let you tip them. If, that is, you tip them."

"Michaels is in love with one of them," Leon confided loudly in Florence's direction. "Her name is Nelly."

"A former aristocrat," Michaels said wistfully. "An unfortunate victim of the Revolution. Such fragile creatures are not made for the daily grind of Soviet work."

"But Nelly won't have anything to do with him," continued Leon. "She specializes in the Japanese."

"He does know that these girls report everything to the secret police," said Essie.

"Know? It's his only hope," said Leon. "He's exhausted from thinking up new state secrets to keep her attention."

These remarks, physically aimed at Essie, seemed also to be intended for Florence, who had hoped that the return to socializing in a group might restore a platonic amity to her and Leon's relations. What she had not counted on was that their physical distance would present not a discouragement but a tantalizing obstacle. Florence was uncomfortably aware of Leon watching her every gesture (and had she not chosen the seat at the table that would offer him the best view of her profile, which he so claimed to admire?).

"It's too bad no one gives a damn about Australia's secrets," concluded Seldon, before getting up from his seat with his drink in hand. "A toast, to our American friends!" he said. And though his knees seemed in danger of giving out under him, he held his glass elegantly from below with a linen napkin. "I propose that we bid a fond farewell to 1934, the first full year that this fine nation which has hosted us was recognized by the United States."

"To no longer living in sin!" Leon exclaimed from his end of the table. "Za nas," he suggested, urging the table to clink glasses, which everyone did happily.

"How much longer do we have for all this nostalgia?" Seldon said.

Michaels consulted his watch. "Twelve minutes left of good old '34."

With this information, Leon bluntly turned to Florence. "Time for a last dance?"

Florence let her napkin drop on the table. Glancing at Essie, she offered a wan smile of apology and stood up, a little languidly, to convey the impression that she was assenting out of politeness. Her efforts at conciliation were pointless; Essie's acquaintance with romance had always been characterized by extravagant hopes and swift concessions. Florence drained her glass of champagne and rose to her feet. A physical sensation of plunging downward accompanied the column of champagne bubbles fizzling upward into her head, their sour effervescence absolving her of accumulated guilt. The unfairness of being allowed to pass ahead of the Russians in line because she'd addressed the Metropol's guards in English. The injustice of abundance in the midst of scarcity. Her failure to discourage the attentions of a young man she couldn't allow herself to be serious about. But it was New Year's Eve, for heaven's sake, and she was tired of feeling bad about everything. She set the glass down decisively and walked on ahead of Leon to the dance floor, not pausing to let him lead her by the hand.

The six-piece band was playing a recognizable number slightly altered by an accordion's minor keys. The song sounded like a Slavic interpretation of an old Guy Lombardo hit, which it was. No words were being sung, but Leon Brink provided them murmuringly in her ear: *Hear me—why you keep foolin', little coquette? Making fun of the one that loves you . . . Breaking hearts you are ruling, little coquette. True hearts, tenderly dreaming of you-oo . . .*

Florence's reluctant smile gave him an opening, but she turned her face sideways just in time to avoid his lips. From the corner of her eye, Florence was watching her friend at the table. Wishing to look enticing, Essie had not worn her glasses. She was gazing about myopically while wetting her lips on the edge of her champagne glass like a kid faking devotion at communion. "Hmm, la dididi, little coquette . . . ," Leon sang. Like a rooting animal, he buried his nose in the fragrant updo at the back of Florence's neck.

"Behave."

"Why?"

"There's people around."

Leon looked about. "Really? I hadn't noticed." For the past three weeks, while he'd been taking her out, Leon had gotten nothing from this girl besides a few stolen smooches on wet park benches. What had been denied him in private he now pursued, like a deprived teenager, on the public arena of the dance floor.

"Stop it!" she said when he licked a bead of sweat from behind her ear.

"What's the matter? You didn't sit down beside me. And now . . . you waiting on some other fellow?"

"It's nothing like that."

Her answer was not, in the strictest sense, true. Being out with Leon, she'd been unable to stop thinking about the irony of her situation: of this forceful, big-talking youngster from Allen Street showing her the beautiful city to which she had hoped Sergey would be her guide. Even as she'd grown fonder of Leon, the ghost of Sergey continued to haunt their encounters. She saw him in the broad backs of the theater audience, in the dull-blond heads of hair at the park, a stock type of which Moscow had no shortage.

"What is it, then—have I got horns on my head?"

"Leon, I feel maybe I've been giving you a wrong impression."

"And that would be . . . ?"

"I'm quite a bit older than you. I'm almost twenty-five."

Her confession generated a lopsided smile. "So what?"

And she realized he already knew.

"I promise," he said, "not to hold your wanton cravenness against you, Madame Comrade, if we can set aside this divide in our generations."

"You see! Even you think it's . . ."

"What?"

"Unbecoming."

"Unbe*coming*?" The word was so quaint it actually caused him to hiccup a laugh.

"Yes, when a woman is older than the man."

"I am genuinely surprised by you, Miss Fein. I didn't think you went in for that sort of petit-bourgeois philistinism."

"Leon, you're . . . you're a boy, practically."

"Now, there's no need to call names. What about Krupskaya and Lenin? Were they *unbecoming*?" He swung Florence around.

"Oh, Leon."

"And Catherine the Great and Potemkin! She had a good ten years on that powdered old queer."

At last Florence gave in and laughed. "But she was the queen!"

Leon gave her a quick glance-over, as if to say, *And this one here is* not?

Not beneath such cheap flattery, Florence blushed. She put her hands around his thin neck. In the smoky mirror that multiplied the dozen other couples on the dance floor, she saw herself laying her head gently down on his shoulder (in her heels, she was the slightly taller of the two). A surprising, not unpleasant smell, the brilliantine in his heavily sleeked hair, accosted her nose. Leon, hoping to devastate Florence in style, had bought the cream that afternoon, from a music store that sold it as a grease for trombones. Waltzing past them, a stout, elegantly turned-out older couple angled their heads and smiled, seeing in the young lovers the happiness of all Soviet youth.

And maybe it was this vision of them that woke Florence with a start. Was it an instinct toward their future life together that she was already sensing, which made her pull back? For what she was seeing suddenly, in her mind's eye, was an image of the two of them dancing on the edge of the world, not realizing they were about to fall off. With the clarity of a premonition, she suddenly understood that all night her discomfort had been running deeper than insincere feminine guilt. What she felt around Leon was a fear so pure it was almost like ecstasy. But here was the strange part: It was fear not for herself, but for *him*. As if, by accepting his love, she would bring about his ruin, make him pay for loving her with nothing less than his life.

How did she know this? She would not have been able to say. The only words that came to her were "Leon, I'd like us to be friends, for now."

But her feeble clairvoyance was no match for his resolve. "Are you trying to make me mad?" he said, studying her face.

"No!"

"You don't want to see me?"

"I'm saying I want to take things . . . more slow, is all."

"How much slower, Florence? Even cold molasses gotta know which way's down."

Between the bursts of laughter and drunken cheers, their song was dissolving into a prolonged rustle from the percussion section, a murmur-ous warning of the countdown to the new year. The carousel of pink and green lights passed over Leon's face as he studied her. "I get it. You're the type that wants a fella to toss her on the floor," he said unpleasantly, "give it to her against a wall somewhere, while you turn your little head away, sniffling 'No, no, no, no,' and loving every minute of it."

His voice had gone brittle with scorn, without any of the old playfulness. "I didn't peg you for one of those frail little clinging vines. . . ."

"Lemme go, you egg!" She turned sideward and gasped as he clenched her forearm.

"You've been giving me the sign ever since we met. Don't think I couldn't have obliged you, if I thought that's all we both wanted."

"Get off me!"

And to her surprise, he did—tossing her arm aside and making her stumble backward on her heels.

She stood holding her sore wrist.

She watched him prowl toward the frosted Palladian doors, which a waiter was just then opening. His "obliged" still hung cruelly between them. But his eyes had spoken a different story; before turning away they had been sparkling like broken shards with humiliation and pain.

The percussive countdown to 1935 had begun.

Florence looked at the faces around the ballroom, certain that they had all been staring at her. But the band had started up once more, playing some nostalgic anthemlike song, and all attention was on the bandleader in his maestro's white tails, delivering a final toast over the throbbing melody—"To the New Year, to the New Happincss!"

Through the clog of bodies, Florence saw Seldon Parker in his half-fogged glasses, bending to light a cigarette off of the sparkler in Essie's hand. Catching sight of her, Seldon wagged his hand. Their faces, the sparklers, the lurid sounds of vodka-laughter no longer seemed real to her. What she'd allowed to happen had diverged so sharply from what she'd set out to do that she was gripped once again by the same painful suspicion about herself that all her efforts to do good and be good couldn't seem to erase: the feeling that, despite her intentions to live honestly and to hurt no one, everything she said and did was a lie; that she was at the mercy of urges—loyalty and rivalry, selflessness but also colossal narcissism—too contrary to be reconciled. She was sure Leon was wrong about her on every count, about being a tease and a slut, but she feared nonetheless that he had torn her open like a sheet of gypsum to expose her wiring. She saw how decisively he could free himself of her, how ruthless he could be if she pushed him too far, and it made her feel with some consolation that everything she'd thought about him was wrong.

She made a sharp turn for the lobby, where Leon had gone.

He was nowhere to be seen.

Under the scattered light of the foyer's chandeliers, the settees were strewn with pensive-looking Russian men leaning together in serious conversations, as well as impatient lovers not waiting for the New Year's bell.

Then she saw him. Coming out of the cloakroom, his coat in hand. He lifted his head and saw her, and before he could look away she called his name, not recognizing the voice that came out of her throat like the dying squeak of a balloon.

He waited, with perceptible reluctance, for her to approach him. The clock's chimes had started; from inside the banquet hall could be heard shouts of "Six! Five! Four!" And then a collective cheer of "*Urrah!*" followed by a burst of music from the band.

Reaching him, she let out a dramatic exhale and hung her head. "You're twenty, Leon, how can you possibly know what you want?"

He didn't seem to want to meet her eyes and looked instead in the direction of the music. "It isn't a choice, Florence. A man isn't free to choose when he walks into an elevator shaft. I walked in—okay—but there were no floors to select, no buttons to push. I just fell right down."

The area where they stood was cold and damp, infused with the musty smells of the *garderobe*. Nothing had warned her about what it might feel like to be cared for this much. He was young, yes, but he spoke like a man. And maybe, she thought, it was youth that made him capable of that kind of certainty. He had no family to abide by. He was not always looking over his shoulder, like Sergey. Tied down to nothing, he was free to love her completely. And she sensed now that such devotion might not come her way again for a long time.

Leon was unprepared for the kiss she planted on his loose mouth, returning it first like a child, with startled confusion, and then with the vigorous force of someone working out a knot of pain. She closed her eyes and let him bury his lips in her temple, press his forehead to hers. There was such a logic to their togetherness that she wondered how she had ever imagined she'd have the strength to pull away. "All right, Potemkin," she said, taking his hand. "Let's go in before they drink all our champagne."

In this way, Leon and Florence began the year 1935.

By the spring, they would be living together in a room of their own— a mighty eleven square meters, which, at the tail end of those still-emancipated times, could occasionally be allotted to a couple living in an unregistered "revolutionary marriage."

A photo of Florence and Leon remains from this period, preserved only because it was sent by Florence to her family in America. Taken on a trip to Crimea—the closest the two came to a honeymoon—it shows them on a pebbly beach, with two other couples. The men kneel in the sand; the women, in bathing costumes, sit perched and laughing on their men's backs, styling their poses after the "sports photography" so popular at that time. Florence, pale in her dark bathing suit, sits on Leon's wiry, sun-blackened shoulders. He stares at the camera, a cigarette hanging from his bottom lip, his eye squinting suspiciously against the sun. On the reverse of the photograph, only the words "Yalta '35."

EVERY YEAR FOR THE next three years, Leon Brink asked Florence Fein to marry him officially, and each time she answered, half jokingly, "You surprise me, Leon Naumovich. I didn't think you went in for that kind of petit-bourgeois philistinism." She did not know what stood behind her reluctance. Perhaps a corner of her heart could not yet accept that the "permanent" part of her life—the marrying and settling down and bearing children—would happen under the crimson-and-yellow flag. And yet, dancing in the buoyant infant hours of the new year, she could not have known that the strand which began to unspool with Kirov's assassination would eventually thread through their lives too. And that her decision to marry Leon would not in the end be separated from a long chain of events begun the day the charismatic Leningrad Party secretary was rewarded for his loyalty with a bullet.

20.

ZA NAS, ZA VAS

THE OLD METROPOL, IT SEEMS, IS STILL OPEN FOR BUSINESS. UNLIKE numberless other establishments in Moscow, it never closed its doors. In fact, in all the years I lived in the city, the hotel remained largely unchanged. Now it's restored in all its Art Nouveau detail—the fairytale mosaics, the plaster friezes, the ornate Deco balconies gleaming in tsarist splendor. The cars parked out front when we arrive are BMWs. Inside, frowning, bald-pated bachelors stand around the jewelry boutique with pouting blondes. "Just like Hollywood," Tom, my boss, observes as we walk past them.

"But with fewer communists," I amend.

Our compatriots from L-Pet are already gathered at a table in the imperial dining room. It is a custom of bilateral dinners such as ours that the first three shots go down smoothly and merrily, and that the repertoire of opening toasts follows a set script: First, to the success of our joint endeavor. Second, to the health of Faraz Abuskalayev, L-Pet's CEO. And, finally, *za nas, za vas, za neft i gaz!*

The libations for this trifecta are poured not from common, lowbrow bottles, but from two civilized crystal carafes set by our waiter at opposite foci of our ovoid banquet table.

Some brief introductions are in order, starting with the honored guest to my right: Ivan Kablukov ("the Boot," as Tom and I lovingly refer to him). Kablukov's official job title at L-Pet is "vice-president of corporate security and communication," though what he actually does there is anyone's guess. He has about fifty kilograms on me and looks ten years my senior, but he claims to have been born in '47, making him four years younger. If this is the case, he was apparently never much of a student, since he didn't manage to graduate from the Gubkin State University of Oil and Gas until 1992. In fact, I've never been able to reliably ascertain *how* the Boot passed the first forty-five years of his life. Given his security post I assume he was connected with the law. Which side of the law I can't say. I *can* say that Kablukov knows not a goddamn thing about either oil or ships. The last time he and I met, in Helsinki, where I was testing our tankers' new propulsion system at the Aker ice pools, he sat beside me through our discussion with the Finnish engineers in assassinlike silence, wearing his Ray-Bans like he was at a poker tournament. Every once in a while he'd turn to me and say, *"Na khera nam vsyo eto nujno?"* "The fuck we need to know all this for?"

And, like the helpful boy I am, I was set and ready to explain to him what the fuck we needed to know it all for, except he disappeared mid-meeting. I didn't see him again until dinner, where he showed up with some *devitsa* two meters tall. A blonde in boots, spilling out of her silver-fox stole. Guffawing like a horse the whole meal. You would have thought he brought her along to show her off, but throughout our three-day trip Kablukov did nothing but complain to me about her. "I have to take this *padlo* shopping again. This heifer won't leave me alone until I buy her two suitcases of fur in Helsinki. Like we don't have our own fur in Russia! Where the hell does she think the Finns get *theirs?"*

We got to know each other a little more intimately the last evening, in the sauna, over chicken cutlets and eighty-proof Finnish Koskenkorva. "It's softer," he tells me. And that's when I notice that our VP of security is a patron of the arts—covered neck to belly in ink. And not those "Never forget mother" tattoos, either, but ones that indicate membership in certain exclusive societies the likes of which simple men like me are better off not knowing about. For two steamy hours I had little else to look at but 118 kilos of tattooed flesh wrapped in a bedsheet. The Boot must have made the same toast twelve times: "Time spent with friends does not get added to one's life span!"

Now that Kablukov and I have done the ritual flogging of each other with birch twigs, he treats me as affectionately as a brother. "How have you been, friend?" he says now at the banquet table, and pours a neat thirty grams into my shot glass. Right up to the top.

"Very fine, Ivan Matveyevich. And you?"

He sighs. "I'd be better off if those two weren't buzzing in my ear."

Seated to Kablukov's left are his first two lieutenants, Mukhov and Serdyuk. Mukhov is a former tanker captain from the merchant marines. Now he heads L-Pet's Department of Safety and Compliance. His idea of protective measures can be summarized in a single phrase: *avos' da nebos'*, which translates roughly into "cross our fingers." As in "It'll get from here to there, cross our fingers," or "It'll stay afloat, let's hope." But I vastly prefer Mukhov's company to Serdyuk's—or "Captain" Serdyuk, as we must call him. He's a former nuclear sub commander, hired by L-Pet ten years ago on the day of his retirement from the navy. Short, stocky, buzz-cut, with a flat mouth that, if it opens, says little. The few sentences I've heard him speak favor the royal "we": "*We* want it like this," "*We* have something to discuss with you." His brows are permanently knit together, like he's Sean Connery still charting his nuclear course beneath the Atlantic.

Besides Tom and me, there are two others at the banquet, young guys about Lenny's age: Valery Gibkov and Steve McGinnis, a Russian and a Canadian who make up the "PolarNeft Working Group." McGinnis and Gibkov work neither for Continental nor for L-Pet, but for the joint-stock company that's been set up to run our mutual venture. They are, so to speak, the house management to L-Pet's landlords, and their presence this evening is a gentle buffer zone. Gibkov in particular strikes me as neither unreasonable nor an imbecile. If there is any hope for Russia's future, it's in this younger breed, who interpret the word "business" according to its primary definition as "making an enterprise profitable," rather than its secondary, local, definition as graft and larceny.

By now we have all praised the smoked Baltic salmon, the sturgeon stew, the remarkably tender veal, and come to the agreement that the vodka (Cîroc? Jewel of Russia?) goes down "very cleanly." Now that the initial six hundred grams have been dispensed with, Kablukov curls a finger at the waiter and orders "the rest."

I've hardly touched my beef Stroganoff before two more decanters materialize on the table. I know it doesn't bode well for my sustained sobriety that every time I glance upward into the restaurant's blue glass ceiling I feel like I'm falling into an enormous swimming pool. But maybe it's just an elemental confusion, a trick not of the eye but of the ear, evoked by the sound of the incontinent tinkle coming from the pissing cherub atop the marble fountain. It's a tinkle suggestive of certain "enhanced interrogation methods" that are currently the topic of conversation between Mukhov and Tom. "Waterboarding—it sounds like summer sport," says Mukhov, grinning ferociously. "You Americans make even torture sound like leisure-time activity."

"Well, now, technically speaking, Oleg, it isn't torture but a simulation," Tom corrects. "The prisoner has the *sensation* of drowning without actually drowning."

"Technically speaking, we have a saying in Russia: 'A chicken is not a bird, and a woman is not a person.' You also have a saying in America: 'Waterboarding is not torture, and a blow job is not sex.' "

"Ha-ha . . . ," Tom objects: "I see your point there, but you might say that the latter is also a kind of, umm, simulation."

This is the point when Kablukov, leaning in close to me, confides in his loose gravel voice, "To hell with all this *politics*. What are they jabbering about like dopes at the G8? Let's have another drink." He refills my shot glass to the rim, not spilling a single drop. "Now, if we only had a little female company," he says, and sinks his drink with a quick jerk of his head before I've even touched mine.

"Speaking of company," I say, "how is your lovely lady friend—what's her name?"

There's an audible grumble beneath Kablukov's chewing that makes me rethink this line of inquiry.

"Those *telki* are all raving mad. My wife's got a rule. She doesn't care who the *telka* is as long as I drop her after three months."

"And every three months a new *telka*!" I say.

"No. I didn't say that. You have to listen. Three months is the *limit*." I can see it's of paramount importance to Kablukov that I understand this rule properly. He's a family man, after all. "Three months is long enough."

"For your protection more than hers."

He nods gravely. "Anyway," he says, "there are more interesting things in life."

Now he's got me curious. What has the Boot discovered to be more interesting than towering blondes? I don't have to wait long for an answer.

"Horses!"

"You race them?"

"What? No! I breed the fuckers!"

"They can't do it alone?"

"I can tell you're joking, Brink, but this is a serious business. The cardinal rule of horse breeding is: no artificial insemination. Otherwise, your horse can't get a passport. That's why they fly the mares to my boy on private jets, so he can give them a proper fuck. He's too valuable to race. His grandpa was some kind of Great Dane. I won't tell you how much I paid for him, but I'll tell you how much I've made on him. Fourteen mil. The life of a retired champion, I'll tell ya. Doesn't do a thing all day but eat and screw, eat and screw. Every sheikh in the Saudi royals flies his mare to my champion so he can shag 'em. The Arabs are fucking nuts about their horses. It's part of their heritage, Arabian nights and all that. All the horses that won the races last year—all his babies. Daddy's got children all over the world he don't even know about." Kablukov drops his voice to a murmur. "I keep him in a special stable, see? Not here in Russia. I'm no idiot. Here he'd be assassinated or kidnapped or both. No, he's safe in England. Only two people know where that stable is—me and the stable keeper."

The infatuation that the Boot has developed for this equine Casanova has evidently supplanted any itch he might develop for a new mistress. In fact, he seems to identify so completely with his Thoroughbred—the thrill of his libertine lifestyle or the risk of his assassination—that for a moment I have to wonder if it isn't himself Kablukov is describing.

But even as I'm giving my full attention to the Boot, it's difficult to ignore the laughter coming from the other end of the table, where Mukhov, our serial joker, has switched back to Russian to regale the young PolarNeft associates with jokes about Mikhail Khodorkovsky, the youthful oil baron who five years ago was arrested on an airport runway and sent to await his sickly fate near the Chinese border. "Berezovsky and Khodorkovsky are sitting together in the *banya*. Berezovsky turns to him and says, 'Misha, really, either lose the cross or put your underpants back on.'" This is followed by laughter, even from Tom, who doesn't understand a damn word but has his Yankee Doodle grin affixed diligently to his face. All in good fun. The only one who isn't smiling is our Captain Serdyuk.

"Now let him sit in Chita Prison, the pilferer," he puts in decisively, sawing into his veal. "Let him sit and think just like ordinary Russians sat."

I eye the still-grinning Tom and decide to spare him a translation. Serdyuk's meaning is clear enough to me: let the *Jew* sit and think, the way ordinary Russians sat. *Velkom home*—I can hear Lenny whispering in my ear. I have a feeling that this is going to be my private refrain for the week. How my son handles this casual anti-Semitism day in and day out, I have no idea.

But, for that matter, how did I?

"That one over there's all right," Kablukov resumes, nodding in Tom's direction. "Usually your Americans need everything neatly laid out on shelves like at a pharmacy." He spreads his thick fingers, talonlike, on my biceps. "That's why it's good to have one of our own here to talk to. Even if"—he sighs again—"Mother Russia isn't good enough for you anymore."

"Life leads us in her own direction, Ivan Matveyevich," I say. By now it's become clear to me that Tom hired me not merely for my engineering prowess but because Continental was looking for a friendly ambassador, someone effortlessly Russian and effortlessly American who could smooth things over to avoid involving lawyers (since ours are more or less useless in this corner of the world). I feel like Kablukov is testing me now, asking for proof of membership. Only, I'm a bit too drunk or jet-lagged to put him in his place. "It's too late for me," I say, mechanically adopting his nostalgic tone. "My son, on the other hand, he won't leave this place for all the salt in the kingdom." I can hear myself speaking before I know what I'm saying. But this confession draws a smile from Kablukov. His furry brows perk up above his Ray-Bans. "Oh? Did he grow up here, your boy?"

"No. He came with us to America when he was six. Moving back here was Lenny's own idea. He wanted to try his hand at the roulette table among the other young Turks. What about your own children?" I say.

But Kablukov ignores my inquiry. "What does he do, your son?"

I tell him he's in finance, but spare the details of Lenny's recent adventures.

"I admire a man who forges out on his own," Kablukov says. "How has his fortune held up?"

I'm surprised at his interest; it's unusual for Kablukov to be curious about *anything* anyone says. I shrug. "You have kids. Do they tell you anything?"

The Boot nods gravely and cuffs my shoulder, then uses it to hoist himself up. "My friends," he announces, "forgive me, but I must leave our cozy gathering."

"So soon, Ivan Matveyevich?" Mukhov objects happily.

"Will you be joining us tomorrow," I say, "for the first round of selections?"

The Boot shakes his head. "I'm afraid pressing business calls for me in Tallin. But my two mates here have assured me that we have *nashi lyudi* among us," he says, addressing me. His warm, abnormally large hand is heavy on my shoulder. "I have complete trust in your good sense," he continues, looking at me. To this he drinks his final bottoms-up, and heads for the glass doors, a cell phone already hanging from his ear.

As soon as Kablukov is out of the room, the good humor of the two lieutenants blossoms. Immediately Mukhov beckons a waiter to replace our dry decanter. Serdyuk loads the remaining veal chops from the silver tray onto his plate. The tactile memory of Kablukov's fingers remains on my collarbone. It occurs to me that he didn't say that he had complete trust in our "expertise," but in our "good sense." I turn to Serdyuk, now fully involved in the work of spearing and swallowing his meat. "So what's so urgent in Tallin?" I say.

Serdyuk continues eating as if he hasn't heard me. I decide I won't repeat the question, and pour myself another drink. Across our *zone détente* of empty carafes and platters, Mukhov's angling in for another joke, this one about a new set of snapshots that have turned up in Abu Ghraib. Rumsfeld has been announcing to the eager press that the recent batch is even hotter than the last. But if the American people want a glimpse, they first have to elect Bush to another term.

McGinnis is translating this dated joke for Tom, on whose face I detect barely suppressed disgust—more physical instinct than emotional state, as if he's just smelled some foul canned meat. I want to tell Mukhov that there are no third terms and Bush has long since retired Rumsfeld. But why bother with clarifications? There's no honor these days in defending America. Three years have passed and the images are still fresh—a chinless girl who looks like a ten-year-old boy in her military pantalons, tugging a naked Iraqi on a leash. America's degeneracy on full display and the world can't get enough of it.

It's almost a surprise when Serdyuk, cleaning off his plate, turns to me.

"The Estonians have a refinery on the coast," he says, finally ready to answer my question. "*We* built it for those *kurad*s back in '82. Then that rat charmer Khodorkovsky got his hands on it. And now it's up for grabs, see? So we made them an offer, but they thought they could do better by selling to the Czechs."

"Are you planning to outbid the Czechs?" I say, though I suspect that's not exactly L-Pet's strategy here.

"Cut it with the idiotic questions. Transneft cut off their tap months ago." I watch Serdyuk's hand twist an invisible pipeline valve. "That showed them how loyal the Czechs are. Now Tallin's mayor is practically begging us to buy that old plant. But guess what—now *we're* going to sit back and think about it."

So that's what it means to be VP of corporate security and communication. Kablukov, the affectionate capo, is being sent to Tallin to wrap up a little unfinished diplomacy *alla famiglia*. Now that L-Pet has conspired with Russia's pipeline monopoly to cut off the refinery's supply, driven it into bankruptcy, sunk its value, and frightened off its foreign suitors—now that it's broken the Estonians' shins—it's finally ready to sell them some crutches. I'm surprised to find myself less disturbed by Kablukov's role as enforcer in this scenario than by Serdyuk's attitude about the whole affair: Who do those cheeky Czechs think they are to buy *our* refinery? And who do these dirty Estonians think they are to sell off what *we* built for them!

"But, really, why all the hysterics and runny noses over a few photos?" Mukhov says, picking up the thread. "We can get some good shots like that from our Chechen brothers in Chernokozovo. The point is, this scandal— what is it about? A myth. What myth? That your American soldiers fight with white gloves on." He's begun to address the table at large, dropping the role of joke teller and coming fully into his own as a propagandist. I prepare my face for what's to come: *Your* military—sadistic brigands! No better than our Spetsnaz. Your *democratiya*, imitation-cheese democracy just like Russia's! And your *supposedly free* press—let's not even start on *that* charade. "Well, guess what? It turns out everyone is exactly the same!" he says, right on cue. "Only *our* State Department doesn't bother with the pretense of publishing an annual report about what it's done for democracy this year." The righteousness of his anti-righteousness is simply too irresistible to contain. He'll have no peace until he's convinced me that every institution in America is a fabrication as elaborate as Russia's own boundless Potemkinville.

And here we are again, dragged by the tide of alcohol into that vast epistemic gulf where every lunatic proposition is self-evident while universal truths are hauled in for questioning. A Logic-Free Zone where I've been, more than once, cornered into testifying that Roosevelt did *not* have advance knowledge of the Pearl Harbor bombing, or challenged to "prove" that smoking really causes cancer.

"Don't forget to mention how Neil Armstrong never set foot on the moon," I suggest. "That it was all a hoax pulled off in some Hollywood studio."

He gives me a sidelong look, trying to gauge my sincerity. But in the end, it's another landing that's of interest to him. "The moon I don't know about," he says. "What I'd rather find out is what happened to the other planes."

"Which planes would those be?" I say.

"Come on, now, the 9/11 planes! There were seven of them."

The PolarNeft guys and I trade looks. "I never heard of any seven," I say.

"Wow." Mukhov looks around the table, aghast. "They really don't report *anything* to you people over there, do they?"

"Well, what's your theory," I say, "the CIA set it up?"

"How should *I* know? Maybe the CIA. Maybe the FBI . . ."

"Or maybe the KGB, right. Let's not go too deep into all the hairy theories tonight."

"Who's talking about theories? You're an intelligent person. I'm only saying, look at who benefits."

"According to that logic," I say, "the Kremlin bombed those apartment buildings and blamed it on the Chechens so your troops could reenter Grozny."

Across barriers of language, Tom is sensing enough explosive tinder in my accusation so that his arm begins to rise toward a defusing toast. But he has no chance to make one, because Mukhov is beaming—not with fury but with jubilation! "*Yasnoye delo!*" he shouts. "*Of course* we did it!" He reaches out his arms as though to give my recalcitrant head a kiss, his face shining with the satisfied glow of a man who's gotten his point across at last.

21.

TRAGIC ERRANDS

MOSCOW,
1936

IT WAS AFTER NINE WHEN FLORENCE AWOKE. LEON WAS LYING BESIDE her with his eyes shut and his mouth open. His arm was thrown over her breasts, gathering her in a half-hug. She took care to untangle herself gently from his embrace, but her ankle nonetheless knocked against the wooden leg of the armchair by their bed.

When she first moved with Leon into their very own eleven-square-meter room, Florence had envisioned the place as a kind of Soviet version of a bohemian Greenwich Village studio. Unlike some of the tiny, plywood-partitioned rooms their neighbors occupied, the quarters she would share with her new common-law husband came with its own fireplace, and a deep window that cast oblongs of light on their walls—golden Moscow light that struck the grain of the naked parquet and infused the room with an air of intellectual and spiritual contemplation. Their limited space, Florence had believed, could be overcome with a charming and spare arrangement of furniture: their bed doing double duty as a couch, her trunk turned on its side to form a bookcase, the deep windowsill serving as a reading area, and Leon's writing desk transformable with a painted kerchief into a table for entertaining. What she had not accounted for was that the common kitchen down the hall would not be nearly big enough for all the people in the apartment to store their food and cooking utensils (and if it had been, Florence would not have trusted her items to remain unsnatched), so, in the end, her contemplative windowsill had been conscripted as a shelf for storing sacks of flour, bread, oil, tomatoes, and jars of pickles and conserves. Leon's writing table was likewise occupied by daily necessities: their kerosene lamp and Primus hot plate, and a basket of linens to iron. From this basket Florence now fished out a dry towel. She threw on her house robe and grabbed her bucket and soap from behind the door, then marched on toward the communal washroom, dismayed to hear already the sounds of someone's scatological efforts from the adjoining toilet.

If living under the iron rule of her old landlady on Petrovka had been like lodging in a strict boarding house, then life in a nine-room *kommunalka* was like residing in the ward of a public hospital: a habitation made humid with haste and confrontation, always tense and always on the verge of a crisis. Everything in their cramped conditions had the capacity to provoke hatred and jealousy. With the worsening of the political situation and the daily newspaper headlines warning of "spies and saboteurs," the hostility had become more apparent. "Not enough that they're nipping at us from outside, the ones here gotta be riding on our backs," a neighbor named Vitkina had said one day in the kitchen, after putting down the paper. She did not look at Florence when she said it. She did not need to.

But Florence was also aware that the real trouble lay not in the prevailing political winds but in her own personality. She did not play the game. She was unwilling to waste time listening to Vitkina complain about her rheumatism, or rehash her old adventures as a partisan in the war rebuffing the proposals from *highly attractive* officers. Nor did Florence have the patience to gossip with whoever happened to interrupt her cooking in the kitchen to conscript her into the latest *entente*. While she understood, in a general way, the unspoken rule of communal living—which was that men could keep a kind of neutrality in conflicts, but women could not—in practice it offended Florence's sense of pride and autonomy to lower herself to the level of these gossipy shrews just to get along.

Not two years earlier, she had wanted to be "among the people," the great Russian *narod*, and now that she was forced into close quarters with this behemoth abstraction, she had to learn to suffer its all-embracing ignorance and malice, the grand scale of its pettiness, its envy. She seemed to have no gift for the sort of deflection Leon could carry off with breezy charm: flirtatiously flattering the old crone who called their corner of the

common kitchen "the kikes' table," responding to the woman's provoca-
tions with theatrical benevolence until the nasty old bitch scuttled out of
the kitchen completely confounded and muttering hateful nonsense to
herself. Nor was Leon beneath having a drink late at night with Garik, the
flabby-cheeked Armenian who worked at the chicken plant. "Putting a
request in at inventory" was what Leon called these late nights over vodka
and pickles, while Florence sat up in bed waiting for him, like some lovesick girl, to come back and lay his hands anywhere on her body. Indeed,
days later, the reward of a young chicken would arrive as promised. But
Florence wasn't fooled: none of his repentant joking about the necessity
of these manly labors could camouflage the fact that Leon seemed, at
heart, to enjoy them.

She was aware of this fundamental difference between them: Leon had
always lived the way they lived now. In tenements, in poverty, in hideous
overcrowding. He had learned early on to make his way through the world
by cajoling and charming and wheedling. Her pity for such a childhood
had played a part in her love for him, and she feared that complaining too
bitterly about their living conditions would expose her vanities. Yet she
could not deny how irritated she was that Leon found nothing wrong with
the way they lived, exposed to so much prying and spite. In America, such
complacency would have signaled a lack of ambition. But here, no amount
of ambition would alter anything. Everyone lived like this, stirred into one
big pot (everyone except of course the big wheels, like Timofeyev). And
that was the whole sickening, unsolvable problem: the fact that Leon
couldn't be blamed for being unable to give her any other kind of life did
not lessen her longing to start afresh. She vowed to take a long walk today,
alone, to clear her head.

Florence returned from her lukewarm shower to find Leon at the table,
peeling an apple into a chipped enamel bowl. He set down his knife when
she removed her robe, then crept up to cradle her from behind, pressing
his lips to the water-warmed skin of her shoulder blade.

"It's half past nine, darling."

"I'll make breakfast after," he offered. His voice was deep and throaty
from sleep.

"Later, I promise. Now I need to get to the stores before the lines get too
long."

So much had changed in the last year. The specialty stores that served expatriates with foreign currency had mostly been shut down. The Insnab ration cards she and her friends enjoyed had been discontinued. A number of their acquaintances had found this reason enough to return home. It was obvious to Florence that these people had never really been committed to the enterprise of genuine equality. To jump ship, now, for lack of caviar and imported wine? She heard Sergey's low warning voice in her head: "Go home, Flora." She dressed hastily and stuffed her documents and keys into her purse.

Leon sighed. "Do you have to go *today?* We never have the same day off."

"Don't be sour. Somebody has to buy you that salty fish you love."

For a moment, his brows perked up with pleasure. "Maybe I'll come with you."

"No, no, sleep in."

The fact was that she had to stop by at the OVIR before the lines got too long. Foreigners were now required to renew their residency permits every three months. It had become her private ordeal, her own little measure of renewed commitment. She could not admit to Leon that she wondered, each time, if this stamp would be her last. "I'll be back in a couple of hours," she said appeasingly before planting a kiss on his head.

Outside, Florence flicked the lamb's-wool collar up over her neck and crossed the leaf-strewn footpath that cut through the back courtyards of the 1st Samotechnaya Lane. She was grateful to be escaping the stuffy apartment and inhaling the raw air under the blue sky of Samotechniy Park, with its tidy pools of grass and flowers. From Samotechnaya Square, she crossed the wide avenue that turned onto Tsvetnoy Boulevard before heading down to the visa registration office. On the front steps of the OVIR, Florence patted down the errant strands of hair under her mohair kerchief and arranged her face in a vacant and submissive expression. Over the past two years, she had learned to dim down the challenging focus of her eyes whenever she entered a public office. She was enough of a Soviet now to know that the most dangerous bureaucrats were not the ones at the top but those patrolling their tiny corners of power at the bottom. She wanted no trouble with the heavyset woman behind the window.

At the counter, Florence slid across her passport, helpfully opened to the page containing her well-thumbed visa. The woman abruptly shut the passport and opened it again to the photo page, then scrutinized Florence's face. She wrote the passport information on a slip, made a second copy, and slid the paper back to Florence without the passport. "Come back next week for your residence permit," she said in a tone just short of a command.

"I'll take that back," Florence said, pointing through the glass to her passport.

"We need to keep it to issue your *propiska*. You'll get it when you come back."

"But you already wrote down all the information."

The clerk shut her eyes in irritation. "This can be *anybody's* information. How do *they* know this isn't some phantom's information, or made up?"

"I was told this isn't necessary." Florence smiled in perfect self-control. "If they want to check that I'm a real person, they should check with my housing committee. I am registered there."

"They told *you* one thing. They told me another. I am following orders. Those are the new rules for resident permits. I cannot issue you a new *propiska* without this document."

A line had formed behind Florence. The clerk glanced over Florence's shoulder and called out, "Next!"

"All right. When will I get it back?"

"I told you: next week," the clerk said. "We'll have the *propiska* by Tuesday."

"You'll have my passport back by Tuesday too?"

But the woman behind the window was already absorbed in someone else's bureaucratic conundrum. At last, Florence allowed herself to take a few steps backward. Her passport was still visible, right there, behind the glass, next to the woman's fat elbow. *Grab it!* a voice pounded in her head. But her movements were already being governed by some other impulse— one so well learned that she no longer recognized it as a recently adopted habit—a wish not to buck the current, not to make a fuss. She took a final glance at the window, but there were too many people now blocking the view. She slowly retied her kerchief on her head and retreated into the morning cold.

22.

———

A CLEAN RECORD

WITH AN HOUR AND A HALF TO SPARE BEFORE MY MEETING AT THE L-Pet headquarters, I descended into the metro and surfaced in the part of Moscow I hate the most. Lubyanka. It's impossible for me to cross it without the ghosts of previous visits haunting me. I can still feel the crick in my neck that I felt as a six-year-old staring up at the prison's nine stories, feeling the morning sludge seep into my shoes and battling an urgent need to urinate. My mother would drag me out of my warm bed at five in the morning and cart me here while the sky was still dark. She hoped that having a child in tow would make it easier to jump the line that had been forming since midnight. The sun would rise on a human archipelago, bodies crouched or sleeping on their gripsacks and canvas bags. Many had traveled for hundreds of miles, all of us waiting to hear some word of loved ones in prison, or else waiting to pass along meager packages of chocolate, money, onions. Sometimes the packages were taken. Often they weren't. Stubbornly, Mama continued coming long after any of the clerks would accept her parcels. And I would be there with her, reliving, each morning, the fresh humiliation of pulling my pants down to pee in the frozen snow.

THE PLACE WAS EASY to miss. It wasn't around the corner from the Lubyanka Prison (now the administrative center of the FSB), as I'd been expecting, but farther down the hill, squeezed in among the glassed storefronts of Kuznetsky Most. I got there by crossing Dzerzhinsky Square, though of course it wasn't called Dzerzhinsky Square anymore. The statue of Iron Felix Dzerzhinsky, the original Chekist, had been removed a while back. And whose cast-iron profile did President Putin replace it with? His mentor, Yuri Andropov, who gave the KGB its ingenious psychiatric diagnosis of "sluggishly progressive schizophrenia." This allowed the state to fill up its asylums with anyone protesting its insanity. But, for the most part, Andropov's philosophy was endearingly primitive: "destruction of dissent in all its forms."

Unlike the prison itself, the warehouse where I hoped to find my parents' dossiers was barely marked. When I located it and at last pushed open the door, I found myself in a linoleum entry hall. The only furnishings, aside from a metal-detector gate, were a folding table and two plastic chairs, one of which was occupied by a pudgy FSB guard in a tan uniform. He rose slowly, as though it were his first physical act of the day. *"Propusk,"* he said, demanding my pass.

It was my first visit. I didn't have a pass. Was I supposed to? I gave him my passport and the letter explaining my intentions. He glanced at the American passport in its maroon Russian holder and handed it back, apparently satisfied. "You'll have to wait for the administrator on duty."

"Is he the archivist?"

"The archivist is out. You'll have to make an appointment with his assistant."

He gestured to the other plastic chair, where, it seemed, I was to sit obediently until such time as the archivist, or the administrator, or his assistant, decided to show up.

I checked my watch. My meeting at L-Pet was starting in twenty-five minutes. I sat down and wiped the sweat from my face. A place like this apparently didn't merit air conditioning. I glanced through the metal detector down into the corridor and saw a few solitary bodies in the reading hall. They had the timeworn, impoverished look of Soviet intellectuals— old shoes, thin sweaters worn in summer and winter. They looked like historians or Ph.D. candidates, each pursuing his esoteric autopsy, whose results would be bound sooner or later in a cardboard portfolio and buried in a vault just like this one. I was suddenly overcome with the ridiculousness of what I was doing. There was something wholly pathetic in sifting for grains of gold in the ash heap of the past.

The guard was picking up the phone— to call the assistant, I hoped. I took a sip from the L-Pet–branded water bottle I'd taken from the welcome package in my hotel room. The FSB guard took a furtive glance at my drink as he cradled the receiver. "Here," I offered, stretching out my arm.

He shook his head.

"It's only water. No radioactive substances, I promise." I got up and set the bottle down on his desk. The L-Pet petroleum-drop logo must have reassured him, because he took a sip.

"The assistant will be here soon," the FSB man now said. "Or, if you don't want to wait, you can drop your request letter in that box over there."

"Is that what you advise?"

"You asking me?"

"Who else?" I smiled.

"I'd wait. Lots of crazies dropping their letters in that box."

I was curious what sort of beef others had with History. "What kind of crazies?"

"The other day, someone came in looking for documentation on a flying saucer the air force shot down near Cheboksary," the guard said. "The assistant has to go through all those letters himself. That's why you're better off handing him your request in person."

"I see."

"People always come in here looking for answers," the FSB man said, leaning back in his chair.

"So—do they *get* answers?"

"Sure they do, just not to the questions they're asking."

Just then, a rail-thin older man walked into the hall.

"This fellow's been waiting for you," the FSB man said unnecessarily.

"Yes. Can I help you?" The assistant spoke with the softly dejected voice of a scholar. I told him I was looking for files relating to my parents, and gave him the years of their arrests. He sighed. "You'll have to write a letter and get it notarized."

"I have everything." I showed him my notarized letter, passport, even a copy of my birth certificate.

"The archivist won't be here until tomorrow afternoon."

"I'm only in Moscow for a few days," I pleaded.

The assistant glanced at the FSB guard, who'd been watching our exchange from behind his desk. "He's come all the way from America," my new friend urged him. His word held weight, it seemed, because the assistant reformed his earlier declaration. "All right, come back by four. You can try to catch the archivist before he takes off for his dacha."

SLINGING AK-74S, THE COMMANDOS patrolling L____ Petroleum's headquarters were substantially better armed than the pudgy FSB man assigned to protect the country's once-secret files. One examined my laminated pass carefully while the other made phone calls from a special glass booth, returning with a second set of passes for me, printed and stamped three times.

I was the last to show. The others (all but Kablukov) were inside, waiting for my arrival to slice open the envelopes with the contract bids. Valery did the honors with an elegant ivory letter opener. He placed each bid on a conference table varnished to such an expensive gleam that it resembled an amber skating rink. The afternoon sunlight filled lead-casement windows that were like lunettes in a French chapel. Were it not for the two-headed Russian eagle that hung over the fireplace, I might have thought the room a library in a venerable university.

Our first order of business was to weed out the obvious losers. Gibkov, the most ostensibly neutral of us, began. "Murmansk Shipping?"

"Solid Arctic experience. And they're giving us the best rate," said Tom.

"But their financials are a mess," said McGinnis. "They might not be in business five years from now."

There were no objections to cutting Murmansk Shipping—surprisingly, I thought, since it was one of L-Pet's hundred or so daughter companies.

McGinnis picked up another envelope. "Jessem. They're Swedish. Can't beat their safety record. Looks like they're doing well, expanding."

Tom objected this time: "They're building a lot of new ships; they're already undercapitalized. We can admire their ambition, but, we all agreed, debt-to-capitalization ratio has to be in the standard range."

Neither of Kablukov's two lieutenants—Serdyuk and Mukhov—had yet to speak. The talkative Mukhov was uncharacteristically quiet.

"Okay. What about this one?" said Gibkov. "Sausen Petroleum. A new company. Based in Geneva. Former oil trader for L-Pet, still does some trading, but moving into shipping."

Mukhov perked up. "We have very good experience with them."

I leafed through the application packet, which didn't take long, since it was about as thin as a communion wafer. "I don't get it," I said. "They have *no* experience. Let them apply once they've chartered a few ships."

Serdyuk shook his head disapprovingly at what I'd said. "Take a closer look. They have a very good reputation."

I lifted the bid and let it drop like a feather. "What reputation?"

"They have never had one oil spill. No accidents. Clean record."

"I'll tell you who else has a clean record," I said. "A doctor that's never operated on a single patient. Tell me what vessels they have in their fleet— a bulk carrier, a container ship, a cruise yacht, even? Anything?"

"They have a very good relationship with the banks in Switzerland," Mukhov put in authoritatively.

"Like every commodity trader in Geneva." Tom smiled.

"The Swiss will give any yo-yo a credit line if they start trading oil," I added, unnecessarily. I cast my eyes around the room for another ally. "And has anyone else noticed they want to charge us more than the others? Sixteen million more a year than the Swedes. What for, exactly?"

Nobody answered.

Serdyuk looked at Mukhov and shook his buzz-cut head like I still didn't get it. "Sausen has a very good relationship with Mr. Abuskalayev."

The air seemed to grow a few degrees cooler at the mention of the name of L-Pet's president. It was not, I knew, a name that got invoked very often, and when it did it was usually spoken solemnly, like one of the seventy-two names of God. It has been said that Abuskalayev, who is half Azeri and half Russian, keeps a Koran in the left drawer of his desk and an Orthodox Bible in the right. He started his business career as the first deputy oil minister of Soviet Azerbaijan, and used his political connections to be named the head of L-Pet. He's not a young oligarch but an old Soviet, which goes a long way to explaining why L-Pet has never been raided or disemboweled. Abuskalayev's balancing act of loyalty to President Putin was, as I saw it, his greatest achievement; in the press, he's given to strategically self-effacing statements such as "On its own, a national company cannot enjoy greater respect abroad than the country itself."

Once more Serdyuk elaborated what a good relationship Sausen had with the CEO, how well they'd done by L-Pet as a broker—all at a sub-audible volume that suggested it was our responsibility to pay heed, not his to persuade.

"We understand they have been a loyal servant to L-Pet for many years," Tom said diplomatically. "But you've done well by them, too, after all."

I checked my watch. Somehow it was already three.

"Let's keep them in the pool for now," Gibkov suggested, sensing tension. "We've got a few other companies to look at."

But I couldn't let the thing go. "Come on, people," I said. "Who are these guys? Are they even real? We've never worked with them. We've never met them." I'd spent three years of my life designing the ships in question. I wasn't about to let a few well-connected amateurs steer them into an iceberg.

"So you will meet them!" said Mukhov cheerfully.

"I thought they were in Geneva."

"Geneva—so what's the problem? We fly them in tomorrow! You meet them here, in this room, at ten o'clock."

Mukhov had a habit, like an actor, of saying something with a straight face, then suddenly smiling, which he did now. "*Nu?*" he said in Russian. "*Vsyo spokoyno?*"

IT WAS TEN MINUTES past four o'clock when I resurfaced at the Lubyanka Station. White cottontail puffs from the topol trees swirled around me, rolling in waves down the cobbled street. At the office on Neglinnaya Street, the security guard was sitting exactly where I'd left him several hours earlier. He looked up at me with a clouded expression.

"Is the archivist here?" I inquired.

In ceremonial disappointment he turned his palms out at his sides. "You just missed him."

23.

———

RECEIPTS

Moscow,
1936

SHE RETURNED TO CLIMB THE STEPS OF THE OVIR THE FOLLOWING WEEK. This time she met a different woman at the window, one who handed Florence her renewed city-residence document and a receipt for the old documents. A pulse of panic, a tectonic quiver, passed through her.

"Where is my passport?"

But the new woman didn't know anything about it. "Here!" She tapped a brittle yellowed nail on the square slip she'd given Florence. "We take your old documents, issue new ones!"

"Yes, but I gave you my *American* passport."

With a facsimile of patience she reserved for the dim-witted, the woman pointed again to the top of the paper. Florence could see the typed-up number of her American passport. With a sensation she wasn't fully sure was relief, she read her name (typed in Russian with a Cyrillic "tz" at the end), and the place and date of the passport's issuance (Nyu Iork, 1933).

"What am I supposed to do with this?"

"You take it to the embassy; they issue you a new one."

"What happened to my old one?"

"How the devil do I know? I'm just giving you what they gave me!"

SHE DIDN'T SEE LEON until evening, when she returned from work. On the way to their room—the farthest down the hall—Florence nearly tripped over the brushes and tins of the old man who cleaned and shined his shoes in the hallway. All the fussy apparatuses of his shoe polishing seemed to have been arranged precisely to get in everyone's way, and yet he had growled at Florence to watch where the hell she was going. Inside, Florence hung her coat on a peg in what Leon jokingly called their "foyer," bounded by the doorjamb and the side of their commode. A tower of folded linens was stacked on the table where Leon stood over them in the act of ironing. With a gentle, almost motherly attention to the task, which Florence admired for having so little of it herself, he finished ironing a crease into his linen trousers and placed the pants in a suitcase that lay open on their folded daybed. "I can't remember—am I supposed to drink sage tea if I get diarrhea, or chamomile?" he said by way of a greeting.

Florence dropped into the armchair and pried off her boots, delaying the moment when she'd have to relate to him the events of the morning.

"I think I'll pack both," Leon said with visible satisfaction. He was embarking on the first epic assignment of his propagandist's career—a project that, he'd explained to Florence, was "not just another banalizing caricature" of the happy lot of Russia's workers. He was once more returning to the East, this time not as a penniless homeless Jew, but as a reporter for the state's official news agency, TASS, on assignment to chronicle the transformation of the national minorities—the Uzbeks, the Kazaks, the Tajiks—from backward illiterates hiding their women under yashmak veils into tractor drivers! Machine operators! Sports fans and amateur thespians! Through his reports, the Western press would bite its knuckles to read of the irrigation schemes that Soviet power was imposing on the arid land, now ripe for growing cotton. Looking at his neatly packed hardboard suitcase and aluminum flask, Florence felt a pinchlike sensation of envy. "You should bring some iodine," she said, getting up and reaching for the top shelf of the commode where she kept the medicines. The loss of her passport still weighed on her chest. Now, still turned away from him, she said, "Something very strange happened to me this morning at OVIR."

She heard the hiss of the iron stop abruptly. She continued without facing him.

"They had my new residence permit. But they didn't seem to have my passport, which I gave the clerk last week. She gave me this. . . ."

Leon came close and stood blinking at the slip in Florence's hand. "My question is," he said at last, "who is *Florentz* Feyn? I'm not sure I know that fellow."

"Leon, you don't think this whole thing is a little odd?"

"You know what's odd? That everyone's telling me to bring cigarettes as palm grease when Uzbekistan is drowning in tobacco." He went back to the table and began to test, one by one, the various tiny cutting, filing, and tweezing implements in his folding knife.

"I'm certain it's a mistake. I'm going back there tomorrow to get some answers."

"Don't fight against the procedure, Florence; you'll just get a chipped tooth. Look"—he unfolded and examined a miniature pliers—"it's got all your information on it, doesn't it?"

"I'm going back, and I'm going to stay there until I talk to whoever's in charge."

At this remark, the canny animation seemed to drain from Leon's face. "Florence, don't do that. It's not the time for that right now. Look, look. . . ." He rummaged through the pile of documents on the bed until he found his leather passport case, then dug into one of the pockets and produced a square of paper very much like the one she'd shown him.

Speechlessly, she took it by the corner as though it were a razor blade. It contained Leon's name, his passport number, place and date of birth, date of issue—in short, the sum of scattered particles that formed his American identity, reassembled and typed out in Cyrillic.

"They gave this to me when I went to renew my visa four months ago. Told me it was too close to the expiration date. That's why they issued me this temporary one here."

"You mean to say you've been walking around with this nothing piece of paper for *four months?*"

It crossed Florence's mind that her impulse to browbeat Leon might be only a natural reaction to the secret worry she'd nursed all day that he would be the one reproaching *her*. This awareness, however, did nothing to diminish her passion for a fight. "You didn't think I'd be curious to know about this *before* I went to OVIR?"

"I didn't know you were heading there that day!"

"Well, it's a little strange that neither one of us has our original passport now."

"All right, it's odd. There's probably some new *nachal'nik* in charge up there who's taken a dislike to the color brown. It's not like America has forgotten we exist."

Florence let herself drop into the armchair and bit her thumbnail. She couldn't be sure if she was more upset about the passports or about the fact that Leon was leaving her all alone.

"How long will you be gone?" she said.

"Only four weeks. And when I come back—oh, baby—I'll bring you some of that turquoise jewelry their harem girls wear in their hair and bellybuttons, *ooh-la-la.*"

"They don't have harem girls, Leon. You're thinking of Turkey."

"Maybe, but I'll tell you what they do have—hashish."

"How will I reach you?"

"Telephones happen to be something the Uzbeks are a little short on, but I'll try to find one where I'm staying."

"Leon, maybe I should stop by the American embassy. Sort this out."

He took a step toward her and knelt down. With the side of his hand he brushed aside a curl on her forehead and smoothed it behind her ear. "We'll take care of it when I get back, okay? We'll do it together. The important thing is not to be in such a hurry all the time." He cupped her head to kiss it the way he might have once kissed, Florence thought, the head of his deranged, tormented mother.

SHE MIGHT HAVE HEEDED Leon's advice were it not for the letter.

Letters from home came less frequently now—two or three times a year—which Florence interpreted as her parents' concession to her choices and not to the failures of the Soviet mail system. This letter, though, included an insert from her brother, who (her mother's portion of the letter informed Florence) was graduating early from Erasmus. In a grousing tone that was nonetheless boastful, Zelda had written, "Sidney is under the impression that he is destined for Yale, but will more likely be attending City College next fall."

Scanning Sid's berserk penmanship, Florence saw that he was not, as she'd once been, under the misty spell of the Ivy League; more practically, he wished to study architecture or civil engineering and become, like his hero Robert Moses (a Yale alum), a "master builder." Two whole paragraphs of scratchy text were devoted to this Robert Moses who was transforming the city of New York from a cluster of disconnected boroughs into a mega-megalopolis spanned by bridges and expressways. Two pictures were tucked into the looseleaf: a four-by-two of Sidney's yearbook photo, his chin propped up self-consciously while he gazed seriously into the distance in a way he no doubt imagined befitted a future "master builder" (his ears nonetheless looking like the open doors of a taxicab careening straight at you), and a photograph of the family in the dining room— Zelda grimacing distrustfully into the camera, Sidney grinning with his eyes closed, Harry and his wife and their baby, now a chubby-kneed four-year-old girl on Solomon's lap. At the end of the letter, her father had added a careful postscript inquiring if Florence would be able to travel to New York to attend Sidney's graduation in June, his circumspect request already anticipating her answer.

Sidney, in spite of his skinny neck and big ears, no longer looked like the kid she remembered. Could two and a half years really have passed this quickly? She missed all of them badly. But more than that she was surprised to feel in herself a belated affection for the family home itself. She was overcome with an almost physical love for the tasseled lampshades in the second photo, the living room's ornamental bric-a-brac, its silver tea tray on the table, the bookshelf in the corner (filled, she knew, with unread Book-of-the-Month selections), her mother's fussy curtains, and all the other unseemly, cozy, bourgeois accessories of which her and Leon's communal-apartment life was supposed to be a principled and conscientious denial.

That night, and several nights following, she went to bed clawed by a restless yearning for some guidance and direction. It was not until the following week that, waking up one morning to the sober light of a white-clouded November, Florence understood that the tangle of her feelings could be distilled into a practical question of housing. Her outlook would improve once she got out of the crush of communal life. Brightly, she remembered that she had once been in line to get her own room from the bank. Now she had a spontaneous urge to ask Timofeyev whether a common-law marriage like hers and Leon's made her ineligible for her own room in a different apartment. With two different rooms to their names, she and Leon would be in a strong position to trade on the gray market for a separate apartment of their own. Surely her mentor would be able to advise her in confidence about which channels to appeal to.

Florence knocked on Timofeyev's door that morning with a renewed sense of courage. She lowered her eyes respectfully when he invited her to sit. "What's the urgent matter?"

Many days had been a brave buildup to this moment, and now she felt tongue-tied.

Florence seemed unable to catch Timofeyev's eye, so she fixated on his collar. She was struck by the way his neck flesh sagged. Once a portly gentleman, he looked now like somebody recovering from a wasting illness. She thought perhaps it was the stress of all the new meetings they had to attend these days, clarifying and reclarifying the implications of the recent trials in which well-regarded Party members had confessed to monstrous crimes against the country.

"Come out with it. I don't have all day, Flora."

"You see, it's my housing situation."

"Ah. The apartment question."

"My husband and I, we weren't officially registered, and I believe my domestic situation is, how can I say it plainly, unworkable."

"And you'd like to apply through the bank for a room of your own, is that it?"

"That's right."

"I'm sorry, but I can't do anything for you, Flora."

"I'm prepared for a long wait."

And now, letting the air out of his lungs, Timofeyev said, "I can't help you because we're cutting your position."

For a moment it seemed to Florence that she'd forgotten some elementary but critical rule of Russian grammar and couldn't decipher the words coming at her.

"You were going to be informed this week," Timofeyev said.

"I suppose I ought to finish typing up the correspondence from last week and organize . . ."

"Flora Solomonovna, your responsibilities have been concluded here."

She could feel herself smiling and blinking at this, blinking and smiling, as if her mind, shocked into paralysis, still needed time to unscramble the signal for her body. Then, slowly, comprehension began to set in. "Grigory Grigorievich, you know I've been tirelessly committed to . . ."

"You'll be issued an official letter so you can apply for work elsewhere."

"Where will I apply?"

He took a moment and, with his face only slightly softened, said, "You have valuable skills. The timing is just poor."

She saw in his face a reflection of her confusion, watched his mustached lips part in preparation, she felt, to give her some clarification. But he seemed at that moment to hesitate, and then, looking her square in the eye, he added, somewhat mysteriously, "It's better this way, Flora, believe me. Who knows what will happen tomorrow."

Under Florence's feet, the parquet rolled like the keel of an unsteady boat as she made her way to her desk and then, gathering her things, left to go home.

And this feeling of vertigo continued all the way into evening as she waited for a telephone call from Leon. But Leon did not telephone that night, or the next. And Florence had no way to reach him in Tashkent or wherever he might be now. In the meantime, her days vacant and idle, she made futile telephone calls of her own. First she called Essie, who was now employed as a copy editor in the Foreign Languages Publishing House, who promised Florence she would ask about any openings in the English-language division. She called back with a reply faster than Florence thought polite or necessary.

"They aren't taking anybody."

"You said they were short-staffed."

"They don't want to hire foreigners."

"It's the *Foreign Languages* Publishing House, for heaven's sake."

"Maybe in the spring."

It was clear to Florence that Essie wouldn't ask again; she was too scared for her own position. Florence made other inquiries, but it was hopeless. The problem was unsolvable. Everybody had to be registered at some place of employment, yet one couldn't get a decent job unless somebody would vouch for you. The newly passed Constitution guaranteed the right to work. In reality this meant that it was against the law *not* to work.

Night after night, she lay awake in a torpor of self-reproach. What had she done to get fired? Why had she not held on more dearly to her passport? When would Leon call? It was the curse of communal apartments that the muffled noises out in the hall were at once too loud and unsettlingly inaudible. Too noisy for her to sleep, too indistinct for her to know what slanders her neighbors were spreading about her. As the days wore on her mental state now vacillated between panic and dread. She had never been a regular smoker, but now, after buying her milk and bread in the morning, she also stopped by the tobacco kiosk. With the window open to the sharp, moist air of early December, she stood trembling in the cold as she chain-smoked Kazbek cigarettes until the nicotine dulled her anxiety and made her tingle with its inviolable aura. She smoked until the world in the window became dove-gray, then fully dark, so that finally the only light in the room was the throbbing ruby of her cigarette ember. If she could only hear Leon's voice! *He* would know just what to say to calm her and mollify whatever demons were pursuing her.

Instead, she crawled into bed with Sidney's photograph as if it were a talisman. She had always been prone to the clarity that extreme loneliness can bring. The alluring beginnings of a new plan now began to take shape in her mind. It wasn't the first time she'd thought about the plan, only the first time she had fully allowed herself to let it take on such a vivid form. Before, her days had been too full of distractions—with work and meetings, and Leon always trying to amuse her and make her feel better about everything. Now, at last, she could think. Again and again the same image came to her: a boat cutting through the waters off the coast of Finland, while out on the deck, standing firm in the spray of cold Baltic waters, she stared resolutely westward. Was there really any shame in going home? Yet now another thought tormented her: Would she be standing alone, or would Leon be by her side?

Cigarettes and brandy-spiked tea carried her through the next four days, until Leon, at last, phoned the apartment.

She darted to the big hallway telephone without having to be called (for two weeks her ears had been alert to every ring). But when Leon's voice came percussively on the line and asked for Flora in Room 6, she spoke indifferently.

"I'd started to lose hope I'd ever hear from you."

"Sorry, darling. I told you it'd be difficult. Can't talk long. I'm making this call on the credit and the good graces of Intourist."

"Is that where you've been staying?"

"No, they've been taking me around the new farms. Last night, I stayed with the chairman of the kolkhoz. The accommodations have been surprisingly pleasant."

"Eastern hospitality."

"Whoever said the Mussulmen are opposed to the drink has never been here. They'll stop at nothing, Florie, to wrangle you into a contest, which I might have a chance at not losing if their refreshments were limited to humble vodka, but do you know what they drink here?"

She let the expensive silence of three time zones go unchecked by her voice.

"I'll tell you," he said, answering his own question. "Fermented camel's milk. I've become quite fond of it. It gives your mouth a strange little kick, almost like champagne."

"When are you coming home?" she said matter-of-factly.

"Scheduled to leave next Monday. The train is three days. Is everything all right?"

She paused, fingering the scraps of paper and store receipts tucked behind the telephone's broad back. "No, it isn't," she said finally. "I lost my job." And when there was silence on his end, she went on: "I can guess who was behind it. The new office manager, Orlova. Timofeyev didn't have the guts to stand up to her. . . ."

"Just like that, with no warning?"

She thought back to a few weeks earlier, when Timofeyev had suggested she take a vacation. He had told her she looked "worn down." But to Leon she said: "And the worst part of it is that no one wants to hire a . . . 'foreigner.' No one will go over their head to put in a good word for me. Even Essie is of no use—never mind everything you've done for her, getting her that job in the first place."

"Listen, Florie, why don't we just talk about this when I get home."

"Everyone's got an Orlova in their office who'll ask, 'Why did you hire some foreigner?' So that's that, Leon. I'm going to the embassy. . . ."

"I can't talk about this now, Florie. . . ."

"I'm still an American citizen, after all."

"All right, take it easy. You don't sound well."

"I can't get to sleep, Leon. I miss my family. . . ." Her final word came out as something between a squeak and a sob. She had been prepared to present her case to him succinctly and decisively, but now she was whimpering and letting mucus run down her nose like a child.

"Shhh . . . shhh . . . Just . . . be quiet, will you? I told you we'll sort it all out when I'm back."

"I can't wait that long."

"Florence, please, just . . . don't do anything or go anywhere. Eight days, sweetheart, that's all I'm asking. Can you do that for me? I'll try to get an earlier train. There's money in a tin box in my shearling on the top shelf."

"We're in for bad luck, Leon."

"Oh, baby, everything's all jumbled in your head right now because you don't have your man with you. It's simple. But I'll be there real soon to take care of my girl. Do you read me?"

"Yes."

"Go on, get some sleep now, you'll feel finer tomorrow."

After a few more stifled simpers, which he seemed to read as a sign of assent, she let him go.

And the funny thing was, he was right. She *did* feel better the next morning. A clean, white, afterlife sort of light awoke her gently at precisely seven. In the window, a thin carpet of silvery snow covered the streets, the trees, the roofs, and the wool shoulders of the street cleaner sweeping the sidewalk with a twig broom.

Consulting the mirror, Florence noticed that sleep had brought a flush back to her cheeks.

What had she expected from Leon? She was ashamed of sounding so weak. The fault was hers. She had allowed herself to indulge in the delusion that he would be on board with her plan, and that they would do together what she now knew with certainty she would have to do alone. Her pain and dismay at this realization began to turn, as she started to get dressed, into a kind of renewal of self-reliance. So he liked how they were living, was grateful for eleven square meters, crammed in like TB patients with total strangers. So let him. He liked turning out his little ditties about how the future was just around the corner—good for him. He liked being sent out to the sticks to be treated like some pasha by the locals and sit around on carpets sipping sour camel's milk—fine with her. She didn't need him to hold her hand; she didn't need anybody's permission to get the hell out of a country that promised to be nothing for her but bad news. Already, the morning seemed to be in full agreement with her plan. The toilet room was miraculously free, the water in the shower pleasantly scalding. In the gloriously empty kitchen Florence brewed herself coffee on the stove. Through the double-pane glass of the kitchen window, the rays had found their way around the clouds and were sending their cold sunshine down in benediction. Back in her room, she put on her downy shawl and her mittens and headed purposefully to the metro.

When she surfaced at Manezh Square, she could just glimpse, under low-lying afternoon clouds, her homeland's rugged little flag flapping against stiff, rapidly cooling Moscow air. In fact, only the flag's tip was visible, a red-and-white wagging tail. To Florence it resembled a shivering finger beckoning from a short height above the U.S. Embassy, whose actual building remained largely hidden behind the ornate Hotel National, and behind its own gates.

Ignoring the moist sponginess that had taken residence in the toes of her stockings, Florence crossed Gorky Street and continued to advance across the plaza toward the yellowed limestone compound. She passed her own reflection in the doors of the Hotel National. In front of a shopwindow, she walked past a man in a caramel-brown coat and fedora who watched her pointedly from behind his round glasses, but didn't alter his expression when she nodded politely.

At each corner of the gates stood a guard in a green overcoat and ursine hat. Bayonetted rifles were strapped assertively across their felt-covered backs. And because one of the guards, on closer inspection, appeared to be an extraordinarily large adolescent, Florence selected the older of the two to approach. He had a beefy peasant's face redeemed by intelligent eyebrows that lifted slightly in readiness to hear what she had come for. Politely, she explained her reasons for needing to enter.

He showed little sign of either understanding or caring about her explanation, and spoke only one word: "Documents."

She dug into her pocket and produced the paper with her passport information.

"This is not valid."

"It is the receipt for my American passport, which was taken by the Housing Office. If you would just read there . . ." She had to rise slightly on her tiptoes to point to her place of birth.

He studied the paper compliantly but blindly, like a child holding a book upside down.

"This is not a passport," he said, handing it back.

"I am aware of that. As I said, I've lost my passport, and this is the only place in this city that I can get a *new* one made. So, if we can solve this problem right here . . ."

"Entry allowed only for official reasons. We need proof that you can enter."

"I just gave you *proof.* . . . Oh, this is too pointless. I need to speak with the *American* guard on duty."

"I am the guard."

"Somebody in *there.*" She pointed behind the gates.

"We have instructions about who may enter."

"*Please*, if you could just go in and talk to somebody, anybody, inside, I'm sure this will all be settled in a few minutes."

"If you keep standing here, we will have to report you to the police.*"

"Oh, for heaven's sake, all I'm asking is for you to *ask* somebody to come out—just to talk to me through the *goddamn gate.*"

"You will have to leave now."

"I am sure you are overstepping your authority by preventing an American from entering her own embassy."

"Vaclav . . . ," the guard said, jerking his head toward the giant teenager, who, after a second of slothful adolescent hesitation, began to approach.

She sensed that her opportunities were numbered. "*Yoohoo-oo!* An American here!" she shouted in English through the metal gates to no one. "*Hello-o-o!* Is anybody there? Can somebody *please* come out and tell these morons . . ."

But here she felt her underarms gripped by upholstered appendages whose embrace, in size and texture, was not unlike that of a comfortable armchair, only that they seemed to be conveying her backward with the torque of a wrecking ball. Her feet, slightly off the ground, beat like weak swimmers in rough tide.

"*Help me, somebody! I am a citizen of the* United States!" she shouted in English. She was deposited roughly on the sidewalk.

The sun had long taken leave behind the clouds. She pulled enough oxygen into her lungs to restore her ability to see and regain control of her limbs. Her ears were still pounding, either from the rush of traffic or from the blood echoing in her eardrums. With an effort, Florence got up on one heel and wiped the dirt off the palms of her hands. She examined the pink flesh, and found it speckled with dents from loose asphalt. She straightened up and fixed her twisted stockings through her skirt, permitting herself one last look back at the guards, who had returned to their posts. Gradually, the pressure in her ears settled and her eyes once again took in the street, the whizzing automobiles, the wedding-cake façade of the National. Only then, as she prepared to cross the avenue, did she again spot the man in the fedora hat. He was at the opposite side of the street from where he'd stood before, but the caramel color of his coat was unmistakable. He was loitering in front of what looked like a Ford V8 parked nose-up on the sidewalk. Florence adjusted her shawl over her shoulders and crossed to the opposite corner of the plaza. When she turned back to look again, he was gone.

SHE HAD NEVER BEEN good at deferring an urge once it manifested itself in her consciousness. She marched the ten blocks back to the OVIR.

"I would like to fill out the papers, please, for an outgoing visa to travel abroad," she announced to the clerk on duty with a confidence that suddenly sounded strained and counterfeit. She presented the receipt for her passport as her form of identification.

The woman behind the pane—the same one as at her first visit there—appraised Florence casually, then picked up the slip and handled it as though it were an item of dubious value that Florence was trying to sell her.

"I am an American citizen, as you can see there." She pointed to the paper through the glass. "I would like to travel to visit my family."

"American citizen? This is a Moscow residency permit. You are a Soviet citizen according to this."

"No, no, you can see." Florence tapped her finger on the pane. "You can see my passport number there."

"This is a permit for a Soviet national living in Moscow, and required of all citizens. All this indicates is that you were given residency permission when you submitted your American passport to the housing office. You were supposed to go to the passport office to get your internal passport."

A Soviet citizen? What in the world was this prune-headed ogre talking about?

"No, no . . . I think you're mistaken. You see, I never went through any
formalities of getting Soviet citizenship. And I have this receipt that I was
given *by your people* for my American passport when I came here to renew
my residency. And *you* told me—very clearly, in fact—that I would have
my passport back within a week."

She was employing the plural "you"—the royal you—to address her
tormentor, though her mannered politeness was obviously doing very little to ingratiate her.

"I told you nothing of the sort," the woman said with an insistence
that veered on threat. "This is not a receipt. It is your identification card."

Florence smiled and shook her head. "I beg your pardon, but I don't
have cotton in my ears, and this is *not* what I was told."

People had collected behind Florence, and it was becoming increasingly obvious to them and to herself, even as she continued to make her
case with deferential hostility, that she was now engaging in what by jun-
gle law might be considered a foolish behavior—prancing with her ass exposed to antagonize a large and threatening rival.

And yet the prospect of backing down felt like an equally impossible
option. "Do you plan to explain to all these people that you've been giving
us inconsistent information?" she found herself saying now. That did the
trick.

"I'm not the one you should be talking to," the woman said, slipping
back the paper. "Sort it out with your own at your embassy."

My own embassy won't help me without it, Florence thought, but strained
to maintain a firm smile. "I will certainly do that, but in the meantime,"
Florence persisted, "I'd like to, as I said before, fill out the paperwork for the
visa."

It was then that the ogre stood up out of her chair to her full, not in-
considerable height and, instead of coming out to do harm to Florence's
physical person, waddled down a short corridor. For a few uncertain minutes Florence stood there with her chin lifted and her jaw set tight against
the mutters behind her ("We'll be here all day"; "An American, she says").
But soon enough, the woman returned with the forms. And Florence,
stepping aside, filled out all the boxes with fingers only slightly shaky from
her triumph. The woman took them back without further words.

LEON RETURNED TO MOSCOW FOUR DAYS EARLY.

It was not the homecoming he was expecting.

No dinner set out on a linen tablecloth. No tea with lemon and sugar. Only his stalking wife pacing up and down the room in a frenzy of psychotic silence.

"Well, that's it. I've called in all my favors. No one will hire me. And you aren't going to ask at TASS, are you? Or you would have offered on the phone. I'm right, aren't I? I can see it in your eyes. You're terrified, like the rest of them."

Tired, unwashed, he walked to the daybed and collapsed on its cluster of scratchy pillows. "I'll ask, Florie," he said weakly. "But there's no point."

"No, of course," she said with unhappy satisfaction. "So what's going to happen to me?"

"Hopefully, nothing tragic, Florence, as long as you manage to keep your goddamn voice down and lie low for a little while. We're entering a difficult time. People are losing their lives and freedom, and you're complaining to me about losing your job."

Her eyes jerked ceaselessly around the room. "It's those careerists, like that Orlova. They're like insects. They use the Party line to get rid of people who are good workers so they can install their own idiots. They're like parasites who lay their own eggs and kill the host." It crossed her mind that the particular phraseology with which she was inveighing against the bank's Party Committee secretary was the same language Orlova herself regularly used to denounce the "wreckers and saboteurs" in the government and elsewhere. But since she couldn't admit to Leon the real reason for her panic, she continued. "This bloodsucking abuse, Leon. It has to be exposed!"

"And how do you plan to expose it?"

"Write to the papers!"

"I'm sure you're familiar with the dispatches we're producing now, Florence. The only letters the papers are going to publish are more bloodthirsty calls for the murder of 'enemies' who no one knows very much about, letters demanding that human beings be 'put down' like dogs. So how about you stop with the hysterics, and use your head."

"I am using my head! I can't not work. It's illegal. As soon as the little snoops around here start asking themselves what I do here all day, I'm leaving myself open to arrest. What do you propose: that I get dressed every morning and wander the streets?"

"We could formalize our marriage. 'Housewife' is a valid profession."

"Housewife?" She pronounced the word as though it were the quintessence of everything she'd ever had contempt for. "How very *kind* of you to try to make an honest woman of me! I should be grateful, shouldn't I? Well, let me tell you something: for such a grand fate I could have stayed in Brooklyn."

She'd never seen him truly angry before, at least not since their first night at the Metropol. He stood absolutely still, expressionless. Only his black eyes, boring into her, assumed a kind of burn, while the rest of his face remained rigid. "Forgive me," he said suddenly, in a sinister, implausibly precious voice. "I almost forgot. The Great Florence Fein! How can they *fail to appreciate* her brilliance, her energy, her valuable service to the Soviet State Bank! Think of the *injustice*. Let's for a minute forget that more important people are being rounded up and sent away to the devil knows *where*. The distinguished Florence Fein has been pushed aside. *Forgive* me for trying to offer you a reasonable way out!"

"Playing wifey in this room all day is not a reasonable way out. . . . We need to leave this place, Leon! Oh God." She began to wail. He clasped her wrist, but even then she couldn't stop. "If only I hadn't given those awful people my passport!" She sunk to her knees as he released her. "That stupid paper they gave me is useless. The guards at the embassy couldn't even read it."

"What are you talking about?" he said, kneeling down close beside her.

"They said it wasn't a valid passport, and I tried to explain that I had to get inside to *get* the new passport, but they turned me away."

She could see the life draining out of his face.

"But I'm going back, and you have to come with me," she continued with a reassuring pressure to his hand. "Like you promised. You're more persuasive. If we can just get past the Russian guards and talk to an actual American, it'll be okay."

He shut his eyes.

"I'll do no such thing, Florence," he said, drawing a breath and raising himself up. "I won't, and neither will you."

"I'm going back to America with or without you."

"Do you even understand what you've done?"

And the trouble was that a part of her *did* understand, had understood all along.

"Did you give the guard your name?" Suddenly he was all business.

"No. He looked at my permit, but briefly."

"Was there anyone else you spoke to?"

"What do you mean?"

"Anyone outside the embassy. Did anyone follow you out?"

She hesitated, remembering the man in the fedora.

"There was this . . . man, loitering outside a shopwindow between the Hotel National and the embassy. I didn't get a good look at him, but . . ."

"What?"

"He was still there when I came out."

"My God, Florence. Next time they see you, they'll stuff you right into one of their automobiles. That whole square is lousy with knockers in plain clothes."

"How do you know all this?" she nearly shouted. "Why are you only telling me this now?"

"Because I didn't think you'd be fool enough to do it!"

And he brought his clenched fist down on the table with a *thwap* so fierce the sugar tin fell to the floor, its pencils scattering.

In the quiet that followed she was keenly aware that the terror she was feeling was misplaced, that Leon's rage was only a drop of water in comparison with the unguessably deep swamp of shit she'd waded into. Florence lifted herself up and clawed out the second-to-last of the cigarettes from a pack in her skirt. But the sight of Leon's chagrined eyes made it hard to stop trembling long enough to light a match.

At last she managed it and took a too-fast, painful drag. She had an urge to press the ember into the meat of her palm.

"All right, let's calm down," he said after a while. "Let's look at this reasonably. . . . Have you filled out any papers—signed your name anywhere?"

Oh, how she wanted to tell him—about going to the OVIR, the ogre whom she'd stared down so tenaciously, the application she'd filled out for an exit visa. She had *planned* to tell him. But now—the way he was looking at her—she couldn't. She threw her head back and blew a gray curl of smoke toward the plaster-mold ceiling. "No," she said.

"Promise me you won't go there again. Not for a while."

"All right. But what about finding a job?"

He shook his head impatiently. "Take any kind of job, Florence."

"You mean work in a factory? A public laundry?"

"What's wrong with that? It's honest labor."

She blew another ring of smoke up at the ceiling. "Now you sound like *them*."

"Maybe I do. But there are plenty of decent folks working all kinds of jobs. Educated people, too. You know I'd switch places with you tomorrow, Florence, if I could."

"You would, wouldn't you?"

"Whatever I had to do to save myself, or you."

She couldn't bear the look on his face. It was one of bottomless devotion, more frightening to her than all of his rage.

BOOK IV

24.

———

THE UTOPIST ALTAR

THERE WERE OTHER REASONS—BESIDES MY FRIEND YASHA'S HINTS ABOUT Mama's unsavory entanglements with the secret police—why I was eager to return to the archives on Neglinnaya Street. For years, another question has riddled me. How was it that my mother survived the twin horrors of prison and the camps, whereas my father, an altogether more charming and resourceful person, perished? If he had succeeded in withstanding the treadmill of interrogation and torture, and the cattle car to Siberia, I am certain Mama and I would have been informed of it. All we were ever told during those freezing, senseless excursions to the Lubyanka Prison at five in the morning was that my father had been given "ten years of corrective labor without the right of correspondence," which everyone, even then, knew was a euphemism for a bullet in the back of the neck. (Only Florence remained unnervingly optimistic about the possible definitions of Papa's penal sentence.) How did someone who willingly imbibed such self-deceptions withstand the brutal realities of the Gulag? In circumstances identical to my father's, how did she manage to get her own crime reduced from treason to a minimal sentence of "agitation"?

Now that I was seeking answers, I could admit to being in the grip of a still more puzzling conundrum, about which I'd never managed to extract a satisfying answer from my mother. It concerned her aborted attempt to escape the Soviet Union. During my college years at the progressive height of Khrushchev's thaw, Florence let slip that she and Papa had tried, quite intrepidly, to leave Russia before it had become "too late." When I later brought it up, she retracted. Heaven knows, Florence had a gift for back-pedaling on all manner of revelations, but this one I could not let rest, in light of her nerve-grating refusal to discuss, in 1978, the subject of our family's emigration. If it were true—if she herself had tried to escape—why not admit it now that we could all leave the country together? And why, after pounding (however briefly) on a locked door, did she decline even to consider stepping across a suddenly open threshold with her own family? Didn't she want to pick up the keys to her cage? What had happened between 1937 and 1978 that made her constitutionally incapable of even discussing it?

I wondered if maybe, very simply, she had finally given up on America the same way America so pitilessly had given up on her.

MY PARENTS WERE HARDLY the only Americans to be stranded in Moscow after 1936. Hundreds like them were cut adrift in the Soviet Union, comprehending too late that they'd fallen from the grace of the American government. The U.S. Embassy seems to have found every excuse to deny or delay reissuing these citizens their American passports—passports they had lost through no fault other than their naïveté. The schemes that the Soviet government employed to strip American expats of citizenship were numerous. Those living outside of Moscow were required to send in their passports for renewal by post, only to be informed that their documents were "lost in the mail"—bundled and repurposed, no doubt, by spies. Muscovites like my mother were required to submit theirs to work- or housing-permit boards. This was how Mama lost hers, though in her whitewashed account the bureaucratic sleight of hand was—her words—an unexpected convenience, as she was planning to apply for Soviet citizenship in any case.

I have since read about those who attempted to seek recourse in the protective fortress of that embassy. If they managed to enter, they were informed by embassy workers that the processing fees for their new passports were to be paid in dollars—currency that was illegal to possess. Other applicants were merely instructed to return again, and again, and again, so that their cases could be "fully investigated"—even as the consular staff that gave these instructions could observe from their office windows that the plaza below was patrolled on all corners by the Soviet secret police, who showed up each morning like fishermen to cast their nets into this reliable pool.

I had always assumed that our embassy's malicious indifference to these castaways must have been a symptom of the anti-Red prejudice that was permeating America at this time and would overtake it completely after the Second World War. Who were these defectors but malcontents and radicals that had turned their backs on their country—on Democracy and Capitalism? They'd made their pink bed, now let them lie in it.

That, at least, was the only explanation that made sense to me. I might have continued to believe it had I not, some years into my new American life, been given the gift of a VHS tape of "a classic American film" bequeathed to my wife and me by one of our patrons at Temple Beth Emet— a friendly, burly psychologist by the name of Harold Greene, who'd taken a special interest in my family's story because he saw in us some sort of missing link to the world of his recent ancestors. With unaccountable pride, Harold once informed me that he came from a long line of socialists, "on both sides," and spoke excitedly of the rally his father and grandfather had attended for Trotsky in the Bronx a thousand years ago. The gift of this VHS tape was only one of Harold's many acts of generosity. (His first present to me and Lucya was a saggy queen-sized spring mattress, which, in bestowing it upon our impoverished household, Harold advertised as "a good Jewish mattress—two terrific Jewish children have been conceived on this mattress!") The video he gave us was called *Mission to Moscow*. Its case still bore the proprietary stamp of the "Library of NYU" and must have found its way to Harold as one more piece of apocrypha from that Red decade for which he nursed such nostalgia. My guess, though, is that he never actually watched it to the end. Had he done so, I suspect that even he, an uncritical sentimentalist, would have recognized it for the watery load of propagandistic Hollywood excrement that it was.

The film was based closely on the memoir of the former U.S. Ambassador to the Soviet Union, Joseph Davies, and produced by Warner Bros. Studios at the request of President Franklin D. Roosevelt himself. After the war—this I learned from Harold—it became the first of the big studio films to be burned on the stake of McCarthy's "un-American" campaign. For good reason, I should say. The list of endless elisions that make up this lying travesty of a movie includes Davies declaring that the confessions made during Moscow's show trials appeared to him "authentic and uncoerced." The film also includes Davies rationalizing Stalin's unprovoked attack on Finland and his pact with the Nazis, and generally whitewashes one of history's bloodiest dictators as some kind of bumbling uncle moving his nation clumsily toward American-style democracy. For me, the height of the film's delusion comes in a scene in which the ambassador gently scolds his staff for being outraged that their embassy is bugged. *But how will the Soviets ever know we mean them no harm,* he lectures his subordinates, *if they can't listen to our private conversations?* At this I wanted to wipe my eyes. Surely, the movie was meant as pure lampoonery, I thought. How could any diplomat be at once so dangerously submissive and so flawlessly arrogant? My disbelief made me curious to learn more about the man under whose aegis my parents had been barred from the one sanctuary that might have given them protection when their lives were so obviously in peril.

Joseph Davies, I would learn, was a liberal Washington lawyer and friend of Roosevelt who had the great ingenuity to marry, at the height of the Depression, the richest woman in America. Marjorie Merriweather Post had inherited the Post Foods empire from her father and expanded it with the help of her second husband. She presided over a kingdom of cereals, cake mixes, coffees, chocolate syrups, cooking powders, and frozen vegetables like a Catherine the Great. Every time an American housewife tore open a box of Grape-Nuts, or brewed a pot of Maxwell House, or chilled a bowl of Jell-O for her children, her domestic gesture contributed another tiny spike to Marjorie Post's prodigious portfolio.

In 1935, Post's divorce of her financier husband and her marriage to Joseph Davies was, along with the trial of the Lindbergh baby's kidnapper, fruitful fodder for the tabloids. Columnists wondered what a woman as regally striking and obscenely rich as Marjorie could find appealing in an antitrust attorney who resembled a cartoon mouse in a bowler hat. Obviously, they underrated the allure of politics for a woman who had everything. Marjorie Post Davies's wedding present to her third husband was a titanic check made out for the reelection campaign of his buddy Franklin D. Roosevelt, a contribution that naturally left a debt to be repaid once the president entered his second term. No doubt Mrs. Davies hoped that her six-figure gift would guarantee her husband an ambassador's post in London or Paris. Instead, the couple got Moscow. And, more relevant to my parents' story, Moscow got them.

The Davieses arrived in Russia unblemished by any knowledge of its language or history. It seemed that Marjorie was worried they might starve there, and so brought with her several boxcars of Post foods, inexhaustible filets and fowls, and four hundred quarts of frozen cream in a dozen freezers, which immediately blew out Spaso House's primitive electrical system, and promptly melted. Needless to say, Moscow failed to offer Marjorie Post Davies much in the way of her preferred entertainment: shopping. And there are only so many evenings a person can go out to the theater and the ballet. Of course, there were other forms of theater to attend, if one counts Stalin's show trials, which Joseph Davies seems to have sat through with the same illiterate appreciation he brought to bear on the operas he watched from his royal box at the Bolshoi.

Ten weeks into their stay the couple was already bored. They sailed their yacht back to America for an extended vacation. At home Davies gave the president and media his diplomatic report: The forced confessions, according to his lifelong experience as a trial lawyer, were "legally credible." The executions of Bolsheviks? "Uprooted conspiracies." Forced collectivization? "A wonderful and stimulating experiment." Stalin? "A fine, upstanding fellow." Nothing was mentioned about the harassments and intimidations suffered by Davies's own diplomatic staff at the hands of the NKVD, and certainly nothing about the hundreds of Americans who were disappearing without a trace. Not long into his tenure, Davies's entire staff threatened to resign in protest of his abysmal stupidity, but lost nerve at the last minute. Afraid of falling on the wrong side of the Russian secret police, they stalled on granting passports to the American nationals whom the Soviets had started claiming as their own.

Was Davies really deaf to all the American citizens banging fruitlessly on his embassy's doors? I refuse to believe that. So—would it have been so hard to intervene on behalf of these marooned souls? The problem was that intervening would have required Davies to perform some actual diplomacy. But how hard could *that* have been? America still exerted no small degree of leverage over the Soviets at this time: Russia still owed the United States hundreds of millions of dollars for all that industrial machinery it had been buying for years on credit. However, Joseph Davies had not been appointed for his moral courage. That mistake Roosevelt had made once already. The former ambassador, William Bullitt, had been replaced as soon as he stopped affirming the president's own convictions about the benevolence of their Soviet friends. No, the fault was not Davies's ignorance, or his cowardice. He had, after all, been sent to Russia to make nice at the cost of everything else. And he carried out his function marvelously. During the 190 days a year they actually spent inside of Russia, the ambassador and his wife were busy throwing costume parties ("Come as your Secret Desire") with gowns and props loaned by the Bolshoi Museum, hosting private screenings of American films for the same NKVD thugs who were bullying his staff, and sailing their four-hundred-foot yacht, *Sea Cloud,* around the Black Sea. Most notably, they spent their free time cruising the Soviet commission stores for prerevolutionary antiques being sold off by a starving populace at bargain-basement prices. Mr. and Mrs. Davies might not have cared to know much about the Soviet Union, but they did make an exhaustive study of Russia's imperial era. By the end of their tenure, they had carted off the biggest collection of paintings, tapestries, Fabergé eggs, silver tea services, religious icons, enameled boxes, royal jewels, porcelain, and liturgical objects ever to be amassed outside of Russia. All of these expropriated treasures are now sheltered in exquisitely lighted display cases inside Marjorie Merriweather Post's Hillwood Estate in Washington, D.C., not far from my office. I once paid a visit there and discovered that, along with a marvelous painting of Catherine the Great, there hangs on one of the walls a portrait of the middle-aged Marjorie Post Davies herself, costumed as Marie Antoinette.

It would be too convenient to conclude that Joseph Davies and his wife were merely two more dupes of Stalin's regime. That would be giving them too little credit. In my experience, those who amass great wealth or power, however fatuous or dim-witted they might appear to the public, possess some mysterious instinct with regard to where their bread is buttered. Joseph Davies, for all his simplemindedness, had a genius for keeping powerful people happy: he pampered his wife, fawned on FDR, and as for Stalin and Litvinov, it seems he adopted the lawyer's posture that they were his clients! Entitled to the best defense that money could buy, regardless of what crimes they had committed.

In turn, it would be giving Roosevelt too little credit to imagine that he chose Ambassador Davies simply on the basis of nepotism and reciprocity. Davies possessed one virtue that every other Russia expert in Washington at the time lacked: he was ready to affirm Roosevelt's own political faith that the Soviet Union shared with the United States a fundamental aim to improve, if by its own peculiar methods, the lot of Everyman. At a time when Europe was drifting toward war, there was a great deal of expediency in this alliance with Russia. But my reading of history suggests that even with America's closest allies there has never been a more uncritical friendship than the one that existed between Roosevelt and Stalin in those years. So let me put forward a different proposition, a heresy for all the FDR idolators who are ready to paint our thirty-second president into *The Last Supper:* somewhere in his heart Roosevelt *admired* that lupine monster! Admired the iron will, the unapologetic social engineering, the politico-economic experiments that were such a potent model for his own expansion of government from a small racket to a big one. Admired, most of all, the conviction that the evolution of great nations was irreversible. Just as the United States was moving from unfettered capitalism to big-government socialism, so, too, Roosevelt might have thought, the U.S.S.R. would evolve from totalitarianism to social democracy. On what basis would he have believed this? On the basis of the same hallucinatory utopism that was so catching in those days among intellectuals. Was FDR a closet communist? Heavens, no. The dispenser of government millions to the biggest corporations in the country was nothing of the sort. He was just a run-of-the-mill utopist. Scratch a utopist and you find a Machiavellian—one who, to achieve his shining vision, must inevitably subscribe to the principle that the ends justify the means.

In short, the trapped Americans, my parents included, were not abandoned. They were not even forgotten. They were *sacrificed* on the common altar of two superpowers.

My only consolation is that history has not been kind to Joseph Davies. He will be remembered as the craven and obsequious ignoramus he was. Meanwhile, Roosevelt, that old patrician, will retreat exonerated into the pantheon of great leaders whose myths only swell with time. For this act of misdirection even I must admit some reluctant admiration. One has to appreciate FDR's deftness in allowing his accommodating old friend Davies to take the fall for his unholy alliances—an act of political cunning in every way worthy of *The Prince.*

25.

CLEANING HOUSE

FLORENCE SURVIVED THE YEAR 1937 WORKING AS A JANITRESS AT THE V____ Theater on Arbat Street, a job she obtained through the theater connections of the wife of her former boss, Timofeyev. It would be his final favor to his American ingénue, not counting the favor she still did not recognize as one, which was to cut off all contact.

And so, in January, while the Party's inner chambers were swept of Stalin's former comrades, Florence pushed a broom down the dusty labyrinth of actors' dressing rooms. In March, when Stalin launched his campaign to rub out deviationist intellectuals like the writers Isaac Babel and Osip Mandelstam, Florence struggled to eradicate muddy boot-prints from the crimson carpets in the old theater lobby. In May, when the Great Leader commenced his purge of the Red Army, liquidating thirty-five thousand officers in a span of eighteen months, she expunged grime from the fibers of velvet cushions. The cleanings would go far into 1938, when the "Father of the Peoples" would order masses of Poles, Koreans, Greeks, and Finns to be rounded up and dumped in Siberia, all while Florence disposed of bucketfuls of cigarette ash and soiled newspaper into rubbish bins along Arbat's crooked alleys. And while Yezhov, the new head of the NKVD, was "cleansing the organs" by executing thousands of his predecessor's agents, thereby setting himself up to be flushed out along with them, Florence chafed her knees scrubbing the porcelain bowls of public toilets.

And yet it would not have been fair to say that she hated the work. Just as a hospital orderly may come to like the smell of chloroform, Florence grew to enjoy the scent of makeup that clung to the carpet runners and drapes after performances. She found herself reawakened to a kind of lonely childhood magic in the company of the empty costumes and abandoned props, the dingy soaring ceiling, the voluptuous curtains that were of a piece with the tattered magnificence of old theaters everywhere. She attended the dress rehearsal of every new production, leaning on her broom like Cinderella in the dark rear corners of the auditorium. She understood perfectly well that she'd been given this job on the tacit condition that she keep herself *tishe vody, nizhe travy,* quieter than water and lower than grass. Watching other dramas unfold onstage, Florence took care not to be noticed, struggling to take comfort in her anonymity.

At night, she came to life in recounting the plays to Leon, scene by scene. She let him knead her tired feet with the heel of his hand while she shut her eyes in raconteurial pleasure at the tales of the characters' tantrums and love affairs, their thwarted aspirations and bitter disappointments—so much easier to speak about than her own. She did not miss a play that season: Arbuzov, Gorky, Chekhov. Sometimes her eyes drifted from the performers to the audience. They too seemed to her like actors, if only because she felt equally apart from them. She interacted with no one unless the cloakroom attendant, Agnessa Artemovna, was ill and Florence sat in her place, stacking moist coats and hats, or wadding scarves into sleeves. Then, after the show, Florence would watch the crowds muscling back toward her in their sharp-elbowed footrace to the cloakroom and would feel, like one of Chekhov's consumptives, shocked at their energy for life. It was the agreeable company of Agnessa Artemovna—a decade and a half older than Florence, but mistakable for Florence's mother if one were to judge from her swollen legs and knuckles—that made Florence's demotion more tolerable. The janitor's closet just off the public cloakroom was Agnessa's private realm, and she tended its clutter of busted chairs, cracked broom handles, scraps of carpet, and chipped pans as neatly as a city sparrow tends her nest of sidewalk trash. After the first act of a play, Agnessa would lock up the cloakroom and invite Florence for a glass of black tea that she brewed with an ancient, calcium-scarred teakettle.

As she depicted herself to Florence, Agnessa had come to Moscow a naïve young woman, traveling from the countryside with other girls in search of factory work. At twenty, she'd married a boy who "drank a little, but seemed gentle." Her mother-in-law thought her a rustic and a yokel and "dragged me around the floor by my hair when I got pregnant." She held Florence's fingers to the bumps and valleys on her scalp where she'd been walloped by the young husband and his mother. Whatever marks the abuse had left on Agnessa's body, they seemed to have spared her spirit, for she spoke of all the violence visited on her in a voice that was buoyant and jolly. She remembered every detail of her younger days—the weather, how much things had cost—which made her stories as gripping as the plays onstage. More so, Florence thought, because they were true. Onstage, the heroes acted out scenes of redemption by joining collectives and subsuming their ambitions to the common will; the leitmotifs of Agnessa's stories always strove in the opposite direction: an almost monomaniacal quest for a room of her own. "I went to work setting type at a printing press and divorced the bastard," she told Florence in the shadow of brooms and brushes. "But we were still living in the same room! I went to the administration and said, 'Give me and my daughter a room.' They tell me: 'Bring us the paper attesting how many square meters you and your former husband have.' I brought them the paper. It was fifteen and a half. They say, 'We can't help you. Everyone gets five meters a person, and the two of you have a half-meter extra. You'll have to exchange it on your own—barter it for two smaller rooms.' 'But he refuses!' I say. 'That's not our problem.' So what am I supposed to do—have another baby by the pig to get my own room? That's when I understood what 'city life' was, girlie. You have to earn *money* here! And put bread in the right palms. So I worked days and took a night job as a cleaner in a morgue. Never slept, never saw my child. I was the living envying the dead. Then I took what I earned and went to the right people. That's how I got my own room at last."

At some point toward the end of Act 2, when it was time to reopen the cloakroom, Agnessa's stories would conclude on some philosophical or wistful note. "Curious how life turns out, isn't it? Look at my hands. I came to the city for an easier life. My sister, she stayed in the country, and hers is the life that turned out better. She became a midwife. She helped me out once. After I divorced, I met a man—a good one, but married. Well, what could I do? Couldn't keep it. Don't look so shocked. She helped many women that way. Got herself a quiet little house in the village. Girls from all over Moscow used to come, even when the deed was legal. And now she's even busier. Her hair is always colored. Fine clothes. Never short in the pocket."

To Florence's relief, Agnessa rarely asked her about herself.

"And how did you end up here?" she once inquired.

Florence had learned by now that simple answers were better than complicated ones. "There was no work in America. So I came here. I met a man, and I stayed."

And Agnessa had nodded in understanding. "That's how it always is."

DURING FLORENCE'S FIRST MONTHS at the theater, she had been forever on the alert for a familiar face, clandestinely peeking into the cloakroom crowds so she might have time to turn away if spotted. But after many months, when no face from her old life had materialized, she eased her vigilance. And so it was an odd thing to hear her own name spoken, one cold April evening in 1939, by a woman handing her a rabbit-fur coat.

Florence squinted as if someone had shined a bright light in her face.

"You don't remember me, do you?" said the woman. "It's Valda."

It wasn't her face but the Baltic name that tripped a wire, and suddenly Florence recalled the well-bred Latvian translator from Nina and Timofeyev's apartment so many years ago. "Valda. Of course!"

The first bell interrupted them, and Florence did not see her old acquaintance again until after the performance. Valda was waiting for her inside the doors of the theater lobby. "Flora, I'm surprised to see you here."

Ancient tides of fear and embarrassment rose up in her, but she steeled herself against them. "Many things are surprising now," she said.

Valda seemed to take the hint. "We ought to talk and catch up," the tall woman suggested in a softer tone.

"Care to stick around until midnight?" Florence offered ironically.

"How about early afternoon? Next Thursday."

And to Florence's surprise, Valda took a slip of paper from her purse and wrote down an address.

UNTIL THE VERY LAST MOMENT, Florence was not at all sure if she would go to meet Valda. It had been a long time since she'd had an occasion to put on a good dress and style her hair. The thought of making herself presentable for the world filled her with a dangerous hope she didn't trust. The address Valda had given her was near Sokolniki Park, at the pine-wooded boundary of Moscow, reachable only by a tram from the very last metro stop. When she arrived, the place turned out to be not a woodsy vista but a student cafeteria at the university where Valda taught—the Institute of Philology, History, and Literature, or IFLI for short. During her self-sequester, the city seemed to have edged outward. In the café, enjoying a bowl of surprisingly delicious soup with Valda, Florence felt like a nocturnal animal awakening to daylight. "You teach here?"

"Yes, in the department of classical philology."

"It must be a delight, this sort of work, discussing literature every day." From the bright sun melting the heaps of snow, from the reviving smell of black soil, from the naked, hatless faces of passing students, Florence felt the intoxication of spring's arrival.

"Yes, I suppose. The students are bright, but . . ." Valda lowered her voice. "I can't discuss the structure of a classical poem anymore without having one of them tell me it's reactionary, or that I'm being a 'formalist.' What can I say? We're supposed to keep up with the times."

But hearing Valda's complaints only made Florence more envious. Not until they were alone, walking at the vacated edge of the park, did Valda say, "To be frank, Flora, I couldn't believe my eyes when I saw you in that little coat box inside the theater."

"Why?"

Valda's eyes grew wide. "What do you mean? I assumed you'd gone back to America or that, well, that you'd been . . . carted off."

"Me?"

"Yes. Because of Timofeyev. Don't look so surprised. Haven't you heard what happened to him? He was picked up after the Pyatakov trial."

"Grigory Grigorievich?" Florence knew that even to speak like this was dangerous, but something in Valda's eyes—the noble plainness of her face—gave Florence confidence to go on. "Goodness! What about Nina?"

"She's gone. Went back to Tbilisi. Heaven knows who's been moved into their beautiful apartment on Prechistenka by now."

She understood now that Valda's link to the glittering world of the Timofeyevs had been severed just as hers had been. They were, both of them, lonely planets who'd lost their orbit.

"You're saying Nina just *left* him?"

"Left him? Oh, Flora, do you think Moscow is any closer to Siberia than Tbilisi is?"

For the first time, Florence learned that Timofeyev, as a young man, had been a part of some opposition group or other. It dawned on her that he had, all along, been prescient about his arrest. He had fired her to spare her from association with him. Again she recalled his glamorous wife's glib advice: "Who are we to think we can fathom everything that goes on up top?"

"Nina's contacts got me work at the theater," she confessed to Valda.

"That little dark theater." Valda shook her head sympathetically. "Of course, it *is* perfectly respectable work," Valda said, backpedaling. "I only meant that with your skills—typing, accounting, your English—you could find very suitable work indeed."

Did Valda have something in mind?

"What about right here at the institute? You could teach English to the advanced philology students."

"Aren't there enough instructors?"

"We've had some shifts in the staff and administration."

Florence didn't ask her to elaborate. She guessed that the institute had not been left untouched by the purge. But now, Valda seemed to suggest, the pendulum was swinging in the other direction. "Overzealousness" was what they called it in the papers. The Politburo had relieved the NKVD chief, Nikolai Yezhov, of his position for doing his work too passionately. Now, with Beria at the helm, the worst certainly had to be over.

She knew what Leon would say to the plan: at the theater no one bothered her. She was safe there. But what was *safe?* She was rotting away inside. The most vital years of her life were being wasted in idleness. Whatever Valda's motives for offering her a different path, Florence had no doubt that Valda's sympathy was real. She was painfully aware that, no matter how proudly and confidently she tried to present herself, her act wasn't fooling anyone. Valda was *genuine* intelligentsia, not one of the new phonies who'd clawed their way into positions of influence. There were still a few people in Moscow, Florence thought, who had a sense of human decency.

"But IFLI is a serious institute. Scholars teach there, and I've never taught."

"That doesn't matter. You have a university degree. And what about those engineers you told me you once tutored in America? You could say you taught *them*." Valda wrote something in her small address book. "I'll speak to the dean. He's a reasonable man. I have a feeling it will work out."

And so it did.

26.

OUR FRIENDS FROM GENEVA

. . . WAS HOW MUKHOV INTRODUCED THE MEN FROM SAUSEN PETRO-leum, though neither fellow struck me as remotely Swiss. Their Slavic mugs, like their names, left no mistake as to their citizenship. Their speech and clothes, however, bespoke a more tangled marriage between North-ern and Southern Europe: Anglicized Russian accents suggestive of Lon-don educations, narrow suits with Italian tailoring. Costumed in Gucci, the two looked terrifically pleased to meet us, indeed. When Gucci Number One pumped my hand, it was with a pleasure so forceful I had the sense he was hoping to squeeze a few squirts of petroleum from my palm.

Our meeting took a while to get started, since every L-Pet executive on the floor wanted to drop in and wish our Geneva friends the best of luck. Clearly no luck was needed. So secure were the Gucci brothers in their confidence that they casually declined all the antiquarian devices we of-fered them for their presentation. They had no use for the pull-down screen or the slide projector, no need of laptops with PowerPoint. Not to suggest they were lacking in manners—quite the opposite. They were as amiable as could be; they delivered the same speech, about their long and loyal service to L-Pet (as its former oil broker), at least twice. It seemed their strategy was to speak as little as possible about what they actually planned to *do* as our oil shipper, and simply let the authority of Abuska-layev's name do the work of persuading. After an hour and a half of this "presentation," almost impressive in its nearly flawless lack of content, the Gucci twins asked if we had any questions for them.

I had a question: How were they planning on operating the ships we were building? Gucci Number Two's knowing smile presaged his answer. "We'll hire professionals, of course."

The professionals they intended to hire turned out to be "the best crew from Sovcomflot"—one of the competing bidders.

I did the math in my head. Sovcomflot was bidding sixty-five thousand a day. Sausen's bid was $111,000. So, building the same ships, at the same shipyard, employing essentially the same operator, they intended to charge us an extra seventeen million dollars per annum for the next ten years. "Your bid is considerably higher than Sovcomflot's," I said. "Do you mind spelling out what this extra money pays for?"

"Certainly. What you are getting is"—and almost in unison our new friends from Geneva uttered a phrase incubated so long ago inside the womb of American capitalism that on their dandy tongues it sounded disarmingly quaint—"quality control."

The only question remaining was the one that couldn't be asked in the open: With whom, among L-Pet's suited ranks, were the Gucci boys planning to split the 170 mil? Was it Mukhov, or Serdyuk, both now bobbing their heads in stern agreement? Was it CEO Abuskalayev himself? Very possibly it was Kablukov, the Boot, though his absence from our meeting suggested ambiguous commitment to his own racketeering—unless he simply didn't like to be present when his orders were executed. I looked over my shoulder at Tom. Surely, he could spot the two-bit swindlers disguised behind all that worldly swank. Since Tom was leading the financial end of this joint venture, I lamely hoped that *he* might have some artful way of broaching the $170-million question. But the Clintonesque squint he flashed me was of no comfort at all. Without acknowledging my wordless plea, Tom allowed his huge hand to squeeze my regular-sized shoulder in a way that seemed to say: *Hold back, tiger. This isn't a fight worth wasting your fangs on.*

I raised my cuff and checked the time. The hour on my Timex was inching closer to three. I had to head to Neglinnaya Street to meet with the archivist before they closed. I continued to dally, hoping the question of Sausen could be put to a speedy and final rest once the Genevans left our conference room, but, to my chagrin, a catered lunch of overstuffed pastrami sandwiches and sauerkraut was rolled in on a silver cart.

When I could stand it no longer, I escaped. Our final vote wasn't until Monday, I told myself. It was still Thursday. I raced to the metro and resurfaced at the Kuznetsky Most station among the parked Benzes and baby-faced smokers in business suits. Against the foot traffic, I bolted toward the anodized double doors of the archive building. It was, blessedly, still open. No sooner had I entered the heel-dimpled linoleum lobby than the FSB man on duty—a new fellow this time—informed me the building was about to close.

"It's a half-hour early," I protested. With an indifferent tilt of his head he indicated a paper sign taped to the wall: SUMMER HOURS.

"The archivist said he'd be here until three."

"He left an hour ago."

I peeked into the reading room. The place was empty. Even impoverished intellectuals had better places to be on a summer afternoon. Then, at the filing closet in the back of the room, I spotted the stoop-shouldered archivist's assistant. "Hey, remember me!" I waved my hand in his peripheral vision. The man turned his head slowly, reluctantly. I took my cue to approach. "I submitted some documents to you regarding my parents' files."

"You're the one from America."

"That's right."

He sized me up with his falcon eyes. "I filed your request," he said.

"Oh, good."

"The personnel will search for it in one of our warehouses. It takes time."

"How long?" I said, trying not to wince at my own infantile tone.

"Who knows? A week. Two."

"But I'm leaving Tuesday," I pleaded.

He considered this. "Have you got someone here who can pick them up for you?"

I paused. I did, of course, have someone, but I was reluctant to have Lenny collect the files on my behalf. Who knew what he'd find in them?

"What if I do?" I said.

"I can give you a form to authorize the receiver. But, mind you, there's photocopying fees."

"How much?"

He gave me the price in rubles. It came to almost fifty cents a page.

"How many pages are in a typical dossier?"

He shrugged. "Could be two hundred. Could be six hundred. Depends on the type of crime."

Now it was my turn to look at him askance. You couldn't move sideways in this city without somebody trying to extort you. I asked him for the necessary forms.

Outside, I stood in the haze of the late afternoon watching as the guard dead-bolted the doors, slamming shut the vault holding my parents' deeds and misdeeds, the repository of my unanswered questions. A tuft of poplar floated into my face. More were tumbling down the sidewalk, plugging the gutters. I began to tramp back uphill. The air felt ionized, barometrically moody. I glanced up and saw that the clouds were curdling, trapping in the remaining daylight. *What are you terrified of?* I thought. That my own son would know the truth about his family? Or know more than I do? Lenny had been nineteen when my mother passed away. He was the only one in the family that Florence had loved with a self-forgetting passion; she spent whole weekends with him after we came to America, something she'd rarely done with Masha, my oldest. Lenny adored Florence, and even into his adulthood continued to harbor certain bizarre romantic notions about the "free-spirited" way she'd lived her life. Though now, recalling the kind of inane advice my mother used to give him—"You shouldn't be too practical in this life," "Leave the thinking to your heart, you'll get fewer headaches"—I wasn't entirely sure that some part of me didn't want to puncture a hole in my son's inflated image of her. "What the hell, we're all grown-ups," I said to no one and took my phone out of my jacket.

After six rings, the call went to Lenny's message service. I tried again. This time it went straight to voice mail. I waited for the beep. "It's me," I said into the electronic silence. "How about an early dinner? Your pick. There's something I want to talk to you about. A favor."

I glanced up once more at the inscrutable sky, then scrolled on my phone until I found the number for Lenny's apartment. The line was busy. I tried again, and this time it trilled twice before a feverish, wet-sounding female voice answered, "About time, where are you?"

"Katya?" I said unsurely.

"Who's this?" It wasn't a question but a demand, though one made in a thin, suspicious tone.

"Yuliy Leontevich. Can I speak to Lenny?"

The voice on the other end seemed to collapse into a distraught incoherence. "Oh, Yuliy Leontevich, oh God, Lenny's not here. They took him an hour ago. I've been calling everyone."

"Slow down, darling. Who took him?"

"Those guys. From the MVD, the Ministry of the Interior. That's what they said. They gave him the paper. They said they were charging him with defrauding the shareholders of some plant in . . . oh, I can't remember. Then they took him." Her voice was trembling on the verge of unintelligibility.

"Where, Katya? Where did they take him?" I was already jogging to the corner, my index finger extending into the street.

"They wouldn't let me go with him. They said they were heading to Holding Facility Nine. In the Kapotnya District, I think. Oh, it's all nonsense. I know it's all to do with those bitches he calls his friends."

At last, a battered blue Lada screeched up to the curb. "Don't go anywhere," I told Katya. "I'm coming over."

27.

LIFE ON THE MISSISSIPPI

Moscow, 1939

LIFE AT THE INSTITUTE OF PHILOLOGY, HISTORY, AND LITERATURE WAS
indeed an improvement over cleaning toilets. Florence's paperwork was
carried out with surprising swiftness, and by fall she was teaching two
classes of intermediate English to undergraduates so deferential and earnest that they rendered her past two years of subservience a forgettable
intermission. The institute was composed of a modest cluster of five-story
buildings. Inside, it was full of crowded landings and noisy halls that reminded Florence of her own student days, with the critical difference
being that she now stood at a distance from all that colliding, permanent
motion.

There had been no need to struggle at composing a curriculum; it was
composed for her. The syllabus consisted of grammar books and approved
authors such as Mark Twain and Upton Sinclair, who stood on the correct
side of the crude classification that divided all Western writers into pro-
gressives and reactionaries. She would have loved to show her brighter
students a paragraph of the Yeats or D. H. Lawrence she'd adored in her
youth. But even if their books had been obtainable, the presence of such
decadent obscurantists on her syllabus would have cost her her job. It was
a relief to be spared such decisions. Teaching a foreign language, one
could remain insulated from the hostile intrigues that ulcerated in other
departments, where professors accused one another of being old-guardists
and reactionary formalists. During Florence's first semester, a professor at

the institute was forced to leave her post after her book received savage reviews in *Izvestia* for its "fetishistic use of aesthetic devices." Not long thereafter, another article came out in the same newspaper *praising* the book. And, just as suddenly, she was reinstated, with her colleagues resuming friendly relations as though nothing had happened. It was not at all clear to Florence what *had* happened—whether the professor had finally repudiated her errors or had simply been the beneficiary of a sudden reversal in policy. Florence had long given up trying to understand the logic of these turnabouts.

Every so often, she met Valda for lunch, but their teaching schedules rarely coincided, and Florence was just as happy to remain aloof from the other faculty members, fearful of entangling herself in any political fray that might toss her pitifully back on her knees, scrubbing footprints off carpets.

One day, toward the end of her first term, the vice-rector called Florence into his office and suggested she raise the grades of several of the working-class students who were members of the Komsomol. There had been complaints, she was informed, about her teaching method after a series of low exam scores.

Watching the rector's beard and mustache twitch around his moving mouth, Florence could feel her skin breaking out in allergic distress. All year she'd applied herself fastidiously to her duties, knowing one mistake could cost her. "I warned the students that from now on a portion of their lectures would be conducted in English," she protested contritely. "I go slowly, but if some of them still don't have a basic grasp of the grammar, perhaps they shouldn't be at this level."

"Maybe they should not be. But . . . ah, allowances must be made, Flora Solomonovna. This is about correcting the injustices that came before. Not all students have had the same opportunities and privileges." The vice-rector seemed to bear her no ill-will. His beard, tinged yellow from pipe smoke, had a stale, benevolent smell. She left his office promising to help the slower students.

This proved easier in theory than in practice. One pupil in particular, who Florence suspected was the one behind her summons, was a tall, horsily pretty girl named Yulia Larina—a shortcut taker who openly fell asleep in class after exhausting herself at Komsomol meetings and parade rallies. Following the vice-rector's directive, Florence gave Yulia her last poor dictation with all the corrections written out carefully to help the girl grasp her errors. "There will be a makeup dictation tomorrow after classes," she suggested. "You will come here to take it, and if you do better on that one, I'll replace your grade." But instead of gratitude, the girl offered her only a look of rude boredom. "I have a newspaper meeting tomorrow after class."

"Then come after that; I will wait."

"After that, I have to go home and cook dinner. I have two younger brothers. Our mother works two shifts." In each of these excuses Florence could sense a suppressed but perceptible challenge. It was clear that Yulia had no intention of redoing this dictation, or any other. She expected Florence to raise her grade simply because of her good standing with the administration.

"You're not the only student with competing priorities," said Florence. But the following afternoon, she was not sure she'd handled things well. Teachers were little more than university servants, a fact that operators like Yulia intuitively grasped. And so it was no surprise that the next day, in her lecture, Florence lost her nerve.

Among the approved texts for her course she had discovered an excerpt from Mark Twain's *Life on the Mississippi* that she was shocked she'd never read before. In it, Twain described the Mississippi River two times: first with the eyes of his youth, as a boy overcome by the river's colossal beauty, and later with the gaze of a seasoned skipper who knew that a golden sunset portended high morning winds, and that graceful ripples in the tide were messengers of mortal hazards. "No, the romance and the beauty were all gone from the river. All the value any feature of it had for me now was the amount of usefulness it could furnish toward compassing the safe piloting of a steamboat." Like a fisherman's hand, the words had grabbed her with a cold, euphoric shiver. The country she'd come to six years earlier—once so romantic and full of possibility—had become for her full of perilous signals.

Florence felt safe in the understanding that her students were unlikely to draw this connection. But she hoped that, with her help, they might still be touched by the words, enough to contemplate that the optimistic certainty stamped on their faces might one day give way to other forms of knowledge.

"What do you think Twain is really talking about?" she asked them the next afternoon, letting her gaze drift from one set of obedient eyes to another. A pale, literal-minded young man named Alexei raised his hand in the front row. "He is disenchanted with the river because it's made him lose his eye for beauty."

"Has it really, though?" She tilted her head as she smiled.

"The quest for knowledge comes with a cost?" murmured a tiny, serious girl Florence had come to think of as "Little Brontë."

"That's very good." Again, Florence looked about encouragingly, waiting for lights to go on in other eyes.

A voice came from the back. "Twain is nostalgic for his own ignorance." Florence knew this voice well, though she'd never before heard Yulia volunteer an answer. "It's just anti-progressive, reactionary romanticism," said the girl, with her usual pointed indifference. Of all the remarks, this was, oddly enough, the most cogent exegesis on the essay so far, enough to confirm for Florence that Yulia's lackluster work had little to do with her intelligence.

"So you don't agree that Mark Twain feels he has lost something unique with his new knowledge?"

The other students watched Yulia alertly now. Even Florence could feel her own face contorting into an appeasing grimace, as if to reassure the girl that her view was as welcome as the others'. Only, the "view" Yulia had to offer was hardly her own: "Writers have to depict life in its revolutionary development," she said confidently, and left it at that. It wasn't an opinion so much as an incantation—specifically, of Zhdanov's official statement from the Soviet Writers Congress of '34. It was a Commandment of a Revealed Truth, and the other students, Florence observed nervously, were all nodding along with it in repentant agreement, as though Yulia were Moses stepping down from Sinai, and they, the shamefaced Hebrews who'd forgotten the Law in their moment of pantheistic abandon. Florence could feel her own advantage slipping. She knew that if she didn't turn things around, she too would be going the way of the golden calf. "And, indeed, Twain spent his life doing just that," she said with smooth elision. "He was a revolutionist not only as a writer of stories, but as an anti-imperialist campaigner and a speaker." And soon Florence found herself launching into a lengthy disquisition on Twain's attacks on organized religion, his critique of slavery, and even his swipes at monarchy through the figures of satiric characters like the duke and the king—

drawing from the information she had read in the institute-approved *Introduction to English Authors*. And she continued in this vein even as class time ran out and the bell rang, adding bits and pieces of her own knowledge, about Twain's rage over America's brutal imperialist seizure of the Philippines, while her students, looking around with shy embarrassment, packed up their notebooks. "Our final dictation will be next week. Those of you who plan to make up previous ones should see me after class," she called with ear-splitting congeniality as they filed out. But Yulia was not among those who lingered to take advantage of this indulgence.

After everything was over and she was left alone, Florence continued to reassure herself that she had handled the situation adroitly. She'd had the good sense to know that to argue with Yulia (whose great rhetorical talent, it seemed, lay in uttering with diabolical timing anything that would put her at an ideological advantage) would have been to play into her snare. Why, then, was her mouth still sour from the anxious way she'd affirmed a point opposite from the one she believed? She could taste the acetic juices of her own fear. She'd come to class hoping to make her students conscious of the more mysterious, philosophical musings of Twain's essay and had succeeded in turning him into just another propagandist. She didn't know if she felt worse about abandoning Twain or abandoning her own courage. Florence sat in the small teachers' lounge with Yulia's error-riddled dictation in front of her. She had not imagined in the vice-rector's office how keenly it would offend her sense of fairness, how supremely painful such a minor capitulation, to have to let this Komsomol bitch off the hook.

The lounge around her resembled nothing so much as a kitchen, with two regular wooden tables, a hand-washing sink, and a couple of ratty armchairs facing a window that looked onto the institute's inner courtyard. Here teachers came to smoke and read between classes, eager to get away from the incessant attention of their students and possibly to get away from another kind of unrelenting gaze—the lounge, being a not quite official space, was the only room unadorned with a portrait of their Great Leader. At the neighboring table, scratching his disheveled balding pate and rubbing his fleshy cheeks, sat Boris Rechok, a professor in the history department. His briefcase, as untidy as his head, was spilling over with papers he seemed to have no interest in straightening. He was distracted by an article in the day's *Pravda*, turning the pages back and forth with a petulance so flamboyant that it had started to distract Florence from the squalid comforts of her own resentment. "Now we're selling them wheat to feed the armies they'll use to attack us!" Rechok muttered loudly to no one. "And they're selling *us* the metal for the shrapnel we'll use to shoot them in the back. Whose genius idea is this?" He looked at Florence and shook his head at the insanity of the new expanded trade policy with Germany, as if importuning some sort of response. Florence pretended not to hear him. She'd seen the same look of confusion and alarm on Leon's face when he'd read about the new protocol of friendliness toward Hitler. "All of Europe blockading Germany, and Russia is sending it provisions. Fifty tons of wheat, rubber, petroleum, a year after the Soviet army is purged of its own suspected fascists!"

"Is a good war better than a bad peace?" she'd asked him in their room, and he'd looked at her strangely. Did she care nothing for what the Germans were doing to the Jews?

But did he really believe those rumors were true?

"How can *you* believe they aren't? When someone says they want to wipe out our people, you can take them at their word." *Our people.* It was the first time she'd heard him use those words. Even in the semi-private confines of their apartment, they unsettled her.

And here, in the open, was Boris Rechok, inquiring out loud: "What am I supposed to get up and tell the students? First historic enemies, now historic friends! Today the dog's a Rottweiler, tomorrow he's a poodle?"

This time, it was harder to ignore him. They weren't alone anymore. Two professors from the faculty of literature—Belkova and Danilova—had strolled into the lounge. Whatever the women were discussing was abruptly aborted at the sound of Rechok's fulminations. Belkova threw the old man a disapproving look he was too preoccupied to notice, then retreated with her colleague to the rear of the lounge to crack open a casement window and light cigarettes. Rechok was still quietly erupting over the new deal with Germany, but Florence was no longer listening to him, eavesdropping instead on Belkova, who was rendering her own tart judgments, albeit on a milder topic—an uninspired performance she'd seen at the theater. Florence listened just long enough to decipher whether the theater in question was the one where she'd worked (it was not), before deciding to pack up her papers and nurse her worries somewhere more solitary.

She might have gone on indulging her preoccupations with Yulia Larina well into the night had something unexpected not happened that evening to replace them.

"You're wanted on the phone," her dyspeptic neighbor announced
from the hall after dinner, before returning to a squatting position on his
shoe-shine stool.

The receiver still smelled of polish when she took hold of it. "Flora
Fein?" said a man's voice.

"Yes. Who's this?"

"We'd like to speak to you about your exit-visa application."

In the stale-smelling hallway the polish fumes were suddenly making
her dizzy. She wondered if she'd heard correctly. She cupped her hand over
the receiver. "Are you calling from the OVIR?"

But the voice at the other end answered smartly, "Come to this address
tomorrow at four, after your classes."

Florence's fingers fumbled for the red pencil she'd dropped in her dress
pocket, and then sought blindly for a scrap of paper among the slips tucked
behind the telephone. She scratched down the street and house number
on the back of a butcher's receipt. "What department did you say this
was?" But whoever had called had already hung up.

"Who was that?" Leon asked when she reentered their room, where he
was clearing the desk for their dinner.

"I'm not sure. . . ." But a buried part of her mind grasped who might
be requesting her presence. "No one important," she said. "Just a secretary from the institute. They're rearranging the exam times again."

THE ADDRESS AT WHICH Florence had been instructed to appear lay on a
quiet patch of streets just inside the inner loop of the Moscow Canal. In
the rapidly dimming light an aura of Tolstoy's genteel Moscow hovered
over the pastel-painted houses and gated courtyards. She searched for the
correct number in the murky light of streetlamps, wary of asking for help.

She told herself that it was best, for now, that Leon didn't know where
she was. Three years had passed since that day she'd attempted to gain
access to the U.S. Embassy (the whole plaza, not to mention the country,
was now sealed off). Leon had been enraged at the risk she'd taken, so

really there had been no point in telling him about her other trip to OVIR to seek a visa to leave the country. Now, as before, she fortified herself with the knowledge that, as long as she kept Leon out of it, he would not need to be "responsible for her" if something unpleasant happened. Had she told him about the mysterious phone call, he would have undermined her plan, convinced her that it was a trap, and turned her hope into torment and worry. And she *did* have hope, a galvanizing hope, even now, after years of half wishing that her foolhardy application had been lost or forgotten. On the wings of this hope she kept her eyes open for the right address, even as another part of her knew perfectly well that the building she was looking for was nowhere near the vicinity of a visa office, or, for that matter, any official government building.

It was a man who came to the door. The first thing Florence noticed about him was his polished black shoes, immaculate despite the slushy weather. Only after she'd followed them into the apartment did Florence take note of the rest of him: an egg-shaped head with side-parted hair presenting a pair of small, precise ears. He looked to be in his thirties, as well groomed as his oxfords, with a set of facial features worked into such a fine alignment that they might have looked effeminate were it not for his stubble and his flat, autocratic mouth.

He introduced himself unceremoniously as Comrade Subotin. The living room to which Subotin led her was, like him, neat and spare, with a touch of the bourgeois. Old-fashioned lace curtains covered the windows, and a lace runner bisected the oval table, anchored there by a potbellied samovar from which Florence half-expected Subotin to offer her tea. He did not. Instead, he moved to the oblong end of the table, where a portfolio of papers lay, evidently in preparation for their meeting. He told Florence to sit. If she had had the composure to do anything other than oblige Comrade Subotin's request, Florence might have noticed, as she would on subsequent visits, the absence of slippers or coats, or books on the shelves—indeed, of any signs of actual habitation.

Hitching the creases of his trousers and taking the seat across from her, Comrade Subotin held up a piece of paper for Florence to examine. It was the visa application she'd filled out at OVIR three years earlier. "Let's take a look at this." He spoke politely but not warmly. "It appears that you did not fully complete your application."

Subotin's hand held a silver fountain pen. "Place of employment," he read aloud. "Here it says the Central State Bank, but in fact you are on staff at the Institute of Philology, History, and Literature."

"Yes, but I wasn't working there at the time I filled out this form."

"But you are now, are you not? Then let's write that down."

Florence followed the movement of his pen as it formed neat, slanted words on a clean form.

"Name of spouse . . . You wrote nothing, but, if I'm not mistaken, you are married."

"We are not registered . . . I mean, officially."

"And yet you've been living together with him for more than four years, which constitutes a civil marriage according to Soviet law. Shall we fill that out?" He repeated the question: "Name of spouse."

Florence could feel a constriction in her chest, the weight of a lead spade where her lungs were supposed to be. She had been foolish enough to hope that whatever she was walking into would affect no one but herself. Now the truth was catching up with her at the speed of her galloping heartbeat. She cast her eyes to the window, its dark mirror obstructed by colorless lace. Had Leon been right—that, as long as she'd worked as a janitress and kept to herself, nobody would have reason to bother her? Now *they* had summoned her. And they knew everything. "Leon Brink," she said.

"Patronym."

"Naumovich."

She tried to steady her pulse with shallow breaths. Subotin continued to fill out the form with his careful hand. Without looking up, he said: "I want to remind you where you are. If you provide the NKVD with inaccurate or incomplete information, you are committing treason, punishable by the full force of the law. It is similarly treasonous for a Soviet citizen to attempt to flee her homeland."

She was tempted to say that whatever jurisdictional alchemy had magically transformed her into a "Soviet citizen" was itself most certainly illegal. Instead, she said: "Are *you* suggesting I was trying to flee my homeland? I went to OVIR openly and filled out a visa application to visit my family, whom I have not seen in six years. All of this I did in broad daylight."

But Subotin's immobile face suggested he was neither convinced nor impressed by this. "And yet," he said, still not looking up, "you neglected to mention that you had a husband."

Florence was silent.

"You *claim* you intended to visit your family. But that is for *us* to decide. Maybe you are intending to go to America to divulge confidential state secrets to its imperialist government?"

"Forgive me, Comrade Subotin. What secrets could I possibly have? I have never been entrusted with any. I am not a Party member."

"Let's not playact, shall we? You worked for the Soviet State Bank for several years, and have knowledge about its methods of obtaining funds, and its other operations. You and I both know that this kind of information has tremendous value to our enemies."

Subotin's smile made a sharp crease around his nose. He obviously did not care about the State Bank and its secrets. Anything could be a state secret. He was simply letting her know that it was not his job to prove her guilt, but hers to demonstrate her innocence. "Economic espionage, no less than fleeing, is a capital offense."

It was important, above all else, to maintain the appearance of calm, of composure and imperturbability. "If you believe I intended to give away state secrets, why have you not arrested me yet?"

"You know where you are, and I have no intention of playing games with you. When we arrest someone we have more than enough evidence. You are here because we would like to give you the benefit of the doubt, and perhaps an opportunity to visit your family in America, after all. Naturally, if we send you, at the state's expense, you will be obliged to do some work for *us*. We hope that as a loyal citizen this is something you could do sincerely."

As the buzzing of his threats faded from her head, an earlier hope started to beat in Florence's chest. Could it be possible? They wanted to send her to America! Why not? She'd never hidden anything from the state; the NKVD had nothing to hang over her. If anything, *she* was valuable to *them*. Of course it was only logical that if they were going to send her to the United States it would be as part of a secret mission of some sort. If that's how it was going to go, she would be ready. "I understand," she said with new solemnity.

"We need to have the highest level of trust in those we send out of the country. To be sure we're dealing with reliable people. Naturally, it is up to you to prove your reliability."

She moistened the roof of her mouth. What did "proving" her reliability entail? Did they intend to give her an immediate assignment? Was this why she had been brought here?

"We need to know, first and foremost, the names of your friends and colleagues, anybody with whom you have regular contact." Subotin ran a delicate finger down the crease of his notebook and tore out a clean sheet. "On the right side, please list any foreign-born acquaintances you and your husband have. On the left side, list any colleagues or acquaintances at the Institute of Philology, History, and Literature." He pushed his fountain pen closer to her.

Rapidly, Florence made a list of everyone she ran into in the course of a day, then wrote a shorter list of those she and Leon knew socially. She had to write quickly because it was important not to think too hard about what she was doing. She took comfort in the idea that the NKVD probably knew with whom she worked and socialized by now anyway. How else had Subotin known when her classes ended? Very well, she'd show them she had nothing to hide. Soon enough they would learn on their own that she had nothing to report, either. In the meantime, she was attesting to her honesty. Still, none of this rationalizing could account for her total absence of shame. And this, she suspected, could only be because some part of her knew why she was doing it. The very sound of the word "America" had gone clean to the tender root of her homesick heart.

Florence slid the paper back toward Subotin and watched him read it. Briefly, she let herself study his face. It was at once handsome and unpleasant. She had the feeling she had seen it before. He slipped the silver pen into his vest pocket and rose from his seat, giving her license to do the same. "You will report here again in exactly three weeks," he said. "I don't need to tell you that you will keep these meetings to yourself."

Outside, early evening had descended. Naked tree limbs twisted in the moist, iodine-colored air. The tram, overcrowded on the way to her meeting with Subotin, was now peopled only by a few pale and listless passengers with bundles at their feet. The bumping trolley jerked her empty stomach as she tried to tell herself that she'd acquitted herself well with Subotin.

Still she could not erase the mental picture of his face, those meticulous features and the narrow build all tugging at some unsettling memory. It wasn't until her trolley crossed the bridge over the Moscow River and was heading toward Manezh Square, beyond which the fortress of the U.S. Embassy stood, as impenetrable as it had been on the fateful day when she'd tried to get past its gates—not until then did Florence's mind come into focus on the memory of the man in owl-framed glasses who'd stood on the sidewalk in front of the Hotel National, watching her as she crossed Gorky Street with the egregious confidence of an American.

28.

A DIGNIFIED EXIT

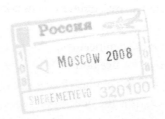

A TASSELED CROSS SWUNG GENTLY FROM THE CABBIE'S MIRROR AS I rode to the detention center where they held my son. Outside, cold summer rain lashed the high-rises that passed us at halting, rush-hour speeds. We were in Kapotnya, in the southeast. Here the building materials were no longer marble and limestone but cinder block and concrete. The naked apartment blocks were anonymous yet familiar; the neighborhood was shorn of all identifying marks save the silos of the local power plant that puffed white sulfur smoke into the rain-darkened sky.

An hour earlier I'd left the cab to wait while I'd run up to Lenny's apartment. With her damp ponytail and smudged mascara, Katya had looked like a lost adolescent, though part of this impression was due to the expensive-looking orthodontia in her mouth (another improvement I suspected Lenny was bankrolling). I hadn't been able to get a complete story out of her, other than that the MVD had spontaneously arrived to detain Lenny over some financial impiety that he'd been only circumstantially connected with two years earlier. Katya, for her part, seemed convinced that Lenny was the victim of a fiendish conspiracy orchestrated by his so-called friends (those *suki*) to take the fall for some nefarious Ponzi-ish maneuver they themselves had managed to dodge. Between the loud percussion of the rain on the roof and Katya's sobs, I could not make heads or tails of her story.

The air inside the jail reception area smelled fermented, suggesting that the place also doubled as a sobering-up station for the local street sludge. I gave my documents to a *militzia* guard and was led through a narrow corridor to an empty room painted hepatitic green. The *militzia* man made me wait for half an hour before he brought Lenny in and ceremoniously uncuffed him.

Lenny's skin was patched with blotches. He smelled, implausibly, of tobacco. "You've been smoking?"

"They've stuffed me in with some skinhead they picked up for harassing Tajik girls on the street. He's always lighting up. I can't fucking breathe in there."

"You look like mincemeat," I said. "How long have you been in here?"

"Four, maybe five hours." He showed me his naked wrists. "They took my watch and my phone. Have you called Mom already?"

"Not yet. How the hell did you get yourself in here?"

"Oh, you think I did this to myself?"

"Did I say that?"

"But it's what you're thinking."

"Just tell me what's happened." I tried to speak at a discreet volume.

"We don't have to whisper, damn it, since I didn't *do* anything." Lenny tossed a challenging look at the guard standing inside the door, who stayed as stoic as a eunuch. As he recited the accusations against him to me in his sour breath, I was unnerved by his supercilious calm, as if he were rolling his eyes at each one of them. It seemed that two years earlier he'd served as one of the brokers on a business deal between an obscure European growth fund and a nickel plant in the southern Urals. After the growth fund had completed its purchase of the factory, it had issued a series of specious bonds backed by the nickel plant but without, it later emerged, the knowledge of the plant's board members. By then most of the bonds had been cashed, bankrupting the plant. A criminal investigation was opened. Old news, said Lenny. The growth fund's managers—Russians with foreign passports—were charged with fraud. Lenny's firm, being only a second-string agent in the dark about their clients' criminal intent, was let off without charge. "It was an ordinary buyout," he said. "All we did was standard analysis. Nobody at Abacus Group had any connection to anything that happened later. Now someone's decided to dig it up again."

I didn't know what to say. "Did someone at your firm get stingy, forget to pay off the right people?"

"Fuck if I know."

Listening to him, I felt sick with despair. It was the second time today I was at, or near, a prison. The street signs changed in this city, but apparently little else. "Have you been charged with anything?" No sooner had I spoken these words than it struck me how hopelessly stupid I sounded to myself.

"No, just 'detained.' "

"What does that mean? How long can they keep you here?"

"A prosecutor is supposed to come in the morning to question me."

"They're planning to keep you here over*night?*" The thought of Lenny having to spend the night in a grim tubercular cell made me so light-headed with anxiety that I had to shut my eyes.

"Trust me, I'm not looking forward to it. I've just spent the past four hours avoiding a guy who's got a manhole cover tattooed on his shaved head, like maybe he wants someone to open it and be impressed by the elaborate sewer system inside."

"You need a lawyer," I said, a bit too frantically. "You can't talk to some apparatchik prosecutor without a lawyer." But Lenny was two steps ahead of me. "I've already told Katya to call Austin. He's getting me a lawyer in the morning."

"You trust those guys? Katya says they're the reason you're in this mess."

"Who else am I supposed to call?" Lenny almost shouted, awakening our eunuch guard.

"I have to call your mother," I said, checking my watch. "It's not even past one at home; there's still time to call around the firms and find you someone good, an American who focuses on this sort of thing."

"Don't you dare."

"This is serious stuff, Lenny."

"Don't call *her.* Call around yourself if you must, but don't get Mom involved or I'll never hear the end of it."

I said nothing.

His eyes surveyed me with grinning suspicion. "I can see what you're thinking—that I got myself into this fucking mess."

"I think no such thing."

"You do. Like maybe I didn't do it intentionally, but by trying to take some shortcut. Isn't that what you tell Mom—that I'm a 'corner cutter'?"

His voice swelled with something almost like satisfaction at forcing me into an acknowledgment of this exquisitely miserable view of him.

But he was wrong about me in one respect: I *did* believe him when he said he'd landed here through no misconduct of his own. What I faulted him for—though I could hardly admit this to Lenny—was the same thing I faulted Mama for: neither of them seemed to have the foggiest idea of how to protect themselves in this country.

"We'll come up with something," I said, though I had no idea what this might be. "I'll be back tomorrow," I told him. "Please, don't open your mouth until then."

Our hooligan-faced young warden was at the gate again, telling us visiting time was over.

Lenny nodded distantly, without commitment, at what I'd just said.

"Please," I pleaded a final time before I was led out.

I SPENT MOST OF THE NIGHT calling various law firms in New York and Washington, writing down names of attorneys who weren't able to take a phone appointment with me until the following day, abandoning myself to this pointless task even as I knew that the "law" had nothing to do with the predicament Lenny was in. What we were dealing with was a simple hostage situation, for which a suitable ransom would have to be worked out sooner or later, perhaps with the intervention of a local negotiator. But where to find a negotiator with enough pull? The answer came the next morning at L-Pet's offices, where, with my eyes desiccated and my head pulsing, I entered in a sleepwalking state and, approaching the conference table, almost spilled coffee on Kablukov, seated in the chair beside mine. "Ivan Matveyevich? You're back so soon," I said.

"Forty-eight hours is quite enough time in Tallin." He spoke in his usual hoarse, semi-bored voice. "And it sounds like there's pressing business to be done here. I hear you've been keeping my lieutenants on their toes."

I painted a grin on my tired face and said we were all trying to choose the best contractor we could.

"I hope all this nonsense hasn't so tied you up that you've neglected to spend time with your son," Kablukov said.

At the mention of Lenny I felt my coffee turn into indigestible sludge in my gut. I could see the desolation on my face reflected in Kablukov's Ray-Bans, and then in the concerned knit of his brows. "You don't look well."

"I could be better," I said, trying to prepare a proper introduction of my request.

"These tedious meetings can give anyone an ulcer. That's why I steer clear."

"The meetings don't bother me, Ivan Matveyevich. It's my son. He's presently sitting in a police station in Kapotnya. There've been some reckless complaints against a firm he worked for—an unfortunate mix-up—some financial delinquency Lenny really has no connection to."

Kablukov removed his sunglasses and rubbed the wide bridge of his nose. "That does sound quite serious." He frowned in sympathy. "Our judiciary system can be . . . careless sometimes."

"You understand. I don't know if Lenny quite understands what he was mixed up in. I'm looking for an *advokat* who can clear this up." My suggestion to find a good lawyer provoked a not unexpected smirk on the old recidivist's face.

"A good *advokat* is worth his weight in gold, certainly. But if one can manage with more informal means of persuasion . . ."

"I'm not opposed to that," I hinted.

"I find it's wise to give one's adversaries a more dignified exit. . . ."

"I feel awkward even bringing this up," I said disingenuously.

"Nonsense. We have quite reliable counsel here at L-Pet, of course. We can place a few phone calls to the Ministry of the Interior. Where did you say they were keeping your son?"

I told him the number of the facility, quickly adding, "But it's not company business."

He took my demurral with a knowing smile.

Our meeting was starting, and I watched nervously through the glass doors as the Boot excused himself to make the phone calls on my behalf. No one besides me seemed to notice his extended absence. My already abraded nerves, in the meantime, were so jittery that I struggled to follow Steve McGinnis's presentation of the work being done on our Varandey terminal. His descriptions of the construction were exhaustingly informative, and to keep them filed in my head seemed a task more Sisyphean than trying to convince myself that Kablukov was intervening on Lenny's behalf out of some fundamental human kindness or charity. No, in my heart

I knew some recompense would be in order. And at this particular moment I did not care; I thought only of Lenny in his cell. Had he been fed? Could he use a toilet? Or were they, as in the old days, making him do his business in a metal pan in the corner?

My grim reveries must have lasted a full hour, or until my phone began buzzing wildly in my jacket. To my spontaneous relief, it was Lenny. I took the call in the hallway, where Kablukov was still nowhere to be found. "I've been released," he informed me with only a slight inflection of pleasure.

"I'll come pick you up," I said.

"Don't worry about that—just come to the apartment."

WHEN I ARRIVED A HALF-HOUR LATER, excusing myself from the meeting on a plea of stomach pain, I found Lenny pacing the living room with a cordless phone in hand. His hair looked greasy, and his eyes, no less bloodshot than mine, were battling sleep with the psychotic mania of the unmedicated. "Don't tell me you don't know anything about it," he was saying loudly into the phone. ". . . Well, you can tell *Ah-lex* I'm not done with *him*. He wants to sell me down this river, I'll pull him into the sewage creek with me—are you listening?" Cradling the phone with his shoulder, Lenny proceeded to the kitchen, where I followed him; he resumed stirring the contents of an enamel pot on the stove. He was still on the phone, telling whatever friend or colleague was on the other end not to blow smoke up his ass, even as he leaned forward with a wooden spoon and took a delicate taste of the pot's contents. He caught my eye and shook his head at the absurdity of it all. The sly, exasperated look tossed my way made me wonder if he really was as outraged as he'd seemed when I'd first walked in, or if this whole display—the tough, manly talk as he unflappably stirred his *alfredo*—was performed for my benefit.

"Did the prosecutor ever come?" I asked once he set the phone on the counter.

"Some *babka* showed up from the prosecutor's office. Clicking heels and a powerbun, full of righteous talk about pilferers like me fleecing 'the people.' I said: Lady, what exactly am I being charged with here?"

"Did she have an answer?"

"She said, 'We have our ways of dealing with abettors of fraud,' and told me I better get used to seeing a lot of her. Two hours later I'm sitting in the same room when the guard opens the door and says I'm free to go. Gives me back my phone and my stuff like nuthin'."

"Did a lawyer show up?"

"No, Austin never sent one over!"

I hesitated. "And no one else came—?"

He cast me a perplexed look. "Who else would come?"

"I don't know." Was it possible Kablukov really had cleared it all up with a mere phone call?

"I've already told you—they have no case," he said conclusively. He set the pot of pasta on the table by the window, where I'd settled myself in preparation for the explanation I planned to give him: that I had intervened and that he still wasn't out of the woods. But in his mania, Lenny seemed unconscious of me again. "Jeez, I stink," he said, taking a strong whiff of himself, and headed for the shower.

I could hear him humming triumphantly under the pummeling water as I searched his fridge for something with which to fix us a more complete lunch. There was hardly anything in it—some bologna and cheese, some wilting tomatoes, grapes going fuzzy with mold, and plenty of beer. At its emptiness I felt an uptick of hope that maybe Katya had moved out after all. In my eagerness to see Lenny, I'd forgotten to ask where she was.

Lenny's kitchen windows were abnormally large for a Russian dwelling; his apartment was in one of the new high-rises on Novy Arbat, whose broad sidewalks, nine stories below me, were adorned with signs for nightclubs and casinos, their neon lights shut off during the day. It seemed fitting that Lenny would perch his nest here—an elevator's distance from the ground zero of fun. I fixed us bologna sandwiches, set the teakettle to boil, and gazed out toward Kudrinskaya Square. Out there, just a few blocks north, still lived our old family friend Ludmila Ostrovsky. I wondered if Lenny ever saw her. She had, after all, once been his mother-in-law. I knew it was unfair of me to persist, so many years later, in connecting Lenny's troubles with the Ostrovskys, but the pathway was, for better or worse, soldered into my mental circuitry. In 1996, Lenny had taken a break from the crushing dullness of his post-college job as a junior business consultant for Arthur Andersen by venturing on a short vacation to the "new" Moscow. And this was when our problems with him really got off the ground. Ludmila, having lost her husband a year earlier to a heart attack, offered Lenny a spare room in her apartment. The room came with an added bonus: her twenty-three-year-old daughter, Irina, would serve as Lenny's guide to the city of his childhood.

Our friendship with the Ostrovskys went back many years—to a time when little Lenny and little Irochka employed her father's old blood-pressure cuff to play doctor on the Ostrovskys' Lithuanian carpet. In '79, we'd stayed in Russia just long enough to witness six-year-old Irina bud into a musical prodigy, displaying her talents on the violin with impromptu chair-top performances to the accompaniment of her mother shouting "More bow!" as the little girl sawed away. In subsequent years, we would learn through letters and phone calls that this early achievement was followed by a string of others, including prizes not only in violin, but also in ice-skating, citywide mathematics competitions, and English. All the talk of Irochka's prodigious talents had led Lenny to remark, before he'd left for his vacation, that he expected to find in Moscow not a girl but a well-trained circus animal. And so Lucya and I were pleased when Lenny reported back that Ludmila's daughter, in spite of her sweatshop childhood, seemed quite "well adjusted," and "not terribly annoying." That year was marked by several perplexing return trips to Moscow and many expensive transatlantic phone calls that concluded with Lenny's announcement that Irina would soon be arriving in the United States on a fiancée visa so the two of them could get married.

It wasn't like I thought that goofy grin on Lenny's face was a result of all those visits he'd made to the Tretyakov Gallery, not like I had no clue about the singular charms of Moscow's girls. But *marriage?* Still, I'd be lying if I said I completely disapproved of this union. Maybe it was the push Lenny needed. And how could I object to Irochka, who, besides being as pretty as a picture, was also mature, impressive, and clever? Impressive enough, apparently, to make Lucya question the virtue of her motives. Not that our son's motives were so virtuous, I reminded her. He was beside himself with his windfall, telling his friends, "A girl like that wouldn't *talk* to me here. A girl like that wouldn't piss on my face if it was on fire." This was Lenny-speak for being in love. In love, and full of hallucinatory visions of childhood nostalgia, though it was plain to see that the girl who bore the weight of all his rapture was, even in her plain jeans and cotton sweater, far more sophisticated and shrewd than our son. For all her wholesome Young Pioneer exuberance, Irina was no kid. In that two-room

flat she shared with her mother, she had lived through a decade of up-
heavals no less disturbing than the American sixties; had watched her father drop dead of a stress-induced infarction and seen her mother go from
Gosplan economist to "redundant state employee" with a vanished pension in a matter of weeks. This would go some way to explaining why, in
1996, while Ludmila was embarking on a late-stage career as an accoun-
tant doctoring the books at a telecom start-up, Irochka was quietly at
work seducing our son on the same Lithuanian carpet where the two of
them had played as children.

Not long after she arrived, it became obvious to me and Lucya that
Irochka had a taste for finer things than the starter apartment our son
was offering. She rolled her eyes coldly at his jokes over Passover dinner.
Two years later, her nitpicking of Lenny's every failing and lack of ambition had become the signs of a woman challenging a man—begging him,
really—to let her go. Some twisted sense of duty kept her from walking out
herself. Through all this searing pain our son held on until Irina finally left
him, taking with her a few possessions and a letter of acceptance from the
Stern School of Business.

And yet the greatest irony was still to come. A week after Lenny signed
the divorce papers, putting his name beside all those tragic little "x"s, he
was on a plane headed to—where else?—Moscow. To make his million and
prove his manhood. To whom? I still wondered.

Lenny came out, wearing a thin bathrobe like Hugh Hefner, then
wolfed down both his lunch and mine.

"You don't think this arrest was accidental, though?" I asked him. I
was trying to summon the courage to tell him about Kablukov, but something prevented me. Knowing Lenny, he would only get mad at me for
meddling. Maybe better to stay quiet.

"The simplest explanation is usually the correct one," he said, chewing. "If there *is* a case against our old client and the Ministry of the Interior wants to finger more people . . . well, that would explain why
Zaparotnik was so eager to seal his deal with WCP and cut me out. Clever
bastard. He dissolves our old firm—so no liability there. Gets himself and
his buddies beamed up to WCP—the fortress. But he leaves one person,
me, in the lurch. So, if the FSB needs to sniff around our old business,
there's always someone to blame. A scapegoat."

"I don't know," I said. "That doesn't exactly sound simple."

He seemed not to hear me. "He's a son of a bitch."

"Maybe it's a sign," I said.

"A sign of what?"

"A sign that it's time to head home."

"Hell, no. I'm not going to let them gaslight me out of here just like that. I'll get to the bottom of it. You want one?" He handed me a Yarpivo from the fridge, and went to find a bottle opener.

"It doesn't pay to get to the bottom of things," I said.

But once again he seemed not to be listening. His phone was ringing. "Yeah, where are you?" he said. I could hear digital bits of a feminine voice in distress. "I'm just here, with my Pop. . . . How much did they ask for the work? I'll talk to them. . . ." He set the phone on the table. "Katya's on her way here," he informed me.

"Where was she?"

"At the orthodontist's office. They're overcharging us again."

Us? I thought. "Since when has she been wearing braces?"

"Since Mom told her—when she visited last summer—that she should get her teeth fixed."

This was pure revisionist history. Katya had already been self-conscious about her teeth. My wife had made a mere suggestion, which she would never have made if she'd known Lenny would be footing the bill.

"I thought you two were through," I said. "What are you doing— making her beautiful for your successor?"

"This is from before. I made her a promise."

My son, the promiscuous promiser. "Lenny," I said, "I think we should start looking for tickets home for you. Today."

But again he was deaf. The door buzzer rang twice, then went flat. "That's her," he said, getting up.

My heart sank a little as Katya came in, carrying two bags of groceries. "Aunt Valya asked me to pick up some eats for tonight," she said, seeing Lenny first. "I thought we could get a head start to the dacha. You're expected too!" She turned to me. "We're giving your boy a big homecoming! Aunt Valya is already there, preparing. And if we leave now, we can beat the weekend traffic."

"Oh crap!" Lenny said, hitting his temple.

"Didn't you tell him? Aunt Valya has been planning for your father's visit for weeks!"

"I forgot! I've been attending to more pressing matters, obviously."

"Well, we better pack," Katya said petulantly.

I stared at Lenny in amazement. What was this dacha nonsense? If he had any wits right now he'd be packing a suitcase for the States, not for a summer outing.

"Katen'ka, Lenny and I have some plans of our own."

"It's going to be boiling here this weekend! The whole city will be empty. And Aunt Valya got a whole calf to grill for us!"

I checked my watch. I was out of time to argue. "I have to get back to a meeting," I said.

"So come after. We'll pick you up at the train station," said Lenny.

"HOW IS EVERYTHING WITH the boy?" Kablukov inquired from his seat in one of L-Pet's overstuffed leather chairs.

"Better, miraculously." I tried to smile. I felt provoked to add that I was in his debt, but hesitated.

"Our friends at the Ministry of the Interior were quite appalled at the way he'd been harassed," he hinted.

"I'm grateful, Ivan Matveyevich."

He seemed satisfied with that. "We're sorry to have missed you. Your colleague there has been rather unpleasant in his cross-examination of the candidates for this contract." He gestured toward Tom, just entering from lunch and giving me a dismayed look that said, *Where the hell have you been?* I gathered he'd been holding the fort against L-Pet for the both of us.

"Mr. Boston is my boss, actually," I said, though Kablukov knew as much.

"We can all see he defers to you."

I tried to assure Kablukov that this wasn't so, that Tom's deferential manner belied his authority, but he wouldn't hear of it. "Listen to me," he said, taking me by the shoulder. I could feel the burn of his gaze even through his dark shades. "You designed these ships, did you not? So you tell your *nachal'nik* over there who *you* think ought to charter them."

"With due respect, Ivan Matveyevich," I said, "I'm not comfortable telling my boss how to do his job."

At this, Kablukov's mutton-colored face split open with a leisurely smile. All of his teeth were fake. *"Comfortable,"* he repeated. "It's an interesting word. In my life, I've had to become comfortable with many things." He lifted the cuff of his jacket sleeve. On his wrist was a white-gold Rolex that I suspected cost more than my car. It wasn't the watch he wanted me to look at, however, but what was just above it—a faded purple tattoo of a card with an upside-down spade. "This I got in Khabarovsk. Now, *that* wasn't comfortable. But wherever we are, we must learn to be comfortable."

I knew that the chill in my arms was only in part on account of the air conditioning. The indigestible lump I'd felt this morning was back, pressing into my lower gut. I recognized it as the sensation I had earlier—an absurd possibility taking the shape of something monstrously certain. And suddenly I knew why I'd been so reluctant to thank Kablukov for his help.

Albert Einstein once wisely said that the formulation of a problem is more essential than its solution. Now these words assaulted me in their most sickeningly literal implication. Nobody, not even Kablukov, could pull strings that quickly. He had devised the problem for which he himself was the solution. This was the simple fact that my worries about Lenny had kept hidden from me. I remembered our dinner at the Metropol several nights prior, my gushing about how much Lenny loved this worm-eaten place. How many hours had it taken Kablukov to find out where Lenny worked and lived? The Boot readjusted his cuff. His gravel voice broke the inertia of my silence. "Now we're singing from the same songbook?" he said pleasantly.

29.

SECRETS

IT WAS ALMOST MARCH BEFORE FLORENCE NOTICED ANYTHING DIFFER-
ent. Her tiredness might have been explained by the heavier course load
she took up in February. The new packed schedule could account for why
she felt so winded walking up a flight of stairs at the institute, or why her
eyes shut spontaneously on the trolley ride home as soon as her forehead
touched the glass. But what about the other signs? The fact that she'd
twice had to flee to the toilets and leave her students alone in the classroom. That her one good brassiere forced her to breathe as heavily as if she
were immersed ten leagues under the sea.

She struggled not to believe it. Her last period had been lighter than
usual. Too light, really, when she thought about it. And now another
month had passed, and nothing. The thing to do was to get it confirmed,
but that, instinct told her, would make the reality of the matter too undeniably permanent.

The trouble, as always, was due to the national shortages. Since September the pharmacies had been out of Prekonsol cream. And then, all
winter, Florence had been trying to replace her old *kafka* cap only to find,
when the new shipment of diaphragms finally arrived on the shelves, that
the one she bought felt too loose. She'd returned to the pharmacy, but all
they sold were the one-size-fits-all models. Unlike dropping off a shirt to be
tailored, she couldn't have this "taken in" unless she planned to waste a
day at the public clinic, sitting in a room packed with mothers of scream-

ing children, waiting to see a doctor who might be able to fit the thing properly (or at least give her something else, maybe one of those Vagilen balloons that were likewise out of stock in the pharmacies), but who would as likely chastise her, like the doctor she'd seen that summer, for her decision to put off motherhood. He warned that at her advanced age (twenty-nine) she was already bound to be a *starorodka,* an old birther, leading to "irremediable problems" for herself and her child later on. The only encouraging thing that jowly dinosaur *had* said was that at this rate it would take her at least five or six months even to conceive.

And now, two months later, here she was.

Florence's mind tried to rifle back to the conception date, which she fixed at just after New Year's. She and Leon had seen in the year 1940 with a wedding—Essie's. Their friend had found love at last, with a slim, reserved Jewish boy who shared Essie's affection for the movies and her nearsighted, protruding eyes. A musician, he'd played clarinet for them at his parents' apartment, where they'd all gone to celebrate after the ten-minute ceremony at the ZAGS marriage bureau, where Essie and her groom had stood alongside four other couples to be joined by the state. Florence had served as witness. That night, walking home in the falling snow, Leon had taken her arm and said, "And what about us—don't you think it's time?"

She'd responded by laughing. "Darling, they only went to that registration bureau because nowadays nobody will give 'em a room of their own without a piece of paper. She doesn't want to live with his parents."

"You don't respect me, Florence. You've never let me be a man."

"That's the silliest thing I've ever heard."

"If Essie can get legally betrothed to someone she's known for five weeks, why must I be barricaded—don't give me that look—yes, *barricaded* from marrying a woman to whom I've given *everything* for five years!"

She couldn't admit that the real reason for her playing hard to get was the other game she was playing with the secret police. A game that had as its eventual aim the severing of all her ties with Russia, maybe Leon included. And so, like an anxious philanderer in a spasm of self-reproach, she gave in to his wish and let Leon have what he most wanted. The very next day, they'd gone out and gotten themselves quietly hitched at the registration bureau. Their honeymoon was just as quiet, with no caviar or clarinets, but two voluptuously restful days and nights wrapped and tangled up in bed. She'd covered Leon's face and body with kisses as if he were a bountiful human shrine. She did this because she loved him and because she needed to ease her conscience, to make up for the ways she had deceived him and was still deceiving him by carrying on private meetings with Comrade Subotin, an entanglement that—bloodless as it was—she knew was more unfaithful than any affair. And so, being scrupulous about hiding her tracks with Subotin, she'd let herself get sloppy where it mattered most.

Her meetings with Subotin took place every three weeks as he'd ordered. For the first few sessions, he had not asked Florence very many difficult questions. He was mostly interested in her colleagues at IFLI: he wanted to know what they said during faculty meetings, who seemed to be on friendly terms and who on strained ones, which professors were allies or friends, and what was the basis of their friendship.

"Belkova and Danilova both love classical music," she reported blandly. "They go to concerts together at the Tchaikovsky. And I think Danilova's son is in the conservatory."

It was gossipy, but not essentially "criminal" information that Florence believed she gave Subotin. She found she had a knack for describing people, getting to the core of their character in a few quick strokes. This one was overly congenial but qualified everything he said with stipulations, just in case, always hedging his bets. That one found a way to disagree with whatever you were saying, even if you were agreeing with him wholeheartedly. Sometimes Florence found herself preparing these little profiles as she set off to meet Subotin, or as she sat listening to her colleagues during interminable meetings. It was only when Subotin began to ask her more pointedly about the "counterrevolutionary" conversations she was privy to, and any "anti-Soviet" activity she observed, that her mind began to gyrate like a creaky, overheated machine. "I am not interested in your personal opinions about these people, Comrade Fein," Subotin said one day. "I want to know why you aren't providing us with any *useful* information."

"Do you want me to make things up? I tell you everything I hear."

"Then find a way to hear more."

"What do you mean?"

"Start conversations."

"Surely you aren't saying I should be a provocateur?"

"I am saying that partial information will be treated as lies. And lies, in your case, Comrade Fein, don't instill in us faith that you can be trusted with a foreign assignment."

But even in her hunger for an exit visa, Florence found she could not bring herself to say anything truly damning about anyone. She knew that what she was doing was sordid enough that she didn't want to tell even Leon about it, but she took some moral comfort in reminding herself that at least she would not dissemble, would not bear false witness against anybody. Subotin could use what she said as he wished, but she would do no more than act as a perfect mirror of her world, making up nothing, adding nothing. If Subotin was genuinely interested in her trustworthiness, then he had people spying on *her*, which meant it behooved her to continue delivering what she knew without slander or embellishment.

But Subotin's persistence was frightening.

He was tired of her "womanly fluff," he told her the following session. This wasn't summer Pioneer camp. He was tired of wasting his time with her pointless gossip and insinuations. Did he have to remind her of the punishment for trying to leave the country illegally? He knew she was withholding—he had other ears to the ground. So, if she wasn't interested in doing her duty by the state, she could prepare to sever their relationship and take her chances.

She came home looking as pale as the ghost of consumption. She had eaten nothing since noon. Her purse seemed as heavy as a spade. Her feet were sore, her spine felt like badly warped steel, her nipples chafed under the caress of starched fabric that might as well have been mosquito netting. "What's happened to you?" Leon said, observing her collapse on the daybed.

Florence cupped her face in her hands and rubbed her aching eyes, then looked at Leon through her slightly spread fingers. The one person who could help her now was the one to whom she was too afraid to tell the truth. Leon, who could talk to anyone, would surely know how to talk his way out of this noose with Subotin. He'd be able to tell her what to say. She dug her thumbs deeper into her sockets to keep her eyes from exploding with tears.

"Florence, has something happened?"

Too many secrets. Too many . . .

"Sit up. There, good. Let me get you some water."

"Leon. I have to tell you something . . . but first you have to promise not to get angry."

He smiled in baffled anticipation. "When have I gotten angry?"

"You have to promise."

Too many secrets.

And so she spilled the wrong one.

Now he was the one cupping his face, his hand wrapped around his mouth, to hide the grin that was spreading from ear to ear. "How long?" he said quietly, through parted fingers.

"About three months. I haven't got it confirmed."

"Oh, baby, how could I ever be angry at you about *that*?"

She shook her head. "Leon, how could we let ourselves get so careless?"

He knelt and took her sunken shoulders. "This is the most tremendous thing, don't you see? Oh, baby, no wonder you've been so worn down. You have to start taking care of yourself, Florie. Tell 'em you can't keep staying late at those faculty meetings anymore."

That he believed her lies about how she spent her afternoons was more tormenting even than his elation. "But, Leon, it's not the time. . . ."

"Shhh, shhh. . . . let me worry about that. Shhh, you just rest now. . . ." And he hurried to the kitchen to cook her up some dinner.

HER PREGNANCY TURNED LEON into an indulgent husband. He began to come home with delicacies: herring, caviar, chocolates.

"How much did you pay for this?"

"Never mind!" he told her. "Eat."

He woke up earlier than usual to cook breakfast, then sat staring at her with a bashful smile while she spooned up her buckwheat and eggs. *Look at him smiling,* she thought. *He is finally getting what he wants: a wife, a real family.* Leon had grown up without a father, and it was plain to see how badly he wanted to be a father himself. She wondered why she had never understood this about him before: under all of his youthful wanderlust and adventuring had been a bottomless craving for a real home.

Her own desires were unreadable even to her. She felt like Dr. Faustus: two souls residing within her breast, each one reacting in its own way to

Leon's tender attentions. She had a real life here—a good job, a loving man. What more was she waiting for? Women her age were already mothers of ten- and twelve-year-olds. The idea that she would be sent to America as some sort of spy was a delusion. What were the chances that she would really be sent abroad on "special assignment"?

Not zero. Possibly it was all a ruse on Subotin's part. But the NKVD didn't need ruses. They could force her to cooperate without this carrot. Certainly their interest in her was long-term. But how long-term? She had to show Subotin that she was ready for the job, and to do it before her pregnancy started showing. A criminal abortion was out of the question—she could get tossed in jail if discovered. No decent doctor would do it, which meant she'd have to find some *babka* in the sticks who might maim her reproductive organs forever, or kill her. It occurred to her that she could take measures to conceal her condition from Subotin. Didn't one hear stories about village girls who kept their pregnancies secret until the end? She'd take out the seams on her dresses, buy a looser coat. Men didn't always take notice of such things. But would she take the risk of getting on a boat to America at, say, eight months? Yes, she would. If only she could just forget the word "America"! Couldn't she choose the reality of her husband's loving touch over the beckoning tide of her dreams?

In the two weeks that followed, her schemes exhausted her more than even her pregnancy. She knew she needed to take some kind of action. And so a plan at last shaped itself in her mind: She would walk into her next meeting with Subotin and announce that she was pregnant. She would inform him that, now that she was going to be a mother, she would, regrettably, be unable to carry out any kind of foreign assignment. She might even have to take indeterminate leave from her job. And since she was no use to the NKVD staying home all day changing nappies, it was best if they terminated their relationship as soon as possible.

But a week later, instead of requesting that he respectfully sever their connection, what she in fact heard herself asking Subotin as soon as they sat down was "Has there been any progress about my foreign assignment?"

He glanced up at her from his papers with curiosity. "Are you in a hurry?"

"No, of course not. But . . . I've been giving some thought to what you said."

"Yes?"

"About faculty whose positions on certain matters of national policy aren't always . . . clear."

"Go on."

"Some of the old guard. Of course, I'm not qualified to interpret their views. . . ."

"Your only qualification is your loyalty."

"There is a Professor Rechok; he's in the history department."

"You've had conversations with him."

"Yes. No. Not really."

"Well, have you or haven't you?"

Under the table, she held her stomach with both hands. A life was growing inside her. She had always viewed herself as an honest, loyal, straightforward person, but what did all that mean now? She had to be loyal to her child.

"We both have a break in our classes at one-thirty. He sometimes spends it in the second-floor lounge, reading the paper. And sometimes he mutters things . . . to himself, mostly."

"What sorts of things?"

She struggled to recall Rechok's reaction to the pact between Hitler and Stalin, the expansion of trade with Germany. What had he said? *So now they're friends, and why not? They understand each other perfectly.* No, that wasn't it. Her imagination was embellishing. What had the old fool said? He was worried about what to tell his students. *Last year the dog's a Rottweiler, this year he's a poodle.* That was it.

"Rechok thinks we may be attacked by the Germans in the future. That Russia is helping them strengthen their military might by selling them materials."

"And you know all this from things he 'mutters.' "

"Yes. He paraphrases what he reads in a way that suggests so."

Subotin took some time to record this with an even, neat hand in his notebook. "A professor on the history faculty promulgating anti-Soviet views among students and other faculty, then."

"Oh no, I don't think he shares his views with the students. I'm sure he doesn't."

"How can you be sure? Do you sit in on his classes?"

"The institute follows a strict program. Violations of the curriculum would be reported at once."

"We don't need you to tell *us* what gets reported. As you said, it's all a matter of tone. In who else's presence has Rechok voiced these opinions?"

"Well, people walk in and out of the lounge."

"Which people?"

She took a siplike breath. Subotin's eyes, she noticed, were almost aquamarine. Like water in a tiled fountain, still and cold. "Sometimes Anna Belkova and Maria Danilova come in."

"Were they present the day he was talking about the Molotov-Ribbentrop Pact?"

"They were."

"And how did they respond to Rechok's anti-Soviet outbursts?"

"Most of the faculty just treats him as an eccentric old man. They generally don't reply to his muttering."

Subotin responded to this answer with a shadow of a smile, a sneer that pulled his lip toward the back and which seemed to say, *You can't have it both ways, golubushka.* "So they said nothing, and allowed him to keep voicing his slander," Subotin clarified.

"I suppose so."

She waited while he wrote a report on a fresh leaf of paper. To her surprise, when Subotin was finished, he gave Florence the transcript to read over.

The facts were as she had told them, but somehow the overall meaning was different. The transcript stated that she'd had anti-Soviet conversations with Boris Rechok, during which Rechok disseminated information about the German threat and contradicted Stalin's economic policy, in the presence of Belkova and Danilova, who had listened to his slanderous statements without contradicting him. The report made it appear almost as though the two women were in agreement with Rechok. It also stated that Boris Rechok promulgated these views in his classes.

"Now, wait," she said. "This makes it seem as though Rechok were *addressing* them. All I said was that he made these statements to himself, while he read the paper."

"If he wanted to say them to himself, he would have spoken them to the wall at home. Obviously, he was expecting reactions."

"But Belkova and Danilova just happened to be in the room. He wasn't conversing with them."

"They were in the room, and they allowed this dissembler to spread his lies unobstructed."

"But your report makes it seem like they share his views."

"Whether they share them or not is for us to determine. The fact remains that they had responsibility, as educators, as citizens, to correct Rechok's lies, and they failed in this responsibility, as did you."

It was an impossible argument to win. The NKVD had their own logic, according to which passive witnesses were no different from conspirators. According to this logic, you bore responsibility not only for your own words, but for the words of all those around you.

"But I never said he promulgated these views among his students," Florence protested. She knew she was grasping at straws.

"If these views are being shared with you, what makes you think they are not being shared elsewhere, with more impressionable minds?"

"But I can't testify to that."

There was a strange flash in Subotin's cool-water eyes. They seemed to go round in surprise for a moment. The grin on his face was almost like the stifled wince of someone who'd had a cheap point scored against him. "Very well," he said. He picked up his pen and crossed out the words "in his courses," keeping only "at the institute."

"Is this better?"

Florence nodded.

He passed her his pen. "Sign it."

She did.

OUTSIDE, IN THE FAMILIAR gated courtyard, the day-melted snow had refrozen to crust. She could see a sickle of moon in the east, but the sky was still lucent, dimming slowly now that the days were getting longer. The moist April air carried smells of boiled meat and onions. Florence felt sick in her stomach. She had to sit down. A shellac of ice covered the green bench. She could feel its cold, melting moisture through her coat, almost down to her ass. She had given them enough to arrest Boris Rechok, a person she barely knew, on charges of "primitive anti-fascism." If they brought him in, would they show him her statement and make him re-

spond? Well, why did he have to say those things around her? What had
she been supposed to do? Lie? Then Belkova and Danilova would have told
the truth in her place, and *then* where would she be? She had finally given
Subotin what he wanted. But he had said nothing afterward about her
going to America. On the contrary, he'd seemed irritated that she hadn't
been more enthusiastic in her denunciation of Rechok! And that look on
his face when she'd objected to parts of his report—she couldn't get it out
of her head. What was that look? She had seen it before. Not on Subotin's
face, no. But—God, to remember it now—on the face of Sergey Sokolov so
many years ago. A look of utter surprise—less emotional state than physical instinct, like a reaction to the smell of something spoiled. They were
memories she had buried—as an animal buries its droppings—so shame-
ful that her mind took great pains not to shed light on them. They came
back now with hallucinatory vividness. She saw herself reflected in her
old boss Scoop's eyes when it was revealed that she'd helped the Russian
engineers, and then in Sergey's eyes when she tracked him down in Moscow. The look they had both given her—as though they had suddenly realized that the intelligent, quick-witted woman in front of them was at
heart a fool. It was this recognition of her foolishness that she thought she
recognized in Subotin's eyes. He honestly *could not believe* she was haggling
with him over the details. Had she forgotten where she was, with *whom*
she was arguing? She still thought she could have it both ways—get into
bed with the NKVD and come out with her slip unwrinkled, her soul clean
and unbesmirched. Too late for that, little dove. She was like a whore haggling over her honor.

The queasiness was overpowering. Florence needed to put her head between her knees just to keep breathing. Beads of sweat slid down between
her breasts. Something percolated in her gut. And then all illusion of control vanished and she was retching, paralyzed by mutinous spasms until
there was nothing left to heave but a thin, watery fluid. It spilled and drib-
bled on her shoes.

The necessity of sitting back up and cleaning herself now proposed a
host of dangers. Somebody was touching her. Florence wiped her mouth
with a corner of her kerchief and turned to see who it was. A tiny old babushka in a lumpy coat was sitting beside her. All the lines in her face
crinkled imploringly. "Are you all right, dearie?" She touched Florence's
shoulder, but this only caused Florence to jerk. Who was this woman? Was

she one of them? Her eyes cast up and around the surrounding buildings. Did one of Subotin's windows face this little quadrangle? Were *they* watching her even now? She flicked her chin at the old woman. "Mind your own damn business," she said and, clutching her bag, made haste out of the courtyard.

30.

VOLGANS

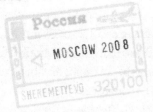

KARL MARX WAS RIGHT: WE ARE NOT THE RULERS OF OUR DESTINIES. FOR all my renouncements of the secular prophet of my youth, I was ready to concede this truth as I sat in helpless silence in the L-Pet conference room. When our meeting came to an end we were down to three bids, two reasonable ones and the hot-air balloon floated by the boys from Geneva. I'd found myself unable to prune Sausen Petroleum out of the running completely. Yet in spite of the pressure from Kablukov I had not been able to mount a convincing defense, either. So I stayed mostly mute through the ceremony of selection, conscious throughout of Kablukov groaning subaudibly in his chair like a disappointed father. Tom looked no less displeased with me when we adjourned (early, so that the men of L-Pet could flee town in their Cherokees and get to their Zhukovka dachas before sunset). With about as much sincerity as I'd brought to our meeting, I told him I had food poisoning, then fled. I also had a dacha to hurry to, if I wanted to lose no time in beating some sense into my offspring.

But, once outside, I found myself unable to work up the will to head straight to my hotel and pack. Instead, I traced a long arc around the Bolshoi, trying not to think about how I'd failed Lenny. I felt plunged in disgrace and ugliness. It was miserably obvious that I had actually believed that my pathetic banter with Kablukov at the Metropol would get him over "to my side." Stupidly, I had only brought more chaos into my child's already exposed life. The only way to get Lenny out of danger was to tell him the truth. This, I knew, was the reason I was in no hurry to get to the dacha to see him. To say what? That I had done the one thing I'd always warned him not to do: opened my mouth? So mired was I in my self-contempt that I suddenly realized I had no idea where I was walking. And here, against a blinding setting sun in Theater Square, I looked up to behold a scene at once ancient and intimately familiar: Beneath the statue of Karl Marx were half a dozen shabbily dressed, graying men—all of them about my age—gathered around open attaché cases and felt display boards to which were mounted hundreds of tiny lapel pins—those antique nickel-and-enamel-painted *znachki* that, like a thousand other amateur collectors, I'd once bought and mounted to felt boards of my own. These falerists had assembled to compare their rare specimens, to trade or to sell them (to *profiteer*, as might say Mr. Marx, in whose shadow all this speculation was happening). The *znachki* caught the five o'clock sun like scraps of gold and touched a deep memory of Lenny at five years old, a demon of childish excitement, jumping at a gift of a new *znachok* I'd brought back from one of my latest research trips to Leningrad. And all at once I was remembering kneeling beside him as he removed the souvenir pin from its acetate pocket—a dime-sized Yuri Gagarin head in a cosmonaut's helmet or a Vostok 2 aircraft hurtling into black space—my fingers helping him affix the small bent pin carefully to the velvet lining of his own collector's case.

As playthings these lapel pins could not have been much fun for a five-year-old. How much of the excitement, I now wondered, was Lenny's, and how much was my own? Of the thousands of pins minted to commemorate every possible enterprise, sports club, city centennial, historical battle, our favorites were those celebrating space travel. Unlike the others, which were merely stylized paeans to socialist construction, the space pins were emblems of a more universal hope—a hope that we could, quite literally, rise above our failings as a species through technology, through science, through optimism. Was I, even then, conveying to him the sort of man I wished him to become—a scientist or an engineer, a believer in the reassurances of steady, incremental achievement? Were these the same expectations that were now at the heart of the belligerent hypersensitivity that reared itself whenever the subject of Lenny's work—or lack of it—arose? I wanted to assure him that no good parent took satisfaction in his child's failures. I happened to know a little something about how crushing defeat can feel, what a near decade of wasted years can do to the soul. Had

I felt it possible to engage in such a conversation without risking some high point of drama or misunderstanding, I would have told my son about May 12, 1977, the day I was flatly deserted by my illusions. The day this beloved city of mine, to which he was still so in thrall, stopped being home.

During the years when I was buying Lenny his *znachki*, I had been working toward my candidate-of-sciences degree—equivalent to a Ph.D.—in hydrodynamics, pursued in between full-time work and minding a young family. Our apartment in those days consisted of two rooms. Our marital bed was a sofa Lucya and I unfolded each night so the children could sleep in a room of their own, and my "study," where I performed calculations late into the night, was a corner of our negligible kitchen. At thirty-four, I already had one brief failed marriage under my belt (made disastrously while I was still a university student). This time around I was "getting it right"— remarried to a smart and devoted girl who was also an adoring mother of our kids, and who heroically bore both shares of the housework to make it possible for me to pursue my dream of a doctorate. Every several months— over a period of six years—I would travel to the wharves in Leningrad to perform studies into gases that might be used to separate ice from its grip on the surface of water. The practical applications of the research were numerous. In those days, the conventional methods of sending ships through ice-cold waters still involved heavy diesel engines to compress massive quantities of air; I was looking into ways to deploy gases from a ship's hull to reduce drag, to reduce the bulk of unnecessary machinery, and to employ redesigned gas turbine engines, diffusers, and expansion chambers to generate hot compressed gas and save fuel. My ambition was nothing short of reshaping the discipline of shipbuilding.

I can no longer remember all the faces of those deciding my fate the day of my doctoral defense, or their questions. I remember that they asked me many. If any member of the review board was especially impressed with my findings, the enthusiasm was well hidden. By the time I left the room, I was covered in sweat. My pulse was still racing a good twenty minutes later, as I waited for the committee's decision in an empty hallway of the Institute of Control Sciences. At last, one of the three came out of the room and approached me. He was short and seemed to be compensating for his small stature with an enormous mustache. During the prolonged interrogation, he had been the most encouraging of my work. "Some interesting ideas there, Brink," he said to me in the corridor. He paused to repeat my name, "Brink," somewhat speculatively. "I saw you were born in Kuibyshev. Your family from there?"

He was suggesting that he was familiar with my passport, which included, of course, the notorious "fifth column" revealing my American nationality and my Jewish last name. But at that moment I was sure that he was suggesting I wasn't a "real Muscovite," so I set him straight. "My parents were both from Moscow," I informed him. "I was born during the war evacuation."

"I'm from Kazan myself," he said. "Not many of us *Volgans* here, are there?" He smiled. I had no idea what he was talking about. At least not then.

"I'll be square with you, Brink," he continued, gazing out the window. "I was hoping you *might* be from Kuibyshev, or someplace far off like that, because here in Moscow we have our production norms, if you will." He pulled a cigarette neatly out of his shirt pocket and lit it. "The trouble is," he said, after taking a hungry drag and clearing his throat, "we can't give *you* a degree until we give it to everyone ahead of you. And in your case, Comrade, it's a clogged pipeline."

He looked at me to see if I understood him. I said nothing.

"So you have a choice," he continued. "Wait six years in our queue, or"—he gestured toward the window, including in the sweep of his hand the whole of the Soviet empire west of the Volga—"you can go somewhere else—say, to Kuibyshev—enroll in their university, and defend your project through a less high-profile institute without our . . . restrictions."

As with all bad news, the meaning of his words failed at first to register. I watched the caterpillar of his mustache flexing, but the message entering my ears was as abstract as a radio broadcast. Possibly a catastrophe, yes, but not necessarily applying to *me*.

I wasn't a complete dolt. I knew about the Jewish quota system in Russia's universities. I had beaten its odds before; maybe I thought I'd go on beating them forever. Whatever handicaps my "nationality" had inflicted on me, I'd been coping with them since I was six with as much patience as lefties cope with the tyranny of right-turning doorknobs, with the monocracy (in those days at least) of right-handed penmanship, scrupulously overcorrecting for my disadvantage with quiet, monumental effort.

But this was a much narrower hoop than the ones I'd jumped through before. This felt like a needle's eye. (Later, I'd learn that fewer than 5 percent of candidate-of-sciences degrees at the institute in any single year were awarded to Jews. But at that moment, at the age of thirty-four, I was once again *little Abrashka* in the children's home, not sure if I was going to sob or throw a punch.) Why had the man come out to speak to me personally? The rejection of my doctorate could have been conveyed by dry official means. Something about him told me that he had come to speak to me not as an emissary of the committee, but out of some private discomfort. In his manner I detected the faintest note of apology.

I walked out, my dissertation manuscript inside my briefcase, out of the sallow lobby and down the grassy median of the boulevard. It was a beautiful day made more brilliant by a recent rain, one of those days when you noticed for the first time that whole limbs of trees had gone green with budding leaves, when telephone wires suddenly swarmed with noisy flocks of swallows. And suddenly all of it—all that beauty, all the scholarly aspiration I'd basked in for seven years—was repellent to me. None of it was any longer mine. The sight of *their* buildings made me sick. The sight of *their* statues, even their *trees*—all of it sent a wave of nausea down my throat. After an hour, I was able to collect myself enough to find a pay phone and call my wife. "Start selling our stuff," I told her. "We're leaving this cursed place."

The first mass migration was still two years away, the first murmurs about the gates being opened only then just spreading. But I already knew that when the day came I'd be ready to leave everything behind. I would cross the border in my underpants if I had to.

31.

LITTLE BIRCH TREE

Moscow, 1940

FLORENCE'S MEETING WITH SUBOTIN HAD LEFT HER BRUTALLY ALTERED.
In the morning, she did not get up until Leon was gone. On the desk by the
bed he had left milk and a pan of groats for her. Both had gone cold.

The day was gelid and bright with spring-melting snow. Florence rolled
up her stockings and put on a hat. It was Friday and she had no classes to
teach. There was only one person she had to go see.

From the nickel-bright street she entered the darkness of the theater;
its smells of dust and powder accosted her with their familiarity. Down a
narrow hall she made her way to the chamber where the attendant sat
with her knees apart, boiling tea on her rusted kettle.

"Flora?"

"Agnessa Artemovna." Florence removed her hat. "I need your help."

TWO KILOMETERS OUT OF Moscow, modern life dropped away as suddenly
as an ocean floor. From the window of the train she watched the muddy
countryside encroach on the city. Three hundred rubles—most of her
month's salary—were stacked inside her coat pocket. Off the main road,
peasant women squatted on muddy banks to wash laundry in a cold
stream. Time hung over everything like a dead weight.

She found the cabin down a dirt road from the village post office, out of sight behind a stand of pines. An old *izba* with carved picture-book windows, it reminded Florence of Baba Yaga's house, except it wasn't standing on chicken legs. The sister was a thickset, imposing woman whose faint resemblance to Agnessa Artemovna was well concealed behind rosacea-complected cheeks and a ruddy nose. She led Florence to an alcove formed by the back wall of a wood stove and a sideboard. In the alcove stood an iron bed, a board on the metal webbing. Florence removed her muddy knee-boots and unrolled her stockings while the woman prepared. The room had a cloying, churchlike smell from the candle that flickered in the sideboard's beveled mirror. She told Florence to undress while she went to boil water in a kettle.

With her head back so the room tilted, Florence could see the chiffonier and the conserves jar of alcohol in which the woman kept the instruments of her trade. Bubbles clung to the inside like fizz in a glass of champagne that was going flat. The sight of them made Florence weak with nausea. The woman brought her a stale-smelling pillow to bite on for the pain. "You can moan," she instructed, "but don't scream."

A small, piercing ache as she inhaled, and then pain that could make you forget your own name. The pillow between her teeth tasted sour with the saliva and sebum of others.

"Steady, steady." Her feet were tied to the bed frame. The woman hummed as she worked—*"Lyuli, Lyuli"*—lullabying while she scooped out the life inside. The flavor of blood filled the air as the daylight grew grainy. The leaping candle on the bureau turned the mirror into a slab of light.

> *On the meadow stood a little birch tree.*
> *Lyuli, Lyuli, there it stood.*

She came to with the stout woman sponging her brow.

"Up, up now."

Her head was still full of echoes. "I can't move."

"Come, off you go."

If the hemorrhaging didn't stop, she was instructed to go to a doctor and tell him she had fallen on the ice and suffered a miscarriage.

She took the evening train back to Moscow, weighed down by the bandages in her underwear as if by sandbags. Every moment, she felt herself losing blood. Around her, figures fluctuated like pulsing ghosts. She told herself she'd been spared more barbaric methods—the carbonate douches and mustard baths. Blood soaked through her stockings and skirt.

Leon found her on the daybed, trembling as if with a chill. He hurried to the kitchen and returned with a bowl of pearl-barley soup and a mug of steaming milk. He sat Florence up and placed the mug to her lips, watching as she made an effort to swallow. Beads of sweat formed on her forehead and upper lip while she sipped. "You're burning up!" He tried to feed her the soup with a spoon, but she refused, pulling the blanket tightly around herself.

"You have to eat."

"I don't want it."

"Then eat for the baby."

"There is no baby."

"You're all hot, Florie. You're confused."

He attempted to remove her blanket. This time she had no strength to stop him.

She had never heard a sound of such anguish come out of a human mouth: "*Oy vey z'mir*, Florence! *Oy mayn gut, oy gu-u-u-t-t . . .*" He was inhaling the words as he howled them, his fists at his temples. Madness had taken hold of him in spasms. He rocked back and forth, clutching at the bloodied sheet. "*Oy mayn gut,* what have you *done?*"

"I couldn't let him know, Leon."

"We have to take you to a hospital."

"No. Let me die here."

"*Tell me who did this!*"

"I couldn't go through with it, Leon. If he found out, I'd be trapped forever. It would have all been for nothing. . . ."

"Who, *goddamn it?*"

Then it all spilled out of her, in incoherent, hopeless sobs: the visit to OVIR, the meetings with Subotin, the long, doomed course of her ruination. "He said he would send me home. He told me I would see my family. . . ." She could hear just how weak, how fatuous these promises sounded. She summoned the strength for the abject confessions, believing them to be her last.

The intensity of his suffering as he listened seemed to turn his black eyes blue, to make them glow like diamonds. He would know now how she'd tried to flee from him. He would recognize at last what kind of whore he'd bound his fate with. On the abortionist's bed, Florence had believed she would die. She had begged Providence to give her another chance among the living. But the world was mechanistic, and now she prepared herself to pay the price. Leon continued to clutch the sheet. Now he buried his face in it, as if to inhale the redolence of its carnage.

But she was wrong about him. When he lifted his eyes again, they were dry. "Florence, listen to me carefully." He squeezed her hand. "Take whatever that agent offers you. Give him what he wants, and don't ask too many questions. Get yourself an exit visa as soon as you can. Then leave! Disappear. Forget this wretched place."

BOOK V

32.

_____

INVISIBLE MAN

PINES AND ROADSIDE SHRUBS AND THE STEEL LATTICEWORK OF RURAL stations streaked by my window on the eastbound train to Alabino. During my hour's commute I'd resolved to come clean to Lenny about my indiscretions with Kablukov. It was for the best. My humbling confession might succeed where other inducements had failed. And yet, when I spotted Lenny in his striped T-shirt, innocently waving his hand from the driver's window of a rusted Lada, I lost all my prepared speeches. The morning seemed too fresh, his smile too genuine to spoil so quickly. Lenny came out to help me with my bag; he looked surprised that I'd actually come. "Get ready to meet the freak parade," he happily warned me as we pulled out onto the empty town road. "There's Alyosha Alcoholic, and Zhorik the Georgian Lothario. One is Aunt Valya's nephew, the other's her husband. They're the same age."

"Are those their formal titles?"

"Zhorik's official title is 'invalid.' Don't ask me how Valya arranged that. Forty-four years old, and he already collects a monthly pension. His informal title is 'househusband.' We're just over down this way."

The house we pulled up to was not the patched-up shack I would have imagined from Lenny's car and dress, but a neat three-story clapboard, with a new coat of cinnamon-colored paint. We entered through the back of the wraparound veranda into the kitchen, where we encountered a towheaded and unshaven young man in rubber slippers. A bony chest was exposed through a mostly unbuttoned shirt. "Alexei, meet my father, Yuliy Leontevich," Lenny said by way of introduction.

Alexei nodded formally. "A little eye-opener for our American guest?" A bottle of Russian Standard stood half empty on the kitchen table.

"Thank you," I told him. "I prefer to start my mornings with cognac."

"Cognac it is." Alexei found a fresh bottle in the cupboard and opened it for me. "The girls have gone mushrooming in the woods, and Zhorik is out getting the meat for our shashlik. Enjoy the quiet while you can."

I adjusted myself to his definition of "quiet." On the counter, a minia-ture radio was tuned at top volume to a news program. We listened to the righteous-voiced female radio host denouncing the continued imprison-ment of another Yukos oil executive rumored to have been denied medical treatments until he signed a confession.

"What station is this?" I asked.

"Ekho Moskvy. The one our gracious president allows us to operate so we can claim to the world that we have a free press."

"Alyosha never turns the radio off," said Lenny.

"You ought to know all about this," said Alyosha. "Aren't you an oil-man?"

"I see only the engineering side," I said. "What line of work are you in, Alexei?"

"Work? I don't work. I'm a freeloader. My occupation is sitting on my mother's neck."

"Well, that's work too."

"He's being modest," Lenny informed me. "Alyosha is a bona-fide money launderer. Just last week, the local police came and raided his of-fice."

"Those crooks overstepped their bounds," the skinny man muttered. "They took five hundred thousand rubles, so I had to call the precinct militzia—my guy there. He sorted it out with a phone call. Ten thousand I might have let pass, but the pigs got greedy."

"So unofficially you're an entrepreneur, and officially you're a dere-lict," I said.

"I'm a nonperson," Alyosha proclaimed proudly. "They have no record of me. I'm not written in anywhere."

"Is that legal?"

"Having no legitimate employment is no longer a crime. All they can do to me is deny me a pension. And I don't need their stinking five hundred rubles a month."

"And, naturally, you don't vote," said Lenny, smiling at me as he needled Alyosha with the reliable bait.

"Voting is a profanation," Alexei replied on cue. "The voters—what are they? There to play the role of the audience who claps."

"Ask him who his hero is," Lenny said, then answered his own question. "Ralph Ellison."

"The Invisible Man is a cipher," Alyosha resumed madly. "He lives in a basement full of lightbulbs, siphoning off electricity from the monopolized energy company. The utility company is unaware of his existence, as is the fraudulent state whose authority he does not recognize. Like the invisible Negro, I choose to have no existence in the eyes of our illegitimate state."

"Show him how you did it, Alyosha."

Alyosha walked to the plug socket above the sink. "It's very easy. You ought to know this as an engineer—you run half the current through a wire attached to a piece of sheet metal, and ground it by sticking it in the earth. I stuck it out there—see?—in the vegetable garden. The electricity runs all year round, without adding a single watt to Valya's meter."

It seemed that, on top of his gifts of oratory and barter, Alyosha had the Russian alcoholic's talent for fixing anything with his hands. "With the heat it's even easier. I just go out into the yard in the winter and pour a kettle of boiling water over the heat meter, and the thing freezes right up. You can heat all three stories of the house without paying a kopek." His voice resounded with pride. "In Russia, we are all thieves," he now declared in English, and then, a few decibels louder than before: "*They* steal from us big! I steal back little!"

"So pleased with himself—the great philosopher." A voice sounded from the hall. A plump bottle-redhead of about sixty entered the kitchen, carrying a large zinc bucket of mushrooms with a curved blade laid on top. She wore sandals and a pair of shorts over heroic thighs that might have belonged to some mythological *kolhoznitsa* gathering sheaves of grain in a Soviet mural. This had to be Valentina, the famous Aunt Valya, Katya's mother's cousin. Behind her trotted Katya, in tight jeans and rubber galoshes.

"So you've met our resident Socrates," Valentina said, spreading a newspaper on the table and dumping out the contents of her and Katya's buckets. She began rapidly sorting the fungi on the newspaper, rejecting the very bad or very dirty ones and tossing them back in the bucket.

"Did you find some good ones?" I inquired.

"A few *chernushki*, and all those little foxes."

"We would've gotten more, but now everyone's discovered our sweet spot," said Katya with her gentle, orthodontal lisp.

"That one's a toadstool," Alyosha pointed out.

"It's a *ryzhik*. You don't know anything."

"Can't you see the thin stem? It's inedible. You'll poison us all, woman."

"Look who's talking! I didn't see you out this morning, poking from glade to glade, bending, picking."

"You're not a mushroomer, Alexei?" I said.

Alyosha reclined in his chair and looked away, like such nonsense was beneath him. "It's too easy here. Last time I went, I got five baskets in one hour. There isn't any challenge. What's the point?"

"Alyosha's enjoyment is complete only when it involves suffering," Lenny said.

I turned to Valentina. "A very nice home you have, Valya. Did your family build it?"

"No, I bought it from the former ambassador to Denmark. The family dacha my papa left to my sister, Nina—this genius's mother. It's down a ways, in Aprelevka. But Nina's vacationing this week on the Black Sea. That's why this one's hanging around here like a stray dog."

"Aprelevka?" I was surprised. "That's where the old military dachas are, or were. Was your father a general?"

"A *komdiv*. Division commander. But there's no trace of the old Gen-shtab anymore. It's been taken over by our new Brahmins. Alyosha! Haven't you shown Yuliy Leontevich to his room yet? Well, what kind of hosts are you? Come along," she said, getting up. "You'll get the tour."

I followed Valya upstairs, with Alyosha carrying my bag like a valet while I admired the furniture. "Sure, I got a few of Papa's things," Valya admitted when I asked her about the carved wood antiques. "Including that little watch," Alyosha said, pointing to a mahogany grandfather clock on the landing. "A real Teutonic treasure, not like the fakes the Germans palmed off after the war on every dumb Vanya in combat boots."

"Your father was an important man if he managed to bring that into the country," I said.

"I can't complain about the way I grew up."

"Regular vacations in Crimea?"

"Yalta. Sochi."

"A family driver."

"You bet. He'd drive Nina and me to our classes at MGIMO. I was so embarrassed by it."

For all my resplendent grades as a boy, I had never even entertained the notion of being admitted to a school like the Moscow State Institute of International Relations, where only the high-ranking Party people could place their sons and daughters, in preparation for diplomatic posts all over the world. The school was not even listed in the regular handbook of Soviet institutions of higher learning. "You couldn't have been the only two students at MGIMO who got driven to class."

"That was more Nina's style. I couldn't stomach that whole clubby atmosphere."

"Is that why you didn't end up a diplomat like your sister?"

"This delegation, that delegation. Not for me. I sat quietly at Vneshtorg."

I was getting a clearer picture of Valya, who, for all her Party pedigree, had the heart of a speculator. I couldn't help admiring her for eschewing the advantages she'd been born into, turning her back on the Soviet career ladder, and instead quietly staking out a mid-level position at the less prestigious Ministry of Foreign Trade, which nonetheless afforded her plenty of opportunities to travel to Hungary, Czechoslovakia, Romania, and return with suitcases full of nightgowns, shoes, and pantyhose that she could peddle, at a profit, among her acquaintances.

Alyosha had set my bag in the guest room.

"You'll sleep like a baby tonight," Valya said. "*I've* never slept on a better mattress. This bed is better than the one Putin sleeps on. Not because he can't afford it, but because his ass wouldn't know the difference."

Alyosha winced as if in pain. "I told you not to speak that devil's name around me!" And then the two of them left me alone.

After visiting the bathroom, I took a look at the music collection on the shelves (Andrea Bocelli, Enrico Caruso, Adelina Patti), as well as the many foreign books. I was certain this was the room Alyosha's mother, Nina, slept in when she spent nights at Valya's. On the small writing desk were notes written in a looping feminine hand. On the wall hung an enlarged black-and-white photograph of a beautiful, bright-eyed angelic boy of five or six. After a moment of looking at the photo I experienced a strange jolt of recognition: it was Alyosha Alcoholic.

I stared at the photo for a long time, thinking, until Valya's auctioneer voice called everyone down to lunch. I followed the smell of grilled meat out through the veranda to the side of the house, where Lenny and Alyosha were standing around a square grill being loaded with pork chops by a broad-shouldered Georgian in a jogging suit. This was evidently Zhorik, in the grip of some ebullient argument with Lenny over the best way to marinate meat. Zhorik was taking the position that the best results came from marinating in vinegar, and Lenny insisted on a concoction of kefir and lemon juice. "What kind of Jew *are* you?" Zhorik challenged. "Don't you know your people don't marinate meat in milk? It degrades the fibers!"

"Here he is, our honored guest!" Zhorik said, spotting me. He shook my hand heartily with his right while holding on to the handle of the weighty grill cage with his left. If he really was an "invalid," then he was the most robust and vigorous of the breed I'd ever met. Valya came out onto the porch. "Alyosha, come in and help me move this table."

But her nephew didn't hear her, or pretended not to. He'd inserted his earbuds deep into his ear canal in order to keep listening to Ekho Moskvy on his portable. "Look at him!" she shouted at the others. "A normal person listens to one, maybe two favorite programs! But this one can't take those things out of his ears. The personality of an addict!"

"Darling, don't be upset; the meat is almost ready," said Zhorik.

Lunch was laid out banquet-style in the dining room. I noticed that Katya was doing all the serving for Lenny, sprinkling dill on his potatoes, refilling his shot glass. He seemed to take for granted that he should be so serviced. He had swallowed down an entire bowl of *pelmeni* dumplings, which Valya had set out as the starter, and was already halfway through another. Whenever Katya heard some subtle grunt of hunger from Lenny's direction, she responded by loading another eight dumplings onto his plate. He caught me looking at him and said, "What?"

I couldn't help myself. "Maybe you should pace yourself," I suggested.

"It's all healthy, it's all natural," Valya objected. "Why aren't *you* eating? What, you don't like it?"

"It's all delicious. I'm just not very hungry."

"What are you, an animal, that you only eat when you're hungry?"
I caught Lenny's eye again. *You're letting them stuff you like a goose,* I
wanted to tell him. But even if I could, there would be no point. In some
kind of protest against me, he seemed to be aggressively plowing through
his second portion of dumplings. Then he dropped his eyes and made a
few meager coughs to suggest he wasn't feeling well. "Poor fellow, you
must have caught a cold in your night in the lockup," said Valya. She
turned to me. "It's a crime, the way they can throw a person in jail for
nothing."

"Well, whoever fucked up and put me there is probably paying for it
now," said Lenny.

"What you need for a cold is a little black pepper with your vodka," said
Alyosha. He reached over and sprinkled some black flakes into Lenny's
shot glass. "Down the hatch—this'll cure everything."

"How do you know it was a mistake?" I said.

"What else was it?"

"I don't know. Maybe someone wanted to teach you a lesson," I hinted,
and thought, *What the hell am I doing?*

Lenny stared at me. "What are you talking about?" He sneezed again.

"Poor pet, let's get you some tea," Valentina said, and Katya was instantly up and on her way to the kitchen for a kettle. Not a moment later,
she set a steaming mug before Lenny and began to stir in an ample spoonful of sugar. *My God,* I thought, *he doesn't even stir his own tea.*

"The danger may not be over," I said. "Maybe it's a little early to celebrate."

"A father worries," said Valentina. "That's the way it should be."

"What are we drinking to?" Zhorik said, lifting his glass.

"To family!" said Valentina. "Lenny is part of our family, and now we
are happy to welcome into our home his charming father—Yuliy Leontevich."

I nodded and drank down my vodka. I had come to terms with the fact
that I couldn't spend a week in this country without having my liver held
up at gunpoint. We all had two more shots once Zhorik brought the pork
chops. First we drank to the women at the table, then to happiness and
prosperity—"in *this* life," Alyosha added mysteriously.

"Alyosha believes in reincarnation," said Zhorik. "He's thrown in his
cards on this lifetime."

Alyosha looked down, accustomed to the eternal abuse. "In my next life, I'll come back as a Siamese cat."

"Why wait until your next life to come back an animal?" Valya said. "Turn your jacket inside out and walk into a zoo. The kids will throw candy at you."

"A toast!" Zhorik announced. "For those who are not with us." We raised our glasses and held them without clinking for this most somber of toasts. Not for the first time I noticed how joylessly an alcoholic drinks. Alyosha seemed to take no pleasure in the shot that had been poured for him. He stared at it for a while, like a person staring at a spoonful of bitter medicine, then swallowed it grimly.

I glimpsed Lenny reaching across Katya for a pork chop. "Here, Katusha, give him this one," Valya said, picking out the biggest, best-glazed piece of meat. There were obviously two roles for men at the dacha: browbeaten little boy or pampered pasha. Alyosha was the first, Lenny the second. Each, in its own way, infantilized.

Lenny murmured that it was stuffy, and Katya leaped up instantly to open a window. I had believed that my son did not come home because he was ashamed to return a failure. I hadn't taken into account the sumptuous passivity to which he'd become accustomed, the voluptuous pampering at which Russian women were so adept.

"Take those things out of your damn ears," Valya shouted spontaneously. Alyosha was again listening to his Ekho Moskvy through earbuds. "Can't you see we have company?" Alyosha reluctantly took out his right earbud, and continued listening to Ekho through his left. "I'm going out for a smoke," he said, getting up, in a posture that said, *To hell with you all.* Just at that moment, Zhorik refilled Alyosha's glass and glanced at me mischievously. Like a marionette whose strings had been released, Alyosha sat back down and swallowed. "You see that!" Zhorik said triumphantly. "Bet you don't have alcoholics like ours in your America!"

"You can't judge by American standards," I answered. "In America, an alcoholic is someone who hasn't picked up a drink in ten years."

Valya looked at me curiously. I did my best to explain to the table the concept of AA. "We had a party, and I offered some cognac to our neighbor, Jim," I said. "He declined. When I asked why, he told me: 'Julian, I'm an alcoholic.' I said, 'Jim, I admire your abstemiousness under the circumstances. How long has it been?' 'Twenty years,' he said."

Valya hooted loudly at this. Lenny looked less entertained.

"For Americans, it's all or nothing," Lenny said. "They all love to talk about their freedoms, but they can't live and let live. *I'll* tell you a story: My mother's first job in New York was in the programming department of Bloomingdale's. She didn't know anything about programming; she was just trying to keep her head above water. I got the flu, and she couldn't take any days off, so my sister stayed home with me while Mama went to work. The school called. Mama told them that I was sick and that my thirteen-year-old sister was staying home to look after me. They sent a cop *and* a social worker to our apartment, and threatened to arrest my mother if she continued to keep Masha out of school. Didn't she know she was supposed to hire a sitter in these situations? A sitter! My mother didn't have money to buy herself new shoes! That was the last time *she* told the truth to Americans."

Valya shook her head. "But Mama kept her job."

"It wasn't an easy time," I said. "My first job was in computers too, but downtown. I'd take the subway every afternoon to Sixty-fourth Street, and we'd meet at a Chinese restaurant across the street from the department store, where I'd help her write up her programming code. She'd take it back upstairs to type it. We survived like that for months."

"What a good husband," Valya said with flattering affection in her eyes.

"Not a good teacher, though," Lenny mumbled. "I remember all the yelling."

"I don't recall any yelling," I said, trying to sound good-natured.

"Oh, come on. Truth only at the dacha. You were *always* yelling at Mom, for being dense, for not picking the programming up fast enough, for not picking up English fast enough. It wasn't like *she'd* grown up speaking it."

I grinned painfully. But Lenny wasn't done.

"You said so yourself, that Mama probably would have divorced you if she hadn't been so dependent on you those early years."

For all his criticism of America, it struck me that Lenny was the most forcibly American one at this table: a gabber, a confessor, an over-sharer. Fishing out desiccated bits of family "dysfunction" from the black holes of memory to vindicate himself. But vindication from what? *You child,* I thought.

But in the bathroom, splashing water on my face, I tried to put the episode at lunch behind me. The important thing was to get Lenny alone. I was in luck: stepping outside, I found him on the veranda, reclining amid the Turkish cushions. I had rehearsed what I'd say to him: *Son, listen, I don't think it was those friends of yours who landed you in jail. . . .* But the words now seemed to possess a grubby hollowness. Observing him among the bright pillowcases, his pale thighs spreading out from his nylon running shorts, I was reminded of the slatternly indifference of a pasha in an opium den. "Have you given some more thought to your exit plan?" I said, sitting down beside him. "If you want, I can go to your apartment and pack your things," I offered in what I hoped was a softer tone. "I don't think we should be losing time."

He looked at me with toil-worn eyes, as if I were the last torment of his afternoon, then propped himself up on his elbows. "You've been here, what, a week? And you're already micromanaging my life?"

"I'm not micromanaging. I'm trying to get you out of danger."

"Why don't you let me decide that, okay? I talked to Austin. He had a lawyer look at our end of the deal—I'm completely untouchable."

Just tell him the truth, I thought. But instead what I said was "Goddamn it, Lenny. Today you're out, tomorrow you'll be back in. And lawyers won't do you any good here. You get on the wrong side of someone and they'll spare no effort to hunt you down."

I knew this outrage was camouflage, but my anger felt real. What Lenny needed now was hardness, disciplined talk, not more softness.

"Cool it," he said.

"I will *not* cool it. . . . You are being *grossly* selfish."

"Selfish?" In his eyes was an expression of chagrin or amusement, or possibly both.

"If you land in jail again, who do you think will bail you out? You want to force me and your mother to mortgage the house? You want to bankrupt us in our old age? Because that's what we'll have to do to save your skin."

Browbeating him, I was so steeped in my pretense that I saw no way out. A confession seemed now like a mistake. Lenny would only add it to the satisfying tally of wrongs I had inflicted on him, and I would lose what little clout I had left.

"Don't worry: calling you for help would be the *last* thing on my mind," he said.

I tried to steady my breathing. "Lenny, I know it's not easy to put so much of yourself in a plan that doesn't turn out the way you want. I lost seven years working on a dissertation that they never gave me any credit for. But you know what I thought when I got denied? I thought, *It's better than losing those years in the camps, like my mother.*"

There was a pinch in his brow when he said, "Baba Flora didn't regret her life. And neither do I. She had a front seat on history."

I thought my jaw might drop. "Is that what she called it?"

"She always said, 'The only way to learn who you are is to leave home.'"

"Did she, now? And who *are* you?" I stared at him. "Do you have any idea?"

Lenny stared back at me. "I do, actually. Not that you'd understand." The chagrined expression had deepened the groove between his eyes. "You act like my time here has been a big waste. You think I regret not having spent all these years sitting in a cubicle with four dudes in monkey suits, looking like a diagram of the Chain of Evolution? Dreaming about how I'm going to retire at forty-five, stash away my cash in a T-bill at seven percent, move to a Tahitian island, and have sex on Viagra for the rest of my life? 'Cause that's how the guys I know in America live. No, thanks. I've been part of something bigger here."

"History?" I said, more mockingly than I'd intended.

"My life's *been* an adventure, is what I'm saying. I know that doesn't mean much to you, but I can honestly say I've experienced things about myself—"

"Adventure?" I said. "That's what they call it when everyone comes back alive. Otherwise it's called a tragedy. That's what my father's life was—a tragedy. And my mother's, too, for that matter."

"Yeah? *She* didn't seem to think so."

"That's because she was a narcissist, Lenny," I said. "She didn't think about anybody but herself. She was a grade-A delusional narcissist. Like you."

These last two words, uttered by mistake, fell hard on the planes of his face. For a moment I thought he might cry. But he only looked at me with bitter, laughing eyes. "I get what you're trying to do, Pa. You think if you can make me feel small enough you can put me in your suitcase and take me home." He stood up. "You think this is the first time I've been threatened? You think it's the first time I've been thrown in jail? It wasn't. Trust me, I've learned to withstand worse than the shit you're flinging."

This came as a surprise to me. I was shocked that Lenny had been able to keep something like this private. But what I said was "Well, you've really become a Russian, then. In love with your suffering."

He stood up. His face, above me, looked merely disappointed, nothing more. "Like I said, I don't expect you to understand."

"You're right. I don't understand." I couldn't stop myself now. "I *can't* understand it, because this 'pioneer of human experience' business is not a model for being a man, Lenny. It's not a model for leaving a mark on the world. What you're describing is just a recipe for"—I couldn't help thinking of my mother again—"for being a leaf on the ripples of life!"

How oddly satisfying it felt to say this, even as it undercut any progress I'd hoped to make with my son. How grimly triumphant, like kicking myself in the groin.

Lenny was at the screen door, his eyes still glistening with indignation, when Valya appeared on the porch. Had she been standing there all along, in the shadows? "Well, what's happening here? Not more politics, I hope. The dacha is for relaxing, not for solving world problems. That's our rule."

I was again at eye level with her mighty, yeomanly thighs, which her blue sweatpants, far from concealing, only demonstrated as capable of overpowering even the loosest of clothes. I watched my son go inside and felt an ancient sadness. Valya held a zinc bucket with that morning's mushroom crop, and over her shoulder was slung a bag through whose plastic netting I could see the outlines of apples, cheese, pickle jars. "I'm off on a walk to Aprelevka to bring some food for a friend," she said. "You wanted to see the damage, didn't you? I wouldn't mind some help." She handed me the canvas bag of food without waiting for an answer. "A walk is good for our old bones."

I CARRIED THE BAG while Valya played the role of tour guide. We were walking down a seventeenth-century road, she said. Peter the Great had given all this land to the Demidov family in reward for manufacturing his army's weapons. Valya pointed off to the right, where one of the dilapidated Demidov mansions still stood, its Arcadian grandeur reduced to a redbrick crumble. Wild growth had reclaimed the rows of classical columns. Slender maples and a riot of saplings sprouted from the roofs of the ancient serfs' barracks. Rain-soaked pornography and green beer bottles littered our path through the woods. "Supposedly, this is all being preserved as a national landmark, but, as you can see, our mentality . . ." Valya nodded at the trash. Farther down the road, we met the "monstrosities" she'd warned me about, new mansions whose enviable views of the forest were blocked by the enormous security walls erected to guard them. I could see only the upper stories of these *novostroiki*, no different from the typical American McMansion except for one detail: they had what looked like garage doors cut into the brick. It took me a startled moment to realize that these were security gates, rolled down over enormous windows.

"It's thieves who are most afraid of other thieves," Valya expounded. "We call these Houses for the Poor. Homeless Shelters. You should be here on a Sunday morning after one of their parties. They stand around, hung over, glancing at everyone who passes like a dog they want to kick. Like '*Kto ty takoy?* Who the hell are you to look at *me?*' They've got that look like in our army: 'We'll *punish* you.'"

"No less punishing than the Party bosses of the old days."

"Oh sure, now everyone lambastes 'the Party.' What was the 'Party'? It was *thousands of people. Millions* of people in the Party. If you wanted to do something, be an activist, improve things, you could find channels through the Party. Now a handful of old KGB-ists run everything. Vladimir Vladimirovich and his judo partners have everyone in a chokehold."

We walked onward with our loads. On our left were the *novostroiki* with their mounted security cameras, and on our right, the old log dachas— faded yellow, peeling green, guarded by yapping, mangy dogs. To our left, paranoid New Russia; to our right the decomposing Soviet Union.

"In 1948, Stalin gave all this land to the army general staff," Valya informed me. "After they'd won the war for him. The generals each got a full hectare. The division commanders got a half-hectare, and so on down the line. Fifteen years ago the developers started buying the big plots and doing four-part splits. If we'd held out, we would have gotten even more for our land. But what we got was enough to buy my house. This friend we're going to see—her family divided the land up long ago among themselves and sold it, but she's the last holdout. Oh, she's gotten offers, of course. But she refuses—only because she's got nowhere else to go, poor soul. I'm surprised no one has set her house on fire yet. Don't look shocked.

That's the way ours do it around here. When they rip up the old fencing and put up their horrible walls, they toss the wire and pickets right into her yard. You'll see for yourself."

"YOO-HOO! INNA IVANOVNA!" VALYA called when we arrived. She let herself in through the open door while I waited on the front steps and observed the sad sight of the yard. Splintered wood and wire lay about as if after a tornado. Mold-rotted bricks protruded from the foundation like teeth from decayed gums. A bathtub with broken feet collected rainwater beside a rusted old *kanistra* of the sort once used to store gasoline. Aside from a meager vegetable garden and some gnarled apple trees, the yard was overrun with weeds.

Descending the steps, Inna Ivanovna finally emerged: a tiny babushka with shorn hair, and hands as arthritic as her apple trees. She wore a ratty gray sweater, sweatpants, and felt slippers.

"Inna Ivanovna, I hope you don't mind us stopping by like this—we were just passing through. This is my friend Yuliy Leontevich. He's come here all the way from *America*."

"Please, come in—just step over that," Inna Ivanovna said, motioning to the piles of cotton insulation littering the floor. She seemed not to care whether I was from America or the moon.

"Some mushrooms for you, from our forest, and berries to make a compote," said Valya, then set out everything, including the cheese, pickles, and vegetables, on the old woman's rickety kitchen table.

"Oh, Valya. You didn't need to."

"We're leaving Sunday, and all this is just going to spoil during the week," she said, though anyone could see the food was fresh from the store.

"Come, come; please, don't mind this mess." The old elfin creature kicked another pile of insulation from the door. "My son brought this over so I could winterize that side of the house. It gets so cold."

Did she really spend the winter in this place? I did not want to believe it. I could not explain how a house like this could remain standing, let alone stay warm. Its walls were water-damaged, its plywood partitions warped. Above the kitchen table hung a round cardboard frame lamp of a sort I had not seen in four decades. The cloth stretched over it like a pair of old bloomers. The wiring that fed it was ancient ceramic-coated circuitry, pinned with staples to the walls because inside the walls the wires would surely catch fire. Inna Ivanovna sat watching Valya put the food into a knee-high refrigerator, her back pressed against an ancient wood-fired wall oven. Was it possible she still used it? Above a low cupboard, like an icon, hung a portrait of young Pushkin.

"How long are you staying in our *posyolok?*" Inna Ivanovna inquired kindly.

Valya answered for me. "Yulik is flying back to America next week. He *lives* there. He's Lenny's father."

"Who?"

"Lenny. Katya's young man."

"Katusha is a sweet girl," the old woman said, smiling at me.

"Yes," I averred.

"HOW CAN THAT WOMAN'S CHILDREN let her live in that death trap?" I asked on our way home.

"Her son lives in her apartment in Moscow. He's a nihilist. That's my diagnosis." Valya snapped her thumb and forefinger against her throat in the sign for a drinker. "Owes everyone money. Makes just enough for a smoke and a bottle."

"I guess even being the grandson of a division commander can't rescue someone from that fate."

"No, it can't. Look at our Alyosha! Didn't lack for anything growing up. Piano lessons, tutors. Ninochka was flying all over the world with her delegations, but there were four grandparents, and just one little miracle between them."

"So what happened?"

"The nineties were hardest of all on Alyosha's generation. Everything collapsed just as they were getting on their feet, and the foreign companies only wanted to hire kids right out of university—before they'd been spoiled by our Soviet system. The ones like Alyosha, who were in their thirties and forties when it all fell down—it was discouraging to watch some of them flounder."

"You're older," I said, "and you've done all right."

"I'd do all right anywhere." And I knew this was true.

It occurred to me that what Valya *had* inherited from her high-Soviet upbringing might be what my son lacked: a sense of discretion, an instinct for keeping her mouth shut. I decided to risk it and ask if among the people she knew there might be a worker at the FSB archives.

"That little place on Neglinnaya?" Valya said, raising a brow. "What do you need there?"

"I want to find my parents' dossiers."

"That's right—weren't they 'enthusiasts'?"

Lenny had clearly briefed her on our family history.

I told her about the trouble I'd run into. "I leave Tuesday morning," I said.

"You can always ask your son to get them on your behalf, can't you? Just go to a notary."

She certainly knew the rules of the place, but it wasn't the response I was hoping for. I didn't want to tell her that I still held out hope that Lenny would be out of the country before I was.

"I don't need to burden him with another task," I said. "He's too busy for that sort of thing. He won't even inform us when he plans to come home for a visit."

"Uh-hm."

Perhaps I did protest too much, because Valya said, "Or maybe you don't want him snooping around what he won't understand. People didn't exactly show their best side in those interrogation rooms, did they?"

I smiled.

"Understood," she said. "Aren't you worried that *I'll* read them?"

"I'd expect nothing less. What honest Russian wouldn't read someone else's file?"

"You're a mean one. Give me your letter; I'll inquire."

"I'll see that you won't take a loss on it," I said, gratefully.

For a while we walked in pleasant silence. And soon, with the sun low but the evening still bright, we were back on the road that led to the house. "I like you, Yuliy," she said, when we passed the sign announcing Alabino, "so I'll be frank. Lenny told me what you've come to talk to him about. It's none of my business, but I know how these arrangements work. If he leaves, it'll be the end of him and Katya. I'm not very objective, I know. I don't want my niece's heart broken. She's a good girl."

"What he decides is up to him," I said.

"But I know what you're thinking: Why is he being so stubborn, why doesn't he take your help?"

I said nothing.

Valya sighed. "I suppose my family thought I was squandering my inheritance too. And now look—my lack of grand ambitions is what saved me."

"I don't want him to blame me for his regrets," I said, and realized it was true.

"Then it's just yourself you're worried about."

"Valya, you've been very hospitable to my son. I want him to feel as at home . . . with his family."

"People feel at home around those who *like* them," she objected.

Maybe as a provocation, or maybe to downplay Lenny as such a prize for her Katya, or maybe because I was curious, I said, "Tell me what you like about him." (Aside from his American passport, I wanted to add, but did not.)

"I like that, in spite of his best efforts, he's a decent guy. There's not enough kindness in our world. Nine years in this country hasn't ruined him. Now that's something."

Decency. Kindness. Things that in our household were taken seriously but not dwelled on as pious notions.

"He was a kind child," I said, looking ahead to Valya's driveway. "Sensitive. It used to upset him visibly when another youngster was crying. The teachers had a nickname for him in preschool: 'the gentleman.' Maybe, if he'd been different," I said, "I wouldn't have warned him about coming to do business here. His mother and I warned him a dozen times."

"Well, aren't you smart for *warning* him," Valya said. She stopped walking in the road. She looked impatient and exasperated. "Anybody can do that. You're in this racket too. You warned him—so what! But you didn't *prepare* him, did you?"

IN MY ROOM, I LAY on the firm bed that was too excellent even for Putin to appreciate. Outside the light had grown dim. I took a few deep, restoring breaths of the pine-scented air. The insects chirped their summer noises. On the writing table, my now charged phone was blinking its green message light.

There was a single message, from Tom.

"It's me. Don't want to rain out your dacha plans, but Kablukov is back in the city. Wants to see us tomorrow afternoon at the Sanduny Baths. Can't imagine what might be on his mind. I'll see you there at noon."

Some choice for a board meeting, I thought—the old city *banya*. All the better to impress us with his prison tattoos. What angle did this old enforcer plan to take now to convince us to rubber-stamp his little kickback scheme?

It meant I would have only tonight with my son, and have to leave in the morning.

I sat and stared for a while at the soft-focus photograph of young Alyosha—the angelic, bright-eyed boy who would evolve into the acrid, afflicted creature downstairs. A nonperson, as he said. It was making me recall a similarly posed photograph of myself that my mother had framed and kept in her room in the communal apartment. The picture had obviously been taken before her arrest. I didn't know how she'd managed to hold on to it during her years of imprisonment, though to me it had always been an emblem of her tight grip on illusions, signifying her inability to see me for who I had become. For this reason, I kept no enlarged angelic photographs of my own children within view.

All these years I had been certain that someday Lenny would have to return home to his family. What I had not accounted for, and what was suddenly plain to me at this dacha with its drunks and misfits, was that Lenny *had* a family—if family meant people who accepted you as you were.

I HEARD A KNOCKING on the door.

"It opens," I called.

It was Lenny, hair moist and combed, in a clean shirt rolled to his elbows. He looked about the room uncertainly. "Did you fall asleep or something?" He looked me in the eye and turned his palms out at his sides. "Come on, everyone's waiting. The shashlik is ready." His lip was curled into a half-smile, which I took as a signal that, at least for the sake of the shashliks, he was willing to put down his weapons.

"Let's eat," I said, putting down mine.

33.

SECOND CHANCES

Kuibyshev, 1943

HER RESCUE ARRIVED IN THE FORM OF A NATIONAL CATASTROPHE. THE
Great Patriotic War got Florence out of Moscow, out of the hands of the
secret police, and once more into the bustle of consequential work that
she craved.

On the Volga River's docks, the dusty summer evening of '43 presents
a ramming chaos of evacuees. The old river city of Samara, since renamed
Kuibyshev, has become the nation's wartime capital. Around the chipped
embankment form serpentine lines for meager wartime rations of sugar,
vegetable oil, kerosene, matches. The only bread available is the roughest
rye. These provisions are ferried into the city on boats or brought on horse-
drawn covered wagons and sold off the wagons and boats themselves. All
of the trucks and automobiles have been recommissioned for the military.
It has occurred to Florence that—were it not for the mounted loudspeakers on every corner, providing constant updates on the war—life in Kuibyshev might resemble the bootstrapping bustle of some nineteenth-century
frontier town. Down at the bottom of the docks, where paddlewheel
steamers deliver more supplies, the mosquitoes have started to swarm.
The terraced hills across the Volga are ablaze with a dissolving sunset. Everyone is in a hurry to get their provisions—which this evening include
salted fish and salami, on account of the recent victory in Kursk—and be
indoors by sundown. At last, Florence, her copious hair tied back in a kerchief to protect it from the dust, obtains her own food parcel swaddled in

newspaper, and is spat out by the same elbowing crowd that's borne her to the front of the line. The fish feels pleasantly heavy under her arm as she squeezes past bodies of every age and variety of sweat—the musky brawl of men, the resinous stink of the old, the grapy tang wafting off the necks of young women—until she is released into the open air, then proceeds down a street littered with oily bits of newsprint, and approaches a brick doorway from which a cold cellar draft emerges to greet her. There is no light—the bulb has been screwed out—and the stairwell windows are covered with dark paper. She navigates by touch until she reaches the top floor and opens the door to the odor of burnt coffee. The first thing she sees is the table, still covered in papers, though she has asked to have it cleared tonight. At either end sit Leon and his friend Seldon Parker, Parker's glasses reflecting the last of the evening's saffron light.

"I thought we were celebrating tonight. Why are you two still working?"

"What am I supposed to do with this?" Parker says, lifting a sheet of paper like it's a dirty undergarment. He begins to read aloud: " 'Hitler's savage hordes set out to overrun the world, rob the toiling people of their last crumb of bread, kill, rape, gouge out eyes, rip off women's breasts, disembowel, chop off heads.' "

"Who wrote that one?" says Leon.

"Our national literary treasure, Dovid Bergelson." He reads on: " 'The most atrocious of all is the cruelty they practice on our Jewish brothers and sisters in all of the countries they overrun. They never tire of inventing new instruments in the forms of torture and execution. . . .' " He pauses to add, "And Dovid Bergelson never tires of ways to describe them. 'All the calamities which have ever beset our long-suffering people—both in ancient times when Nero drove Jews into circus arenas to be devoured by lions, and in the Middle Ages when Jews donning shrouds went to die at the stake or themselves applied sharp knives to the throats of their children in order to save them from a more horrible death that awaited them— all these calamities pale before Hitler's cruelties. . . . Day and night their blood, splattered against fences, running over the pavement, calls out to us. It flows and flows in ditches and sewers, and no Mother Rachel will rise from her grave and cry out for Justice.' "

"He hasn't left anything out, has he?" says Florence.

"Nero's circuses, lions, disembowelments, Mother Rachel—oh my!"

Seldon clutches his hair. "Give a Jew a pen and he'll maul you with it. Doesn't he understand that no paper in England or America is going to print this?"

"You can't expect a great novelist to conform to the dictates of the Western capitalist press," says Leon.

"Great novelist, ha! He's become a bigger hack than Ehrenburg."

"Then cut something," says Florence, starting to clear the papers from the table herself.

"We're translators, not editors," Parker says helplessly. "And if you haven't noticed, we have a mountain of these masterpieces to finish."

Which, in fact, is the case. Stacked on the chairs and windowsill are piles of dispatches: articles and essays documenting Nazi atrocities against the Jews, profiles of Jewish officers and pilots, biographical sketches of scientists and engineers in the defense industry—all to be prepared for publication. But not in the Soviet papers, where they are useless and unwelcome. These communiqués must be translated into flawless English, with no ounce of poignancy lost, and made suitable for the foreign bourgeois presses: the Chicago *Daily Herald, The Boston Globe, The New York Times,* the *Evening Standard.* For all their purple prose, the aim of these articles is simple: to help the Red Army raise money in America and England. At last, Florence is doing the Important Work she has waited all her life to perform. Every morning, she and Leon—comrades-in-arms on the ideological front—walk together to the office of the SovInformBuro on Vantsek Street to translate the dispatches that have been approved by the editorial board and military censors for consumption by American and European readers.

The theme of international friendship is stressed at every turn. The Volga, which Hitler's troops are threatening to cut off, is referred to as "the Soviet Mississippi." If a successful attack has employed British Hurricanes or Spitfires, or American bombers, the article is to follow this formula: First profile the heroic Soviet pilot, then go on to praise the machinery and make note of its manufacturer. If an American company has sent a donation of blood transfusion kits or portable X-rays to a Soviet field hospital, the article should first mention the brave and skillful nurses, then the ways in which the medical equipment has eased the pain of the wounded soldier; finally, the name of the company and country that sent the supplies must be noted. Every gift deserves a thank-you card. In charge of generating this mountain of propaganda are a number of anti-fascist committees—one for women, another for scientists, yet another for youths, one more for Slavs—each producing editorial content to milk a different segment of the foreign public. But it is no secret inside the offices of the SovInformBuro that the most lucrative wartime agitprop by far is being exported by the Jewish Anti-Fascist Committee. Its members are Yiddish writers, poets, and actors, some of them celebrities even beyond the Soviet Union. There is the poet Peretz Markish, wild-haired prophet of the avant-garde; David Hofshteyn, poet-elegist and compatriot of Marc Chagall; Leyb Kvitko, beloved author of children's verse; and the novelist Dovid Bergelson, perhaps the best-known Yiddish story writer besides Babel. All of these men once left Russia to live abroad, to wander through Warsaw and Berlin, Paris and New York, London, Vienna, Palestine. Each one of them, unable to support himself with his writing in a world indifferent to the *mame loshn*, has since returned to the Soviet Union, lured by promises of publication and of a Yiddish renaissance funded by the government. Unbeknownst to their humble translators, each of these celebrities feels as trapped as Leon and Florence. (Markish, in a secret letter to a Warsaw friend, has written: "We don't know what world we're in. In this atmosphere of trying to be terribly proletarian and one hundred percent kosher, much falseness, cowardice, and vacillation have manifested themselves and it has become impossible to work.") But now, after years of evading peacetime terror, they too have emerged into the relative safety of war. Like Florence and Leon, they have been granted a second chance.

At the helm of the Jewish Anti-Fascist Committee is Solomon Mikhoels—renowned actor and director of the State Yiddish Theater. His five-foot-tall jester's body and pugilist's face are instantly recognized by Moscow's audiences from his role as "the Jewish King Lear." A little-known fact: just before war broke out, Mikhoels feared for his life, and with good reason. The NKVD had been planning to link him to the arrested Isaac Babel. But when a thief is needed, he is brought back from the gallows. Spared, for the time being, the eminent performer is entrusted with the task of squeezing dollars out of foreign Jews to fight the Nazi scourge. At the very moment when Florence is clearing away papers to set the table in honor of Leon's twenty-ninth birthday, Solomon Mikhoels is breakfasting on a sunny veranda in Los Angeles with Charlie Chaplin, who has helped him raise money among the Jews of Hollywood.

Months earlier, Mikhoels and the poet Itzik Feffer were put on an ocean liner bound for New York. Everywhere they went, great swarms of people gathered. At a rally at the Polo Grounds, Mayor Fiorello La Guardia greeted them as old friends while American and Soviet flags snapped in the wind. The head of their welcome committee was none other than Albert Einstein. Privately, Mikhoels and Feffer could not stand each other, but onstage, with the red carpet rolled out for them, they became blood brothers. From below, one hundred thousand American eyes watched Mikhoels carefully lift up a crystal urn filled with yellow and black dirt, but no flowers. At the raised rostrum he addressed his American brethren: "Before I came, some friends from the Moscow Theater and I bought this vase. Our soldiers filled it with some earth from Ukraine, which holds the screams of mothers and fathers, of the young boys and girls who did not live to grow up. Look at this. You will see laces from a child's shoes, tied by little Sara who fell with her mother. Look carefully and you will see the tears of an old Jewish woman. . . . Look closely and you will see your fathers who are crying 'Sh'ma Israel' and beseeching heaven for a rescuing angel. . . . I have brought you this soil of sorrow. Throw into it some of your flowers so they will grow symbolically for our people. . . . In spite of our enemies, we shall live."

Cheers burst forth from the crowd. Men in felt fedoras stood at quivering attention. Women wept into their fur stoles. They had been primed for the arrival of Mikhoels and Feffer by articles and essays in American newspapers, translated from tragic Yiddish into galvanizing English by none other than Leon Brink and Seldon Parker. Offstage, Mikhoels's secret police escorts took note of the actor's tear-streaked face. He was, of course, an orator of the first rank, the obvious choice for this important trip. To his left stood Itzik Feffer. In Russia he was known for his tepid, satirical verse. Among his literary comrades in the Jewish Anti-Fascist Committee were those who thought him undeserving of being selected to accompany Mikhoels on such a glamorous voyage. Each believed he ought to have been chosen in Feffer's place. All of them, having lived abroad, knew they would never be allowed to set foot outside the Soviet Union again. It was the shared opinion among them that Feffer's great talent was not for poetry but for tacking with the political winds. On this score they were correct: it would be Feffer's testimony, after the war, that would lead to their roundup and arrests. But now, standing beside Mikhoels, Feffer was taken aback by the violent affection of the crowd. The air in the open stadium smelled of corn dogs and the fusillade of camera flashes. He looked down into the audience as if into an abyss. The faces of the American Jews were hardly distinguishable from those of Russian ones. Only their eyes were different. The absence of fear in them alarmed him. He felt disturbed by their untamed goodwill, already sensing how this public ceremony of adoration would be repaid with a private ceremony of vengeance once they returned home. Feffer approached the rostrum and, speaking in Yiddish and Russian, urged their support for the heroic Red Army.

Leon and Florence, confined to the boundaries of the country that had forcibly adopted them, did not witness any of this, though they were able to read in the foreign presses about the trip's success. Hadassah, the Jewish National Fund, and B'nai B'rith all welcomed Mikhoels and Feffer with profound enthusiasm. Fund-raising dinners were held for them in Boston, New York, Pittsburgh, and Detroit. Everywhere they went, Jews opened their purses. At an event in Chicago, so many people rushed the stage that it collapsed under Mikhoels's feet. He would complete his tour on crutches.

Beneath this froth of giving was a cataract of genuine feeling, a common pulse tapped by Soviet writers who, for a decade or more, had been prohibited from any open talk of Jewish unity or Jewish suffering. The fight against fascism had loosened their shackles—or, rather, made their proclamations a matter of military necessity. "I grew up in a Russian city," wrote Ilya Ehrenburg, the most prominent journalist of his time, and Stalin's own court Jew. "My mother tongue is Russian. I am a Russian writer. Like all Russians, I am now defending my homeland. But the Nazis have reminded me of something else: my mother's name was Hannah. I am a Jew. I say this proudly. Hitler hates us more than anyone else, and this makes us proud."

And what about Florence and Leon—were they immune to the force of these once-forbidden sentiments? For Florence, watching Leon translate dispatches day and night was no less startling than noting the changes in her own body. Leon's identity as a Jew was maturing from a nomadic wanderlust born in the tenements to a full-on national consciousness. Years later she would wonder if the Biblical echoes in Markish's poems were responsible for her husband's surreptitious attendance at the Moscow Choral Synagogue on the eve of Yom Kippur, if the reports of Jewish soldiers fighting bravely in Stalingrad were what nursed his budding interest in the mechanics of shortwave radio, by which he would follow the secret transmissions broadcasting the struggles of a new state being formed in the desert.

But all that is in the future. For now, Florence finishes clearing the table of papers and lays out on chipped enamel dishes her bounty of salted fish, kielbasa, and black bread. The men are less than helpful in setting the table, lost in talk of the recent military turnaround at Kursk. If the bloody triumph at Stalingrad was mainly an accident of climate (the same brutal Russian winter that had stymied Napoleon's armies a century earlier), then the strategic offensive on the Eastern Front this summer has been more reliable proof of the Red Army's mettle. The tide of war has turned. "It won't be long," says Leon, "before all the fighting is over."

"Pure bosh," objects Seldon, rolling himself a cigarette of cheap *makhorka*, the only tobacco available. "Nothing's going to be over until the Allies open a second front in Europe. We'll provide them with cannon fodder until everyone's exhausted or dead, and then the squire of Hyde Park and that pompous pair of jowls will finally grace us with a few battalions. And just in time, deus ex machina, to get all the bloody credit."

"Roosevelt wants to enter, he's only waiting for a decision from Churchill."

"You sweet soul. Those two gentlemen sausages are in it together. If Germany were winning, they'd help Russia. But if Russia is winning, they'll help Germany by doing nothing. Just as long as they're getting as many dead bodies as possible on both sides."

Since their evacuation to Kuibyshev, the three of them have been living and working side by side in this tiny attic flat. Staying up and talking late into the nights. Their domestic arrangement makes Florence think of Seldon as their ward, though more often it's Seldon, with his mix of Yiddish and East London inflections, who sounds like their guardian. When he gets his teeth into a topic, he won't let go, and he keeps sounding off about Roosevelt and Churchill even as the siren wail from the loudspeakers announces curfew. Florence squints through the window. Everywhere, lights are being turned off, gas lamps extinguished, cigarettes snuffed out. She gets on her knees and fetches the thick black-painted paper they keep behind the wardrobe. She drags a chair to the window and carefully mounts it, her movements becoming more deliberate and cautious as, on her tiptoes, she begins to tape the paper to the top of the window. By now the street below is practically invisible, quarantined in a darkness meant to protect the city from German air-raid bombs. For the past two years they have lived in a constant state of emergency, and still, during most of that time, Florence has been unaccountably happy. So happy, in fact, that she can hardly admit it to herself without a momentary twinge of shame. All over the Eastern Front, men are falling dead—being slaughtered, as they say, in the flower of their youth. Wives have been separated from their husbands, sweethearts from lovers. And every morning, she wakes afresh into a state of guilt and gratitude to find Leon asleep (alive!) beside her. It is like a miracle. All over the country, mothers and wives are opening envelopes with death notices. Essie, back in Moscow, has already received a *pokhoronka* of her own. In a letter, she has informed Florence that her young husband perished during the assault on Rostov. At the age of twenty-six, Essie is already a widow, her grief tempered only by the fact that she has "no orphan mouth to feed at a time like this." It is while Florence is balanced on top of the wooden chair, thinking about her friend, that she suddenly feels it. A brief flutter in the slightly gas-distended balloon of her abdomen. But this time it is not indigestion from the Lend-Lease gelatinized meat Leon brought home a few days earlier (a delicacy donated by the Americans, with the letters SPAM printed on the can). What she feels is a disturbance not at all gastronomical: a flapping of butterfly wings, a tiny somersault. For the first time, the new life, quarantined in a protective darkness all its own, announces itself. For a moment, Florence loses her balance.

Leon jumps up, hearing the chair's scrape. "What are you doing up there! You shouldn't be doing that."

"You were too busy strategizing our victory."

"Put that paper down. I'll glue it."

"That's right," pipes in Seldon. "Your woman's been on her feet long enough. Come and have a drink, Florie. We're celebrating tonight. Your boy's a man. Almost thirty years old!"

"I'll put the kettle on," she says.

"Enough, you teetotaler. A little homespun spirit won't kill you."

Leon attaches the last piece of rolled paper to the window and glances at Florence as if asking permission. She gives a happy shrug.

"Seldon, Florie's going to have a baby."

Seldon's eyes, growing wide, turn from one to the other. "You're having me on."

"No, it's true."

"Fancy that—she's up the duff! How long?"

"Going on six months," Florence says, almost demurely. The wartime rations have kept her alarmingly skinny. And this time, she thinks, there won't be any stupid abortions. She has been given a second chance. This child, when he is born—God willing—she will cherish to the end of her days.

"Well, well," says Parker. "Keeping your little secret all this time from Uncle Seldon."

From his green bottle he pours a bit of moonshine into their mismatched glasses. He always seems to have a supply, in spite of the deficits, procuring it through his own secret channels. "A little bit for Mama," he says, pouring a drop into Florence's teacup ("It's bad luck to toast with water"), and then raises his own glass. "From now on," Seldon announces, "may it be only the baby's cries that keep us up in the dark."

She raises her cup, satisfyingly heavy in her hand, and takes a drink.

34.

LIFE VS. PRAVDA

THE ACTOR'S FUNERAL TOOK PLACE ON AN OVERCAST DAY IN JANUARY and was held in the grand style accorded to state heroes. Mourners met the coffin at the Belorusskaya railway station as it was being removed from the Minsk concourse. A polished motorcade ferried the casket through the snowy streets of Moscow into the open courtyard of the Moscow State Jewish Theater where thousands had gathered on the surrounding streets to say their goodbyes. The casket was laid open in the Russian style. Inside, ensconced in a froth of satin and smothered by flowers, lay the great Solomon Mikhoels, his mutilated features made up with greasepaint as if for one last role. His body had been found days earlier in an ice-scabbed snowbank on a side street in Minsk, where Mikhoels had been summoned to judge a play for the Stalin Prize. An apparent hit-and-run. Pressed into his flesh by the wheels of an automobile was the solid-gold cigarette case given to him by the Jews of America during his tour of their continent—the souvenir of his propaganda work.

Overhead, the telephone wires sagged with sheaths of ice. Tears froze on faces before they could be wiped away. Among the mourners were Mikhoels's compatriots from the theater. The Yiddish actors of Minsk had followed the body in its casket to Moscow. Two evenings earlier, they had taken turns lingering like inconspicuous bodyguards outside Mikhoels's hotel room, alert to a foreboding they could not themselves explain. That evening was dark and windy. Mikhoels was paged to the hotel telephone.

The caller invited him to a dacha belonging to the Belorussian minister of state security. Snow was falling when a taxi arrived for him. On the road to the city outskirts its headlamps were trained on the softly sifting flakes. At the dacha, agents held back Mikhoels's balding head and beat him unconscious. He was taken to the ruins of the old Minsk ghetto and run over by a truck. The snow continued to fall well into the morning.

The theater building was too small to hold the crowd, which spilled out into the courtyard and alleys. In the great congress of mourners stood writers and associates of Mikhoels from the Jewish Anti-Fascist Committee. At the foot of the casket was gathered the triumvirate of Yiddish lyrical poets: Markish, Kvitko, and Hofshteyn. It had been agreed that Markish would give the eulogy. Mounting the speaker's platform, the poet wore no hat. His hair stood up, stiff and unruly, as if suggesting the tormented outrage of his being. His voice rang through the brittle air with the clang of bronze.

> *Snow covered the wounds on your face,*
> *so the shadows of darkness couldn't touch you*
> *but the pain rages in your dark eyes,*
> *and cries out from your trampled heart.*

A stir passed through the crowd. The poem was the first sign given during the carefully orchestrated ceremony that Mikhoels's death was not accidental. Markish continued to read from his slip of paper, taking no notice of the crowd.

> *I want to come, eternity, before your defiled door*
> *with the stigmata of murder and blasphemy upon my face,*
> *just as my people walk five-sixths of the globe,*
> *a testimony to axe and hatred for you to recognize.*

Standing pressed in the throng, Florence felt the charge pass through the bodies like an electric current. Her Russian, though capable and quick, was not attuned to the coded clairvoyance of poetry. She tried to read the faces around her. Beside Markish stood the actor Benjamin Zuskin, who had played the Fool to Mikhoels's Lear. The two had been the great acting duo of Moscow's Yiddish theater. In the past two days Zuskin had taken

Mikhoels's place as the head of the Jewish Anti-Fascist Committee, which had been moved to Moscow at the end of the war. Now his comic face seemed seized by a kind of physical pathology. His promotion to this top office had made him unable to sleep. He did not expect to live to see 1949. On the other side of the speaker's podium stood the poet Hofshteyn, who had lived in Palestine but returned to Kiev before the war to care for his two sons, left motherless by the death of his first wife. He was as bald as a rook. His black eyes gazed into the distance in front of him so intensely they appeared to cross. It occurred to Florence that all of them had the look of chess pieces left vulnerable by the capture of their queen. The only exception to this was Solomon Lozovsky, the chairman of the SovInform-Buro, to whom Florence herself reported. The old revolutionist had been a compatriot of Lenin's. At seventy, he was still physically imposing. He had once worked as a blacksmith in the railroad town of Lozovaya, Ukraine—which was how he'd gotten his name. Now every breath Lozovsky took left a crystal residue on the hairs of his spade-shaped beard. His eyes seemed to flash a terrible Biblical judgment at Markish's reckless push against the limits of caution.

Florence and Essie stood together, holding each other's gloved hands. Leon and Seldon Parker were stationed closer to the casket, among the important people, having been the official translators for the JAFC. The ceremony was drawing to a close. One by one, people began to approach the casket, lay their lips on the waxen forehead. But it was Seldon who now drew Florence's attention. Standing beside Lozovsky's middle-aged secretary, Olivia Bern, he was whispering something in her ear. The lenses of his steel-rimmed spectacles flashed as he pointed a finger up to the roof of the theater building, where, as if out of nowhere, a man had material-ized.

Undaunted by the cold, the man wore no coat. His shirt, open to his thin chest, flapped in the wind. His only concessions to the climate, Flor-ence saw as he raised his violin, were the fingerless gloves with which he held his instrument. And then, spontaneously, the music ruptured the tight air like a rip in a bolt of fabric. Gathering into a melody, it seemed to erase its own pattern with each new note. The violinist appeared to play as if through no effort of his own, the dirge pulling him to and fro with the wind. Florence could feel the melody's precarious grip on her frightened heart. She had met Mikhoels in Kuibyshev but had not known the great man closely. Now she experienced the music as a thin torch throwing its light on the steps of a spiraling scaffoldless stairwell, ascending even as it illuminated the cavernous depths below. Among Mikhoels's gallery of characters had been Tevye the Dairyman. And now the fiddler's song was heard by those below as an ode to that role. There seemed to be no definition of grief other than the one announced by his tune.

Slowly, the cortege of people began to disperse, some following the casket to its burial, others heading homeward. The fiddler, whoever he was, continued to play his strange requiem into the evening, long after the last of the mourners was gone.

ALL DAY THEY HAD STOOD outside on their feet. Now strong tea and cognac were the means by which the four of them, in Leon and Florence's room, revived themselves from the cold. The dark window was spattered with icy rain, and neither Essie nor Seldon seemed to want to be the first to leave.

"Wouldn't you say it was as grand as Kirov's funeral?" said Essie, addressing Florence in a confectionary voice intended to lift everybody's spirits. From his place in the old armchair, Seldon took a deep suck of cognac. The contraction on his face was too slight for Essie to notice. "Well, maybe not as fancy as Kirov's," she pursued, "but certainly as grand as Maxim Gorky's."

"Grand, grand, grand," intoned Seldon. "Funerals are to the Russians what carnivals are to the Portuguese."

"Well, I thought it was rather somber, not festive at all," said Essie.

Seldon turned to her. "Do you know what the definition of a carnival is, Essie?"

Leon, who had been gazing off into space, turned to give Seldon a look of mute warning. Essie didn't reply. "It's a ritual of sanctioned absurdity," Seldon continued. "Everyday rules are suspended for its duration so that everybody can temporarily indulge in pretending things are the opposite of what they are." Seldon's voice had grown rich and heavy with drink.

"Essie, why don't you and I collect Yulik from Aunt Dunya's room," Florence suggested. "I shouldn't have left him napping into the evening."

"Yes, the time. I'd better be scurrying," said Seldon, though he made no move to get out of his chair.

———

YULIK WAS AWAKE. HE was sitting with his stockinged feet curled under him on the bed, playing with some mismatched buttons and knickknacks in a rusty tin. Seeing his mother, the boy abandoned his project and hopped off the bed to run into Florence's arms. She gathered him and lifted him up on her hip. "Have you had a good day with Aunt Dunya, *bubala?*" The boy didn't answer. He continued to stare at Florence, as if to verify the reality of his mother's presence.

"We went to the children's park, and now he's helping me sort out my sewing kit," said Aunt Dunya, who was nobody's aunt. Avdotya Grigorievna had been a servant to the apartment's original owners, before they had fled to Paris. She'd managed to appropriate for her room some of their better furnishings, including a mirrored vanity, a rosewood armoire, and an intricate house-shaped cuckoo clock, all of which she kept as polished as when she'd been the family maid. She had contrived to get herself a disability certificate and enjoyed the official status of "invalid." Nonetheless, her disability pension was small, and in spite of its valuable bric-a-brac, her room always emitted a mildewed smell, possibly because all of Aunt Dunya's clothes and underwear dated from the same period as the furniture. What money she lived on came from looking after the building's small children when their parents were at work.

"How about a kiss for Aunt Essie?"

The boy acknowledged Essie but hung on to his mother's neck with the grip of a primate. "Has he been fed?"

"We had some nice cabbage soup, but he only ate half the bowl."

"It had boiled onions," the boy finally spoke, in his defense.

IN THE HALLWAY THE BOY watched the pattern of shadows cast by his mother's and Essie's moving bodies on the floorboards. He was tugging his mother's hand, trying to lead her back toward their room, while her friend held on to her other wrist, forcing her motion in the opposite direction. They were speaking in quiet, secretive tones.

"Any chance you might be bringing any more magazines around?"

"Essie, hush."

"Oh, there's no one here. It's been months. I miss our 'reading nights.'"

"I do too, but they've gotten so strict at work, even with the old issues. I'd have to stay late to get them, after everyone's gone."

"Just do it like before. Slip one into a *Pravda* and stick it in your coat. I don't even care if it's in English, honey, as long as it's got some pictures."

The boy tugged harder on his mother's arm, to no avail.

"Is there something else?"

"No. Well, yes," said Essie. "I wanted to ask you about Seldon. . . ."

"Our Seldon?"

"You'd tell me if he's . . . got somebody."

"What do you mean?"

"A woman."

"Oh. If he does, it's no one he's told us about."

"It's just . . . I saw him chatting with Olivia Bern, Lozovsky's secretary, after the funeral. They were standing together a long time."

Florence had an impulse to smile. She knew Bern from Kuibyshev, a Swiss émigrée who'd come to Russia in the twenties. As secretary to the head of SovInformBuro, she was dry and humorless, dispensing assignments in a clipped manner, one of those Bolshevik old maids who were married to their work. "Olivia's too old for him by fifteen years. They're friendly, as far as I know."

"You're right. She's so plain and unattractive. I don't know why I asked. . . . Please don't mention it."

"Essie, I'd *never*."

"I know you wouldn't breathe a word."

"I'll see you tomorrow, dear."

IN THE KITCHEN, FLORENCE found her galvanized tin tub and warmed some water on the stove. She brought the tub and water back into the room and found a starched linen towel in their wardrobe. Leon had Yulik on his lap, and Seldon was still sitting in the old armchair, his long legs crossed, exactly as when she'd left.

"If they wanted him d-e-a-d, why the hero's funeral?" Leon said.

"Would it be the first time?"

"Accidents happen."

"Is he an old drunk that he'd be walking around at night, freezing in a snowbank? They wanted him out of the way."

"But what for?"

Over the armrests of the chair, Seldon's hands hung as if severed at the joints. He was a willowy man with an absence of bony definition in his limbs. Without quite knowing why, Florence found it puzzling and amusing that Essie should take a sudden interest in him. Above the bed in Essie's room hung an enlarged portrait of the dead young man to whom she'd been briefly married. The corners of the frame were festooned with artificial lilies. She and her young man had been husband and wife for twenty-three months—most of that time spent apart—but Essie had taken so ardently to her mourning that she still spoke of "my Misha" with vocal trembling that suggested a lifetime of love. However, every widow had a right to her grief, and Florence, counting her own blessings, kept quiet whenever Essie dwelled rapturously on her sorrow. Perhaps her shy curiosity about Seldon suggested a positive change. He might not be a dashing officer, but the war's losses had left eligible men in short supply. Yet Florence could not help feeling something . . . misguided, perhaps, in the attraction, if only because Seldon had never shown any interest in Essie apart from the elaborate irony with which he frequently treated her. Florence took Yulik out of her husband's arms. "Raise your hands," she said, and lifted his shirt over his head. She knelt and slid his ribbed wool stockings down his four-year-old legs.

"I don't know. I think something's being cooked up," said Seldon.

"Inside the committee or the whole bureau?"

"All the staff changes—the twat of a section editor they brought in. We've been preparing a series on 'Great Inventions.' Mostly culling from old years' encyclopedias. I let the words 'Nobel's dynamite' slip past the copy controls, and she went at me like a bag of ferrets. Didn't I know Nobel had nothing to do with dynamite? He only stole the patent from Zinin and Petrusevski!"

Florence sat Yulik down in the zinc tub and bathed him in the water, scooping it up with a cup and letting it fall like rain around his pale shoulders. She felt deep discomfort with the direction of the conversation.

"I told her, 'I ain't the writer, ma'am. I just translate what I'm given.' 'We all have to be vigilant about inaccuracies,' she says. 'Inaccuracies, distortions, and political errors.'"

Leon took no notice of Florence's displeasure. He permitted himself a laugh. "Lucky thing you weren't making an entry on Edison's incandes-

cent lamp or she'd have charged you with maligning the name of Vladimir Ilyich Lenin, inventor of the Lenin lightbulb."

Florence ordered the little boy to step out of the tub and patted him
down with a kitchen towel. She found Leon's total faith in Seldon smug
and disconcerting. Abandoning oneself to this kind of joking was impru-
dent even with one's best friend. "Seldon. It's late," she reminded their
guest. "We have to put Yulik to bed."

"I'm feeling pretty knackered myself. Come on over here," he said, addressing the boy, who was now dressed in a fresh nightshirt. "I got something for you."

Yulik came up and was lifted onto Seldon's knee. Seldon took the last
two *papirosi* out of his pack of Kazbek and handed the empty pack to the
boy. "A new stallion for you," he said, as Yulik studied the picture of the
horse and rider.

"We'll cut it out tomorrow," said Leon. "You can add it to your stable.
What do you say to Uncle Seldon?"

"Thank you."

Seldon roughed the boy's hair as he stood up. "And thank you, Florie,
for the libations."

She nodded as Leon walked Seldon to the door. "Good night, family,"
he said. "Sleep innocently."

ALL IN ALL, FLORENCE THOUGHT, THE WAR AND ITS END HAD LEFT THEM
better off than before. When they returned from evacuation with their
small son, she and Leon had continued to work for the SovInformBuro,
the broadcast network, with its peacetime staff moved into a vast new
maze of offices on Leontievsky Lane. Like Leon, she had stayed on as a
translator. Her job now entailed scanning select American periodicals for
news items that could be plucked out and repackaged for the Soviet press.
With a glance at an American paper, she could pick out a story about the
acquittal of a lynch mob in South Carolina and enlarge it to a feature that
demonstrated the corruption of the American court system. Or rewrite a
report on a coal mine explosion in Centralia, Illinois, to illustrate the disre-
gard of mine owners for the oppressed worker class. It was not enough

merely to translate a story. One had to translate it in a way that gave the correct depiction of events. A short news item on an auto manufacturer's offer to replace its car owners' tire rims with new, unscuffable metal rims could be restyled in a way that suggested that American capitalist firms regularly duped consumers with flimsy and dangerous products and were forced to replace those products only when their abuses were discovered. Even a story about a natural disaster, like a tornado that had leveled eighty houses in Woodward, Oklahoma, could be reworked to emphasize the low quality of houses constructed by corner-cutting capitalists who cared for nothing so much as the almighty dollar.

Such interpretive sorcery was a labor for which Florence was well suited. Her lifelong talent for flagging injustices large and small, which had left her feeling misunderstood by her teachers and fellow students when she was a schoolgirl, had finally found its ideal expression. For Florence it required no more mental limbo to interpret the foreign news in this reproachful light than it took to square her own daily life with the utopia promised by the Soviet press. Among her co-workers, she was not unique in this respect. Within the sealed offices of the SovInformBuro, the journalists and translators who every morning read and discussed the foreign dispatches, which were denied and forbidden to the rest of the population, treated these stories as wholly reliable, whereas the Soviet press reports chronicling bountiful harvests and anniversaries, unanimous votes of approval, uninterrupted workers' achievements, and fulminations against imperialists were treated as fiction. To hold these two premises was merely necessary for the work and did not make one unpatriotic.

Aside from access to bountiful reading material, the job's more utilitarian benefits included a larger room for Florence and Leon, in a better apartment that was also closer to the city center. Through the bureau's channels Florence had also managed to help widowed Essie trade her double room and move into the single spare room at the end of their hall. The act had not been entirely altruistic. The discomfort of living in a *kommunalka* without allies still haunted Florence's memory. Now she would have a friend who was like a sister just down the hall, to take her side in apartment divisions and disputes.

As a young woman, she had bristled at the lack of privacy. As a mother, Florence discovered the advantage of always having a neighbor nearby to watch Julian in a bind. Motherhood had recomposed her life along new lines, and helped drive from her memory the last of her nostalgia for home. Of course, she wished her parents could meet their grandson. But from the moment Julian entered the world, Florence had begun to conceive of life as separate from the aspects of its outward circumstances. Over and over, life renewed itself. Over and over, it made itself blind to the death and destruction of the past. Every morning, she gazed into her son's small face and marveled at the alert, inquisitive intelligence she saw in it, his bottomless, frequently manic delight in the sensate world—a song his father might make up, the free association of words, the taste of a sesame candy.

And so, for his sake, she resolved to accept things as they were. She did not care to remember her despair before the war, her nervous exhaustion, her wild and foolish attempt at escape. She was arriving at a revelation that the secret to living was simply forgetting. Besides, the war was over. The country was at peace—with itself, too. The immeasurable toll of the war seemed to have satiated Russia's enraged cannibal heart at last.

She no longer experienced homesickness as a great ache in her bones but as a manageable prickle that could pass with time. At her desk at the SovInformBuro, while her eyes scanned headlines from Cleveland or New York, Florence might carefully allow a little of the old malady to rise up inside her, but only enough—as she translated the climbing tally of injustices—to remind herself that she'd done right to leave. Only occasionally did she permit America to occupy her full consciousness, and that was when, in the seclusion of Essie's room, the two of them paged through the glossy stock of foreign magazines that Florence managed to sneak out of the office.

Every now and then, there circulated among the translators' desks issues of *Time, Newsweek,* and *Life.* Strict procedures were in place for signing out magazines to one's desk. But Florence had discovered that if one of these periodicals found its way to you through another desk, and if the issue was not recent, it could go absent for a night, a whole day sometimes, without causing a great eruption of suspicion from the inventory librarians. And though no one would admit to it, Florence was sure she was not the only one who now and again left the SovInformBuro office with an American magazine hidden inside the creased newsprint of her *Pravda.*

It had become a ritual: once Yulik was tucked into his cot, Florence would take the magazine, still concealed by newsprint, across the hall to

Essie's room, where Essie would have prepared a pot of tea in anticipation of their reading, along with a plate of wafer cakes, the only treat they could indulge in without the risk of staining the magazine's filmy pages.

One evening some months after Mikhoels's funeral, and after weeks on the lookout, Florence was able to get her hands on a recent issue of *Newsweek* with youthful Soviet troops on the cover, and the headline "Could the Red Army Overrun Europe?" bannered alarmingly across it. While Essie fussed with pouring the tea, Florence sat at the small table Essie employed as a vanity, leafing through pages. It was their unspoken agreement that she would get first look at whatever she brought into the apartment. Some of the corners were already frayed and bent. A few of the pages were torn out at the root, to expunge, Florence presumed, the most forbidden material. And yet on the page right in front of her was a political cartoon— a caricature of a mustachioed Stalin holding a bird rifle and trying to shoot down cranes carrying bags of food labeled "Marshall Plan" to beleaguered Berliners. The man they were all sworn to love and fear was here pictured as a buffoon, a sloppy, spiteful poacher. Florence tore the page out and stuffed it into her apron pocket. She did not care to look at this cartoon in the presence of another person, even Essie. It served only to remind her of the risks she was taking in sneaking the magazine home and showing it to others.

"Enough hogging," Essie said, sidling up in her chair beside Florence. With the corner of her blouse she wiped the lenses of her horn-rimmed glasses. "Jeez Louise, what's that?"

"Says here it's the Westinghouse automatic clothes washer."

"Looks like some sort of jukebox radio with that window. Where the heck does it go, in the kitchen?"

"I guess so."

Essie ran her fingertips over the wide glossy page. She adjusted the glasses that enlarged her pale eyes and suggested constant awe and bewilderment at whatever she saw.

A fact that didn't need to be stated: it wasn't for the articles they lusted but for the advertisements. Here, between the "serious" stories, were all manner of whimsical new inventions: "pressure cookers" that never burned a meal, "duplex refrigerators" that kept meat fresh from June until October, electric ovens that could roast thirty-pound turkeys, Hoovers that sucked dust from drapes and blinds, "pop-up toasters" in which one could behold one's own reflection. Looking at these colorful illustrations, Florence was struck by the vision of the birth of a new era, one in which the technological ingenuity perfected during the war was now being turned toward a singular aim: the easing of the housewife's burdens, a brawny project of domestication on a national scale. The high gloss of modern kitchens illustrated a life that was at once familiar in her memories, and not at all believable: a sumptuous, sunlit dream of the future.

"Look at the dresses they wear nowadays," said Essie, "with the bow at the back—and that's just at home?"

"Oh, Essie, I don't think anybody washes the dishes wearing a dress like that, here *or* in America."

"I wouldn't mind my own 'sink bowl' to wash the linens in, never mind one of those machines. And a desk telephone like that, instead of that enormous thing always ringing outside my door. I'm the only one who ever picks up, you know, because I can't bear to have it ringing all the time."

"You'd rather seven telephones be ringing in seven rooms?"

"At least they'd get picked up once in a while."

Whenever they got together like this, Florence had noticed, Essie got into the habit of ebullient complaining, speaking in helpless response to whatever happened to pop into her head. Outside this room there would be a dangerous edge to such innocence. And yet, in a peculiar way, Essie's glib deprecations of their Soviet reality were the only appropriate response to Florence's sharing the magazines with her. It was a kind of routine they had perfected: spurred on by Florence's feeble defenses of their quotidian lives, Essie would go on to issue ever more mounting grievances. Sure, on New Year's they got subsidized caviar and champagne. But who needed cheap aristocratic delicacies one day a year when they couldn't reliably obtain fresh meat or cheese the other 364? Or fish that didn't smell like it had been thawed and refrozen half a dozen times? Or when they couldn't see the nose-and-throat doctor without bribing the nurse first? And Florence let her go on, let Essie's mouth run with all the things she too was thinking but wouldn't say.

If Florence had still been in communication with Captain Subotin, she might have begrudged her friend for exposing her ears to such damning anti-Soviet talk. After all, this was the very sort of colloquy the secret police would be keen to know about and surely punish her for withholding.

And if she withheld it, who could say that Essie herself would not some-day be hauled in and forced to describe it? Such were the perils that ad-hered to any group of more than one. But Essie herself surely was aware of these dangers. It occurred to Florence that her friend's candor was served up as a sort of collateral of trust in compensation for the risk Flor-ence herself was undertaking in smuggling forbidden loot out of Sov-InformBuro's quarantined offices. Likewise, Florence was aware that there would be little pleasure for her in perusing these magazines alone. Essie was all that stood between her and the bitter despair that seized her when-ever she opened their pages by herself. The diabolical paradox of her life was that her escape from America had been fueled by an ambition to flee the servitude of domesticity. And yet, at thirty-eight, after a day of work-ing as an equal alongside men, her liberation took the form of evenings spent elbowing in lines for food, arguing with her neighbors over every square centimeter of ledge space and scrubbing her child's linens on an old washboard in the common tub. Come morning, there was more wait-ing, this time outside the common toilet to flush the chamber pot from the night before. Her crockery and plates were all chipped. She felt deserted by America, and enraged with herself for the nostalgia that gripped her heart; and, still, she could not stop looking at the pictures.

She was glad when Essie changed the subject.

"You think Seldon might notice if I wore a dress like that, with a cut up the leg?"

Seldon again. It amused her how much Essie despaired of getting his attention.

"Honey, I don't think he'd notice if that slit went up to the waist."

Essie's eyes met Florence's in the mirror on the vanity table. "What makes you say that? It's a rather mean thing to say."

Florence glanced down, back at the magazine. "Essie, don't fish for compliments. You know you're perfectly cute without any fancy frocks."

"Then what were you trying to say?"

"Oh, I don't know. He's an odd duck, Seldon. How about some more tea?"

"Sometimes I get a feeling he has a wrong impression of me."

"What's that?"

"That I'm a silly or a trifling sort of person. It's only because I'm a little nervous around him. And he always seems to be testing me to see if I get the joke."

"Well, I've never heard him say anything of the sort about you."

"And, see, that's the trouble. Most of the time he doesn't notice me at all. You could help change that."

"How?"

Essie smiled. "By inviting me in more often when he comes over."

"It's Leon he comes to see, not me."

"Still, considering everything," Essie said, modestly glancing away, "it would be a nice thing to do."

Considering everything Essie did for little Yulik was what she meant. Watching him and warming up meals when Florence was out. Essie adjusted her glasses and turned the page to a silverware advertisement that read "The happiest brides have Community."

"All right."

"Thank you," said Essie without looking up.

LATER, FLORENCE WOULD WONDER if everything might have turned out differently if she'd only made more of an effort to keep her promise to Essie. The image of the two of them turning the pages of *Newsweek* would come back to her vividly, like the last clear memory before the onset of a savage illness that turned everything into a malarial hallucination. Only then would Florence recognize Essie's wish to be invited into their company less as an expression of lust for Seldon Parker than as a longing to embed herself once more into the warm crucible of Florence's own intimacy, to be welcomed in as a fourth into their tight little trio.

When she remembered the weeks of that summer and fall—weeks that raced by so quickly they seemed to her like slippery leaves falling and skidding underfoot—the only part of the story she would recall with clarity was the beginning, which was also the story of the radio, the real and secret fourth member of their quartet.

It had taken Leon all winter and part of the spring of '48 to collect the necessary pieces to build his device. Shortwave parts were hard to come by. For months he had loitered around the electric exchange shops on the margins of the city's outdoor bazaars, until he'd collected everything he needed. And then, to Florence's wonder, he brought his autodidactic capacities to bear on a whole new set of skills—on the logic of circuits, pentodes, power transformers, and endless mechanical minutiae of which he spoke at length to Seldon Parker. With pieces of mounting wire and insulated wire, he managed to rig an antenna capacitor. With parts of an old Radiofront set, he tooled together a converter which made it possible to switch their longwave radio reception to the greatly expanded number of shortwave stations. Stacked together, the whole setup resembled a tiered cake, a miniature Rockefeller Center made of receiver, converter, and amplifier. Its completion precipitated more visits from Seldon, late evenings whose memory for Florence became a continuous wall of scratchy white noise, of sputtering and hissing, of jammed signals, and occasional rewards for patience: the high nasalities of BBC English, or the midcontinental drawl of the Voice of America.

And then came May 14, and their already fervid gatherings around the radio acquired a new, exhilarated preoccupation. To Leon and Seldon, all scraps of news from Europe and America became secondary in importance to Israel's progress against its foes: Egyptians in the Negev, Syrians in the Galilee. For weeks, Florence listened to her husband talk about the capture of Nazareth, the strategic value of Beersheba—places whose names she had not heard since her little brother Sidney had been studying Biblical history in preparation for his Bar Mitzvah.

One hot evening in July, when the light outside was still as pale as at noontime, she sat at the open window, mending the scalloped edge of a tablecloth as feeble snatches of sound issued from the rubber military headphones Leon liked to cup to one ear while catching a signal. Out in the hall could be heard the squeals and the screech of Yulik's new training bike as he rolled it down the parquet floor with the neighbor boy, Yasha. Florence felt a headache blooming in her temple.

"They're trying to jam it," Leon said hopelessly.

"Bugger, we just had it!" complained Seldon. He rubbed Leon's shoulder. "The important thing is not to let the Old City fall to the Arabs now. We'll take it back, won't we, Florie?"

We. Us. An unsettling sense of collectivity was creeping into Seldon's normally egocentric speech, as if he and Leon had personally fought off first the British, then the Arabs from her apartment. She looped a knot.

"Why, so they can die guarding a few shrines?" she said, and bit the remaining thread off with her back teeth.

Leon put the rubber headset down and looked at her. "We're talking about the Old City of Jerusalem. Aside from what those words may or may not mean to you, it's of vital strategic importance."

She folded the tablecloth and got up. "Some of us have things of vital importance around here too, like mending your linens and making some dinner for our child." She went to the door.

"If you're going to the kitchen, darling, pop a kettle on the stove, will you?" said Seldon.

She didn't answer him. "Turn the volume down," she said to Leon.

She too had rejoiced when the Soviet Union had cast its vote in favor of an independent Jewish State. That didn't mean she was going to let her enthusiasm overwhelm her common sense. *Their* Jews weren't *our* Jews.

Every evening after dinner she opened *Pravda* to learn about *ours*. Composers, critics, directors who had abandoned their duty to the people or had "infiltrated" the Soviet theaters, the professional journals, the academies, with the aim of impeding the progress of Soviet drama, or literature, or art. There seemed to be no common thread, aesthetic or ideological, to those being exposed. Only the charge of "nationalism," and their names bearing a distressing contiguity: Abramov, Adler, Kalmanovich, Pinsker, Segal. Were there any doubts, the original family name was printed in parentheses after the changed one: Gankin (Kagan), Lisov (Lifshitz), Bonderenko (Berdichievsky). Nobody at the SovInformBuro was unmindful of this new current. The Anti-Fascist Committee's Yiddish journal, *Einkayt,* had been shut down. The committee's signboard had been removed from its office.

In the wide hallway, Yulik and the stout Yasha Gendler were still riding around on Julian's new wheelie. Or rather, Yasha was pumping the pedals while her son chased after him on foot.

"Mama, it's *mine,*" the child cried in helpless appeal when he saw her.

"Yasha, why don't you give Yulik his turn."

"Just one minute, I wanna test the bell first," called the boy, trilling the metal bell.

Florence did not dislike Yasha, but privately she disapproved of the way he was being brought up. His mother, Rosa Gendler, always fearful that he would not have enough to eat, still followed him around the kitchen with a spoon.

In the common kitchen Florence set a pot of water to boil and got a couple of potatoes from where she stored them under a square table. She rinsed a knife and began to peel them, then did the same with some carrots, and tossed everything into the pot. Down the long hallway, she heard the big front door clatter and open. Everybody had his own way of unlocking it, and Essie's was always a key-jangling, winded, sighing entrance. Still in her coat, Essie entered the kitchen carrying groceries—some bruised tomatoes and canned sardines in her string bag, and a paper-wrapped kielbasa. "Mmm. What are you making?" She peered into the pot, the curiosity in her eyes enlarged by her glasses.

"A little *salat Olivier*, that's all. Have to finish this can of peas."

"Expecting company?"

Florence glanced quickly in the direction of her closed door. "Seldon was just leaving." She wished she hadn't spoken. But what if Essie saw him on his way out? Essie set her woven bag down on the table and stood watching Florence chop vegetables.

"Well, that won't be enough," she said finally. "What you need is a side dish. How about a little *doktorskaya* kielbasa? It's finally back in the stores. Smell this, just like perfume."

Florence took an obligatory sniff.

"I'll slice it up and join you."

The headache was reaching around to her other temple, like a snail peeking its head in and out of its shell. The thought of a crowd in her room tonight was giving the throbbing snail permission to come out of hiding. Florence pushed back. "Not tonight, Essie. I'm just too beat. And I have to feed Yulik and put him to bed. Next time."

A well-worn disappointment gathered around Essie's mouth. "Well, I won't ask twice," she said.

Florence stood staring into her pot of boiling water. She tried to reassure herself that Essie really wasn't as hurt as she appeared. She was aware, nonetheless, that she'd have no problem inviting Essie in were it not for Seldon's petulant suspicion of her friend. Whenever Essie knocked while the radio was on, Leon would turn it off and cover it before she entered, then endure her small talk kindly, eyes darting with longing at the radio. But it was Seldon who, of late, radiated toward Essie a silence that was openly rude. When Florence looked up from her pot, Essie was gone.

Florence left the kitchen with a metallic aftertaste of guilt in her mouth. She made a mental note to sit down and have a conversation with Seldon. If she could trust Essie enough to share foreign magazines with her, they could trust her to be present while they listened to these foreign transmissions.

But, on entering her room, she found not the men but lumps under a tartan blanket. They'd gotten a signal. Florence set her salad on the table and lifted up the blanket to stick her head in. Leon and Seldon were huddled together in the warm dark, their ears cocked to the broadcast coming scratchily out of the speakers. The announcer was talking about an assassination in Italy, which was inciting communist-organized strikes.

"What are you two fools smiling about?"

Leon turned the dial to the off position and pulled down the tartan. "You won't believe it, Florie. Golda Meyerson is coming here, to Moscow in seven weeks."

"The woman from Palestine?"

"She's leading the first diplomatic legation, they've announced it."

"She's coming to speak at the Choral Synagogue," said Seldon.

"When?"

"During the Jewish holidays."

Florence looked at Leon quizzically.

"We'll all go and see her!" Seldon announced with incautious triumph.

Florence stood up and went to the window. The summer daylight was dimming at last. "I don't know. I haven't set foot inside one of those places since I was eighteen."

"You don't have to go inside," Seldon reassured her. "It'll be outdoors, I'm certain. If Mikhoels's funeral was any indication, there'll be thousands." He turned to Leon. "We'll need to get there early."

Florence glanced back at Leon. He looked completely on board with the plan. "What do you say, Florie?"

She heard herself give a simpering laugh. "Well, now we know how you like them, Seldon," she said. "Built like a bulldozer with legs like tree trunks."

Seldon did not look impressed by her snideness. "Meyerson may be no beauty, but she's one hell of a woman."

"That's how they grow 'em on those kibbutzes," Leon chimed in.

"They've done what we couldn't: manage to turn our Jews into regular peasants after all."

"Go and listen to her speak; you'll hear she's no peasant," objected Seldon.

Florence said, "Thousands of people—all the more reason to stay home."

"Fine, then I'll take Yulik," said Leon, as if he'd expected her answer.

Florence bored her eyes into her husband. Did she really need to remind him, in front of Seldon, that the last thing they ought to be doing was showing up on the street of the central synagogue, sure to be crawling with NKVD agents? Was he so dense he couldn't understand this? No, he understood. He didn't care. With Seldon around he became like a boy, hungry for risk and adventure.

"If you think I'll let you take my son into that mad crowd . . ."

"*Our* son. And he'll be fine. He'll sit on my shoulders like the other children. I want him to see it and remember it."

There had been a time, she wanted to remind Leon, when he would have forbidden her to expose herself to such foolish danger, restrained her with the force of a prison warden. When had he become the one who threw caution to the wind?

Seldon, in his chair, was watching their exchange hungrily. Her face-off with Leon seemed to have kindled in their guest an amused if guilty enjoyment. No doubt he'd primed Leon for it.

"We'll see," she said.

IT WASN'T LONG BEFORE ESSIE'S FEELINGS ABOUT FLORENCE'S SLIGHT showed themselves. At first Florence did not perceive any change. Whenever she saw Essie, her friend looked cheerful—joking and making small talk, or carelessly laughing with Yasha's mother, Rosa. If Florence entered the conversation, Essie excused herself. In the hallway Essie acknowledged Florence's greeting by raising her chin only slightly in a cool salute. It occurred to Florence that Essie's new closeness with Rosa Gendler was a demonstration of her social self-reliance, her loud laughter a display for Florence. She stayed alert for a moment when she could approach Essie with a lighthearted apology, a jokingly remorseful defense of herself that would restore feelings on both sides. At last, she found Essie alone in the kitchen, trying to retrieve a hanging bag of onions from a hook inside the storm window.

"You need some help with that?"

"No, I'm fine."

Florence slipped off her shoes, hoisted herself onto the windowsill, and untwined the snagged strings of the bag from the hook. "There you go."

"Thanks," Essie said quietly without much gratitude.

Florence hesitated for a moment. She had prepared a whole spiel, but now the words escaped her. "Seldon will be coming tomorrow evening," she hinted. "Why don't you drop in? You know, make an appearance."

"Thank you, I have plans."

"Oh, Essie—I'm sorry for the other time. I had a crushing headache and . . ."

"I appreciate the invitation, Florence, but I'd rather not."

"Oh, come off it, you know you don't need an 'invitation' to knock on our door."

"Don't I?"

"I feel bad. I want everyone to get along. You'd be doing me a favor." Essie sighed.

"What did I say?"

"I accept your apology, Florence. I just don't want to."

"Can you at least tell me why?"

Essie squinted out the window. "I realized you were right, is all."

"About what?"

"Seldon. Let's face it, he has as much interest in me as a horse does in a wheelbarrow."

"I never said that."

But Essie seemed not to hear this. "I was chatting about it with Rosa and it struck me smack between the eyes that I'd been wasting beans of time on a man who doesn't care for our kind anyhow."

"*Our* kind. What kind's that?"

"Oh, you know what I'm talking about."

"I promise I don't."

"You said yourself he's an odd duck. Well, Rosa thinks so too." Essie's voice fell to a whisper. "He reminded me of one of those swishy fellas the

Workmen's Circle would hire to help us put on plays. In the Bronx . . . Oh, don't look so startled. That's what you were trying to tell me."

Florence felt the glow of humiliation spreading up her neck. "I wasn't."

"Well, then," Essie said, turning away again, "maybe it's that dandy way the English have. All their men got a touch of purple on them, don't they?"

Florence could feel the shock gathering like palsy in her face, her mouth paralyzed in its alarm. She pictured Seldon touching Leon's wrist. She pictured the two of them in the breath-filled, warm darkness under the tartan blanket with the radio. Suddenly she had the feeling she was looking at Essie through the wrong end of a telescope, with Essie appearing remote and horribly small. "Why must you utter every stupid thing that comes into your silly head?" she sputtered. "Only children and idiots do that."

Essie narrowed her eyes. "I'm sorry I said anything at all." But she didn't look very sorry.

FOR SEVERAL WEEKS, FLORENCE attempted to forget Essie's malicious insinuation. But the distasteful notion had taken semi-official residence in Florence's mind, and renewed its lease the morning when Leon and Seldon left for the Choral Synagogue to hear the ambassador from Israel, Golda Meyerson, speak. (The only centimeter of ground Florence had won was in forbidding Leon to take little Yulik along with them.) It stayed in her head when Leon came home alone that evening, intoxicated by what he'd witnessed. He didn't even remove his aviator's jacket, merely hung his flat cap on the hook by the door before gathering Florence in his arms and gripping her waist. "Florie, I've never seen anything like it. The whole street, it was like a river of bodies: students, old folks, men in uniform, mothers and kids! Thousands of people! I didn't know there *were* so many Jews in Moscow. Oh, and the most amazing part—do you know the first thing Meyerson said when she got up to speak? 'A dank ir zai giblybn idyn'— 'Thank you for remaining Jews.' "

Yulik, whom she'd been getting ready for bed, ran up in his stockinged feet to his father. Leon lifted the boy to his shoulder and gave his son a moist kiss on the head.

"Papa, you're wet!"

It was true. Leon was glistening. His hair—cut short now, so that only a bit of curl showed—was matted to his head by the sweat of his excitement. He set the boy down and wiped his forehead. "Oh, you should've seen it!" His hands were on Florence's hips again. "Right in the open, they were calling out *Am Yisrael chai!*' When she came down, everyone was crowding around her. People were trying to touch the hem of her dress and kiss it. She's speaking again on Yom Kippur, and this time we're all going."

"I wanna go!" cried Yulik.

"That's right. You'll go with your dad. I'll teach you a new song, *Am Yisrael, am Yisrael, am Yisrael chai!*'" Leon sang.

Yulik started hopping. *"Ha misraim, ha misraim . . ."* He was chanting it louder than Florence thought advisable. The smart thing—the wifely thing, she knew—was to pretend to share Leon's excitement. Later, in bed, she could tell him quietly of her misgivings. And yet something about his grotesquely happy face warned her that he was in the thrall of a new love affair—not with Seldon Parker, as Essie had implied, but with something still more dangerous.

"Is she the Messiah, that people need to kiss the hem of her gown?" Florence heard herself say.

She could tell from the unpleasant bitterness around Leon's mouth that she'd bruised something delicate. "So clever, Florie. So it doesn't mean *any*thing to you?"

"It means something," she said. "It means all the ones who touched her holy robe will be called in for questioning next week. And I hope, for your sake, it was well worth it when they ask you to explain, inside the 'Special Department' at the SovInformBuro, what you were doing there."

"Ha misraim, ha misraim!" Yulik continued chanting in his high voice.

"Enough making that noise already!"

The boy stopped singing, startled. He glanced at his father.

"Don't shout at him."

"Go wash your face, and get some water for your teeth," she ordered Yulik.

"There were thousands of people. Nobody saw who was who," said Leon.

"Don't be so sure."

"If they call me in, then they'll call in Seldon too, and dozens of others."

"What happens to them or to Seldon Parker is of no concern to me," she said, getting the child's toothbrush off the windowsill. "You can be sure that crowd was crawling with agents."

"So was Mikhoels's funeral, for heaven's sake! What do you expect me to do—stop living my life? I can't worry about *them* every minute. Tell me, what are you frightened of: that the word 'Jew' was said in public today? Not any more than it was said at all those rallies the committee held during the war."

"That was *the war*! There was a reason for it—we were raising money for the army."

"Understood. It was fine to say it when *they* told us to say it. But not now, not when people actually believe it."

"Are those your words or Mr. Parker's?" she said.

He gazed at her uncertainly, as though he didn't know her. Then he spun around and took his cap off its hook. Florence followed him. "Where are you off to—back to boozing with that windbag?"

But Leon didn't seem to hear her. "Don't stay up," he said.

TEN DAYS LATER, an article appeared in *Pravda*. The Party flack, Ilya Ehrenburg, had written up an opinion piece laying out the official policy to dictate how Soviet Jews were to regard Israel. "Is Israel the solution to the Jewish question?" No, was the emphatic answer. The injection of Anglo-American capital was as dangerous to Israel as were the Arab legions. The solution to the Jewish problem would depend not on military success in Palestine but on the triumph of socialism over capitalism, principles of the working class over nationalism. If there was no choice but for some victims of Nazi atrocities to leave demolished Europe and make their way to Palestine, this was by no means the case for Jews within the borders of the Soviet Union, where the oppression of money, lies, and superstition had long been conquered.

"There've been rumors, coming out of Birobidzhan," Seldon informed them late one evening. It was nearly nine when he pressed the apartment buzzer, ringing three times for their room.

"What rumors?" said Leon.

"That the Jewish Party members are being arrested for receiving aid packages from the U.S."

"Receiving packages? Hell, everybody did that. It was all done through the Red Cross."

Florence insisted they talk more quietly. She could hear Yulik stirring in his cot. "By taking those packages, they were encouraging the impression that the U.S. was responsible for victory," whispered Seldon.

"Mama?" the boy was calling out from behind the floral curtain that partitioned his side of the room from the grown-ups.

"That's absurd. What were people supposed to eat?" said Leon.

Florence said, "Where did you hear that, Seldon?"

"I'd rather not say."

"Mama?" Julian had gotten up from his cot and parted the curtain.

"Go back to sleep, monkey."

"I *can't*. I want to sleep with you."

"All right, lovey, just get back in your bed. I'll lie down with you as soon as Uncle Seldon leaves. Seldon, can't this wait till morning?"

"There's more. The articles we were translating—for the American press—now they're being called bourgeois nationalist propaganda."

"That's got to be a joke," said Leon.

"Especially any articles that mentioned the names of American companies—the ones that sent rubber heating pads, syringes, those sorts of things. They're saying that by praising those companies, the writers were encouraging American businessmen to make deals over the blood of Soviet boys."

"Seldon, who's saying all this?"

"But it was in the protocol," insisted Leon. "To mention the name of the company. We were *told* to show gratitude."

"Apparently, we bowed too deeply."

IN THE DARK BEHIND the floral curtain, Florence lay on the cot beside her son. Light from the moon illuminated his downy neck and the curve of his shoulder in its cotton pajama top. Curled up he looked like a little swan. For a long time she rubbed his back and hummed softly; finally, she could hear the deep, slow breathing that meant he was asleep. She tiptoed back to their daybed, then lay on her back for a long time and stared at the ceiling. Above her the plaster molding, slightly peeling, had a pattern of leaves and lilies. There were birds, too, whose wings had been cropped by the wooded partition that had divided the once-large room into several smaller ones. It was like looking up into a world of myth, as different from the world around them as the sky was from life on earth. She could feel the heavy turn of Leon's body beside her. "Why does he always come around so late?" she said, trying to gather anger into her whisper. "He knows we have a child. Yulik needs to be put to bed at a normal hour."

"It's never bothered you before."

"How does he get his information? Yes, I know. . . . He makes his rounds . . . eats and drinks at a different apartment every night. Never refuses a free meal or drink. How do we know this Birobidzhan gossip isn't just empty noise?"

"I imagine he heard it from Olivia Bern. She processes all the letters the Jewish Committee receives."

"He hears a rumor, then runs over here to frighten us."

"Perhaps he's frightened himself, Florence. We're the closest thing he has to family." She felt him turn toward the wall. "Why must you be so hard on people?"

THE TELEPHONE CALL CAME when she was at work. Florence was summoned by one of the typists who sat at the other end of the large, partitioned room.

"Flora Solomonovna?"

"Yes."

"I'm glad to get hold of you at last."

She recognized the voice. Its casual tone hit her like a whiff of something sour. A rotting smell from another life. Black and smooth, the telephone in her hand felt as heavy as a piece of obsidian about to pull her to the bottom of a lake.

"It's been a long time, Flora Solomonovna. Don't you recognize who this is?"

She could hear a smile behind the words.

"Yes, you remember me after all," said Subotin. "Well, this is no time for chatting. You're at work. A real move up from that silly institute. I could never picture you among all those gabbing, effete intellectuals. Now, propaganda work, serving the country—that's more like it. Keep up the good work, and we'll chat when you're free. Four o'clock tomorrow, say, at our old spot."

Florence glanced behind her. She could not stay on the phone for much longer without drawing stares. "I'm sorry, but that won't be possible, not tomorrow at four or any other time." No, she would not march into the trap so obediently this time. She had a child to think of.

Almost as if he'd read her mind, Subotin said: "I promise I won't keep you long. If you can help me with what I'm looking for, you can be out in time to pick up your little boy from his kindergarten."

That he would know the ordinary schedule of her day did not shock Florence. The Chekists knew everything. It was how he had said "your little boy" that sent gooseflesh down her arms. They never mentioned anything by accident. Subotin gave her the address, as though she could ever forget it.

NO ONE CAME TO THE DOOR when she knocked. Florence tried the knob and let herself in. How familiar the place looked. The same striped wallpaper, the same lace curtains. She approached the window, which looked bigger than she remembered. Below, the street cleaners were already out, pushing their brooms. Florence touched her fingers to the cool pane.

"It's a shame, isn't it?"

She turned around.

"That stained-glass panel, it was quite pretty. Brought a certain old charm. The whole window shattered in one of the bombing raids, is my guess—this building being so close to the water. That's what their planes aimed for during blackouts. No matter how dark it gets, it's impossible to make a river completely invisible. Sit down."

He hadn't changed much, either. The war had been merciful to him, Florence was sorry to say. No missing limbs or mutilated eyes. With his graying hair he looked as groomed and banally elegant as ever.

"Please state your full name."

She couldn't suppress a laugh. "Flora Solomonovna Brink."

"Your husband's full name."

"Haven't you got all this?"

Subotin looked up and repeated the question.

"Brink, Leon Naumovich."

"Nationality."

"American, both of us."

"*Amerikantsi*," Subotin said as he wrote it down. He was smiling to himself, a smile that suggested he knew just as well as Florence did that—American or not—they had the double blessing of being Jews.

"Talk about the work you and your husband carried out for the criminal organization known as the Jewish Anti-Fascist Committee."

So it was true, then, what Seldon had predicted: a case being stitched against the committee. At this moment she wondered if their lives were perhaps no longer under their control at all. She considered the paths available to her. To say that she did not think the committee's work was criminal in nature would be to appear to be defending it, and therefore to admit involvement. Any knowledge or involvement of any kind had to be denied. "Neither my husband nor I was ever employed by the Jewish Anti-Fascist Committee."

This answer sounded confident enough and had the added advantage of being true, if only technically.

"I'd like you not to forget where you are. We know for a fact that you both served the Jewish Committee as translators."

"The committee did not have its own translation bureau. We were assigned to translate materials produced by all five committees in the SovInformBuro—the Committee for Scientists, for Youth, for Slavs—"

"I am now asking you about your work for the Jewish Committee, not the others. Answer the question."

"I was not a specialized translator. My husband did some translation of articles that had been written for *Einkayt*, the JAFC's magazine."

"Why was your husband given these assignments?"

"He could read Yiddish as well as English, obviously."

"And what did you and he make of the materials you were translating?"

"We were told they were necessary to raise money for the Red Army."

"And were they not about the special achievements of Jews, separate from the achievements of the Russian people?"

"Perhaps a few. I don't remember. I did not write them."

"And so, consequently, you were in agreement with the exaggerated and false claims being made."

"I wouldn't dare to think that an unimportant person like myself could differ with those higher up on anything, least of all on questions of wartime propaganda."

"You are avoiding my question. Answer concretely. Did you take no issue with the materials you were handling?"

"Like I said, I am always in agreement with the government's policy."

She didn't avoid Subotin's gaze. It wasn't 1937 anymore, or 1940. It was 1948. If he was going to play this game, then she'd show him she knew the rules.

He smiled slyly.

"So you had no feelings about the blatantly nationalistic material you were translating?"

"We were doing our jobs."

"And were you also doing your jobs when you attended the Zionist rally to support the Israeli ambassador, Golda Meyerson?"

"I did not attend this rally."

Subotin glanced down at his papers, quickly but not imperceptibly. "There are witnesses. . . ."

"Your witnesses misperceived. You can check. I was in my room that day."

Subotin's face flushed red, betraying his irritation.

"There are witnesses who saw Leon Brink and others. . . ."

If he was guessing about her, could he have been guessing about Leon too? She didn't want to take the risk. "I did not attend this rally. I had no interest in it. My husband went out of curiosity. He had heard about the lady from Palestine and wanted to see for himself what kind of person she was."

"And a thousand other people also went out of curiosity, yes? And they also called her name and toadied to her staff out of simple curiosity. And shouted Zionist slogans out of curiosity!"

"But what slogans?"

" 'Next year in Jerusalem!' "

She wanted to laugh. "That's no slogan. Jews have been saying it since they were expelled from Babylon. It's just something that gets said on their holy days. It means nothing."

"Outbursts of crude and zealous nationalism being made in the thirty-second year of the Revolution are not nothing. I am forced to think you are less than forthcoming if you insist such a nationalistic frenzy was not whipped up by a band of Zionist scoundrels."

How to tell him that no whipping up needed to have been done? That Jews would have gone on their own to take a look at Meyerson, with no prompting?

"I am insisting on nothing of the sort," she said. "How would I know? I wasn't on the Jewish Committee."

"But you spent three years in Kuibyshev among these people, and around those who worked closely with them. Discussions and conversations transpired that you heard—things whose meaning you may not fully appreciate now."

She was almost tempted to smile. In spite of Subotin's recriminating tone, Florence understood these words as a retreat. He wasn't accusing *her* anymore. If it weren't for his total power over her, she'd even say he was wheedling, trying to enlist her help. Perhaps, he was suggesting, she was too naïve to really understand what went on inside the scoundrels' den. Nevertheless, she could help them.

"It was five years ago," Florence said. "More. If anything got said then, too much time has passed for me to recall it now."

"I'm sure, with a little time, you'll remember," said Subotin.

WITH ESSIE SHE WAS now on the most abbreviated speaking terms. In the common areas, they ignored each other with an almost polite formality, like guests at a resort. Florence despaired of keeping up this posture with her old friend. It was simply a routine her body had fallen into, independent of any hurt feelings. Nevertheless, she felt, under the circumstances, that Essie ought to be the one to make amends. And so it continued.

One Sunday afternoon, Florence came into the room and found Yulik whimpering and sobbing in the niche under her sewing machine. Through his mucus-filled sobs, it took her some time to ascertain the cause of his suffering. That morning, while Florence had gone to buy food, Essie had taken Yasha to the new miniature railroad at the children's park. Yulik had tried to come along, but Yasha had told him arrogantly that he was too small. The two had come back from the park laughing loudly and talking of what great fun they'd had riding in the miniature wagons all morning.

"Aunt Essie doesn't like me anymore."

"No, it isn't that, bunny. *I'll* take you."

"No! It's too late!"

"We'll go next week."

"No, I wanted to go with *them*."

FLORENCE GAVE A STOUT rap on Essie's door. She could endure Essie's silent treatment without getting unsettled, but moving this combat into civilian territory—taking it out on Yulik—that was something else entirely.

"What were you thinking?" she said when Essie opened the door. Essie stood in her kimono robe with its flowers and birds of paradise. Florence walked past her into the room. "I found Yulik crying his eyes out. He said that you and Yasha didn't take him to some railroad."

Essie inhaled sharply through her nostrils and smoothed her hair. "Yasha asked me to go a long time ago. He wanted us to go—just the two of us. I couldn't take them both, you know. I'm not a hired nanny."

"But you had to come back talking and laughing so the whole apartment could hear. You could have made a little less of a show about it."

"We all live in one apartment, Florence, whether we like it or not. What do you expect me to do? Stop talking to people? Stop laughing? Should I walk on my tippy toes? Sometimes people feel left out and that's just a fact."

"He's a child!"

"Oh God, Florence. I didn't know if you *wanted* me to take him."

"You could have asked me."

"Forgive me, but every time I try to so much as say hello, you hurry away. You're busy or you shrug and turn your back on me. I've been trying and trying, but I know where I'm not wanted."

Essie's eyes were shining with bitter tears. Florence's jaw hurt from holding back her own.

"Essie, I haven't meant to be aloof. I thought you were still mad over . . . Oh, this is too silly. I don't know why anybody needs to apologize, or for what."

"I wasn't holding out hope," said Essie. "But I'm sorry it upset Yulik. That wasn't my intention." She tightened the belt of her robe, as if suddenly embarrassed to be caught in such a disheveled state.

"Let's just forget it. Listen, I've been trying to get ahold of some magazines for us, but the new section editor they brought in, she's . . . a real wolverine."

"They all are nowadays. Do you want to sit?"

"Maybe I will. It's unnerving. The first thing she did when she walked into our translators' room was read aloud all the names—'Vainberg, Feinberg'—in this disgusted voice, and said, 'What is this, a synagogue?' "

Essie sat down on her bed, nodding. "I know, I know. I borrowed the typist's colored pencil this week and broke the tip. I went to ask her for a razor to sharpen it, and she grabs it back and says, 'I'll do it myself; you people break everything you touch!' "

"I don't know what's happening."

"After all these years, I thought I was finally . . ."

"One of them," said Florence.

Essie nodded, her eyes dry now. "But we never will be, will we?"

35.

———

ESCAPE

Moscow,
1948

NOT LONG THEREAFTER, FLORENCE MADE GOOD ON HER PROMISE TO Essie, knocking on her door with an issue of *Life* magazine in her hand. On the cover was Ingrid Bergman, costumed in her role as Joan of Arc.

"Florence! How did you manage to—"

Florence placed a finger on her lips. "There was more than one copy. Now, put it away quickly, before I change my mind."

"Oh, let's look at it together," Essie said, blushing in gratitude.

"Not tonight—I have somewhere to be. You hold on to it."

"You're sure?" Essie held the magazine tightly.

"Just don't wrinkle the corners or get any marmalade on it."

IN SPITE OF THE NAGGING WORRIES on the margins of her consciousness, Florence felt agreeably magnanimous toward Essie all the next morning. Sharing the magazine was the best thing she could have done for their long-standing friendship. She assured herself that Essie could be trusted to keep it well hidden. But the pleasure she took in her own high-mindedness began to dwindle later in the day when Seldon showed up out of the blue, unshaved and smelling of alcohol. His hair was uncombed and his clothes were crumpled, as if they'd been slept in.

"Feffer's missing."

"What do you mean, missing?" Leon asked.

"Missing. And still no word about Hofshteyn."

David Hofshteyn's disappearance in Kiev had occurred in September. People had thought him ill and in a sanatorium. Now word came that the poet's wife was in Moscow, searching for him at Lefortovo Prison. Stalking their floor as he informed them of these developments, all six gangling feet of Seldon seemed to Florence raw and almost physically menacing, making her want to get Yulik out of the room as quickly as possible.

She put *valenki* on the boy's feet, bundled his capped head in her scarf, and herded him to Avdotya Grigorievna's room, giving the old woman a ruble in advance to take him outside. She returned to a room quickly growing thick with the acrid smell of Kazbek shag tobacco. Seldon was pacing back and forth, spilling ash from a cigarette that smoldered neglected between his fingers. He was talking too quickly to have time to smoke. "An organization with any independent political strength can't be *his* tool, you see? The personnel are too cemented, too interconnected. That's why the cadres are constantly being 'cleansed,' as they say. It's the permanent revolution, see, so no personal ties can form that are stronger than *his* authority. I've thought a lot about this."

Florence looked at Leon in panic. A terrible force had entered their life in the form of Seldon. All she could think now was that it must not drag them down, too.

"Seldon, sit down," Leon urged softly.

"I'd rather stand." He stuck a finger into his collar as though suffocating. "They're cooking up something. Have you been reading the paper? 'Glorification of alien culture,' 'rootless cosmopolitanism'—who do you think they're talking about? They're trying to brand the Jewish Committee a nest of saboteurs. I'll wager for a big show; they're just painting the stage now."

It took a long time to make sense of Seldon's staccato speech but eventually Leon and Florence unpacked his disturbing intuition: The press was merely ahead of the police; the recent disappearances were only the tip of a monstrous case being fashioned somewhere in the bowels of the NKVD. More and more people would be pulled under; no one was safe. "Wherever Feffer is now, I can only imagine what that second-rate bastard has already told them."

"You don't know that for sure," Florence heard herself saying, but she found she couldn't meet his eye. "Anyway, why would they care about *us*? We only translated. What did we do?"

He peered at her as though she, not he, was the one in need of a psychiatric examination. "What did we do?" He mimicked her voice in a cruel falsetto. "Flora Solomonovna, what did *they* do?"

"For chrissake, Florie," said Leon, turning on her, "you're asking the wrong goddamn question!"

"Well, what should I be asking?"

"What is there in this room that we ought to be getting rid of!" Leon said, as if stating the obvious.

"That's it, man!" With that Seldon began pulling volumes off their bookshelf, unsettling the dust of their notebooks and papers. "What's this?"

"Theodore Dreiser."

"To the fireplace. The dictionaries, too. Get rid of everything." He upturned a crate of back issues of *Einkayt* that stood at the end of their daybed.

"Stop it, don't touch them!" She flung herself at Seldon's arm, knocking the books out of his hand, and then fell to her knees before the pile scattered on the floor.

What she did not expect was Seldon bending down on his knees to help her. "I'm sorry, Florie. I'm so sorry." He took her hand and held it with such alarming tenderness that she felt it like an electric charge. He helped her up. Stripped of the demonic will that had possessed him just a moment earlier, he collapsed in their sagging armchair. "All right," he said, forcibly pressing his eye and forehead with the heel of his hand as if kneading the flesh of thoughts behind his skull. "All right," he repeated. "We can't sit and wait for them to come for us." There was a certainty in his voice now, a deadpan calm that chilled Florence even more than his hysteria a few minutes before. He stared out at her and Leon but also beyond them into some permanent elsewhere. What followed—what he said then—might have been the reason he had knocked on their door that morning, or it might as easily have burst forth from some sudden protective impulse to which he had succumbed. There was a man, he said quietly, a worker at the British Foreign Office here in Moscow, who knew his brother.

Leon: "Your brother?"

"Half-brother. From my father's first marriage." A half-brother nine years older who had started working at the Royal Treasury before the war. A friend of his in the Foreign Service had recently been rotated to Moscow. Somehow the man had tracked Seldon down and delivered to him a letter from the brother in England.

"Where is it?" said Florence.

"I got rid of it. I'm not mad."

"You've been meeting this man!"

He had, but he was careful. They met only in crowded places—in the metro, or at the fountain by the Bolshoi.

It didn't mean they weren't being watched, Florence objected.

They had a system, said Seldon, a system consisting of writing a note on thin typing paper and rolling it inside a cigarette. The man, whose name was Hank Kelly, Seldon said, would light up a regular cigarette and take a few puffs until he saw Seldon. Then he'd put out his cigarette and drop it on the ground. The one he actually dropped on the ground was, of course, the clean one with the note, which Seldon would pick up to learn any news, and the location of their next meeting. "It's always a different place. We go back and forth like that. He knows the situation in the country. He says he wants to help me leave."

"Escape?"

"Yes. The key is getting past security and into the British Embassy. Once we're inside, they can doctor any documents." He looked at Leon. "They can do it for us all."

She looked at him in amazement. What was he proposing?

"Seldon, it won't work," said Leon. "They abandoned us years ago. The American embassy is as sealed as a fortress. Nobody goes in or out except by automobile. The guards won't let you in even if you're American-born. Why is it that none of the embassy workers have ever made any contact with the likes of us?"

"That's right," she said. "We're trash to them. Absconders. Traitors. We left and good riddance. They despise us, and that's the truth. It's no different with the English. I don't know who this man is, but you need to stop this, Seldon. The punishment for attempting to escape the country now is execution."

Seldon looked at her but didn't seem to hear what she'd said. He was in the thrall of his plan. "Yes—if I was just anyone, that might be true. But I told you, my brother works for the United Kingdom! He is an important person. Just listen. All this fellow has to do is get himself a car without the official driver. They're all rats, naturally. But if he can drive the car himself, we can get into the embassy undetected."

She got up to stand by the window. She thought if she could catch a glimpse of her little boy outside, even for an instant, her heart might be better able to bear this conversation. Below, she saw Julian, a small bundled figure, chaperoned by the larger bundled figure of Avdotya Grigorievna, playing among the other children in the iron-fenced inner yard.

Leon now ventured the honest question, proposing it gently, like someone talking to a madman. "But why us, Seldon? Surely, this is a risky proposition to take on your own?"

But it was Seldon—his eyes full of that painful tenderness again as they flickered between Florence and Leon—who spoke to them as though they were the mad ones. "Don't you know? Because you will perish here. Even as we talk they are signing your death warrants."

And now Florence glanced at her husband, to find that he was looking at her for an answer.

"And what about Julian?" she said.

"All of us. I'll talk to him. I'll tell Kelly I'll only go if he takes you, too. But you have to make the decision."

She looked at Leon. Hadn't he told her that they had to accept their life here, had to accept the lot they'd drawn? Hadn't Leon made her abandon all her hopes of escape? And now he was looking at *her* for the answer. He wanted *her* to tell him what to do.

"I need to know if you're in," Seldon said.

She closed her eyes and waited for her husband to break the silence.

"We're in," Leon said.

TWO SLEEPLESS NIGHTS LATER, in bed, she said, "Do you believe him?"

"He's our only hope, Florence."

"It's too odd, his whole story," she whispered. "The cigarettes, the brother, or half-brother or whoever."

"I don't know. If anyone's going to pursue a plan like this, make contacts on the outside, Seldon would be the man."

"All right," she said, sitting up in bed. "Suppose it's true. Why would the British Embassy give two copper pennies about us? They don't get their own people out."

"He said his brother is an important person."

"Oh, Leon, how much do we know about Seldon? He said himself they were raised by different mothers. He seems to think he's important enough to be rescued, when . . ."

He cut her off. "I don't think he'd be telling us all of this if they were just empty words."

"He imagines things, Leon."

"He embroiders things, maybe, but . . ."

"Not just this. I can see it in his eyes, the way he looks at you."

There was a long silence in the darkness.

"I don't know what you're talking about."

"Oh, but I think you do know."

Even in the darkness Leon's body exerted a powerful force over her—his smooth shoulder and the bones of his large hands, the muscle of his naked calf jutting out from under the blanket.

"Don't pretend you're blind," she said, her voice sounding exactly like Essie's.

"You're speaking nonsense, Florie. Let's both go to sleep."

But once started she could not stop. "Am I? That love-struck look he gives you every time you say something encouraging to him. Putting his hands on your arm like some debutante when he's loosened up after a drink."

"I think maybe you should learn to watch your mouth."

"Is that so? Watch my mouth while I let that queer eat my food and ogle *my* husband on the courage of *my* vodka? You know what *I* think? I think he would be perfectly glad if he could take you with him—only you—and leave us here to rot."

And then her head was pressed to the wall, the fibers of the hanging carpet above their daybed stabbing into her back and ass through her nightgown as he pinned her hip with his knee.

"You never get it, do you?" Her hair was in his fist, her head jacked back. In the white luminescence from a streetlamp she could see the contorted lineaments of his repulsed face.

"Let me go," she whispered, her voice hoarse and stifled.

He released his grip from her hair and rolled heavily off of her. "God-damn you." He balled his hand into a fist. She winced as he swung his clenched fist into the stout torso of the pillow. "Goddamn you, Florence. Why do you think I want us to do this? We can't live how we're living, like trapped animals, bound, gagged. Maybe before the war I could, because I dreamed things would get better. But we can never be free here." He turned his head toward the pale floral curtain behind which their son slept. "I don't want him to grow up hearing the word 'kike' every day."

She steadied herself against the wall to regain some composure and tried to make her voice sound reasonable. "You think he won't hear it in America, or England?"

"Maybe. But once we're out, we can go anywhere . . . even to Pales-tine."

It was then that she felt sorriest for him—for his falling prey to his own dreams of flight, for the way he had nurtured them in secret as she once had. "Is that your plan now?" She could not resist punishing him for them. "Didn't manage to get yourself killed in the last war, so you want to pick up a rifle in the desert, huh? Get us killed by the Arabs instead?"

"At least there the Jews fight out in the open—they don't quiver like sitting ducks, which is what we are, Florence, make no mistake. Things are getting bad."

"You think I don't know that? You think *I* don't know they're getting bad. *You* don't have to tell me! Subotin called me in again."

Silence.

She couldn't summon the will to look at him.

"When?"

"Last week."

"How could you? How could you not tell me?"

And suddenly he was off the bed, snatching the blanket off her as though to see what else she was hiding. Giving her that look like he didn't know who she was.

"I meant to, I promise. I was *waiting* to, and then Seldon came and . . ."

"What have you told him already?"

"God, don't act so suspicious. What makes you think I've told him any-thing important? You don't trust me."

"What does he want now?"

"He knows things. He knew you and Seldon were at that rally for Meyerson. He thought I'd gone, too, tried to pin it on me. *Damn it*, I *told* you not to go. Every minute you spend with Seldon shortens your life by a day."

"Be quiet, you'll wake up the boy. What else?"

"He wants reports from Kuibyshev. Conversations. Anything involving the Jewish Committee."

He lowered himself back down on the bed. "So it's true."

"I think if I just tell him what he wants he'll leave us alone."

"And what do you think he wants?"

"The truth! That it was a nest of saboteurs and spies . . . !"

"Do you believe that?"

"What does it matter? Oh, darling." Gently, experimentally, she touched his shoulder. "*We* didn't do anything. We only translated what *they* gave us."

He stiffened at her touch. "Don't fool yourself. Everybody's tied together with the same rope."

"What else do you expect me to do, Leon? We have a *child*."

But her sob-strained voice, her lachrymal nasal breathing had no effect on him.

"If you think you're helping yourself, or us, you're making a mistake, Florence. Once you've given him what he wants, it's over. Their attitude toward informers is no better than toward the ones being informed on."

"Don't call me that! You think I want to be doing this? I *need* to give him something. I have to wiggle my way out of this. Don't berate me, for chrissake, *help* me."

It was as if she had said, "Open sesame."

He turned to face her. None of her bullying ever exerted the same force on him as her raw need.

He rested his face in his hands. "I have to think."

For a long time he sat like that, as if staring down into a lake. At last he said, "All right, tell him anything about Mikhoels. Whatever you give Subotin about him, it's just more dirt on his coffin."

"Subotin is smarter than that—it's too convenient."

"Name someone who's already in prison. Feffer. He's finished anyway. He'll be the first one shot. I don't know about the others. Seldon said Hofshteyn was sick when he disappeared. Maybe he's dead now."

"My God, how can we be talking like this? So calmly! It's so horrible. I can't."

"Hold it together. If you lose your composure like this you're in his hands. You need a strategy, Florence, not just tactics. It's the only way. The important thing is not to name anyone who hasn't been taken."

"Yes. Yes."

"We can't tell Seldon."

"Of course not." She gave Leon another pleading look. "I don't want him coming here at all hours. . . . He presses the buzzer and the whole apartment knows he's here."

"Where should we talk then? At the SovInformBuro all the walls have ears."

"On the street, in a park."

"And do what—drop cigarettes with notes for one another? What if he's on to something? We need somewhere we can really talk, Florence."

"All right. But he can't just show up unannounced and press our buzzer anytime he wants. Tell him he has to tell us in advance, and to come after it's dark, and stay down below, on the street, and you'll come down for him."

"I'll tell him," he said, "if that's what you want."

AT THEIR NEXT MEETING she sat watching Subotin write in his blank notebook. His hair had thinned up top. That was the other change in him, one she'd failed to notice the first time because his hair had been cropped so short and because she had been so nervous. Now she let her eyes stare at the balding forehead above that hateful, elegant face.

For several days she had rehearsed the testimony she would give Subotin. She would "recall" conversations she had heard in which Mikhoels had voiced "nationalistic views." She would tell him that after the war Mikhoels had spoken to his staff about the situation the Jews were facing in the U.S.S.R.: the evacuees coming back after the war and finding their houses occupied, the ongoing discrimination in hiring, and so on. He had insisted that it was the job of the Jewish Committee to intervene on their behalf. This, some of the personnel had felt, was a brazen overstepping of the committee's clear role as a propaganda organ.

Of all of this she now spoke to Subotin confidently, having the inner assurance that it happened to be true. As he recorded her testimony, his expression remained inscrutable. "And did Mikhoels implicate the Soviet government in this?"

"He said not enough attention was being paid to the problem."

"He voiced the view that the Soviet government was negligent in its duties. . . ."

"Yes."

"And he felt it was within the scope of his duties to take over the work of the government."

"No . . . Well, he only wanted to draw the attention of important people to the fact that Jews had lost their homes when they'd been evacuated. . . ."

Subotin cocked a groomed eyebrow.

She bit her lip. Why was she relapsing into defending Mikhoels, when she was supposed to be condemning him? The truth was that she had not at the time seen what Mikhoels was doing as wrong. He had been deluged by letters from suffering people. How could the man who had served as the heart and voice of Jews in the Soviet Union all through the war refuse to help them once the war had ended? But to defend him wouldn't cause his resurrection, would it? It would only bring harm to her. How long ago, it seemed, had she told herself that she "would not distort or exaggerate," that she would be a clear mirror and say nothing that might imperil another person. Now she knew all those airy promises were worthless. Whatever information she gave him, Subotin would rework to serve his version, just as she herself had reworked articles in the American press for her bulletins. Leon was right: better to throw dirt on a covered grave.

On the subject of Itzik Feffer, she allowed herself a harsher tone. She told Subotin that Feffer had treated being selected to sail to America with Mikhoels as a personal triumph rather than an assignment. That he'd lorded this "achievement" over other members of the JAFC. She was careful not to accuse Feffer of any actual crimes—he might still be alive. But no matter how much she disparaged his character, quoting gossip she had heard from others, Subotin did not look satisfied. His expression was bored as he continued to record what she said. Then he brought up the Crimean Plot. As Subotin described it, the conspiracy involved leaders of the JAFC who "promised" parts of the Crimean Peninsula as a beachhead for imperialist military actions to the Americans with whom they had contact. According to "information possessed by the investigation," the leaders of the Jewish cabal had already started distributing key positions of this imperialist foothold among themselves. He now expected Florence to tell him which positions had been distributed secretly, and who would hold them.

She wanted to press a hand to her mouth. Why, the idea would make a cat laugh! She had never heard of such a plot. It implied that a tiny group of poets had coordinated a plan to topple the mighty Soviet government. She'd known only of a suggestion, floated briefly and entirely publicly, of settling Jewish refugees who'd lost their homes in Crimea. She tried to study Subotin's face to determine if he believed what he was saying. If he did, he was surely a fanatic willing to believe anything; but if he didn't, it meant only that he was a total cynic, and so her efforts to dissuade him would be just as pointless. As all of these thoughts darted through her head at lightning speeds, strategy and philosophy became mixed. Who was more dangerous, a fanatic who believed hideous falsehoods, or a cynic who only pretended but was willing to make them true if it was necessary? She reminded herself that she could not get embroiled now in a denial of the existence of this alleged plot. Her only way out was to claim to know nothing of it, to tell Subotin that the Jewish Committee members were a cozy little gang, and if such a plot existed, she would have had no knowledge of it.

As soon as she said as much, Florence could see that her answer was less than pleasing.

"I see," he said, without putting down his steel pen, "you tell me they carp and backstab and elbow each other for power out in the open, yet when it comes to this plot you suddenly claim they were 'a cozy little gang.'"

He was telling her that he'd given her rope to play dumb long enough.

"I only meant I know nothing about it. I'm not ruling out that they talked of this plan to others."

"Others, such as . . . Seldon Parker?"

She'd heard the name in her head even before he spoke it. How could she have been so stupid as to think he would demand nothing of her if she continued to act foolish and naïve? Of course, Subotin had had a target picked out for her all along.

"Yes, it's true," she said, "that we shared two small rooms in Kuibyshev with Seldon Parker, in evacuation. We did not do this by choice. As you can guess, housing was nearly impossible to come by in Kuibyshev. We were assigned our quarters. When we were evacuated, we were living twenty to a room in a frozen schoolhouse. So when the SovInformBuro offered us the two rooms, we were grateful. Seldon lived in the smaller of the two. We saw him every day, shared meals and so on. As for how well we came to know him—that is a different question. He's a difficult person to get to know. He is very private and plays his cards close to his vest. What I mean is, he's quite gregarious, well spoken, and so on; he can give a good toast, tell a joke. But sometimes I had the feeling I did not know him very well at all. I am not sure how to explain this."

But her denials would not save her, that much she knew. She needed strategy, as Leon said, not just tactics. She could hear Leon's words in her head. They were all tied with the same rope and would all get pulled into the same noose.

At this moment, Seldon's plan for escape no longer struck Florence as mad. It offered as much chance for survival as would doing nothing. The question now—and this was the only part of the game over which, she believed, she still had any control—was how to stall Parker's arrest. How to suggest to Subotin that she might wheedle out of Seldon Parker the necessary information he was after.

"He did have a . . . special talent," she said now, and permitted a small smile to cross her face.

She could see, under Subotin's immobile mask, a subtle but not imperceptible uptick in interest. "What was it?" he said, sternly.

"He could always obtain alcohol. You may think this was easy, but vodka was quite expensive in evacuation, and no one could get his hands on wine. At the bazaar it was five hundred rubles a bottle! One could get it by other than the official means, but that isn't something I've ever known very much about. In any case, *he* always had a way of getting it—vodka, Georgian wine, even sherry. I don't know how, but it made him very popular among the higher-ups in the committee. I'm sure *they* weren't suffering from any lack of rations. But Seldon was always good for a bottle."

"You're saying he drank with them."

"He did, occasionally. He liked the good life. In this way he made friends inside the committee. I know he liked to stay up drinking with some of them. What sorts of things got spoken during those wet hours, I can't say exactly. Sometimes he dropped hints. Once, he said that Feffer told him he was finally going to 'get a little relief, see a little paradise,' when he visited America. He'd quote little things people might say when they drank."

"And you never asked him more?"

"He prided himself on knowing these people personally, calling them friends. I'm no gossip, and I don't like to flatter people by rising to their bait when they show off."

"It seems to me that a person who talks that way is *asking* you to ask."

Hook. Bait. Swallow. She'd gotten him.

It was a risk, she knew, to suggest that Seldon might have inside information on any plot—real or imagined—hatched up by the committee. A suggestion like that was cause enough for the NKVD to move in and arrest him. And yet her instincts told Florence that if they'd wanted to arrest Seldon they would have done it by now. No, whatever elaborate fraud this "investigation" was concocting, it still needed some credible information with which to pry out further confessions. It alarmed her how instinctively she'd started to understand how this crude and unsophisticated game was played. Great lies would be ransomed with small truths.

"I suppose," she said, "I could ask him now. It was three years ago. It would take some work for me to get Parker to talk about those times. But, then, he does enjoy telling stories."

"How you do it is up to you," Subotin said flatly. Still, she perceived an undertone of encouragement in his affected indifference.

She had bought herself time.

FOR SEVERAL DAYS THERE was no light in the stairwell. It seemed to Florence that every few weeks the naked bulb in their building's entry got unscrewed and stolen, either by the inhabitants or by the courtyard adolescents. After a while, the housing committee simply ceased replacing it. The February nights were long and she had to maneuver her way home through the courtyard in grainy darkness. This evening, with the shadows of the trees darkening the entrance further, her only means of navigation was touching her toe to the snow-crusted footpath. She managed warily, clutching her two string bags of groceries and regretting having gone out so late to the outdoor market to buy the bruised vegetables that were sold off cheaply at the end of the day. She crossed the threshold of the vestibule, her eyes still unadjusted to the near-perfect gloom. Florence stopped. Inside the vestibule's damp cavern, she had a sense she was not alone. She strained to hear what she'd thought was the rasping of a shoe, a breath. But in the predatory stillness could be heard only her own shallow, frightened breathing. No, she had not been mistaken. Whoever was lurking at the edge of the darkness had chosen this moment to break his inertness and move toward her.

She sought an escape—the door or else the stairs—but could not tell which way was which. The person was clutching her arm. An instinctive spasm took hold of her: the string bag full of onions in her free hand traced an arc in the air like the shot of a medieval mace. Her scream broke the breath-heavy silence and she lashed again with her bag of onions at the intruder. She felt him let go of her arm and she scrambled as fast as she could, falling up and over the first two stairs until she was able to grip the railing and lift herself up to the first landing.

It was then that Florence heard the whimper. She glanced down, and there, in a streak of weak moonlight, she saw the lean figure crumpled at the bottom of the stairs.

"Seldon?"

A groan.

Her footsteps clattered back down the stairs. "Oh heavens, have I hurt you?"

"My gut will recover. Not sure about my pride." He had on a fur cap with the ear flaps pulled down.

"Why didn't you say it was you?"

"I might have, if you hadn't belted me with that sack of . . . what are these?"

"Our dinner." On her hands and knees Florence tried to pat around for the onions that had rolled away.

"Leon told me not to come strolling in unannounced anymore. I said I would be down here at half past seven. I've been standing here for close to an hour."

Now Florence remembered her own directive to Leon. "I left him with Yulik. He must have forgotten," she said guiltily.

Seldon held what loose onions he'd found as, half limping, he followed Florence up the stairs. She fit the key into the lock and opened the door to the common hall. No one was in the corridor, thank goodness. A light was burning in the kitchen, at the corridor's end. Someone was there, clinking pans and pots. Seldon set his load down and began to slip off his boots.

"Oh, for heaven's sake, don't bother!" she hissed.

She ought to have said nothing at all, because just then Essie stuck her head out and peered into the corridor. Her apron was dusted with flour.

"Florence! Just who I want to see."

"You're up late baking," she said, trying with all her power to sound like a person whose nerves were not flayed and raw.

"I completely forgot that I promised to make a napoleon torte for one of the girls at work. She's leaving on maternity. And I ran out of condensed milk. Oh, hello, Seldon," Essie said, spotting him by the cloak rack. Her eyes squinted suspiciously behind her slightly flour-dusted glasses. "Haven't seen you here in a while."

"Good evening, Essie."

To Florence she said, "You wouldn't have a can of the condensed stuff in your cupboard?"

"I'll take a look."

Florence tried to hide her impatience as she looked for the condensed milk, with Essie waiting in the doorway. Standing on a chair, she felt around on the top shelf where she kept the dry foods, macaroni, sugar, soap. Yulik was turning in his cot, sleeping fitfully. Seldon had joined Leon, and the two were lighting cigarettes by the window, which they'd cracked open. She found the can and gave it to Essie.

"You saved me. I'll get you *two* cans next week."

"One will do."

"Well, then." She looked around and smiled wanly at the men. "*Ciao.*"

Florence dropped the hook in the eye and latched the door. They were all aware of the child asleep, and talked quietly. There was a new development in the plan Seldon had worked out with Hank Kelly, the man from the embassy, who had promised to help him. There was to be a party in about seven weeks for all of the embassy staff and their families, at a lodge in the village of Uspenskoye, where some of the foreign embassies apparently had their dachas. To this rural outing, the embassy staffs would be shuttled by turns in official cars. Kelly predicted that, with so many guests being ferried and some of the drivers off duty, he would be able to take the wheel of his own car as a volunteer driver. On the afternoon of the party, they would all dress in their best clothing—"your Sunday finest"—and take a trolley out as far as they could to the station of Usovo, and wait there for Kelly to pick them up in his automobile on the way from Uspenskoye. He would drive them back to the embassy compound. Kelly would provide them with the names of several embassy workers, including an actual staff couple and their child. Kelly's official ID should suffice at the security point. Once everyone was behind the safety of the embassy walls, an appeal on their behalf could begin.

"But what if the guards stop us and ask for documents?"

Kelly had told Seldon that it was unlikely that the guard would check anyone's papers but his. If, however, theirs were requested, Seldon and Florence were to begin arguing like a married couple, in the queen's best English, about who had been entrusted to bring the family's documents.

"Speak like you have a fat plum in your mouth and they'll never suspect you're not English," he advised her.

"What about Yulik?"

"Best that he not say a word. Dress him in a foppy little sailor suit. Something starched and fresh. That goes for the rest of us. Flora, get a new dress made if you have to, and buy new shoes."

"Shall I get a set of tails?" Leon said with a sense of doom. But Seldon did not blanch at this. "Some fresh trouser braces and a new hat would be advisable," he said, then added, "Now, listen to me carefully. You are to pack only the essentials. A day bag. No suitcases."

"Wait, wait," Florence interrupted. "How can we know—even if everything goes as this . . . this Kelly says, how can we be sure the embassy won't toss us back out? We're Soviet nationals, after all."

"According to this country's laws, yes. But we were all issued our new passports illegally, which means we never stripped ourselves of our previous citizenships. It was chicanery. They poached our passports and that's that. You have a child, for heaven's sake! It would be heartless for them to toss you out."

"People will know we're missing."

"Leave everything in the apartment just as it is. Tell your neighbors you're taking a short holiday. By the time anyone notices, we'll be on a train to Finland with new papers."

They sat talking over the plan in cautious whispers meant less to keep the child from waking up than to keep themselves from being alarmed by their own audacity. They spoke calmly, as though they were discussing the plans and fates of other people. Even after Seldon gave them all the information he had, they went over the details for the better part of two hours, until a light knocking on the door finally broke the inertia.

Florence tiptoed to the door and in Russian inquired who was there. "Me," came the taut treble of Essie's voice. Florence unlatched the lock and found Essie holding a platter with several pieces of napoleon torte, her eyes scanning the room. "Oh, Seldon, you're still here." Essie's surprise seemed as feigned as the occasion of her visit. She made an effort to smile. "I thought if you were still up, you might have a taste. I made more than I need."

As though waking from a trance, Seldon rose to his feet. He donned his coat and took a square of torte off Essie's tray. Turning to address Leon and Florence, he said, "I ought to be out of your hair at this hour." Then, taking a bite of the torte, he looked with surprise at Essie. "Umm. Terrifically tasty."

"I put rum in, just a splash."

"That must be it."

And bending his head in salute, he took his leave.

IN THE UNINTERRUPTED FLOW of days that followed, Florence went out and bought new clothes and fabrics. For herself she purchased a pleated tartan skirt, which she hemmed to below the knee, a wide-brimmed hat, and short matching gloves. For Leon she was able to find a button-up vest and striped tie. For Yulik she bought a pair of checkered flannel pants, which she intended to shorten on her sewing machine into a pair of knickerbockers like those she'd seen in foreign magazines, a style she had decided fit the pampered child of English diplomats. She worried about Yulik's role in their scheme but told him nothing of the plan, allowing herself to hope that when the time came he would be prepared to play along. He understood English, after all, though at the age of five he already knew better than to speak it outside their room. Still, in private, Florence began speaking to him exclusively in English, correcting his pronunciation more forcibly than she ever had in the past, with an insistence he found odd and stifling at first, but that with time he began to accept in his usual good-natured way. In her mind she was now daily rehearsing the testimony she would give if the car was stopped by a Russian guard—

"Why, on a short outing? I hardly imagined we'd need *documents.*" Alone in front of the small mirror by the door, she pronounced each word as crisply and carelessly as she imagined an Englishwoman might speak it. In this way she girded herself for their departure and at the same time tried not to think about the future. The whole thing could be called off at any moment. And yet, several times during the course of a day, she found herself slipping unconsciously across that invisible border between reality and fantasy, the present and the future—she and Leon, in the costumes she was so scrupulously assembling, and Julian still in his English schoolboy's getup, with their new papers in hand, crossing into Latvia, then Finland, the lashing wind on the ship, the final passage across the ocean. The worst-case scenario she did not dare let herself imagine. If harrowing and unbearable punishments lay in store, there was no sense in trying to anticipate them. Strangely, it was no longer their imminent escape (still a month away) but her impending meeting with Subotin that kept Florence awake at night.

Her current strategy now consisted of stalling when it came to the question of Seldon Parker, and yet at the same time convincing Subotin that she was getting Parker to open up about what he'd been told in devious confidence by the members of the Jewish Anti-Fascist Committee, in wartime and after. But what was there to disclose? She needed to feed Subotin's paranoid fiction with little scraps, just enough to keep him hungry for more testimony. And now the only shred of incriminating testimony she had to offer was something Leon had told her to say, a phrase Mikhoels was rumored to have spoken in defense of starting a Jewish republic in Crimea: "You can live wherever you like, but you need to have your own house and roof." That was it, and so she served it as her meager catch from working over Seldon Parker.

Subotin's pen stopped making its scratching sound. "So Mikhoels was preparing," he said, "to settle Crimea with Jews who would help America seize it for their imperialist purposes."

"Well, I don't think his aim was to wrest Crimea away from Soviet power. That wouldn't even be *possible.*"

"I am not interested in your opinions but in facts," said Subotin.

She would have thought he'd be intrigued by such an inculpatory quote from the head of the committee, but ever since she had walked into the apartment and taken a seat, Subotin had been visibly impatient, scratching down something with his pen, then crossing it out when she contradicted the testimony he sought.

"The fact is," she said, trying to sound conciliatory, "that a plan to settle Crimea was discussed. According to Parker, it was the kind of romantic idea that only actors or poets would come up with." She was on her own now, making it up as she went along. "I can't say for sure how far it went. I'd need to work on Comrade Parker a little longer to be able to know."

"You've had many weeks."

"To prompt someone about conversations that took place years ago is not a straightforward matter. One has to create the right atmosphere of . . . reminiscence."

She could give Subotin the "version" he wanted. She could do it now: say that the top brass of the Jewish Committee were preparing to wrest Crimea away from the Soviet Union with aid from America, and so on. Claim that Seldon Parker had been aware of all this, was in cahoots with it. It would lead to Seldon's arrest, certainly, but it might leave her and Leon spared. Her offering would buy them their lives, would leave her family intact. Wasn't that all she wanted? To protect them, to protect Yulik? Who was Seldon to her? Not her blood. A friend? What was a friend? A deviant was what he was, a *shicker* with an unsound mind.

But she could not do it. Maybe his plan was nothing but a castle in the air. Maybe this Hank Kelly did not exist. Maybe he did exist but would lose his nerve at the last moment, get them all thrown in the basement of the Lubyanka Prison. And yet. And yet Seldon had confidence. And because he did, so did she. Whatever pure or unwholesome motives had stirred him into coming to their aid, the plan he had conceived—the pact to which all three of them had bound their fates, their lives—was all she had now. It was the one hope she still safeguarded from all the broken promises of her fifteen years in Russia.

"You've had more than a month to 'set the mood,'" Subotin said.

"Please, I'm getting closer. Last time Parker dropped by for a drink I got him talking but he would only stay for a short time."

Subotin recorded this and said, "This was when? The Thursday before last?" He seemed to be consulting something in his notes.

"Yes, I believe so." She pretended to think. Had she told him the precise day Seldon had visited?

"And how long do you consider to be 'a short time'?"

"Pardon me?"

"Would you say an hour is a 'short' time? Two hours?"

His pale-blue eyes had fixed on her. Was this a theoretical question? What was he asking her?

And then, suddenly, her mind caught the meaning of his words.

Two hours.

For a moment, it was like Russian was again a foreign tongue to her and she had grasped the essence of the question at the last possible second.

Two hours. It was not theoretical. He knew. He knew that Seldon had been in their room two Thursdays ago for two hours. That was what he was telling her, in the guise of a question.

He was watching to see how she would respond. But *how* did he know? Nobody in the apartment had seen Seldon walk in or out. He had hidden in the shadows for just this reason. Only Essie, when she'd brought them the napoleon torte. Essie, of whom Seldon had harbored suspicions all along. Florence had never considered the possibility that her best friend could have occupied this very room with Subotin, or someone like him. Why not? An assumption so fleeting and vain that she had not even registered it as a thought—that she, Florence, had been singled out in some way for her insight and intelligence. Yes, a part of her had taken a depraved kind of pride in this venal, repellent work they forced her to do. This violation of herself, which sullied and antagonized her every waking moment, had sustained in her some shabby illusion: that she was shrewd, that she was, in some way, special. And now she did not even have that. An idiot was what she was, to think that Essie had sought entry into their company out of desire for Seldon. The blushing-girl act had been a ruse to worm her way into all the secret talk going on in Florence's room. Essie running her mouth off about those magazines—what was it but a provocation? To get Florence to start yapping. Did anything else even make sense? *Two hours.* Those two words were all it took. They were enough. And now it was no longer Subotin who sat across that polished oak table from her, staring her down across the lace runner heaped with papers— his deck of cards. The reflection in the burnished, shining surface of that samovar from which no tea was ever poured was no longer of her and Subotin. It was of her and Essie. Subotin now was only the repository for whatever Essie had told him, or had told somebody else who had told him.

But he had been informed wrong before. She knew that. His sources made mistakes, or lied.

It's your word or mine, little girl.

"The last time Seldon Parker stopped by my room," she said, "I did get him talking. He wanted to talk, I could sense it. But, unfortunately, we were interrupted."

"Interrupted by what?"

"By whom. My neighbor, Esther Frank. Seldon never talks openly when she's around."

"Why is that?"

Florence permitted herself a shrug. "Doesn't trust her. Finds her irritating, and also . . . provocative."

If Essie's eagerness had been her asset, it could also be her liability.

"Provocative in what way?"

"She gripes. About the rations, the shortages. That the government is ignoring ordinary people." At last, Florence found she could meet Subotin's gaze head-on. "She tries to draw people into discussions, arguments they don't want to have."

A talentless informant, was what she was telling him.

"Yet you have never reported her anti-Soviet talk before."

"You have never been interested in Esther Frank before."

"You've listened to her outbursts and said nothing."

"What can I say to a person who is determined to be unsatisfied? I suppose she compares her life here unfavorably to the one she had before, in America."

She flinched as Subotin brought his fist down hard on the table, causing two sheets of paper to fly off onto the floor.

"You *suppose*. You *presume*. It appears to me that most of your purported 'information' is just that: Supposition. Presumption. More of your womanly prattle! You have been trying to elude this investigation."

"But I tell you everything I know!"

She could feel the tears welling in her eyes. Her nerves were worn raw. She could not stand to be in this room one minute longer. "Everything I know. I have *nothing* to hide." She let the film of tears fill her eyes. Let him think she was crying because he had wounded her honor.

"You have yet to provide me with any validatable information about concrete plans or activities of anybody in your circle."

"But I *can*. If you just give me more time."

He pointed a finger at the ceiling. "I also have orders, and I need results."

Florence swallowed. The words, when she spoke them, did not sound like they were coming out of her mouth. "You want something concrete. She keeps foreign magazines in her room." She could not look at him, though she was aware of his looking at her, aware of the silence.

"What magazines?"

"*Noosveek. Laif* . . . I don't remember." She wiped her eyes. "That is why Esther Frank slanders our Soviet reality, because she compares it to gaudy tinsel she sees in capitalist propaganda."

Let him call Florence a liar. If Essie was reporting the opposite story from her end, let Subotin now sort it out. *Your word against mine, girlie.*

"Where does she get those magazines?"

"She works at the Foreign Languages Publishing House of TASS. Maybe there, or maybe from her foreign contacts."

"You've seen these magazines."

"I'm afraid I have."

"Why haven't you reported it before?"

"It's vulgar frippery, nothing I considered substantive compared to the treasonous activities of the JAFC."

She could hear him tapping his pen on the paper, perhaps struggling to decide where this all fit in. "You leave it for us to decide what's substantive," he said. She watched the top of Subotin's balding forehead as he moved his pen across the paper. It would be her last memory of him.

FOR TWO NIGHTS SHE did not sleep. Yulik was sick again. The icebound Moscow winter, which lasted into April, had left him weakened with bronchitis. Once again he was plagued with fevers and the expectorant wet cough that kept him from sleeping for more than a few hours. Nursing a sick child left time for little else, and gave her reason to withdraw from the communal life of the apartment—to keep her distance from Essie without exciting suspicion. It was past midnight when she went to the kitchen to make mustard plasters to lay on the boy's back and draw out his congestion. She was standing at the stove, heating the water, when she heard it—the voice of the building janitor, wheedling and slightly drunk. She set the pot on the table, beside the plasters dusted with flour and dry mustard. "I don't know nothing about those ones, them's all foreigners," he was telling someone, the slurred words pitching higher as the voices ascended the stairs. She thought of running back to their room, to alert Leon, to gather her son in his blanket and take him . . . where? She tried the door to the unlit back staircase—the old servants' entrance—and found it miraculously open. But what could she do—take her son's heat-radiating, feverish body out of bed and into the stairwell's dank cold? And then what? She had not seriously thought of running until now, did not think of it because she knew it was pointless. There was nowhere to go. And it was already too late. She could hear the footsteps on the landing, the janitor with his chain of keys leading the men in boots inside. They were already here, out in the hallway. And she, hidden just inside the door of the servants' entrance to the kitchen, could not see them. But she could hear. A gruff voice demanding, "Which room is it?"

Please, don't let it be ours.

"Who's in the kitchen?" The squeaking slap of their boots coming closer.

"Here it is," said the janitor in his raspy voice. The boots stopped just outside the kitchen door.

And then she knew.

They were knocking on the last door in the hall. Essie's room. Three insistent knocks, and then an impatient fourth. The commotion was drawing the other neighbors out of their rooms. At last, the door creaked open. "Yes?" Essie's voice was as weak as a child's. They were demanding her papers.

"What do you want with her?" Florence recognized it as Avdotya Grigorievna's voice—that old woman was afraid of no one.

"Back in your rooms," a voice was ordering them. They had a warrant for a search and arrest.

And Florence, concealed behind the kitchen door, was too terrified to move. She could not see Essie in her battered house slippers, in that loud florid robe hastily thrown over her nightgown. She did not see her blinking myopically, blind to this ghoulish surprise, as she was blind to everything. Florence was spared the sight of her friend's face—the terror mingling for an instant with female embarrassment at being caught in her slatternly state in the middle of the night. She did not need to see it. She knew it.

But she had not believed—not really—that anyone would come after Essie. Not if Essie was the apartment's real informer. Because what she had said to Subotin, about the magazine, in her moment of fright, she had said only to cover herself, being sure that Essie had already whistled on *her*. But what had made her sure? Florence could not remember anymore. *Two hours.* Yes. The disquieting vision of Essie with her napoleon torte. But what if Essie was not the conniving one? What if someone else was watching the house—someone outside, watching whoever came in and who went out? Or the janitor himself. Or anyone. She had fooled herself into thinking she knew the whole dark clockwork of how it worked. *Would you say an hour is a "short" time? Two hours?* Nothing more than a goading conjecture intended to rile her. And she, out of her mind with fear, had risen to the bait. On animal impulse, she had abandoned all the safeguards of her "strategy" in order to defend herself against a cunning provocation behind which stood possibly nothing. Defending herself—with a reckless disclosure, with a lie!

Her back against the wall, she pressed her hand to her mouth to keep herself from saying the words aloud: *What have I done?*

But it was too late. No amount of doubting would alter the course of what was taking place on the other side of the door. The police had pushed themselves past Essie into her room, where they were bound to find, behind the bureau or under the bed, the magazine Essie had not yet given back—Florence's gift, the final memento of their truce.

FLORENCE'S LIAISONS WITH SUBOTIN ended as suddenly as they had begun, with the telephone. At work the following day, she picked up the heavy receiver and was told that she was to be rotated to another handler, who would make contact with her in time. As the days wore on and the week of their departure approached, she waited in a state of agitation for a contact that did not come. Whatever distress the meetings with Subotin had caused her, Florence found this new, uncertain period of waiting an even greater strain on her nerves. She had no way now to assess the conditions in which they found themselves. At night, she was seized with a feeling of calamity and awoke in alarm at the slightest noise. Leon too saw the break in contact as a bad sign and told her they needed to be prepared. They both kept packed and ready a rucksack with clean underwear and a tin of tooth powder, some money, and a pencil, in case the police knocked on the door. They had rid themselves of most of what they believed could compromise them. At Seldon's suggestion, Leon had dismantled the radio, throwing pieces of it away in different trash bins around the neighborhood. They had long ago disposed of their Hemingway and Twain, and their tattered issues of *Einkayt*. Now even old editions of Lenin's writing were no longer safe, Leon claimed. One by one, they tore out pages from their books and ripped them into scraps to be flushed down the common toilet. Disposing of these scraps at night, Florence imagined all of Moscow clogging the network of pipes beneath itself with forbidden literature. Leon had told her to tear up her brother's letters, but this single thing she could not bring herself to do. Instead, she preserved them rolled up inside a tin full of flour; she just couldn't rip up the brittle, yellowed pages, her last link to a universe beyond their tumorous world of fear.

Only her resolute determination not to transmit her feelings to her young son—to allow Yulik to go on as if everything were normal—carried her through the weeks. But the boy, sensitive to every change, seemed to become afraid of separating from her even for short periods, as though he sensed that if he let her out of his sight just once she might disappear forever.

She kept him home from school and let him spend his days looking at picture books in his cot. His favorites were the books that showed how to make models out of cardboard, with pages whose figures could be cut out with scissors to make parachutes or toy windmills, grain elevators, lighthouses. She sat up reading to him from books about aircraft and sea vessels, locomotives and steamships overcoming great distances. She let him nap late into the evening, while the red sun was setting behind snow-covered roofs. At night the boy would wake up and find his mother sitting on a chair beside his cot, leaning over him, her thick curls falling on her shoulders, her warm hand petting his cold, moist forehead. She would shush-shush him and tell him to go back to sleep. Watching her son breathe heavily while he slept, she experienced for the first time an acute sense of her mortality. She tried not to anticipate what might happen to the three of them. She could no longer picture a future.

36.

WITH GOOD STEAM

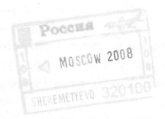

I FELT LIKE ALICE IN WONDERLAND. THE CAT TATTOOED ON THE SIDE OF Kablukov's breast grinned homicidally as it vanished and reappeared through a veil of floating steam. I tried not to stare too pointedly at Kablukov's flesh while the three of us—Tom, Kablukov, and I—lounged like Roman senators with bedsheets draped around our laps.

Kablukov had left his Ray-Bans in the locker room, but his eyes were half hooded in the attitude of someone accepting obeisance. "Do you know why I like doing business with Americans?"

"Please, Ivan Matveyevich, do tell us," I said. My throat ached from the steam, or maybe from the effort of having to be civil.

"Enough with the formalities. Please, call me Vanya. I like Americans because you are like us. Simple. Not like those complicated French, or the chilly Germans, or the Japanese—who the hell can read their faces, they all look alike to me."

I translated for Tom, who did a fair imitation of looking amused as Kablukov set aside his beer glass and leaned across the stone bench to squeeze his hand, as though to seal the mutual understanding.

Around us, grown men were sprawled or slouched on marble slabs, breathing through their mouths, absorbed in the grave business of their health-inducing stupor. A few squatted against the Turkish tiles by the polished spigots, scrubbing one another's hides or thrashing them with dried birch leaves before banishing the toxins in bursts of cold water. If I closed my eyes, I might have been in a tannery. The vapor seemed to turn all conversations into a mutter, save the cries of "Harder! Harder!" that occasionally rose above the echoes of thwacking and thrashing.

"A man can be a 'professional,' a good worker. But what is work? It is only . . . a *thing*." Kablukov signaled for an attendant. "What matters is what is on the inside." He hit his fist against the strangely shaped cross etched on his chest. "A man's spirit. Take care of him," he ordered the ancient-looking attendant, motioning at Tom. The wiry little man gestured for Tom to prostrate himself on the bench and then proceeded to whack Tom's back and legs with birch twigs, gently at first and then, after a few nods from Kablukov, with more vigor, flagellating Tom's smooth Midwestern flesh in rhythm to his poorly suppressed grunts of pain.

"Easy there," Tom warned the man sheepishly, between groans.

Kablukov adjusted his loincloth and took a few heavy swallows of steam, then ordered the attendant to bring two fresh beers, which the man did with disturbing efficiency. Kablukov released a gurgle of air as he popped each cap. "There's no point spending less than three hours in a *banya*," he advised us, upending his beer bottle, then waiting for me to take a drink. "You Americans go to your doctors and buy your pills, pills, pills, and we"—he spread his arms and planted the bottle on the bench—"we take care of our bodies right here!"

As an advertisement for the *banya*'s salubrious benefits, Kablukov hardly struck me as a model specimen. The first time I met him, he'd appeared to me a physically powerful man. But that first impression was a testament to the value of an expensive suit. When he was naked, it was plain to see that, like a walrus, he had no shoulders. All his formidable bulk was concentrated in front of him. Decades of lard and vodka consumption had coarsened his tapered frame and bloated his face into that of a veteran pimp or public official.

"You're selling me a horse I already own," I said, a bit too irascibly. I was impatient to know what Kablukov was after. "I mean, I used to come here to Sanduny," I amended.

"Ah, before we lost you to the Americans."

"Even as a boy," I said. "With my father."

"Is that so?"

It was, in fact. I *had* come here with Papa, though only one time. I'd retained the fading memory in glimmering patches all of my life. It was the last image I had of my father.

"My own father was Armenian. You see this?" He tapped the tattoo on his chest. "People think it's some ordinary cross. It ain't. It's the Holy Lance. It's the spear they used to stick Christ Himself." With his index finger Kablukov made a slow surgical swipe along his left rib. "The Holy Lance was brought to Armenia by Saint Gregory the Illuminator."

"You learned that from your father."

Kablukov looked at me like I was nuts. "My father? If I spotted that bastard walking down the street, I'd pop him. However"—he raised a finger—"I believe in the importance of remembering one's heritage. That's why I have this." He pointed to a faded blue inscription on his forearm. "He who's been thrown in the water is not afraid of the rain."

Kablukov now ordered the wiry attendant to give peace to Tom's abused flesh and come service his own. I tilted my head back and dozed to the murmur of men's voices. The muffled *banya* noises formed a braid of sound around me as I faded in and out of mental acuity. I had tried to fight sleep, but the intervals between my conscious moments were diminishing, while slabs of memory rose up like stepping-stones in a streambed.

WITHOUT QUITE BEING AWARE of it, I was remembering my father—his thin frame, his ropy muscles, the hair on his toes—as we made our way up the tiled stairs to the Sanduny *banya*'s second floor. At my eye level was his flapping penis. Already I was aware of its being different from my own—not only in size, but in the prominence of the polished bulb of the tip. It would be another ten years before I would learn about the mark of Abraham that I and the rest of my Jewish peers were missing—sons born after the war, who, for fear of the fascists, had entered manhood with our foreskins intact.

The Sanduny *banya* was older and hotter than the municipal facilities I'd gone to with Mama, those plain and dingy public baths that lacked the atmosphere of departed imperial glory which lingered everywhere amid Sanduny's carved and gilded walls, its peeling moldings, the chipped marble staircases and vast clouded mirrors. A ruined paradise, a shipwreck of ghosts flogging themselves and one another like penitents. Upstairs, where the steam was densest, the real enthusiasts congregated in their peaked felt hats and slippers. There the air was barely breathable. From somewhere, Papa obtained a big zinc tub and filled it with cold water from a spigot.

"What's that for?"

"You'll see."

Naked, he carried it to the wooden benches at the rear while I followed behind, afraid of losing him in the forest of legs. The floor under my feet was covered in slippery leaves.

"Now, when it gets too hot for you, you just bend down and inhale the air right up above this tub, see? The moment you feel your lungs burning, put your face right by this cold water and breathe. You got it, boss?"

"Got it."

I did as he instructed, while he scraped his back and shoulders with a scrubber. Every time someone opened the oven door and tossed more water on the glowing bricks, I dipped my head down to the zinc tub. As soon as I was able to breathe again I'd look around furtively at the other boys in the baths. Some were just a little older than I was, and a few were younger. All of them strutted beside their fathers, confidently withstanding the heat. I felt myself growing jealous of them, embarrassed every time I needed to kneel down and drink in the cool air above the tub. The boy who had gone to the *banya* each week with Mama—surrounded there by white-skinned, milky creatures, mountains of old flesh and mounds of ripe bellies, patronized by kindly female smiles—seemed to me now a distant person, a little child. My mother was always reminding me to clean this spot and that, "so nothing gets stuck between." Papa, handing me the soap, seemed to trust me to take care of this business on my own.

I tried not to linger above the tank of icy water, where it was easier to stay. Each time I stood up, I tried to hold out against the heat a little longer. The floor scalded my feet. Somewhere in the haze above me, the men were calling for the attendant to "Toss on more!" I could hear the creak of the boiler door, the water being hurled against the bricks and exploding in hissing steam, filling the room with fog as I struggled to breathe.

———

KABLUKOV'S VOICE WHIPPED ME back into the present.

"I couldn't fail to notice you put our boys from Sausen through their paces at their presentation."

Our side of the steam room had emptied out, and the vapor had subsided. I saw Tom get out of his cold shower and wrap himself in a towel. Scrubbed and refreshed, he sat down beside me. "What's the man saying?"

"That we ask a lot of questions."

"Tell him we asked them the same questions we would ask any potential contractor."

But Kablukov seemed to understand without translation. "And it's right well that you did! I told those boys they should know this shipping is a serious business. When they start this job, they have to be prepared for everything."

It took some self-control for me not to raise my eyebrow. I turned and translated for Tom.

"We haven't made our decision yet, Mr. Kablukov," he said respectfully. "There are still a few other contractors to consider."

Kablukov shut one eye and nodded gravely to show he understood without need of an interpreter, and to signal, it seemed, that he had no intention of meddling in our selection process. "It's your consideration that we're depending on." He set his elbows firmly on his toweled thighs, leaning in and lowering his voice to a throaty whisper. "I didn't set up our meeting for no good reason."

I did my best to convey the gist of this, though I wasn't sure where it was heading.

"Our Sausen friends, whether you give the contract to them or to somebody else"—Kablukov shrugged his narrow shoulders—"over the long run, it won't make a big difference."

So why all the fuss? I thought.

"That is not the reason I wanted us to talk like this—person to person. I did not wish to make it an official meeting, because what I have to say is still very early news. In six months, L-Pet will make an announcement that it is putting up for auction twelve percent of L-Pet stock, with an option to buy another three percent."

He motioned with his fleshy arm for me to translate for Tom, and sat back patiently as I did.

I watched Tom perk up out of his vaporous stupor. "Ask him if they'll be selling those shares on the open market."

Once more Kablukov seemed to understand the question without my help, and answered: "Who becomes a successful bidder in this auction will depend on many things. We expect Exxon and Chevron will try to offer us bags of lucre for our reserves. But we have no desire to tie ourselves up with a behemoth. As Mr. Khodorkovsky discovered, the bigger your partners, the bigger your problems. What matters to us is what's in here." He jerked his thumb toward the hairy flesh straining to hold in his gut. "We like doing business with people who like doing business with us. You understand?"

Through the fog and chiming anxiety in my own head, I understood that Kablukov was attempting to do me a favor: he was smoothing the road for Tom.

"We have preferred buyers," Kablukov continued. "Just as we have preferred partners."

I had expected a stick, but instead he was dangling a carrot. I did not believe him. I did not trust him. But I saw no way around all that flesh. Kablukov nodded at me and reclined politely. He was handing me the script.

I translated obediently. What else was there to do? I could taste the sourness of my expression. Four years of work, the gem of my life's labor— surrendered to the gluttony of a sweating, geriatric gangster. But studying my reaction Kablukov only smiled. He seemed to read my smirk as a show of our alliance. "Does our friend over here understand what I've just shared with you?"

"Wait a minute, wait a minute," Tom said, leaning toward Kablukov's bench. "You're talking about Continental becoming the preferred buyer of twelve percent of L-Pet stock?"

His eyelids still at half-mast, Kablukov nodded.

"With an option to buy another three."

"In two or three years, you could raise that share to twenty percent," Kablukov suggested to me.

When I translated for Tom, he said, in astonishment, "That's a fifth of the company! It would make us a strategic equity investor."

"Little by little," Kablukov said, smiling at us like an elder. "There will be many interested parties, but we are looking for a partner who understands our way of doing business. You see?"

I did. Perfectly. Kablukov had not needed me to pressure Tom; he only had to blackmail me into keeping my mouth shut. He could get to Tom on his own. Tom had dollar signs flashing in his eyes. It occurred to me that this was the essence of the Boot's criminal genius: to exert his influence on each link in the chain.

"The companies we work with . . . we think of them all as family."

Tom said, "Ask him what guarantee Continental will have that we will be the preferred buyer."

Reduced again to being a translator—a courtier—I did as told. Kablukov patted his hands on his bare chest as if searching his pockets. "What guarantee can anyone give you here? There are no guarantees. There is only trust."

WHAT I REMEMBERED WAS the hot and suffocating embrace of the steam. Sounds of voices reached me from a distance. I lay on my back on the hot tiled floor. Above me, still naked, crouched my father, splashing cold water on my face. He shouted to someone over his shoulder: "Tell them to stop tossing water on that stove! My kid's fainted."

"They've been here three hours!" a skinny old man sitting beside him said with high-pitched indignation. "Don't they see the sign says you gotta leave after two?"

My father picked me up and carried me to a cooler part of the room.

I struggled to keep my eyes open. "What happened?"

"Nothing, sport. Just a little too much steam. Lemme see your head." He sounded nervous. I could feel a cord of shame creeping through my confusion as the bodies parted to let us pass. "You've had enough? Me too, boss," my father said. "Let's get out of here."

AFTER WE PARTED WAYS with Kablukov, Tom said he wanted to talk to me alone, at dinner. We met an hour later at a phony Irish pub of Tom's choosing. He was waiting for me at one of the wide wooden tables under green felt bunting. "Do you understand what the Boot was dangling in our faces back there?"

I said I thought so.

Our waitress brought us two draft beers. She was bound in a corset, like a medieval wench. Most of the other diners were pallid, doughy expatriates from Britain and its former colonies. We fit right in.

"If Continental becomes the preferred buyer for twenty percent of L-Pet stock, it means we put our own man on the board, get him voting on key decisions." He was looking at me pointedly, as if anticipating astonishment, or an objection.

"It's a very appealing offer," I made myself say.

"Hmm." Tom was letting his gaze drift into the dim, paneled corners of the pub. "Too appealing. L-Pet's practically state-owned. I can't imagine the Kremlin giving away one-fifth of the company to a single partner."

I considered the courses of action available to me. "But they do seem to like doing business with us, don't they? Like Kablukov said, it's a matter of trust. Two more." I tapped on my empty beer glass as the waitress walked by. I hoped a refill might make the task of praising L-Pet go more smoothly. But Tom shook his head. "None for me," he told our wench. "They haven't offered us any assurance in writing."

I wanted to suggest that we could ask them to, but I had the sense that this wasn't the tack Kablukov intended for me to take. "You're the one who told me that in this business you wait for the press announcement and you miss the boat," I said, and tried to smile. I had excrement all over my mouth.

"So we open our legs and cross our fingers?" Tom was tapping his fingernails against the table in a way that looked involuntary and painful. "We have protocols. We set up strict guidelines to keep this whole process . . . aboveboard."

"And following those same protocols we've led them exactly where we want them, haven't we? You always said that this deal was more of a strategic move than a commercial one. We were just buying access to their fields. So here you go—the door is being cracked open." There was a degrading kind of satisfaction in making all this up as I went along. My stein of beer arrived, and I drained it fast.

"I'm going to have to defend this decision in D.C. This isn't Monopoly money we're tossing around. The numbers have to make some sense."

I did an impression of giving this question serious thought, then said, "If you want to talk about numbers, we can talk about numbers. You told me the only thing that matters for stock prices in this business is future reserves. We'll have a one-fifth stake in a company that's got its ass up against the Barents Sea—biggest gas field in the world. Not to mention all of western Siberia. Continental has a problem with taking a loss on a hundred and seventy mil? Sorry, Tom—but I figure you'd be the first to say we shouldn't give up the farm because one fox wants to grab a couple of our chickens."

"All right, all right."

"You don't get a do-over with some things. You can be sorry or you can be right."

I watched Tom's meaty face arrange itself into the shape of reluctant agreement. He was peering into his half-empty beer glass and nodding. "You're right, we should be taking the long view."

I was flooded with relief and disgust in equal measure. *He's been ready to take Kablukov's bait all along*, I told myself. *It's just my blessing he wanted.*

When he looked at me again it was with confusion and pity. "But what about you? You've worked on those ships for years. Doesn't it rankle you? Two days ago you wanted to run these Sausen guys out of town, and now you're ready to hand the keys to these chiselers?"

"There's something bigger at stake than my pride." For the first time, I said something that wasn't a complete lie.

"I'm just surprised," Tom said. "As long as I've known you, Julian, you've had no patience for cheap shortcuts or tricks. I've always admired your sense of fair play."

It shouldn't have hurt me to hear this, and yet it cut like a bullwhip. The faith Tom had in me was more painful than his suspicion. I had, for most of my life, tried to steer clear of any Just Causes—paving the road to hell and all that. And yet my eschewing of the noble path had never been without a shade of moral ambition: I would at least do no harm, I told myself, would decline to add my drop to the world's copious sum of pretense and crookedness. But how ready I was now to defile all that for the sake of Lenny's safety. "Maybe I'm starting to see the big picture," I said.

I ENDED UP WALKING back to the hotel alone. It was past eight. The sky was overcast but still full of light. I found myself wandering along the near-empty streets around Bolshaya Nikitskaya. I let my eyes gaze upward at the old mansions, inhabited long ago by writers and their characters—old nobility and the newly rich—and now occupied mostly by embassies and branches of cultural institutions. Some of these estates had been slicked up since my day, with elegant new doors and smart plaques. Others were in advanced stages of disrepair, the pastels of their stucco paint scabbed and freckled with age. A tiered spire of one of Stalin's Seven Sisters peeked out over the tops of the sand-colored apartment towers, but I was at a loss to say which sister it was. I wanted to get Kablukov's image out of my mind—the stretched and faded tattoos, the gray hair sprouting from his narrow shoulders, the smile oiling his face. What did it matter to me? It wasn't my money. But my sense of disgust and restlessness only multiplied as I walked. Along these quiet streets I thought I could walk myself back into sanity, but instead I felt a loneliness settle in my heart. The Sanduny Baths had made me recall my father—the last day I would ever spend with him. I'd gone with him at the request of my mother, who was preparing for some kind of event or trip we were all to be taking in the next couple of days. She had sewn me a pair of knee pants and had made me walk around in them that morning in our room, while she adjusted the suspender straps with her needle. The knee pants were supposed to make me look like "a real English boy." I did not understand what that was or why I needed to look like one. I had been warned not to say anything about this to anyone in our communal apartment. For the sake of this "trip," my mother had spoken only English to me for several weeks. We practiced words, her finger on my lips so that nobody would hear. The arrangements were all shrouded in vagueness and innuendo. Their mysterious logic dictated that I learn to pronounce words like a British citizen, and to this end my father's friend Uncle Seldon had come over one night to instruct me in proper English elocution. I was told to sit up and forward when I spoke, to keep my tongue where it could almost touch my front teeth and imagine that I was speaking through the crack in a door. At some point, Seldon gave me a hard candy to put on the bottom of my tongue and hold there while I said things like "We surely shall see the sun shine soon." It was a kind of game, but one I knew not to talk about. Going to the baths with Papa was part of the game. We were getting ourselves fresh and clean in preparation for the adventure.

It was while I walked up Nikitsky Boulevard that I remembered it. I could hear Papa's voice come back to me, welling up from the bottom of my mind.

"Maybe best not to tell your mother about the fainting," he said as we strolled home.

I told him I wouldn't. I was too embarrassed anyway.

"We don't want her to get any more nervous than she is."

"All right."

The sky had become clotted with thunderclouds. Drops of rain were starting to fall on our noses and fingers. We hurried home as the horizon grew dark and the trolley lines over our heads swayed in the sharp bursts of wind.

It was a squalling downpour by the time my father, carrying me on his back, got to our building. The big black and white tiles in our lobby were wet and smeared with footprints. The lift, as always, was broken. We took the stairs.

Old Baba Ksenia, who was nobody's grandma, was in the hallway when we walked in. "Wipe your feet! You're tracking in mud."

Papa, as always, was clownishly deferential to her, dramatically wiping his shoes on the floor mat and inquiring about her health. Irritated by his compliance, she grunted and waddled back to her room. We paused briefly in the common kitchen, where Papa pulled a dry cloth from the clothesline and toweled me off. Through the double-paned windows, I watched the storm clouds. The glass of the outer pane was attacked by wind. Water slid down in a trembling pearl-gray wall behind the glass jars of conserves between the panes. I felt clutched by a fear I couldn't explain. Or was this fear only something added to my memory later on?

There were others in the kitchen: the apartment's drunk, Tolik, and the heavyset woman who worked as a cook at a popular café in town. She was accusing him of replacing her new tangerines with rotten ones.

"They rotted. What's it got to do with me?" he said.

"Some people consider it their duty to steal something."

Mama was in our room, stitching flowers onto a hat.

"Where have you been?"

"Got stuck in the rain."

She shook her head and glanced nervously out the window. "What if the whole thing's canceled? Then what will we do?"

"No, it'll clear up by tomorrow," Papa reassured her. He got me changed into my flannel pajamas. The clouds in the sky formed a witches' brew.

"Why are his cheeks so red?" My mother tested my forehead. "Is he sick?"

"He's fine," Papa said, and gave me a wink to ensure I'd keep our secret.

"Maybe we better call it off. . . ."

I could feel her panic. It boomed and rumbled through me like the thunder outside.

Papa came over to her. "You worry for nothing." But even he did not sound convinced.

"I don't want to go," I said.

They both stared at me.

"Do you want me to read from *Treasure Island?*" my father said.

I shook my head.

"Don't be scared."

"I'm not."

"There's nothing to be frightened of, I'll show you." He got up and opened our curtains all the way. "The storm is still far away. Do you know how I know that? Sit up, I'll tell you."

He went to his writing table for a sheet of paper and a pen. "Here. Lightning travels faster than thunder, and why is that?"

"Because light travels faster than sound."

"Smart boy. But do you know how fast sound travels? About one-third of a kilometer every second! I'll teach you a trick. Count the number of seconds between the lightning and the next thunderbolt." He found his Voltan gold-plated watch and gave it to me. "Are you ready? When I say 'count,' you start counting. Okay. Count."

I held the cold, heavy watch in my palms. Its second hand seemed to tick slowly.

"What have you got?"

"Twelve."

"All right, now let's divide that by three. What do we get now?"

He drew three rows of four dots on the paper. Finally, I held up four fingers.

"Which means the storm is still four kilometers away. Now, if you hear that loud lightning snap followed immediately by thunder, then you can hide under your pillow. The storm is exactly where you're standing."

I felt myself relaxing under the spell of one of his lectures. "You want to keep counting? Okay. When you understand something, you don't have to be scared of it. It's called electromagnetism, what I just taught you. And when you get older, maybe you'll learn all about it at some place like . . . the Technion. Or MIT." He looked at Mama and smiled.

"Why are you filling his head with this?"

"He should know there are places other than this paradise."

"Where is Technion?" I said.

"Stop," Mama said.

"Are we going there?"

"I'm not sure, but *greyt zah tsi* and knock wood."

A MEMORY IS A DIFFICULT THING to judge from a distance. Did the details unfold as the child perceived them? Years later my mother used to tell me that my father, Leon, was full of fantasies. Had the Technion been one more of them? Did he have a suspicion that his life was being counted in days and not in years?

By morning he would be gone. Taken away during the night, while I lay in my cot, behind my little curtain, blithely sleeping through his arrest. Uncle Seldon, who had taught me to speak with a hard candy under my tongue, would be gone too. All this I would learn in the coming weeks, when my mother would wake me in the black just before dawn and drag me with her to unmarked buildings around Lubyanka Square, where the sun was already rising over the multitudes who, perched atop their parcels, had come to scour the rosters for the names of their sons and brothers and fathers.

But all this would happen later. What I remember from that evening is my father sitting beside me with his watch, the two of us counting the seconds between the lightning and the thunder, quietly waiting for the coming storm.

THE CONCIERGE STOPPED ME on my way to the hotel elevator. There was a package waiting for me at the desk, he informed me. I knew what it was as soon as I saw it. A large cardboard box, the sort for storing office papers in warehouses. It had been dropped off an hour earlier, the clerk said. I looked at the note attached:

> *Some light reading for your flight home.*
>
> *A friend in the ministry helped me track it down . . . says the warehouse only had your mama's papers. No trace of papa's.*
>
> *Don't thank me with a bottle of perfume. Come see us again at the dacha when you return.*

> *—Valya*

SAVAGES WITH CHRONOMETERS

THE BOX MUST HAVE WEIGHED A GOOD THREE POUNDS, AS MUCH AS A ripe pineapple. Its heft conveyed its own message—*Here, you fool,* the box seemed to be saying. *If it's the truth you're after, better have some muscle for it.*

Sweat pooled under my arm as I rode the elevator, seeping down to where the sharp corner of the box pressed into my rib. I slid my key card in its lock and dropped the load on the hotel bed. After dragging an enormous rococo armchair across the room, I carefully removed the cardboard lid. A stout stack of photocopied pages defiantly presented itself. I removed the thing whole. It had the feel of a single stone slab, an ancient tablet with damning Biblical judgments etched upon it. And suddenly, having waited so long to hold it in my hands, I felt paralyzed to read it. Certainly I was unable to read it like any normal manuscript—starting with page 1, then moving to page 2, 3, and so on. I was seized with a terrifying feeling that here in my possession was something that could do me physical harm the longer I held on to it—a radioactive item—even though my mind continued to reassure me it was just an inert, dead stack of papers. And so, out of rapacious curiosity or immobilizing fear, I undertook to devour the entire thing at once, thumbing through pages and skimming my eyes haphazardly over random words.

We have incontrovertible evidence.

Your refusal to confess will cause you only anguish.

I was poisoned with bourgeois nationalism.

You admit to your hostile, vicious thoughts but deny
the criminal acts that are a natural consequence
of them.

I supported him; thus a criminal tie grew between us.

You will not evade moral responsibility.

Your slanderous fabrications shall not go unpunished.

I trusted these people and lost my vigilance.

Your denials are futile.

I admit that I adopted a slanderous orientation.

Do not try to conceal your hostile activity.

You will turn yourself inside out and tell the
truth yet.

I state until my last breath that I consider myself
an honorable Soviet person.

We want only sincere confessions.

Page after page, my eyes scanned over near-identical accusations, interminable denials, and redundant "sincere" confessions. Were I a film
producer I would instantly fling into the dustbin this shopworn script,
stitched from stock phrases that even the lowliest hack in Hollywood

would have avoided out of professional self-respect. Try as I might, I could not imagine my mother—or any normal human being—uttering a phrase such as "Since I read these articles and studied their content, it follows that I was an accomplice to their slanderous nationalistic character." Or saying of a colleague: "She did not wish to sever herself from these views." And yet one out of every few pages of these interrogation "protocols" bore the authentic signature of one "Flora Solomonovna Brink." Anemic and abbreviated, her signature crouched humbly beneath the valiant autographs of her interrogators, one Senior Lieutenant Andrey Antonov and one Captain Viktor Bykov.

It took me a while to slow down long enough to focus on a single page. And when I did, reading through a few of the protocols consecutively, the first thing I noticed was that almost all of my mother's interrogations took place between ten-thirty at night and six in the morning.

I know from my perusals of penal literature that jail cell bulbs burned all day and night, to keep the prisoners from getting a decent night's rest. Now I tried to contemplate the brightly lit hell into which my mother had descended. I imagined her nodding off for a few minutes at a time between midnight interrogations and being awakened sharply to shouts of a guard behind the latch: "No sleeping during the day!"

I recalled again our years of living together while I was in high school—Mother's ability to doze off into deep slumber even when I kept on all the lights in our common room to study for my exams.

I pictured the metal plate across the peephole being pushed aside. An eye appearing and disappearing. The glint of a key as thick as a gun barrel. I imagined her long shuffle to her interrogations. Walking in her loose boots, the laces no doubt removed so the prisoner would not attempt suicide. The elastic of her underpants pulled out as well.

The nocturnal interrogations, some of which lasted as long as ten hours, rarely produced more than a few lines of testimony: a short paragraph or two recorded in some mawkish, mechanical mimicry of human speech. These supposedly sworn statements of my mother's were recorded by hand by her inquisitors—Captain Bykov and Senior Lieutenant Antonov—whose rabid vitriol consisted of roughly patched-together Soviet slogans and countrified yokelisms that I had not heard in at least fifty years. I never had to consult the signature at the bottom of the page to know when my mother was in Antonov's hands. Rarely did he accuse her of lying. The word he used instead—*lukavit'*—possessed a softer, folksier flavor, hinting at the *lukaviy dyavol*, the sly devil who prowled the countryside tricking the people. Frequently, Antonov swore to "expose" her similarly *lukaviye*, or "devilishly cunning," intentions. I marveled at the word, which I couldn't remember encountering in a context outside of Baba Yaga folktales. I had a similar reaction to Antonov's use of *kleveta*, which, narrowly speaking, meant simply "slander" or "denigration," but which also sounded a vaguely folkloric note, connoting a world inhabited by mudslinging hobgoblins hell-bent on molesting innocent mortals. Both struck me as rather marvelous pre-Soviet words that, like many Russian superstitions, had obligingly taken on the forms of politics. Better still was the word *zapiratel'stvo*, which meant "denial" or "hostile secrecy," but whose sound suggested something closer to "constipated silence." And so, when Antonov repeatedly threatened my mother that her *zapiratel'stvo* was futile, his fulminations seemed to have a scatological echo, as though he was warning her not to "constipate the truth!"

Under the Soviet Criminal Code, the charges against her were as follows: Article 58.1, for espionage, under which the punishment was twenty-five years with confiscation of all property, and Article 58.10, for anti-Soviet propaganda and agitation, for which the penalty was seven years in prison or labor camps. The evidence for the spying charge consisted largely of her wartime work for the Jewish Anti-Fascist Committee— ironically, the same work for which she had been issued a "Medal for Outstanding Labor in the Great Patriotic War of 1941–1945, with Certificate of Authenticity," which (I would soon discover) had been confiscated, along with the rest of her possessions, during the arrest and search.

It was Antonov who demanded of my mother "sincere and honest confessions" even as he accused her of the absurd crimes she could not have possibly committed—sending classified state secrets to American and British spies, establishing contacts with "reactionary circles" in the United States, meeting with people she had never met in locations to which she could never have had access. It was a mock investigation, false from beginning to end, only legitimate if they forced her to take part in this theater, to play the role of villain and foreign spy, to put her authentic signature on this sham of a production.

But to fool whom? That I could not answer.

I was not, of course, a total virgin to the written records of the Soviet penal system or the Gulag. Since my mid-twenties, when such chronicles first began to circulate in samizdat form, I'd been stealthily and haphazardly reading whatever forbidden literature I could get my hands on. The two volumes of Evgenia Ginzburg's memoirs I read many months apart on well-thumbed pages of blurry mimeographed text. The grimly bewitching stories of Varlam Shalamov I was given only forty-eight hours to complete before I was to pass them on to the next underground reader. Solzhenitsyn's *The First Circle* I first encountered in a friend's darkroom, where we spent the night adjusting his photo enlarger in order to read page after page of tiny projected text (he had the book stored on a roll of film). But now, with my mother's interrogation papers in my hands, it was not Solzhenitsyn I found myself thinking about but Vasily Grossman, a writer I hadn't read until my late thirties, but who had summarized for me, better than anyone I'd read before, the unique political pathology of the Russians:

> The thousand-year-old principle nurtured by the Russia of the boyars, by Ivan the Terrible, by Peter the Great and Catherine the Great, the principle according to which Russian enlightenment, science, and industrial power develop by virtue of a general increase in the degree of human non-freedom—this principle achieved its most absolute triumph under Stalin.
>
> And it is truly astonishing that Stalin, after so totally destroying freedom, continued to be afraid of it.
>
> Perhaps it was this fear that caused Stalin to display such an astonishing degree of hypocrisy.
>
> Stalin's hypocrisy was a clear expression of the hypocrisy of his State. And it was expressed, first and foremost, in his demand that people play at being free. The State did not openly spit on the corpse of freedom—certainly not! Instead, after the precious, living, radioactive content of freedom and democracy had been done away with, the corpse was turned into a stuffed dummy, into a shell of words. It was like the way savages, after getting their hands on the most delicate of sextants and chronometers, use them as jewelry.

Here, in my hands, were dispatches from the orderly precinct of this phony justice: each page meticulously numbered and wreathed in the accoutrements of legality—seals, stamps, signatures. All the while eviscerated of any law. The subtle instruments of logic and reasoning were turned to cudgels in the hands of brutes. They could harass her, shake her, prod her, maybe even beat her into signing her death sentence. And yet some compulsory tribute to the principle of human freedom prevented my mother's captors from forging her signature.

Her investigation had the imprimatur of a classic snowball case, with the interrogators doing their best to connect Florence to a broad conspiracy that inculpated more famous personalities. To that end, they were claiming she had passed secret materials to foreign agents by means of articles she had not written, but *translated* into English—articles containing classified information about agriculture and wartime industries. Whether any actual articles were submitted into the record was unclear to me. A representative sample of the deposition:

BYKOV: Do you deny the accusation that you translated into English classified materials by the orders of Epshteyn and Mikhoels?

F. BRINK: I deny that I was aware that the materials assigned to me were classified. They were all examined beforehand by Soviet censors.

BYKOV: Since you examined them and studied their content it follows that you were an accomplice to the articles' undercover character. Testify to the hostile nationalist orientation you developed in Kuibyshev.

F. BRINK: I admit, in part, that while working for the Jewish Anti-Fascist Committee I fell under the influence of those around me. I absorbed their hostile anti-Soviet attitudes and found myself acquiring a nationalistic stance.

BYKOV: And you held anti-Soviet discussions and invented lies against the Soviet Union.

F. BRINK: I categorically deny this. I never expressed dissatisfaction with Soviet government policy.

BYKOV: You admit to being poisoned by bourgeois Jewish nationalism but deny the criminal acts that are the natural consequence of it.

F. BRINK: I allow that I experienced some nationalis-
    tic deviation. It was not manifested externally.
BYKOV: But you admit that it existed in your soul?

Her *soul?* What business did they have asking about her *soul?* What was this, I thought, a trial or an exorcism?

The final verdict read:

The fact that you listened to anti-Soviet outbursts
and did not rebuke others for their nationalist
remarks means that you became a co-conspirator
and nationalist.

Savages with chronometers. It was not merely that her interrogators had no understanding of logic. Their questions and conclusions were underwritten by an essentially primordial worldview: one's thoughts and actions are either holy or sinful, pro-Soviet or anti-Soviet, with us or against us. This crude cosmology left no room for neutrality. Even the medieval Catholics of Europe had surmised, between heaven and hell, the zone of purgatory, from which salvation was still possible. Russian Orthodoxy had never accepted such a notion—its consciousness was incapable of recognizing anything but immaculate piety or irredeemable guilt.

I suspected Valya had not been able to retrieve my father's documents for the same reason Mama had not been able to pass to him any parcels: my father had been killed too soon after his arrest. Was that, I suddenly wondered, his punishment for refusing to sign any of the papers given him? I felt sure he'd refused to play his part in the sham production in order to spare us. To protect Mama and me, he'd given no testimony that could implicate Florence in any way. I was likewise certain that, in some sane portion of her mind, Florence must have known this all along. Her refusal to leave Moscow after his arrest only made me angrier.

My suspicion was substantiated when I scavenged my mother's documents for my father's name and found it appearing in the testimony not in the capacity of "your husband Leon Brink," but as "the spy and slanderer Brink," and even, occasionally, "your accomplice Leon Brink." It would seem, according to these papers, that my mother *had* no friends or intimates, only accomplices, conspirators, and collaborators. Every now and again she was accused of being, along with some other felonious character, a *yedinomyshlennitsa*—a word I'm at a loss to translate into English, because the concept would be a paradox in the American vernacular. It means, simply, a creature of identical single-mindedness with another. If such conformity of the mind were possible, the list of my mother's *yedinomyshlennikov* included my father, various members of the Jewish Committee, and "the spy and slanderer Seldon Parker," who after some confusion I recognized as my father's friend "Uncle Seldon," whose nicotine-stained fingers I associated in my child's mind with matchbook horses and aluminum fish that he promised could tell my fortune.

It was in the midst of my scavenger hunt for something recognizable—something that matched my own jumbled, painful childhood recollections of the year 1949—that I came upon a thing that stopped me cold. I didn't know how I could have missed it on my first perusal of the archives, since it was so close to the top of the monstrous stack. It was a list, three pages long, appended to my mother's Order of Arrest, containing nearly every item seized on that terrible night when two uniformed officers of the MGB barged into the room in which my mother and I had been living on our own since my father's arrest, seven months earlier.

TAKEN FOR DELIVERY TO MGB THE FOLLOWING:

1. Passport no. XXIII-CU no. 599812, issued 25 September 1936 by the 64th department of militia of the city of Moscow to the name of Brink, F. S.

2. Medal for Outstanding Labor in the Great Patriotic War of 1941-1945, and Certificate of Authenticity.

3. Bank savings book no.___ with remaining 1,024.45 rubles.

4. Wristwatch of foreign firm Voltan in yellow metal, no. 5648891 (on cap). Working, without a second hand.

5. Assorted documents in a foreign language—7 items.

6. Assorted photographs—16 items.

7. Assorted notebooks—4 items.

8. Forms and certificates—7 items.

9. Cutouts of geographic maps from Soviet newspapers—4 items.

10. Carbon copy paper—used. 1 pack.

11. Anglo-Franco-German dictionary.

SIGNED BY SUPERINTENDENT OF HOUSE,
TALKOVSKAYA, VARVARA ARTUROVNA,
WITNESS TO SEIZURE.

HOUSEHOLD ITEMS:

1. Dinner table—1, good condition, previously owned
2. Cabinet chairs—2, PO
3. Soft chair—1, old
4. Table servante—1, PO
5. Wardrobe closet—1, PO
6. Commode—1
7. Assorted metal beds—2
8. Book étagère—1
9. Assorted suitcases—2
10. Storage trunk—1
11. Photo camera, Komsomolets brand—1
12. Photo camera, foreign brand—1, broken
13. Assorted porcelain statuettes—3
14. Bronze bust of V. I. Lenin—1
15. Assorted table lamps—2
16. Reproducer radio—1
17. Assorted autopens—2, broken
18. Footstools—2
19. Daybed with springs—1
20. Mattresses, cotton—2
21. Bedspread, cotton—2
22. Blanket, wool, gray—1
23. Blankets, cotton—2
24. Sheets—6
25. Alarm clock, round—1, fixed

26. Suit, children's, gray wool—1
27. Suit, children's, brown wool—1
28. Pants, gray wool, children's—1
29. Coat, children's, semi-seasonal, mouse-colored—1
30. Jacket, children's, wool, with lining—1
31. Jacket, men's, brown leather—1
32. Jacket, men's, canvas—1
33. Robes, women's, assorted—2
34. Jacket, women's, gray wool—1
35. Suit, women's, steel-colored wool—1
36. Shirts, women's, assorted—3
37. Summer coat, women's, dark-blue wool—1
38. Shirts, women's—tricotage and silk—2
39. Dress, checkered linen—1
40. Dress, black crepe de chine—1
41. Dress, blue silk—1
42. Silk pajamas, women's, birch pattern—1
43. Netted table oilcloth—1
44. Jacket, men's, canvas with fur lining—1
45. Military jacket, men's, wool—1
46. Underwear, men's, white wool—3
47. Shirts, men's, assorted wool—2
48. Undershirts, men's—2
49. Button-downs, men's—8
50. Sweaters, children's, assorted—3
51. Button-downs, children's, assorted—3
52. Pants, children's, assorted—4
53. Underpants, children's—9
54. Tablecloths, assorted—3
55. Undershirts, children's—4
56. Towels, assorted—3
57. Pillowcases—3
58. Blankets, cotton—3
59. Feather pillows, assorted—3
60. Ice skates with boots—3 pairs
61. Boots, children's, assorted leather—2 pairs
62. Demi-boots, men's—1 pair

63. Shoes, women's—2 pairs
64. Galoshes, men's—1 pair
65. Galoshes, children's—1 pair
66. Galoshes, women's—1 pair
67. School briefcases, children's,
    leather—2 pairs, old
68. Violin, children's—1
69. Metal box with drafting tools—1
70. Electric iron—1
71. Ties, men's—9
72. Bowls, metal—3
73. Soup dishes, assorted—12
74. Bread box, clay—1
75. Small dishes—20
76. Pots—2
77. Milk pot, enameled—1
78. Teacups, assorted—10
79. Saucers, assorted—12
80. Vases, assorted—3
81. Shot glasses—6
82. Rinsers—2
83. Tablespoons—6
84. Forks—5
85. Teaspoons—3
86. Teapot, small, porcelain—1
87. Frying pans—2
88. Kitchen knives—4
89. Sugar bowl—1

Apartment has been sealed and all
    items given for safekeeping to
    Talkovskaya, Varvara Arturovna,
    superintendent of housing.

I ran my hand over the words like a blind person reading with his fingers, as if attempting to touch those shabby, precious, lost items. How quickly they returned to me in every poignant, awful, nostalgic detail. My mother's "checkered" dress, of brown-and-green plaid, which brushed against me as, holding hands, she and I walked to the bread kiosk. My father's aviator jacket, its collar savory with Shipr cologne. My own "mouse-colored" coat and battered school satchel, bought off another kid in the building, along with the violin my mother had maneuvered to obtain in the hope that I would become the next David Oistrakh. Even my little booties—two pairs—had been included in this criminal seizure. I could scarcely read the list without having my chest fill with the pressure of agony. Where had it all gone? The undershirts and porcelain figurines and ice skates and sugar bowl! For "safekeeping" to Talkovskaya, Varvara Arturovna, whoever the hell *she* was (the name brought to mind absolutely nothing). And where, then, was my mother's jewelry—her pins and clip-on earrings and amber necklace and scarves? Where were her *gloves*? Pilferers! Thieves! Writing up our life like it was up for auction.

And at that instant, I was six and a half years old again, watching the two arresting officers—a man and a woman dressed in quasi-military olive-drab uniforms—opening the door of our wardrobe, running their hands over every hanging item of clothing, palpating the linings, sticking their busy fingers in the pockets before flinging every one of my mother's possessions on the floor.

They'd taken down a framed photograph hanging above my parents' bed, a studio shot of the three of us: my jug-eared one-year-old self seated between my young papa in his pulpy suit and my pompadoured mother, her lips cinched in a dark Cupid's bow. They had taken the picture down to check that nothing was concealed behind it, and then, to make perfectly sure, they ripped open the back of the frame, while my mother—her face blanched and sleepless, her dry lips armored in nothing like the darkly painted heart in the picture—made some tactful imploring protest. And where was I? Seated on my little cot by the radiator, the floral curtain dividing my side of the room from that of my parents jerked open. What time was it? Four-thirty or five A.M.—the violet of the November morning just beginning to creep in through the drapes. I couldn't move. A heavy hand was weighing down on my shoulder. It belonged to our neighbor down the hall, Avdotya Grigorievna—old "Aunt Dunya"—who cooked me barley soup after school while my mother worked. In the hubbub she had forced her way in the door and refused to leave—to intercede on my behalf, I imagine, though, given the way that trembling paw bore down on my shoulder, I might as well have been a bedpost holding her up. I was surrounded by her scent—the distillation of everything aged and sour and sleepy—while the pudgy young woman in a soldier's uniform ransacked my mother's closet. My bladder was held tight against the reality of this moment; I did not dare open my mouth to ask if I could leave the room to relieve myself, and instead concentrated all my focus on the discolored square of wallpaper where the photograph of my family had hung. And now the female officer paused in her scrutiny of our étagère to examine, with a sort of sardonic admiration, the small brass bust of Lenin on the top shelf. It was the same bust—I realized with a mute sense of catastrophe— that Mama took down from the shelf whenever she brought home walnuts. Where had she gotten this statuette, whose impressive bald head fit so perfectly into the curled palm of her hand while she smashed the nuts open with the base of V. I. Lenin's thorax? Probably it was a reward for services well performed at some place of employ.

A corner of my heart had always suspected that Mama would one day be punished for her misuse of the bust of the grandfather of our nation. Moreover, I was convinced that only I could come to her rescue. I would redeem her incomplete loyalty to Lenin, just as soon as I could shake off Aunt Dunya's leaden paw, with my full-throated recitation of the Pioneer Oath, which I had seen pasted to the classroom wall:

The Pioneer is true to the work of Lenin and Stalin. The Pioneer loves his motherland and hates her enemies. The Pioneer is honest and truthful. His word is firmer than steel! The Pioneer is as brave as an eagle. He despises a coward.

I imagined the male officer, who in his handling of our stuff seemed the more businesslike and less spiteful of the two, remarking that no one whose child could recite the oath so flawlessly could be an enemy. They'd instantly know they'd barged into the wrong apartment, would be very contrite (perhaps the man would give me his cap), and would leave us, with hearty handshakes, in peace. And then, almost as if I had willed it with the magic of my hope, the male officer, who had been sorting through a mess of papers on the table, scanned the room until his eyes fixed on me.

"Tell the kid to get up," he commanded Avdotya Grigorievna. I stood up without prompting: It was my chance to get out from under Aunt

Dunya's henlike guard. I tried to will myself to clear my throat in preparation for my recitation. But he walked past me to the metal cot and, bending down to strip it of my flannel sheet and wool blanket, flipped the cushion mattress over to reveal its dingy bottom, overturning my pillow.

"That's the child's bed—can't you see there's nothing there?" came the warbling remonstrations of Aunt Dunya.

The officer ignored her and, taking out a large pocketknife, slashed the striped pallet along its belly like a fish.

More shrill, frightened protests arose from the old woman as the man stuck his arm inside the mattress, looking for God knows what; the clots of stuffing fell like New Year's cotton snow at my feet. I could not speak. I had begun to tremble. My wool stockings grew warm with an abasing wetness.

The situation was so chaotic that for some time no one noticed that I had pissed myself. The male guard was giving special attention to the space behind the radiator, while the girl in uniform, like a hawk, watched my mother packing a small suitcase. Aunt Dunya watched the guards, and the old Tatar janitor who had led the two upstairs now stood in the doorway, a ghostly witness, wearing the same sullen, impervious mask he always wore, no doubt having been made to play the official spectator to this scene many times before. And then my secret was out. "He's wet himself!" my nanny nearly shouted, causing my mother to leap toward me.

"Stay where you are!" the uniformed girl brayed.

"Please, let me change him."

Aunt Dunya was now trying to push down my wet bottoms. I hung on to the elastic, resisting. I refused to be unclothed, my shame compounded with terror at being stripped naked in front of these hostile strangers.

"Someone make him stop hollering," the man shouted.

I was choking with snot.

Again, my mother's voice: "Leave him alone. Let me change him."

At last they permitted her to rifle through the disarrayed wardrobe for a pair of dry underwear and wool pants for me. I was in such a state by then that my mother's efforts to peel off my wet stockings and change me must have been something like trying to clean the scales off a leaping trout. I don't know how we managed it; I know only that when she had me dressed again she told me—with what sounded to me like a scolding, bruising me all the more—to leave the room with Aunt Dunya.

I refused. I would not let go of her neck. I hung on, howling and sobbing, shredding my vocal cords, while they attempted to pry me off her, until, exhausting even our captors' endurance, I was allowed to stay in the room while Mama packed her little bag and dressed herself.

"Hurry up," the female guard ordered. "You aren't going to the theater."

I remember Mama's hair, wiry and disheveled, when she buttoned her coat. She pulled it back in front of the small mirror by the door and attempted to pin it up into a bun with her carved herringbone comb.

"You can't take that!" her female guard informed her. What was the reason? Maybe because it was sharp and could constitute a weapon. Mother looked stricken by this—as though not being permitted to make herself presentable was the final injustice of all the other injuries she was being made to suffer. The girl held out her hand for the comb, but Mama would not let go. She held on to the carved blond tortoiseshell as though it was the last possession she had left, something too precious to hand over to this covetous, barbarous creature. She came over to me and knelt, placing the comb in my palm and closing my fingers with her own. "Don't chew your nails," she said, sucking back tears in her nose. "Tell Aunt Dunya to cut them." She rubbed my fingers, took my head in her hands.

"I want to go with you, Mama."

"No, no. I'll be back in a few days."

We had been speaking Russian, and then, as if she saw something terrible in my face, a wild despair came over her, lighting up her eyes like sapphires, and she uttered in hoarse English, "Whatever they tell you about me, know it isn't true."

"Speak Russian!" the girl at the door barked.

"Don't make trouble, and don't believe what they say."

And then she was pulled away. She allowed herself to be dragged to the door roughly by the elbow. I wanted to run after her, but I was stopped by a male MGB officer in the hall, where Aunt Dunya gathered me into her deep, sour bosom as I bleated and screamed. "Quiet, now, don't make trouble," she said, echoing Mama's request, though she could not have understood the English. Over her shoulder, I caught the brown of Mama's coat and the top of her blue headscarf disappearing below the landing banister—the last I would see of her for seven years.

And now I sat, a sixty-four-year-old man on a hotel bed, a stack of Xeroxed papers in my hand, feeling crushed with the shame of my six-year-old self, who'd wet his pants and didn't even manage to say a proper goodbye. My mama. The bewilderment and defenselessness, the incapacity and *rage* of that abandoned child now overcame the last of my vitality and strength at the end of an exhausting day. I put the papers to rest on the paisley coverlet and shut my eyes. *No more tonight*, I said to myself. If I kept on, I knew I would have no strength left to perform, come morning, the distasteful task of obeisance that was required of me. That obligation was already making me as sick to my stomach as the contents of these disinterred pages.

I lay on my back, but sleep would not come; I was too agitated to give myself over to its oblivion. The lines of handwritten text were running together in my head. November, December, January. Months of torture. And then whole weeks passing with no recorded interactions at all, as if she'd been forgotten by her jailers. I marveled at the sheer waste of resources, human and material, that it took to propagate this tremendous industry of imprisonment and interrogation. A whole perverse manufactory in which human beings composed the raw material, and where the final products were . . . what? Signed and stamped bits of paper. And, of course, slaves. The prison cells were only the first stage of an operation whose ultimate aim was the harvesting and replenishment of slave labor.

It struck me with new vividness that places like Lubyanka, Butyrka, Lefortovo were mills in which a person freely walking the streets (if such a "free" creature actually existed in Russia) could be turned into a beast of burden, plunged into mines, sent to fell trees and dig canals and generally kill himself on starvation rations while contributing to the great enterprise of socialism. But here too I knew I was wrong—they were *not* to be turned into beasts of burden, for beasts could be made to work only eight or at most ten hours a day, whereas slaves could be made to labor to exhaustion for sixteen hours or more. Beasts could not be stuffed into cattle cars or onto hulls of steamers without food or water and be expected to survive the journey. It would, in the end, be far too expensive to treat animals in this way, because the breeding of more animals to replenish the dead or unproductive ones would itself require some degree of care and resources; human beings, at least under this system, were endlessly replenishable, and thereby completely expendable.

I didn't know if I was more horrified by the cruelty or by the shortsightedness. The Russian camp guards, camp commandants, and numerous layers of bureaucrats had not even sufficient respect for *humans as beasts*. Brooding on it, I imagined that the most sadistic slaver in the American South might have figured human endurance into his calculations in order to ensure, at least, his slaves' ongoing exploitation (if not the fate of his own Christian soul). The most mercenary obligation to keep the slave fed and sheltered well enough so he wouldn't keel over from disease or exhaustion—that, too, was dispensed with by the Gulag administration. And this was because, even in the most benighted county of the American South, a human life was still usually worth at least the gold it took to purchase it, whereas in communist Russia it was worth nothing at all.

There would be no sleep tonight. I switched on the bedside lamp and pulled another stack of pages from the cardboard box. Again they seemed to run together, so repetitive was their format: strident, preposterous accusations followed by a qualified admission of guilt, a paragraph at most, distilled from hours of interrogation, offering only a vague contour of what really went on inside those dungeon rooms. And then, after a few months—January, February, March—I noted a change. Previously recorded by hand, the protocols suddenly became typewritten. Apparently, a stenographer had been obtained, and one who evidently possessed a level of schooling higher than that of the two alternating hammerheads, Bykov and Antonov. I gathered this from the fact that the transcriptions were now marred with fewer spelling and grammatical errors, though a rustic phrase or two ("don't try to drown the question with your water-muddying tactics . . .") continued to pepper the otherwise sloganizing banalities.

Were the stenographers on some sort of rotation system, and my mother's turn had finally come up? Or had her case become elevated in stature, so that she now merited one? The pages gave me little clue, but the record of interrogation suddenly grew more elaborate, and, maybe for the same reason, more absurd, involving not only other employees of the SovInformBuro and the notorious "Jewish Committee" but her personal correspondence with, of all people, Uncle Sid. A sample:

ANTONOV: Testify to your criminal relationship with
    the American Ceed-ney Fein.
F. BRINK: He is my brother.
BYKOV: We have uncovered evidence proving he was dis-

tributing secret messages, which you sent back to
your espionage cell in New York.

F. BRINK: I deny this.

ANTONOV: There are communications taken from your own
room that you hid abominably in a tin of flour.

F. BRINK: I cannot speak to what I'm not shown.

BYKOV: We have a translation right here: I have passed
ahead your messages to the group. . . . "Glad we've
reestablished contact. I should not write this—but
we hope the whole cell will be reunited soon."

The words, cast in a language of diabolical formulae, struck me as
even less plausibly likely to issue from Sidney's pen than were my mother's
responses. Bykov and Antonov had to be desperate if they were introducing letters from Florence's brother as evidence of spying.

ANTONOV: Testify to your involvement in the Mish-Pok
espionage ring.

F. BRINK: I've never heard of this ring.

BYKOV: I quote: "I've passed your messages to the crew.
The whole Mish-Pok thinks of you."

The answer came a few lines later, after, it seemed, my mother had requested to see the original letter.

F. BRINK: *Mishpucha*. It's a Yiddish word. It simply
means "family."

I imagined the original, pre-translated letter must have read something like: "I've passed on the messages you sent to the crew. The whole
mishpucha thinks about you. . . . So glad we are finally in touch after such
a long lapse. Probably oughtn't write this, but everyone hopes you will be
reunited with us one day."

I almost giggled when I tried to imagine these Ivan bumpkins attempting to pronounce the word *mishpucha*. It was like some cheap borscht-belt
gag, a hopelessly corny joke about cultural misunderstanding between
Gentiles and Jews. Only this wasn't the Catskills. It was the basement of

the Lubyanka. Whatever scene I imagined taking place was closer to Dante than to Jackie Mason.

The interrogation got stranger still a few pages later when the accusations became phrased once more in language that defied translation. Bykov, now in charge, harassed her to admit her *"pristrastie"* for hostile bourgeois literature, *pristrastie* being a variation on the word for "passion," though it might be better captured as a sinful, habitual craving. As far as I knew, one could have such a depraved appetite for only three things: drink, cards, and sex. Not, typically, for hostile bourgeois literature.

BYKOV: On December 23, 1948, you disseminated anti-Soviet materials to your accomplice Esther Frank, while the two of you held vicious discussions and invented slanderous fabrications against the Soviet Union.

F. BRINK: I deny categorically sharing slanderous materials with Frank or engaging in anti-Soviet conversation.

BYKOV: The magazine *Life*, which Frank has already admitted you shared with her, contained slanderous statements and pasquinades of figures in the Soviet government.

F. BRINK: I am guilty of this, in part. My intention was not to disseminate libelous images.

BYKOV: With what counterrevolutionary aim were you showing the magazine?

F. BRINK: I was not sharing it with any counterrevolutionary aim. I wanted to read about an American actress who had recently appeared in a movie, and to learn more about this film.

BYKOV: What film?

F. BRINK: *Saint Joan of Arc.*

BYKOV: This is a Christian saint?

F. BRINK: Yes. It was not a theological film.

BYKOV: What sort of film was it?

F. BRINK: Historical.

BYKOV: A historical film about a religious martyr.
F. BRINK: Yes.

Here followed a brief dispute as to whether Joan of Arc was a religious figure, a revolutionary one, or a *counter*revolutionary one, with Florence favoring the interpretation of Joan as a patriot and daughter of "the people," and Bykov conceding this point to her but insisting that a film about a martyr produced in America nonetheless constituted religious propaganda. I was, however, impressed with Bykov's readiness to engage in such an existential debate over Saint Joan's varied roles. After Antonov's dim-wittedness, Bykov came across as a bona-fide intellectual. Drawn as I was into this exegesis, I almost missed, toward the bottom of the page, the following exchange:

BYKOV: You yourself informed us that it was Esther
    Frank who was disseminating this information.
E. FRANK: I never did such a thing.
BYKOV: You will have your chance to respond to the
    prisoner.

What was this? Had I missed something? It seemed that Bykov and my mother were not the only people in the room. There was another witness (aside from the invisible stenographer)—this "E. Frank," who was not only an onlooker to the whole exchange, but a participant. When in the course of her imprisonment had my mother mentioned an Esther Frank? I had not seen it mentioned until now. And then a sickening thought arrested me.

BYKOV: Did you not inform to Captain Subotin of the
    NKVD that Frank was disseminating vicious anti-
    Soviet propaganda?
F. BRINK: I said that we had looked at the magazine
    together.
BYKOV: And that Frank attacked our Soviet reality.
E. FRANK: It is she herself, not I, who attacked it.
F. BRINK: I did not say she expressed dissatisfaction
    with Soviet government policy. Frank did not share

with me these views. It is true that I said she compared the Soviet living standard to the images in
the magazine.

E. FRANK: I never asked to see this magazine, or others. It is Brink who foisted them on me in her actions as a provocateur.

F. BRINK: This is not true. At the time I had the
magazine I did not see anything slanderous about it.

BYKOV: Yet you reported that the magazine belonged to
Frank.

F. BRINK: Yes, I do not deny it.

BYKOV: If you saw nothing hostile in the magazine, why
did you deny your possession of it to Captain Subotin?

F. BRINK: I was led to believe that Esther Frank was
an informer who had arranged our meetings so as to
provoke me into sharing with her the materials I
used for my classified work.

E. FRANK: This is a lie. I was not an informer of the
NKVD. It was Brink who had this honor.

The hotel room's air conditioning could not account for the chill I suddenly felt up and down my limbs. It was as though some metabolic engine
keeping me warm had sputtered and ground to a halt. My arms were
breaking out in gooseflesh. I got up and turned off the thermostat, then
opened the doors of the narrow balcony for some warm air. I knew that
what I had just read, if it wasn't fire, was at least smoke.

Esther Frank. Earlier in the interrogation, Florence had been questioned about a number of people, most of them other translators and writers for the JAFC, their names indistinctly known to me from history and
books. But the name Esther Frank shocked me now with its instant familiarity. Could it be . . . Aunt Essie from down the hall? Aunt Essie with
glasses a foot thick and silk paisley bathrobes? The apartment's middle-
aged spinster (though maybe not; I recalled now a portrait of a man in
military uniform hanging above her bed). Yasha Gendler and I had both
spent many hours in Aunt Essie's room, playing on her iron post bed. She
had a foldout card table beside it, on which we'd play games of *Durak*, with

me often trying to convince her that my sixes were really nines, which I could sometimes succeed in doing if her glasses were off.

I scanned the rest of the stack in search of mentions of Essie's name, but found nothing.

Here were the facts I was left with: (1) Florence had confessed, or lied, to a previous interrogator, "Captain Subotin," that Esther Frank had been the purveyor of bourgeois propaganda; (2) she was now *not denying* that she had (i) informed on Esther Frank and (ii) was herself the purveyor of said propaganda.

My heart beat maniacally. Was this it—the evidence I had been hoping not to find? Was this the proof that my mother had informed on her friends and neighbors, as Yasha had insinuated with such self-satisfaction?

Rapidly I read through twenty or thirty more pages for more evidence, or names of other people that my mother had informed on. I could not find any. It didn't matter. Perhaps there had been ten others, perhaps only Essie. N = 1 made this proof no less true than N = 10. What I had discovered amid this terrible treasure I was holding was my mother's betrayal of a real-life person I had known.

And suddenly I pictured Aunt Essie through Mama's eyes, felt the chill that must have run down her body at the sight of her friend, ill and emaciated and laid low by prison's indignities. The same friend who had shared her berth and her secrets on the steamer, the two of them vibrating with girlish expectation on their way to Russia. Essie, for whom she must have felt some trace of affection even in this hell. Had she found it necessary to steel herself against these tender ghosts even as the two of them kept up this ceremony of mutual denunciation? I could feel all the madness of it suffocating me. In spite of the warm night breeze coming in through the balcony, the hotel room with its tidily made bed and plush carpet felt as confining as a jail cell. And so, leaving the papers on the spread, I fled. Downstairs and out the front door and into the warm night, until I was walking down along the brightly lit avenue of Tverskaya, still exploding with traffic and blinding billboards at one-thirty in the morning, with people avidly strolling in pairs and sitting in restaurants and drinking black coffee behind the radiant glass of all-night cafés. Whoever said New York was the city that never sleeps has not strolled at 2:00 A.M. in Moscow. I walked until I came to a kiosk, manned by a young leather-clad Tajik, and did something I hadn't done in decades: I bought a pack of cigarettes.

Then, after pulling one from the pack and lighting it with a match from the hotel matchbook, I walked several more blocks, smoking my throat-scratching Marlboro in the clammy night warmth, until I circled back around to the rear entrance of the Marriott Grand.

It was my first cigarette in twenty-nine years. The last had been a savory goodbye puff on a footbridge over the Wien River in Vienna, where my family was marooned, as penniless sightseers, during the months when we were stateless refugees. It was not our transient poverty alone that induced me to quit. I had wanted, I think, to become a wholly new person in every way. In America I planned to start fresh, free from whatever fierce attachments had kept me imprisoned in physical and mental stagnation. Now, reentering my hotel room, I accepted the narcotic invitation of a second cigarette on the balcony, really no more than a fenced ledge hanging five stories above Tverskaya's nocturnal activity. The smoke burned my throat. I leaned over the railing and flicked my ash down onto the heads of whoever might be below. I needed to think. I needed not to think. I needed to know what to feel about those papers on the bed I'd been so eager to read. To stall, I allowed myself to indulge in some self-pity. Such a mode came easily to one who had been orphaned, so to speak, as young as I had. Though I've never visited the office of any practicing psychoanalyst, I had skimmed enough of my wife's self-help literature to understand my own abiding "sense of inferiority"—the chip on my shoulder, as the Americans would call it, that made it impossible not to rise to Yasha Gendler's bait, to prove to him that I was not what he accused me of being: a son of a snitch.

Now that I had expended so much energy and come so far to take on his challenge, my reaction—or lack of one—nearly shocked me in its strangeness. *Okay, Yashka,* I said to him in my head. *You've won this one.*

And then, a second surprise: for the first time in my adult life I was not leaping to become my mother's judge, or her defense attorney. For so many years, those had been the only two roles I could play. Prosecutor was the default—there was always an abundance of her qualities to criticize and impugn—but the prosecutor's costume could be instantly traded for the defender's if, and only if, I was in the docket along with her. Neither posture carried much meaning now.

The clock on the nightstand read 2:37. On the wall above hung a winter scene by Savrasov—crows roosting in naked branches. There was no denying the grief that had come upon me, a grief almost greater than that which possessed me the day of her funeral sixteen years before. I mourned now because when she had been alive I had not understood her. To the end, she frustrated my understanding, defied it with her own silences, her suppressions and elisions. Not about her past in the camps, per se. I was careful not to probe too hard into her tour through the bowels of hell, respecting her silence on the subject. No, what I blamed her for was another kind of silence. What I could not abide was her unwillingness to condemn the very system that had destroyed our family. Her refusal to impugn the evil that had deprived me of a father and left me motherless in those years when a boy most needs a mother's love. I am not a crybaby. I am not one to nurse old wounds. Others suffered more, God knows. It would have been enough for me if she had said, just one time, *Yes, what they did to you, to me, to our family—that was unforgivable.* But she did not say those words, and her muteness—her apologism for the system that she insisted—to me!—"would always take care of the children"—became a second, no less painful, abandonment. In the sixties and seventies, when I was compulsively reading samizdat, I wanted her to be as cynical and disillusioned as I was. I wanted her to be angry for the miseries that *she* had endured: the murder of her husband, the forcible separation from her child, seven years of bondage and humiliation and hunger. That all this failed to enrage her infuriated *me* all the more. For it left me to carry the anger for both of us.

That she wore the habitual submissiveness of the slave made me pity her as a victim of her times, of her political beliefs, a victim of her stubbornness and of her illusions. And, certainly, she *had been* a victim, but until this night I had not considered how she might also have been something else. An accomplice to that very same system that preyed on her. Only now did I allow myself to consider the alternate explanation: that her muteness was not the submissiveness of a slave but the silence of an accessory. I wondered now if her refusal to condemn the whole machine in which she herself had been a cog, however small, was not—as I once believed—the consequence of lifelong brainwashing, but an appropriate, even honest, response in the face of her own abiding guilt.

Was she apprehensive about decrying what she herself had done, however unwittingly? Reading through the text once more, I saw that the reason she'd given for bearing false witness against Esther Frank was very odd: she was convinced that the same charge had been leveled by Essie against her. If this excuse was to be believed, it spoke to her terrorized state of mind: a hall of mirrors full of goblins.

But if she believed that Essie had it in for her, why would she come so belatedly to her former friend's defense? Why did she admit to possessing the forbidden magazine? I reread for the nth time the list of seized items. It did not include any foreign magazines or other foreign bourgeois literature for which she was accused of having such a passionate craving. They wouldn't have missed recording such a jewel of evidence. Perhaps she had gotten rid of it before her arrest. Why then admit to having possessed it at all? In the basement of the Lubyanka it would have been my mother's word against Essie's. Was it her conscience that made her fess up to spare her friend? I would have liked to believe it, but I didn't think so. I tossed the charred filter of my cigarette down the shaft of balconies and stepped back in to resume my inquiry.

I was nearing the bottom of the pile when something occurred to me. My mother had been accused on *two* charges, of which the propagandaand-agitation charge (58.10) carried the relatively lighter punishment of seven years. If she had been found guilty of espionage, the punishment would have been twenty-five years, or more likely, as it had been with my father, a bullet in the back of the head. Was it possible, I wondered, that her "confession" to sharing the magazine was strategic? That she was pleading, as it were, to the lesser charge because she sensed there were only two ways out of the Lubyanka—via Siberia or via a body bag—and she was holding out hope for the former?

I need to admit that it was on the hotel toilet that this thought came to me. Whatever calming effects I'd expected the cigarettes to have on my nerves, they'd had the opposite effect on my bowels. No sooner had I finished the second Marlboro than I felt my gut seizing up in spasms. I fled to the bathroom, archives in hand, determined to piece together the last days of my mother's imprisonment even as my body was intent on expelling all the *zakuski* I had been forced to devour at the *banya* with my own tattooed tormentor. Or maybe it was nerves, after all; my overwhelmed organism seemed unable to process anything new until it had purged itself completely of everything dispensable.

By the time I was finished on the john I felt as light and immaterial as a yogi. There were black circles under my eyes, and my exhausted, ravaged reflection looked like it had lost a solid fifteen pounds. I was at last a hollow vessel ready to receive my spiritual nourishment. This was around the point when I got to the bottom of the stack. All along, I had kept reading. Based on her contacts alone, the case for my mother's being found guilty of spying was a strong one. She had worked with and known spies at the Jewish Committee. Her husband, "the spy Brink," had, according to her interrogators, already confessed to forwarding industrial and military materials to American spies, like the journalists Paul Novick and B. Z. Goldberg, who'd come to the Soviet Union to prowl around for state secrets. According to the logic of association, she was bound for a thirty-year term or worse. Which was why it shocked me when, in the second-to-last protocol, I discovered this:

POSTANOVLENIE O PEREKVALIFIKATSII OBVINENIIA

PROPOSAL TO RE-QUALIFY THE CHARGES
----

30 April 1950—Brink, F. has been accused of being an
    agent of foreign reconnaissance, and for an ex-
    tended time of engaging in spy work against the
    Soviet Union.

We did not find adequate proof of espionage in the in-
    vestigation.

But along with this—being anti-Soviet oriented,
    Brink, F. kept up ties with enemies of the people,
    concealed their and her own enemy work, and voiced
    her anti-Soviet views to them, as well as kept and
    distributed anti-Soviet literature.

We propose changing the charge 58-1(a), according to
    statute 204, to charge 58-10.

I reread it because I couldn't believe my eyes. Just like that, with no buildup, her interrogators had dropped the espionage charge.

Had her gambit worked?

How could it have? Most of the seven-month-long interrogation had been devoted to "unearthing" her contact with "known spies" and espionage cells. In contrast, the only so-called evidence to support her being a dispenser of anti-Soviet propaganda was the temporary possession of an anodyne magazine that featured as its main story a flattering puff piece about a movie star—Ingrid Bergman in the role of Joan of Arc, hardly a symbol of capitalist decadence. Furthermore, it was a magazine she had had in her possession because she worked as a translator for the foreign press. Could they really argue that showing a friend an article about an actress could constitute "distributing propaganda"?

I was fully aware that I was attempting to use logic in a logic-free zone. And yet it was undeniable that—if measured by correlation and volume alone—the weight of so-called evidence in my mother's case fell much more heavily on the spying charge than on that of propaganda. How, then, I was forced to wonder, had the second charge been so abruptly dropped by her eager executioners? I inspected the protocols once more for an answer. There was no clue.

THE CLOCK ON MY BED stand flashed 3:12 A.M. I opened the mini-fridge and poured myself a club soda, then sat in the armchair, sipping it from a whiskey glass, gazing down at the white tunnel of Xeroxed papers on the bed. I'd have to clear them off soon if I planned to get any sleep. I finished my drink and rose slowly. With great effort I started putting the protocols back together. My eyes fell once more on the "Mish-Pok" page, which staggered me anew with its outrageousness. But now another thought arrested me: all this time my mother had never stopped communicating with her brother. She had kept writing to him, and he to her, through a Great Depression, two sets of purges, a world war, through the numerous trials and setbacks of her life. No doubt the letters had been heavily self-censored, and yet . . . in spite of the various pressures she must have been under, in spite of the various disruptions in their communication, she had never completely severed the thread of their correspondence! It was amazing, really. When I thought about it, there was no one else with whom she had shared such unbroken intimacy, not even me. I recalled now my mother's final years, when I had installed her in her own Section 8 apartment in Brooklyn, in a largely Russian neighborhood off Ocean Parkway. She was happy to have her independence again after living with us in Bensonhurst. On Saturdays, when I would drive over with a carful of groceries, I'd often find her with Sidney, who would come from New Jersey to see her; the two of them would stroll slowly along the tree-lined median of the parkway. Sidney would hold my mother's elbow as she pressed ahead with the help of her new rubber-tipped cane. I'd roll along past them in my car, unnoticed, before parking in front of her apartment building. It always surprised me how animated and unguarded her face looked in those moments. By the time I parked and walked over to them, they'd be sitting down on a bench, in mid-conversation, my mother chatting away as I rarely saw her do. Seeing me walk up, she'd stop talking and smile, happily but slyly, like a gossiping schoolgirl spotting an approaching teacher. I never bothered to ask myself what the two of them spent so much time discussing. They had their whole lives to catch up on, after all. And yet she *was* different around Sidney, more candid and innocent somehow, almost—I thought now—like the *young Florie* before all kinds of calamities had befallen her. A girl arrested in time.

I CHECKED THE CLOCK. Almost 3:30 A.M. in Moscow. I counted back the hours: 7:30 P.M. in New Jersey. I took my phone out to the balcony and dialed Sidney's number.

He picked up on the first ring.

"Uncle Sidney?"

"Julian! Back so quick?"

"No, still in Moscow. Am I disturbing you? It's probably dinnertime there."

"Nah. They feed us all at six."

"So early?"

"Doctor's regimen. They're as strict as the army with a quarter of the portions. It must be the middle of the night for you. What's up?"

"Couldn't sleep."

"What's the trouble? Work?"

Now I paused. "I have new respect," I said, "for women who give lap dances to fat men for money. It's not easy to put on a smile and pretend to enjoy it."

I was glad to get a laugh out of him. "Welcome to the corporate world," he said.

"I've been thinking a lot about Mama."

He didn't say anything.

"I passed the Lubyanka the other day," I continued. "You know, they've declassified a lot of those old dossiers."

"It was no picnic" was all he said. I thought maybe he hadn't understood me.

"Did Florence ever talk to you about it?"

There was a long pause, and then a sigh. "Some. Toward the end."

I didn't know how else to broach the subject, so I said simply, "I got hold of her file. I've been reading it over."

A pause, and then, "Good for you."

I couldn't tell in what spirit he meant this, so I continued, somewhat faux-naïvely. "I've been trying to piece it together—her time in the prison. Some of it doesn't make a lot of sense. I thought . . . I don't know, maybe, if she told you something, you could help me get a better picture."

"I don't know what I'd be able to tell you."

"Well, for one thing, they were charging her with spying *and* spreading propaganda. . . ."

"It was all nonsense. She wasn't any kind of spy or . . ."

"I know that. But see, they'd connected her to all these rings—these fake conspiracies—and then, all of a sudden, they dropped the spying charge. Dropped the questioning altogether. I can't figure it out."

I waited awhile for him to answer. From below came the sound of an occasional whooshing automobile along the night-abandoned avenue. I thought I'd lost the connection. "Uncle Sid?"

"Those weren't her shining moments, Julian," he said suddenly.

And I knew. She had told him. If not everything, then more than I'd imagined.

"I'm only interested in knowing what happened. It won't make a difference to me. She's still my mother. Did she give someone up? Did she make a deal?"

"No. It was too late for deals once you were inside that place." On the other side, I could hear a raspy intake of breath. "See—there were two guys . . . questioning her."

"Right. It's here in the papers. Bykov and Antonov."

"I don't know the names. One of them she called the Hayseed."

Antonov, I thought immediately.

"Half the time she didn't understand what he was roaring at her. And he was always threatening her with *rass-treyol.*"

"With what?"

"You know—paint a little rubbing alcohol on her third-eye and bang! Bang!"

"Oh, *rasstrel*. A bullet in the head. But why the alcohol?"

"To prevent a blood infection."

I smiled to myself and let him continue.

"Also, he was a real frothing anti-Semite. Of course, a lot of them were, but he was always shouting at her, 'You ungrateful hag. You ate Russian bread. The Soviet government gave you a roof and now you betray it. For your people I fought on the front lines. For your ilk my brother lost his leg in the war . . .' and so on. He'd keep her awake all night, then hand her over to the other one. And *that* one would make her sit in a chair against the wall for hours—no sleeping, of course—while he shuffled around his papers. He'd even make phone calls home while she was there. Ask his kid if he'd done his homework. Tell his wife he was going to be late again. 'Hi, honey, long evening at the inquisition office again, don't stay up.' That kind of thing."

"Why?"

"Who knows with them. Maybe to remind her that there was an outside world."

"Maybe to show he wasn't a bad guy—loved his wife and family? Good cop, bad cop?"

"Sure. The classic strategy. He was the one who'd tell her your father was still alive, that they were holding him somewhere in another part of the building. He'd say, 'I'll be frank with you, lady—your husband's not in good shape. He's been here a long time. We could make things easier for him with your help—confirm such and such and I'll see to it that you get to see him. Maybe we can even arrange a conjugal visit, hee-hee.'"

"Was any of it true?"

"No, all lies! He was just trying to rattle her. He was taunting her. He'd say, 'The question is whether your husband would be interested. After all, if he saw you now . . .' This sadist, he'd look her up and down and say, 'Yes, I can see you were once not a bad-looking woman.' He'd put his hand on her knee and shake his head. 'You've turned into a real hag here, Flora Solomonovna. You've really let yourself go.' Of course, she hadn't seen herself in the mirror in months. Her hair had gone gray and she didn't even know it."

"But I mean, did she believe him? About my father. Did she fall for it?"

"No, she didn't. Stop asking questions. That's not important."

How could it be not important? I wondered. But I had no time to pick an argument. It was 3:50 A.M. in Moscow. I had New Jersey on the phone. I did as I was told.

"Anyway, this guy—he got his kicks from talking like that to the women. They called him Karman—the Pocket."

"Who did?"

"The women in her jail cell. There were about fifteen of them."

"In one cell?"

"Yes. His left hand never left the pocket of his military trousers."

"He had a reputation among the women?"

"You could say that. There was a girl in her cell—the pretty daughter of some disgraced big-time communist. Whenever the Pocket called her in, she'd return to the cell in tears. Evidently, he made her describe in minute detail all her past sexual experiences. Florence, I think, got spared because maybe she was too old. She was maybe thirty-nine."

"So he didn't touch her."

"As far as I know, aside from the knee patting, his mode was that he just listened and kept that hand inside his pocket. That's how he got his kicks."

"Wow."

"So, one time, the Hayseed, he walked in while the Pocket was doing his routine about the conjugal visit, his hand on her thigh. Well, he was disgusted by it. Maybe he said something, maybe he just gave a smirking look—but the message was the same: *Even this hag?*"

"So they weren't exactly comrades?"

"They couldn't stand each other. More important, they were *afraid* of each other."

"Afraid how?"

"In that world, you know, nobody was safe. Today you're on one side of the table, tomorrow you're on the other. Those KGB guys got cleaned out like everybody else. They all stooled on each other. It's like life in the Mafia.

Good while it lasts, but sooner or later it's your ass hanging from the meat hook."

"They distrusted each other."

"Right. Well, then at some point they started her on the conveyor belt—you know what that is?"

"Of course."

"A hundred hours and more of uninterrupted questioning by rapid rotation. She was already very weak, and now the total lack of sleep—she was probably ready to fess up to being the Pope's sister-in-law, but she did everything she could to avoid getting this bum rap for spying. It was only her lack of imagination that saved her. She'd tell them, 'If you know so much about conspiracies, write up the story yourselves and sign it.' But they'd shout, 'You must tell us yourself! You must sign. We want only the truth!'"

Again I thought of Vasily Grossman. They had to make my mother a willing participant in the charade. They had to make the corpse of freedom dance like a clown.

"She wouldn't give them what they wanted. Kept dozing off in her chair. They'd wake her up by shining big reflector lamps in her face. Or they'd shake her awake."

"Did they ever beat her?"

Sidney paused. "The problem was that crazy motherfucker—not the Pocket, the other one—he was a loose cannon. Always hyped up from tooting that blow . . ."

"Wait—Antonov? You're saying he was doing drugs?"

"Bolivian marching powder."

"*Cocaine?*"

"Yes, that's it. He snorted it to keep himself going all night. That's what a lot of those bastards did, kept themselves juiced while working over the prisoners."

"He snorted in front of Mama?"

"Most of the time, she'd be dozing off. She'd crack an eyeball and see him at the desk, powdering his nose. He carried the stuff in a little tin. Like a lady."

"Hell," I said.

"Guy had a permanent cold from it, always sniffing. Nose as pink as a poodle's. The Pocket would come in and tell him to wipe his nose, very contemptuously."

"They each had something on the other."

"I'm sure he was happy to have this coke fiend do his dirty work, as long as he could keep the violent stuff from getting out of control. So they were going at her, sometimes both at once. And now she's just answering by rote: 'I do not plead guilty to espionage or conspiracy. I never expressed dissatisfaction with the Soviet Union.' She must have fallen asleep chanting this stuff. Next thing she knows, she's being woken up with a kick to her kidney. Her chair's on the floor. She's being punched and hit in the side. She's on the floor with those damn lamps aimed at her, and all she can see is the Hayseed's black boot. So what does she do? She starts shouting, 'Terrorists! You can't beat me! This isn't 1937. You can't extract false confessions with beatings!'

"So now the other one—he's in the room too—he steps in and says: 'Too bad you're not in the hands of the Gestapo, you kike bitch. You know what *they'd* do to you? They knew how to handle traitors.'

"And she says to him, 'Are *you* comparing yourselves with the Gestapo? Is that where you learned your methods? How unpleasant it would be for you if your superiors heard you proudly modeling yourselves after the fascists.'"

"Hold on," I said. "She said that, to *them?*"

"I don't think she knew what she was saying. It was just impulse. But that was it. The next day, they gave her a document to sign. All the espionage charges were dropped. Neither of those guys apparently wanted the investigation to go on a day longer. They wanted her shipped off before she ended up in the hands of another investigator, or before one of them ratted on the other. That Gestapo comment—it spooked them enough that they wrapped things up quick."

I rubbed my forehead. I was feeling achy and feverish from the lack of sleep. The balcony height was making me queasy. "Why didn't she tell me this?" I said. "Frankly, I would have been impressed."

"Well . . . once you uncork the bottle . . . you start talking about one thing, and before you know it a lot of other stuff starts coming out. You weren't the easiest guy to tell stories to."

"What do you mean by that?"

"I don't want to overstep. I don't know what it was between you two."

"Say what you were going to say."

"Your mother thought you had a lot of . . . virtue."

"Me."

"Yes. You were always very uncompromising."

I couldn't believe this. I had to laugh—to regain my sense of myself. "She thought *I* was the idealist?"

"She knew you didn't just listen. You'd try to catch her on inconsistencies. That's just how your mind turned."

"Julian Brink, the purist," I said.

"Look, you probe enough in anyone's history and you're bound to reach some less-than-sublime conclusions. It was hard enough for her that you had paid the price for so many of her choices."

This I had not been expecting. But before I could answer, Sidney said, "It's late. For you and me both. I don't want to talk myself hoarse."

"Of course. Thanks for talking to me, Uncle Sid."

"When you're done shaking your tail for the fat men over there, you come pay me a visit."

"I will. Good night."

I waited for him to hang up and set down my phone.

I FINISHED CLEARING THE PAPERS, still under the spell of the scene Sidney had narrated. My mother's brazenness. The audacity of such an accusation. There had been a certain shrewdness in it, however inadvertent. She had done to her interrogators what they were attempting to do to her: pry open their allegiances, divide and conquer. Even in that near-perfect darkness, she'd felt around and found a chink.

I put the papers on the nightstand and set the alarm for seven. And then I tried to get some sleep.

38.

———

COMRADE BRINK

I SLEPT FITFULLY AND WOKE UP TO ICY AIR SLICING IN BETWEEN THE folds of my comforter. The room was completely dark aside for a seam of daylight cutting in between the heavy hotel curtains. I could hear the air conditioner going full-blast. I had no memory of turning down the thermostat, which I felt sure was possessed by demons.

I'd been having a dream, and the temperature offered an explanation. The setting was an unspecified polar region. The dream itself had had the grainy quality of an old cinema reel, a war film out of my childhood. There was a ship, setting sail down a channel. It looked like the cruiser *Aurora*, but I knew that beneath this historic cover it was one of my own ships, because of the specific pattern with which it cut through ice. In the dream I was steering, but also watching myself steer. And though there were no others, at least that I could see, I felt enveloped in an aura of approval from my crew, full of my somber contribution to the heroic effort—a feeling of virtue that I was enjoying very much until I cared to look down at the helm, and found upon the polished wooden wheel not my own hands but a pair of fat paws covered in tattoo ink. From here on the dream became a scene from the *Titanic*. Recklessly, and possibly deliberately, the tattooed hands piloted my *Aurora* right into an invisible iceberg that materialized out of the night. I could hear a scraping, a slicing of metal skin, which continued in dream time until, auspiciously enough, tufts of stuffing began falling out of the hull and dropped at my feet like cotton snow.

My heart was still pounding when I awoke. My shoulders and neck were stiff. I felt more exhausted than when I had gone to sleep. At last I got up and drew the curtains just enough not to burn my retinas. Six floors beneath me Tverskaya was astream with vehicles, clogged in one direction with honking traffic. I let my body go through the motions of employing the toilet and showering. Under the pummel of the hot water, I thought about the two young guys, Gibkov and McGinnis, who were going to take over the work of managing the Varandey project after we were done. I'd liked them for not being sewn out of L-Pet's adulterated cloth. I'd had the impression they'd liked me too, for my directness and expertise. Now they would no doubt view me as just another old hypocrite. I was already adjusting myself to the loss of esteem, the downgrading of expectation.

In the dimly lit mirror above the mini-bar I watched my hands shake as I looped a tie around my neck, cinched it up, and folded down the collar. I stirred my soluble crystal Nescafé and drank it down beside the nightstand, where Mama's documents still lay. Daylight touched the mimeographed signatures of those who'd signed Florence's prison sentence. I was surprised to see that, aside from Bykov's and Antonov's, there were three other names—though not so surprised when I gave it some thought. The bowels of hell were nothing if not the precinct of bureaucratic order. I instantly beheld an image of these pages moving from desk to desk, making their way up the chain, farther and farther away from my mother's cold jail cell, acquiring more patina of officialdom with each signature and stamp. It was likely that the figures who'd signed this order, which had so clemently committed my mother to seven years of hard labor, had never even laid eyes on her. I rested my cup down on the page, pleased with the brown coffee ring it left when I picked it up again—my very own rubber stamp added to the three official seals of the NKVD. What a lust for procedure all these tidy forms were meant to convey! And all the while: splintered allegiances, private agendas, mutual loathing. What unanimity, or, to borrow the NKVD's own language, "identical-mindedness," these neat ranks of signatures suggested. But that too was a falsehood. The NKVD was cannibalizing itself even as it set its teeth on the world outside. How had my mother known—in this deep circle of Hades—to sic those two dogs, Antonov and Bykov, upon each other? To pry apart their loyalties just as they had tried to pry apart hers and Essie's? Was she studying their tricks even as they worked her over? Or had she simply seen beyond the obvious: that nobody was invulnerable. That there were no united fronts. That it was rot all the way through—the rot of fear and envy.

And now another image of orderly signatures struck me. Instinctively, my eyes went to my computer case, sitting half forgotten on the carpet in a slanting rectangle of light from the curtains. I went over to it and removed from the briefcase the sheaf of documents connected to the joint venture. It was part of the "welcome packet" I'd had to read on starting the Varandey terminal project. Composed in a slick PR style by Continental's press department, it was intended for the oil trade journals that exist to cover such things. I had opened it and closed it the day they'd given it to us. Now I pulled the papers out of the folder one by one. I scanned the pages: orderly, dull corporate prose, unshadowed by any hint of internal discord. I knew my plan was delirious, but my fingers would not stop their busy turning. They leafed to the end of a long-winded mission statement, on the final page of which I discovered at long last, toward the bottom, a list of signatures. They were arrayed in two pillars: Russians on the right, Americans on the left, like dancers at a debutante ball. My own name appeared toward the middle of the American column, above my vague title: "Director of Project Services." On the right were Mukhov's, Serdyuk's, and Kablukov's names and signatures. And directly beneath Kablukov's half-literate chicken scrawl, a neat, slightly right-tilting, unflamboyant, but nevertheless magisterial signature I had not seen before. Underneath it was typewritten "A. Kozlovsky, Head of Foreign Partnerships." I had never laid eyes on the man. Whoever he was, he'd been too otherwise occupied to favor us with his presence in our mahogany conference room. Evidently, he was one of those faceless executives every company has, across whose desk documents must pass on their mysterious way up, to be approved at the very top before being sent down again. I knew that there weren't very many people in the chain above the Boot. Yet this Kozlovsky fellow's name was beneath Kablukov's, signifying his higher status. There were no mistakes made when it came to where a name fell on a page. Mistakes regarding lives lost, fathers killed, mothers imprisoned—sure. But the placement of signatures on a document—never.

BY NINE I WAS at L-Pet headquarters, hoping not to be spotted by anybody from our project, anyone who would want to walk with me to the conference room for our concluding meeting. I found the elevator blessedly empty and rode it as far as it would take me, to the twenty-first floor. I could taste the acid washback from the instant coffee sloshing around in my empty stomach. Thanks to the crystals of sweetened caffeine, my hands were no longer shaking, though I was jittery in other ways, pre- pared to wander the labyrinths of L-Pet until somebody pointed me to A. Kozlovsky's office.

It turned out to be in the east wing of the complex, as I learned from a young man in a trim suit who displayed a wonderful lack of suspicion of my question after I showed him the official badge hanging from my neck, and who in fact walked me all the way down a side hall to another set of elevators that took me where I needed to go. Thus I emerged at last in a glass-and-steel part of the building that seemed to be a separate tower. For a suspended moment I couldn't place where I had come from or where I was. The view below me was no longer of the grassy median of Sretensky Boulevard but a block entirely torn up by construction, apart from a small yellow-painted church and attached parish house stranded in the midst of this violent modernization. I approached a set of glass doors through which was visible an open area like the VIP lounge in an airport. Oblong leather couches and potted trees were illuminated by invisible light fix- tures tucked into recesses in the ceiling. No weighty mahogany or unused fireplaces here. It was as though I had escaped one century and ascended to another—though this lighter, neoteric world was still out of reach on the other side of the glass doors, closed by some strong magnetic grip that could only be released electronically, but not by my pass. I spotted what looked like a reception desk, but there was no one there.

The closed glass doors were an obvious invitation for me to turn myself around and wander back down the footbridge. It was nine-fifteen. The meeting would be starting in a few minutes, and I could still divert myself from this present course. I had no idea how I would get into that closed gallery, how I would manage to find Kozlovsky, or even what I would say to him if I did. But when I opened my eyes, I saw a woman walking to the desk that had previously been empty, a middle-aged brunette with a severe haircut like the writer Ayn Rand's. There were others coming down the hall behind her, a group of three loudly chatting men, strolling toward the doors behind which I stood. One of them pressed a button on the inside to release the magnetic lock and waited while the other two walked out, holding the door for me, so that I might enter. I stepped in confidently, all at once aware that I was approaching the desk with my toes pointed out, the cowboy walk that afflicted some of our Texas colleagues around the halls of Continental. I felt light-headed with my brazenness.

Ayn Rand gave me an indifferent look when I smiled at her. I continued grinning until, finally, she addressed me in Russian with a cool *"Zdrav-stvuyte"* and a "Can I help you?"

I was about to answer with my own *zdravstvuyte*, to try to get on familiar ground with this creature, when something made me pause. Clearly, this woman had identified me as a fellow countryman, from somewhere below deck, to be addressed with appropriate contempt. I did not like the way things were starting off.

"Yes, hello," I said, in English, and smiled an even broader smile. I did not believe that my accented English could really have fooled her, or that she had accepted it over the glaring evidence of my Russian mug. But she blinked and looked at me again, uncertainly, as if trying to recalculate a sum, yet with a face composed into a more obliging expression.

They can never think they know who you are, were in fact the words in my head. And hearing them I thought: The only way to get the balance back in my favor was to keep them off theirs.

I told her I was here to see a "Mr. . . . Cuz-luv-sky," pretending to have some trouble with the name. I lifted up my security pass, on which my own name was simply written as "Julian Brink, Continental Oil," title omitted, and told her I was the technical director of the Varandey project, which was an amplification of the truth, if not quite a bald lie. She picked up the phone, then pointed a finger at one of the oblong couches, a directive for me to go sit down. I took a few paces back, but didn't sit.

"*Kto-to* from Continental," I heard her say into the phone, and then to me, more loudly in English, "You have appointment?"

"My secretary should have made one. . . . I am flying back to Washington tonight, and I need to . . ."

Her expression indicated that she didn't much care when I was flying back, or where. She slid a paper across the desk. "Write your business here. Mr. Kozlovsky will call you."

The dame did not even give me a pen. No problem. From my shirt pocket I took out my phony Mont Blanc. I waited for her to put down the receiver. "One question," I said.

She offered up an agitated face, on guard for new surprises.

"Is your family from Norilsk?"

"Why Norilsk?"

"I worked there last year and met a lady who looked *just* like you. You have such white skin." I heard my voice, my unsanitized articulation of the English language, my preposterous act, and I continued. "This lady . . . she told me there are two reasons for such lovely white skin: the White Nights, and, because the Mongols never reached them in Norilsk, that they are the *real* Russians. And you are, yes?"

It would have taken a truly heroic effort for her to stifle her smile, though she tried. "No. My family is from Novgorod," she said. "But we also did not have any Mongols, either."

"Ah!" I went to take my seat on the leather couch.

"Wait here," she said, and picked up the phone again. When she hung up, she gestured with her finger. "You have ten minutes."

ANTON KOZLOVSKY WAS A tall man in a pale-gray suit with neat hair and pale eyes set widely apart on a face that bore the pitted pockmarks of some childhood affliction. He did not shake my hand when I walked in, and glanced at his watch almost as soon as I sat down.

"What can I do for you?" he said.

I introduced myself, said I was a representative of Continental Oil for the Varandey project—all of this in Russian. I had no pretensions about fooling him. With his wide-set eyes he looked at me, not quite coldly but . . . factually, and for a moment I wondered if he had learned to stare people down in this way in his childhood, whenever they gazed at his pitted cheeks.

Behind his head was a map of the world with brown pins on every L-Pet field, and blue pins that I thought might indicate future fields to develop.

"In a half-hour, our joint team will be making final selections for our shipping company. There are some last . . . unanswered questions about one of the candidates for the contract."

"What questions?"

"Questions of competency and . . . cost."

"So voice them with my team. Why are you coming to me with these technical matters?" He fixed me with the same challenging, factual look. I cast about for the right thing to say. I felt there had to be some perfect ordering of words that could be pulled down from somewhere—words contrived for just this use. But they eluded me.

"Respectfully, you'll be signing off on the deal," I said. But I could hear these words losing exigency, my voice sounding wheedling. Whatever force of certainty had brought me this far had abandoned me.

"I'll sign whatever my team decides." Kozlovsky checked his watch again, quickly but deliberately. I pictured Tom and the others waiting for me in the heavily paneled room four floors below. Maybe they had started the meeting without me. And yet I could not get up and leave now without showing myself to be a stoolie and a coward. I tried to study Kozlovsky's face, to guess if he was in on Kablukov's graft deal or not. I had assumed, without quite realizing it, that with one look at him I would be able to answer this question and know what to do. His face gave nothing away.

"I'm sorry to waste your time," I said. "It's my mistake for not listening to Ivan Matveyevich. He did say your signature was only a formality."

"*Who* said that?"

"Kablukov. He said your signature was a formality and that the decision has already been made . . . above you."

I shrugged my shoulder regretfully, my thumb rubbing the phony Mont Blanc in my sweating hand. Kozlovsky did not look happy to hear what I'd just said. He was not a man who took well to being taunted. With those few words I had done the equivalent of pulling down my pants and showing him my behind.

"I don't know what Kablukov told you, but there *are* no decisions made above me."

"So, then, you must be familiar with the particular details of this deal?" Kozlovsky shook his head at my game. "You are really something. *Nu.* Talk already, Comrade . . . Brink."

"At this moment, in Conference Room 14A, we are choosing a shipper for the Varandey oil project. Mr. Kablukov and his team are insisting on a company with no experience, and that will charge the project—and us—seventeen million more a year."

"And you, Comrade Brink, you have come here to ask *me* for the reason."

"Not at all." I tried to sound lighthearted. "It doesn't matter to me what the reason is. Whatever it is, we will sign with whatever shipper you want. Only . . . it's a question of risks and . . . let's say, *rewards.* In this industry we are, by nature, in the business of assuming risk. Sometimes you don't know what kind of risk you are underwriting, or"—I turned my palm out—"if *you* are necessarily sharing in the rewards."

I looked at the map above his head. A few of the blue pennants were in the middle of the sea, near the Arctic. Offshore. The future.

"You are proposing something to me?"

I snapped to. Kozlovsky had the face of a traffic cop I'd erred in trying to bribe. He'd misunderstood me. This was not at all what I had hoped would happen.

"Of course, I am not talking about our side," I said rapidly. "What matters to Continental is a continued collaboration with L-Pet. . . ." But this too had the wrong sound to it: bootlicking and asinine.

"Yet you've troubled yourself to come here on behalf of Continental. . . ."

"No, only on behalf of myself," I corrected. "I have a son here, as your Mr. Kablukov well knows. My son is trying to make his own way in the world. I respectfully request that he be free to do his business, without interference, and L-Pet will be free to do theirs."

Kozlovsky blinked a few times. Something was quietly registering in him. He was an organization man who liked to do his work cleanly. No doubt he was aware of Kablukov's tactics, and tolerated them. But he also hated to be made to answer for Kablukov's gluttony, the messes he left. I was now sure he hated Kablukov no less than Bykov had hated Antonov.

He stood up, indicating that our time was over. I kept sitting. I wasn't going to leave this room without a guarantee. Kozlovsky studied me silently, moving his pale eyes from my face to my shoulders to my hands, as though deciding whether or not to fling me out of his plate-glass window. "You don't need to worry yourself over this anymore," he said finally. He consulted the pass hanging from my neck. "Dzhuli-*yan,* we verify everything here."

EVERYBODY WAS ASSEMBLED AROUND the Olympic-sized conference table. I apologized and took my seat near Tom and a seat away from Kablukov. They had been drinking coffee from the dispensers set up along the back wall, but now both their cups were empty. In his shades, Kablukov nodded at me in a gesture of seriousness that seemed somehow ludicrous.

"Gentlemen, I think we can begin now," Tom said, looking displeased with me.

I busied myself removing my laptop from its case. It seemed to be stuck between some papers, and I realized with a shock that I had accidentally stuffed my bag not with L-Pet documents but pages of my mother's files! And then the absurdity of my predicament became clear to me. I had just performed an act of foolishness rivaling any of my mother's, and why? To protect Lenny? To take down the Boot? Or was my suicide mission, in the end, done for that same childish principle for which my mother had lost so much blood—the hopeless cause of Fairness?

At last I extricated my laptop from the wrinkled pages of Florence's file, taking care not to let any of them slip out. I had no idea what to do next. I felt a pedant's urge to draw up the spreadsheet on which I'd been logging the faults and virtues of the charter candidates, though I knew it now to be inane and worthless.

It was at that moment that the door opened and Anton Kozlovsky walked in.

Mukhov gazed at Serdyuk, as though he of all people was likely to know the cause for this unexpected visitation. I gazed at Kablukov. "Anton Yevgenevich . . ." Kablukov rose slightly out of his chair, followed by Mukhov. "We weren't expecting you today."

"My trip to Ufa was moved."

Kozlovsky did not introduce himself. He let his underlings at L-Pet do the honors.

I prepared myself for the imminent scenario in which Kozlovsky would announce that I had gone to see him. Was it regret I felt? No, not regret. My mind was blank. What I was experiencing was a sense of inescapability, the Nietzschean feeling that all this had happened before and would happen again. In a matter of minutes Tom would know I had broken ranks. The process would go on as predestined. The fruit of my work would be irreparably separated from its labor, never again to be brought under my control. My suicide mission was complete. I was already dead, I just hadn't been informed of it yet.

Kozlovsky did not look at me. He said merely, "Please, sit," to the others. Between me and Kablukov was an empty chair, and here was where

Kozlovsky planted himself. "Please, friends, continue as you were. I won't be disturbing you. I know your work here is almost over. I only wish to sit in and hear the merits of our various contenders for this important charter."

I did not glance in Tom's direction—though I could feel him looking at me. I was certain he was waiting for me to take some action now. This would be my valiant moment of self-abasement. Before things got out of hand, I was to make my announcement and inform Kablukov, and now Kozlovsky, that all of the bids had been carefully weighed in the past several days and that our contractor—Sausen Petroleum—had been selected. This morning, we were only going to dispense with the formalities of paperwork.

But how could I say any of this after what I had done? Over my shoulder I could smell the aroma of a freshly smoked cigarette still lingering on Kozlovsky's suit. I could not will myself to begin. I would sound like a psychopath.

"*Nu?*" Kozlovsky addressed me impatiently.

I touched my closed laptop. "We have a matrix," I said limply.

Focused on me, his pale irises had the effect of a cattle prod. *I am here. Now what do you have to show me?* those eyes said.

And so that he wouldn't utter another word, I opened my Dell and drew up the spreadsheet.

KOZLOVSKY HANDLED HIMSELF BEAUTIFULLY. For much of the discussion he sat politely in the background, listening to our brief account of the merits of the top three choices—Jessem, Sovcomflot, and the Geneva-based Sausen Petroleum. Mukhov did much of the talking, making such smooth transitions that it was difficult, at times even for me, to distinguish which company he was talking about. But Kozlovsky seemed to assimilate all this knowledge instantly, keeping one eye on my screen while pausing to ask questions heavy with common sense.

"What do our Americans think?" he said at last.

"We will defer to your judgment," Tom said with the easygoing smile I recognized as the grin of a shit eater.

Kozlovsky, feigning innocence of our conversation, asked to see the original proposals of the top three bidders. He studied them for some time, blind to the nervous smirks around the room. I watched Kablukov. Under his dark glasses, he appeared to be entering some kind of vascular distress. He loosened his necktie and wiped his head with a handkerchief.

"One of these seems to want to charge us quite a steep rate," Kozlovsky pointed out.

It was Mukhov, good foot soldier, who jumped first to the defense of Sausen. All the old arguments tumbled out again—they had a superior relationship with the Swiss banks, a clean safety record, blah blah blah. "It appears they have *no* record," Kozlovsky suggested calmly. Only one argument was not raised in Kozlovsky's presence, and that was the excellent relations Sausen Petroleum had with the company president, Mr. Abuskalayev. On this matter, neither Mukhov nor Serdyuk, and not even Kablukov, spoke a word.

"It looks like the real choice here is between Jessem and Sovcomflot. Of course, I would naturally favor one of ours, *nashih*, but that," Kozlovsky said, "is only my own prejudice, and I know that you will make your own decision."

He waited until we did. Sovcomflot it was, after a unanimous, if not entirely eager, show of hands.

OUTSIDE, I LOOKED UP and was surprised to find the sky as blue as I had ever seen it.

"What happened in there?" Tom said, his hand shielding his eyes from the sun, which bounced off in streaks from the obsidian shine of the L-Pet complex.

"A mystery wrapped in an enigma," I said.

"I still can't get my head around it. I thought Kablukov had the final word."

"Every thief has a boss."

"Well, we got what we wanted, I suppose."

So now it was *we*. "I guess we were courting the wrong asshole," I said.

"Let them sort it out," he said. For the first time since I knew him, Tom seemed not to be certain what his next words would be. He rubbed his smooth chin distractedly. "Who can figure it out with these goddamn Russians," he finally concluded. He seemed to want to change the topic. "We were all waiting for you. Why were you late?"

I contemplated telling him where I'd been fifteen minutes prior to the meeting. But it was better, I decided, to let the doggies sleep. Tom suggested we go take in some sights in the hours left before our flight, check off a box from the tourist column. But I excused myself from playing tour guide. I had more pressing business to take care of. I crossed the street to the other side of Sretensky Boulevard and entered a coffee shop housed in a building of dingy pink brick. And that was when I called Lenny.

It took two tries before he picked up. "Sorry, Pop, I was on the toilet," he confessed with typical Lenny bluntness. "Is it time for your flight already?" I felt relieved to hear his voice. Things had wrapped up early, I said. Then I proposed that we take our promised trip to Izmailovsky Market. Hunt for some classic *sovietskii* junk.

Long pause. "Um, Pa. I think we sort of missed that boat. Most of the booths are closed on weekdays."

"Oh, I'm sure there'll be some desperate auctioneer trying to unload his old Leica. Maybe we'll find something worth some real money."

He seemed to be hesitating.

"Please come with me," I said. "It would make me happy."

And as I said it, I realized it was true. But I was unprepared for the rush of gladness that flooded my heart when he said, "Okay, I'll meet you there."

MUZHCHINA

THE FLEA MARKET WAS MOSTLY DESERTED, AS LENNY HAD PREDICTED. But I thought I liked it better this way, the two of us wandering along an empty street of open-air stalls in the shadow of a tsar's wooden fortress painted like Disneyland. Lenny picked up a porcelain panda, then set it down again. I caught him checking his watch. "Help me pick a gift for your mother," I suggested.

"How about this?" He held up a green rubber gas mask.

"It'll be from you, not from me," I warned.

I wanted Lenny to catch my treasure-hunting fever, but it was true that we'd missed our chance. Only a fraction of the shops were open, and those that were did their business in the most touristy gimmicks: Yeltsin matryoshka dolls and military paraphernalia. My eyes were still gritty from my lack of sleep, but I felt an enlivening rush knowing Lenny wasn't due for trouble anytime soon.

"Mom hates this kind of shlock," Lenny informed me as we walked into a stall full of books and posters.

"That isn't entirely true," I said. "She can appreciate a good piece of kitsch as much as anybody." By way of example I approached the vendor, a fellow with a stringy beard and a long face that resembled those on the religious icons (of dubious origin) that lined the back wall of his stall. "Do you have any anti-capitalist art?" I said.

The man knitted his brow as though I'd just asked him to drop his pants. *"Cho?"* he said.

"Posters," I clarified, "with fat capitalists—you know, in top hats, puffing on cigars."

"What kind of store do people think this is?" he said, offended. Lenny and I exchanged looks. Amid the literature spread out on the tables around us was a catalogue of paintings by Marc Chagall, an *Almanac of Mushrooms*, Lenin's *The Emancipation of Women* (penned by his wife, Nadezhda Krupskaya), an illustrated pamphlet of the Protocols of Zion, an Estonian album of *Forbidden Erotica*, and the autobiography of Bill Clinton. "I have absolutely *no* idea," I said.

"LET'S GET SOMETHING TO eat," I suggested, interrupting Lenny's reading of an American serviceman's phrase book dated from 1962 (the same year, I noted with curiosity, as the Cuban Missile Crisis). He lifted his eyes and gazed out toward the Disneyfied Izmailovo fortress. "I used to really hate coming to places like this," he said suddenly.

"You did?"

"Yeah, they made me think of *her*."

I knew right away whom he meant. "Irochka."

He gave me a smirking smile.

I hadn't meant to be coy. That was simply what I'd always called her—the daughter of my old friends, and later, of course, Lenny's ex-wife. Not Irina, but *our* Irochka was what *all of us* had called her, first tenderly, then with an edge of irony and malice that could never quite negate the original tenderness.

"That first summer I came back here," he said, "it was '96, she'd take me around the city. All these pensioners selling their heirlooms laid out neatly on newspapers. Their lifetime collections of little pins or porcelain cups, or crystal bowls."

"They still do that."

"No, not like then. The inflation was out of control. They were selling off anything just to eat. It was so fucking depressing, and here I was with my wallet stuffed full of American dollars."

"And you wanted to spend it on Irina."

"Well, that's the thing. There was this old guy, I remember, trying to sell an antique silver tea set for maybe twenty bucks. I could see he wasn't one of these professional hawkers, just a desperate old pensioner. She bargained him down to nothing—eight dollars, maybe. I would have been happy to pay twenty. But it was like . . . I was afraid she'd think I was a sucker."

"Life isn't meant for you to squeeze every last drop out of a stone," I offered.

He looked at me dubiously. "But you always liked how practical Irina was. How tough. You used to say I could learn a lot from her."

"Did I?"

"You'd say, 'Here's one girl who doesn't forget to check the weather report.'"

I said nothing. Whatever errors of mine he'd logged, whatever critical implications about himself—I couldn't repair them now with a petition for a proper audit. The past could never be remedied like that. Looking at him, I knew that.

"Do you still think about her?" I said. I was still cautious, but now I realized I was no longer afraid that our conversation might head in the wrong direction—toward some place of misunderstanding, or blame, or fractiousness.

"Not really. I should have seen it coming."

"Come on. You were twenty-three, blinded by love. Happens to the best of us."

"You know what she used to say to me by the end, when we were living together in that apartment she couldn't stand? She'd joke about how I wasn't a full *muzhchina*. She'd say: '*Muzh ti muzh, da china nyet.*'"

He laughed, imitating Ira's drawling Moscow accent as he repeated her cruel little pun on *muzhchina*, the word for "man." I'd never before paused to consider how it was made of two shorter words: *muzh*, which meant "husband," and *cheen*, the word for "rank," or "title." *A husband you are, but no title.* I wondered to myself if Irina had made it up. I'd never been surprised by her cleverness, though I was now surprised that she could have been so casually cruel.

"For years I wondered what would have happened if our family had stayed here, you know? Never emigrated? Maybe I would have grown up tougher, not so soft and guilty all the time. But the thing is, I'm *not* one of them. I'm not like Irina, or like Sasha Zaparotnik. I'm . . ."

"American," I said.

"Yeah." He and I had never talked like this. Now I wished we had.

"So you wanted to try out the alternative?"

He looked at me. "It sounds crazy, right?"

"It doesn't." How many times had I wondered who *I* would have been had I grown up in America, the son of a mother who'd never left? "Look, you haven't had it easy," I said. "I faced some stern blows in my life, but when I failed I always had an ennobling excuse: The system was rigged. I had the Soviets to blame. It gives you a less critical view of yourself."

I'd never exactly recognized this before, but now, saying it, I thought about how it might be true. In my own circumscribed youth, I—and so many of us—had been allowed to retain a sufficient sense of our own virtue, even if the constrictions we faced couldn't be overcome—*especially* if they couldn't. "The thing America doesn't tell you about a life of freedom," I said, "is that sooner or later you're bound to feel like your problems are all your own fault. Even if maybe you just got unlucky."

"They should put that on the warning label," Lenny offered.

I remembered Valentina's words on the road back to the dacha: I had *warned* Lenny, but failed to prepare him. Could I honestly claim she was wrong? What I'd up to now failed to see was that, in issuing all my warnings, I had struck a devil's bargain against his success. Standing on the sidelines of his struggle, my arms crossed, I had been waiting all these years for the moment when he would fall on his face. So that when he got up again, humbled by his defeats, he would at last be ready to be converted to my fatherly wisdom.

But if this was the path that I'd imagined for my son, what place was there in it for me? By attributing his problems to his stubbornness, I had released myself from a greater responsibility to stand by his side.

We passed a kiosk of toys for sale. Lenny picked up one of the stuffed animals and said, "You know those toy bunnies with long arms and Velcro paws that hug each other? That was how Ira and I were when we were six. We'd run into the bathroom and hide under the sink when you and Mom were getting ready to leave the Ostrovskys' apartment. We'd hide in the bathroom like that, hugging each other so you couldn't separate us."

"First love," I said.

"But it was more than that. She really knew me. I didn't need to be cool or cynical or anything with her. I could be who I was. And, yeah, on some level I knew she was using me to come to New York, but I didn't think it would end like *that*. With her coming home at midnight smelling of Calvin Klein while I stayed awake on the couch playing video games. She was screwing her boss right under my nose and I didn't have the guts to let go of her. It's like I knew I couldn't walk away from that with anything, not even two percent of my self-worth. So I just held on."

He gazed out at the mostly vacant shops again. "I always do that."

"Do what?" I said.

"Hold on to whatever it is, past the expiration date. Even with all the distress signals, I stay in that boat to the bitter end. I know that sounds very fatalistic to you." He gave me a brief scoffing smile.

I was tempted to smile back. That had long been my own estimation of his predicament, the root of so many of his struggles. Even so, I was happy that he was coming to his own conclusion about it, and that I had done nothing to prompt it except to listen.

BOOK VI

40.

THE PILOT

ON THE BITTER, BLUE NOVEMBER MORNING WHEN CAPTAIN HENRY ROB-
bins landed in Seoul, he recognized almost no one. Reservists were distributed piecemeal among the regular units. The men who were to be his
fellow pilots were all young. They were boys in their twenties who, having
missed their first chance at a war, had eagerly signed up for the next one.
They had come of age in a time of ticker tape parades and welcome bands.
Everything they'd learned about battle came from Sunday matinees star-
ring Robert Mitchum and John Wayne.

In the years since the war, Robbins had worked to grow his small portrait studio into a full camera shop, selling lenses and easels, projectors
and timers—a business finally beginning to turn profitable just as he was
recalled. His renewed invitation from Uncle Sam caused a storm of distress
in his soul that he was at a loss to put into words. If asked, he would not
have admitted to feeling cheated. When his young wife pointed out that
Mr. Truman's new Selective Service rules permitted thousands to elude
military service while he was being summoned a second time, Robbins did
not indulge her. That he was not permitted to defer his enrollment because, unlike many of his GI friends, he'd gone to work instead of to college, was a point that likewise failed to elicit his outspoken bitterness.
Though there were no more ticker tape parades, patriotism was still an
inviolate sentiment in 1951, and Robbins was a man of his generation,
accepting his privilege to disagree but not to disobey.

And yet from the time he arrived at his Reserve Center in Charlotte, and even after he got to Korea, he found himself in the grip of foreboding. He'd had to scrape and hustle just to get his camera shop off the ground. Now he worried that in his absence his business would collapse, and his equipment and tools would be repossessed by the bank. He had a wife and a three-year-old, and another child on the way. His father was dead; his mother was old. He did not know how long this war would go on or if it was even a war. The generals called it "a police action," which suggested he was being sent over to handcuff folks or hand out speeding tickets, when in fact he knew full well it was just going to be more killing.

In spite of the jadedness creeping into his spirit, Robbins did not consider his sentiments political in nature. Over a decade would have to pass before Americans would begin burning up their draft cards in public for lesser grievances, and national sentiment would begin to swing in the opposite direction from sacrifice and duty. He tried to muster up old courageous feelings but all he could summon was a vague sense that he was being punished for his loyalty to his country.

Then again, there was the jet. The F-86 Sabre had nothing in common with the B-24 he'd flown in the last war. Her takeoff was smoother than the fur of a cat, her wings tapering to the razor width of a Ritz-Carlton sandwich. Her new curved design got her racing almost to the speed of sound. In the anterior of the cockpit was hidden a trio of computers that let her radar eye aim at targets at night or in bad weather. Instead of aiming at the enemy manually, all Robbins had to do was center the target, correct for mirror tilt, and wait for the Sabre's magic eye to supply range, deflection, and lead time, everything necessary for a good shot. If civilian life had taken the will of the warrior out of him, the jet was giving it back.

Officially, Robbins's squadron had been told they'd be flying against Korean and Chinese pilots. This was not so. It took Robbins two missions to understand what everyone knew: that the MiGs he was up against were being piloted by Russian aces who'd cut their teeth in the last war fighting the same enemy he had. In spite of the Sabre's advantages, the lighter MiGs could climb faster and escape at the first signs of a good fight. At a distance, their contrails were like the waving cape of a matador taunting a bull in an open arena, luring the F-86s deep into enemy territory, until the moment the MiGs dropped their noses and disappeared over the Manchurian horizon.

It was on Robbins's sixth patrol mission, while flying wingman to a young commanding officer and getting another good look at the snowy mountainous Korean terrain (no decent markers, and nowhere flat enough to land in a pinch), that he saw them: a dozen MiGs speeding southward to where the American fighter-bombers were carrying out low-key operations against the communist communication lines. A cold moon was fading in one corner of the sky while the sun in the other made the Yalu River flash like a mirror.

Robbins did not have time to be surprised about what happened next. Ignoring the numerical superiority of the MiGs, the lead pilot, a twenty-five-year-old wild buck from Idaho, did then what might be described, in a history text or an obituary, with words like "indomitable valor" or "heroic spirit against formidable odds," but which Robbins might have called, had he had time to think of any words while he turned the velvety controls to follow, "pointlessly dooming vanity."

COLONEL TIMUR KACHAK WAS HAVING A BAD YEAR. A GEORGIAN OF IN-different, but not irrational, brutality, Kachak considered his appointment to the top security post of Perm—made up of 150-odd labor camps near the Siberian border—a vicious insult. He had worked as a detective in the Cheka before being cherry-picked by Beria for interrogation work. He was not, in his own opinion, a dumb fuck who could be relegated overnight to being a glorified security guard in an Arctic wasteland from which nobody could escape if they were stupid enough to try.

Kachak (previously Kachakhidze) was one of Beria's boys—recruited and groomed by Lavrenti himself. But Beria had fallen out of grace. Stalin had appointed Abakumov, another member of the Georgian Mafia, to curb Beria's power. Now a battle for control was raging inside the secret police. An upstart by the name of Ryumin had bypassed both Beria and Abakumov and gone directly to Stalin with the report of something called the Jewish Doctors' Plot—an expediently ingenious concoction that was certain to get Abakumov tried and brutally killed for "inaction." Kachak had been transferred to Perm while Beria waited for the smoke to clear and tried to rebuild his position; if there was going to be a purge of the old

guard, he needed a few of his men a good distance away from the guillo-
tine.

In Moscow, Kachak had had a three-room apartment overlooking
Chistiye Prudi and access to a second flat, where he met with informants
and screwed his girlfriends, one of whom was Abakumov's wife. This, he
believed, was the real reason he'd been sent to the end of nowhere. Now,
instead of seeing the Clean Ponds out of his window, he woke to the sight
of slag heaps and coal mines, enjoyed three hours of sunlight a day, and
supervised men outfitted only slightly better than the slave-prisoners they
were mandated to guard.

The call came from Beria himself. A Sabrejet pilot had crash-landed
near the Yellow Sea but had eluded capture by poisoning himself inside his
cockpit. A hundred Chinamen had been conscripted to haul the plane out
of the water, saw off its wings, and, under the cover of an overcast night sky,
roll the wingless aircraft to a control center, where it was dismantled further
and loaded in pieces onto a convoy. Now, the security organs believed, another American F-86 pilot had been sent as a prisoner to one of Kachak's
labor camps. Kachak's job was to find him and send him to Moscow. Kachak
watched the sun setting outside his office window as he listened to Beria's
voice. It was 2:00 P.M. He smiled. "Do you think I know each *zek* personally?" he told his old boss over the phone. "We get three dead Americans a
week here. Let them come and search at the bottom of the mine shafts."

"I think you understand the consequence of this."

"If they wanted him so much, why didn't they bring him straight to
Moscow from Andong?"

"They didn't know the type of plane he was in."

"And now they do."

"The unit combed the hills and found parts. He'd been moved out by
then."

"So the military let him slip through their fingers. Why should *we* pay
for their mistake?"

"This isn't me you're jerking around, Timur—it's Koba himself. Stalin's ordered the jet transported in pieces to the MiG design bureau."

"Then what do those geniuses need the pilot for?"

"The dashboard is destroyed. Whoever was in there took a rock to the
controls before he did himself in. They'll need help reconstructing the
panels."

"So Koba has a plane without a pilot, and *we* might have a pilot without a plane. But let me ask you this. . . . If he told them nothing in Andong, what makes the MGB think he'll talk in Moscow?"

"What are you saying?"

"Nobody even knows if he's still alive. . . ."

"Paperwork says a shipment of Americans was sent through Vladivostok, then to you."

"*If* he's alive, let me work on him here."

"This isn't your specialty."

"I'll find a way."

CAPTAIN HENRY ROBBINS FIRST REFUSED TO TALK AND, LATER, TO EAT. The food brought by the guards to his cell remained untouched. After five days the American pilot lacked the strength to get up from his pallet and was carried to the interrogation room and tied to a chair. He knew from his army training that if one had no food it was still wise to keep one's body mobilized, to do calisthenics and massage the limbs, in order to delay muscular deterioration. But he was under the reign of a single goal now, and that was to die. Robbins did not expect his requests to be granted by the filthy Russians, but he continued to repeat them with an unremitting insistence calculated to infuriate his captors. Day and night had started to replace each other without his noticing. His chest pains and weak pulse he read as promising signs that death was nearby. What he had not counted on was the prolonged, creeping tow of time. The same feebleness that pinned him to his pallet made the minutes like hours, the hours like days. Time was an impossibly heavy stone raking him underneath it as it scraped on endlessly. Robbins was discovering the great cosmic mystery that only the dying know: the closer a man is to the moment of finality, the slower time's drag. This, his final test and torture.

HE'D BEEN PICKED UP still wearing his G-suit, a holster strapped around his thigh, his suit pockets now almost empty of the candies he'd packed and sealed with friction tape in the event he would ever need to pull the ejection lever and punch out of the plane. For three days, he'd crawled down the rocky path that snaked east along the shrub-covered mountain. He tried to follow his wrist compass southward but could not be sure if he was in North Korea or across the Chinese border. He knew one phrase in Korean, *nam amu jeongboga eobs-seubnida*, which he believed declared a refusal to answer any questions apart from name, rank, and serial number. But the faces of the men of the anti-aircraft artillery unit that greeted him when he reached the bottom of the mountain path were neither Korean nor Chinese. The pistol strapped to his thigh was there to protect him in case he ran across a predator or an enemy soldier. But when he saw their number, Robbins understood that the gun was issued to him for a much simpler end—one he'd been too cowardly to take.

ON THE EIGHTH DAY his jailers arrived bearing strange instruments. From his bed, Robbins caught a glimpse of murky liquid sloshing around in a deep dish. A man in a white coat held a rubber tube in his hand. The guards sat him up. A warfare of faces swarmed around him. They were trying to squeeze the hose into his mouth. With an incomprehensible store of strength, he reached for the tube, but they twisted his wrists behind his back and grabbed his head in an armlock to keep him from shaking it. The man in the white coat pinched his nose, forced his mouth open with a spoon. They would let him neither live nor die. He was handcuffed and tossed on his stomach. His pants were pulled down, and the hose bearing life-giving nutrients was wedged up his rectum. He relaxed his muscles and thought, *Let them*, and soon after felt the wet, stinging comfort of his first shit in a week.

Shortly afterward, the doctor returned with new implements. Robbins's lips were pulled back, and clamps like small stirrups were jammed between his molars, rotated up and down until his jaw could be pried open enough to slide in the gagging tube. Slowly, it was pushed down, like a fishing line being lowered by a child. Robbins felt himself gagging—a pain more violent than anything before. But the tube was undeterred by the spasms in his throat and stomach. Like a drowning man he drew in air through his nose; above him, the doctor's redshot face went black, like a cinder turning to ash.

When Robbins came to, many hours later, it was with a cramp in his guts and the disappointing sensation that he was still alive. He sensed he was not alone. Somebody was seated beside him on the berth. "Captain," he heard, in a voice clearly that of an American, and even more surprisingly, a woman. "I've brought you a little tea. It'll make you feel better."

THERE WERE NO THERMOMETERS IN PERM'S LOGGING CAMP ITSK-2. They weren't needed. You knew the temperature by the density of the mist, which began to form at forty degrees below zero. It hung suspended like a new element, one you drew in with the pain of a thousand tiny needles and exhaled with a moist rasp. At such low temperatures there was always the threat of frostbite: Moisture on the tip of the nose froze as soon as it touched the atmosphere. One did not dare urinate in the snow. The trickle from Florence's nose had been freezing over for a week now, and it was only November. She possessed no handkerchief or anything resembling one, and was forced to wipe it ceaselessly with the sleeve of her jacket while she steered her body behind the others along the now familiar four-kilometer path into the forest. Her regulation-issue rubber galoshes did nothing to protect her feet from the cold. Inside them, her toes were wrapped in rags tied with strips of other rags. The mug around her waist was a tin that had once contained Lend-Lease pork—SPAM—which the American allies had donated, along with grain and tractors, during the war. It had long lost its shape and been rubbed clean of the letters. It was her only possession and she guarded it fiercely.

Walking the packed-down snow, Florence hoped it might still be dark when they reached the clearing. Then they would be allowed to hold off sawing and go instead to gather dead branches for a bonfire, which would give her a chance to rest a bit and warm herself with a cup of hot melted snow. But the winter sun was already filling the space between the trees with its scarlet aura when they arrived.

As soon as she was in the woods with Inga, her partner, Florence again found her strength ebbing. The breakfast ration of watery porridge had sustained her only through the difficult walk. She tried not to think about the pain in her right foot, the ankle flesh swelling up against the rubber, blackening her vision with each step. It was like stepping on a bayonet with your heel.

Florence's job was to hold the box saw steady while Inga did the sawing. But even this proved an impossible task, since it required her, if nothing else, to keep both feet planted firmly on the ground. Inga's strength was at once a salvation and a malediction: it had kept Florence from slipping into the penal food category, but had forced her to keep up with Inga's movements even as her own muscles trembled. Inga's effort, diligent and tragic, reminded Florence of when she had first arrived in Perm and tried to work "honestly and conscientiously," in order to be rewarded with an extra food ration. Before long she'd come to understand that it was working toward the extra ration that would kill you—help starve you quicker on an extra four hundred grams a day. She had only survived her first winter in Perm thanks to their brigade leader, an old *kolkhoznitsa* who knew all the tricks and let them gather old timber, cut the winter before, to add to their incomplete norms, and taught Florence to stack her wood in loose piles that looked full from the outside. She'd manipulated the books to show full quotas until some higher-ups got wise to it and assigned them a new gang leader indifferent to their fortunes.

"You'll have to work faster than this," Inga said.

Florence felt dizzy. The nausea of hunger had been assailing her earlier and earlier each day since the pain in her leg had started. She smiled. "Work isn't a wolf. It won't run off into the woods." She'd heard this joke herself when she arrived, and now she repeated it. There was nothing new to say in this place.

Inga glared at her with her flat Estonian face, flushed with exasperated effort. None of the women in the brigade were "true" Russians, aside from a few who'd been ordered by the army to serve in the Nazi-occupied areas and, as a reward for their loyalty, were accused of being collaborators. They were referred to as "fascists," as were all the politicals indicted under Article 58, including Florence.

"Keep it steady," Inga warned.

Florence had come across only a handful of women who'd worked in the forests for more than two years—that was how long it took for the quotas to turn a convict into a corpse. This was Florence's second winter.

Fresh prisoners like Inga were shipped in seasonally to replenish the living corpses, and were themselves replaced the following winter. This knowledge slid across Florence's consciousness like a worn proverb; she could not find in herself the will to be either outraged or consoled by it.

The pain in her boot continued to slice into the thin meat of her leg. It cut deeper still. It refused to be ignored.

"What is it now?" said Inga.

"My leg. I can't move it."

"Which one?"

"It's probably the frostbite. But it's swelling."

"That don't swell. Let's see it."

"It's stuck in the boot."

"What do you mean, 'stuck'?" Inga glanced through the pine trunks toward the clearing, where a guard's cigarette smoke hung in a dirty gray cloud above the snow. She pulled the boot off while Florence sat on a log. Florence's torn footrags were caked with blood and pus from her frostbitten toe, but the pain was elsewhere. The middle-lower portion of her calf was purple.

"Holy mother!" She knew what it was before Inga said it. "That's a scurvy ulcer, it is."

For two weeks she had been touching the tenderness at night and praying it away. Now it was as hard as a winter apple. Florence pressed her finger into the bruised flesh. The white indentation remained and did not go away.

"You'll need a raw onion," said Inga.

"Where do I get that?"

"Put that thing back in the boot before you freeze."

"It doesn't fit. I told you. It's too swollen."

"Jesus. We'll need to cut the boot."

"My boot! I can't! What with?"

Inga walked deeper into the forest and returned with a sharp rock. She threw her coat on Florence's leg and split the rubber with the stone blade. It wasn't hard to slice; these boots were summer footwear. "It'll fit now. Then you can go to the infirmary."

"I've gone, I've gone. You don't get a bed unless you've got a 'septic' temperature."

Inga placed her rough naked hand on Florence's forehead and shook her head. "All you need is a raw onion. A raw potato will do fine. Drive off the scurvy."

But Florence had not spoken the full truth, which was that the female doctor had all but spat on her and told her she was lucky they were feeding her at the state's expense. The fifty-eighters didn't get beds.

IN THE AFTERNOON THE prisoners built two bonfires, one for themselves and another for the guards. Like primitives they stared in silence into the fire. The dribble from their noses hissed as it fell into the cinders. From a pocket she'd sewn into her jacket, Florence removed the remains of her morning's ration, forty grams of bread, frozen solid. She gnawed and sucked on the bread, then spat out a wad of bloody saliva on the snow. Her teeth were shaky in their gums. It was another sign. She didn't know where she would get a raw onion, or a raw potato. A simple, terrifying thought came into her head: the descent toward death was an escarpment drop to which she had finally been delivered. In a matter of weeks she would be one of the disgraced—too weak to keep her cap from being stolen off her head, indifferent to the lice that sucked her blood, abused for the amusements of the criminals, eating penal rations and searching for rotten scraps in the frozen-over urine behind the mess hall. She would enter the ranks of the "wicks"—those who'd come to the end of life's sorry candle.

In truth she had no desire to live, and yet she continued to go on living. She thought of nothing but food. According to an arithmetic only the mind of the starving has the will to pursue, she measured the distance to death in grams of black bread and pieces of herring floating in her soup. Once demonstrative and exuberant, she'd become a miser of movement, expending as little as possible of her energy, physical and mental. Living, Florence had come to understand, was only another habit. The most stubborn and difficult to break.

Animals survived because they possessed no memory. She too had made herself dead to the past. Here it was not hard to believe that her old life had never existed. If this sinister cold and weak fire was where all those previous lives had led her to, then they could not have been real, but only canceled dreams yearning for an expired god. Forgetting had always been her great talent. She had forgotten everything. Moscow. America. The voice of her thoughts was no longer English, for she no longer grappled with the sort of thoughts that required the tangle of language. From time to time she remembered that she had a son. This painful knowledge would burrow through the metastasized sheathing of her mind and settle there like a small hungry animal. Florence told herself that Yulik was being taken care of, well fed. She had been allowed to receive letters, in which he had written, "I am dressed appropriately for the season." She believed this, for it was her only comfort. Other times, the idea that she had a son who was alive somewhere was as remote to her as the thought of spring.

To forget meant to discard the future as well as the past.

The Perm winter had sucked her dry of all affection, had poisoned her soul with overwhelming indifference. She was conscious of this and powerless to alter it. It was, in its own narcotic way, a kind of spiritual peace.

AT SUNSET THEY MARCHED back to the camp with their tools. Less than a mile out one of the women in the group collapsed in the snow. She was an old, frail Armenian who had been in the brigade for only a few months. For the past week she'd had difficulty making herself understood, not because of her Caucasian inflections but because of her swollen tongue and dementia. She was believed to be suffering from pellagra, a vitamin deficiency that the *natsmen* of the warmer climates always fell prey to first. Florence and another prisoner were given the ignoble but not difficult task of carrying the Armenian back to the zone. By the time they arrived, she had no pulse.

The woman had slept on a berth below Florence's, and now Florence felt afflicted by the unfortunate circumstances of her death. Had the woman expired in the night in their barracks, Florence and the others would have contrived a way to arrange her body so that they could keep receiving her portion of bread for at least a day or two. The death had been a waste.

IN THE MORNING SHE was pulled out of roll call by the gang forewoman. "You're to see Scherbakov," she said in an amused tone that might have been sinister or congratulatory.

"Who's Scherbakov?"

"Who's Scherbakov? He's the commander of the guards, you imbecile." She pointed to the guard who was already there to escort her, his rifle barrel gleaming.

Fat Scherbakov sat at his desk when she arrived. With him was another man in uniform, slender and younger, whom he introduced as Lieutenant Something. (Florence's sheer amazement and fear at being called in made her forget his name as soon as it was spoken.) "Name, statute, date of birth," Scherbakov said, hardly looking at her. On the corner of his desk was a cup of tea in a saucer that held the rind of a slice of lemon. "Is she the one?" said the young lieutenant. He seemed disbelieving. The distaste on his face was more physical instinct than emotion, like pain or sleepiness. He took a handkerchief out of his pocket and drew it to his nose. "I'm not taking her like this. Send her to the bathhouse. Commandant Kachak doesn't like the smell of these convicts."

The lieutenant was waiting when she came out of the bath hut, wearing the same clothes she'd had on before, only damp now from the disinfection chamber and no more deloused. "Get in the truck." A guard threw back the canvas tarp from the pickup truck's bed.

"Where are you taking me?"

The lieutenant gave no sign of hearing her.

THE ICE ON THE ROAD was dirty and packed down. The desolate landscape was barely visible in the windblown snow. She sensed she was being driven in the direction of one of the main labor camps. Every five or ten kilometers a watchtower on stilts peered out through the fresh blizzard. It was like leaving one's planet and learning there were dozens more like it in the solar system, each with its own planetary rings of barbed wire. After a while, just north of a very large camp, the truck turned off the highway. They had entered the especially high-security zone known only to select guards as the Zone of Silence, so called because it held British and American soldiers captured in Korea, and even those kidnapped by the Soviets from divided Berlin. Florence, of course, did not know any of this. What she saw when the driver slowed the truck was a stone building that looked like a monastery. It had once been one. Converted by the Bolsheviks to a transit prison, the building had since become too small for that purpose and now served as the headquarters of the secret police for all the camps in the area of Molotov. Its frozen basement, once the monks' cells of the friary, was a gallery of interrogation rooms whose vaulted ceilings sucked up and sealed for eternity the wails of the condemned.

The room Florence was led to had a heavy wooden door with a low barred window used for observation by two guards. She was told to wait outside while the young lieutenant took his leave. She glanced through the bars. The creature inside the cell sat on a wooden chair in the center of the small room, wearing a dull and listless expression on his angular features. His shaved hair was growing back in a pale stubble. There was little time to look at him, as the lieutenant strode back with another man, a person of obviously higher rank, neatly uniformed and closely shaved, but with a crop of black hair sprouting from under his military blouse, open to the chest as though he were a Mediterranean lover. In this dank basement of a prison he carried with him a formidable odor of eau de cologne and real tobacco, of health, serenity, and contempt. A tetrad of brass knuckles glinted like jewelry on his hairy fist. This, no doubt, was Kachak, the commandant the lieutenant had spoken of earlier.

"This one will repeat what I say to the spy," he said, addressing a third man, who, in spite of the pulpy suit that hung from his bones, Florence immediately recognized as a prisoner-slave like herself. It took Florence a full moment, however, to realize that the commandant was speaking about *her*. "Yes, yes, yes," said the suited convict, eyeballing Florence curiously. His eyes glistened with the faithfulness of a beaten dog. This, Florence would soon learn, was Finkleman, a former "engineer-physicist" plucked from the bottomless jaws much like herself, called on to assist the Motherland one last time.

"*Nu, chto!*" the commandant barked at her. "You've forgotten Russian already?"

"I haven't," she denied, though every word roared at her today had been unintelligible in its suggestion of a turn of luck too good to be anything but another delusion. "You will repeat to the spy what I say in English. No more, no less," the commandant said. "If you don't understand his responses, explain to *him*." He meant the convict in the suit. In the convict's hand Florence glimpsed a sheaf of graph paper and the most prized of all possessions in the camps: the stub of a graphite pencil. An undercurrent in her mind was wondering how she might get her hands on the pencil stub and trade it among the criminal element for an onion or a pair of socks; she was fantasizing about this even as far greater riches were being dangled before her in the form of the spy, now slumped sideways like a cripple, with his hands roped to the chair he sat upon. The commandant opened the big door and led the two of them into the room, but it was only when he sat down across from the tied-up man and launched into an artillery of questions that the coma of Florence's astonishment was broken by a more frightening mental paralysis. "Tell us which controls on the gunsight supply the correct deflection for the radar eye," Kachak demanded, expecting her to translate. "Is this done by the pilot or by means of cybernetic feedback?" There seemed to be a touch of hysterical impatience in his voice, barely suppressed, as if he had already asked this inconceivable question a dozen times and was now only daring the half-dead man instead of questioning him. Florence could not comprehend, let alone translate, the question. The exertion of keeping the words together in her head brought on a hunger-nausea as vicious as when she had marched half starved in the snow. But there was only one way forward. She had believed that, in her almost two years in the camp, she'd driven English out of her memory, along with everything else. But here it was, emerging from the thawing permafrost of her frozen brain.

"The commandant would like to know about a radar eye," she said, too fearful to ask what a radar eye was. With ridiculous courtesy, she inquired about the "air-to-ground shooting range" and the "autopilot program." But none of this prompted the most basic acknowledgment from the prisoner. She was starting to grasp the situation, which was not turning in her favor. "Does he really understand English?" she said, turning to the withered engineer-physicist, the one person in the cell she felt entitled to address with such a doubt. It was then that the prisoner opened his mouth and spoke as might a wind-up toy: "United States Air Force Cap'n Henry Robbins. I request that my government be notified of my status as a Prisoner of War in the Sof-yut Union. I thereto request to be returned to the company of my fellow officers in captiv'ty."

And once more he was silent, as though he hadn't spoken at all.

Speechless, she felt the white scorch of his words singeing into her consciousness. *Prisoner of war?* What war? The last one? That would mean he had been in captivity longer than she had—at least five years! But how could that be? Why would an *American* be a prisoner of war—hadn't they been fighting on the same side? And what of his request to be reunited with his fellow officers? How many others were there? She was now entering her second winter in Perm and had heard nothing about any captured Americans. Florence now felt seasick, as she would feel once more almost thirty years later, stepping off the chartered plane at JFK Airport, the sensation of having come unmoored in the dimension of time, of having been sealed away while the world had sped on without her.

She quickly launched into a translation of Captain Robbins's request. But Kachak needed no help comprehending it. Before she was through, his metal knuckles struck the side of Robbins's cheek, making the prisoner's head twist on his neck like a ribbon around a maypole. "No requests granted to spies," he said and removed a handkerchief from his pocket to wipe the blood off his fingers.

SHE WAS GIVEN DINNER: A FULL BOWL OF THICK PEA PORRIDGE AND half a loaf—almost six hundred grams—of bread, baked so recently that it had not yet turned to stone. It all but melted in her mouth and was gone before she'd even gotten used to the spongy taste. Afterward she was led through to another part of the monastery, where the commandant had his office.

"Sit," he told her. He himself remained standing, gazing through the frost-shaggy window while he smoked. The sky had acquired the carmine aura of premature evening. Florence could feel blood pulsing in her leg. She had dragged it behind her like a rotted hoe. She was appalled at her body's lack of gratitude. Here she was, out of the biting cold for the first time, and what had the abscess done but use the respite to blossom into glory! It throbbed viciously, in sudden rivets of pain.

"You will speak to nobody about today," the commandant said finally, turning to face her. "You will not mention it to prisoners or anyone in the administration of your camp."

Florence said she understood.

He ground his cigarette out on a saucer on his desk. "Even in a task like this you are entirely replaceable. Remember that."

Florence listened as the commandant spoke about the importance of secrecy when dealing with captured spies. And still, she remembered that the man had said he was a POW. She noted that Kachak was no longer wearing his brass knuckles.

"What is it?" said Kachak.

Only then did she realize that her mouth was open. She had no idea what she'd meant to say. Her only thought now was to ask him to obtain for her a raw onion, or potato, or a lemon—anything for her scurvy. But to bring up something so beggarly with the commandant would show her as homely and ill-bred. It would suggest she did not appreciate the significance of the topic at hand. And then there was this: If she admitted to being sick, would he find someone to replace her with immediately?

"Well!"

"Where shall I say I go?" she blurted.

"What?"

"What do I do when I leave the camp? I need a story."

Kachak rapped the nail of his middle finger on the desk. Was it possible he had not thought through this far? "You've been assigned to a mineral prospecting team," he said finally, "because of your training in geology. The rest is classified."

THE YOUNG LIEUTENANT USHERED her out. The truck was waiting in the snowy road, and, seeing it, she knew the terrible mistake she'd made. Her frostbitten cheeks and fingers began to throb, as did the toes wrapped in her threadbare footrags. She was being returned to hunger, to the coldness of the barracks, the boot kicks of the guards. The thought made the ache in her leg seize up in a spasm.

"Get moving," said the lieutenant, who was walking behind her.

Her leg could not move.

"Go on!"

She was an animal, trapped, and now only the instincts of an animal could point to a way out. She let herself fall like a beast into the snow.

"Get up!"

"I'm unable!"

She waited for the lieutenant to kick her, and when he didn't, she undid her boot as quickly as she could and pulled up her pant leg. His face winced at the sight of her flesh. In the dimming light, her leg looked fully blue. "It's atrophied," she pleaded.

"You can settle it when you get to your camp. Go to the infirmary."

"The nurse won't give me a bed."

"Nonsense. Get up!"

"They don't give beds to politicals. Unless it's a quarantine. You know that."

"So—what do you want me to do? Take it up with your authorities."

"I beg you. Keep me nearby. A day or two. Once I get a septic fever I'll be of no use to you, or to your commandant. I'll get the prisoner to talk. I can."

"Keep your voice down, you louse," he said. And then: "Don't leave this spot!"

The cold snow burned her cheek. She shut her lids and it gave way under her body like a down comforter.

FLORENCE AWOKE AT DAWN on a real cot, in a hospital room with white-painted window frames. Her clothes were nowhere in sight. The flannel gown on her body was so thin and worn that it looked transparent in the cold light. Somebody must have changed her. She tried to rouse up some feeling of shame, but that too had long been driven out of her. All she could conjure was a dim memory of voices during the night.

Take her to the fourth ward.

No. Upstairs. He doesn't want her near the criminals.

She's a hag.

They'll screw a hundred-year-old crone if you let 'em. She touched her leg. Someone had bandaged it tightly. Her fatigue was more powerful than the pain. She curled herself around the pillow like a sea creature and fell asleep.

FOR THE NEXT THREE DAYS she stayed in the main camp's infirmary and was taken out during the day to assist with the interrogation of the pilot. Each day Robbins was asked anew about radars and gunsights, and each time he gave the same responses—requesting that his government be notified of his status as a POW, and that he be reunited with his fellow officers inside the camp. Her only contribution to the interrogation was to make out from his slurring, Southern-inflected speech the same repeated request, which became less intelligible by the day.

Florence had gathered from the chatter of the guards that Robbins had commenced on a hunger strike—that he was refusing to eat as well as to talk. She marveled at the dying man's fierce will to let go of his last grasp on life. Having herself resolved to end her life many times, she knew that carrying out a plan to die—even in death's own chamber—was not as easy as promised. Some small bit of joy or fortune—a sudden warming of the weather, the arrival of a letter from the orphanage—could undercut one's will to end it all. She had seen fellow prisoners swallow too much snow in order to make themselves bloated and sick. Engineer nosebleeds. Rub dirt into a sore to get blood poisoning and spike their temperature to a fever. Urinate on their hands and feet to catch frostbite. But none of these inducements of illness was performed with the wish of dying. The aim was always to obtain admission to the hospital for some desperately needed rest. Self-mutilation was self-preservation. Few had the courage for the real thing. What little thought camp life had not driven from the mind was subordinated entirely to a dogged clinging to life.

With Robbins it was the opposite—he'd become wise to the authorities' desire to keep him alive, and so bedeviled them by trying to die. For some period of time each afternoon Florence stood peeking through the barred window of Robbins's cell as Kachak bent over him, whispering menacingly or shouting threats. Each day the man in the chair became even more of a fragile ghost, his reddish hair growing longer as his graying skin hung looser on his bones. Like an old man's, Florence thought, though he was obviously young. Her only hope now was that he would not die. If he did, she would be sent back to general labor in the women's camp, sent back to toil and deteriorate and meet, at last, her own end.

In a small upstairs ward of the infirmary, she was allowed to lie prone all day. On the fourth day of her stay she discovered, with some amazement, that her leg was improving. There was real herring in her soup instead of just fish bones. On that and a mere bowl of cereal the body could begin to revive itself, as long as it did not have to be sent to work. Twice inside her loaf of black bread she had found, hidden like a coin, a hard, sour pill of vitamin C. It had been hidden there by the camp doctor (himself a prisoner), the same one who had rescued Robbins by prying open his jaw and working a rubber tube down into his stomach. Florence would not know about these force-feedings until they were over. For four days, she would live in limbo, neither called into interrogations nor sent back to the women's camp. It was on the fourth and final day of this stretch that the doctor came to alert her that he was certain of bad news. Robbins's health was worsening; he was slipping in and out of consciousness. His throat and stomach had continued to react to the force-feedings with convulsive spasms, and he had begun spitting up blood. The doctor slipped Florence a vial of amber liquid. She was not, he advised, to trade or sell it for anything back at her camp. She understood this to mean he expected her to be sent back any day. The liquid was a vitamin-filled syrup. Florence was speechless as she held it. The doctor had acted toward her with more kindness than she thought imaginable in a place like this. Surely, she could not ask more.

And yet she had to. The vitamin elixir, as precious as life itself, would not save her. She would have to sell it the very first day and use the money to buy bread. If she held on to it, it would get thieved immediately. One of the criminals would knock her over the head and rob her on the first day she was back.

She looked into the doctor's pitying eyes. They reflected what he saw: a haggard, reduced "wick," her face covered in blood clots, her skin bitten by lice. Florence had known this moment would come; she'd planned to throw herself at the doctor's mercy, offer herself up as an orderly who could clean latrines and mop blood, do anything if it meant she could extend her stay a bit longer. But looking into his eyes she understood that such imploring was useless and completely idiotic. He had no jurisdiction over her. If she wanted to live she had to appeal to a higher force. Not God. The only god who reigned here was the cannibal god of human sacrifice, the black beating heart of the monstrous machine that had started devouring her years ago. Only from such a god, she thought desolately, could she ever seek her salvation. No sooner did she think this than she felt a flash of light showing her a way through the darkness. She gripped the syrup and gazed at the doctor. The idea she had to sell him was, after all, in his favor.

Even as she uttered it, Florence did not really believe she was proposing the things that came out of her mouth. Yet the doctor listened.

HOW HAD SHE PULLED IT OFF? SHE HAD CONVINCED THE DOCTOR, AND he, in his turn, had convinced the commandant. "So you want to worm the hook yourself, eh?" Kachak said, before the door to Robbins's cell was opened for her. "Well, why the devil not?" He spoke in a voice of pure satire. The force-feedings had become a burlesque. The smile on Kachak's face looked, to Florence, slightly deranged. He had been drinking. Maybe he thought he had little to lose.

She sat down beside Robbins's cot with a tray in her lap. She didn't look toward the grate in the door, but was distressfully aware of the commandant's eyes observing her. What she had proposed would have been the highest order of impertinence coming from her mouth; the doctor had presented it as his own idea, telling Kachak, "He won't take the food from the guards, or any of us. He won't touch it if we're even in the room." She, a fellow countryman, would bring it to him, persuade him to take some bites. Now she turned to Robbins's back and spoke. "Captain—I've brought you a little tea. It'll make you feel better."

He lay turned away, facing the wall.

"There's a nice bowl of fish soup here for you, with barley. Maybe you'd like some bread?" The tray had two slices of actual white bread, something she didn't believe existed in the zone. "I promise I won't try to make you talk," she said. She glanced toward the barred window. "Unless you want to. You can probably say anything you like here—to be honest, I don't think the commandant understands a word you say."

She stared at his scrub of reddish stubble. She felt she was talking to a dead body. Or to herself. This was insane.

"You're from the South."

No answer.

"Yes, I could hear it in your voice earlier. Georgia? Alabama?"

Nothing.

"I know this isn't bacon or collards." She tried to make her voice lilt. "But you're getting a feast by any measure of ours. I wouldn't pass it up if I were—"

Before she could finish, he'd lifted his arm and with whiplash speed delivered a swift strike that sent the enamel bowl of soup flying off her tray. It hit the floor with a crash and metallic ping; its contents splashed on the wall. A piece of herring lay on the floor, not far from her foot. She glanced backward at the little barred window. Kachak was not visible, but a guard stood in a posture suggesting readiness to put an end to the whole experiment. Florence raised a palm to indicate there was no need for distress.

She breathed through her mouth to collect herself. "The farthest south I've ever been was Washington. I'm from Detroit myself," she lied. "That was a long time ago, of course. Funny, you always think you'll come back home." Gently, she placed her fingers on the back of his shoulder. "You need to eat, Mr. Robbins. Or they'll come and pry your cheeks open again. I don't think you want that."

"You don't know what I want."

She seized up. His voice was no more than a coarse whisper.

"You're right. I don't know," she said.

"I got no business with traitors," Robbins said, louder this time, but still without looking at her.

"That's where you're wrong, Captain. Neither of us is here on our own recognizance." The story she told him then was one she'd told before. Her daddy had been a bootlegger during Prohibition. Being a stubborn man, and a greedy one, he never got with the county program by letting the police in on a cut of his profits. He was arrested and sentenced to an unjust term, but somehow managed to escape with the aid of his criminal friends. He'd been born in Russia, and was given citizenship on his return here, before calling for his wife and daughter to join him. "I was nothing but a babe. Turned seventeen on the ship," Florence said. This story had served her well. She'd concocted it in prison, where she'd quickly wised up to the fact that the most reviled and punished group—among not just prisoners but also warders and interrogators—were the true believers. A special contempt was reserved for these earnest adherents, always the first to lose their grip on reality and start scratching at the walls. To admit that *she* had come to Russia voluntarily, out of political sympathies, would have been as suicidal as admitting she'd worked for the secret police. The truth was so ludicrous, Florence couldn't even believe it herself anymore.

"My daddy used to say he wished he'd stayed in prison in America," she now said to the prostrate body beside her. "Would've been no different than here, except with better food."

He made a noise that sounded like a grunt. Or was it a laugh? Florence looked down at the tray. The bread was still there, and the sugared tea, getting cold. "Well, Mr. Robbins. If you're not going to touch this sumptuous meal, I might have to. Even if they do accuse me of being in cahoots with a real live spy."

"I ain't any kind of spy. I am an air force officer."

He'd spoken in a quiet but resolute tone of voice. Florence looked at the spot where his skeletal shoulder suggested itself through his tunic shirt. "Then how did you get here?"

He turned, rolling slightly over on his pallet. His eyes were gray-blue and redshot. They burned with rage. "How'd I get here? You playing me for a fool, lady? There's a war on."

Her eyes widened. It was true, then.

"So it's happened? America has dropped the bomb at last," she whispered. "Oh mercy."

Robbins studied her for a moment—some kind of mordant delight dancing in his eyes. Florence sensed they were reacting to something in her face, some magisterial ignorance on her part.

"Shit—you really don't have any idea, do you?"

She stared at him.

And for the first time that she'd seen, he laughed, helplessly, each gasp swallowing up the next as if he were struggling for air.

SHE'D BEEN LED OUT BY THE GUARD THEN, BUT SHE LEARNED FROM THE doctor that, except for the overturned soup, Robbins had eaten what she'd brought him. So the commandant, in spite of himself, was persuaded to let Florence back in the following day instead of the force-feeding team. Unbeknownst to her, Robbins had refused to touch any food unless she brought it. Though giving in to such a request caused the commandant inexpressible indignity, he had no choice. Florence had no way of knowing this, but Kachak had already taken a great personal risk in not handing the pilot over to MGB headquarters in Moscow. Beria would look the other way only as long as it served him. And if Kachak produced no results or, worse yet, let the man die on his watch, his earlier "insubordination" would be rapidly uncovered, and his exile in Perm, such as it was, would last a very long time indeed. Or be served out on the other side of the barbed-wire fence. Such things were known to happen.

Kachak had taken this gamble knowingly. In Moscow he'd tortured confessions out of hundreds of people. But this was different—not the usual "stitch work" of writing up the right version beforehand and having the prisoner corroborate it while his fingernails were being pulled off. Getting a *real* confession—real *intelligence*—now, that was a more delicate operation. Kachak had no idea what he was hoping to find; he didn't know a thing about gyros or radars or optics. Whatever the pilot confessed would have to be intelligible to the brains up at the MiG Aviation Design Bureau, with their plagiaristic lust for the F-86's technology. It would have to be solid, verifiable, not the usual bullshit. Kachak didn't approve of this Robbins, lying on his cot like a dying king and giving *him* orders. But he'd have to stick to soft tactics until the time came again for hard ones.

Inside his monk's cell, Robbins allowed himself to be fed by the old woman's hand. Spooning pea porridge into his mouth, Florence could not prevent herself from staring at the prisoner's bristle-covered chewing cheeks, the rise and fall of his Adam's apple as he swallowed. It was the cruel irony of recovery that the more she herself was fed at the infirmary, the more she wanted to eat.

"How old are you anyhow?" Robbins said, as if he'd been holding the question in for a while.

"Forty-one."

His face got cloudy. He didn't try to suppress his shock. Florence tried to guess from his expression how old he'd thought she was. Fifty? Maybe sixty.

"Jeez." He was looking at her hands, their gray scaly skin. The blistered, frostbitten tips of her middle and ring fingers had darkened and thickened while she'd been at the infirmary. She still had some trouble bending them. "What've they got you doing?"

"Sawing trees in the forest, most of the time. Carrying wood."

"You don't look like you could pull a twig."

Florence shrugged.

"And you mean you really didn't know about this war?"

"I hardly know what month it is."

"Well, it ain't like a real war anyway, more like a knife fight where you'll swipe at your opponent's arms and legs all day without being allowed to stab him in the vitals."

She did not exactly understand what he meant. Robbins still sounded delirious from his exhaustion and depletion. Florence glanced toward the bars in the door. The guard wasn't visible. "You said there were other American officers with you . . . ," she whispered.

"Five of us. Two other guys from Korea. Two from East Berlin. They were stationed there. Not POWs like us—kidnapped by your secret police. One guy they just picked up in a bar in the eastern zone, visiting his girl. Stuffed him in a car, and that was it for him. They claim we're all spies. It's against every international law. POWs they're supposed to declare to our countries. But no one knows we're here."

She scraped up the last spoonful of porridge and fed it to him. "The commandant won't allow me to meet with you alone for much longer, Captain."

"It's Henry."

"I need to tell him something."

"You can tell him I got nothing to say to him until my government is informed of my status as a Prisoner of War in the U.S.S.R."

"SUGAR?"

"Please." She was stunned to be sitting across the desk from Kachak, to have him offering her tea.

"How many teaspoons?"

"Two," she said, just as though she were back at home.

He had a meaty, striking if not exactly handsome face. His shirt was buttoned up to the neck this time.

"You've made progress."

Florence couldn't tell if this was a question or praise. "Yes," she said. "He's been eating. In a few days, I believe he'll have much of his strength back."

"We'll resume questioning tomorrow."

"No." She'd spoken before she could stop herself.

Kachak blinked. "No?"

"I only mean," she corrected, "I don't think he'll give in under strain. He hasn't before. And he still insists that his request to alert the American government be carried out."

"I see," said Kachak. "So he's found himself an advocate."

She felt her two frostbitten fingertips begin to throb. Or was it only her fear? "I am nothing more than an interpreter," she said.

"Is that what you are?" He was staring at her, one of his abundant eyebrows lifted challengingly. He slid a cigarette from his front pocket without taking out the pack and lit it. "I have a *dozen* interpreters here. I have enough Ivan Ivanoviches to translate all of Shakespeare." He took a small drag to get the cherry glow going, then let the smoke out silently through his nose. His eyes were not telling her what he had; they were asking what *she* had.

And still she had nothing.

Or did she?

She had once, so long ago, studied mathematics, logic. All she'd retained from that now was a single insight: a negative outcome could be as useful to a problem as a positive one. Florence experienced this knowledge so fleetingly she did not even recognize it as a thought. But she said to Kachak: "It seems to me that Robbins's conditions have changed. It's true that his request to have his government alerted remains unaltered, but he is no longer asking to be reunited with the other Americans."

Kachak let the smoke drift out of his mouth and nose. He was listening. "He is in no position to be making *any* demands."

"Perhaps not. But I suspect his earlier request to be reunited with his fellow officers had to do with his isolation. Solitary confinement will make a man desperate for any contact with human beings."

"And what do you suggest?"

"Just to keep him talking . . ."

"With you?"

"Yes, for the time being. He badly wants someone to talk to. I sense this."

Kachak gazed up into the vaulted ceiling and smiled. " 'And the woman said, The serpent beguiled me, and I did eat. . . .' "

He gave her until the end of the week.

HER ASSOCIATION WITH THE CRIMINAL WORLD—EVEN IF IT WAS THE imaginary criminal world of America—had been useful in the camp, too. She was, of course, still a "fascist," but when word got around that she was a bootlegger's daughter, she was told to come to the barracks occupied by the *blatnye*, where the criminal women reclined on their bunks, undressed to their dirty bras in a barracks made cozily warm by fires or stoves stoked regularly by their court of prisoner-lackeys—civils or politicals like herself—who served the criminals' every whim in exchange for a crust of bread or some protection. She was asked if she'd ever met Bonnie Parker. Or seen Al Capone. Somehow, the legends of these felons had made their way here without losing any of their glamour. She admitted frankly that she'd never seen any of these criminals face-to-face but related the stories she'd read in the papers, describing the string of heists and murders pulled off by Bonnie and Clyde as they darted around the country in stolen cars. With as much detail as Florence could recall after twenty years, she retold of the bloody battles between the Italian gangs of Capone and the Irish gangs of Bugs Moran, and how Capone's men, luring the Irish crew to a warehouse full of cut-rate Canadian whiskey, unleashed a hail of bullets and then escaped in the guise of policemen—staging the massacre on the American holiday celebrating love.

After that, she was invited back to tell them about other gangsters, John Dillinger and Baby Face Nelson. The half-undressed *dyevka*s listened while they slapped cards on their greasy pillows or picked lice out of their armpits like monkeys and tossed them to crackle in the fire. The guards, tenderly or sardonically, called them "girls," and some of them indeed had the bodies of girls, and the faces of old women. They'd sometimes interrupt Florence's stories with profanity-laced commentary of their own, spoken in shouts, of which Florence understood hardly a word. Outside, she was more or less left alone, for she had entered the dubious ranks of the camp's "novelists"—the ones who entertained the criminals with recitations of the great classics, Dumas or Dostoyevsky. In her case, though, the "novels" were really double features she had seen years ago, with Sidney, at the Brooklyn Paramount or the RKO Albee—*Tarzan, Mantrap, Flesh and the Devil, The Public Enemy*—gangster films and sappy romances that the criminals ate up in equal measure. Half the time she had to improvise the plot, composing the script as she went along, just as she was doing now with Robbins and Kachak, adding colorful touches that might entertain or please in the moment.

When she wasn't with Robbins, Florence stayed in the infirmary, firing the stoves, washing latrines, swabbing blood from the floor—the privileged, easy duties she would never have been given in the women's camp. She was almost sure that once they'd used her up as a translator, they would pin another ten years on her for "fraternizing with the enemy." Or simply shoot her. She did not care. As long as she was kept in soft work and fed eight hundred grams of bread a day, with some soup and fish on the side, as long as she could stay warm and not be out in the frozen woods, she would do whatever was asked.

"YOU'RE LOOKING FINE, MISS FEIN," Robbins said unexpectedly almost two weeks later. He knew her by her maiden name. "Got a little color back in your cheeks."

Florence could feel her forehead flush. She had an urge to tell him it was all thanks to him. He had bought her a month of life, at least. Instead, she said, "You didn't tell me how old you were."

"I'm thirty-four. Maybe thirty-five by now. Hard to tick off time where there ain't no calendars or windows."

"Not so young for your common air force pilot."

"Oh, I see what you're thinking. They told you I'm a spy. Well, I ain't no more a spy than you are a lumberjack. It's not my first barbecue, is all."

"You were a flyer in the last war?"

"The 254th Fighter Division," Robbins said with some pride. He was cleaning out the remains of his bowl with the bread, strong enough to eat on his own now.

"Must have really liked all that fighting to volunteer again," she said.

"Who said I volunteered?"

"Didn't you?"

"I was a reservist. Would be out for good by now if I'd read the fine print. . . . Just never thought we'd get into a new conflict this soon."

This was something. So the patriot had a bone to pick with Uncle Sam, after all. Florence probed this sore. "*That* doesn't sound quite fair. . . ."

"Fair's a place where pigs win ribbons."

She had heard such sentiments before. Robbins had marched willingly, but not happily. This gave her hope. The hope felt like a valuable gemstone she had discovered in her pocket and was now secretly keeping warm.

After a while, Robbins said, "Anyway, when it's all over, if the communists or anyone else learns they can't git away with invadin' and takin' over another country, then some good will have come out of it all."

She arranged her face into a likeness of kindness. "Does it make it easier to believe that?"

"What?"

"That America believes in the freedom of other nations to determine their own destinies? Because, if it does, well"—she smiled disarmingly—"then it believes in such a freedom selectively. Manila? Mexico? Hawaii, for that matter?"

She herself believed only selectively in what she was saying. Long ago, she'd stopped caring about politics, and now her words sounded only like echoes of some ghost of her prior self. Still, she sensed that Robbins was tired of suffering, that he only needed permission to put aside his obedience and duty. She would give that to him. "I'm not convinced that the lives and futures of young men like yourself," she said, "have been forfeited for any reason other than to bring glory and profits to the few. And I don't think you're convinced of it, either."

The captain appeared to be weighing what she'd said. "My, my," he said finally. "Aren't you well informed?" His missing teeth gave him a sinister smile. "How's that worked out for you, being so well informed?"

She could think of nothing to say.

"I don't know what kind of religion you're trying to peddle, Miss Fein, but I've heard better pastoring from a two-day drunk preacher."

He thought she was ridiculous. Of course he did.

"Here's a little more information for you," Robbins said. "America's got no interest in some squalid, insignificant scrap of Asia called Korea. We're in this mess on account of your Soviets having the A-bomb now. Didn't know that, did you? Yup. A few things have changed since you got here, Sleeping Beauty. Ain't you curious how the Russians got their hands on it? 'Course you are. A couple of clever Yankee Yids like yourself—husband-and-wife duo—sold 'em the recipe for a bag of magic beans. Thought they'd balance the scales. And now here you and me are. So how's about you take your red mouthwash and sell it somewhere else."

WHAT AN IDIOT SHE'D been. What a *stupe*, with her phony indoctrination session, as though he were some adolescent YCL-er. As soon as she arrived in the Zone of Silence, she knew she could afford no errors, and now it had been four days since she'd been called to see Robbins.

Don't let them send me back. Please, don't let them. . . . Her own childish pleas to the fates ran in her mind all the time now. What a fraud she was. All her life she'd been praying in this scattered hectic way in spite of her total lack of belief. *Why have you plucked me from the abyss only to throw me back in again?* From the gutters of memory she was recovering lost prayers of her childhood. *Barukh atah Adonai Eloheinu, melekh ha'olam, hagomel lahayavim tovot, sheg'molani kol tov.* But such prayers for her were not the language of faith or aspiration, they were the cry of a trapped beast. At night, awake in the agitating lunar light, she could hear her heart raising its muzzle to the moon to release its high-pitched wail.

If she could only be pardoned for all she had done . . .

FLORENCE DID NOT KNOW about the phone calls being made, back and forth, between Kachak and Beria. Nor could she have known that the unmarked train bearing the partially shattered and disassembled F-86 Sabrejet was nearing Moscow. She could not have suspected, as yet, Kachak's growing desperation to wring some valuable information from Robbins before he would be obliged to hand the pilot over to his seniors in Moscow.

And so it happened that when Kachak did again call Florence into the interrogation room, the sudden shift in his offer and tone struck her as some sort of supernatural turn of events. "Tell him I am planning to send him to Moscow," he told Florence, who sat, along with Kachak, at the table facing the silent Robbins. "I am quite through with wringing water from this stone. I trust"—he turned to Robbins—"that my fellows in the Lubyanka will have more success with you."

Obediently, Florence translated. Robbins could not know what the Lubyanka Prison was, and she had no opportunity to tell him now, exactly. Florence sensed Kachak's message was intended for her as much as for Robbins.

"You ought to know, however, that if you expect kinder treatment at their hands than you've had here, you're quite mistaken. This is a children's park compared to the handling you'll receive there."

Again, she translated. It produced no response in Robbins.

"You'd be wrong to think it gratifies me to hand you over into less merciful hands. You could say I've even come to admire your . . . tenacity. It will not serve you, of course. In keeping you here I have tried to spare you the worst that you are bound to encounter. I've never been partial to the tortures and sadistic habits the Mongols introduced into the Russian temperament." He paused, giving Florence an opportunity to convey all this. She fully expected Kachak to go on and describe which Mongol tortures Robbins could look forward to, but he didn't, trusting Robbins to imagine them.

"If you persist in being silent on the matter of the F-86, that is your business. You are no longer my responsibility. If, however, you decide to come to a realistic understanding of your situation and give me what I am after"—he now turned to Florence as though what he had to offer up next had to be mediated across a bridge firmer than mere language—"then I will personally advocate for him. He will get an apartment. Medical care. *If* this information proves to be worthwhile, arrangements can be made. A new identity. He can even teach at our Air Force Academy—air battle techniques, tactics—the MVD could open those doors."

His tone was gamely and (she thought this later) alarmingly accommodating, as though Kachak could not quite believe he was saying these things himself. Florence interpreted to the best of her ability.

Then Robbins spoke: "All right, then why not ship me on to Moscow tonight?"

It was a taunt. A dangerous one. She had no wish to translate it for the commandant, whose offers had the scent of desperation. Robbins could smell it just as well as she. But there was more to Florence's hesitancy: She did not want Robbins sent to Moscow; with him would be gone her only hope of staying out of the ravages of the camp.

In the end she did not have to translate; Kachak understood the gist quite easily himself. He said, "It isn't so simple. He must show he is serious. Give me information I can verify with experts. Then I will give my word."

The commandant told Robbins to think it over. A new life, if he wanted it.

But the following morning, having "thought it over," Robbins put in a request to speak not with Kachak but with Florence, alone.

THIS TIME KACHAK DID not offer Florence tea.

"You've had quite a vacation, haven't you?"

"I'm grateful with all my being to be of any use to you, Commandant."

"So you are." He stood up to take in the view of the soiled, muddied snow outside. There were rocks in the courtyard of the monastery, pieces of a fallen wall. Florence could see the spot where she had first fallen, deliberately, in front of the truck set to take her back to the women's camp. "I loathe this place." He spoke as though to himself. "Kolyma would have been better. The ground is frozen solid all year round there too, but the question of what to do with all these bodies wouldn't be so irritating. There would be the mine shafts."

She realized that by "bodies" he meant corpses.

"Abandoned mine shafts—perfectly suited for disposing of the dead. Here the pits get filled up as soon as they're dug. I've been saddled with undertaker's work. It's quite dreary."

His complaint was strategic. She had become used to Kachak's bruised, flamboyant air. It occurred to her that he would not have been a bad stage actor, though this thought made Florence no less frightened of him. He turned around to face her. "I expect the right answer from Robbins. Do you understand?"

She gave a weak nod.

"I've given you ample opportunities to appeal to his reason," he said now very straightforwardly. "And you have shown yourself less ingenious than promised. Or should I say, less committed to your persuasion of him than of me?" There was a rich hint of whiskey on his breath.

"That isn't so. I have tried. I *am* trying!"

"It isn't only the dead, you know, that we throw into shafts! Ours may not be as deep as Kolyma's, but no one's yet plowed themselves out with two broken arms!"

Her eyes had welled up. She was weeping, shamelessly, disastrously.

"Stop your blubbering!"

There was no handkerchief to speak of. She did not want him to see her wiping her nose with her sleeve. "I will try harder," she said, nodding frantically, servilely.

But it was not the threat of dying with her arms broken atop a pit of corpses that had sent her into hysterics. It was something she could hardly acknowledge without exploding into more waterworks: she would *never* be done with this torment. Until her last gasp she would be appeasing, informing, cajoling, betraying, acceding to whatever nasty and impossible demands they gave her next. All she had ever wanted in her life was to breathe her own air! And all she had gotten in return was enslavement. Because she was not like Robbins. Because she lacked the courage of refusal—the price to be paid for true freedom.

"Enough!" Kachak said. "Go. You know what your job is."

WHEN SHE WAS LED IN, Robbins was lying on his back, looking up into the ceiling. The stone bricks, Florence noticed, got smaller and narrower as they rose up the wall, and were thinnest along the vaults of the ceiling, almost like parquet tiles, scorched and blackened there—no doubt, by the nightly fires that the monks had lit.

She was fortunate that he spoke first. "Do you have children, Florence?"

She felt a voltaic jolt at the question. "Yes," she said calmly. "A boy. He's eight. You?"

He didn't answer. "Is he with your people?"

"I have no people here, Henry. I don't anymore," she clarified, remembering what she'd told him about her made-up bootlegger father. "My son is in a children's home."

"What's that, an orphanage?"

"More or less."

"Must be a mean way to come up, without your mama."

"I know how you're feeling, Henry. You miss your family."

"You don't know a thing," he said sharply, but without any real malice. He still didn't look at her. "My wife, Judith—her mama and daddy died when she was ten. She was passed around among relations. It was never exactly high cotton. We got a little girl, Bertha. We were expecting another when I got called up. Going to name him Virgil if he was a boy. I guess I'll never know now. This *plan* that Kachak's got . . . It's all prevarication, isn't it?"

"I don't know, Henry. It could be a real chance."

"You believe him?"

"I believe," she said, "that Kachak wants to get out of this place as much as anyone. If you do your part, then . . ."

"Hell!"

"A new life. In Moscow . . ."

"Not *my* life. I'd never see my family again. . . . They'd never know what happened. . . ."

"They'll know you died honorably as Captain Henry Robbins. And it'll be true. Here you'll be somebody else."

"If I turn . . ."

"Don't think of it that way. Whatever knowledge you have about that plane, they'll have it too, sooner or later. Time will march on. Get on that bus 'fore it's gone."

"I'm an American, Florence. . . ."

Rage was prickling up her neck and ears. He was like she'd been seventeen years ago, unable to see the situation clearly, blinkered by his principles. "Henry, listen to me," she said, taking his icy hand. "I tried to leave for years—I did. I looked for every way to come back home. I thought Russia was barricading us in. But I couldn't even get a foot in through the American embassy. And that's when I learned something about our great land of liberty. . . . America didn't want us back—deserters were all we were to it. You think it's different with you 'cause you're a soldier. But I am telling you, Henry, even if they knew where you were . . . we're flotsam now. We're lost to our people."

He studied her, the expression in his hooded, bruised eye stern, and the one in his good eye curiously bemused. "You can tell your commandant I ain't saying another word to him until he informs the United States government that U.S. Air Force Captain Henry Robbins is a Prisoner of War in the Soviet Union."

"God*damn* you, Henry!" Her whole despairing will was being annihilated by his pigheaded refusal. "Damn, *damn* you, Henry. It won't matter a whit if the You-Nahted States knows you're a POW," she said, mercilessly mimicking his inflections. "Even if this war ever ends, *you* won't be re-

turning home. Not after what you've seen of our network of health re-
sorts. *This*—right here—is the secret to the Soviet miracle. You think
they'll ever let that little piece of propaganda slip out?" She didn't care if
her voice was rising to a screech. "But you can live *now*. You've got the
power over them *now*. . . . Use it, for heaven's sake!"

He watched her with his cadaverous Anglo-Saxon face. And finally, he
said, "You still don't get it. I don't care about being *returned*. Don't you
think I know I'm never going back to Carolina again, or seeing my family?
Goddamn it, I don't care about *livin'*—can't you see that? Them's whom
I'm thinking of—Judy and my kids will never know what happened to me.
She'll be waiting, and waiting on it. 'Missing in action' is all she'll be told.
I can't leave her in the darkness like that. I don't expect you to understand,
but I ain't opening my mouth to say another word till I see that confirma-
tion letter from Uncle Sam."

"As you wish," she said.

"WELL," SAID KACHAK. "What answer are we to receive today?"

"He wants the Americans to be informed. He wants his family to
know," she said. She did not care if he broke her arms and tossed her atop
corpses. She was obliged to die here, so let it be. "He wants confirmation,"
she said. "An official letter back from his government."

"So write one."

She permitted herself to look up into his eyes. They were lucid and serene. Had he sobered up? "You can type it up yourself," he said, grinning.

"You don't mean . . ."

"There must be standard wording. . . . Our security organs can find
you some official American stationery. But let me ask you, what do you
think will happen once he gets his 'confirmation,' umm? Do you think
he'll talk *then*?"

"He only wants his wife to know what became of him."

"Touching." Kachak shook his head. "You silly old bitch. He will *never*
talk once he is persuaded that the Americans know he's being held here!
Whatever information we collect from him—his government will then
know its source. Certainly. His *family*? The only fact of which they'll be
informed is that Robbins was a traitor. He's been playing you for a cow,

you sentimental biddy. I should have handled this myself from the beginning. Now I will."

She wanted to speak but found she could not now form words without addressing the trembling muscles in her lips. It had been a helpless struggle from the beginning, and the absurd weight of her hopes had only clouded her mind to this possibility. Yes, she was a fool. But not a fool in the way Kachak believed. It was not the sentimentalism in Robbins's doomed demand that had lit a dark corner of her soul, but an echo in it of something familiar—something she'd once felt herself, when, with eyes wide open, she had forsaken Essie, her closest friend. In her animal devotion to her family she had been ready to cross any line.

But she had made a mistake. She had spoken to Kachak of "country" and "family" as if they were one and the same to Robbins. That had been her error. She had misunderstood him. He wasn't as blindly principled as she'd thought. He would do wrong by his country before he ever did wrong by his family. All along, that's what he'd been trying to tell her, even if he didn't know it himself yet.

"Give me one more chance to talk to him," she said. "I know how to make him change his mind."

"You've done enough." Kachak motioned to the guard behind the door.

But Florence didn't get up. "I can offer him something you can't."

Kachak looked irritated for having to rise to her bait. "And what's that?"

"It's not something I can say. You'll have to trust me."

Her insolence was bringing a hard glow to his eyes. His face said he was a man who could shoot her between sips of his tea. And yet, she persisted. "If he goes to Moscow now," she said, "you never will."

SHE WAS ALLOWED INTO Robbins's cell to say her goodbye. He did not look up when she entered but repeated his unaltered request by rote, like an incantation.

"It won't happen, Henry," she said. "They'll promise you anything, and tell your government you're dead anyway. And soon enough, if you go on like this, you will be."

"Well, ma'am." He grinned at her unpleasantly. "One way or another, I'm not ever getting out of here alive, am I?"

She didn't speak.

"You can tell me the truth, Florence."

"No. You aren't."

"Thank you," he said. "Thank you for that. It's all I want. The truth. For my family too."

"You aren't," she spoke again, "but I am."

He fixed his eyes on her. His left one, almost healed.

"I can get out of here. And I will. I'll get out and I'll find your family—I'll write them and tell them what happened to you. It won't be soon, but I'll find a way. But I can't do it myself. If you don't want to help yourself, help *me*. Tell me *something*. Something I can give the commandant. I'm only alive, Henry, because you're still talking to me. And when you stop"—she coughed—"they'll throw me back into that pit of torture and filth . . . into that shore of corpses. And I will die. And any chance you have of your family ever learning what really became of you, it'll be gone with me. But if you talk—drag it out for my sake and keep me alive—I'll make contact, I'll tell them whatever you want me to."

IN THE EVENING SHE packed away what few miserable, priceless objects she'd scavenged in her weeks in the infirmary. Rolls of cheesecloth bandage for her feet. A dull syringe needle with which she'd maneuvered to patch up her padded jacket and boots. A tiny vial with a few drops left of iodine. A flask half full of rubbing alcohol. An aluminum spoon she'd swiped from the hospital kitchen. The vitamin syrup she still hoarded. Bits of cotton. This was her treasure to sell or trade when she returned to the women's camp. The rubbing alcohol she'd offer up first to the top *blatnye*, who'd drink it up right away and after that, she hoped, leave her alone. She allowed these nervous, tactical plans to flick away the agony of her other thoughts—thoughts of her foreshortened future, such as it was. And thoughts of Robbins, who'd given no response to her madcap offer.

A guard came for her in the morning and Florence did her best to tell herself that she'd done all she could. Outside the ice fog was so thick she could barely see the guard's olive-clad back a few paces ahead of her. Her rasping breath told her it was fifty below. But instead of the truck, she was led once more to the interrogation room in the monastery. Her eyes, watery from the cold, took a moment to recognize the thin man who was there with Kachak. Once she blinked the frozen tears from her eyes she saw that it had to be Finkleman, the engineer-physicist. Robbins was there too, seated with his hands unshackled, limp like bait on the wooden table. "Let's begin," Kachak said.

EVERY DAY FOR THE NEXT ten weeks she arrived to translate for the commandant as he, with surprising patience and knowledge, extracted from Robbins the mysteries of the Sabrejet's radar gunsight. The sight was designed to compute leads at ranges of up to fifteen hundred yards. The extensive time of flight needed for the sight's computer caused the sight to be very sensitive to aircraft motion at long ranges, which made it hard for pilots to keep the "pipper on the target" as they maneuvered close to the enemy. Much of what Henry said sounded barely like English to her, but after some time Florence began to understand his qualified extolment of the plane's potency and even his tender gripes about its bad habits. She was nothing if not a good pupil, and within a few weeks she was as versed as the engineer-physicist in phrases like "ballistic solutions," "range selector," "radar value" fed to the "computer." Out of Robbins's memory, diagrams of the destroyed control panels of the F-86 were reconstructed. And when these were sent to Moscow, where the captured Sabrejet was being disassembled and copied, Robbins told them of the multitude of maintenance problems they were to expect, the power of rough runways to jar the delicate electronic components, what kinds of ground clutter could cause the radar to fail to work below six thousand feet. He did not have to tell them all this, Florence supposed. She suspected he was adding to the list of technical details for her sake, dragging things out to ensure her survival through the winter. She found herself imagining Robbins's young family, out of loyalty to whom all his enthusiastic disloyalty was being transacted through her. With her own American family she'd had no written contact in almost five years. Ten months ago, her father had died of a heart attack, going to sleep and never waking up. This fact Florence would not learn for years to come.

AND THEN ONE DAY in April, when the sun's radiance on the snow was almost blinding, she was summoned once more to Kachak's office. She found him wearing his military cap, set at an informal angle meant to keep the sun out of his eyes, but that also seemed of a piece with his jaunty mood. It seemed that, like her, he could not prevent himself from feeling that spring was near. "Get ready to say goodbye to your American," he announced, appearing to take pleasure in the worry on her face. "I am taking your pilot to Moscow. He will be assisting the engineers at the MiG bureau with the testing of their new planes. He is starting a new life, as am I. You do not look very happy, Flora."

"I am only surprised, Colonel."

"You did not think I was a man of my word? You insult me, Flora Solomonovna. Robbins has kept his part of the bargain, and I am keeping mine. It would be a lie to say it is a terrible sacrifice. I will be taking over the post on technological intelligence in Moscow. I am leaving this wasteland for good, in no small part thanks to you. I should like to thank you."

"Thank me?"

"For your service to the country. It shall be noted when you apply for probation, once your sentence is up."

Her heart sank again.

"It is not in my power to commute the sentence of a political traitor such as yourself. But I should like to do something for you so that your effort does not go unrewarded."

"Let me keep working in the clinic. As an orderly. I have learned to make myself useful there."

"You don't want to be sent back to your old camp?"

"I would rather not."

"Very well. We can arrange to keep things as they are."

"Thank you, Colonel," she said, standing up as he did.

"One more thing."

"Yes."

"You can go and say goodbye to your friend Robbins, if you like."

"Yes."

"He is, after all, your comrade now, such as things are."

Kachak was still smiling at this when Florence stepped out.

———

HENRY'S EYES, THOUGH FULLY healed now, looked bloodshot. He made a motion for the guard to stay outside his room while he and Florence had their last moment.

"Hello, Henry."

"Florence."

"The commandant says you'll be on your way tomorrow."

His eyes stayed down, not meeting hers.

"Henry." She touched his hand. "It's very good. Please don't be miserable."

"I've done a terrible wrong, Florence."

"No."

"I'm a traitor. I've betrayed my country."

"Go and don't look back. I have great hope for you."

He shook his head as if trying to dislodge this very idea from his brain. "I did what I'd sworn never to do." He gripped her hands hard. "Promise me you will not tell them what I done—only what became of me. When you get out, you tell 'em I died an American. 'Cause it's the end of the line for Henry Robbins here."

She believed he meant that now he would have a new name. His old identity would be erased, communication with the past made impossible.

"Of course."

"You remember the address."

"I couldn't forget it."

"Lord bless you with a long life." He placed his rough bony hands atop her head as though administering a blessing, but kept them there longer than any clergyman, holding on to her until his eyes, and hers, flooded with tears. "Goodbye, Florence."

THE NEWS OF WHAT HAPPENED thereafter Florence did not learn for several more days. It was Konstantin, one of the male nurses, the one who on the doctor's orders had begun to teach her how to find a vein on the arms of tuberculosis patients before injecting them with calcium chlorate, who delivered the news.

"Your American is dead," he said. They were in the room where the corpses were collected for fingerprinting before they were taken to the morgue.

Florence struggled to feign incomprehension. She had been warned never to talk about what had happened. How did they know?

"Dead, dead," said Konstantin the nurse. "Shot himself up right through the roof of his mouth . . . Oh, you knew him, all right."

"But . . . he was going to Moscow."

"All I heard is he was all packed up to be sent *somewhere*. The guard was escorting him out of his cell into the corridor. They hadn't walked a few paces when he turned right around and grabbed at that rifle, plain overpowered the guard, then shot himself in the mouth. Blew out his brains."

She felt a black hole open in her heart, a conical void with no bottom. "He couldn't have had the strength."

"Must have been planning it for some time. Waiting for the right moment. No one else was in the corridor to stop him. It helped that the guard was just some kid. Even so, he had enough strength to wrestle that weapon right out of his hands."

"It can't be so."

But it was. The news had come from the driver who took the bodies from the morgue and dumped them in common graves. The driver had seen the body himself. "But don't you say nothing about it," said Konstantin. "He mention anything to you about it?"

"Who?"

"The American!"

"Heavens, no!"

. . . *Promise me you will not tell them what I done—only what became of me.*

She shook her head furiously.

'Cause it's the end of the line for Henry Robbins here.

But hadn't he been talking about the American skin he was shedding and leaving in Perm before he became a different man in the capital? Oh, how stupid she was. He *had* alerted her, made his plan perfectly clear.

"He didn't tell me anything."

"Better not have," said Konstantin. "The commandant is fired up like fifty pitchforks, questioning everybody."

She understood that Konstantin was telling her this to warn her.

But the questioning didn't come. By some grace, she was once more spared.

For weeks thereafter Florence worried that the incident would cost Kachak his escape from Perm to Moscow, and the reprieve he'd promised her. But whatever promotion he had exacted from the big wheels inside the MGB was honored. He kept his pledge to her. She stayed on the books as an orderly in the clinic. Until one day in March of the following year she heard, on the radio loudspeaker mounted in the main patient ward, a sound her ears had forgotten. Classical music! Not the celebratory marching kind, but a solemn and pristine movement, like the voice of angels. Was it Beethoven? Handel? The music was followed by a medical announcement, a complete report on Stalin's vital signs, including an analysis of his urine. His urine! Like the music, the voices proclaimed grief but rang with ecstasy—speaking of a God who pissed and shat like all the rest of dirty humanity. And she knew it would not be long now.

THE MAGIC FLIGHT

BY THE SIXTIES, MOSCOW, LIKE AN OAK, HAD ADDED ANOTHER RING TO her center—the Automobile Ring Road. If you happened to find yourself driving along one of its four asphalt lanes in 1975, you would bear witness to a luminous sight: white outcroppings like a new species of meadow mushroom had sprouted in semicircles around preplanned courtyards, imposing their lucid, indelicate physiques over territories marked for future construction. Our new residential districts—the *mikrorayoni*—once villages of a hundred inhabitants, were now being zoned for a hundred thousand.

The people were saying goodbye to their crowded, peeling *kommunalki*, abandoning their dowdy one-room flats in pockmarked, cinderblock Khrushchevkas, moving out to the city's nine-, sixteen-, twenty-five-storied frontier! And in 1975 my family was moving with them. Lucya, the kids, and I joined the tide of optimists picking out Yugoslavian wall units, Polish bedroom suites, Bulgarian kitchen cabinets to fill up the expanse of three whole rooms. In the kitchen, atop the new semi-automatic washing machine that Lucya tried to domesticate with a piece of macramé, stood our German Grundig shortwave radio. A Japanese stereo set squatted proudly behind the glass of the Yugoslavian *stenka*. Trade relations between the Eastern and Western blocs were on the up. The word "détente" was on everybody's lips. Out in orbit, the astronauts of the Apollo mission and the cosmonauts of Soyuz linked up their two spinning crafts in a weightless space tango. News of this great cooperation was broadcast to us on our Horizon television set, on which months later we would watch Ford and Brezhnev, speaking as if his mouth were stuffed with sausage, fail to reach an agreement on cruise missiles and backfire bombers. It couldn't last, of course, all this mutual cheek kissing in Helsinki. By the end of the decade the party would be moved to Afghanistan.

But all that was still years ahead. In the summer of 1975, I had a different sort of fragile détente to attend to. For years now my mother and I had adhered to a delicate truce of our own—which is to say we were "getting along," which is to say we were not discussing politics. Florence no longer remarked that socialism was a wonderful idea in theory, and I no longer answered that so was flapping your arms and flying around the house for exercise before breakfast. In the end, the schism of our truce was precipitated not by affairs of state but by that most Muscovite of impasses: the apartment question.

"Not for me" was what she said. "I'm perfectly fine where I am. I can manage."

I can manage. A phrase much favored by my mother, along with *There's no need to make trouble.*

"No, you can't manage," I said. "Or maybe you can, but why should you have to?" I reminded her of the previous month, when I had twice taken her to the hospital after a herniated disk, acquired in the camps, had induced near paralysis in her leg. "And if the pain comes back and you can't move?"

"I won't be any closer to the doctors if I'm out there in the sticks."

"You'll be closer to *us*, to me—that's what I'm telling you."

She was still occupying the same cramped communal apartment that the two of us had lived in since 1956—when she'd returned from the camps, and I from the children's home.

"I can't walk up all those stairs."

"The buildings have elevators!"

"No, no . . . I've seen those places. Very low ceilings. I've lived my whole life with high ceilings."

"But, Mother, you'll have *more* space, not less. You live in a high-ceilinged *closet*. Everything's stacked on top of everything else. There's no room to hang a picture! Two steps between the lavatory and the kitchen. How can you think?"

"It suits me fine."

If it was the money, I told her, I would be more than happy to put down a payment for a one-bedroom cooperative for her in our building. The offer was disingenuous, I admit. Not because I wasn't willing to pay for a co-op for Mama, but because I knew perfectly well that she had money for it herself. I knew this because, two years earlier, when I'd asked to borrow a little cash for our own down payment, Florence had stunned me by producing, as if by the rub of a genie's lamp, half a dozen fat rolls of hundred-ruble notes—almost four thousand rubles—spooled so tightly and rubber-banded with such asphyxiating force that to get all that paper flat again required the use of a hot iron. She told me firmly that it was not a loan. "Am I an Egyptian that I need to be buried with it?" she said of my promise to pay her back.

How had a sixty-five-year-old retiree living on a skimpy state pension maneuvered to save such wads? *She* would have claimed it was by living on nothing but sardines and black coffee, and almost never buying a new coat, and getting the same pair of shoes resoled winter after winter. But how had she *obtained* the money in the first place? That is a more interesting question, and the best way I can begin to answer it is to say that, after two decades in post-Stalin Moscow, my mother had built up for herself a rather lucrative sideline.

Her day job, until she formally retired at the age of fifty-five, was that of a third-level sales clerk in a bookshop, the House of the Book—or, more specifically, the smaller annex that winged it, known as the House of the Foreign Book. It happened to be one of the only spots in the city where one could obtain foreign literature—dictionaries, English translations of Pasternak and Chekhov, as well as popular paperbacks by Jack London, Ernest Hemingway, Arthur Hailey, Erich Maria Remarque. Also, English textbooks of the kind much in demand by the ambitious mothers of a new generation of adolescents, the MGIMO set who were driven to class in black Volgas. The overdressed, competitive wives of the new *nomenklatura*, eager to launch their children into diplomatic posts and careers that would require them to know "proper English" unbutchered by the national schoolteachers, who taught it without ever having heard it spoken aloud.

The job in the bookshop paid next to nothing, but it gave Mama a chance to show off her skills. She always knew how to spot them, the women in imported knee boots strutting in for the first time in search of primers and phrase books, and Florence would lead them politely to the dim back of the store where she could wax on about the advantages and quality of various textbooks, allowing herself to demonstrate by reading a few lines from the books in her flawless English, until the mothers ventured to ask about her "history" and she, smilingly, gave them the very abbreviated version—along with her telephone number, should they "have any questions" about the book they'd bought. After that would come first the invitation to tea. Before long she was tutoring students privately every night of the week, with a waiting list growing longer by the month. On Sundays, while I sat cramming for my own college entrance exams, my mother was making her rounds of the well-appointed apartments atop the Lenin Hills, arriving with mimeographed lessons and leaving with cash. Her vinegary verdicts on the homes she visited were always delivered in proportion to the solicitous attention she received from her clients. Privately, she mocked her patrons' offers of French cognac and Dutch chocolates, ridiculed the husbands' peasant habits and the wives' lyceum pretensions, rolled her eyes at their lacquered furniture sets and their *ikebana* flower arrangements. Of one client, an approved Kremlin physician, I recall her remarking, "I can't say much about her medical skills, though her doctor's coat is specially tailored so the pockets are nice and deep." None of these people were, in her opinion, "real communists." All the real ones were dead.

But even these tart judgments—shared, I'm sure, only with me—were really a measure of nothing more than her own delight at her long-belated independence. She was not these people's servant anymore; she set her own hours, chose the kids she worked with, and quit if a student did not apply appropriate seriousness to his studies, all the while rolling up her blue, purple, and apricot ruble notes into tight little bundles that she stuffed in her wardrobe between the bedsheets and towels. Her Americanness—the very difference that had once set her so fatally apart—was now the key to her freedom.

Was it this freedom she thought I was trying to deprive her of?

"I don't want to move out of the city."

"But we aren't trying to move you to some *village*, just closer to us. Closer to *your own family*. Aren't you tired of sharing a bathroom with eleven people?"

THE PATRIOTS

"I've lived through worse."

"If anything happens to you, I can't promise that I can be there every day. Not if we're on opposite sides of the city. I work! Lucya does too."

"I have my neighbors. They're decent people. No one yells, no one drinks. And I don't like the kinds of people who roam around those outer districts."

"What kind of people? They're regular people, like us."

"You don't have to tell me. . . . I've seen them . . . ordinary workers, drunkards . . . those whole neighborhoods . . . a complete absence of culture. No theaters, no bookstores—it isn't living, it's vegetating. It's some kind of punishment."

"You won't be much farther from the center than you are now. We live right by a metro stop. And neighbors are not the same thing as family. This is a good time to buy—and let me remind you, Mama, you are not getting younger."

"Do you plan to bury me already?"

I talked myself hoarse, to no avail.

ALL OF THIS SHOULD have given me ample warning of the territory I'd be entering two years later, when we went from discussing my mother's move to the exurbs to a journey of far greater distance. A few things had changed by then. I had gone from being a promising doctoral candidate to being another Jew denied a degree, and I had finally understood that whatever fresh breezes of cultural change I'd whiffed would never mask the stench of my country's rot. Like many, I had allowed myself to hope, and had been made to pay for my optimism.

And then, just as fast as my horizons collapsed, they opened up again. Bushels of American grain, imported to shore up the embarrassments of our kolkhozes, were now ensuring my family's unmolested passage out of our suffocating confinement. Never could I have imagined that my mother would pose the greatest barrier to my departure.

"Hasn't everything already been discussed?" she said, innocent-eyed, each time I asked her if she planned to come with us to America, or, as she called it, "that place." So consistent was her avoidance of the word that anyone listening might have thought she and I were still arguing about deporting her to Moscow's suburbs. "Mama, we're not leaving without you."

"No, no." A curt head-shaking dismissal. "My life is where it is."

"I can't just let you stay here, all by yourself."

"I can manage."

"That isn't the point! We're applying for the documents. We're set on leaving. Do you understand what that means?"

"I'm not planning to get in your way," she said, as if all of this was just an unpleasant misunderstanding. "Whatever papers you need me to sign, I won't put up a fight."

This last ludicrous barrier to immigration was still on the Soviet law books: every grown adult wishing to emigrate needed his or her mommy's or daddy's permission in writing. I had her consent but not her cooperation. One afternoon, she arrived at our apartment to sign the papers that would allow Lucya and me to leave the country.

"Mother, this is your last chance," I said. "You'll be parted from me—from the kids—forever. Is that what you really want?"

I could see she was visibly aquiver, in spite of all her restraint. I didn't care. I was done playing nice. I wanted to rattle her.

"Is it?" I demanded.

The Berlin Wall was still eleven years away from falling. Jimmy Carter was president. There was no Gorbachev yet, no perestroika, no porous borders, no Skype, no frequent-flyer miles. To leave was to leave. To go was to stay gone.

But from Mama I got the silent maneuver again.

Fury was not the feeling it provoked in me. Not rage, either. Something deeper than rage. Something unleashing itself from under all the civilizing restraints of upbringing. I tried to cover it up with empathetic listening. "What am I asking you to do that is so horrible?" I asked her.

"What—tell me—will I do *there*?"

"You'll have a pension, just as here."

"Sit on the dole, twiddling my thumbs. Here I have my work, my students."

"You're sixty-seven! How many more years of work do you have left? There's more to life than work, Mama. I'll take care of all of us."

"It was never my intention for you to take care of me!"

"But I want to!"

"Why are you persecuting me like this?"

"What am I doing?"

"You want to turn me into an invalid!"

"I don't want to *turn* you into anything."

"You want to make me *useless*. So that no one will need me."

"That's not true—*I* need you, that's what I'm trying to tell you."

"Trying to take away my independence. Do I not deserve at least this, after everything? Have I not earned the right to a little freedom in this world?"

"You call this being *free*? Living in this country, with its lies and hypocrisy, these execrable quotas . . ."

She knew, of course, of my being denied my doctorate, and her eyes were powerless not to show it even as her lips could not help uttering their beloved phrase: "I've lived through worse."

I could hear the kids in the living room, where my wife was keeping them away, my daughter asking why Papa was yelling at Grandma. Panicked, Lucya came in and tried to make a hasty peace between us, but we were careening blindly now, not to be stopped. "—This garbage," I continued shouting, "that we are told to eat from morning to night . . . eat with a big grin on our faces . . . I am throwing away my *life* here!" I screamed. "My life!"

"It was never my plan to prevent you from leaving. . . ."

"You're afraid to go back, is that it?"

"Stop it!"

I could see I'd hit an artery.

"You threw away your life, and you can't bear it. . . ."

"I will *not* listen to this. . . ."

You can't bear going back a failure! I wanted to shout at her. *You can't bear admitting that all your exalted ideals, your so-called principles, all your struggles, everything you gave up—that it was all for nothing!*

This was not, however, what I said as I stared into my mother's frightened blue eyes—those bottomless eyes that in spite of having lost some of their vividness with age remained the focal point of her face. To say all this would have required a callousness and cruelty of which even I was not capable.

What I did in fact say was less courageous, though possibly no less hurtful to a woman in an already fragile state of mind.

"Do you want to die alone, Mama? Because this is what is going to happen. You will die alone in that miserable little room you love so much, a stone's throw from your 'theaters' and your 'culture'—die just the same, and no one will notice, or knock on the door, until someone's cat begins scratching on your door because of the smell. Do you hear me?"

"I will not let you!" Her voice was trembling now, as her eyes began to brim with angry tears. "I will not let you force me to give up everything I . . . I . . ." But she couldn't go on. She fled from the room, from me, out the front door, before I could think to run after her.

She didn't wait for the elevator. How fast was she bounding down those stairs to get away from me?

When I heard the hubbub a few landings below, I did not at first understand what had happened. From the echo of voices in the stairwell, I did not immediately make out the stifled moans of my mother.

By the time I reached the landing on the seventh floor, there were two people trying to help her up—a couple about to enter their apartment. The bearded husband was lifting her by the underarms, while the wife held Mama's right foot in her hands as though she were picking up a cracked egg.

It had been a bad tumble, though Mama herself did not seem to realize this. "I'm perfectly all right," she was insisting between growls of pain. Maybe she thought her fall, frightening and painful as it was, was only an embarrassing slip. She would not meet my eyes. I came in on the other side of her and draped her arm around me. It was as weightless as a child's. "It doesn't look right at all," the woman said, releasing her ankle. Inside the torn nylon casing, Mama's foot was swelling like a frankfurter on a skillet. When I touched her heel, she let out a loose howl of pain.

The ancient Greeks believed it was the effort to escape one's fate that led one directly to it. And so it was with Mama. Her worst nightmare had arrived at last: she'd become an invalid.

42.

THE DIALECTICS OF FLORENCE FEIN

IN THE FIRST WEEKS OF FLORENCE'S RECOVERY, THE ACT OF HOISTING herself up onto crutches parked by the foot of the sofabed was an ordeal of such backbreaking labor that there was no chance of her returning to her old room on Chekhovskaya. They couldn't risk it. In his living room, already in the midst of being dismantled and packed, Julian had made a semi-permanent bed for her on the foldout couch. Here she would remain encamped like a refugee while the family prepared for their own wandering journey without her.

In spite of this inconvenience, everybody in the apartment was solicitous and accommodating. In the mornings, her nine-year-old granddaughter brought her breakfast on a tray—buckwheat grains, black tea, pain pills. Julian, defeated, no longer hassled her about coming with them. His eyes still flickered with frustration and guilt whenever he asked her how her foot was healing. The same went for Lucya. All that awkward doting attention made Florence feel like a patient in a mental ward. Only little Lenny, diving into her lap on the armchair, gleefully making noise while his mother tried to hush him "so Grandma could sleep," was immune to all that enfeebling politeness. And so she loved him the most.

Still she was glad when, after the flurry of morning activity, the hair brushing and feeding and getting-the-kids-ready-for-school, they finally hurried off and left her alone. Through the kitchen window, sipping her tea, Florence watched autumn dissolve the last of the summer warmth with endless rains. A moist haze covered the towering buildings in this featureless new neighborhood. The rain washed the potholed streets while the new metro, nine stories below, swallowed and disgorged commuters. With her fractured ankle healing in its cast, she'd been obliged to cancel most of her lessons. For a time, some of her students agreed to come to Julian's apartment, to be tutored at the tiny laminate table in the minuscule kitchen where she now sat alone. But in the permanent disorder of a home teeming with two small children, it was impossible for her to do her work properly.

All her life she had managed to keep herself busy, to stay one pace ahead of unwanted thoughts. But now, with no responsibilities aside from recuperating, Florence was left with little else besides her ruminations. Her frailty and the pain pills made her tired in the afternoons. In those dead hours she welcomed the ablutions of synthetic sleep. But the enforced rest also did something strange to her. Sometimes, coming out of the mists of a chemical nap, she would experience an unmoored sensation in her throat or stomach, as if she'd just been standing at the railing of an undulating ship. Other times, she would wake with a start, hearing a voice in her dreams. "How can a girl leave her family?" it asked her. "Who in their right mind would do such a thing?" It had been a long time since she'd had such a powerful memory of her father's voice. In the apartment's failing afternoon light it was not her son's but her father's disappointment that she felt most keenly.

But she'd *had* to leave. In that place, so long ago, fettered by all the ancestral guilt, she'd refused to let her own desires be cramped by all that mindless rectitude. It was not that she hadn't believed things would change in America—they *were* changing, even then, all around her. But who could have foreseen what was bound to come: the schisms, the wars, the race struggle, the whole age of "sexual politics" they wrote about nowadays. The women libbers. Who could have predicted the Pill— unburdening girls from the weight of millennia. Yes, she could have stayed and waited for all the changes to happen—the decades-long march toward progress. She could have stayed and become part of that march. But she'd had no patience for all that. She had wanted to skip past all those prohibitions and obstructions, all the prejudice and correctness, and leap straight into the future. That's what the Soviet Union had meant to her back then—a place where the future was already being lived. And so she had fled the Land of the Free to *feel* free. She'd had to make the decision unilaterally or she would never have made it at all.

How can a girl leave her family? She hadn't given thought, back then, to what it meant to have a child of your own. Or what it meant to lose your child. She would learn all that later.

More and more she thought about Leon. Had she known how little time they'd have together, would she still have been so restless, so penny-pinching with her affections? A poor wife she had been to him, who was so steadfast with his love, who forgave her the unforgivable, justified the mess she got herself into with the secret police, entanglements she could hardly find the strength anymore to justify to herself. They'd had no peace in those days, those years of humiliations and terrors. But how much more terrible would they have been without Leon by her side? Would he still have perished had she been wiser? Had not spoken to Subotin about the rally for Meyerson, said nothing of their friend Seldon? Yes, sometimes she wondered about this too. Had her embroilments delayed their fates or sped them all faster to the season of their deaths?

It was impossible to know. Old age made you discover that it wasn't the big mistakes but the small ones that laid claim to your regrets. That she had not brought more pleasure into Leon's life—this now caused her more heartache than anything she could or could not have done to save his life. How stingy she'd been to rush off somewhere when he wanted her to sit and listen to a joke. How she'd rolled her eyes at his entertainments, his "frivolity," when all along it was only her he wanted to make laugh. How parsimonious not to make love more often, to turn away from his desire because she was too tired, not to tell him at every opportunity how much he meant to her.

For all her misfortunes, life had done right by her in some ways—it had given her, above all else, a good child. When she came back from the camps, without Leon, she'd longed for nothing so much as to make up for lost time, to raise and protect Julian as she knew a mother ought to. Only, by then, he didn't need her protection. He was used to taking care of himself. He made his own bed in the mornings, sewed buttons on his shirts, polished his own shoes like a soldier. Already like a little man—all elbows and knees—cooking macaroni for himself after school. All those years she had missed had made of him a contained and self-sufficient boy. At thirteen, he was cordial to her, addressing her as "Mama" out of respect, though the word fell so awkwardly from his lips. And on her part, it had not been easy to be a mother again after those solitary years. Some of his memories of her had remained intact. But it would take time for any affection to grow again naturally. Still, he didn't seem to hold anything against her. Not for a while, at least. The friction would erupt later, in his final year of high school, when the Great Reaction set in, camouflaged in his political and philosophical opinions, rhetorical challenges, a contempt for anything she dared to defend or even treat neutrally. Whatever hurts had taken root during those missing years had finally broken earth.

Perhaps it was her just deserts after the contempt she'd shown her own parents. Her son seemed to take pleasure in pointing out her every ideological "contradiction," as he called it. If she so much as complained about the kerosene breath of a bus driver or cashier, he'd say sardonically, "You mean *the working people*, Mama?" When he spoke with disgust about how he and other college students were forced to go around the neighborhood on election day with their wooden ballot boxes, knocking on doors and imploring people to cast their one-candidate ballots into the hole to assure a 99-percent voter turnout, she would tell him that at least he was giving everyone an opportunity to vote. He would look at her like she was out of her mind. He could not stop laughing when she mentioned (just once!) that he ought to be proud his country had no unemployment. "You know where else had zero unemployment, Ma?" he'd said, needling her. "Bergen-Belsen." When she told him he might at least be grateful for the free college education that was teaching him to be such a matador of logic, he reminded her of the three years of forced residency he'd have to serve in some backwater town, and how, as a scientist-engineer, he'd still spend his life being paid less than a drunken assembly-line worker.

Of course she knew that parents and children argued, but with Julian there was something different. He would not admit how much he blamed her for abandoning him as a child. To a child's heart, the reasons for the abandonment made no difference. Yet the mind of the grown man could not perceive this simple truth. He wanted her to atone for leaving him by repudiating the whole system that had torn her away from him. It wasn't enough for him to be *right* and for her to be *wrong*. If that was all he needed, she could have obliged. But no. He wanted her to reject *all* of it, renounce every beautiful idea she'd ever cherished. And this need seemed to her so bottomless, so much deeper than a simple desire to best her intellectually, that she was at a loss as to how to fulfill it.

Those were the times she experienced the loss of Leon most acutely. Leon would have known how to talk to Julian. He would have transmuted to comedic gold the base metal of Yulik's hard sarcasm. But she did not know how to summon such beautiful words. "Your tongue is hung on two swivel hinges, I can't keep up with you," she'd say whenever he'd try to back her rhetorically against the wall. Eventually the best they could learn to do for each other was respect each other's silences.

Now, with Julian no longer bringing up the name of the place he was going, it was only the slow emptying out of the apartment that stood to remind Florence of the unalterable fact of his leaving.

They were selling off their things. In the evenings, she watched her son write up lists of books and records to sell or give away to friends, his fingers stained by the purple ink of the mimeograph paper underneath. Over the course of several weeks the bookshelf in the living room where Florence slept was evacuated of the authors who'd been her irreproachable, loyal friends during her recuperation. Out went the bound volumes of Tolstoy and Pushkin. Gone were the Gogol and Lermontov. Out went the record player on which she'd listened to Stravinsky and the poems of Tsvetaeva. The shelves began to fill up with something else: black-lacquered wooden dishes hand-painted with gold leaves and red berries, wooden spoons and saltshakers rendered with green-and-gold petals and patches of strawberries—decorative *Khokhloma* that, in all her years in Russia, Florence had never been tempted to buy. It was her daughter-in-law's idea. A high-strung, practical girl, Lucya intended to wrap all these peasant tchotchkes in shirts and socks inside their suitcases and drag them to America as gifts to be distributed in gratitude to anyone who might help them along the way. What else would they have to offer to their American benefactors? How odd it was, Florence thought, to picture her own son arriving, in the place of her birth, a Russian bearing gifts of the Old World.

SHE THOUGHT THAT HER FATHER'S VOICE would stop haunting her once she ceased taking the sleeping pills, but it only seemed to grow in resolve as she recovered and began to maneuver on her own around the apartment. Once more she was severing the cord between herself and her family. A part of her had always known this day would come. She'd prayed for the day of Julian's release, steeled herself to let him go. Couldn't he understand that it was because of everything she'd had to deny him—because she could not now bequeath to him anything substantial—that she wanted to spare her son the burden of her old age in his new life in America? *I can't, Papa,* she told Solomon. *I can't oblige him to look after me forever.* But what her father said next stunned her: *He is the one who needs looking after, don't you see? It's not enough you left him once?* It was then that she knew: not in word but in deed could she atone herself with Julian.

Yet what right did she have to escape the soil that had swallowed up Leon, Seldon, Essie? As long as she knew that her bones were destined to be buried along with theirs, she could hold off the reckoning. As long as she went nowhere, she could continue to tell herself that it was this cursed land that had swallowed them all, and not she who had sacrificed them for her own deliverance. After forty years in the desert, even old Moses hadn't been permitted to cross into the Promised Land.

With her students no longer keeping her busy, she began to practice English with her grandchildren, reading to Masha from some of the British storybooks that Lucya had managed to find. Masha was a quick, attentive child, just as Julian had been, but it was curly-headed Lyonya, little Lenny, whom Florence adored, the child they had named after her Leon. It was he who nuzzled up to her on the sofabed, sitting with his legs in wool stockings folded beneath him, his rosebud lips hanging open while he listened to her tell him about the crocodiles who prowled the New York subways.

"But should I be scared of them?" he asked her.

"Only if you're by yourself, which you won't be."

"Because Baba will be there with me."

She was at a loss what to tell him. "Your father and mother will be with you, bunny."

But he looked unconvinced, as if he intuited even then how disoriented his immigrant parents would be in the grim labyrinth of the subway.

His grandmother, though—she wouldn't be lost anywhere. "But you'll be there too," he said again with more certainty.

And she found she couldn't muster the strength to tell him no.

43.

AVALON

THE STAFF AT THE AVALON RETIREMENT COMMUNITY HAD FOLDED UP and packed away all the deck chairs save our own. Down on the grass, Sidney and I sat on our lounges, observing the last of the sun's brightness. The blue turned to pale amber, almost exactly the color of the Amstel Lights we were sipping. I'd been nervous about the effects of the beer on my uncle's intestines, but he assured me he was doing much better since his surgery, and in any case he seemed to take only one sip for every five of mine. Though his wrists were still unsettlingly thin, I was relieved to see that Sidney's face no longer had the hollowed-out look that had so worried me last time.

It was late September in New Jersey, the weather still warm enough for us to linger, the air smelling of longleaf pines, which were just now shedding their needles, and also, more faintly, of a sour and slightly feculent whiff of algae that carpeted a pond on the edge of the grounds. Sidney had been asking about the family and I told him that Lenny was now applying for jobs in private equity firms around the globe, from Prague to Pretoria, anywhere that might reasonably be called an emerging market.

"No dishonor in following the money." Sidney nodded. "None at all. But no plans to come home soon, huh?"

Maybe, I said, Lenny's staying away would induce me and Lucya to finally take a real vacation. It was time we became more like American baby boomers and learned to leverage every phase of life for pleasure. "Maybe we'll all be taking a safari in Cape Town," I suggested.

"How about you? Any plans to return to Moscow?"

I wasn't sure how to answer. "I don't know," I said, truthfully. The joint venture had been put into motion; I'd done my part, such as it was. And then I told him my other news: I'd gotten back in touch with my colleagues at Herbert Engineering, where I'd worked before I'd been poached by Continental Oil. The news was that in six months an icebreaker I had worked on would be sailing from New Zealand to Antarctica to escort supply vessels to the McMurdo polar station, a trip that happened only once a year. The NSF was, as usual, sponsoring this science mission, and this year the project's manager had called to ask if I wanted to be on board with the other researchers and eccentrics. It was an opportunity to test the ship in real conditions. The only hitch, of course, was that I'd need to go in the capacity of an independent engineer, not as an executive on the payroll of a big oil company.

"So you want to cut your paycheck in half for a chance to see some polar bears?" Sidney said.

"There're no polar bears, but . . ." I could hear my voice growing high with excitement. "It's a whole other world down there, Uncle Sid." I told him I'd been reading about the professional dreamers and oddballs who worked in Antarctica for months at a time. They seemed like my kind of people. I would go see the outposts of the great explorers, Scott and Shackleton, the hero-adventurers whose stories I'd devoured as a boy. Everything in their huts had been left just as it was a hundred years ago—all preserved forever in the perfect cold. "It's the very bottom of the world," I said, trying not to sound too adolescent. "A place where time stands still."

Sidney nodded sympathetically. "And your own explorations? Did you find what you went for?"

I knew he was talking about our last conversation, when I'd called him at three in the morning. "Not everything," I said.

Somebody on the second floor switched on the radio to a local jazz-and-blues hour, and for a few moments Sidney and I were both quiet while dissonant and tender piano chords finally resolved themselves into a silvery downtempo melody.

"Uncle Sidney, when exactly did you know that she tried to escape the country?"

"I knew." Sidney closed his eyes. "By '47, I knew. Maybe even before the war happened, only I was too young to understand then. She wrote to the family."

I stared at him. "She put her intention in *letters?*"

"The language was very Aesopian. You had to read between the lines, which was something my parents were not experts at doing."

"What do you mean?" I couldn't believe it.

"Well, there'd be hints. She wrote me a letter once where she talked about a time when we were kids on the farm and she fell down a well, and I ran to town to get help and rescue her, and that she always knew I'd do that again for her."

"Did that really happen?"

"What are you talking about? What fucking farm? We lived in Brooklyn!"

"You mean it was code?"

"Well, that's what I realized after I went through the war and got some brains in me. It was encrypted. She knew the censors read all the letters." Sidney breathed hard. The labor of remembering seemed to take some strength out of him. "Then, after the war, I wrote to Secretary of State Byrnes, then Marshall. I wrote a handwritten letter stating that my sister, Florence Fein Brink, who had lived in Russia since 1934, was being held in the Soviet Union against her will. I asked could the State Department please look into the matter through our embassy in Moscow."

"Did you get a response?"

"After the second letter, yes."

"What was it?"

"It was very curt. It said, 'Since your sister no longer has the status of an American citizen, the Department of State is not able to take any steps to assist in obtaining information with respect to her.' I still remember the wording."

"That's it?"

"Yup."

Now it was my turn to exhale. "You couldn't have done anything more." It seemed to be the least fraught thing I could say given the enervated tone of Sidney's voice.

"Maybe I couldn't, maybe I could."

He paused, as if to listen to a few more chords of the music. "Anyway," he said a moment later, "that was *my* failure of courage. I got their response and I didn't pursue it further. I was twenty-nine years old, starting a career, starting a family—in the thick of my own life. The American government said to lay off, so I did.

"I knew a fellow at the State Department, a friend from school. I could have called him, pressed the subject. But it was 1948. McCarthy already had his fingers in everything. The whole country was watching Alger Hiss on TV, testifying before Congress that he wasn't a communist. This was a man who'd been very high in Roosevelt's administration. Nobody was untouchable. The blacklisting had started. My firm had big contracts with the government. Everybody had to take loyalty oaths. What did I need the trouble for? Making phone calls blabbing about my pinko sister over there in the Soviet Union . . . They wrote me that letter and I let it go."

"It wouldn't have changed things," I said, and knew instantly that it was the wrong thing to have said, to try to assuage whatever storms had brewed in his heart all those years.

"The point, my friend," Sidney said sharply, "is we're all leashed pretty tightly to the era we're living through. To the tyranny of our time. Even me. Even you. We're none of us as free as we'd like to think. I'm not saying it as an excuse. But very few of us can push up against the weight of all that probability. And those that do—who's to say their lives are any better for it?"

I knew he meant Florence—unpinning herself from one set of circumstances, only to be pinned down by another.

"But enough . . . ," he said. He was exhausted from wading into these philosophical depths and wished, I sensed, to move on to something else.

Only I couldn't. "Leashed is right," I said. "When she finally had a chance to leave, she was so goddamn intractable."

"You've been bludgeoning your poor dead mother with that for years. It's not such an interesting question. She had her life there! Her theaters, her students. More interesting is why she finally agreed."

"That's easy," I said. "She was fragile. She'd had that accident. She didn't want to be left to care for herself on her own."

"Is that what you think—us old people, we're all frightened of having no one to bury us? Come *on*. After all she'd been through, being left alone was the *last* thing she was worried about."

"Then why?"

"For you, dummy! Because you'd never have forgiven her if she didn't go."

I looked at the sharp, fragile contours of his face, harder to see now in the dark. "Is that what she told you?"

"Not in so many words. She said to me, 'I was a bad daughter, Sidney, and I wasn't any kind of wife. I didn't understand the meaning of the word "duty." I wanted to be a real mother, but I didn't have a choice then.' She was calling me long-distance from Moscow to tell me this. Of course I was thrilled to learn she was coming to the U.S. with the rest of the family. I said, 'Florie, what's changed?' She said: 'I already orphaned my boy once, Sidney. I can't do it to him twice.' "

I could feel her words suddenly in my body, rattling my veins, swelling into a clot in my throat. The sensation I'd felt that night in my hotel room, of how little I'd allowed myself to understand her all those years, returned to me now in the form of a fresh and tormenting grief. "I was thirty-six," I said, my voice growing thin. "I had kids of my own. I wouldn't have been devastated if Mama hadn't . . ."

"Don't you tell *me*," Sidney said, not letting me finish.

He was right. I took a deep breath of the pine-scented air. I understood better than I wanted to what she'd meant. Sidney and I had never spoken like this before. He had never told me about the girl who'd turned her back on "duty" and the old woman who'd renounced her freedom for the duty she'd once forsaken.

Sidney sat with his eyes shut. The lawn had gotten louder as darkness descended. The symphony of insects was vying with the music floating down from the window. Whoever was listening had turned it up to be heard above the intruding noises of nature, but the frogs and crickets, not to be outdone, had raised their volume. I sat in the near darkness, listening to the horn and piano mix with the hissing percussion of the cicadas, the frogs keeping time—the whole pulsing orchestration of the natural world that knew nothing and cared nothing of the suffering and resplendence of our short lives.

Sidney's eyes were still closed, and for a moment I thought he had fallen completely asleep in his cushioned chair, that our conversation had taken the last of the day's vitality out of him, and that I would now have to shake him awake. But when I spoke his name, softly, his eyes popped open again, their slightly protuberant whites flashing like the peepers of some alert nocturnal animal.

I helped him up, taking his elbow, and guided him through almost total darkness along the steps to the back porch, where the sliding doors had been left open. "Don't dawdle too long at the South Pole," he warned me. "Time might stand still there, but from where I'm sitting it flies fast."

I made him a promise that I would come back to visit him soon. I watched him walk slowly inside until he'd closed the sliding door behind him, and then I walked the ten moist, grassy yards back to my car and took the uncrowded nighttime highways home.

44.

BROOKLYN

Brooklyn

EVERY WEEK, NAVIGATING THE STRANGE NEW CITY, SHE DISCOVERED what was not there. The Polo Grounds. The soaring glass cathedral of Penn Station. The splendid Gothic spire of the Singer Building, replaced by the chubby functionality of another skyscraper. The Brooklyn Bridge trolley service. Sidney's beloved Dodgers and their old stadium at Ebbets Field, now a swarm of housing projects.

There were neighborhoods into which she could not venture alone. Brownsville, Bedford-Stuy, South Brooklyn. Places where the streets had been gutted by arson and something called "smack." Graffiti mauled the buildings where she'd once taken her typing classes. Gone were the elevated tracks raining soot on pedestrians below. Fulton Street was not girdled by metal tracks but abandoned to light and foliage. Even the street signs had upgraded their drab yellow and gray to a bright, assertive, chemical green.

In the first months, Florence had felt assaulted by the changes, but soon she came to like that there was so little Old Brooklyn left to remind her of her past. She prided herself that she'd never been vulnerable to nostalgia. The soddenness of this destitute borough no longer had the power to disillusion her.

It was funny, Florence sometimes thought, sitting in her kitchen and looking down through the fire-escape window onto Ocean Parkway, that, after having accomplished the great act of her escape from it so young, it was to Brooklyn that she'd ultimately returned.

She'd been granted her U.S. citizenship upon arrival (her reward for being born an American). The other privileges had taken more effort. With the help of Sidney and Julian, she'd filed paperwork with the state of New York and the city to get her SSI benefits, and her Section 8 housing, and her own Jamaican home attendant, who came twice a week to help her cook and clean, to measure her blood pressure, to take her to the doctor and the hair salon. But aside from this weekly help, she was living on her own again, in a one-bedroom on the corner of Avenue C, where car alarms howled all day and night, and where each Saturday she watched black-hatted Jews, like ghosts of an ancient era, walking with their legions of children to shul.

She found that, in spite of her fears, she was not useless. At all hours of the day her new neighbors—those from Odessa and Kiev, with spilling décolletages and pumpkin-colored hair; Georgians who spoke Russian with thicker accents than her own; Tats from Azerbaijan who wore headscarves and skirts long enough to sweep up the grime off their tiled tenement floors—found reason to knock on her door, seeking translation help with the confusing paperwork that arrived every week in envelopes from Social Security, Medicaid, and the Publishers Clearing House. The elderly among them came to her for intercession with their impossible-to-understand home attendants, whom they persisted in calling "foreigners," though these women from Jamaica and Barbados had been in the country far longer than they.

But the knock on her door she most looked forward to was her brother's. It was Sidney who got Florence out of the house and to the old parts of Brooklyn where, fifty years ago, they'd gone in search of petty treasures: cake cutters, pencil charms, police whistles, sucking candies, parakeets. Of course there were no more Woolworths and five-and-dimes where one could scout for such cheap gems. Nothing could be bought for a nickel or a dime anymore. Even the pay telephones now cost a quarter. And there was nowhere to go that made a decent egg-cream soda. And so, instead, brother and sister sat on benches in the parks, talking while they watched the lanes of traffic, talking until the thread of words pulled a circle around them that made the past half-century vanish. Remember! Remember!

"Remember when you tried to get a job like Eliza Weiss, selling clocks up at Martin's all Christmas?"

"Eliza—dear God, could that poor girl even *tell* time?"

"Remember when Mama took us walking past the Menkens' mansion so she could peek at their new 'oriental room'?"

"Sure. She couldn't stop talking about those paper fans and silk damask wallpaper! Word was, Mr. Menken had a lot of apologizing to do."

"A scandal?"

"*That's* what everyone was talking about, silly. You were too young to get it."

"So who told you?"

"Nobody told me, but I heard. As our nanny Sissy used to say: A rich man can't say sorry with daisies any more than a poor one can ask forgiveness with jewels."

TODAY THEY'D MOVED PAST their favorite bench, taking care to walk slowly so that Florence could favor her good leg. She hung on to Sidney's arm, her purse hanging between them, so no hoodlum would be tempted to snatch it, though there were no valuables in it, aside from twenty dollars and a handful of bus tokens. Nothing important, besides the letter.

Her brother was the only one who'd ever known about the original letter. The one that, after five years of writing in her head, Florence had finally committed to paper in July 1959. It was the month when Sidney had visited them in Moscow, maneuvering to arrive as a delegate for the American National Exhibition hosted by Khrushchev.

In all these years she had never forgotten her pilot, the man who'd dropped down out of the sky like an angel to give her a chance at a second life. Yet, in making the promise to tell Henry's family of his fate, she had committed another falsehood. Years after the camps, struggling to rebuild her life and raise her son, she'd continued to tell herself that her offer could not, under the circumstances, have been binding. A promise forged in the crucible of hunger and desperation, made while one could not even intuit a future in which one was alive—surely it had to be null and void. If such a letter were mailed from the Soviet Union and opened by authorities, she could expect an immediate and unpleasant visit from the kind of people who still had the power to do her, and her son, enormous harm.

She wondered if she would have had the courage to write the letter had her daring brother not volunteered to slip it out in his briefcase. Seeing Sidney that afternoon in Sokolniki, so outwardly changed—standing at his full height in a sports jacket and sunglasses, his bristly hair now a gelled wave, on his hand a plain gold band—made her panic. How sure of himself and of life he was. How *American*, with his glow of health and certainty. A stranger. But she'd misjudged: The same love and loyalty burned in him as always. He'd brought along a thick stack of photographs—of their parents, of her older brother, of the nieces and nephews they knew she'd never see—and spoke to her for hours about all the life she'd missed. In the end, it was he who suggested that she sew the letter to Robbins's family into the breast lining of his flannel suit. Sidney encouraged her to use her real name, but she was still too cautious. And it had not gratified Florence to realize, the day she and Julian saw Sidney off at the Moscow airport, that the promise she'd made in bad faith to Robbins was the one promise in her life she'd been able to keep.

Up on Albemarle Road was the Baptist church that had once been their synagogue, its Star of David still visible on the railing of the gate as the doors emptied out. The accents she heard now were Creole instead of Yiddish. These were neighborhoods into which Julian didn't like her venturing, even with Sidney by her side. As quickly as he'd been able, her son had left New York and made the move to Westchester. What he didn't know wouldn't kill him. Besides, not everything had changed. Erasmus Hall was still the white Gothic fortress she remembered, the pines in front now tall enough to hide its upper windows. The Loew's Kings Theatre still stood on Flatbush Avenue like a grand old opera palace, the dilapidated grandeur of its baroque façade soot-stained and water-damaged. The post office too was exactly where she remembered it, inside a venerable old brick building that aside from some graffiti scrawl had escaped the ravages of time.

The letter she planned to send today had more details than the one she'd penned in '59. Her real name, for instance, which she'd been too terrified to include the first time around. The details of the camp where she'd come across Henry. If they wanted to know more, they could call her. She included her telephone number.

She still felt queasy and light-headed at the thought of revealing so much information about herself, especially since Sidney had urged her to mail a second copy to the Veterans Department missing-persons office in

Washington. If her years in Russia had taught her anything, it was that there would always be a dear price to pay for giving away too much.

Yet what a relief it was to ignore those lessons. To break the penitential silences.

There was no line inside the post office. The postal clerk, a heavyset woman in thick glasses, took Florence's envelopes, stamped them, and summarily handed her a receipt.

Outside, an April wind tossed about litter of orange rind and wet newspaper. In the brightness of high noon, Florence lifted her chin and let the sun warm her face. She could still picture him—the man whose eyes, black and bruised, had shone with such constant, implausible, and incorruptible faith in her. Robbins had called her Sleeping Beauty, and she felt now that she was at long last waking up.

Sidney was waiting for her at the curb. "Ready to head home, Florie?" His dry hand was warm on her elbow.

"Yes," she said, "let's."

ACKNOWLEDGMENTS

———

THERE ARE PEOPLE WITHOUT WHOM THIS BOOK WOULD NOT EXIST, whose stories and insights were the soil from which my characters could grow: Timothy Friedman, Aleksandr Iyerusalimskiy, Ilya Ponorovsky—my heroes in every sense of the word. I'm grateful to my family, who never let me compromise this book's vision: Sophia Krasikov, my mother and fellow creative seer, who read every page and let no falsehood pass her doorstep; Gregory Warner, my husband and compañero in life and storytelling, and my finest editor.

I'm grateful for the sharp-eyed friends who read the original manuscript and gave fabulous advice: Alexis Calice, Aoife Naughton, and Laura Starecheski. Thanks to my dad, Jacob Krasikov, for his merciless cuts, and to my sister, Tatiana, my anchor. To the friends who have become my extended family over years of writing: Natasha Iyerusalimskaya and Olga and Anya Ponorovsky. To my friends and guides in Moscow: Olga Ladygina, Olga Osnovskaja, Sergey Zhuravlev, and Tatiana Smirnova. I am indebted to the Rohr Family Foundation for the priceless gift of time and to Carolyn Hessel for her enthusiastic support of this work as it evolved from talk to prose. Thanks to my editor, Cindy Spiegel, to my agent, Richard Abate, and to the early thoughtful readers: Judy Sternlight, Laura Van der Veer, Caitlin McKenna, Louis Pelosi, Jackie Stapleton, Lynn Lovett, Michael Meyer, Walter and Betty Grey, Carol Christian, Robert Herz, and Rosalind Fink.

I owe a debt of gratitude to the hundreds of papers, interviews, and books that aided my knowledge of the turbulent and tragic Stalinist era and helped me fill the interstices of my characters' lives. Two volumes were especially helpful in understanding the political context of their plight: Tim Tzouliadis's excellent *The Forsaken: An American Tragedy in Sta-*

lin's *Russia* and *Stalin's Secret Pogrom: The Postwar Inquisition of the Jewish Anti-Fascist Committee*, edited by Joshua Rubenstein and Vladimir P. Naumov.

And finally, my thanks to the guiding spirit of Pauline Friedman, one of the daring women who made the world go round.

ABOUT THE TYPE

This book was set in Photina, a typeface designed by José Mendoza in 1971. It is a very elegant design with high legibility, and its close character fit has made it a popular choice for use in quality magazines and art gallery publications.